GW00362613

EXIL]

CORPORATION

Truth can be stranger than fiction
Fiction can sometimes come true

A novel by
Mark D. McClafferty

Exile Corporation © 2010 Mark McClafferty
All Rights Reserved
WGA Registered Works ® R692-14919
ISBN: 978-0-9567304-1-1

Publisher: NVS Group
PO BOX 7490
Bournemouth, Dorset
BH1 9TP England

Book purchases available at:
www.exilecorporation.com

Cover designed by: R J G Ink
A Paperback Original 2010: First Edition

For Jane

My first true love, my last true friend
You will always be the wind beneath my wings

Acknowledgements

To say thank you; those two words are not enough to describe how thankful I am to have been born into such a great family. I am thankful that my Mum, Maggie and Dad, Danny, have been such good fun as parents and that they have taken the time to participate in my life. I am thankful that I have been able to enjoy them for so long.

My big sister, Sue and her kids, Dolly and Harry, you have always brought a smile in my darkest days.

My eldest brother Steve; thank you for being my co-pilot and my rock, encouraging me to soar and for bringing me back to earth as my guide and conscience, always there for me in my time of need. You can never be replaced and the world is a better place for having you in it. I will forever be your little brother, looking up to you in so many ways. Lynn, my surrogate sister, always bubbly, bringing laughter to so many, you are a star. Thank you for never judging me and for always giving me the benefit of the doubt. Ruby, Molly and Tommy, my nieces and nephew, you give so much unconditional love, thank you for giving me so many great memories from watching you all grow up.

Dan the man, my brother and my soldier, you have always been The Man, lifting everyone's spirits, the first to stand up to protect me and the last to fall down. Never give up on who you are and never forget the person you were. 'You know how we do.' Thank you for just being you.

My son, my boy, my main man, Luke; you faced so many hurdles, doubts and fears growing up without me in your young life. I am thankful everyday for the love, friendship and good times that we share. I am so proud of the man you have become and I look forward to seeing you rise into becoming a great man. You will do great things. Thank you for ridin' hard with me.

There are so many people who have touched my life in different ways; I have tried to include you in this book so that you will know how much you have meant to me. Most have been good, some have been bad and there are a few that have just been plain ugly!

I want to thank all of my friends for being in my life. A life I have watched myself live and have had to look in the mirror and question, why I am living it, and why do I deserve so many good people in it. From the past to the present, you have all helped to shape me and influence me. This is my story but it is also your story, for you have all helped in writing it. Be proud of it, as I hope you can be proud of me. A diamond with a flaw is worth more than a pebble without imperfections.

If You Believe It, You Can Achieve It

As we grow up, we learn that the one person who was not supposed to let us down probably will. You will have your heart broken probably more than once, and you will break hearts too, so remember how it felt when yours was broken. You will fight with your best friend. You will blame a new love for the things an old one did. You will cry at times, because time itself seems to be passing you by all too fast. Eventually, you will lose someone you love.

So take too many pictures, laugh too much and love like you have never been hurt by anyone or anything in your life, because every sixty seconds that you spend being upset, feeling let down, angry or filled with revenge is a minute of happiness you can never get back.

Dare to dream and dream to do. The difference between the dreaming and the doing is in you.

Do not be afraid that your life will end.

Be afraid that it will never even begin.

- Mark Knoxx
Chief Executive Officer
Exile Corporation

Hollywood Homicide

1

Present Day: November 17

Launching the black Porsche Cayman S forward from the stoplight while giving the hot, blonde-haired woman behind him in her BMW a cursory wave, the executive drove along the soft camber of Sunset Boulevard towards his morning destination. Standing before him, gleaming in the mid-November balmy morning sunshine, was the Sunset Tower Hotel.

Guiding the Porsche into the hotel's driveway, he brought it to an abrupt halt as the parking attendant stepped up to the new arrival. Getting out from the car, he straightened his canary yellow linen jacket, which he wore with a white shirt and dark blue Rock & Republic jeans. The executive looked at the parking attendant, both of them in their mid-twenties, telling him, 'Keep it up front, okay. I'll be about fifteen minutes.'

He palmed a crisp, fifty-dollar bill into the attendant's hand.

'Sure thing,' the parking attendant answered enthusiastically, as he got into the car to drive it up farther along the hotel's driveway.

Standing for a brief moment in front of the hotel, the driver swept his eyes up and down The Strip, his eyes shaded by his Armani sunglasses. He was twenty-seven years old, six foot tall, with sun-bleached blonde hair and every inch a Hollywood player.

Walking up the entrance steps, he pulled back his shirt cuff to check his watch; it was 8:54 a.m.

'In and out Smooth,' was all his lips betrayed as he sauntered nonchalantly into the lobby.

The cool lobby came as a welcome break from the sun-soaked morning outside. Locating the elevators, he walked over to them, noticing the well-dressed concierge – James, he recalled - who gave him a slight nod in acknowledgement while he continued his conversation with a guest.

Padding his way across the highly polished marble floor, the executive's leather loafers hardly made a sound. Arriving at the elevator, he viewed himself in the reflection of the polished chrome doors, and for a moment, insecurity and doubt flashed across his face. He was now only two minutes away from his nine o'clock appointment. He had been specially chosen, because of his expertise in getting the job done.

The ping from the elevator's arrival brought him back from his thoughts. The doors opened, revealing a mirrored interior as he casually glided in and turned to face the lobby. Raising his left hand, he pulled off his shades and pressed PH for the penthouse.

2

'Hmmm, let's see. I'll have the Hollywood Shuffle with a side of toast and two eggs over eeaassyy,' Dan McGann said, letting the last word roll off his tongue in a flirtatious way that caused the waitress, Amanda Linsay, to laugh sarcastically. She had heard it all too many times before.

Amanda turned her attention to the other side of the booth, trying to get the two cops to cooperate in telling her what they wanted to eat for breakfast. Joining in with the morning's antics, she playfully admonished them both by saying, 'I don't know why I even bother with you two, and for you, Richie babes?'

'Oh, so it's babe, is it? I told you I was Amanda's favorite.'

Richie Keets smiled back across at Dan to see if he was taking the bait, but Dan just stared at him with a look that was impenetrable. Amanda jumped back in to clarify her remark. 'Well, when I say babes, Richie, I mean in the sense that you are a baby, especially when it comes to women. Look, I got some real men to serve here, so what's it gonna be, or shall I just bring you some warm milk to suck on?'

Dan cracked, and laughed with Amanda, knowing she'd gotten one over on Richie. Amanda hovered over Richie with her pen now static on her notepad, listening to him reply, 'Just give me the same with a V8, and hurry up with a refill, will ya? We got places to go and people to see, babes. This ain't no social club; I've been sucking on this empty cup for ten minutes.'

Richie lifted his empty coffee cup, doing his best to get in one last jab while Amanda looked back at him as she began to walk away. Quick as a flash, she held down a Heinz ketchup bottle as if she held a dick in her hand, motioning it up and down suggestively while she replied, 'Yeah, yeah, suck on this.'

Dan and Amanda both erupted into a fit of laughter, along with a few nearby patrons. Everyone now looked at Richie, his mood changing, knowing she had caught him again. Dan hit Richie with a wise crack that set them both off into a tirade of arguing with each other. Dan McGann and Richie Keets, the Los Angeles Police Department detectives continued berating each other, which had been their way of working together for the past eight years in the L.A.P.D.'s Robbery and Homicide Division. They were partners, best friends, and like brothers, they squabbled, but they each knew their own life often lay in the gun hand of the other.

Seated at their favorite window booth in Edie's Diner on Sunset Boulevard, the two cops got down to the day's work

11

.d. They were working a case regarding a string of rders over the past eighteen months, involving young nale prostitutes and exotic dancers throughout Hollywood. They had also picked up a case that had intrigued some of the country's finest police officers from coast to coast. The Club Bangers had taken down a string of strip clubs, bars and nightclubs in a series of strong-armed robberies around Hollywood, having worked their way across the country. The Club Bangers were a group of young gun mafia-affiliated hitters, who had finally reached Dan and Richie's turf. Another day had started just like every other for the boys in Los Angeles.

Digging into their breakfasts, Dan listened as Richie unloaded the latest word on what was going down on The Strip while he breezed over a magazine article that covered his favorite movie star, slumped over the seat of her Mercedes-Benz, taking a hit of cocaine. It was an actress that Dan knew Richie had had a schoolboy crush on for years. Richie let fly by saying, 'Man, I should tell these rags what really goes down in this town. I'd make a bundle selling my stories.'

Dan took a swig of his coffee, not paying attention to Richie, while he lazily gazed out the window, taking in the view of all the beautiful people beginning their day on the Sunset Strip. His eyes caught something as he focused on a black Porsche that had pulled up across the street at a hotel. *A fine-ass ride*, he thought, while he watched some guy posing in front of it. *Here's some young hot shot standing in front of his hundred-grand ride, without a care in the world, and here's me, barely making ends meet.* He sucked down the last of his coffee, and then turned his focus back to Richie. 'We'll probably have to back Caron up on this Club Banger thing tonight, okay?' He said. 'Or has your old lady finally put her foot down and not letting you out?' With a smirk on his face, he did his best to get a rise out of Richie.

Richie leaned back against the high-backed booth, rubbing his hands hard on his face. 'Man, I don't need this shit right now,' he answered coldly. Lowering his face with a hard look, telegraphing that the subject was closed, Richie changed the subject by asking, 'So, what time's this guy showing up with this earth shattering info' on who our serial killer is, and what does he want for this inside scoop anyway?'

Dan's expression turned just as serious. 'I have no idea. All the guy said was he'd meet us here around nine, saying he knew we'd be here anyway. Said he'd give us all the evidence we'd need to put our serial killer away. He didn't give his name, and I couldn't trace the call. It sounded like he had an Australian accent, though. Other than that, I have no clue what he wants for telling us.' Dan followed up quickly by saying, sarcastically, 'But at least I won't have to ask for permission to go out tonight.'

Richie snapped back, 'Fuck you! At least I got someone to check in with. What about you? Who gives a shit about you? You're like a fighter, always wanting to go one more round. Hey, don't kill the messenger, Dan The Man, all you seem to be doing lately is the checking out and I haven't seen anyone wanting to check in.'

Their tirade began to get more personal as Amanda approached with fresh coffee. She heard Dan say, 'Yeah, well, when was the last time you laid some pipe with Jo, huh? Tell me that? You're always out on the town with me, and then going home dog-ass drunk.'

They continued jabbing at each other over breakfast, keeping it real.

Richie Keets had been raised on the mean streets of East L.A. without a father and barely a mom. He had hustled a number of hot items and got involved in illegal activities from an early age in order to survive, until one day, he got caught by a young, hot, sexy mama, named Jo. After a year of dating, they got married and within a year of that, Jo gave birth to their daughter Elenoor. From that day on, Richie gave up his days of moving bricks on the street and started to build a future for his family by finding his calling within the ranks of the thin blue line of the L.A.P.D.

Unlike Richie, Dan was part of a happy family. He was the captain of the swim team and a member of the gymnastics team. Growing up in Marco Island, Florida, Dan had plenty of girls chasing him. He entered the military after college and became a Navy SEAL before retiring and becoming an L.A.P.D. cop. Dan McGann was now forty-seven years old and a veteran of the Gulf War, but he was still fighting on the streets of L.A. for every dime he earned. Dan was a weapon, ready for war. They came from different upbringings, but they had found in each other, qualities that made them unbeatable. They believed in each other, and they loved each other, knowing each would give his life to save the other. They believed in making the world a better place, even if that meant they could only do it during their ten-hour shift in Hollywood each day.

Richie carried an air of danger about him that came from his early life on the streets. He had a street edge to him that he used well, working the streets for information. The raw reality was, that he respected those people who lived in the streets, but if you crossed him or disrespected him then you had better lie down or be prepared to get down.

Dan carried himself with an easy air and a freewheeling spirit, always handing out a warm smile to those he met. Confident and self-assured, he knew who he was and what he was about. Relaxed intensity he liked to call it. Dan was that guy for a reason. It had never been pretty, but someone had to do it, and he'd done it for God and Country.

Nothing that the drug dealers or murderers did could sway their convictions about getting the job done. Dan and Richie were six foot two, packed with muscle, and battle-hardened. They were ready to bring the pain to anyone who tried to bring it to them. Dan had an all-American look with his blond hair and blue eyes, flashing his million-dollar smile to get things done. Richie used his hazel hair, dark hazel eyes and dark dimensions to intimidate people. They complimented each other: being known comically by their peers as the dynamic duo. None of their fellow officers knew how or what they did to get the results they did, but everyone agreed on one thing: in a fourth down with thirty-five yards to go and three seconds on the clock, they were the go-to-guys who could close out the show.

They were different, but they were the same. Dan and Richie were both killers.

3

'Boom! Boom! Boom!' The heavy banging on the door echoed throughout the penthouse. 'Boom! Boom!'

Lifting himself up onto his right elbow, Chris Wright looked lazily across the bed at the two party chicks he had used and abused the night before. It had been a fun-filled Hollywood night that included sex, drugs and rock and roll. Letting out a small chuckle, Wright amusingly said, 'What the fuuckk?'

Pulling his hand through his long, greasy, black mane of hair, and then pulling down on his goatee, he shook his head, trying to shake off his hangover. Looking at the girls again, and thinking it was a good thing he'd been woken up, Wright now turned his attention to the reason that he was awake. Someone was beating on the door, and now the morning sun was beating down hard into the penthouse suite's bedroom and boring into his skull.

'Alright, alright, you fuck! I'll be there in a minute!' he shouted, as he began to look for something to throw on. Rubbing his belly for comfort, he found the hotel's bathrobe lying on the floor. As he picked it up, Wright thought to himself, *what were the names of those bitches anyway?* His hangover was going into overdrive and beginning to kick his ass, which was exactly what he was thinking of doing to the person on the other side of the door, who was still pounding on it. Walking over to it, Bezerk hollered, 'This place better be on fuckin' fire, asshole, or I'm gonna light a fire under your ass for waking me up. You best belieeve thaatt!'

Arriving at the door and the source of the incessant banging, he looked at the clock hanging in the foyer. That enraged him even more, as it told him that it was the ungodly hour of nine o'clock.

4

Staring at the PH on the door, the executive had decided to bang on it once he realized that the doorbell was not going to wake those inside. He allowed himself a wry smile, knowing what to expect next. He stayed focused on the door, not paying any attention to the booming voice shouting from inside as he literally felt the hinges of the door begin to open. Pumping his legs hard and fast, he lowered his shoulder into the door. He bolted through it, knocking Chris Wright to the ground with a violent backhanded whip of his nickel-plated Glock nine millimeter pistol across his face. The butt of the gun's handle cut a jagged slash across Wright's nose and forehead. Bleeding profusely, he fell backwards onto the marble floor in instant shock and pain, which forced him to curl up on the floor, while a stream of blood pissed out of his head.

Taking control of Wright, the assailant methodically pulled off the bathrobe's belt strap and used it to tie Wright's hands behind his back. He then grabbed him up by his long mane of hair, pulling him up to his knees. Wright growled from the pain that raced through his body, his face taught from his body weight being pulled up by his hair. The assailant roughly pulled down both sides of Wright's bathrobe to restrict his mobility, exposing his thick shoulders and chest. All Chris Wright could think about was filling his lungs with hot air that helped to move his chest up and out, on which was a big thick, black inked tattoo that read: THUG.

Spitting blood across the pearl white floor tiles, Wright managed to gain some venom in his voice and shouted at his attacker, 'You're one dead mutherfuckaa homes, you hear me? I'm gonna kill you myself.' He spat out the blood that was filling up his mouth and continued, 'Believe that, fag boy. You're dead!'

His eyes were bloodshot, his nose and forehead were spewing out blood, and he thought he'd had one hell of a hangover minutes earlier.

The assailant did not take up any debate with him as he coolly went about his work.

Taking stock of what was happening, Wright's rage built up and he defiantly pulled his head away from his assailant's grip. He immediately felt more pain as he took a hard knee to his back that winded him. He noticed the clear latex gloves that the attacker was wearing as he picked him back up from the floor. Wright instantly thought, *Shit, I might not walk away from this one.* He tried to reason with the attacker, saying, 'Listen, man, whoever's sent you has got this all fucked up.

What the fuck's this about? Whatever they've told you, you're gonna be making one big fuckin' mistake, fool!'

There was no answer from behind. The assailant was screwing a silencer onto the pistol's barrel.

Wright spat out more blood onto a floor that was now spattered with blood, feathered out in all directions. He asked, 'Tell me what this is about! You're a professional and so am I. We can work this out. Hey man, do you know who you're fuckin' with? Do you know who I am?' His deep baritone voice boomed throughout the suite.

'You are right, Mr. Wright. I am a professional, and I do know who you are,' the assailant answered with a dash of sarcasm in his broken English accent. With one last tightening down on his silencer, he said, 'And that is why I have been sent –.'

Turning his torso to his left while he raised his gun hand, the assailant instinctively squeezed off a round that caused his pistol to kick up, spitting out its deadly cargo. It hit the sheen of a body that had caught his peripheral vision, while it was running towards the penthouse's balcony. The body dropped instantly and a naked girl now lay across the threshold of the balcony's doorway. The warm morning sun softly stroked her hair, as she lay there with her eyes open, dead.

The gunman belted Wright across the back of his head for the inconvenience of the additional kill. Following up with a heavy kick for good measure, he left him writhing on the floor in agony, realizing he had better clear the other rooms before continuing. He hissed in a heavy foreign accent, 'Don't go anywhere, cowboy. I'll be right back.'

He sidled over to the master bedroom's door and his cold, gray eyes swept the room, dissecting it inch by inch for the smallest detail. He noticed that on either side of the bed sat numerous types of glasses, empty beer and wine bottles, and cigarettes. On the bedside table nearest to him, three lines of cocaine were laid out.

'Party hard and live each day like it's your last,' he muttered.

Sliding further into the room with his back against the wall, he noticed a detail that was out of place. On the wine glasses, there were two different shades of lipstick. Looking at the floor there seemed to be too many items of clothing for one woman. This meant one thing. He was not alone. He checked over his shoulder to make sure that Wright was still on the floor where he had left him.

The gunman placed his hand on the door handle of the bathroom. Pushing down on it, the door opened smoothly, swinging open to reveal the glass-encased shower and Jacuzzi tub, agonizingly revealing more of the bathroom. The gunman looked along the sightline of his gun while he followed the swing of the door until his eyes fell upon her between the pearl white toilet and the washbasin cabinetry, sitting in silence and shaking in terror. She sat there, naked, with her knees pulled up tight to her chest. Her big, round, doe eyes finally met his when she realized she wasn't invisible and he had found her. Her red hair lay down one side of her face, covering one breast. The gunman realized how beautiful she was, probably no more than twenty years old. He stood away from the doorjamb and gazed in wonder at her beautiful face while a long, lone, single tear ran down her cheek. All the fire left him as he wished that he could have met her under better circumstances. Now she would never have the opportunity to know him, or to understand why he had to kill her. He lowered his pistol while they looked at each other, lost for a moment in time and space. She was willing him with her very soul to let her go, begging him for mercy in her mind. He seemed to have heard her pleas as his eyes seemed to soften. He could hear a muffled sound next to her.

'Ma'am, stay on the line with me. Is there someone in the room? Can you tell me where he is now?' The telephone cord hung down beside her with the telephone's handset sitting on the floor. 'Ma'am, hold on, okay? Police units are just a few minutes away.' The police dispatcher repeated the information over the phone, doing her best to stay composed.

The gunman understood. How could she have known? He looked at her with a look that told her everything would be okay and her eyes radiated back at him with the heat of new hope. The searing heat of happiness and the bright light of freedom were draped over her as warm as the sun, shining outside. With a quick flick of his shoulder, it was the exact opposite, as darkness suffocated her before her brain could register what had just happened. She suffered no pain; there was no sound, no thought, only the darkness.

'Ma'am, hang on, okay? Just a few more minutes, officers will be there with you. Stay with me,' the police dispatcher said, sounding like she was pleading now, not realizing that she was speaking to a corpse.

The gunman envied her lying there so serene and at peace. She was beautiful as she lay there on the floor. He quietly closed the bathroom door, leaving her as if she were asleep.

5

'Jo and me would like to have you round for dinner, Wednesday night around seven thirty, okay?'

'Sure, what's up?' Dan asked.

'Nothing, we just want to see you and Elenoor would love to see you too,' Richie answered; his face betraying him.

Dan replied, 'Aahh shiitt, have I got to cover your ass? I told you, you'd been out too much lately. Anyone would think you were the single one out of the two of us Pikey, the way you've been out partying with me.'

Richie didn't respond, seemingly lost in his thoughts.

Dan picked up on his vibe and decided to make light of it. Changing his tack, he said, 'Whatever you need me to do, no problem. I got your back, bud, you know that. I'll tell you what; I'll even pick up the check. How's that grab ya?'

'By the nuts!' Richie joked, putting it back to him.

'Just chill. Everything will work out, you'll see.' Dan said, trying to lift Richie's spirits as he left him in the booth.

'Everything okay?' Amanda asked Dan, while he rummaged through his cash, standing at the register.

'I'll let you know when I know,' Dan replied.

Amanda held his hand in hers as he passed her the bills, asking, 'And when will that be?'

He looked up into her bright, deep brown eyes that were screaming at him to give her the answer she wanted to hear. He hesitated, and so, she carried on probing, asking further, 'You still have your key, right?'

Dan answered, 'Yeah,' but not in the enthusiastic way that Amanda had been hoping for. She soldiered on, embarrassed and flushed in the face, saying, 'Well, you can stop by anytime, you know, if you'd like.' She continued getting Dan his change from the register and then said, 'I hope I see you soon, babes. That's all I mean, you know?'

Clasping her hands around his, Dan felt his mouth forming the words to begin explaining that they needed to talk when his radio sprang into life with his call sign, causing him to turn his attention away from Amanda.

'Richmond 2, Richmond 2, all units, be advised a possible 187 in progress at 1965 Sunset Boulevard, the Sunset Tower Hotel, please respond.'

Dan snatched up his radio off his belt to answer the dispatcher. As he did, he looked over at Richie who was also listening to the call. Both of them understood its meaning: a homicide was possibly taking place right now, right across the street from them at the Sunset Tower Hotel.

6

Having been inside the penthouse for only a few minutes now, the gunman had killed two people unnecessarily. Such were the spoils of war. But this killer lived by his own credo: it's either you or him, but it's not going to be me. It had served him well over the years, which was why he was the best, and in such demand as a highly paid assassin. He grabbed Chris Wright up from the floor by his hair again. Wright let out a wail of pain and spat out more blood across the floor. The assassin bent down to hiss in his left ear, scowling hard in it, 'Listen up Bezerk.'

For the first time, he used Wright's street name, as he was known throughout Southern California. Bezerk was a shotcaller for the Southsiders, one of the most feared and ruthless Mexican gangs in America. He was one bad motherfucker, and all day long, he was a Thug.

'Let's not make this any harder than we have to, shall we?'

'Fuuckk yoouu!' Bezerk answered hard.

The assassin laughed while he pulled out a cell phone from his jacket pocket. 'You're going to get a kick out of this.' He pulled Bezerk's head up to his face by his hair; Bezerk let out a low-pitched growl. The assassin pressed the speed dial and spoke into the phone, saying ominously, 'I have the man of the hour here now.' He went quiet and seemed to be taking instructions over the phone. He then answered, 'And if he chooses to not comply? I understand completely. Please hold one minute.'

Turning his attention to Bezerk, he yanked back on Bezerk's hair and practically lifted him off his knees as he spoke in a harsh tone, saying, 'Listen carefully. Make no mistake, you are dying here today, you hear me? I'll kill you quick and painless, no bullshitting around. You understand me? Fuck around, and I'm going to make it hurt like a mutherfuckaa and it'll be real slow. Trust me, cowboy, this is the end of the line for you. Answer some questions and I'll kill you quick.'

Bezerk replied just as hard, shouting, 'I guess you're gonna have to earn your money today boy, coz I ain't sayin' shit!'

The assassin let go of Bezerk and smiled briefly while he took a small step away from him. He lowered his pistol and fired a hot round into the back of Bezerk's knee. A wild howl came out of Bezerk in acute agony, making its way out past the penthouse door that stood ajar into the hallway. All of Bezerk's bravery and fight left him, now that his life force was beginning to drain out of his body. The floor around him was now a sea of blood, snot and tears, while he fought to gulp down air and maintain his life. The assassin bent down and pulled him up from the floor by his hair again; only this time, Bezerk did not feel any pain. The gunman disregarded the fact that he was on his way to dying, as he pulled Bezerk up to his face to say, 'Answer some questions and I will put you out of your misery and end this miserable life of yours. I can, and I will end it for you quickly. I give you my word bro,' saying it with a hint of humor in his voice at how his fake American accent sounded to him.

A small nod in the affirmative from Bezerk was all he needed to see. He wasted no time speaking back into the cell phone, saying, 'I am putting you on with him now, sir. No problem, I will check back with you in approximately three minutes for further instructions, should they be required. I am putting you on now.'

He lowered the cell phone to Bezerk's ear. Bezerk was holding on for his life, and now he was holding on for someone to speak. It felt like an eternity. All there was, on the other end of the line, was silence.

'L.A.P.D. Detective's McGann and Keets, Robbery and Homicide,' McGann barked as he and Keets entered the lobby of the Sunset Tower Hotel. Dan raised his detective's gold shield. They had immediately come upon the concierge, who introduced himself as James Bronson. A number of police black and whites were pulling up in the driveway; two of them blocked in a black Porsche that had been parked in the driveway.

'Secure the perimeter and lock down all public access points, restaurants and bars. No one in or out from this point on until we have ascertained and contained the situation, understood?'

Detective McGann fired off further instructions to the police officers who then went off in all directions to carry them out. Dan and Richie were now in full metal jacket mode. Dan turned his attention to James Bronson again, telling him, 'Contact every guest and tell them to stay in their rooms, no matter what they hear outside. Tell them to only open their doors to a uniformed police officer, got it?'

James nodded in agreement and took up his own radio to pass along the instructions. Walking away from McGann with a colleague, looking a little dazed and confused by all the action that was unfolding this morning, he said to him, 'Things like this just don't happen here.'

Detective Keets was now marching back across the lobby towards McGann, having been in the hotel's security office to watch the morning's surveillance tapes. He fired out at Dan, saying, 'Any word from the penthouse yet?'

'Nothing, what you got?'

'No one's been in or out of the penthouse since nine o'clock,' Richie stated in an agitated way. Dan mulled it over and somberly answered, 'Well, we're gonna have to establish some kind of communication with whoever's up there soon, to find out if this is a robbery gone bad.'

'Or a murder,' Richie added matter-of-factly, standing squarely to Dan.

Every fiber in his body cried out to be put out of its misery, but he held on, defiant.

'Long time no talk, Bezerk.'

The voice on the phone gave Bezerk a shot of adrenaline and drove his senses into overload as he processed the voice he was hearing, the voice of his friend that was so distinctive because of its English accent, saying in a mocking tone, 'How you doing? Not so good, huh?'

'What the fuuu -?'

Bezerk tried to reply, but the voice cut him off and continued, 'Let me ask you, when you're fucking one of your dumb, skanky ho's, how do you know that it's you who's doing the fucking? Are you fucking her or is she fucking you? So I'm going to ask you straight up, did you really think you could fuck me and get away with it? Knowing you all these years, and now I finally know why they call you Bezerk, because you are berserk. You must be mad to think you could fuck me and get away with it. You were my dog, man, and by that, I mean you were my dog for real, and I was your master. You're just a stupid, mangy dog to me now Bezerk. And like a dog, when it does well, it gets thrown a bone, and you've had your choice of juicy bones thrown your way over the years, you piece of shit, haven't you!'

All Bezerk felt was hatred and betrayal. The voice's words were draining him like the blood draining out from him onto the floor.

Not waiting for any reply, the voice reached a fast frenetic pace while Bezerk began to fade away, as he heard it say, 'I made you dog! But once that dog goes bad and bites the hand that feeds him, well then, no matter how much his master loves his dog, he's got no choice but to put him down, and that's what I'm doing with you boy, putting down a rabid dog, yeess siirr.' The voice mimicked Bezerk's deep baritone voice and then laughed, clearly enjoying the torture he knew Bezerk was enduring. Continuing, he said, 'Your time's up boy, and you're being put down. You finally fucked with the wrong guy. I just never thought it would end up being me, but then I never thought you'd fuck me over the way you have either. You and I were soldiers man, but now you got to go, you hear me?'

There was no response from Bezerk.

After a moment, the voice spoke up again, saying, 'Maybe this will help you pay attention, as it'll have some bearing on whether your family in Del Sol lives or dies.'

Bezerk was dying and didn't care. He'd lived the life of a

dope-slinger and a hired gun for the Sureños, the Southern Mexicans, in the streets of San Diego, moving up the Southsiders' ranks to become an international drug trafficker. He knew he would die sooner or later; it had just turned out to be a little later, that was all. But upon hearing these words, he regained some of his fire in his belly. He forced his massive tattooed chest up and out once more, replying hard, 'I'm gonna kill you, you hear me? You're dead! No matter where you go, my crew'll find you and gut you like that piece of shit, Guerro. You remember what I did to him? Believe it homes, I'm gonna come get mine!' Bezerk spat out his venom, meaning every word like it was his last.

The voice retorted, 'Your people, your crew. You really are a stupid dog, you know that. How the fuck have you got so far in this game, anyway? Oh yeah, that's right, because of me! I gave you your life and now I'm gonna take your life. If I don't get what I want from you, then I'm gonna take your whole pathetic family's lives too!'

The voice laughed while Bezerk began crying, imagining his family being murdered. He answered fast and furiously, 'Aah, aah, I'm gonna fuckin' kill you, you piece of shit. You'll get what's coming to you, and I'll be waiting for you in Hell, belieeve thaatt!'

Laughing, the voice responded, 'Yeah, I know. I'll see you there, asshole. Be sure to hold me down a spot. Tell me what I want to know, then it can all be over and I'll consider letting them live.'

Only heavy breathing could be heard once Bezerk realized he couldn't find the words. He was falling from this world to the next, hallucinating and beginning to mumble incoherently. The assassin found it difficult to hold him up by his hair. Bezerk's mind hadn't registered what he'd just been told. He just felt content that he would soon be gone from this world and all its pain.

The voice's tirade picked up on the phone, taunting him again by saying, 'Hey Bezerk, your boys Beaver and Tavo, Coco and Jester are on the other line with me. You wanna listen to me giving them the order to take your family out? You can listen to the gunshots and all the screaming if you like or you can just tell me what I want to know. Tell me what you've done with my guest list. Were is it? I already know about the two of you, you fuck. You're dead and so is she. I hope she was worth it. You've ruined my life and that's why I'm taking everything you love from you, and then just like me, you're gonna lose everything. This is how you repay me after everything I've given you. Why'd you do it? Why'd you have to fuck everything up?'

In a child-like voice, the answer came, sounding hoarse over the phone, 'I don't know why. I just wanted to be like you, you know. That's all, just, I suppose, be you. Don't kill 'em. They're all I have. They're good people. They've got nothing to do with this. Please Mark, don't do it.'

The voice could be heard instructing others to ready themselves in a commanding English accent, talking to people that Bezerk knew all too well. The assassin began to ready himself for his final shot while Bezerk's mind filtered in and out of consciousness on his way to dying, feeling no further pain from his wounds. The voice said, 'I'm going to count from ten, and if I don't hear what I need to know, then you're going to be hearing your mom and dad, your sister, her husband and your cute little niece,all being taken out. I give you my mutherfuckin' word I'll kill 'em, and it'll be because of your cheatin', double-crossing ass, doogg! Five ... four ... you know how it works Chris, everybody dies. Shiitt, you were the one who taught me that. I don't give a shit anymore. Your family's gonna get ghosted right now and you're gonna listen while it goes down, so listen up, fool.'

'Wait, wait! Just wait a minute. I'll tell you what you need to know, please wait, don't do it! I'll tell you, just don't kill 'em, aah, aah, fuuckk, don't do it.'

There's a saying that the truth shall set you free, and Christopher Lee Wright was being set free for the first and last time in his life.

9

Having taken the service elevator up to the sixteenth floor, McGann and Keets were now standing in the fire exit stairwell. Richie keyed his radio to speak with hotel security, who confirmed that no one had left the penthouse suite.

Dan looked into the hallway to clear it. He then walked deftly to the far wall with his eyes locked on the door, his gun locked and loaded to neutralize any threat that came from that direction. Richie came out from the stairwell and picked his way along the near wall, until he came up opposite Dan. The penthouse door stood ajar, and from their position, they could hear sounds from someone clearly in distress. Giving each other hand signals, they moved nearer to the door. Richie dropped down onto his belly and began to inch his way up to it while Dan covered him, standing in a firing stance in the center of the hallway. Richie lowered his face and rested it against the threshold of the door, where there was a gap between the plush hallway carpeting and the lower marble-tiled floor inside. He made out the outline of a man on his knees with a man standing over him. Richie squeezed in further to the door to get an idea of what was being said. He heard, 'And if he chooses to not comply? I understand completely. Please hold one minute.'

Richie inched his way back away from the door. He estimated that the two men were approximately ten feet from the door, about four feet to the left. Richie and Dan backed away until they reached the fire exit stairwell again, so they could talk and assess the situation.

After telling Dan what he had seen and heard. 'What do you think?' Richie asked.

As the senior officer on scene and Richie's elder by six years, Dan replied with some menace, 'It doesn't look like we're going to need a negotiator and S.W.A.T.'s too far away to help. Sounds like it's a hit all right, and this guy's gonna off the dude any minute, so I guess it's bust and bang time, bud. You still got it in ya?'

Richie answered, 'Yeah,' in a resigned way, while Dan smirked at his expression. Dan then keyed his radio to notify the police officers on scene that, as commanding officer, he had made the decision to go in and take the perpetrator down now.

They discussed their final approach in hushed tones, and then moved back out into the hallway. Dan knew he would have the element of surprise. He focused on the positioning of his target and stated in a hard way to reassure himself, 'Someone's dying today.'

Getting his mind sharp, he took up his position as far to the right as he could in the hallway, standing about four feet away from the door with Richie crouched beside him. A silenced gun shot rang out. They heard someone crying out in pain. Seconds now meant the difference between life and death. Dan began to count down softly, saying, 'Ten, nine, eight ...'

Richie was on one knee, getting ready to run at the door. He nodded with the count, thinking, *Man, I hope I don't end up catching some lead in my ass.* The element of surprise was on their side. That and Dan's training in the art of war, one shot, one kill. Dan mouthed out, quietly counting down, 'Four, three ...'

10

'Okay then, tell me without bringing shame to the game. Tell me now!' The voice shouted.

Bezerk jerked his head back against the barrel of the gun, trying to knock the assassin off balance. 'I'd rather die on my feet like a man than live on my knees like a coward!' Bezerk roared, determined to end his life as he had lived it, going hard in the paint, one last time. The assassin quickly regained his composure and got back into his triangular shooting stance while Bezerk tried to stand up. The assassin took aim. Knowing his orders were clear from the start when he took on the contract. He screamed, 'Consider your ticket to Heaven revoked!'

Bezerk could literally feel the tightening of the trigger on the assassin's gun from behind. The door exploded open and a body rolled into Bezerk's field of vision. His eyes popped out of his skull as he desperately tried to indicate the position of the gunman. Bezerk's heart was killing him with every heartbeat, and now, in the dying seconds of his life, he was about to be saved. He saw a muzzle flash from another gunman out in the hallway. The flash blinded him and the loud boom deafened him. Then in one fluid motion, he fell onto the floor into his own pool of blood, while his nerve endings sent out an S.O.S. that registered nothing. The flash he had seen had been nothing more than his life flashing before him. A millisecond of the life he had lived. Now, his lifeless body lay crumpled on top of his brains, having just been blown out by the assassin. McGann had been forced to adjust his targeting before he could shoot, due to the assassin having to change his stance. The irony of it was that Bezerk had caused his own death in the split second timing between the shots being fired between the two gunmen. Before Bezerk's corpse had even caught up to his brains on the floor, Dan had taken out the assassin, who never knew he had him in his sights. One shot, one kill. Dan exhaled and lowered his Smith and Wesson nine millimeter to his side.

Richie rolled up onto one knee with his gun raised. He quickly realized that both men in the room were dead. The body on the floor was all twisted up in a patchwork of blood, brains and bone. He looked over at the assassin's corpse, which was sitting against the wall with no expression on its face. A thin, single bloodline ran down behind the assassin's ear. Taking a deep breath and exhaling, Richie shouted out, 'Clear!'

Dan came into the suite with uniformed officers running up behind him from the stairwell. In quick succession, the uniformed officers secured the penthouse with crescendos of, 'Clear! ... Clear! Clear!'

Richie crouched down and leaned over the slain corpse to look at the dead man's face, and then he quickly looked up at Dan in surprise and said, 'Dan, it's Bezerk.'

McGann responded succinctly in a long, pissed drawl, 'Shiitt.'

An officer came back into the room, remarking, 'We got two dead Jane Doe's: one known street thug, and one big question mark.'

Dan then looked over at the dead assassin for the first time, and instantly realized that it was the same man he had seen from the coffee shop, standing outside the hotel only some ten, fifteen minutes earlier. He'd been thinking *that should've been me living the high life*. Only, it had turned out that he was a low-life and was not having such a good day after all, getting tagged and bagged. The cops looked at each other. Neither one said anything to the other, but they sure were thinking the same thing. Dan spoke up first and said, 'This is really gonna fuck some shit up. Bezerk getting iced will push this case to the top of the heap. I guess we'll be putting' in some late nights after all.'

There was no hint of sarcasm on Dan's face as he said it this time. Richie looked as if he was about to respond, when he looked past Dan over his shoulder at the penthouse door, and Dan heard a voice from behind him say, 'Looks like the Westside Pimps have struck again!'

Detective Ray Tombs spoke sarcastically as he and his partner, Detective Dave Blisset, entered the suite, aiming his dead panned smile at Dan. Blisset laughed with him as they walked up to Bezerk's body.

Blisset said, 'can I get a yo?' laughing at his own greeting. 'Man, it sure looks like you guys have had one hell of a cookout in here and everyone's done over crispy. So what's this we hear? You two were conveniently across the street while this was going down and just happened to get in here and take the perp' out before S.W.A.T. arrived?'

'Yeah, all neat and tidy, man, you boys sure do work quick. You two knew him pretty good, right? So who took Bezerk out, the perp', or you guys?' Tombs' words had stung as they were intended, backing up his partner to seal the deal on their thinly veiled accusations.

Keets reacted sharply by saying sternly, 'Fuck yoouu!'

Richie got up in his face and stood toe-to-toe with Tombs. Both cops were running hot, standing over Bezerk's cold body, getting ready to throw down. Tombs gave Keets a small smirk and followed that up with a knowing look to his partner. They opted to walk into the master bedroom where they then began to talk in hushed tones. Some uniformed officers chose not to make eye contact with Dan or Richie, while others seemed to hang about the suite, unsure of what to do next. A few officers stole a quick look at them as they continued with their work. The air was thick with tension from Tomb's and Blisset's accusations that had left a nasty stench hanging in the room like six-day-old pork bellies.

Dan focused his thoughts and began to take back control by dishing out some instructions. He turned his attention to the uniformed sergeant, saying, 'There's a black Porsche parked downstairs in the driveway belonging to the perp'. I want it sealed and readied for C.S.I. There's a parking attendant who spoke to the perp' too, hang on to him.'

With that, the suite came alive again, as all the officers got back to business. Crime Scene Investigation officers arrived and began their work, while two coroner vans pulled up at the hotel's rear entrance to take four dead bodies to the morgue.

Danny McGann and Richie Keets stood by the penthouse door in preparation for leaving. They both surveyed the room one more time. Then they both took one last look at Bezerk's body lying on the floor. Dan bore his eyes into Richie, and Richie did the same back at Dan in an understanding way. Not a word was spoken. They left the penthouse, leaving the carnage and the past in their wake.

11

The temperature in Miami was a blistering ninety-eight degrees with a humidity factor of about eighty-five, but at least there was an intermittent warm, crisp, breeze that swam into the large, austere home office through the open patio doors.

The deep, cherry brown, high-backed leather chair swung around to face the view of the one hundred and thirty foot long Sunseeker Predator moored at the bottom of the pristine, manicured garden. An electric blue circle of thick cigar smoke rose up from the front of the chair, a perfect circle every time. A voice could be heard coming from the chair. 'Get it done and make it messy. You know how we do. Yeah, he's gone, been a long time coming.' Carrying on after a pause, 'Now he's got to go, too. Yeah well, that's how it is. Tell Beaver not to worry about getting out; it's all been arranged in Mexicali. He's just got to get there, and then they can all disappear from there. Yeah okay bud. Speak to you later, Adrian. Thanks for taking care of this last thing for me.'

He hung up the phone and drew hard on his Avo cigar, savoring its taste while savoring the spoils of war, thinking about what had gone down this morning. The man sitting in the chair was a happy guy. Swinging his chair around to face the cabinet behind his desk, he bent over, placed his encrypted SWIFT cell phone in the safe, and shut its heavy door. Spinning the dial to lock it, he then kicked the chair back around. He then noticed one of his favorite songs by Sade playing on the radio. It made him think about her, and the life he'd chosen. That got him thinking, *Mi vida loca*. He muttered to himself, 'My crazy life,' but then he said determinedly, 'Bad things happen to bad people.'

He had made his mind up years ago that he would go hard, all the way to make it. He had dared to dream and now this life he was living was his reality. He had money, power and respect, and he worked hard to keep all three by going the extra mile. He had realized a long time ago that by just going a few extra inches made all the difference. That had got him to where he was today. His legacy would soon be complete, securing his place in history. Content, he pulled on his cigar, thinking about his next moves. Learn from yesterday, focus on today and prepare for tomorrow - was how he lived his life, living in the details of it.

The phone on his desk rang. He answered it in a soft, warm tone, 'Yeah, Janey? Okay thanks, hun, it's about time he called. I got it, go get some sleep babe, okay?'

The girl questioned him about the caller with some

concern.

He listened for a minute and then, in a rich English accent that sounded soothing, he answered by saying, 'It'll all work out babe, no problem. You worry too much. Now go get some sleep. I'll see you later.'

The girl's voice on the other end of the line said something that made him laugh.

He answered, 'Yeah, I'm glad you're home, too. Okay, little pop, don't worry. Love you too. Put him through.' He stiffened up in his chair and straightened his back. He was the first to speak once he realized the caller was on the line, having heard him cough over the phone. He greeted the caller by saying, 'Good afternoon, Mr. Vice President, how are you today?'

'Great thank you. I'm just lovin' life and livin' it large,' he replied sarcastically.

Mark Knoxx gave the caller his complete attention as they got around to discussing what had happened back in Los Angeles.

12

'Listen up, all of you. This is one of those high profile murders that the media just loves to blow up out of all proportion. They've already given it a cozy headline for the six o'clock news, The Bezerk Murders for Christ's sake!'

For the third time in the past hour, Captain Pete Wyatt had worked himself up into a heated frenzy. He was now stalking up and down the rows of the twenty or so seated detective's, making sure each one got the message loud and clear.

He said with some concern, 'And here you all are, my crack squad of detectives, and what do you have? Nothing, zip, nada, you've got no leads, is that what I'm expected to believe? Well, you can be sure that if the media's all over this case, that means they'll be all over this department, and, if they're all over this department, then they'll be all over me. So guess what? That means I'm gonna be all over you guys like a hundred dollar hooker on a cheap suit. Got it?'

Returning to the podium and smacking down his folder, he looked back at the detectives filling the briefing room, demanding, 'No one's to give any interviews without my authorization. No leaks and no exclusive exposé's, do I make myself clear ladies and gentlemen?'

Leaning his elbows on the podium, he tried a different approach, skilfully rallying his troops; Captain Wyatt spoke a little softer, 'Look guys, I don't have to tell you how this one looks. Shiitt, this is Hollywood! Everyone just pull together on this one, okay? Get out there and do the job that I know you can all do and wrap this up fast. Make me and this department proud.'

Richie filled the void left by Captain Wyatt, 'We had no choice. The perp' wasn't going to let us bring him in. We had to take him out. He was clearly a professional hit man. We just got lucky that we were across the street in the diner. Otherwise, he might have got away clean.'

'I don't need to hear that!' Wyatt retorted, jumping all over Richie. 'That's old news. What I want to know is who sent a hit man and why? And we have no leads, is that what I'm hearing? Bullshit! Don't feed me that.'

Seeing his opportunity, Ray Tombs jumped into the deep end and interjected, 'The Porsche was stolen from an office parking lot in Beverly Hills. Early reports on the perp' are that there are no prints on file. We're running him through Interpol. Obviously, it would have helped if he'd been brought in alive, but hey, what you gonna do?'

All the other detectives looked grim, understanding Ray's accusation.

'What the fuck's that supposed to mean, Tombser!' McGann spat his words scathingly from his seat at Tombs.

Ray Tombs stuck to his guns, answering, 'Come on, guys, we all know Bezerk was your favorite gangbanger. You had something going on with him, right? And you two are conveniently across the street when this is going down and end up taking the hit man out who killed Bezerk?' Tombs pushed hard on the Westside Pimps, trying to take them down a few notches in front of the squad.

Dan jumped out of his seat with his face like thunder. Ready to rip out Tombs' throat, shouted, 'You piece of shit!'

Wyatt got in the thick of things, trying to keep the two of them apart, while Tombs shouted, 'I'm just putting it out there! It's what we're all thinking. I'm just the one saying it, that's all.'

Putting his hands on their chests, keeping them at bay, Wyatt barked, 'Look, you two, this better not start stinking up my office, you hear me? I don't care what the two of you've got going on, but I'm telling you this. If there's something I need to know, then one of you had better tell me now, because if I get a whiff of something not right about these murders, then I'll have your badges and your asses. And if I hear about you two going at each other's throats again, the same goes, got it?'

The squad looked on in silence, knowing what was going on. It was common knowledge that Dan and Richie had been out on the town most nights in search of the serial killer who was doing the prostitutes and strippers throughout Hollywood. They all knew that, for some reason, Bezerk had been off limits as The Westside Pimps had him locked down. He was Dan and Richie's number one boy, and the number one club of choice that they liked to hang out in was NVS, and it was only a matter of time before the media found out.

'I got a call from a guy saying he had information on our serial killer. We were supposed to meet him in Edie's Diner at nine o'clock. I noticed the perp' pull up across the street while I was waiting for the informant. I had no idea what he was there for.' Dan paused to collect his thoughts, and then said, 'You know the rest. It's in my report.'

'Well, what's not in your report is who the trigger man was, who was he talking too on his phone and why was Wright taken out? So let's go after the person on the other end of the call. Focus on who ordered the hit and why!' Wyatt growled with resolve, while he looked for some hint of ideas from the detectives.

'Wright, we know all about,' Richie said, while he thumbed through his notes. He continued, 'A history of violence, grand theft auto, home invasions, drug trafficking and a soldier for the Southsiders. We've been banging heads with him since he came up from San Diego to run NVS.'

'Yeah, he moved up in the world there,' Dan said, following up. 'I checked the F.B.I. and the D.E.A.'s database and both came back as restricted files.'

Wyatt sat down at their desk and took on an inquiring tone, replying, 'Really?' He gave Dan the briefest of waves, indicating for him to continue.

Dan said, 'Every time I entered the names for Christopher Wright and his a.k.a. Bezerk, it kept coming back as restricted access with a contact name for the F.B.I. in La Jolla.' Looking through his notes, Dan found the name he had been looking for and called it out, 'A special agent, Maxine Dobro from the F.B.I.'

'Damn it! And I suppose you went ahead and called her to ask her why, right?' Wyatt replied, looking frustrated.

'Hell no! I'm leaving that for you,' Dan answered.

Wyatt seemingly brightened and said, 'Give me her number and I'll see what she has on him. What about this guy Bezerk running this club NVS. How did a guy like him end up running that prime piece of real estate?'

Richie threw it out there, asking him, 'You've heard of NVS?'

'Of course I've heard of it,' Wyatt answered him coldly, not having such a humorous day today.

'I know all about NVS,' Tombs offered up from his seat.

'Why don't you enlighten us all, please, Detective Tombs.'

Wyatt's tone of voice let everyone know that he was mocking him, while Tombs rolled right on through it by saying, matter-of-factly, 'The Envious Group's owned by an offshore entity based in the British Virgin Islands.'

'Okay, go on Ray.' Wyatt's tone now turned more respectful.

'Well, the Envious Group is wholly owned by a man who's a star on Wall Street. I own stock in one of his companies that's going public next week,' Tombs said coyly, flushing up while Wyatt frowned at how he sounded.

'That's great, Ray. Is there any point to this?' Wyatt asked, reversing his tone.

Tombs got back on track, explaining, 'The Envious Group owns around a hundred and fifty bars and clubs across the country, but it's only a division of a much larger holding company called Exile and that company's worth billions.' Looking pleased with himself, he kept everyone hanging, waiting on the punch line.

'Aannd?' Wyatt asked.

'Mark Knoxx is a billionaire and he'll be making a few hundred million dollars more after next week. So how did a drug dealer like Bezerk get inside a multibillion-dollar corporation like Exile? Or maybe, more to the point is why?'

Wyatt, now finally getting what Tombs was implying, looked at the blank faces staring back at him, asking them, 'Anyone?'

With no one offering anything, Wyatt came back to Tombs, asking him, 'Do you think Mark Knoxx could be involved?'

'No way, Knoxx is too big a player to be wrapped up in something like this. He's all about corporate mergers and acquisitions, Wall Street stuff. He's one of the power players and into the lifestyles of the rich and famous. He's from England, you know.'

Wyatt simply released a small 'aah,' as if that explained it all perfectly.

'Damn, dude, is that a woody in your shorts?' Detective Richard Groome, known as Groomie, shouted his one-liner from across the squad room and even captain Wyatt could not resist laughing with the others.

Wyatt took up a commanding position behind the podium again, and put his hands up to reason with them by saying, 'Alright, alright, settle down, guys. Here's what we're gonna do. McGann and Keets, along with Groomie and Bowen, you'll follow up on Wright and his known associates. Let's see how this thug got inside a multibillion corporation. I also want to know if this billionaire boy's club member, Mark Knoxx, had any direct ties to him, got it?' Wyatt looked at his detectives. They were with him every step of the way. Then he looked at Tombs and continued, 'And you and Blisset, along with Smart and Adwell, will work the paper trail on Exile and Knoxx, and Ray. Since you have such a hard on for Knoxx, you can call him and get a statement.'

A collective round of 'Woo hoo!' went up at Tombs' expense.

'Man, go hump a chair or something!' Groomie shouted, getting in one more stab as another round of laughter resonated around the room. The cops began to collect up their paperwork as the briefing came to a close.

Tombs couldn't help himself, even though none too many cops chose to listen to him, exclaiming, 'Yeah, laugh it up! Laugh all you like, but I'll be getting some insider tips from a guy who moves markets. I'm invested in his new IPO that's coming out next week.'

'You do that, playa'. Maybe you'll get a date out of it,' Richie replied fast, hitting him back hard. That caused another ripple of laughter to chime out throughout the room. Detective Caron Smart' infectious laugh helped to ignite the room in raucous laughter even further.

'Dan,' Wyatt remarked, motioning for him to walk with him, 'come to my office for a minute.' He left behind more rounds of laughter at Tombs' expense. Pete Wyatt wasted no time as he closed his office door, having barely sat down, he asked, 'So what do you have on Bezerk?' Exhaling a long drawn breath as he relaxed in his chair, he looked at Dan. Dan looked back and was about to speak when Wyatt's phone rang. He picked it up, looking frustrated at the interruption. 'Yeah Ang'?'

He looked out of his windowed office at Angie Thorley, the attractive five foot eight inches tall, long-legged, brown-eyed, super-neat and super-efficient personal assistant. She looked at him while she was talking. Wyatt took on a severe pain-in-the-ass look on his face, Dan noticed.

'Get outta here!' Wyatt exclaimed. Looking at Dan, he moved the phone's mouthpiece away for a second, to say, 'I got a Maxine Dobro from the F.B.I. on the line says she wants to speak to me.' He went back and spoke to Angie Thorley, saying, 'Yeah okay, Ang', put her on hold a minute.' Wyatt turned his attention back to Dan. While his phone line blinked, he asked flat out, 'Do I need to worry about this murder linking you and Richie to anything you two shouldn't have been involved in?'

'Nothing, Pete, we're clean. Wright was helping us take down a crew called The Club Bangers. My guess is he was taken out by one of the Cartels setting an old score. He's a big homey with the Southsiders. He had connections to the Mexican Mafia and he's been hands-on with the rest of L.A.'s finest gene pool.'

Wyatt leaned forward in his chair and, looking energized, barked, 'Well, get out there and come back with someone's ass tied to the front of your car's grill. Go do what it is you do.' Waving him off, he said, 'I'll see what the Feds know about this Bezerk guy.'

Dan made a hasty retreat, leaving Wyatt to fend off the F.B.I. agent who had got the jump on him. Walking down the corridor, he could hear the melee gathering steam. 'Wall Street's built on suckers like you, Tombser. You might as well just put it all on red in Vegas!'

Keets, Tombs and Blisset were going at it as Dan approached them. Carrying a mean-ass look on his face, he pulled at Richie once he'd caught up to them, telling him, 'Come on, let's go do some real police work and leave these wanna-be's to pimpin' the streets!'

The four of them picked up some pace while they walked along the corridor towards the exit, while Richie asked, 'How much have you got in this deal of yours with Knoxx anyway?'

'Forty grand,' Tombs answered.

'One good deed deserves another. Don't forget us when you're all moneyed up, will ya?' Richie asked, doing his best to make it sound petty, playing Ray as he held the door open for him. Richie laughed sarcastically as he walked through the door.

'Yeah, yeah, whatever. You two smart-asses remember this day. I have a life and a future. I intend to spend it wisely when I hit the big time with Knoxx's new deal next week.'

Both groups separated as they made for their cars in the parking lot, with Dan shouting back, 'Is that right? Oh yeah, we'll remember this day all right. You can be sure of that, the day you get your ass handed to you from your pal Knoxx, suckaa!'

They were rolling with laughter as they walked to the car. Ray was laughing too as he turned back around to face them. He walked backwards with his arms spread wide, and now some distance from them, he shouted back, 'Yeah, you'll remember this day sucker's, 'cause by this time next week, I'll be the one laughing all the way to the bank, baby. I've bought my ticket to Heaven!'

Spinning back around on his heel to catch up to Blisset, Tombs sauntered off happy in the knowledge that the shares he'd bought were a lock and Knoxx's new deal would pay off tenfold. Tombs was all in with Exile Corporation.

Dan started up his Ford Mustang.

'What a prick!' Dan remarked. Both of them laughed.

'No doubt, more like buying a ticket to Hell and back,' Richie confirmed. 'Man, once those Wall Street vultures start picking at your bones, it's over, dude.' He pictured Ray coming back to the station after his I.P.O. deal, broke.

'I heeaarrdd thaatt. Yeess siirr!' Dan replied in a deep, baritone voice, imitating Bezerk. They fell about in fits of laughter in the car. Dan then peeled out of the police headquarters parking lot and headed out onto the Sunset Strip. They drove towards Sunset Boulevard and Vine Street. They were headed for NVS.

13

Arriving outside the NVS nightclub, Dan and Richie were immediately surrounded by a mob of reporters and camera crews clamoring for sound bites. McGann gave a statement, saying that a press conference would be held later in the afternoon at police headquarters. Dan gave the two uniformed officers a cursory nod as they entered NVS. They were pointed in the direction of the club's office and told the person they needed to see was still on her way in to the club. Entering the office, they were impressed by the opulence of it. With floor-to-ceiling mirrored windows that looked out over all the dance floors, it had a conference table off to the left and a large teak office desk at the back wall. Behind the desk was an large fish tank with an array of tropical fish swimming lazily around. In the rear corner stood a fully stocked bar, with the centerpiece being a large, blood red, L-shaped couch.

'Pretty cool shiitt,' Richie remarked, as they strolled around the office.

From the window, Dan looked down at the cavern of the empty dance floor and replied, 'Yeaahh, pretty cool shiitt.'

Richie strolled over to the inside wall and sang out, 'Man, I like these.'

They both stood there admiring the pictures that had been drawn in pencil and pen. Each picture was a collage drawing that had a theme to it: European, Aztec, South American, an Italian period piece, an Asian Dynasty theme, and the last one closest to the door, was of a Russian Revolution. Richie asked Dan, as they studied them more closely, 'These must be worth some dough, huh?'

'They are nice pieces, aren't they?'

Looking at the door, Dan answered, 'Uh, yeah, they're exceptional.' Feeling caught off guard, he walked away from the pictures back to the middle of the office. He also felt uneasy as he was looking at a stunning young woman.

She walked over towards Dan and extended her hand.

Taking her hand in his, he asked, 'Thanks for coming in.'

'Hi, that's okay. My name's Olivia Marbela. Pleasure to meet you.'

'My name's Dan McGann, Detective Dan McGann, and this is Detective Richard Keets. We're with LAPD Robbery and Homicide.'

'How much are these worth?' Richie asked her, stepping in, breaking the uneasy atmosphere that Dan had created for himself.

Looking at Marbela, Dan was wishing he had showered

this morning.

Olivia Marbela answered, 'Oh, I don't know. Chris drew them. He said he liked to draw them because it reminded him of prison.'

They all agreed on one thing: Wright certainly had a talent for drawing. Talking about the pictures for a few minutes helped them bond with Olivia and melt away any tension in the air. Dan then waved towards the conference table, indicating that he wanted the interview to begin. They all sat down and got comfortable. Dan offered Olivia a number of drinks to convey that they were her friends and on her side. He also wanted to put on his best performance, as Olivia was definitely his type, being young, beautiful and exotic.

Olivia Marbela looked relaxed in a professional manner, sitting straight in her chair, dressed in a simple gray pinstripe business suit that looked anything but simple. With long, dark curly hair, jet black eyes and full lips, her face was exceptional. She looked and acted the consummate professional during her opening statements, speaking in detail about the background of the Envious Group and its relationship to the holding company, Exile Corporation. At twenty-nine, Olivia Marbela was knowledgeable and insightful in describing the inner workings of Envious and Exile to Dan and Richie. During the first forty-five minutes of the interview, Dan asked Olivia relatively easy questions, gradually working up to the harder ones as he went along.

He resigned himself to the fact that she was out of his league, having noticed the disconnected manner in the way she spoke to him. That, and the diamond bezel Rolex watch she stole a quick glance at, gave him a clue too. He decided it was time to step it up a notch. Richie sat beside him, knowing the routine; he sat with his pen poised to continue taking his notes.

'You said earlier; you've been with Exile for about three years now?' Dan asked.

Olivia nodded, saying succinctly, 'Yes, that's right.'

'Do you know if Wright ever had any direct communications with Mark?'

She stared back at Dan like a startled deer caught in the headlights of an oncoming car. 'During the time I've worked for Exile, I've never heard Mark speak to Chris, or of him, to anyone.'

'Do you happen to know how Wright came about getting his position in the Envious Group?'

'No, I don't.'

Olivia's eyes moistened, realizing the questions were getting more focused on Chris's relationship with Knoxx. Marbela was a company girl all the way but this seemed to be getting too weird and a little scary for her.

Dan's set up complete, he pushed on by enquiring, 'Let's come back to you for a moment, Olivia. How much are you paid by Exile?'

'I'm paid a hundred and eighty-five thousand a year, plus benefits.'

Dan had a newfound admiration for Olivia, but he kept his momentum, asking, 'As you stated earlier, your position in Exile is the V.P. of marketing and promotions?'

Olivia, motioning her head, confirmed, 'Yes, it is.'

'And what was Wright's position in Envious Group? I mean, you know, what did he do?'

Marbela seemed to stay on script, answering assuredly, 'Chris handled the security for all of the clubs, coast to coast, and managed the guest list for all our VIP's, making sure they all had a good time and had everything they needed.'

'Yeah, I'm sure he did,' McGann said in an off-handed way. He continued ploughing ahead, asking, 'And what was Chris paid?'

'I'm not sure if I can answer that. I've signed a confidentiality agreement. I think I'd better consult with our in-house legal counsel.' Clearly stumbling, Marbela now looked uneasy and her voice sounded a little distressed.

Dan sensed that he had hit a roadblock and offered her a way out, saying in a friendly manner, 'I'll tell you what. Give me a ballpark figure without saying the actual amount. Can you do that?'

Olivia released a hint of a nervous smile, showing her bright, white teeth in appreciation. She left Dan and Richie hanging while she thought about her answer. She then let out a nervous, 'I'd saayy ... aboouutt ...' Looking up above them, thinking, she finally said, 'Around fifteen times what I earn.'

Richie scratched it out on his notepad, doing the math. It came to two million, seven-hundred thousand dollars. Dan and Richie glanced at each other while Richie exhaled a small whistle. Dan knew he had hit something solid. He just had to dig a little deeper to find out what and he needed to get to it sometime in this lifetime. He questioned her hard now, asking, 'Who'd have the authority to approve that?'

His mind raced ahead of his question, expecting the answer he thought he already knew would come out from those luscious lips glistening back at him from across the table.

Olivia replied, 'Exile would.'

Not quite what Dan wanted as his answer. He carried on, by asking, 'Yeah, but who in Exile could okay it?'

'I guess Mark would be the one to approve it.'

Dan fired back, asking, 'Are you actually guessing, or do you know for sure?'

'I'm not guessing. I'd say Mark would be the only person who could approve such a salary.'

Dan ended their meeting, feeling Olivia was reaching for her answers. The hour had flown by in her presence. Walking out through NVS, Richie asked in an uninterested way, 'So are you all ready for the public offering next week?'

Olivia looked at them, somewhat bemused, answering, 'We're not actually the one's going public next week. I'm not involved in it.'

Dan tried his luck, asking her, 'But I thought it was all over the news that Mark was taking his company public next week? We have a friend who's invested in it.'

Olivia looked at them, with no apparent reason for knowing why they were asking her about it.

'Well, we're not. I mean, Exile's not. It's for one of Mark's companies that he's spun out from the Exile group. He's raising eighty billion dollars for it next week.'

Stopping in their tracks, Dan and Richie looked at each other and kind of laughed. Richie, checked that he had heard her right, asking, 'Did you say eighty billion with a B?'

Dan watched how Olivia was acting. By his estimation, she seemed quite genuine, relaxed and frank in her remarks, as if she wanted to win them over. So Dan asked away. 'Give us a run down on this billion dollar deal would you, Olivia?'

The three of them stood in the doorway of NVS on Hollywood and Vine, and just like that, all the missing pieces fell into place. Olivia didn't even know that she knew important pieces of information, and that had been the best part of the plan. As she explained Knoxx's project, she filled in the blanks, just like the drawings up in the office; a blank canvas was being drawn on.

The two Westside Pimps who were regular, hard charging, everyday street cops who earned their forty-six grand a year the hard way, they were now getting schooled in one of the most complex, billion dollar deals of the last decade that sounded exciting, visionary and deadly. And while a beautiful, unwitting twenty-nine-year-old explained it to them she unlocked all its secrets. Olivia Marbela had just blown The Bezerk Murders wide open. The Hollywood detectives had now stumbled onto a motive and, more importantly, they now had a prime suspect.

14

'Thanks for coming in on short notice guys.' Dan stood at the podium in briefing room B19 at police headquarters, the morning after The Bezerk Murders. It was a full house with some of the top brass sitting in on it. Dan was all business, as was Richie, looking dressed for success. The other officers knew something was up, but as to what, no one knew yet. They all sat quietly, or spoke in hushed tones, while they waited for things to get started. Dan opened with, 'Ladies and gentlemen, we are all here this morning to get to the bottom of the murders that we know as The Bezerk Murders. From here on out, our investigation will be known as The Enterprise.'

It was too irresistible, as most of the room cracked into laughter with a number of Vulcan salutes going up around the room.

Dan did his best to stay on script. He said firmly, but with a ring of humor, 'Our investigation's being called The Enterprise because we'll be going where no one has gone before.' His line helped to release some tension inside the briefing room.

'All right, my man Dan!' Big black Mike Adwell said, from the corner of his mouth while he chewed a toothpick.

His petite and pert blonde partner, Caron Smart, was seated on her ass that you could snap a quarter off. She laughed with Mike, bright as a button, and happily responded, 'Oh yeah, this is gonna be good.'

Standing firm at the podium and looking somberly back at the cops, Dan did his best to continue in as simple a fashion as possible by saying, 'Yeah it is what it is, so let's just get down to catching the bad guys, shall we? From here on, you'll all need to be on your best behavior.' Scanning the room, he looked at the likely suspects.

'If you'll just give me a minute?'

He then walked away from the podium and left the room.

Caron Smart and Richard Groome threw up Vulcan salutes to each other while everyone began to speculate in muffled tones about what might be going on. A door opened and Dan walked back into the briefing room with two women and captain Wyatt, who were shown to their seats while Wyatt walked up to the podium.

'I'd like to introduce you to the head of the F.B.I. Southern California Drug and Organized Crime Taskforce, special agent Maxine Dobro.' Wyatt indicated who she was with a sweep of his arm. She smiled radiantly at a few detectives with an air of confidence, sitting tall in her chair, emphasizing that she was a major player in all of this. Dobro mouthed the words, 'Hi.'

She looked sleek and slender in her designer cut business suit that accentuated her darkened features of long brown hair, hazel eyes and manicured talons. She chose to cross her long legs and point her toe towards the cops. She wore her age well, which was estimated by some in the room to be around fifty. Next to Dobro sat the other female, who Wyatt introduced as special agent Teresa Hadley from New York's FinCEN, telling the group that FinCEN stood for Financial Crimes and Enforcement Network. Wyatt explained that special agent Hadley monitored the world's banks, searching for irregularities and fraud. Hadley's slight but demure features hid a mesmerizing stare from her chocolate eyes. She smiled somewhat shyly in the general direction of the audience.

Captain Wyatt then looked at the Sheriff standing by the side door who, on cue, opened it. A girl in her late twenties stepped into the room accompanied by a plainclothes police officer that none of the detectives recognized. She was stunning in every way, looking like she had a mixture of black and Asian descent. Her long shiny black hair glistened under the hot lights as she looked at all the cops wide-eyed, not used to being the center of attention. She was shown to her seat and sat down next to Dobro who paternally patted her thigh, asking her, 'Are you alright, Olivia? Don't worry. Everything will be okay.'

Wyatt began his opening speech regally, saying, 'As you're all aware, this case has been given the highest priority. For those who have lost their loved ones, the City of Hollywood is asking the one question that we're unable to answer. Why? We must find the answer to this question. We must work together to bring down those involved and they must be brought to justice.' Wyatt scanned the room and carried on. 'No matter who's involved in this murder, our message must be a clear one. No one's above the law. Dan, would you please come up here?'

Wyatt gave way to McGann, who opened his segment respectfully if somewhat nervously, greeting the group, 'Hi guys.' Dan then nodded at a few faces as he gripped the sides of the podium to stifle his nerves and said, 'You're the best at what you do. I know this's true because I have the privilege of working with you all every day. The papers being passed back are for all of you to sign. If you don't want to sign them then you're excused from this briefing and from this case.' He watched the various expressions on faces as it all sunk in while they read the page, continuing, 'You're required to sign the National Security Act of 1947 that states that any information disclosed to you must be held in secret at all times and in the future. Failure to do so could result in prosecution.'

Everyone blinked hard, realizing that any fun they'd been having at the beginning of the meeting had now turned more serious. They signed the forms and sat in silence. Ray Tombs leaned into his partner, quickly saying, 'I had a feeling this was going to be big.'

Dave Blisset nodded. 'Don't get any bigger, bud,' he quipped back.

Dan then said matter-of-factly, 'I'd like to introduce to you to Maxine Dobro. She'll be able to provide some background on this case. Maxine.'

Stepping across to the podium, she instantly took control of the room by filling it with the poise and finesse of a seasoned speaker. Holding eye contact and looking around the room to make sure she held everyone's attention, she then spoke in a loud and confident tone, 'We have the execution of a well-known, high-ranking drug dealer, Chris Wright, in a high profile hotel in Hollywood. The murder of Wright's family members in Del Sol was carried out almost in unison. Wright's parents, sister, her husband and their eight-year-old daughter were murdered.'

Scanning the room, no one was fidgeting in their seat. The cops looked mortified as she continued, 'We also have confirmation, that in Mexicali, Mexico, in the early hours of this morning, two cars carrying seven males, fitting the descriptions of those who carried out the murders on Wright's family, were found dead. Their bodies were riddled with bullets and the cars they were in were set alight. The Mexican Federales will keep us posted on their I.D.'s when they're able to identify the bodies. This is clearly sending a message to someone, but by whom and more importantly why, we don't know. You may be asking yourselves, why's the F.B.I. here? Well, I'm here to represent the F.B.I. but I'm not officially involved yet.' She lifted herself up on her toes and raised her voice at the podium, saying, 'Just like in all those bad-ass cop movies, I get to say the line, "You've got forty-eight hours to get me something before the Feds take over the case!"'

The room rang-out with some light relief, as Dobro had said it in good humor.

She then said, 'I believe that by letting you guys work the streets of L.A, you'll break this case open, and then we can go public. As you'll soon see, it can only be done this way because we're looking for specific information. You'll soon realize that we're up against some worthy adversaries on an international level. Whatever support you need, I'll be happy to provide you with any assistance I can. Good luck, ladies and gentlemen, but remember, the clock is running.' Dobro then looked to her left and said, 'Teresa. Everyone, Teresa Hadley with FinCEN.'

Special agent Hadley rose quietly, not making eye contact as she picked her way across to the podium. Dan caught her scent and felt himself instantly attracted to her. She caught the eye of several of the detectives in the room. Dan watched as she walked intently on her five foot seven inches tall, slim, dark olive-complexioned frame, topped off with shoulder-length chestnut hair. He caught her smooth rhythm as she passed by him.

'Hi everyone.' She opened her speech as if a little unsure of herself, saying, 'I hope I have the opportunity to get to know you all a little better over the next few days.' She seemed to catch herself. 'Although I know you don't like the Feds in your business, so maybe not too much getting to know you then,' she quipped with a timid smile that managed to get everyone to laugh with her politely, helping to break the ice.

Deciding that it was time to get professional, she hit the button on a laptop computer that had been placed on the podium. A PowerPoint presentation lit up on the back wall, magnifying the first page for everyone to read. She glanced at the screen too. Hadley then turned back to the room while everyone was reading it. The screen showed a family tree with boxes connected by lines, leading to other boxes, all of which led up to one box and one name at the top:

The Enterprise

'This is The Enterprise,' Hadley stated coldly.

This time, no one laughed or made Vulcan signs. Everyone's eyes were fixed on the screen. She explained in detail what each name inside each box did and how it was connected to the next name in the next box above it. Some of the company names were known, and some weren't. Some were names of individuals who were known, and some were not. Hadley kept the room enraptured with her savvy financial presentation. All the cops were getting an inside look into the inner workings of high finance, when most could not even balance their own check book.

'The Enterprise is involved in hostile takeovers, mergers and acquisitions, all of which is legal. The Enterprise has a global reach. The companies and the individuals shown here have a global reach inside everyone's lives; yours and mine,' she said, standing firm, having found her poise. Comfortable in the realm of her own expertise, she continued strong, 'The Enterprise is everywhere we eat, drink, shop and sleep. They communicate to each other across the world through shell companies, consultants, and straw man C.E.O.'s, and that is illegal. The Enterprise monitors all of your purchases, and

46

then they figure out how you bought what you did and why you bought it, cross-referencing all the data within their databases.'

Teresa Hadley was then peppered with questions coming from concerned citizens, not from police officers. She answered each one with as much information as she was prepared to provide, knowing there was so much more she was not telling them. During her presentation, everyone waited while they all ventured a look at the name at the top of the chart that headlined it. It was all too much to comprehend, because everyone knew that companies maintained their private information on databases. It had, in a way, become the normal procedure; it was simply accepted. No one had any idea what was really going on with their personal information that was being used to manipulate and control them. All the boxes led to one name at the top, a company that controlled them all. A name they all knew well:

Exile Corporation.

Hadley completed her presentation, having explained each company's position and its relationship to Exile Corporation. She then explained why her bosses in New York had brought her into the investigation, because they were frustrated that the F.B.I. in California weren't able to crack the code for The Enterprise. The F.B.I. still had ways to rein in perceived criminal organizations, and special agent Hadley was it. She was an expert in International Tax Law and Forensic Taxation and Accounting. Just like in the 1920's when the Feds brought down Capone on tax evasion charges, she was going to do the same to The Enterprise.

Taking her time, she made sure everyone in the room was on the same page, before taking one last look at them, and then saying, 'This is why we're talking to you and why we need your help.'

Hitting the button on the laptop, another chart appeared on the screen. This chart had its own set of boxes that were all linked by lines. Much like the chart before, they all led up to the box at the top.

Seeing the name in the top box, the hairs on the backs of Danny and Richie's necks stood on end. Ray Tombs felt a flush of excitement and anxiety run through his body as he absorbed it all. Olivia Marbela became familiarized with the names, while Maxine whispered in her ear to confirm that what they were looking at was all in order and correct. A chill ran through the room, along with another hush from all the assembled cops waiting to see what this all meant. Their eyes were fixed on the one name that looked back down on them with such contempt in gold block lettering:

HEAVEN

'That's what I've invested in. I know all about HEAVEN,' Ray quipped.

Dave, responding quickly, replied, 'I don't think so, buddy.'

Teresa stood off from the podium, while more papers were passed around. Moving back to the podium, Hadley slowly and succinctly spelled out the word so everyone would have a full understanding of what each letter stood for. Saying in a slow manner, she said, 'HEAVEN: Hospital Evaluation and Authenticated Vitals Encoded Navigator. It's a revolutionary piece of electronic software that's been designed by Mark Knoxx. The hardware, being the Navigators themselves, is also being produced in-house by Exile Corporation.' Moving out from the podium, finding her rhythm, her flow continued, 'HEAVEN is fully funded by Exile Corporation, and hospitals throughout the world will benefit from it lowering the risks from overworked doctors working under stress, making wrong decisions when diagnosing a patient.' Looking strong, she made eye contact with her audience. 'Look, let's face it, doctors are only human and they make mistakes, only their mistakes often lead to innocent people dying. Patients dying in hospital leads to wrongful death suits and that leads to higher insurance rates for the rest of us. It doesn't look good, does it? Remind me to never be on the front line with you guys. I don't want to get shot, thank you very much,' she said, bringing the room to a convergence of giggling.

Caron Smart nudged her partner, Mike Adwell, asking him, 'You'd take a bullet for me, wouldn't you, honey?'

Both laughing, Mike replied, 'Yeah, sure I would, babe, anytime.'

Hadley carried on, stating bluntly, 'The insurance companies are haemorrhaging hundreds of millions a year from wrongful death suit insurance claims, and death rates in hospitals are around sixty thousand a year. Pretty scary, huh? Over the next twenty-five years, there will be around ten thousand baby boomers retiring each day, totaling around seventy-five million people.' Now looking intently at the cops, she asked them, 'Can you all see where I'm going with this?'

Their faces told her that they did. They were now beginning to see the magnitude of this case, realizing the scope and depth of Knoxx's empire. The genius of it.

Hadley then said, 'So, in steps Mark Knoxx to save the day with HEAVEN. Having successfully completed its trials, it will be distributed to hospitals throughout the world in a matter of days. Hospitals that have used it in the trials are saying that it's nothing short of a miracle. A miracle sent from Heaven, no less.'

A three-dimensional picture now began playing on the wall as she spoke further, 'HEAVEN can provide real time, zero tolerance diagnoses for patients by accessing their records and then cross-referencing them with other patients' records who've been treated successfully for the same disease or ailment. All this is done through the Navigator in a matter of seconds, telling the doctor the precise amount of drugs to administer and in what order. Mr. Knoxx is so confident it will be a success that he's offered to underwrite any lawsuit or insurance claim being filed, arising from any failure associated with the use of HEAVEN.'

Moving across to make eye contact with Dan personally, as if to get her point across, she said, 'I've estimated that Knoxx will earn around eight hundred million from the sale of Navigators and further billions from licensing fees.'

She calmly sipped some water. Tombs was the first to speak up, asking nervously, 'All these boxes that are linked to Knoxx, some are known crime families. I'm invested in HEAVEN, so I'm set, right? He said it would be a global killer. What's up with Knoxx? Do these guys want to kill him because it's going to be so successful?'

Ray got animated and Teresa got irritated. Tombs had asked his question with some genuine concern for Knoxx's safety. Hadley's contempt overflowed, just as her glass of water did when she put it down on the podium. For the first time showing her inner strength, she retorted, 'No, detective, Mr. Knoxx isn't in any danger, at least not from the names listed here. We're the ones in danger. Make no mistake, there is a global killer in all of this, and his name is Mark Knoxx, and we are going to take him down!'

15

A tangerine glow engulfed the downtown skyscrapers, the sun's glow mixing in with the night sky that was slowly but surely creeping up over South Beach, Miami. The beach scene was beginning to pick up, as happy hour kicked in around town. The markets were closed and the only items that consumed the news were the multiple homicides that had taken place in California, the reporters referring to them as The Bezerk Murders.

Knoxx watched the news reports with amusement, taking care to watch the interviews with detective Dan McGann and a certain special agent, Teresa Hadley. He took great delight in hearing McGann state that they were following up on all leads, which was code for the fact that they had none. He laughed, watching McGann explain how he'd had no choice but to take the gunman out, shooting him dead.

'That's why I picked you, my man Dan,' Knoxx said quietly, while he drank from a glass.

Watching a virtual game play out in real time, he felt a rush of sexual heat run through him. He was the puppet master and his puppets were doing what they were meant to do, whether they knew it or not. Mark Knoxx lived in the details. Death waited in the middle ground and mediocrity thrived in the vastness of living day to day. Fail to prepare, then prepare to fail. He had prepared for this final game. All the right people were now in play, using lessons that he had learned on his way up the ranks of Wall Street, reading the lessons in *The Art of War* to guide him. If you didn't play the game his way, then he would instruct his army of stockbrokers to march up and down Wall Street and kill you off. He would buy you out or buy your company out. He had built an empire over a few short years, and with one phone call he could make or break any deal as he pleased.

He was a smooth operator and charming to all who came in contact with him. He was a buccaneer, a visionary and a leader, but he seemed like he was a man who carried himself with an air of danger. Knoxx had walked the line in more ways than one a few years back. There's a fine line between genius and madness, and now he was walking on a knife's edge where one slip and it would be his last. He had once been quoted in *Time* magazine as saying, 'I don't need to be the smartest guy in the room, just the richest.' When he had been asked about his meteoric rise to wealth, fame and power, Knoxx had explained that it was due in part to the amazingly talented team he had around him. He was the poster boy for the American Dream, whether he was promoting himself or one of his companies. At six foot two, two hundred and twenty-two pounds, with dark brown hair and blue eyes, wrapped in a muscular build, the media loved him. He was the Wall Street killer and the darling of Main Street, always being photographed with the actress or model of the moment. Women wanted to be with him and men just wanted to be him.

He had arrived from England with the three ingredients for success that were curiosity, passion and ambition. He hunted for high net worth investors. He gained their trust by offering them first look deals in his companies; Knoxx had learned his craft well. He was known as the best in the venture capital field, being known as the man who could move markets. He'd become an enigma, having recently immersed himself within his core group of trusted friends.

His best friend, Jane, the gatekeeper holding his secrets safe worked as his personal assistant. Alisha Ellington, who he had dated but remained friends with, came on board as his media coordinator. He also had his legal counsel, Matthew Tamban. And last but not least, Olivia Marbela, who was the vice president of marketing and promotions. Everyone played their role and everyone knew the score. When Mark Knoxx knocked, opportunity knocked.

Always finding time to meet with prospective clients no matter where they were in the world, he would be there to close the deal, using whatever means at his disposal to get the job done. Entertaining clients in his Gulfstream jet or on his Predator super yacht, in any of the NVS clubs, he thought local while working global, living life in the details. This was Mark Knoxx's life, his life in Exile.

He finished an evening meal of peppercorn steak wraps with a Niçoise salad, sautéed mushrooms and seasoned, crispy curly fries, washing it down with a red Chianti wine brought up from the wine cellar. It was finally time to dial it down and reflect, while he sat out on the patio by the infinity pool. Listening to the bubbling brook of the Jacuzzi, he found comfort in reflecting back on his life and on what he had accomplished to date. Life is full of choices and to make no choice is to have made a choice, but every choice has its consequences. He had made his choice a few years back from which there was no getting out now. His past choices provided him with all of his wealth, fame and power. His choices had also led him to this night.

As the lights flickered, bouncing off the shimmering pool, he reflected on what his life might have been like, had he taken a different course and had he made a different choice. Because tonight, he could only think about how he would be murdered too.

16

Having signed off on his e-mails and finished his phone calls for the day, Knoxx laid back on a sun lounger. He lit up a Cusano 18 Maduro cigar and savored its taste while he reveled in delight at how his meticulous planning had worked out on schedule. The murder of a drug dealer in Los Angeles had ignited the media's imagination about why it had taken place just as he'd hoped it would. It was clear that even though Dobro was Hadley's boss, Hadley had now taken the lead in the investigation. Knoxx had watched as agent Hadley said, 'In the course of our conducting an ongoing multi-department investigation, we have determined that one of the victims, Christopher Wright, was linked to organized crime on an international level. This murder has led to FinCEN, the Financial Crimes and Enforcement Network, to uncover ties linking Wright to numerous offshore bank accounts whose account holders may be involved in criminal activities.'

When Dobro did make a statement, she had said succinctly, 'Heaven only knows where this investigation will lead us, but mark my words, those of you who've perpetrated this heinous crime; you will be brought to justice. I guarantee you that.'

Having finished watching the evening news, it was clear to him that he would have to take one more step before he had any chance of living a normal life again. Taking a long draw on his cigar and then filling his mouth with a finger of Jack and Coke, Mark now knew that they knew. They knew about him. Something he'd known for some time, but now he had to know what they really knew. They already knew too much, but it was amusing to watch it all unfold as he had anticipated. The stakes were too high to let it all fall into their laps, as they were hoping it would. Hope was not a strategy. They obviously had their game plan, and so did he, and his was always in motion. The difference between decision and action is motion and now he had concluded that it was time to put his final play in the game. Knoxx was a Scorpio, and his tail would really sting when he struck back.

There was also an unexpected comedic moment when it came to the business segment of the evening news. It was as if a self-fulfiling prophecy had taken divine intervention and opened a conundrum, wrapped inside an enigma, sealed inside Pandora's Box. The business analyst began by saying, 'And in other news, the world will sleep a little more soundly next week, knowing that Heaven watches over all of us, when Exile Corporation unveils its new medical Internet program called HEAVEN. It will provide up-to-the-minute medical diagnoses for millions of patients by accessing hospital records to administer the precise dosage of drugs. The Internet program, developed by Exile, is being taken public in an Initial Public Offering on the New York Stock Exchange next week.'

The news analyst then described the design and the applications of HEAVEN. He signed off with a final philosophical summary. 'It makes one wonder. We have become so dependent on technology in our lives, and now our very lives could hang in the balance, depending on it. Who is truly the master of whom? If history has taught us anything, it's that what has been dreamt up for the good of mankind has so often made its way into the hands of those wishing to bring harm to mankind. Let us all hope and pray that there is a God in Heaven, because after next week, thanks to Mark Knoxx, HEAVEN will really be watching over all of us.'

Genius or madness, the world would know soon enough. Closing his eyes, he drifted off into a dreamscape with the aroma of cigar smoke in his nose and the taste of whisky on his breath, a content smile on his face and a warm glow in his heart. Where the heart leads, the mind follows, and at this point in time, he was leading and the rest were following.

An electric shock ran through him from a touch. Knowing that touch well, it gave him an instant arousal that sent a bolt of animal instincts through him.

Keeping his eyes closed, he inhaled her perfume while her long, toned legs enveloped him. Her warm skin rubbed hard against him as she sat across him, pushing her ass down into his lap to feel how hard he had become. Her long legs easily reached across him, planting themselves on either side of the sun lounger. She smelled sexy and hot to the touch, as she let out a low-pitched hum in excitement.

Her open sheer, chiffon robe kept her body humming at just the right temperature, while she tossed her large mass of long, bouncy, curly blonde hair over his face. Her lips touched his, so very soft and seductively, while he played along with her, pretending to be asleep. He felt a slight push in his mouth while she worked her tongue into it. Beginning to force herself on him while her hair fell about his face, she began to smother him in hard passionate kisses. The tingling, tap dancing sensation from her kisses helped to make him harder, causing him to want her even more. Knoxx opened his eyes just a touch and seductively sighed, 'Aahh ... Nicky.'

Finally giving into her, he pushed his tongue into her mouth, while he grabbed her tight, hard ass that was so round and full. Digging his fingernails into her hard ass, she moaned in delight and released a small whimper of excitement, followed by a naughty giggle that gurgled up from deep inside. Mark tore into her in a fit of hard, passionate kissing, and then in an instant, they pulled away from each other and looked deep into each other's eyes. Nicky's teal green eyes were filled with lust, shining with a warm sheen of love, but tears were welling up in them as she looked into his ocean blue eyes. They fell into another kiss that was longer, deeper and harder, with Nicky pushing her hips down deeper onto his hard, pulsing manhood. He ravenously worked his hands inside Nicole's robe and began to pull aside her pink, lace panties, while she became more excited and wet, thinking about the two of them fucking right there on the patio. Nicky pulled at him and started to bite him, while he pulled on her long hair and bit her red-hot, lipsticked bottom lip. She got to work, riding him hard and putting him away wet. The night's moon danced across the bay, lighting their way to the heights of ecstasy like Japanese lanterns festooned across the bay. Lighting each other's fuse, they exploded inside each other, bringing Nicole to a happy, tear-filled crescendo.

Nicole Young had been the cabaret act at NVS in New York that Knoxx had hosted fourteen months earlier. She had brought the guests to their feet, but with just one look at her, she had brought Mark to his knees. He would have paid any price to win her heart. She just didn't know how much of a price he had already paid.

17

Miami was in full swing, as it was seven nights a week with all the bars, restaurants and nightclubs banging and full to the brim. A smoky gray Rolls Royce Phantom pulled up to the curb. Its rear windows were blacked out, not allowing anyone to see who was riding hard inside; It was rolling on Hipnotics gun gray metallic, twenty-two inch rims. The car kept its engine purring and the air conditioning blasting. All eyes flashed along the line outside the club, trying to figure out who might be inside the car, while they patiently waited for the red velvet rope to rise. The sea of people around the entrance quickly parted when a giant hulk rose up from the front passenger seat. His skyscraper mass of bulging biceps flexed as his charcoal skin went taught. His eyes trailed along the line of onlookers to see if anyone wanted any action, because if they did, then it was going to go real bad, real quick. Quincy Taylor stood in front of the rear door on point. The elusive red velvet rope was lifted up and everyone outside the club knew to back away from the aircraft carrier that was parked up out front.

NVS was ready to accept them.

With one final sweep, Quincy opened the rear suicide door, and out stepped Mark Knoxx. He quickly turned back to the inside of the car to offer his hand, and then Nicole Young stepped out. Her long, shiny toned legs, garnered admiring glances from all the young Turks in line because she just made it all look so effortless, oozing sex appeal. Having had sex a short time earlier, she looked radiant in her little black, Vivian Westwood number, while Mark whispered in her ear, 'You look stunning, babe.'

Putting his hand on the small of her back, she smiled at him and her eyes glowed. Knoxx was rocking in a white on white, Versace ensemble, which was the dress code for South Beach. As he led her into the club, Nicky looked hot and Mark looked cool, Yin and Yang.

Corporate raider by day and badass playboy by night, he was a good guy but he was bad-boy, and he could rock in both worlds. He had EXILE tattooed along the back of his triceps and a tribal Scorpion wrapped around his left bicep. On his right bicep, he had a fighting dragon, symbolizing wisdom; it breathed fire across a shield that read 'One Life One Love'. A banner draped across the shield with the name 'Jane' on it, as a tribute to his first true love and his last true friend, Jane Mears. He was letting the world know that he could and would throw down if you wanted to test him.

NVS was jumping in Miami, like the rest of the clubs

throughout the Envious Group, and Knoxx was the number one baller at the number one club, as they entered it.

Gliding through the club, shaking hands and handing out kisses, they arrived at the V.I.P. lounge where a heavy throng of people were already busy enjoying the music and socializing. Mark instantly looked for Jane Mears, and once he had spotted her, proceeded to make his way over. After giving her a big hug, he bought her a well-deserved drink and then listened to her as she filled him in on the details of what had happened back in Los Angeles the night before.

From where Mark ate and slept right now, the air was filled with a feeling of invincibility that was intoxicating and all-consuming. Regardless of what his inner voice was telling him: it's all over.

In the V.I.P. lounge, the clubbers looked down periodically at the huge dance floor below filled with dancers having a good time. Knoxx and his party had everything at their beck and call, sipping on the best champagne, wine and liquor, while the dancers on the dance floor looked up at them periodically throughout the night, looking envious.

Nicole and Alisha spent most of the evening drinking and dancing, having a great time in each other's company. Nicky got up on stage and sang a few songs, singing one of Mark's favorite Alicia Keys tracks that brought the house down. Mark had realized some time ago that he had grown tired of tasting the Baskin Robbins 31 flavors of models and actresses. He had found his mirror image in this girl, Nicole Young, and he had been the man to fix the girl with the broken smile. Now they were both content just being in each other's arms. Nicole was the box of matches and Mark was the box of fireworks, and when they got together, it was like the Fourth of July. In spite of what he was dealing with in his life, against all odds, they had found each other and fixed each other's lives. In spite of himself, he had fallen in love with her. They had been separated only a handful of times since falling in love, when Mark had taken meetings that he could never tell Nicky about. But since their last separation a couple of weeks ago, she hadn't even wanted him to touch her. She had been crying most days, and he had been relentless in trying to find out why. Everyone answers to someone in the end, even a president, and Knoxx was no different. He answered to people who monitored his every move. Just as he had received help to achieve his goals, so he was helping others to achieve theirs.

Having noticed Mark on his own at the bar, Alisha saw her chance to begin peppering him with questions, trying to make sense of what had happened over the past two days. Knoxx answered her questions cryptically, knowing she probably knew. But he knew that Alisha knew what was best for her, which was keeping her thoughts to herself. He knew he could trust her to do just that, which was why she was on the team, and in any case, Jane would tip him off if anyone was falling out of line.

Alisha had been questioned a few days earlier about why Nicole had been crying so often. She had given him the answer he had been searching for. Even though it was something he hadn't wanted to hear, he had rewarded her with a Porsche Cayman for telling him the brutal truth. She knew what she had told him and how he had taken it. He had told her what he wanted to do to them to get revenge once she had told him what she knew, and it had been playing on her mind ever since. But she knew not to push it. She knew how he handled his business.

After having a disjointed conversation with him, she reassured Mark in an intimate way, saying, 'You know I love you, right? Whatever happens, no matter what, I'm here for you, okay? If you need to talk to someone, make sure it's to me. Just be careful, honey, please.'

Her eyes projected a lust-filled look that confirmed her intentions and desires. Letting him know she meant it with all her heart, she held Mark's arm to pull him closer, while he replied, 'Everything's under control. I'm okay. Trust me, I know what to do from here on out, and if I do need to talk to anyone, I'll make sure it's you.'

He glanced away to make sure they weren't being watched, realizing they were probably closer together than he would have liked; thinking it probably looked like they were having more than a casual conversation. Breaking away from Alisha's hold, he broke off from his thoughts and instinctively looked across the V.I.P. lounge, and his eyes immediately found Nicky. Their eyes met and Nicole blew an exaggerated air kiss at him before she smiled and waved happily. He walked away from Alisha, and waved for her to come and join him as he sat down in a chair. Watching her as she sauntered over to him seductively swinging her hips, he thought, *it'll all turn out all right on the night.* No matter how dirty Knoxx's hands were, he held everything and everyone in them, and tonight, it had all been worth it.

18

'Hi babbyy,' Nicole said, handing him a chilled glass of Perrier-Jouet champagne. She planted a wet kiss on his lips that tasted crisp and sweet. As she wrapped her long, taught arm around him and got settled on his lap, she said, coyly, 'How've you been, baby? Have you missed me?'

He replied, 'Baby, I've been missing you my whole life.'

'Aahh ...' Nicky answered. They laughed and then they kissed, playfully nuzzling. Afterwards, she said, 'I love you, Mark.'

Nicky's eyes flashed with a wet sheen in them as a serious signal. Feeling the heat from the despair in her voice, he answered, 'You're like the sun and the moon to me, babe.'

Nicole's eyes welled up, about to overflow in a torrent of tears again, just as she had been doing regularly over the past two weeks. The first hint of a tear ran down her cheek, the dam about to burst.

Pulling her in, taking her in his arms and holding her tight, Mark said reassuringly, 'You're my warmth in the winter and my shade in the summer, honey. You are my world.' Hugging her tighter, he looked into her eyes with all his soul, letting her know his truth. He said, 'Nicola, I know.' He said it menacingly, accentuating the word 'know' and using her real name.

Nicky could only wipe away a falling tear while she hovered on his lap like a child. She nodded aggressively, choosing not to open her mouth for fear of saying the wrong thing. She fell into his chest to nuzzle her face into it for the protection he gave her.

As he held her tight, his words sounded ominous, as he remarked, 'I'll always love you, Nicky. I'm trying to do the right thing, babe, but it always ends up being the wrong thing, or I'm mixed up with the wrong people, you know, trusting the wrong people. I'm not scared of anyone or anything, you know that, right?'

Nicole raised her head to look into his eyes. His words seemed to be encouraging, but they also sounded like a warning. She kissed him, giving him everything she had to give him in her soul, not knowing he'd already sold his for her. Nicole Young knew what Mark was capable of; she knew some of his past and had heard most of the rumors. She had accepted his habits, mood swings and his killer instincts. All she knew was that she simply loved him. Mark then joked, saying, 'You know what? I'm gonna take you home and fuck you like a porn star, babe, and then tomorrow, we're gonna go shopping and live life like a rock star!'

That brought Nicky back to a fit of tear-filled giggles. While she dabbed at her eyes to dry them, she answered, 'Hmm, yes please, I like the sound of that.'

They both laughed hard and then kissed just as hard, remembering how it had been on the patio earlier in the evening. Mark then said softly, 'I'll be right back, honey. I need to use the phone in the office.'

Knoxx waved over at his bodyguard, Quincy Taylor, and when he got over to him, Mark spoke in his ear. Quincy then stood tall and barked at the crowd nearest them, 'Make a hole, people.'

'I need the room.' Knoxx said coldly to the staff working in the office. Quincy threw off a look of bad intentions that helped them vacate it as quickly as possible.

Looking at his watch, checking the time zone difference, Mark knew he had made his mind up. It was time to put his final play in the game or risk losing everything. To not take a risk is the biggest risk of all. He sat at the desk and looked at the phone before picking it up, calculating how it would play out. Nicky's words hung in his mind, knowing how she meant it. 'Don't be too long, baby.' She was hungry for him. That had spurred him on. He was a lion when it came to protecting her, but it's the lioness that gets to choose which lion it wants to mate with and she had chosen him. To succeed, one has to be willing to fail. He had defended Nicole. Now he had to defend himself. Alone with his decision, he would be the only person to know what he was about to do. He knew he had to make the call. He knew the one person back in Los Angeles who would give him what he needed: inside information.

19

The press conferences had finally wound down and had helped drain everyone's enthusiasm for talking about the case back at police headquarters. The day was drawing to a close. Special agent Hadley was assigned a special desk to work from that sat opposite the door to the men's room. The cops thought it was highly amusing to watch her trying not to look as the door swung open every few minutes. Dan and Richie had spoken about her, and Dan had mentioned that he had respect for the way she had conducted herself in the press conferences. He had also realized during the day, that he had been looking in all the wrong places for a potential mate. Now, from where he was sitting, his potential mate wasn't too far away. Teresa had been giving as good as she got from the cops and took it in her stride. She was smart, funny and attractive, and she had been glancing Dan's way periodically throughout the day. Richie, as usual, put Dan in a tight spot. Richie stood at her desk as he dropped a file on it, asking her, 'So what time have you got to get back to your special agent man?'

Flashing a quick glance Dan's way, she tried to sound casual, replying, 'No G-Man waiting at home for me, I'm afraid, and you?'

Dan jumped in on that one, trying to get back at Richie, 'Oh yeah, you better believe it. As long as I write him a note, he's able to stay out at night.'

The two of them got into it in front of Teresa, firing a torrent of abuse and quick fire banter at each other, taking vicious, deeper cuts with every line they traded. She fell about laughing with them, and at them, as they fought like two little boys. After they had finished taking lumps out of each other, Richie finally got back to questioning Teresa, asking her where she was staying while she was in L.A. She told him that she and Maxine were staying at the Sunset Marquis Hotel on Alta Loma Road, which was not too far from the Sunset Tower Hotel.

Edging down on the corner of her desk, Richie asked, 'So what's Maxine's story?'

'If I tell you, will that get me a better desk?' she playfully answered.

Dan was taking to her more and more. She was cool and had a good sense of humor. He got in on the action again by saying it depended on how good her Intel' was, but said that he had enough weight in the division to get her moved. The two of them locked eyes for the first time. Neither one looked away until Dan had to, when he felt his face flush up.

She looked around the room, and it seemed that nearly every detective in the room was working on cases except them. But then, Dan and Richie were the Westside Pimps, and they had their own way of working a case. Teresa looked over at Maxine who had either been in meetings with Wyatt in his office, using his office, or talking on her cell phone. Teresa began by telling them, 'Maxine's a machine and she's relentless in keeping the Exile case moving forward, and she's definitely got a thing for Mark Knoxx.'

Teresa went on to tell them that Maxine had lost a handful of colleagues over the years. Some Maxine thought were murdered while investigating Exile Corporation, either to protect Knoxx or on his orders. Maxine was a single mother of two children, one boy and one girl. Dobro's daughter, Danielle, was a student at UCLA, studying law. Teresa mentioned that she had three children, a boy, and two girls. She checked Dan's reaction after managing to get that piece of information out in the open. Dan gave her a smile in a way that told her that it was cool with him. She then continued, and said, 'Maxine can be a ball buster, but she always comes through with the goods. She's got a big heart and she's fearless in her pursuit of what's right.'

All of them seemed to gaze over at her at the same time. Maxine was on her cell phone in Wyatt's office and she was already looking at them. She turned away once she realized they were looking at her, and continued her conversation behind closed doors. Dan gave Teresa a break by saying she'd done enough to get herself moved from the men's room desk.

'Thank God!' she exclaimed in mock excitement at having been accepted by them.

'Watch out Trace, it looks like you're in Dan The Man, McGann's sights now, and he always gets his man, or girl,' Richie jokingly said, doing his best to shake things up between them.

They did their best to laugh it off while they wore a school kid crush on their faces. Dan then helped Teresa set up her things at a desk next to his.

Having spent most of the day compiling the files that both departments had on Christopher Wright and Exile, Maxine called a meeting in the conference room in five minutes. Dan and Teresa caught a little alone time, and this time, Dan got a little more intimate, as it was becoming clear that whatever was going on between them was mutual.

Richie gave Dan a look of, 'oh man', when he walked into the conference room with Teresa. Dan's shot back a look of, 'what?' They sat next to each other, which didn't go unnoticed by Maxine as she managed her own disapproving look.

'I'd like to know what we have on any links tying Wright to Knoxx. Did they know each other earlier or was it a miracle that Wright just happened to end up running NVS?'

Dobro's eyes fell on Ray Tombs.

'I've been working the phones. I've left several messages with his personal assistant, Jane Mears, who's assured me that once she manages to contact him she'll have him call me. I've left the same message with his attorney, Matthew Tamban. I guess Knoxx is pretty busy with his I.P.O.'

Maxine's face summed it up. Being known to not suffer fools well, she quickly moved on, asking, 'Anything on why Wright was being paid so much?'

She looked at her star.

Thumbing her notes in her file, Teresa replied, 'Wright wasn't paid directly from the Envious Group. He was paid from an account in London. It appears that another company based in Andorra called Envoy Developments. Exile has received seventy-five million pounds from an unknown source to underwrite a building project in London. These funds were then used to secure insurance on the manufacturing of HEAVEN Navigators. The funds haven't been disclosed as debt financing or as earned income to either Exile or Envoy. The funds weren't generated from the sale of Navigators, as they aren't available for sale yet, so the big question is, where's this money coming from and why is someone investing seventy-five million in cash into Envoy?'

'Very good,' Maxine said, and gloated at the other detectives.

Dan had his mind set on asking Teresa out on a date. He just hoped he could rise to the challenge, having just heard her mind at work.

'Why do you think someone would?' Maxine then went on to ask, 'C'mon, give it a shot. Let's see where it takes us.'

They all looked at Teresa, waiting to see what kind of ride she was going to take them on. Teresa seemed to take a minute to gather her thoughts, knowing that none of them could see the relevance of what she'd told them and what she'd had on her mind for a few weeks now. She knew she had been held back by Maxine recently, but now Maxine seemed to have gotten her second wind, and so Hadley felt she could at last get her thoughts off her chest.

She explained, 'I believe Knoxx and Wright have met before somewhere in the past. By my calculations the research and development costs for HEAVEN are running at around eighty to a hundred million a year, and that kind of money leaves a long paper trail. Yet Knoxx's net worth and the income price per earnings for Exile haven't been affected, which tells me the money's coming from a foreign source that both parties want to keep a secret. And as you might be aware, all bank wires that are transacted in U.S. dollars pass through New York's Federal Reserve for clearing and tracking the money's path from one bank's source code to the recipient bank. The money that Envoy Developments received didn't pass through New York, indicating that the money originated from somewhere outside the U.S. For now, it's out of my jurisdiction.'

Everyone looked suitably impressed but confused about what she was explaining, so she summarized, 'So why does Knoxx have secret offshore accounts taking in huge amounts of money practically on a monthly basis? From what entity the money's coming from is anyone's guess. One thing I can say with some certainty is that the money's being used for the development of HEAVEN Navigators, but why is it so important for them to be made in record time? Who knows?'

Richie's phone rang and he quickly took the call. He said in a lowered voice that he would phone the caller back. He looked at Dan, cold as ice.

Hadley had continued. Saying in a tone that meant she was ready to take it to Knoxx, she said, 'So let's bring in the I.R.S. and have them do an audit at Exile's offices to review the books for the Envious Group. I like to say that the I.R.S. can't make you do anything; it can only make you sorry that you didn't.'

Her line brought the room to a rousing chuckle and ended the meeting.

'What was that about?' Dan asked, regarding the inconvenient timing of Richie's phone call.

Richie remained stone-faced and kept his pace up as he walked with Dan along the corridor, replying, 'Nothin', bud, I got something I gotta handle.'

Dan read hard and fast that whatever he had on his mind, he didn't want to share it. As they entered the squad room, Maxine walked in and pulled the detective's' attention away from smiling and dialing, working the phones. She said, 'Let's take some time out and get something to eat at Barney's Beanery, is it? We can get to know each other a little better, and then we can come back and hit the phones again.'

By the various reactions from the cops around the room, they were all down with that, replying positively with a round of 'ok.'

Maxine answered, 'Okay then, I'll see you all there in about twenty minutes,' and confirmed it was a go. Caron Smart picked up her phone to call her husband, Jeremy, while singing out to the cops around her, 'Yeah, it's karaoke night too!'

She then told Jeremy in no uncertain terms to get his ass down to Barney's Beanery pronto, to meet her there at the favorite cop hangout bar on Santa Monica Boulevard in West

Hollywood. Jeremy said politely in his smooth English accent that he would see her there. Hadley also made a quick phone call to her kids, Lauren, Alex, and to check in one her baby girl, Lulu. Dan looked around the squad room for Richie and found him off on his own at the far side of the room on his cell phone immersed in a private conversation.

It then occurred to Dan, thinking back to what Richie had said to him the previous morning, that he didn't have anyone to call and no one who would miss him. It gave him pause for thought, while he watched Teresa beam with radiance while she spoke warmly on the phone, laughing with her kids. Dan thought about Richie, his wife Jo and their daughter Elenoor, realizing that, besides them, who did he really have?

Getting up from his desk, he walked into Captain Wyatt's office to see Maxine, telling her that she could invite her daughter, Danielle, who she'd referred to in an earlier conversation as Dolly. She was living in Westwood Village while she was studying at UCLA. Maxine thanked him for the offer, saying she would ask her. Dan sat with her, talking for a while, feeling a mutual admiration and camaraderie for the job they did. They had both paid their respective dues, he thought, doing their jobs as police officers. Dan made sure Richie drove while Maxine called shotgun, securing the front passenger seat as the four of them began making their way across Hollywood to Barney's Beanery restaurant and bar.

20

Hadley had spent most of the car ride over to Barney's explaining how she tracked international bank transactions. It was clear to Dan and Richie that she was the lynchpin to the Exile case, and possibly The Bezerk Murders. Teresa had openly questioned Maxine about why she hadn't been given the green light to bring Knoxx in for questioning. Maxine had answered that because he had a number of high profile friends in the political world, unless they secured evidence tying him to improprieties, it would be futile to try to subpoena him. The ride got heated when Maxine, clearly aggravated, confirmed that she was in charge. No matter what people thought they knew about the Exile case, they were wrong. Tears seemed to well up as she forcefully said, 'I have to win this thing!'

Everyone moved on to other topics, willing Richie to get them there in record time. He winced at the moves he heard Dan putting on Teresa from the back seat, saying, 'Oh pulleeasse,' at how corny Dan was sounding, while Teresa giggled like a love-struck puppy.

The cops were in full swing at Barney's Beanery when Dan, Richie, Maxine, and Teresa walked in. Caron had held down some seats at her table, where she introduced her husband Jeremy to them. As Jeremy was not on the job, he was already downing some iced cold ones from the bar. The first rounds of drinks and chicken wings came to the table and everyone got down to taking a break from police work.

Dan put his hand on Teresa's arm and leaned in to say something, causing her to laugh. She caught Richie's eye. Richie winked at her, and a cold chill raced through her like a bolt of electricity. She shuddered, like someone had just walked over her grave. The cool, late November evening soon became night. There was something in the air, with everyone having fun and making new friends. The case was picking up new vigor and Hadley sensed that she was on her way to being given the go ahead to indict Knoxx. Dan felt he'd been given the go ahead to ask Teresa out on a real second date.

Caron's name was called from the stage. She walked through the bar to get up on stage to sing one of her favorite karaoke songs.

'Oh man, here we go!' Mike Adwell drawled out, laughing, as all the cops began to whistle and shout at Caron, clearly knowing something Teresa and Maxine didn't.

Caron proceeded to slay the song *I Will Survive* and all the cops in the immediate area felt that they were lucky to have survived. She arrived back at the table. After picking up her drink, she waited for the verdict, looking at Mike first. He opened up with, 'Yeah, babe, you killed 'em. I was feelin' it, girl!' Mike gave her a high five and a big smile, knowing what his partner needed to hear.

Teresa sat in the middle of Mike and Jeremy. She clearly felt it was appropriate to take the middle of the road with her new friend by remarking, 'Caron wow! Who knew? What a voice, honey, well done.'

Caron moved on, unfazed, and looked at Jeremy, who said, 'What can I say, hun? It sounded like two puppies humping in a plastic bag. Good job the room's full of cops, or I might have had to shoot you, or myself!'

Jem's English accent was tinged with a slur from the beers he'd drank. The three judges exploded into a fit of laughter that caused Caron to yell back, 'Guess who's not getting any humping tonight, you pompous fuck!'

Mike was laughing, but he still tried to support his girl, saying, 'Don't worry 'bout him girl, you got skills!'

Teresa asked Caron to sit next to her, providing Caron with some much-needed praise and support. Soon, they were back into girl talk.

Dan had got up from his chair to go and sit with Maxine. They talked about Knoxx, with Maxine explaining how she'd been assigned to the Exile case a few years back. It had cost her, her marriage and, she went on to say, she'd been on Chris Wright and the Southsider's trail for what felt like half her career. Her career was all-consuming, and it had, it seemed to Dan, eaten her up. Her kids were growing up faster than she liked and she hadn't had as much time as she'd like to spend with them, she told him.

Dan noticed the disdain she was showing for the job while she spoke to him. She clearly felt embittered from the years of being on the grind and what it had done to her and her family. Maxine said she would be visiting Dolly while she was in Los Angeles, as she had every few days over the past few weeks. She seemed to dwell on that, as he kept eye contact with her, waiting for her to say more, but she turned her head away and took a deep breath. What Dan felt from this exchange, he wasn't sure?

Then he heard, from a couple tables away, 'I like her!'

Caron's raised voice snapped him back from his inner voice, telling him that something wasn't right. He let it wash over him and left Maxine's table to join the girls back at theirs. Maxine followed him with her eyes, tracking his every step as he made his way back over to sit with Teresa.

21

'I guess your partner'll be pumping her for information all night, then?' Maxine said sarcastically to Richie.

He choked on that one, laughing, he answered, 'Yeah, Dan's like that. No job too small, he's real dedicated.'

Tombs, Blisset, Bowen, and Groomie were all ganging up on Dan, having realized he had a thing for Teresa. They couldn't resist the playful banter at his expense. Dan felt like he'd been caught with his hand in the cookie jar, stealing a quick look at her; the two of them smiled at each other like two teenage school kids. Ray did his best to antagonize Dan until he had a call on his cell phone that he had to take in private. Teresa did her best to keep the conversation light, but Dan knew what he wanted to do, which was to lean across the table and kiss her. She let it slip that she was pleased she'd been assigned the Exile case and sent to California. Dan ruefully quipped, 'Well, I'll be sure to thank Mark Knoxx for that if I ever get to meet him.'

Looking deeper into her eyes, her eyes glinted. It seemed she hadn't been put off in the slightest by all the ribbing. She had even helped to fan the flames by teasing Dan in front of the other cops in the worst way. Tonight had been a good idea. A night Dan would never forget.

Having become comfortable with Dan, Teresa aired her thoughts by confiding in him about what had been troubling her regarding The Bezerk Murders. 'The assassin had used multiple identities before entering the United States,' she confided, knowing this information was to be held in the strictest of confidence, as instructed by her superiors at the State Department. She went on telling him, 'He'd been tracked back to England where he'd used the name Luke Watson to board a plane for the U.S. MI6 had discovered he'd been a Spetznaz Special Forces operative. The cell phone he'd used was a throw away. The call ended up at First Waste Management, a waste disposal firm in Chicago that had checked out and been cleared of any involvement. Someone had the connections to piggyback on their phone line for the killer to place an untraceable call to the as yet, unknown mystery man.' She then asked Dan, 'Who has access to that kind of firepower?'

Dan answered that he didn't know.

Holding Dan's gaze, she said, 'Whatever we're beginning to get close to, the people involved have huge resources at their disposal to cover their tracks and stop us dead in ours.'

Sitting at her table, Maxine checked her watch and decided that it was time for the evening's fun to end. The night had moved on quickly and had helped them bond with the L.A. cops. Everyone was taking something away from their night spent in Barney's Beanery.

Maxine asked Dan if he and Richie would escort them back to their hotel. Dan answered nonchalantly, saying that it would be okay, while relishing the thought of a night-time stroll with Teresa hanging off his arm. Richie had his partner's back by saying that it was cool with him too. He knew he'd be keeping Maxine occupied so Dan could put his moves on Teresa while they walked them back to their hotel.

Mike said he was heading home to give his ears a rest. Caron's husband Jeremy had already been sent home. She was still pissed at him for what he had said to her about her singing, so for some time to come, he would probably be living his life in exile from their bedroom.

Mike stood at the valet stand waiting for his car, while Ray and Dave stood off to the side, lighting up their cigarettes, shooting the breeze with Groomie and Bowen. Mike chuckled as he watched Caron take up Teresa and Richie in her arms, with Richie in the middle and Teresa at the curb, to begin one more rendition of *I Will Survive.*

'Yeah, you go girl!' Mike shouted after them, laughing hard at what he was watching. Maxine and Dan began to laugh too, walking some 20 yards behind them as they all began to make their way along Santa Monica Boulevard before turning up towards Sunset Boulevard. Everyone walked together, with Teresa, Richie and Caron frog stepping in time past the Niketown's store window. They laughed hysterically while they tried to sing, with every note off key, '*I will survive, hey, hey!*'

*   *   *

'I say again, coach. Eighteen seconds until the receiver is out of the pocket. Does the quarterback take the shot?'

Four blocks east of Barney's Beanery, approximately seven hundred yards away, they had been waiting for this moment for over two hours. The black-cladded sniper was locked on target and tracking his quarry with every step through his night vision scope. His spotter barely made any audible sounds as he spoke in his throat-mike over the secure satellite communications link back to his commanding officer. All they needed to hear were three words. The sniper soon heard them in his earpiece: 'Take the shot.'

Destiny

22

Stirring from a deep, booze fuelled sleep and squinting out from under the duvet, Mark's eyes focused on Nicole sleeping contently. He watched her as if she were a little girl, listening to her faint breathing. Every day, it seemed as if he was seeing her for the first and the last time.

They had arrived home early, which in Miami meant before midday from the night before. This was the life that Nicole had become accustomed to, living in Mark's life. Her life was filled with attending parties and events, but behind this was the life she was living with her man. He was more than the media-generated persona. For all the light that shone on them as a power couple, there was also a dark light, and Nicky understood her place beside Mark. He was a shining star that shone as bright as the sun, fuelled by the intensity of his own burning ambition. She knew that if she got too close, she'd get burned, and she had come to know the safe distance from where she could live in his world. Nicole had learned of the deals she should know about and the ones she shouldn't. She loved her life with him and she knew she loved him without question. Mark leaned in and kissed Nicky lightly on her head. He then nuzzled in, softly kissing her lips and whispered, 'Love you, baby.'

Nicky returned a soft whimper of agreement as she snuggled in deeper under the duvet to carry on sleeping. The scent of sex still lingered on them both and she still felt the afterglow from the hard, passionate sex they had launched into when they had returned home from NVS.

He dropped away from her and got out of bed. Standing naked in the vast master bedroom, he checked the bedside clock that read 6:15 a.m. The morning's sun was already rising over the endless horizon. Standing at the window, he stood in awe, feeling its heat, remembering. *Old habits die hard*, he thought, allowing the curl of a small smile. He then waded across the plush carpet that caused his feet to bounce as he made his way to the master bathroom. Standing over the toilet to take his early morning piss, he thought, *what the fuck have I done?* His eyes stared at a picture on the wall above the toilet. Standing there in another place and time, he finally let a thought fall from his lips, saying in a hard way, 'Mutherfuckaa.'

He muttered it, not in a harsh way, as it should have been,

but almost with admiration, in a way that meant, 'Damn, I miss you, boy.' The drawing was of a small, fat kid in schoolboy clothes with his oversized belly protruding over his shorts. His fly was undone and the naughty boy was peeing into a swimming pool. His big head and big, bushy hair exaggerated his look as he looked back over his left shoulder with his index finger raised up to his pursed lips; he knew it was wrong, but he couldn't help it and he had been caught in the act. Mark always laughed at it, seeing something new in it each time. The caption at the bottom of the drawing read: Is It So Wrong?

Shaking off the last droplets from his piss, he quietly said, with some remorse in his voice and in his heart, 'Fucking Bezerk.' There was no turning back now and nothing could change what he'd done, saying with conviction in his voice, he said, 'You know how we do.'

He stood in the peace and quiet alone thinking of how it had all began, nearly five years earlier.

*   *   *

The rattling of the keys woke Mark up around 6:15 in the morning as each cell door was being unlocked by the correctional officer who was making the rounds to open up for breakfast, not that Knoxx or his cellie ever got up for it. He always got up to take a piss, slipping into his shower shoes from his lower bunk to shuffle the five paces or so to the steel urinal next to the door of Cell One on K-Unit. He finished and hit the flush button, causing the vacuum of flushing water to wake his cellmate, just as it had most mornings for the past seven months.

'Fuckin' fag, Pinche puto,' his cellmate said, as he rolled over to face the wall on the top bunk. Both of them would sleep on through the morning until lunchtime chow was called at around eleven o'clock. A Mexican gangbanger would bring their breakfasts to their cell.

'Fuuckk yoouu,' Knoxx replied as he got settled back in under his white cotton blanket. The clanking of the keys continued around the floor on K-Unit as another day was beginning just like any other in M.C.C., Metropolitan Correctional Center, which was known as the Mexican Country Club.

Mark Knoxx was in prison awaiting trial for investment securities violations. It involved the insider trading of shares in Internet companies, which he had not disclosed to investors that he had controlled. He had been denied bail as the U.S. prosecutor had told the judge that she believed him to be a flight risk and that she thought Knoxx had access to millions in offshore bank accounts that hadn't, as yet, been repatriated. The U.S. Prosecutor had stated, 'Mr. Knoxx is a financial threat to the good people of the United States, Your Honor.'

He had been housed on the Maximum Security floor at M.C.C. in San Diego. This was K-Unit, and he had landed in Cell One on Range One, where he was to sit until he began a lengthy prison sentence or was set free. The former was the more likely event because the Feds had a confidential informant who was not that confidential at all. Knoxx knew who they had; they had a rat. The feds had an old friend of his who had approached him years earlier, telling him that he wanted to work for him doing whatever it took to live like he was: living large and loving life.

The plan was for Jason Burne to be at the bank every Thursday at ten o'clock to sign the payroll bank wires to Knoxx's offices. After that was done he was free to spend his twelve thousand dollars a week, and that's exactly what Burne did, spending his money on parties, clubbing, whores, drink and drugs. He became hooked on cocaine, and when Knoxx found out and assessed him to be a liability, he ended his deal with Burne, cutting him off from the money. This in turn cut Burne off from the sex, drugs and rock and roll lifestyle. No more high life and no more getting high, so Jason Burne turned into a low-life rat who wanted to get revenge. Due to him being a spineless, limp-dick-prick, along with the many weaknesses he had, he knew he could not win in any situation going up against Knoxx. He went to the F.B.I. and had them do his dirty work for him in exchange for immunity. Then he let Knoxx know he had turned him in by taunting him with voicemails. Low-life rat.

'Tough times come and go but tough guys are around forever,' his old cellmate had said when Mark had told him his story.

K-Unit held the baddest of the bad in it. They were all gladiators and K-Unit was The Coliseum that housed murderers, terrorists, drug traffickers, bank robbers, and gangbangers. The elevators taking the inmates up and down the tower block were called The Bus, taking inmates to and from the court to seal their fate. Knoxx had been brought to this place, this Hell that these men called home. It was like being washed ashore upon a New World, working his way up the beach, getting to know the inmates fast, and be accepted by them. Was this going to be his ending, or a new beginning? Was this bad luck, fate or his destiny?

Upon his arrival at M.C.C., Knoxx met the shotcaller for the white race; The White Car. A bad-ass barrel-chested gunslinger and dope dealer called Pauley. Paul Ybarra was a five foot eight, two hundred and fifty-five pound monster who ran with the Hells Angels, San Diego Chapter. There were twenty-two of them housed in M.C.C. on conspiracy to murder and distribute controlled substances. Pauley explained that they were protecting their business interests that were worth one billion dollars a year in drugs distributed along the West Coast from Mexico to Canada.

'Well sir, you have any problems, you come see me, okay?' Ybarra had told Mark.

Pauley let the correctional officer's know that he didn't want his current cellie living in his cell and within forty eight hours of Knoxx's arrival, Ybarra's cellie was being carried out on a stretcher, dead. Later that morning, Knoxx was told by a C.O. to roll up and take his belongings over to Pauley's cell, which consisted of a plastic, finger toothbrush, a small tube of toothpaste and a bar of Dove soap in a small plastic bag. He carried his things across to Cell One, with a hand towel and his bunk's bedding.

When he got to Pauley's cell, he said, 'Well, I figured I can't get any whiter, nor any more of gentlemen than a gent from England now, can I?' The Swastika tattooed on his stomach made it crystal clear what Pauley was all about.

From that day on, his schooling on how to do his prison time, known as a bid, got underway. Pauley ruled the whites, and in doing so, he let them know that Knoxx wasn't to be fucked with, having his nineteen-inch biceps to back it up. Tattooed on his right inside bicep was OUT, and LAW was tattooed on the inside of his left bicep, because that was what he was, an outlaw. His life was lived enthralled in reading Louis L'Amour books about the old days of the Wild West. Ybarra's problem was that he was born a hundred and fifty years too late. His horse was a one thousand and fifty c.c. horsepowered, hard tail Harley Davidson and his dream was to ride shotgun with civilians through the deserts of Mexico. The life he wanted to live was a simple life that involved hard riding, hard drinking, hard living, and putting hard lickin' on his women. Pauley had the deepest, darkest eyes and a long ponytail, with a long handlebar moustache and sleeved-up tattoos that accentuated his look. He carried his weight well and all the rough riders of K-Unit knew he carried weight on the floor too. He had one way of doing time, one that he drilled into Knoxx first thing in the morning and last thing at night, telling him, 'Trust no one.'

Knoxx got into the routine of prison life, known as The Program. Pauley told Mark, 'You do the time, don't let the time do you.'

Falling back on his stockbroker training, he remembered that it's not what you know or who you know, but who knows you. Getting down to the business of letting the other inmates get to know him sooner rather than later was the order of the day. Back to basics, just like days gone past when

72

he was in basic training in England.

Knoxx made it known that he would be starting 'How to Start a Small Business' classes in the Law Library, and soon after he started, his classes were full every Friday morning. Inmates soon sent word out that the man to see on issues involving business, and life on the street, was the guy from England with the knowledge. It was not too long before Knoxx became known and referred to as, 'Knowledge.'

Pauley had it sweet in M.C.C. Cell One's window faced north up to Point Loma, overlooking Coronado Bay. The two of them stood at the window watching the sun fall from the sky most evenings. Their cell also looked down on numerous hotels along Union Street that had rooftop swimming pools, which helped keep his head in the game, watching the people chill by the pool.

Their lockers were always full with supplies from the commissary store. They had it better than most, having the best seats at the chow hall benches and at the front of the television. The White Car had some strong soldiers in it, and most nights were spent bullshitting, with each guy getting down on how they had caught their case.

Pauley was a junkyard dog, as mean as they come, and he kept The White Car in line. Everyone knew their rank in it, and it soon became apparent that Knoxx had taken his place as second in command. They ate and watched television together, played cards and worked out together, calling it, 'Getting your money.' Knoxx was Pauley's dog and Pauley was his soldier, holding him down. They ate a jailhouse spread of Pauley's making most nights, which helped to keep Knoxx's weight up. After lockdown each night, Pauley would often finish the night off in their cell by telling an old war story, removing his round-rimmed glasses while he pulled down on his long Fu-Manchu goatee. Ybarra was relatively uneducated, but he had two things in spades that Knoxx admired: heart and honor. Having done many a rodeo in prison, his words helped to shape Knoxx, with Ybarra telling him, 'Handle your business, youngin'.' Pauley imparted this most nights before his time ran out.

23

The Japanese have a saying that when a butterfly beats its wings, the waves can spread out across oceans to cause a typhoon on the other side of the world. The time he spent as Ybarra's cellie, under the circumstances, had been time well spent. The devil is in the details. Ybarra's nightly anecdotes, stories and pointers had helped to fine tune and ignite what Knoxx knew he already carried inside him: his killer instinct in the art of closing the deal.

Mark handled his business by fending off the prison hustlers, trying to work him out of his shit. Ybarra helped to keep his mind strong, along with his body and soul, by keeping him straight, making sure he did his Prison Program the right way each day. Knoxx hardened to prison life and to beating the system by not letting the meat grinder grind him down.

Days rolled into months and new fish rolled onto K-Unit. Inmates were rolled up off the floor to move on to other prisons, or they were carried out on stretchers or in body bags. Knoxx had his Program down cold, just as his emotions were now about being banged up.

Each range had its own crew and routine each day. All the top tiers were for the convicts who had power and juice in the Joint. Range One had the woodpile, the whites. Range Three had the shines, the blacks. Range Five and Seven was for the Southsiders. All the lower ranges with even numbers were for the Mexican peisas and all the maggots who didn't have enough juice to sit up top. Range One had everyone getting in on the jailhouse spreads most nights, which consisted of Tap Ramen soups, mixed with tuna, melted cheese, Summer Sausage and crushed Doritos nacho chips laid on top. Pauley, Knoxx, Bones, Iverson, Malton, Keville, Cardillo, Meserve, Matthews, and Truelove all held down Range One. Nothing went down on the range that Pauley hadn't either approved or didn't take a piece of, and nothing ever went down that would bring down heat from The Man: the cops.

'You got me fucked up. Don't get it twisted!' This was the usual line heard coming off Range One as another heated discussion got underway, usually involving Meserve, Keville a.k.a. Hot Sauce, and Andrew the Knacker Matthews. They always had something going on whether they were using a stinger to heat up water or making hooch. They were the go-to-guys on Range One and they had the hustle on whatever you needed.

'You racin' today booyy?' Meserve asked, pushing up on

74

inmates come Sunday, NASCAR race day. Meserve was a hard charging bull of a man from Maine. His hustle was running the NASCAR book. Two mackerels, known as Money Mac's that were worth one dollar per car running race day. Winner take all, that came to around thirty-five Macs, minus Meserve's management fee of course, for the collection of the bets, which was Meserve's forte on the block as the white's enforcer. It's one thing to take bets or to gamble, that's the easy part. It's another thing to collect, and that's where Meserve came in.

'NASCAR, biggest sport in the world!' Meserve always loved to say proudly. Knoxx and Meserve spent many days and nights debating that one once he had introduced Meserve to The Beautiful Game, the worldwide sport of soccer.

The Program continued each day with most of the inmate's playing card games such as Pinochle, Spades, Texas Hold 'em or playing checkers, dominoes and chess. They made various gifts from chip bags or drawing pictures for their loved ones back home. Some guys kicked back in their cells, reading, or watched television on the range, while a few cons were busy getting their money, working out. Everyone had their own Program in how they got their time done. The convicts operated on a 'one up one down' policy, where if a guy needed to catch some shuteye during the day, his bunky would watch their house, making sure no one dropped anything into the cell and then went and dropped a dime to The Man. This would get the inmate rolled up to the bucket, known as the SHU, the Secured Housing Unit, or best known as The Hole. 'Bunky love,' the cons called it, and each cellie had his bunky's back.

Knoxx had learned to do his time the convict way, thanks to Pauley. He had been down for around eleven months and still wasn't playing it the way the Feds wanted him to. He still had game that he wanted to run on them. He just didn't know how to do it. The Shotcallers knew they were never leaving; this was their life, and this was their house. Inside the big house, the guards knew who really called the shots. They knew not to disrespect the Shotcallers, because if they did, then they might not get to go home that night after catching a hot one from a con, which meant they could get some cold steel or a pointed plexie twisted deep into their liver or kidney for getting it twisted in thinking that they called the shots.

Pauley was moving on to Lompoc, California to start his thirty seven-year bid. Meserve had been sent to The Hole for fucking up an inmate who hadn't understood the terms of gambling and Eric Keville had been transferred back east to Fort Dix, New Jersey. This left a power vacuum on Range One. Most of the range's crews cycled over, losing good soldiers and earners. But with each Tuesday evening, just like Knoxx had eleven months earlier, walking in with a bed roll under one arm, a small plastic bag with washroom supplies in the other hand and an oh so familiar, 'holy shit. What a shit hole. What the fuck have I just walked into', look on their faces, new fish rolled onto K-Unit.

One guy strolled in dressed in the prison issue, tan jumpsuit and blue and white boating slippers like he was coming home. Within an hour, he was set up in a cell next to the high power Mexican Mafia Shotcallers. Being a high-ranking Southsider, they supplied him with new Reebok tennis shoes and a radio and headset. All of these were high ticket items in the Joint, which indicated that this guy was a somebody that Knoxx needed to get to know, and someone who needed to know him. Over the next few weeks Knoxx noticed the Southsider had stayed low-pro' and had opted to eat his meals up on Range Five, working out, getting his money up there too, choosing to work out with a select few Sureños. Knoxx had heard that this guy had put work in, dishing out some discipline within their ranks. He took note of how the Southsider did his daily Program and who he favored hanging out with. He watched from across the floor, noticing when the Southsider was walking back from the showers, that his long mane of black hair nearly covered a tattoo of Del Sol across his shoulders with the Virgin Guadalupe tattooed on his back. His arms carried sleeved tattoos, and Knoxx saw the tattoo he had across his chest in thick, black bold lettering that read: THUG.

Walking his usual fifty-four paces around the perimeter of K-Unit one Saturday morning, listening to his headset radio, thinking of life on the outside, Knoxx realized the Southsider was sitting at one of the chow hall benches that he had to pass by. He knew that to walk by and not acknowledge him could be seen as disrespecting him and that could become a problem. He quickly surmised that this guy must know who he was, just as Mark knew who he was by now, since he had been asking about him, and he figured the same of this Southsider.

So today was going to be the day they were going to introduce themselves. At least today, he was going to introduce himself and see how it played out. Slowing down, he moved up, filling the void but still keeping a respectful distance, mindful of carrying an easy air about him. He sensed the Sureño had a bead on him, even though he did not look up. As he approached, Mark said confidently, 'Hey man, how you doin'?'

The Southsider looked up at him, mad-doggin' him with a sideways look, and then replied, 'I 'is all 'iight.' Sucking on his lip, he added, 'Just killin' time, you know how we do. You know what I mean?'

'Yeah, I know what you mean,' Knoxx replied innocently enough. He moved in closer to see what the Sureño was drawing. Life, it's so often made up of the choices we make. A small choice can end up making such a big difference, even something that seems insignificant at the time, like a butterfly beating its wings. Leaning in to view the drawing, he saw it was of a stone wall within a sun that had a face set in the middle of it. The drawing was a real work of art.

'Man, that's really good. Is it for sale?'

Knoxx had realized early on that money was a fast way to making friends, but this guy did not seem to be biting on the bait.

'I'm hookin' this up for one of my homeys, but hey, I guess I can hook you up on the next one. Everything has its price, you know what I mean? Yeess siirr.' He broke into a chuckle. Whatever he was laughing at, it was funny to him.

Knoxx asked, 'So you think you can hook me up?'

He was met with a sucking sound from the Sureño sucking on his lip. Thinking about it, he replied, 'Al'iight, I'll get at ya when I'm done with this joint.'

Knoxx moved closer to give him a pound, which was a clenched knuckle-to-knuckle greeting, as a way of showing friendship and mutual respect.

'Guys call me, Knowledge,' he said, feeling stupid as he said it.

'I'll get back at ya,' the Southsider replied, looking at his drawing. He seemed deep in thought while Knoxx took his cue and began to resume his walk. The gangbanger did not seem to be offering up his name. As Knoxx walked away, he heard him say, 'Fools call me Bezerk.'

Because Knoxx's case had been in the newspapers, the prison reps who controlled each gang, called the Shotcallers, or the high power, knew who he was and what he was. A Baller, a guy who had the balls to go get his money. The Shotcallers gave him respect for having played his game tight on the street where he had amassed one hundred and seventeen million dollars from a number of pump and dump stock schemes, and Knoxx gave them respect for the game they ran inside. Having an English accent lent him some notoriety amongst them too. The White Car was in the minority. The Black Car held an uneasy truce between the Bloods and the Crips. The real power was with the Southsiders, called Sureños in Spanish, and their overlords, the Mexican Mafia called the EME. The Southsiders were the largest Mexican street and prison gang throughout Southern California. They ran drugs, people, guns, cars and everything else in between, across the border from Tijuana into San Diego and on up to central California. Knoxx had been given a pass to walk among them, as he was a real live millionaire and someone who might be of use to them on the street some day. He was 'Knowledge' and he began passing along his knowledge by teaching the high power how to set up fronts, shell corporations, blind trust accounts, and tax evasion strategies for their drug businesses. He held it down with the Southsiders, who in turn provided soldiers to do his laundry, his allocated job, and to smuggle him food from the kitchen. Word was sent out that he wasn't a punk and that he had juice with them. Mark Knoxx now had power because he had the Southsiders.

Knoxx had come into prison from Beverly Hills as an elitist and his game was in the deals he could make with built-in percentage points, management fees additional hidden commissions. Fees that could nickel and dime to death any deal but the way he had it down, he was quartering the deals to death in their millions. He had been trained in the art of closing the deal, and he knew that knowledge was power. What he was now getting was an insight into a whole new form of power, as life came cheap in prison. The shotcaller held absolute power over their gang members who obeyed them unquestionably, referring to it as 'you know how we do', and they did. In prison the real power lay in the power of the numbers and one thing Knoxx knew was numbers. He got comfortable at the seat of power next to his new allies, the Southsiders. He appreciated the awesome power the shotcallers wielded from inside their eight-by-twelve cells. Each shotcaller had an army of convicts at his disposal, who were all loyal to their general. From the maximum-security floor, the general gave orders to his troops in a war against law enforcement agencies and rival gangs, each fighting for territory, drugs, money, power, and respect, keeping his army fighting on the streets every day.

Mark had an ally in his fight against the Feds and she came to visit him like a soldier every other week. His soul mate and best friend, Jane Mears. Mark gave Jane his orders that were sent out to his army of stockbrokers and corporate lawyers so as to keep his empire running. Jane was his sanity from this world that he had been dropped into. He had come from the life of Wall Street to live on Jump Street. If he were to lose his case, then his life would pretty much be over. Jane had found out where Jason Burne was living, on Manchester Avenue in Mar Vista, close to LAX airport in a nondescript suburb of Los Angeles. He was living his life like nothing had ever happened, waiting on the day when he would be called up to send his old friend down. Pauley had once told him, 'A coward dies a thousand deaths, a soldier only dies once.'

Knoxx was soldiering on. He had been reading the newspapers and watching the news on television, taking notes and forming an idea. Sitting at his bunk by the window, looking out over his million dollar view of Coronado Bay for motivation, he decided he wanted to buy up a number of bars, nightclubs and strip clubs and then combine them under one operating company. By his estimation the land leases and liquor licenses would more than cover the acquisition price. Work went on. It was business as usual, as surveys and financial reports were submitted, with updates being relayed to him in the visiting room by Jane. Any relevant information went back out via legal mail to Knoxx's criminal law firm and passed onto his corporate legal team, headed up by Matt Tamban. Two roadblocks stood in his way, according to Jane. One, he needed to be out of prison and two; he couldn't have a criminal record if he hoped to operate the group of clubs as a publicly traded company. He had two problems and he needed one solution.

24

'C'mon guys get your asses up for chow!' Iverson shouted in their cell. Knoxx and Bezerk had slipped a sleeping pill the night before, which they had gotten from a guy in the pill line. Mark Knoxx and Christopher Wright, who was known throughout prison as Bezerk, had become fast friends since their first meeting at the chow hall bench almost seven months earlier. The Mexican Mafia had determined that a Sureño soldier would be moved into Knoxx's cell to keep an eye on him and keep the peace on Range One after the Hells Angels had moved on, and he had picked Bezerk. As it turned out, Chris Wright had been born to an American father and a Mexican mother while they were living in England, when his father had been on military duty there. This allowed Bezerk to have a United Kingdom birth certificate that helped to seal their bond. The two of them finding each other here in this place, was it luck, fate or destiny? Mark would soon find out.

Bezerk had grown up in a suburb of San Diego called Del Sol. At the age of thirteen, he had to choose between the 18th Street or the Southsiders gang. His destiny was to join the Sureños. He got schooled real quick by his handlers and soon, school was out, and runnin' and gunnin' was in. He held down his block, by being plain berserk. Nowadays, slinging dope and throwing torpedoes was all he knew to do, but once the cell doors locked for the night, Mark saw the thirteen-year-old come out in Bezerk: before he had made his choice and had suffered the consequences. Mark had come to know Bezerk as Chris during the nights they shared; but once the cell doors opened each morning, Bezerk was definitely in the house. Mark knew one thing about Chris, though, which was that no job was too big or small, no matter how long it took, when it came to getting one over on The Man. Mark would be at the window reading papers on his case or reading a newspaper, and there would be Bezerk, ranting on about how he was going to pull off his latest and greatest coup. And more often than not, thanks to his unrelenting will, he did pull it off. Life locked down was like sucking diesel every day, but for the two hombres, Knowledge and Bezerk, doing what they could for each other made breathing each day a little easier.

'You my dog!' Knoxx would playfully shout out when Bezerk had come back into the cell to show off his winnings, or with something he had hustled for them.

'You know how we do!' was Bezerk's cheerful response.

'C'mon, dog, hurry up. Are you gonna flush that thing or

what?' Knoxx shouted out from the tier of Range One while he was watching the morning edition of *American Chopper*. Everyone joined in the fun, shouting at Bezerk,

'Aqua! Aqua! Put some water on that thing. Flush, God damn it!'

The guys laughed hard while each one pulled his t-shirt up over his nose. Knoxx got up from his chair and walked over to their cell to pull open the door so everyone could see the culprit. Bezerk continued reading his morning paper while he dropped the kids off at the pool.

'Yeess siirr, I'm gettin' mine this morning!' he shouted, while he laughed hysterically. The daily game of playing one another had begun. The one thing about Bezerk that Mark knew he could count on was that Bezerk loved to win at whatever he was doing. Most things he did had something riding on it, whether it was push-ups on demand or having to forfeit some of his store. It did not matter to Bezerk, even if he was betting on the sky not being blue. In Bezerk's world everyone and everything had its place and each day had an order to how it got done. He was always joking, 'You do you and I'll do me.' That was how it ran each day.

'Dance with the devil. The devil don't change. The devil changes you, dog,' Bezerk had told Mark, when they were in lock for the night, the night before.

Just as Pauley and Knoxx had done when they were cellies, so Chris and Mark now talked about numerous subjects and about their own lives. Everyone knew El Diablo, The Devil. He lived with the cons every day, whispering in their ear, 'You gotta take this fool out. He's clowning you, man,' or 'you gonna let this bitch punk you out like that?'

Anything could set it off, and then each race would jump off, with everyone getting busy fighting. It was as easy as bumping another inmate and not apologizing.

'You got to give respect to get respect,' Bezerk had told him. The devil lived in the details of everyone's lives, keeping everyone in check. Knoxx would often be the voice of reason for Bezerk, taking up the same role that Pauley had with him. The two of them realized they had forged a genuine friendship inside this Hell where everything had a price and everything was a hustle. And today would be the day that Knowledge would break it down for Bezerk, having thought about it during the night; he'd be giving Bezerk the opportunity to get his hustle on.

Knoxx had hardened in his resolve over the past eighteen months, and not caving into the prosecutor's latest offer to sign a plea-bargain agreement of serving ten years and one month. At thirty-eight, that might as well have meant a life sentence. He couldn't allow himself to be broken off for ten years because of the testimony provided by a pathetic, low life, scum-sucking rat. He could never give Jason Burne the satisfaction of being the one who put him away.

He had two people in his life who would stay strong for him, who he knew would go to bat for him and do whatever had to be done to see him get out. Jane Mears desperately wanted him out, growing up and growing apart, was the only thing that had gotten in the way of them getting married. She loved him unconditionally, and he knew he would give his life to save hers. He needed her as his communications wire to the outside world, sending word out through her. Jane had been a tortured soul growing up and Mark had fought his own demons too. They loved each other without question, and together, they slept in an Angel's arms. Their love for each other entwined them forever; having each other kept them safe from themselves. Mark was her boy and she would do whatever was necessary to get him back out in the world next to her. Jane would protect and defend her perfect Mark, her friends always joked, to the end of her last breath. Jane gave Mark his very purpose in life, which was his driving will to succeed in life and he loved to put a smile on her face, letting her know that she was needed in his world, and that she was loved unconditionally by him too.

A few rule over the many, and generals give orders to soldiers. He had found himself sitting in the middle of this Hell with an army at his disposal and a soldier sleeping in his house. Everything he needed was right in front of him. All he had to do was reach out and raise an army.

People on the street were faking it to make it. Mark realized he could lead these men to the gates of Hell and take it all. Knoxx's dog, Bezerk had the heart of a lion and if he wanted to take something from you, then he would push up on you and take it. He had respect for the cons, because they gave respect to get respect, and he had a heartfelt admiration for the way they held it down for each other. But if it had to go down, then they got down and handled their business. All Bezerk needed was leadership and direction, but Christopher Lee Wright also needed an out from the life of being a gangbanger. Given the opportunity, Bezerk would ride hard. He'd ride 'til he died. He looked out for Mark, backing him up in every situation against anyone, always saying, 'You know how we do.'

Knoxx knew the day had come. The time was right to break it down for Bezerk and tell him how they were both going to win their lives back and get out.

25

'Hey doogg, they're getting ready to serve up some ass this morning. Maybe you wanna get out there and give 'em a hand, coz it smells like you've been servin' up some ass in here.' Mark said, as he arrived back in the cell after his morning's speed walking session.

Still lying on his top bunk, Bezerk replied, 'Yeah well, they can come up in here and speak to my squeaky lips that have no tongue, mutherfuuckaa's! Yeess siirr!'

Rolling over and facing the mustard-colored wall, curling up tighter under his thin white cotton blanket, he let out a booming low-pitched grumbling laugh. Knoxx paid him no mind while he made a cup of coffee, having heard the same routine too many times.

'Your ass stinks, man. It felt like it smacked me in the face when I walked in here,' Knoxx said.

'Yeah dog, and that's all you'll see, is my ass jumping down and smacking you on your face if you make me have to get down off this here rack.' Bezerk replied.

Mark slammed his locker door closed on purpose, ensuring his movement would keep Bezerk awake. Mark answered, saying, 'Yeah, and I'll smoke your ass right off your fat feet before they hit the floor, fool. C'mon, get up, chow's up in ten minutes, Schnook 'ems.'

Bezerk pulled himself tighter under his blanket, replying in a child-like voice, 'Whateveerr.'

Leaving the cell he left the heavy steel cell door open so the drone from the floor of K-Unit would come into the cell.

His steps were quickly followed by, 'Fuckin' faagg! Uh huh, just wait, real fuckin' funny, doogg!'

Bezerk's loud, deep baritone voice boomed out after Mark, indicating another day had begun as laughter rippled out around Range One.

'Fuckin' Bezerk,' the guys said while they laughed.

'Range One! Line it up!' Correctional Officer Tarver shouted up at the tier. Everyone began to walk down from Range One to walk the line. All the cons walked the line, three times a day for chow. Each car had its spot where they liked to sit. The shotcallers sat and ate first; soldiers second, and on down the line. No matter what the chef's surprise was, it was accompanied by dry, black refried beans and caked, dry rice. Life on the outside provided two certainties, which were death and taxes, but in prison, it's that the four o'clock count will always come at the wrong time and the meals served up will always be a mystery meal. And because the M.C.C. stood for Mexican Country Club there was always a soggy orange Taco to go with the fare. Each day got into swing during lunchtime chow when each Range got to sit down together and talk for the first time.

'Knowledge, Bezerk, how you doin'?'

Range One's crew greeted Mark and Bezerk much the same way each day. Not much ever changed in the Joint. While the seasons changed outside, the temperature invariably stayed the same, being in lock on the block. As they sat down to eat their lunch at the chow hall bench, the rest of the cons were already covering a number of topics and having a laugh. Jimmy Cardillo brightened up as Mark sat down opposite him. In his thick Boston accent, Cardillo sang out, 'Hey, I came up with a cool idea for you last night. You can use it if you like, I don't mind, but I'd rather be working on it with you.'

The guys at the bench began to laugh, as they knew what to expect. Cardillo had been pitching ideas to Knoxx over the past two months or so, with each idea getting worse than the one before. Knoxx laughed along while he mashed his mystery meal into a pulp, and enthusiastically replied, 'Yeah? Let's hear it.'

Cardillo was already working hard to get it right in his head, and started, 'Yeah well, I've been thinking see, I know how to talk to women, maybe not the standard of broads you're used to, but I can hold my own.'

His bald, chrome dome bobbed along as he tried to maintain his composure, while everyone around him began to fall about in fits of giggles. Even Cardillo broke down, giggling as he tried to continue, saying, 'Believe me, Mark, I've broken the backs on some smokers.'

An eruption of laughter broke out around him.

'Man, you are one fucked-up individual, dude.' Dominic Truelove snorted beside Cardillo as he tried to eat with his young bank-robbing partner, Corey Stalely, nudging him as they laughed.

Jimmy carried on, undeterred. 'Look, guys, check it out. I can go into bars and clubs ahead of you Mark to check out the babe front. Think about it, can't you see?' Jimmy now began to play his own role and that of a chick in a bar, saying, 'Check this out, hey waassuupp? Excuse me, have you heard of Mark Knoxx? Oh you have, have you, well, guess what? He's going to be here in a couple of days and I can arrange for you to meet him if you'd like?'

Everyone seated around him fell about in hard laughter.

'Damn dude, say it don't spray it!' Truelove said while laughing. The nineteen-year-old bank robber bandit was famous for saying his tagline, 'have a nice day', as he was leaving the bank he'd just robbed.

He laughed hard while Jimmy did his best to continue on,

saying, 'Check it out. I have his phone number. Me and Mark, we're like this.' Cardillo crossed his fingers. His Boston accent was in overdrive as guys from other chow benches now began to look over at them.

Bezerk, mad-doggin' the other cons, kept them in check. 'Mind your own, fool. You might live longer.'

Jimmy let it be known that he would, of course, have to try out the merchandise first to assess the girl on Knoxx's behalf, which was, of course, the deal killer.

'Yeah Jimmy, I'll have my people call your people, okay?' Mark replied once Jimmy had finished his pitch, openly laughing with the rest of the guys as he finished his lunch. He then went onto say, 'Well fella's, we might be here for a long time, but we're damn sure making it a good time.'

With a double rapping of his knuckles on the chow hall bench, he indicated that he was finished eating. The rest of the guys double tapped the bench in response. Another inmate who had been waiting for his turn to eat at the bench, then took up his spot

Walking up the stairs to Range One, Bezerk caught up with Mark, saying, 'Listen fool, I wanna get with you on something, you know what I mean?'

Bezerk was using his patented remark, 'you know what I mean' Mark had come to understand, he used it most when he was either excited, nervous, deep in thought, or anytime he felt like it.

'Tarver'll be busy runnin' chow for an hour or so, so let's get to it in the house,' Mark replied.

They sauntered into the cell. Closing the cell door meant they didn't want to be disturbed. They pulled out two Coca-Colas and sat down on the plastic chairs assigned to their cell. There was barely room for the two of them. Knoxx sat in front of the two glass slats that served as the window, while Bezerk sat next to the steel countertop that doubled up as the sink. Bezerk leaned onto his elbows and began pulling on his goatee, which meant that he was thinking about how to begin. Mark sat quiet, giving his young protégé his props, letting him begin in his own time and in his own way, giving him some bunky love. He had been watching Bezerk's transformation for a while now, slowly coming back around to being a well-read, bright, enthusiastic and insightful Chris Wright. He had come to realize that Bezerk, or rather, Chris, had a bright future. He could sell fire in Hell, ice in winter and bring the pain like the rain. Knoxx was hoping that today's topic was going to be about the one he had surreptitiously been working on Chris for some weeks now.

Within a few minutes, he was not disappointed, hearing Bezerk say, 'Look dog, you havin' a problem means I got a problem, which ain't good for you and ain't good for me, you know what I mean?'

Mark knew exactly what he meant, and it meant something was going to be done about it.

'You mean on my case?' he replied innocently enough, putting it back to him as if he was not sure what Bezerk was asking him. He hoped Bezerk would take the bait, as he threw the ball back at him, praying Chris would catch it and run with it.

Never one to mince his words when he had something on his mind, Bezerk replied, 'Yeah, dog, your case and this piece of shit rat you got on it. This fool's got to go.'

'I'm holding my own, but there isn't anything I can do about him.'

'Yeah, well listen, no one gets out from under these Feds once they're onto you, dog. You know what I mean. There's only one way to beat 'em, and that's to beat 'em at their own game. You got to go hard at 'em and fuck 'em up real good! Yeess siirr, real good.' Bezerk laughed, imagining the Feds case on Mark coming undone, and said, 'this thing you got going on out in the world, is it for reals?'

'Yeah, bud, I'm calling the group of clubs 'The Envious Group', and each bar and nightclub is going to be called 'Envious', spelled N V S, get it?'

Painting a visual scene, Mark guided Bezerk through it. Like a heat-seeking missile he hit the target. Bezerk fell into a big belly laugh, 'Por Serio, for real? Oh, you're good, boy, damn that's cool, dog, NVS. Yeah, that's gonna work real good. Oh yeah, boy, this fool's gotta go. We're gonna green light this culo's ass for sure.'

He had mischief on his mind as he continued to seriously pull on his goatee while he sat there thinking.

Knoxx just smiled and took a deep swig of his Coca-Cola while Bezerk carried on, 'Yeess siirr, this guy's dead, belieeve thaatt.'

Mark swigged back hard on his Coke again, thinking, *was it done? Was this how things got done?* Knoxx's mind was racing with delight, relief, and fear. Had a decision been reached over a Coke and a smile and just like that, a man's life was going to be taken? Could it be this simple? He finally met Bezerk's eyes and listened as he said, 'Listen Mark, I've been thinking things over some on how best to get it done, with no back trail.'

Knoxx had learned his craft well, but while he listened to Bezerk get into how he was going to get it done, Mark realized he knew his craft well too. How to commit a murder and get away with it. Any plan to get out of prison was a good plan, but Bezerk's plan happened to be a rock solid plan and he could not believe how simple Bezerk's plan was. They got down to business, planning it and running through the pros and cons of it. After that, there was only one more thing to discuss. Payment. The air inside the cell had been thick with conspiracy to commit murder all afternoon. They ran through different versions of how it would all play out in the minds of the Feds, the cops, the media, and whether it would actually improve his chances of getting out or end up making it worse. One thing Mark knew was that once Bezerk had something on his mind, he was determined to find a way to get it done. He knew that once Bezerk was back on the streets in Del Sol, reppin' his block and slinging dope, he'd end up right back in prison, if he was lucky. The more likely outcome would be that he would get himself killed on the streets, going down hard, just as he had lived his life as a Sureño, a Southsider, and a Thug. It seemed easier to talk about murdering a guy than it did about getting paid for it.

Knoxx had been badgering Bezerk about how much it would cost and he continued cajoling him by saying, 'Whatever the amount, dog, I'm sure I've got it covered. I got you, bro, believe thaatt.'

Imitating Bezerk's voice, he helped alleviate some of the tension, causing them to laugh about it. Mark had learned this trick, years ago, mirroring his audience, winning them over to his way of thinking and then closing them, doing whatever it took to stack the cash high on his side of the table. Knoxx had stacked his chips so deep that he could be called Hewlett Packard. Getting his money for Bezerk was probably handling ten grand a month, but for Mark that was a day. And today, there wasn't enough money in the world he wasn't prepared to pay, but the question was: could he bring himself to pay an amount in exchange for a man's murder so that he could go free? Hell yeah, he could.

'C'mon, vato, whatever's on your mind, B'. I got you, dog. You know what I mean?'

Knoxx said, repeating Bezerk's favorite saying while imitating his voice again, helping them to laugh.

But then, after a minute, the cell fell quiet, until Bezerk said quietly, 'Shiitt, I dunno Mark.'

'Just say the number that's in your head. Everyone has a number, Chris, and you know yours, right? I'll tell you what, how 'bout I go first with a number and you tell me if that'll work?' Knoxx said softly, slowly pulling it out of Chris, walking him along with him to close him. He was lying on his bunk and Bezerk was leaning against the wall on his plastic chair. They looked like they were bullshitting the day away when anyone came in for a shot of coffee or some other shit, or when the correctional officer on duty looked in on them during his rounds, while all the time, they had been plotting to exterminate a rat.

26

'Yo, count these nuts!' Bezerk shouted at the correctional officers. Bezerk was being Bezerk while they worked their way around K-Unit, taking the four o'clock count. He taunted them as they looked in on them through the cell door window. Every day was the same and every day, it was the same jibe, and every day, it made them laugh. Every prison in the United States undertakes a stand up four o'clock head count to ensure that every inmate is alive and present.

'Like we do about this time,' he said as they returned to flopping back down on their bunks. It would be another forty-five minutes or more until the four o'clock count cleared and they would be unlocked in preparation for dinner to begin. The whole block was quiet as all the cons were, for the most part, enjoying an afternoon siesta. Throughout lockdown, they heard someone shouting, or screaming, the sounds of arguing or raucous laughter coming from the other cells. Knoxx had made his offer earlier in the day, and Bezerk had said he would think on it in his own noncommittal way. Yet, he hadn't said if the offer of twenty-five thousand dollars was acceptable for murdering a man, exterminating a rat. He had barely given it any thought since he had made the offer, thinking it was unlikely that anything would happen anyway. Everything seemed surreal to him, even now, after all this time in prison. No matter what he thought of the punk-ass bitch, Jason Burne, he knew he was not a murderer. Even though he had always thought about fucking him up or having him taken out, Knoxx knew, in his heart, he didn't want him dead. Anyway, nothing would probably come of it. It felt good to talk about it with Bezerk and fantasize about getting some revenge, but the reality was, just like the rest of the guys in lock on the block he would have to man the fuck up and get on with doing his time. A ten-year sentence was considered a short time, anyway, and Mark was close to being down for eighteen months now. So by the time he got to signing his plea-bargain, and, taking into account his good time, he'd have to serve around six and a half years. That's how all the cons broke their bid down, by justifying the time one day at a time, another day down.

'So what you gonna do when you finally get to bounce outta here, bro'?' Mark asked, putting it to Bezerk while he lay up on his top bunk.

'Shiitt, same as I always do. Go handle my business, dog, you know, back to slingin' dope and throwing some chuck 'ems. Del Sol, mutherfuuckaa's!'

Bezerk sounded empty as he sang it out, trying to make light of it, but Mark knew that he secretly wished that things had been different in his life. Bezerk had resigned himself to being a drug dealer, knowing his destiny was set. Coming back to prison or dying on the streets in a hail of bullets, death being his only solace, he hadn't prepared himself for the afterlife, thinking, *Why ruin the surprise?* After a minute, some words filtered down; he said, 'I'd like to start my own ink shop someday, you know what I mean?' There was a moment of silence. Bezerk then said solemnly, 'I doubt I'd be able to, though, not with my jacket.'

Mark could tell Chris was thinking back to his life. A life lost. Then he heard, 'Fuckin' faaggss.' Bezerk was back.

'What if I had something for you?' Knoxx said, even though his offer sounded hollow. Bezerk leaned over from his top bunk to look down at him and replied, 'Serio, for reals? You know I can turn my hand to anything. Shiitt, you know how I get my hustle on. I'd love to be able to tell my mom's I had something for real, you know what I mean. Man, I'd love to be able to spend a Christmas with my folks. You know, my little Chica, Jessica, my niece, is getting all grown up without me. Damn man, I'd love to get a real start in life. I've been slingin' dope and chuckin' my fists all my life, homes. It's all I know. These fools in here, they got me for life. There ain't no way I'm gonna break out from under them.'

Knoxx nodded, holding Bezerk's gaze. He knew someone's always selling and someone's always buying, and right now, he had to let Chris sell himself on the idea of a fresh start with him. He reassured him by saying, 'Listen, you do this, what we've been talking about, and I'll tell your life will be set; you'll be my dog for life. I can and I will take care of everything for you and your family. I got your back, for real.'

This was his time. Time to close the deal or it would seal his fate. Ten or more years down, doing hard time. Knoxx said, 'Check this out. I ain't ever gonna have you putting in any work on anyone. I'll put you in charge of security for all the clubs. You can manage the guest list and get to hang with all the high rollers.'

Bezerk's face began to light up, imagining how his life in Envious would be, and how all his homeys would be envious of him.

Mark continued, saying, 'Think about it. I can make it happen. You hanging out with all the celebrities, man, how much are you gonna be getting laid? You'd be The Man for real! I need someone who I can trust to run this shit for me, someone who I know is my dog. If you get this thing done for me, well then, I'll know you're my soldier for life. I'll be throwing millions your way. You make it happen for me, and I'll make it happen for you. Easy money, bro'.'

Classic Knoxx, classic pitch, classic close. He flashed the

beginnings of a smile and then Bezerk heard him say, 'Yeess siirr, I heeaardd thaatt!'

Bezerk laughed at the thought of them working together, and then said, 'I don't know shit about running no clubs.'

'Don't worry about that I'll hire all the right people to get all that shit done. You just handle the security and manage the V.I.P. guest list and I'll handle the rest,' he answered, picking up some pace, closing him hard. He sensed that Bezerk was beginning to believe it could happen and, if he thought it could happen, then the other thing would have to happen first.

Bezerk ventured a question, asking, 'What would I be paid for runnin' the security for the clubs?'

'It'll be a whole lot more than you've seen in your life,' Mark replied, imitating his bunky's voice, 'You can belieeve thaatt, yeess shirr.' They giggled, and then Mark went onto explain, 'I'll set you up with some flash cash, some wheels, and a pad when you get out, in how long now, about six months, right?'

'Yeah booyy,' Bezerk answered happily.

Knoxx continued painting his picture for the future, brighter and in more vivid colors, continuing, 'Dude, the day you walk out of the Joint will be the day you start living a real life. I'll show you how to love life and live it large, baabbyy!'

Both of them laughed again, hearing the C.O. shout, 'Clear!'

They heard the clanking of keys in the cell doors, meaning the four o'clock count was over. The cell doors opened and Mark had closed Bezerk. One bad chapter was closing in his life and he would get his life back, he hoped, real soon. After evening chow, all the crew got down to watching the evening news. The War on Terror was spiraling out of control and hundreds of lives were being lost. President Blackmoor said things would improve over time and insisted that he knew best. As a country, he was staying the course in Iraq and Afghanistan. It was common knowledge it seemed, in the United States, that the real power came from the man standing at the left shoulder of President John Blackmoor. Vice President Mr. Stephen Tasker. The consensus flying around Range One was that he called the shots in the administration. It was reported that Vice President Tasker had business ties in Dubai, interests in various companies throughout the world and offshore bank accounts in a number of countries. He was always being filmed at parties with billionaire businessmen and international industrialists. He was later filmed flying off with Karl Musrapt, Andrew Pierce, Darrel Self and Roger Greene. These individuals and their companies had been covered in numerous investigative reports.

Knoxx's evening prison program consisted of watching the CBS Nightly News and then the BBC World News, followed by Entertainment Tonight. None of Range One's crew had any say in what they could watch but Mark still had to shout them down sometimes, shouting, 'Listen up, maggots, if I want to learn anything, I'll listen to myself. Can it! Shut the fuck up!'

Bezerk was getting his hustle on, playing Pinochle at the back of Range One with his O.G. crew, who had all done hard time in various prisons; the old gangsta's still had game and still thrived on the action. Knoxx sat in front of the television, poppin' and looking fresh in an ironed jumpsuit as he had a visitor coming to see him tonight. Jane Mears.

'Knoxx visit!' Officer Tarver shouted up at him while she sauntered across the day room floor to open the hard steel door of K-Unit.

The hour's visit flew by, with them swapping some gossip, some funny stories and then they traded news on what was happening on the street. Jane always asked how his mom and dad, Maggie and Danny, were doing. They had been like surrogate parents to her when they had dated. Mark always said he would let them know that she had asked after them. Jane did her best to put on a brave face for her perfect Mark, especially when their time ended in the dank, stark visiting room.

Mark began said, laced with emotion, 'Honey, no matter how it all turns out, I want you to know that I love you and I always will. Forever, honey. You're my first true love and my last true friend.'

He paused, taking up Jane's hands, which were hot and moist to the touch. She was doing her best to keep it all together for him and not cry as she replied, asking, 'I don't care what you've done, I just want you back out here with me. This isn't you. Whatever you have to do to get out, you have to do it. Whatever you need me to do, just tell me.'

'You know, I dreamed of being rich. Dreams are where we figure out where we want to go in life, and life is just how we get there. Be sure to allow for traffic,' he quipped, trying to bring a small smile out of Jane.

She dabbed at her eyes, asking, 'What is it? Please tell me?'

The only thing Mark could ever tell Jane was the truth. He replied, 'I just want to be a good person, you know? Do good, but I guess in order for me to do that, I think I'm going to have to sell my soul to the devil.'

Jane's sharp, green eyes glinted under the white lights, moist with pain, but she regained her composure. She straightened up in the plastic chair to look Mark in his eyes, saying sternly, 'Whatever you have to do, do it.'

27

Knoxx returned from his visit in a mood that told everyone to stay clear of him. After a quiet couple of hours, he called Jane to make sure she had arrived safely back at her apartment in Santa Monica. Jane again, stressed her point over the phone that time was running out. When Knoxx stepped in front of the judge again, that would be all he would have in front of him at his sentencing. Time.

Bezerk had been shouting from the card table for him to make the night's spread. He had ignored him while he watched the late news covering the war in Iraq, and then the gang violence in the streets of L.A. and in Tijuana, Mexico. A report came on the news about the latest government scandal where it had been caught wiretapping U.S. citizens' homes and cellular phone calls without approved wiretap warrants. The report went further by suggesting the same thing might be happening with individual's' bank accounts too. The reporter questioned, 'And all of this is in the defense against global terrorism?'

It seemed Vice President Tasker might be responsible for approving the illegal wiretapping and surveillance. While he watched, Knoxx garnered an admiration for the man because he was obviously a man who made things happen. Rumors were that he had tens of millions tucked away in offshore bank accounts held in blind trusts. They were earnings generated from his global powerhouse company, Macbine, which had, in turn, made him bulletproof from lobbyists' influences. Knoxx had determined that this guy had so much juice in Washington that he did not give a shit what anyone thought of him. He was King-fucking-Kong along The Beltway. In the mood he was in, it was just what Knoxx needed to see and hear, and it helped to steel him to his task. The United States pushed people around - hell, even countries around - to get its way, so why not him? There and then, Knoxx decided he wanted in on the biggest game in the world. Sitting in this hellhole, in his white t-shirt and gray flannel shorts, with shower shoes on his feet, he knew his destiny lay somewhere else. Not here, not in this place, not now, not ever. Bezerk had been putting the spread together in between hands of Pinochle, while he and his boys routinely shouted, 'Bet! Bet!' from the card table. One of them had to drop to the floor every few minutes to give up twenty push-ups if they lost a hand.

As he left his seat in front of the television, Andrew the Knacker Matthews, commented to him about what he thought he'd heard, 'What was that?'

Knoxx repeated in a dark tone, saying, 'Destiny, bro'.'

Later that night, correctional officer, Miss Tarver, gave a shout out to her favorite hoods on the block, as she locked down K-Unit for the night, telling them, 'Good night fella's. You be good now you hear?'

'Like we do about this time, you know how we do,' Bezerk said ruefully.

Bezerk handed Mark his jailhouse spread. It was in a small plastic container filled with Tap Ramen soup, refried beans, chopped up Summer Sausage, topped off with squeeze cheese and Doritos nacho chips, washed down with an ice cold Coca-Cola. He then launched into his play-by-play on how he'd cleaned up in Pinochle while they ate. Each day was the same routine, and each day finished the same. This was their life. The two of them ate and bullshitted some more while the ten o'clock count rolled by, and then Knoxx began the real conversation, carrying some bad intentions on his face when he said, 'You thought on it anymore? You know, about what we talked about earlier?'

'Yeah, I got you, dog,' was all Bezerk offered as his response.

Watching Bezerk stick his plastic fork into his spread, Mark felt that wasn't good enough. He answered, 'That ain't what I want to hear. You know what I mean? I got to know and I need to know now.'

Leaning in and closing the gap, pushing up on him. Bezerk noticed the intent in Knoxx's eyes and was quick to extinguish the blaze by answering him, 'I know what you're sayin' and I'm sayin' I got it handled. It's getting done, belieeve thaatt.'

Regaining his composure, Mark continued in a more controlled manner, explaining, 'Look, I've done my part and arranged to get you ten grand. I just want the return on my investment, that's all I'm saying. I'm just nervous, I guess, you know. About what I'm a part of, I can't believe I could be capable of something like this.'

Bezerk sounding like he was softening too. He lowered his voice and his demeanor, replying, 'Yeah I know. Just keep your head in the game and keep doing what you do best. You do you, and I'll do me. We both know what's at stake and what needs to happen. Just know, dog, this fool's gone for reals. He's like dust in the wind, and just like dust in the wind, he's gonna get blown away, you'll see. Yeess siirrr, this mutherfuckaa's gone!' he proceeded to explain that the message he'd sent out of the prison, known as 'a kite', had been received and understood.

It was all just a matter of time.

28

It was now eleven thirty and lights out had passed some time ago, but they were still pumped, talking about what they wanted to do once they were back on the streets. There was no more talk about what had to be done for this to happen, as there was nothing they could do about it. All they could do was lie on their bunks and bullshit the night away. Periodically, they'd get up to scope out the view at the hotel's pool across the street, where a drunken, horny couple had come up for some night time activities unaware that they were being watched. Mark had spent so much time sitting by the window, gazing out at the world below him that he felt he knew everyone's daily routine within a seven block radius. Looking down, searching for inspiration while he worked on his plans, he knew the delivery times of the U.P.S. guy, and most of the times when people went to and returned from work.

They also knew what else was coming around midnight. It was the only outside noise they ever heard. The Santa Fe Cruiser, the midnight train that rolled north from Mexico along the coast to Los Angeles delivering goods, grain, and fresh fruits. Blowing its foghorn, approaching downtown San Diego. The railway crossing gates lowered, shutting off each street. The thunder from the locomotive shook the streets below as its heavy engines pulled anywhere from ninety-five to one hundred and seventeen train cars through. It took around sixteen minutes to pass through downtown, with its huge night light burning up the track ahead of it, making this a spectacle that the two of them did not like to miss. It gave them something to bet on, and argue about who had lost the bet, while the train still rumbled through town below them. Tonight's bet had been to dance an Irish Jig, when the twelve o'clock count came by. Sure enough, when their flashlights shined into Cell One, there was Bezerk, having lost the bet by nine cars, doing the Jig like a man possessed, in his white boxers, with one white tube sock hanging off his right foot. Both of them were laughing their asses off. The two prison guards looked in, laughing their asses off too.

After things had dialed down, Mark signed off for the night. 'Another day down, dog.'

Bezerk sleepily replied, 'Like we do about this time.'

29

'What? What? You wanna go?'

Wap! Wap! Wap! Bezerk had gone, well, berserk.

Gamble, lie, cheat, steal and worse, snitch in the Joint, then there's only one way it's going to end. Ugly. If you did any one of these things, then you had better be good at two things: paying up or getting down.

Bezerk was going hard at it at 6:40 in the morning, throwing down in their cell doorway, standing in his boxer shorts, with his shower shoes on with a black, Crip gangbanger. The gangbanger had decided he would push up on Bezerk first thing, thinking there was a discrepancy on his loss from the Pinochle card game the night before. Things had quickly gone from bad to worse. The gangsta said he didn't want to pay anything, clearly miscalculating the resolve of Bezerk, even at 6:40 in the morning. Bezerk wanted what was his and he was sure as shit going to get it. 'Make me wait, punk, see what happens, yeah right, fuck yoouu! I'm comin' to get mine and you'd better have it, or see how I'm gonna fuck you up!'

The O. G. slid back across the floor of Range One, flat on his ass from a right hook. Bezerk slammed the cell door shut and jumped back up on his perch above Mark, who duly got up and turned out the light. He grumbled as he rolled over to go back to sleep on his top bunk. 'Fuckin' faaggss.'

Knoxx, reinforcing the mood, showing Bezerk some bunky love, said, 'Let 'em come get some.'

Another day had begun. The rules of doing time the right way was to 'roll along to get along'. The shotcallers held their power by brute force. If you're a piece of shit on the streets then the cons inside are going to figure out real quick that you're a piece of shit inside. If they're in to your shit, and word is put out on you, 'He's no good', then you had better be a ghost or roll up and check your ass into the hole. Civilians, punks, snitches and fags were the game the lions in the Joint preyed upon every day. The lions roamed the plains of the unit and the yard, looking to fuck someone up or take their shit. Pay your dues. If you want to stay out of harm's way, then you had better stay out of their way. Plain and simple, easy money. Do your bid right, you can repay your debt to society and you might even get to live to talk about it.

The days rolled on and so did the boys on K-Unit. Knoxx played Texas Hold 'Em with some of his friends, Matthews, Iverson, Malton and Ivan the Russian Zarchovic. Matthews was in on for money laundering four million dollars worth of bogus telephone calling cards. Iverson was in on a drug trafficking charge, bringing in drugs from Mexico. Malton ran prostitutes and Coyotes, people who smuggled illegal immigrants, stowed away inside cars and any other forms of transport, across the Mexico border. The U.S. Coastguard had arrested Zarchovic off the coast of Peru. The Coastguard had come to their aid, since it looked like their boat was sinking because it was loaded down with seventeen tons of cocaine. He'd posted the twenty million dollars for the bail, but the judge then had a change of heart, saying, 'Anyone who can come up with that kind of money can definitely disappear if he chooses to.'

Matthews, Iverson, Malton and Zarchovic passed on their contact details and their friends' contact details to Knoxx for future reference.

Knowledge and Bezerk only made a few references to their discussion, and they both knew not to push it as they had a lot riding on it. They had placed their bets and they were all in. Bezerk went about his daily routine, getting his hustle on while Knoxx read the newspapers and discussed the state of the world's affairs with his posse. They both took time out in the day, getting their money, working out together.

'Get the fuck off me, you assholes! Fuuckk yoouu!' Sam Malton shouted from the floor, followed up with laughter. He had his jumpsuit pulled up over his head, while both Mark and Bezerk playfully kicked him in his groin and in his back, dropping on him with their elbows, WWE Wrestling style. Malton was at their mercy, having had the audacity to walk into their house when they were talking privately. What he had needed was a shot of coffee, but what he ended up getting was a shot to the balls. Back on his feet and red in the face but in one piece, Malton managed to put on a brave face, saying, 'Nah, fuck you guys, you wait 'til you're in Tijuana, then I'll fuck you guys up. TJ's my fucking town. You'll see; I'm gonna kick your ass!'

Everyone laughed.

Bezerk, getting his breath back, replied in fits of laughter, 'Naa fuck that fool. I'm gonna come down there and I'm taking all your shit, and I'm gonna take me a piece of your ass too, while I'm at it.'

Whatever the games, stunts, scams and plots, they all helped pass the time by a little easier. Prison is built tough because it holds tough guys, and everyone in it is doing time for a good reason. They're bad guys with bad intentions and just because they looked like a pride of lions, lazing the days away, didn't mean they were all pussycats, because they weren't. K-Unit housed killers.

30

Like most Tuesday nights, it was movie night, and the night that new fish were on the line, coming onto K-Unit. New guys coming in off the street always caused a commotion, getting assigned their cells, with everyone checking them out. One guy rolled in, walking off to Cell Three on Range Four, and his name was Calvin Boozy Dedrick. He stood five foot ten inches, and he weighed in at around two hundred and thirty-eight pounds. Forged from hardened steel, he carried a look of murder on his face. Sheriffs had taken him down in a running gun battle while he made a break for the Mexican border, having been on the run across the United States since gunning down three rival drug dealers eight days earlier back in Dorchester, Boston. At thirty-eight years old, and like most of K-Unit, Dedrick had been in and out of juvenile prisons and mainline prisons for over half of his life. Only this time, coming into M.C.C., that was what he was looking at: life in prison.

The Piru Bloods' shotcaller, called T.C., Top Cat, up on Range Three, already had his crew on high alert. They knew this guy's rep from the news stations that had been following the story, and this shotcaller knew he could not allow Dedrick to stay on K-Unit for even five minutes. Word on the tier was the gangbangers he had slain back in Boston were some of their own Bloods. It would be an eye for an eye. Even inside the Joint, the war still raged. T.C. took up counsel with his captains on the upper tier, while his troops kept a close eye below. Knoxx had noticed the commotion from across the floor and sent word over to Bezerk for him to get comfortable up front on Range One. Things looked like they were about to heat up and something was about to go down. He was right.

Within twelve minutes of Dedrick's arrival, the Bloods sent down a scout named Sleepy, built like a tall, thin, cool glass of water and no threat to anyone. Boozy stood in his cell with the meanest, banging headache, his whole body aching from the past few days' events. Confronted by Sleepy, Boozy turned him out in such a way and with such disrespect that it became clear to T.C. that it was on for real. They were going to have to check this guy into the hole. What Boozy Dedrick wanted was a large pepperoni pizza, chicken wings, a six-pack of Buds and a suite at the Marriott with two fine-ass bitches waiting for him in bed. What he had was a cold, hard cell with a cold steel bunk in it, a paper cup in his hand, a plastic bag full of washroom items and a cold realization that this was going to be his future. He was starting life without parole and he was in no mood to play nice or make friends tonight.

Meanwhile, up on Range Three, T.C. had decided that this guy wasn't going to be getting settled in on K-Unit, for even one night. They were going to go handle their business right away and get this dude to roll up off the floor. Dedrick was going to be checked into the SHU: Secured Housing Unit; The Hole, one way or another. The task of doing that fell to big Ray, who was a big, kettle black, militant, shiny, bald-headed brother. He was a little slow, but that didn't matter, because that's how he broke you down, slow and steady. Standing at around six foot five and weighing at around two hundred and eighty pounds, few men could stand in his way. T.C. dispatched some of his soldiers down onto the dayroom floor. Knoxx was watching it all unfold from his seat on Range One, deciding that this was better than watching a movie. They both settled in for the show, Bezerk explaining that it was going to be a rival gang jump off. An East Coast West Coast thing, so it was cool; no one else's crew had to be on point.

Boozy casually strolled up onto the dayroom floor to get a taste of cool water, and then sat down at the nearest seat at the end of chow benches, closest to his cell. Ray got up from his chair above on Range Three, telling one of his boys, 'Hold down my spot, I'll be back in a few.'

He took off his radio and headset and began to make his way down the stairs to walk onto the dayroom floor. Sleepy kept the evening shift C.O. busy by shooting the shit about last night's basketball game.

Boozy quietly took another sip, paying no mind to anyone, with no thoughts in particular. No one got the chance to find out if he had poetry or murder on his mind.

The four top tiers were now on red alert and most of the O.G.'s and shotcallers were all watching the two of them without really watching. This was the most dangerous time as anyone who got in the way could spark off a race war. The enemy of my enemy is my friend, and none of the other crews wanted these two teaming up in a war against them.

Ray's black dome glistened as he leaned over Boozy from across the chow bench. Boozy simply stared back up at him with a look of amusement on his face. Ray started to get his blood flow up, getting more animated as his big, bobble head began to move from side to side, getting crazier by the second. In his slow way, he had gotten his point across as he stared Boozy down, waiting for the reply to his command, 'Roll the fuck up, bitch.'

That was the last thing Range Three heard Ray say. Boozy had pushed himself out from under the chow bench to get his own point across. He delivered five quick jabs to Ray's throat, with the point of a pencil he'd had strapped into the palm of his hand. It worked like a piston. Boozy's hand fired one shot after another, the pencil going in deeper and deeper with every piston-like pump. Blood spurted out from Ray's neck. He didn't shout out and he didn't look up to his Range for any help, because he couldn't. He was headed for the deck with Boozy holding him firmly in his grip, wailing away on him. Ray was already dying from his wounds. All the peisas, inmates and maggots jumped up from their seats and began shouting and hollering as everyone became aware of these two guys fighting to the death. The correctional officer immediately came out onto the dayroom floor and pushed the panic button on his radio. Catching Boozy's eye, he shouted, 'Lockdown! Lockdown! Everyone to your cell!'

Boozy Dedrick seemed to hesitate, looking at the cop, before he looked down at Ray, helpless in his hands, gasping and wheezing for air. Dedrick made his final choice between life and death. Knoxx never forgot what he witnessed and he never forgot Calvin Dedrick, watching him drive the pencil into Ray's left eye. He released him from his grip, and Ray's lifeless body slumped to the floor between his feet, while Boozy's arm was covered in blood. He looked across the floor to two Blood gangsta's, looking ready to take up the next wave of attack.

Knoxx was now standing up, leaning against the railing on Range One, saying excitedly to Bezerk, 'Holy shiitt!' Taking in the surreal action in front of him.

Like a proud father, Bezerk answered, 'Yeess siirrr, that's how things get done. He handled his business all right.'

Boozy waited. The Bloods stood ready. T.C. stood on top of Range Three. He gave the nod for them to stand down, thinking he had lost one too many soldiers for one night.

The whole floor was in turmoil as everyone went wild, howling, yelping, shouting and whistling. This was Hell. The pencil had done its work; Boozy's sword was still strapped into the palm of his hand as the heavy, steel door to K-Unit opened and the riot squad moved in to take him down. He managed to get off two big hooks that deflected off the shields as they took him to the floor, hogtying him with zip ties. They began to carry him out. The lions roared in unison throughout the floor as the guards took him out of K-Unit. No matter what the beef was, all the cons knew they had one thing in common: they hated the cops. The cops knew it too, and so they formed a skirmish line facing each upper tier, banging on their shields with their nightsticks as intimidation. None of the shotcallers or their soldiers moved into their cells on the top tiers. The pride of lions was deciding what their next move would be.

'First one in the tube's a rubber bullet; from then on, it's all live rounds gentleman!' The Captain's voice boomed out over the blow horn. The guards stood firm with their shotguns at the ready, seconds ticking by. Outnumbered and outgunned, the lions returned to their dens, one by one, deciding to take up the fight another day. All the ranges were locked down for the night. Range One got settled in for the long haul, which ended up being for two weeks. All of K-Unit enjoyed room service as each inmate was given their meals through the slats in the cell doors and let out, one cell at a time, for showers.

No one had gotten to know Dedrick, and yet, all the cons admired him for the way he had handled his business. Knoxx would never forget the way Dedrick handled his business in such a clear minded, definitive way. He had read later in the newspaper that Calvin Dedrick received four life sentences and was sent to ADX super max prison in Florence, Colorado. He was quoted at his sentencing, defiantly saying, 'The problem ain't the problem. The problem is your attitude towards the problem.'

During lockdown, no one had any contact with the outside world. Time, it seemed, stood still. Cell One on Range One just laid it down for two weeks, taking power naps, playing chess, cards, betting on the Santa Fe Train at midnight, and every afternoon was spent working out in the cell, getting their money. For the most part, Chris read books and Mark sat by the window, working on an idea that had come to mind over the past few weeks from watching the news. An idea had taken shape that gnawed at him throughout the lockdown. He had to write it down or go insane.

They spoke about the role Bezerk would play in the Envious Group, with Mark describing his dreams for it. He consistently drilled into Chris how he wanted him to speak, and explained how to become Christopher Wright again. Bezerk slowly came around to the idea that this might be the time to finally give up his violent past and start over. He realized he had been talking about getting out of The Life, for probably half his life and now. Here it was. Now he had the chance to change his life. He had The Out, but the funny thing was that he had fought for everything in his life with the heart of a lion, but for the first time in his life, he was scared, and the one thing that scared him was change.

Knoxx had sprinkled some of his magic on Bezerk. That magic dust had made Bezerk disappear, and Chris Wright appeared before his eyes. Now the two of them were as thick as thieves, planning their future. Bezerk sat at the steel countertop most days, drawing, listening to his radio. This time, he had drawn a Southsider, with shades on and a long moustache, looking back over razor wire across the border from Mexico into California. The caption read No Quiero Trabajar. It meant: I Don't Wanna Work. Bezerk, eyeing his work, said that he would put it up on the wall in the NVS office to remind him of where he'd come from and to remind himself that he needed to do what Mark had said. Laughing hard, he went a step further, saying he would look at it while he'd be fucking all the hot Hollywood babes in his office, as that would not be any work for him either. Bezerk then got busy on another picture, laughing hysterically at times, which brought tears to his eyes as he saw it taking shape. He didn't let Mark see it until later, when it was finished. He shouted for him to come into the cell to check it out. When Mark arrived, he told him, 'Yeah booyy, this is what I'm gonna do when I come over to your pad, bro'.'

Mark stood over Bezerk and, in a fun, joking way, replied, 'Then there's no way you're coming to my house, faagg.'

He looked at it and began laughing uncontrollably. The drawing was of Chris as a young schoolboy, when he was thirteen, with a fat belly poking out over his pants, peeing into Knoxx's swimming pool. A caption at the bottom read: Is It So Wrong?

Knoxx found that he could not sleep. The quiet of the days and nights only fuelled his dormant rage further, fanning his hatred for the cops, the government, the outside world and, himself. His idea was strewn about his bunk on crumpled bits of paper. Then, early one morning, while he was looking out over the bay at the golden hues of yellows, reds and oranges, the morning sky gave him the gift of clarity of mind, filling his spirit and giving him the outline of his vision. It came to him in an instant. It spoke to his soul and it gave him one word: HEAVEN.

He shared his vision, his nightmare, his dream and his plan with Chris throughout the day, while they sat in their white boxer shorts and white tube socks, sipping on the last of their Coca-Cola's. They discussed the ramifications of the idea that he had come up with, both thinking about it in their own way, finalizing its meaning. HEAVEN, he then on to explain, it stood for Hospital Evaluation and Authenticated Vitals Encoded Navigator. Mark explained that it could provide a service to patients who needed it the most; the sick, the poor and the elderly. He could use the income streams generated from the Envious Group to pay for the research and development of it, supplying the Navigators to hospitals throughout the United States and then, who knows, maybe the world, charging a monthly fee for the downloads from HEAVEN's database.

He finally said, 'This is my chance to finally do something good, you know? A chance to right my wrongs. I have some sort of destiny, I know I do. Maybe this is it, and you know what? Someone's probably going to think it up anyway, so why not me? It's like this. I either watch someone else do it or you do it with me. This is gonna take us so high, we'll be looking down on Heaven!'

Cracking a smile, they broke into laughter. Mark continued selling himself on his wild idea, which was wild because they were sitting in a prison cell and he was facing a minimum of ten years in prison. Bezerk had a hint of hope in his eyes and the burning light of freedom was shining hot and bright in him as he looked at Mark, saying, 'Shiitt, doogg, you're either one of the smartest dudes I've ever met or you're one of the craziest fuckaa's, for reals.'

Laughing some more at how it all sounded, the two just sat there looking to each other, checking for doubt in each other's face. The cell went quiet with quiet confidence as they began to see it all for what it was. Genius. It was just madness to think that they could be the guys to pull it off.

'Another day down, dog.' Knoxx remarked, as another night ended.

Bezerk answered, 'Like we do about this time.'

The stifled sound of 'ding, ding, ding, ding,' from the railroad tracks' crossing gates let them know that the Santa Fe Train was rolling through. Letting Bezerk and Knowledge know that it was midnight. Neither one of them wanted to play tonight. All they wanted was to be out of this place, just for one night. They both realized their time had come, while they lay on their bunks thinking about their future. Everything had its place in time, and Mark now realized his place in time was to have been here, in prison.

31

'The greatest competition in life is the competition you should be having with yourself, bro'. Run when you can, walk if you have to and crawl if you must, but never give up. Form a strategy, build a routine and execute the plan, and then repeat. That's how I want to build Envious and develop my HEAVEN program. HEAVEN can revolutionize the way drugs are administered, reducing the risks from doctors under stress. It can all be run through the Internet in real time. That's the beauty of it. I can run it from anywhere in the world, so why not do some good for a change.' Knoxx stated, idly chatting, passing along his knowledge to Bezerk as they laid it down on their bunks. Another early morning sun was beginning to light up the dark light from the previous night's sky.

The silence was deafening until Chris spoke up with real clarity, having real concern for his well-being he said, 'Shiitt, doogg, you think they'll actually let you develop it? You know what I mean? Those guys out there don't fuck around, man, and they got the biggest gang on the block. Man, look at all the shit the U.S.'s into, all the wiretapping and monitoring of everyone's bank accounts. They ain't gonna let you fuck them around.'

They both realized the threat it would pose to the pharmaceutical companies if he were to develop HEAVEN. He then reflected on Bezerk's words and replied, 'Never get too settled. When you spend too much time resting on your laurels, all you'll get is a sore ass. Before I came into prison, I only had two goals in life. One was to drink in every bar and drink it dry, and two, was to sleep with every woman in the world. Yeah boy, all I got now are these bars, and I'm getting fucked alright by these punk-ass bitch cops!'

The two of them broke into a long chuckle on that one. Bezerk added to the fun when he rolled over from his top bunk laughing, to say, 'Open your eyes boy, I'm a blessing in disguise. Don't get it twisted and don't let these fucks beat you down. Otherwise it'll feel like you're doin' your time sittin' on an inner tube in the ocean with a slow leak, mutherfuckaa's! Like we do about this time.'

They heard the familiar sound of the keys rattling on the correctional officer's chain. It was around twelve minutes past six in the morning, when Mark got to taking his piss when their cell door was unlocked. Lockdown was over and K-Unit exploded into life as all the cons came out of their cells to see who was still around. It was good to be back out on the floor after having no outside contact for two weeks.

Everyone immediately got down to business, getting caught up on the CNN, the Compound News Network.

'C'mon, doogg, I got's to blow it up for reals.' It was Bezerk's way of telling him that he needed to go to toilet in a big way.

Knoxx took his time getting their cups of coffee on purpose, just to taunt Bezerk one more time. They had laid it down for two weeks straight and now the games and stunts were back in play. Another day had begun, just like the last five hundred and fifty-two days before them, for Mark.

Bezerk, getting all mad, said, 'Uh huh, try me, fool! Very funny, doogg! Go on, bet me and see if I don't just drop right here in front of you. I'll just sit here and poop, right now, and you can watch me if you like. Go on, BET!' He stood by the cell door as Mark made his way out past him, laughing. He then shouted back as the cell door slammed behind him, 'BET!'

He got in line for some hot water behind Larry Kirkpatric, also known as Bones, the shooter for the Hells Angels. Being the shooter, he was facing the most time, and so would be the last one to go down for sentencing. Bones greeted him in a friendly way, asking him, 'Hey Mayhem, are they still together?' he was calling Knoxx by his pet nickname.

Knoxx looked blankly at him, replying, 'Who?'

'Your butt cheeks,' Bones answered, proud of himself for trapping Mark on his joke.

'Oh yeah, nice one, fool. I'll be on you, you can belieeve thaatt!' Knoxx replied, mimicking Bezerk's voice.

They both sniggered, while Bones replied, as he moved off, 'Yeah, I know you will, Mayhem.'

Knoxx spent the best part of two hours watching the morning news. The White House seemed in turmoil with the wiretapping scandal having expanded to twelve billion dollars in cash that had gone missing in Iraq. The Senate was trying to approve subpoenas to find out what was going on. He was enthralled, glancing across at his partner Bezerk, knowing the ramifications for Knoxx's new venture. It all seemed so surreal, being in prison, sitting on something with such power and global appeal.

There was that man again, controlling the flow of information, the Vice President of the United States, Stephen Tasker, taking a sip from a glass of water before he read out a prepared statement. 'I can assure the citizens of this nation that every avenue of investigation will be exhausted. I shall personally oversee the investigation into any misuse of power within this administration, and in any misuse of federal resources in the illegal activities of what is essentially spying on our own people. I send this warning out to those who may be subpoenaed: It is easier to tell the truth; that way you do not have to remember what you've said in the past.'

Tasker finished strong, standing presidential at the podium in the Rose Garden. Having taken the media's questions, he finished with a polite nod and a said a quick 'thank you' as he then walked back into the White House. Slim, six foot two and bald, Tasker portrayed himself in the most professional and controlled manner. Every word, every movement, his body language was honed to convey money, power and respect. He was the three hundred pound gorilla in the White House administration, known for being the thinker, the strategist and the doer.

Mark checked the time. It was finally a respectable time to call Jane. Taking his plastic chair over to the phone, he sat down at it and dialed her number. He heard her answer on the second ring. After the recording initiated, letting the recipient know the call was from Federal prison, Jane hit the number five button to allow it to connect. Mark opened up in his casual way, saying, 'Hi ya honey.'

Upon hearing his voice, Jane immediately broke into uncontrollable tears, muttering and mumbling.

'What, honey? Slow down. I'm okay; it was nothing to do with me. We were all in lockdown for two weeks in our cells. I couldn't call you. What's that? Breathe, hun, slow down.'

The words came in a torrent over the phone, and finally hit home like a sledgehammer. Jane's voice was shaking and nervous, but she had managed to relay the important part of what she needed to tell him. She laid it out for him and he felt his whole body go numb. His mind was numb and his toes were numb as he fought for each breath, trying to keep his own words steady, easy and smooth, as if disengaged from their conversation. He did his level best to shut Jane down, shut her up and get her off the phone as fast as possible. Jane had told him that Jason Burne, the rat, was dead. He'd been carjacked on his way home. Two Mexican gangbangers who had just robbed a gas station, needed a car for their getaway and they had run over to his and shot him dead to take it.

32

'How do you feel? Are you okay with all of this?'

Knoxx was in the visiting room with his lawyer, Simon Pike. He had been telling Knoxx that, in three days, he would be out of prison.

The U.S. prosecutor's case had crumbled because of the premature death of their witness, Jason Burne. He was the only guy who could tie Knoxx to their case, having been the only person who had information on the bank account transactions. There were no other eyewitness accounts or documents to support the government's claims and they had no bank accounts linking Knoxx to the money. What they did have was a lot of circumstantial evidence and one deflated U.S. District Attorney. The words falling from his mouth, Mark casually replied, 'Funny how it all works out. I guess what goes around comes around.'

Holding Pike's stare, Pike seemed to know its meaning, but they both opted to leave it at that.

'Yeah, I guess it's a good piece of luck or fate on your part, hey?' Pike retorted, as he picked up his papers. Knoxx held his tongue and gave Pike the opportunity to change the subject. Pike then said, 'So I'll see you in court in three days. District Attorney Bergman has assured me that if you pay your fine and plead No Contest to the indictment, she'll drop the embezzlement and money laundering charges as part of a global deal. We'll be in Judge York's court for the hearing and she's pretty sympathetic to defendant's rights, so there shouldn't be any problems.' Squaring off his papers and loading them into his briefcase, he remarked, 'So that's it, Mark. You're out. Stay out of trouble, and please, stay off the phone,' he said, as if imparting some kind of hidden message.

Knoxx then stood up to shake hands, and asked, 'One last thing,'

'Yes?'

'Will I have any type of record, you know, criminal record?'

'No, you'll have a civil judgment against you on the fifteen and a half million dollar fine. The charges are dropped, so no; you'll have nothing on you as far as the federal government is concerned. You're a free man both in character and in the ledger of keeping score.'

'It's always about the money isn't it?' Mark said with an ironic smile.

Pike replied, joking, 'Yes, Mark. You mean you haven't figured that one out yet?'

Knoxx stripped out in the strip out tanks one last time. The cop looked bored as he ran through the routine, looking

106

at nuts and butts as he lifted his up real high, showing off his big balls of steel. Walking back onto K-Unit, he could hardly contain himself as he looked up at some of the top tiers, where some of the shotcallers were railing up off them, bullshitting, passing the time. They gave Knoxx their sign of respect with a look of 'waassuup', and, 'good lookin'', nodding their heads at him and pursing their lips. There was respect and props for their nigga' Knoxx, as word went around that he was out. He had handled his business. No one came up to speak to him about it. Only in passing, did they congratulate him, in such a way that hinted at them knowing. For now, they did know. He had come into prison a civilian, but now he was leaving them as a lion, as one of their own.

Mark and his boy Bezerk stayed in their cell for the best part of the next three days, having only one thing left to do. Getting Knoxx inked up. Bezerk gave him an awesome jailhouse tattoo that Mark had envisioned and roughly drawn, with Bezerk working on him relentlessly, getting it down. He had chosen a fighting dragon to symbolize wisdom and courage, as well as a hurricane of vengeance and a shield with 'One Life One Love', written across it and the name 'Jane' draped over it. The skull behind it meant that he would protect her until his dying day, wrapped around his right bicep. Bezerk finished the half-sleeve tattoo off with his own mark of allegiance and respect, with a tattoo of the Southsiders membership inked on him. 'Mi Vida Loca', the three ink dots symbolized, 'My Crazy Life'. Mark chose to go the whole way, getting a tribal scorpion, as he was a Scorpio, wrapped around his left bicep, along with EXILE tattooed on his left triceps. Exile Corporation had now been formed as the company that would own both the Envious Group and HEAVEN. He was ready.

In nature, it comes down to kill to survive. The gazelle wakes up in the morning, knowing it has to run faster than the slowest gazelle to survive. When the lion wakes up, it knows it also has to run faster than the slowest gazelle to survive. When the sun comes up, you had better start running. As the sun came up on this final morning, he knew that by sundown, he would be a free man. He had faced down his demons and had come to terms with fact that he had taken one life to win one back. His own.

'Nuts to butts, guys, find a friend,' the correctional officer was saying to the cons coming back up on The Bus from the court, some of the U.S. Marshals and C.O.'s on the court run. They had their fun at Knoxx's expense, knowing he was done with his bid in the big house. They thought he'd probably had something to do with having won his freedom, making remarks on the way to, and from, the court. He didn't rise to any of it, as his mind was already on what flavor pussy he'd be eating later that night. Cutting him out from the mainline chain, he stood waiting for K-Unit's door to open one last time. He walked into the unit and there they were. His posse were all waiting for him, expectantly, and had put together one last jailhouse spread for him. All the shotcallers came over and Range One cleared out as all the high power congregated as a sign of respect for their new soldier. Everyone was making light of the fact that he was on his way out, giving him messages to pass on and telling him, again, to write them.

They all respected the fact that he was a man of his word, and he was Knowledge to them. They knew he was driven, motivated, and ruthless. A leader is not measured by the position he holds, but by the actions he takes, and they knew the action he had taken. He'd had the money, he was given the power, and now he had earned their respect. Knoxx had paid the entrance fee into a very exclusive club, he was in a crime family now, his seat in power, safe and secure.

Mark pulled Bezerk into their house, where he gave him his entire store from his locker and headset radio to pass on or sell. The two of them embraced, and for a moment, looked into each other's eyes as brothers.

From the many, they were one. They were brothers in arms. Bezerk gave him a large manila envelope, from which he pulled out a drawing of a young schoolboy peeing in a swimming pool. Bezerk choked back, saying heavily, 'I'm gonna do it for reals, doogg.'

'Yeah boy, I don't doubt it,' Mark replied, feeling some emotion too as Bezerk took the picture from him and then laid it down on the countertop.

Bezerk said, 'I put something else in it for you, too.'

'Yeah?'

'Yeah, look here, it's our Southsider codes. I've hidden it in the picture for you; it's the phone number for my boss on the street, Big Smoke.'

A number of dots were hidden in the drawing that read like a telephone keypad.

'Call him dog, okay. He'll hook you up; tell him you're with me.'

Mark just chose to look at Chris for a moment, before he finally summed it all up, saying, 'You know what Chris? You and me meeting, it was destiny.'

Get Back

33

Having spent most of the day working his way through the strip out tanks, Knoxx found it amusing that most of the cops thought it odd he was leaving with only an envelope. They opened it and pulled out a picture of a fat kid peeing into a swimming pool, looking over his shoulder with his index finger pursed at his lips. Each cop laughed and made his own comment about it. Mark laughed to, knowing it had the phone number for the Southsiders' big homey encoded in it and he was walking it out right under their noses. The best place to hide something was out in the open, he knew, having been trained a long time ago in the art of deception. After what seemed like the longest and most anxiety-filled day of his life, he pushed through the huge, heavy brass and glass doors to breathe his first breath of free air in nearly nineteen months. Union Street in downtown San Diego was all hustle and bustle with everyone going about their business. They were mainly lawyers, district attorneys and inmate's visitors pushing their way up the street, all wanting to get into M.C.C., while Knoxx had been dreaming of getting out of it. Now here he was, covering his eyes from the sun to get a better look at the world, which was a menagerie of colors, sounds and people all talking and walking. None of them had a clue who he was or where he had just come from, or what he had done to get out. Standing tall and wide-eyed on the sidewalk, absorbing it all, he realized that he had the choice of taking a left or a right, as it didn't matter one ounce where he went today, because today was the first day of his new life as a free man.

Rounding the corner and marching towards him, not wanting to miss him, wanting to be his welcoming party, she laid eyes on him and picked up her excited step. She began to shout and wave, like a crazed band groupie. She ran up to him, shouting, 'Mark! Mark! Hello daarliing! Aah, it's so good to see yoouu.' Jane Mears kissed him and then hugged him repeatedly, while she began to cry tears of joy. They were both happy at being reunited, safe in each other's arms. Mark joked, 'Come on, let's get outta here, Janey. All I want right now is a pizza and a beer.'

They laughed continually and strode away from the tower of pain with him not looking back at it once. The

Metropolitan Correctional Center was in his rear view mirror now, and only sunny skies lay ahead. Mark and Jane spent the afternoon in the Gas Lamp District of downtown San Diego, walking around, just window shopping and talking. Jane stopped walking sometimes to break into tears, thinking about how Mark had first gotten himself into prison, and then how he had got himself out. Even though he had not told her specifically about how it had happened, he was sure she knew.

He spent some time reassuring her that everything would be okay and there would be no more prison for him in the future. He told her, 'We'll be together forever, Jane. You've always been there for me and no matter what we do, or where we go from now on, we'll do it together, honey, okay? Forever, Jane, and don't forget, forever's a long time.' Giving her a big hug, while he rubbed her arms for comfort, he then looked deep into her sharp, green eyes. Finally dragging a smile out of her, Mark quickly said, 'Come on, let's get a room for the night and freshen up. Then we'll go out and do some partying. We're gonna party like there's no tomorrow.'

The night flew by as Mark and Jane, did what they did best when they were together. Loved life and lived it large. Once the night had wound down early, since Mark was not up to the task of an all-night rebel rousing just yet, Jane helped get him back to the hotel. He got into bed, with a lot of help from her, and slept his first night as if he'd never want to wake up again. He was in Heaven.

Waking up, but now with a hangover, he got up to take his early morning piss, and then it came to him: he was out. He was free. He was free to do whatever he wanted to do today, and his first thought was to make a phone call. He came back into the bedroom. After drinking some ice water and then running himself a hot bubble bath, he picked up the phone and dialed a number he had been looking forward to dialing once he was out.

She answered sleepily as it was still before eight o'clock in the morning, but he did not care, as he could not wait to hear her voice on the phone. Mark and Angelica spoke on the phone for the better part of forty-five minutes, making plans for that evening. He playfully teased her about all the things he wanted to do to her later that night, while she giggled, clearly enjoying everything she was hearing, and enjoying the thought of it all coming true. Her rich, deep voice stimulated him as he lay on the bed, looking forward to getting to grips with Angelica. She was a light-skinned black chick he had met when she had been singing in a hotel bar, where he'd had a business meeting a few years back. It was a relaxed relationship, but it was always intense when they got together. They may have had feelings that were strong enough to take it to the next level, but the bar had been set too high maybe, as that elusive next step never seemed to come up in any serious conversation between them.

Mark hung up the phone and then dripped himself into the hot tub, He had a different type of time now, he thought, not the type of time he'd had to do inside. He was only a few blocks away from M.C.C., but he was as far away as his mind could take him. Once he had got out of the bath, he fell back onto the bed and fell asleep. No more Bezerk snoring and farting from his top rack, and no more four o'clock count. All he had now was the quiet of the suite and his own time to dream about his future, and what he was going to make of it. The whine of the commercial jets taking off and landing at Lindbergh Field airport, ten blocks to the east, helped to ease him into a deep sleep. All he dreamt of was some get back. He needed to get back some of his lost time, while he was in prison knowing that money does not sleep and money does not care who it sits with; you got to go get it and he wanted to go get his money. As he slept blissfully, he dreamt about how he was going do it. 'Come and get your money' had a different meaning now that he was back on the street.

Having arrived back in Los Angeles, he spent most of the week hanging out with Angelica, taking walks along the beach and going to the movies, having dinners at home and getting caught up in the bedroom. Angelica got him back in the game, working her five foot eight, slender frame up and down his toned body, working him hard until he was trained right. Every inch and every minute of it, he loved it, the touch, the smell, and the taste.

'Yeah, boy, it's good to be the king,' Mark jokingly said to her each day. Another day down brought another day of wonder, taking in all the different colors and smells, the variety of food and drinks that all had their unique tastes. Everything inside prison was a bland; white on white, wrapped in plain vanilla with no smell, no taste - just plain white paste. Knoxx had all of his senses back, with one that was rapidly coming back into play this particular week, which was getting back in the money.

After spending time with Angelica and Jane, it was time for him to be seen back in a suit, doing the rounds in and around Beverly Hills. Time waits for no one, and his time had come to pick up the phone to dial the phone number for Matthew Tamban, his corporate lawyer, to make an appointment. After some polite small talk, the appointment was set for the following morning. It was Matthew Tamban's last appointment before lunch, so they could then go to lunch together and catch up on what Mark really wanted to talk to Matt about. After hanging up, he called Jane to let her know that it was time for them to hit the stores. He needed some new clothes, and who better to help him spray some of his cash around, than Jane. It had been an awesome week and he hadn't once given the previous week a thought, as there was no point because it was all behind him now. As fast as he had hit the gate at M.C.C., he stepped on the accelerator pedal of Angelica's blue Corvette to pick up Jane. Time, it seemed, was flying by, and now he had time to laugh, hug and just simply smile. Everything tasted good and nothing, and no one, could change that now.

He arrived at Jane's apartment and rang the doorbell. When it opened, his day, and the ones to come, went back to being cloudy days again. A man he did not recognize, opened the door, opening it as if Knoxx was entering his home, not Jane's. He was around forty-seven years old, about six foot tall but on the thin side, with a big hooknose that seemed too big for his face, and a short cut of thin, gray hair. Mark quickly caught the scene and kept his wits about him as the man introduced himself as Dave. Mark asked him his full name and he said it was Dave Kenshaw. He did not look too impressed and the man sensed it as he put out a limp handshake that Mark crushed. Impatient and annoyed, he did his level best to keep the conversation light and breezy, but he was already bristling from the man's opening questions, asking him about his time in prison. Knoxx's instincts were honed from prison, and right now, they were telling him. 'This guy's no good.' Both men felt uncomfortable in each other's company with Mark just wanting to get back into the warm sunlight, back in the car, and as far away from this fish-eyed fool as possible.

Jane came out from the bedroom, giving her lame apologies. Mark made it clear that he wanted to leave and tried to push Jane along to get her things together for leaving. Jane then gave Dave Kenshaw a kiss goodbye, while Mark watched, not moving from the couch. She said she'd see him later and then she looked at Mark, as if she'd been the one waiting on him. She made for the door, saying, 'Come on then, whoop, whoop, let's get going, darling. The shops'll be closed in only nine hours, dear. Lots of shopping to do, and so little time.'

'See you, Mark,' Kenshaw threw out, while he got comfortable on the couch, getting back to watching television.

Knoxx replied hard, 'Yeah.'

Pulling the door shut behind him, Mark felt angry but didn't know if it was out of jealousy or the fact that Jane had kept Kenshaw from him. Feelings are like that. Another thing that was coming back to him now was feelings. Everything seemed the same, but they were different too. When they arrived at Century City Shopping Mall, all the stores were as he had left them. The people walking around were the same, but he felt different somehow, feeling he'd changed. As he sat down for lunch with Jane, he had a thought, it felt strange, and, he could not understand it. He realized that he missed the boys in K-Unit. He missed the days inside.

34

The following day, Mark strutted into the law offices where Tamban worked. Letting the receptionist know he was there to meet with him, he waited in reception for Matt to send word that he was ready for him. Mark had met Matt during a business negotiation, with Tamban representing the other side, but after the deal had gone through, however, he had taken to Mark in a big way and they had become good friends. Tamban was five years older, but he felt younger than Mark, because he always had a story to tell him about what he'd been up to in Hollywood each time they met. Matt was five foot six inches tall, built on a slight frame and wore the classic black horn-rimmed glasses, which made him look like the classic nerdy, Jewish lawyer. Whenever they were out of the office, Matt took great delight in watching Mark talk the ladies into joining them at their table for drinks.

Matt Tamban had been working in a partnership law firm for around eight years. He hadn't made partner, but Mark worked with Matt because he was more than competent in all aspects of corporate law. He had a sizable office, but still had documents, prospectuses and contracts on the floor piled up high against the walls. Yet whatever he needed, he could put his hands on it at a moment's notice.

Knoxx was told by the receptionist that he could go in now. He wove his way through the eighteenth floor on Century Park East, in Century City, which sat comfortably on the cusp of Beverly Hills. Most of the office doors were open. He saw that the lawyers were busy racking up their billable hours, while their personal assistants and paralegals were busy typing transcripts. Walking along the hall to Matt's office, all of his intimate desires ran wild as he passed by each work station and checked out each girl's rack and then her face, as each one lifted it up to glance at him as he stepped by.

Turning the corner to walk the hallway down to Matt's office, he caught a glimpse of an intern working at a photocopier; she looked every inch a movie star and porn star rolled into one. He could not help himself as he veered off course to walk by the young woman. Mark stopped and introduced himself in an easy, friendly way. She responded in kind, telling him that her name was Olivia Marbela. Her look was dark, demure and enticing, and she cut him down to size with her own brand of humor, responding in kind to every line he laid on her. Mark took an instant liking to her; he liked her look and he liked her personality. She was professional in the manner of doing her work. She had an air of having a higher level of class in the way she held her head and her gaze, never once feeling threatened or embarrassed by his flirtatious advances, taking them in the fun way they were meant.

Tamban had come out of his office to find Mark standing with Olivia, helping her collate reams of papers, happy to just wile away the day, as he helped her with her work.

'Will you ever stop?' Matt said as he walked up to them. Mark flashed a million dollar smile, while Olivia continued her work. Knoxx countered, 'I'm getting reamed, steamed and cleaned, thanks to the hourly rates you charge, so I'd rather get my money's worth being in the company of Olivia, and she's way better looking than you Matty boy.'

They all laughed, while Matt stood with his hands on his hips, looking at Mark as if he was a naughty schoolboy late for class. He admonished him by saying, 'Come on, we've got some serious business to get through today.'

'Until next time, Olivia, it was a pleasure to meet you, and if you ever get tired of working here, be sure to let Matt know and get him to call me.'

Olivia looked at Mark and while smiling a radiant smile, she confidently replied, 'That might be sooner than you think.'

Matt took her cue and guided Mark to the conference room, doing his best to talk about business, while Mark only wanted to talk about Olivia. Mark said, 'She's the one, Matt. Damn, she's fine. She's the next ex-Mrs. Knoxx.'

Matt summarily dismissed it as he laid out some papers on the conference table, replying curtly, 'You always say that about some hot chick you meet.'

'Make sure you call for some coffee, while I'm here and get Olivia to bring it in.'

Tamban was not finding any humor in Knoxx's new-found school boy crush. He just nodded accompanied by a tutting sound. Matt then settled into talking about the documents that had been sent to him via Jane Mears, about Mark's idea for acquiring a number of nightclubs, bars and strip clubs. This group of Envious clubs would be held in a larger holding company that would then be taken public on the stock exchange in an Initial Public Offering, calling that company Exile Corporation. Matt talked about the formation of the companies and how each of them would work in relation to the other, but his mood seemed to change when he pulled a single sheet of paper out that held Mark's destiny on it. Scanning it, Matt began to talk about it, while Mark sat firmly in his leather chair, listening. 'I've been talking to Irv Einhorn and he believes your idea can work. As long as the land and the liquor licenses for all the targeted properties stack up, he said you could pull it off, but I think it's a long shot.'

'So why the long face, Matt? You don't look too happy,' Knoxx replied, spinning his pen in his hand. He was really only waiting for the coffees to arrive, thinking about his next move on Olivia.

Matt pushed back on his black horn-rimmed glasses, which Mark recognized as a sign of bad news. Matt looked at the spreadsheet again, and then pushed it across the table for him to review. As he did, he said, 'As you'll see, according to Irv's calculations, you've leveraged everything you have, and taking into account all the second mortgages on the properties and the investor financing, it seems you're still twenty million dollars short.'

The door opened and Mark got up from his chair to assist Olivia with her tray, seemingly more interested in helping her than listening to any bad news that Matt had for him.

Matt asked him, 'Did you hear me?'

Mark helped her set the tray down. 'Yeah, I heard you,' he replied, while he looked at Olivia, and asked her. 'You can stay a while, if you'd like?'

Olivia looked awkwardly at Matt, who just brushed it off and gave up, waving her to a chair. Olivia Marbela hesitated, not knowing what game was being played at her expense, while Mark held her stare. She then found a place at the same side of the table next to Matt, with both of them at a loss as to what was going to happen next. He looked at them with a sly smile and a cheeky grin. Classic Knoxx. With a hint of mischief in his eyes, in a polite and disarming way, he began by asking, 'Olivia, do you mind if I ask you a couple of questions about you and your goals, and what you think about what I'm trying to do?'

Olivia's curiosity was peeked. She looked over to Matt, who simply looked back at her with a blank look. She answered timidly, 'Okay.'

'Great,' Knoxx replied enthusiastically, while he poured out a cup of coffee. He then began to explain his thoughts by painting the picture of what he had envisioned, 'I'd like to know what you think of a nightclub chain being called Envious. All the clubs and bars would attract all the V.I.P.'s and would become known as the number one place to be seen. All the people who couldn't get into them would all be envious. The clubs will host all the best after parties for things like The Oscars and The Grammy's and all the stars in L.A., New York and Miami will want to be seen in Envious. I'm going to spell it N V S, what you think of that?'

Calmly sitting back in his chair, he then sipped his coffee, while Matt spoke up, saying he didn't think it was fair to be asking Olivia such an open-ended question. Mark simply smiled and waited for Olivia to find her courage, her confidence and her voice. She finally found all three, saying, 'Well, I think it's a big undertaking. It sounds like it would be exciting to be in, I mean, going to, you know, going to the clubs. I like the name NVS, it sounds cool. I think it'll be a hit alright, if you can get the movie stars, music people and athletes to go there.'

Mark chimed in, saying to Tamban in an enthusiastic manner, 'See Matt, that's what I've been banging onto you about. If you build it, they will come, bud. All I need to do is to get someone to promote the clubs who's hip, happening and drop dead gorgeous.'

Letting out a cheerful, bright smile, he then turned it into an all out laugh as Matt caught onto what he was up to. Matt said in an annoyed voice, 'No Mark, come on, you can't be serious.'

Matt laughed at the nerve of it, recruiting one of the staff right in front of him. Recruiting a girl he'd just met minutes earlier into a company he didn't even have yet. Mark and Matt were laughing, which now made Olivia feel like she had said something wrong, or worse, that they were laughing at her. Was this a game they played on all the interns? Knoxx felt her uneasiness as her deep, black eyes shone, waiting for the punch line. She sat quietly and somewhat regally, taking him in, trying to decide if he was a genius in disguise or just a madman in the open.

Mark then asked her, 'So let me ask you this, Olivia. What if you had a position in this company where you could promote all the events that would attract the stars, you wouldn't only get to see them, but they would all be contacting you to promote their star-studded events. You wouldn't be going to premieres, Olivia; the premieres would be coming to you. Would you be interested in that? Think about it, all those celebrity parties you read about in magazines. You'd be hosting parties from coast to coast, and you'd be flying around the country in first class, until I get us our corporate jet.'

Not seeing the fun in it anymore, Matt jumped into scold Mark, cutting him off, boring his eyes into him, saying firmly, 'Come on, really, this is madness. First off, you don't have all the money you need to pull this off, and secondly, what corporate jet?'

Mark replied just as firm, telling him, 'If you're gonna dream, dream big, buddy. Watch me do it or do it with me, because I am going to make it happen. You either make things happen or you watch them happen. Look at you, Matt, how long have you been working here and you still haven't been made partner yet?' Seeing his opportunity to embarrass Matt in front of Olivia, he continued, 'Wouldn't you like to be in the middle of all the action, Matt? Come on, think about it. What an opportunity for both of you. Things happen for a reason, Matt and that's the reason we're all in this room right here, right now. You can continue being my lawyer and bill me your hourly rates for doing the same amount of work, or you can have a piece of the company, and then have a share in the profits. You'll have the added bonus of being The Man, and not just working for the man. You'll be amongst all the movers and the shakers, bud, all the hottest babes in the movie industry, and who knows, maybe you'll get to meet Halle Berry one day?' He knew Matt's weakness for Halle Berry; he was pulling out all the stops to close him.

Matt quickly retorted, 'Mark, you don't have enough money to buy all the clubs you need, and if you don't buy them all, then the numbers don't pencil out. You're stuck in a Catch-22. How can you even think about taking us on when you don't have a company and you don't even have a business to run?'

'Oh Matt, if that's all that's stopping us, you may as well stay here and then, in five years, you can look me up in Forbes' One Hundred Richest People list. Dare to dream, Matt. The difference in the dreaming and in the doing is in you. Just ask yourself, 'What do I really want from life?''

Knoxx shut his mouth, keeping his eyes on Matt, who looked straight back at his, looking as if he was searching his face and searching inside himself at the same time. Matt then said, 'You really think you can pull this off? You have to find twenty million and if it's in debt financing then the numbers don't work. You need to find someone who's willing to take this on with equity participation. That's the only way it will work.'

Sweeping right past his official tone, Mark answered by asking his own question, 'So you're in then?'

'If you can come up with the money,' Matt answered.

Mark waved him off. Breaking into a devilish smile, he replied with some humor, 'Aahh the money. Don't worry about that, I got it covered. Listen, bud, the adventure doesn't begin until something goes wrong.'

'Yeah well, it went real wrong for you last time around, and you only just managed to pull yourself out of that one by the skin of your teeth. Things have a way of coming back around. Just be careful this time. You don't want a repeat of your last mistake, or worse, do you?'

They both knew the meaning behind what Matt was saying.

Mark hit back like the crack of a whip, 'That's why I need you on the team Matt. You always worry too much. Now, are you in or not? Don't think about the money for now. I'll get the money.' Quickly changing his approach, while Matt stalled, He turned to Olivia, asking her, 'What'd you say to me doubling your salary, whatever that is, and you come and work for me to build a string of clubs? You can promote to all the stars, starting with a club here in L.A. and then in New York and Miami. Does that sound like something you'd want to be involved in?' He was willing her to give him the right answer.

She took a beat to think, and said, 'Well yeah, I mean, who wouldn't want that?'

The third party close had just come off smooth as silk. He looked at Tamban, knowing he had him now. Looking him squarely in his eyes, Knoxx quietly said, 'Yeah Matt, who wouldn't want that, huh?'

Matt and Olivia let out a nervous laugh as Mark began to laugh with them. Matt realized that Mark had him cold. Everyone in the conference room realized they were in.

Mark then playfully added, 'If you say you're in, then I'll buy lunch.'

Matt finally smiled and then giggled, replying, 'You always buy lunch.'

35

Days turned into weeks, while the three of them, Mark Knoxx, Matthew Tamban and Olivia Marbela worked on forming the Envious Group and Exile Corporation. They began hiring staff in preparation of opening the first NVS nightclub in Hollywood.

There was still one small problem of Mark being twenty million dollars light on his end. No matter how many meetings he had with Matt and the accountant, Irv Einhorn, the numbers just would not stack up. Despite that he could pull together enough investors in time to close the real estate deals, the fact was that he was running out of time. Always time. Working for you or working against you. He had invested his time and millions in capital, paying for valuations, deposits, architects and interior designers for the majority of the properties. Einhorn had been firm in his estimation that it was twenty million or nothing. And nothing really meant nothing. If this deal did not go through, he would be left with nothing in the bank and nothing in his future, and that was just unacceptable. There was always a way. The problem isn't the problem; it's your attitude towards the problem. Mark remembered what Dedrick had said, realizing that a problem could be solved with a decision being made. *Going with a half-ass plan is better than having no plan at all,* he thought.

The future had caught up with Knoxx. The time he'd spent in meetings and socializing had meant he'd forgotten about the time that was ending for someone else. Bezerk had hit the gate. He had called Mark to let him know he was out. True to his word, Mark sent down a package containing ten thousand dollars, telling him he'd come down to San Diego to visit him in a week or two. He arranged for a car to be delivered the following week, so Chris wouldn't have to go out and steal one. Keeping Bezerk on the down-low was a priority right now, as he had to pull together twenty million in ten days or the deal, his vision, and his destiny, along with his money, would all be lost.

'Come on, fool, I'm losing it down here. You gotta come down so we can get something going.' Bezerk had said on his last call.

His phone calls were only adding to Mark's stress levels, while he was doing his best to massage the numbers one more time in preparation for yet another business meeting with yet another potential investor. He did his best to put him off without sounding too condescending, even though he was being a royal pain in the ass, acting like a spoilt child needing attention. Bezerk had no idea what to do on the street unless he was runnin' and gunnin' with his crew. Knoxx finally gave in and said he would fly down to see him Friday afternoon. Bezerk drilled him repeatedly on the phone that he'd better not let him down or he would hunt him down and kick his ass. He then asked Mark something that he had forgotten about, since being back out in the world, 'Did you call Big Smoke, vato?'

Mark answered that he hadn't, much to Bezerk's annoyance. Why would he have any reason to contact a gangbanger thug like this Big Smoke guy? Mark went back to working and didn't give it any more thought. It was just Bezerk being Bezerk, wanting to get back in with his boys, wanting to show off his buddy from the Joint, Knowledge. But Mark had no time for playing gangsta' in the hood right now. He had some serious business to take care of and he had millions hanging out in the wind. For all the power lunches and wine-filled dinners with potential investors, the outcome always seemed to be the same, for whatever reason. It became apparent that the elusive twenty million shortfall was going to stay that way, elusive.

'Maybe later,' 'some other time,' or 'twenty million seems like too much to invest into nightclubs right now,' was all he'd heard. Whatever the reasons, it wasn't what he needed to hear.

'Not this time, maybe next time around,' one potential investor summed up, but for Knoxx, within a week there wouldn't be any next time. He'd be out of time and out of money. He needed an act of God to turn his life around, but next to needing God, he needed to go down to San Diego to see his boy, his dog, Bezerk.

36

'Waassuupp, fool?' Bezerk said, while the two of them hugged and got a good look at each other for the first time since they were in M.C.C. It had been around seven months since they'd parted ways. Now, they had to get used to seeing each other in street clothes, and see how different they really were from each other. Bezerk was sitting on a bar stool in a white, triple-extra-large t-shirt on his thick chest, with Capri jeans on, his socks pulled up to just under his kneecaps and basketball sneakers on. To cap this all off, he had a tight, number one-buzzed haircut that accentuated his long goatee. Mark sat on his bar stool in a coordinated ensemble of a dark Polo shirt and dark jeans and soft leather loafers, with a gold Rolex Daytona watch shackled to his wrist and if he hadn't known Bezerk better he would have sworn Bezerk looked like he wanted to roll him for all his shit. They got caught up on old times and Mark then suggested that they move things up to his suite, feeling embarrassed by Bezerk's look while they sat in the bar at the W Hotel. Bezerk made matters worse by suggesting they should call up some hookers and score some action. Knoxx, however, had another kind of action on his mind.

After ordering up room service, with enough beers to keep them going all night, Mark started out by giving Bezerk a pep talk on how he had dressed for their meeting. He tactfully said that if he was to be a part of the Envious Group, then he would have to step up his game in the wardrobe department. Again, he felt it prudent to highlight Bezerk's role that he wanted him to play. Thankfully, Bezerk sat quietly listening, while Mark laid out what he had in mind for him and what he had planned for NVS. Mark then changed the game and got around to the problem that was holding up the plan: a small matter of him being twenty million dollars short. He reminded Bezerk that everything he had just described would be pure fantasy if he could not come up with it. 'No money no honey,' was how he'd wrapped it up. Then Mark got around to what he had been thinking about for the past couple of days, and the name he wanted to bring up to Bezerk to see if there was any action to be had there: Big Smoke.

Mark explained that he was prepared to wash the Southsiders' drug money through the nightclubs. In return, they'd get a piece of the action from the clubs and be able to have their guys employed as security at all the clubs. All he required was an investment of a cool, twenty million dollars. The way he explained it, he thought it made good business sense. They sat in their comfortable chairs in the suite, drinking some cold buds. Mark felt his flow was strong and his case for the Southsiders' involvement had been even stronger. He finished strong, telling Bezerk that he could vouch for him, having done time together. Besides, he had a decent track record in the investment game and had all the right banking connections, ensuring the laundering of the drug money would go smoothly. Mark then pointed out that the Southsiders would be running the security at all the clubs, so it would be suicidal for him to fuck around with the money. He knew he had made a great case for their involvement and knew he had covered all the bases in his brief. Mark then sat back and drank hard on his beer, checking his bro' for any reaction.

Bezerk looked like he had been kicked in the balls. He was doing his best to comprehend the whole go-around of millions of dollars being washed through various accounts. He'd had one thing on his mind, while Mark had been explaining the deal, and now it was his turn to share some information.

'We got a problem, dog,' he simply announced, and Mark thought, *Not again*. If this wasn't going to work out, then he was out. Out of time, out of money and out of business.

He reacted sharply by admonishing Bezerk. 'I don't need to hear, there's a problem. What've I been telling you? All problems can be solved. You just have to see them for what they are. They're hidden opportunities, disguised as a problem, that's all.' Doing his best to look as confident and self-assured as he could under the intense pressure, he calmly put his beer bottle down, and asked, 'What's the problem?'

Bezerk pulled on his goatee, thinking about how to begin, and how to frame it all in as clear a way as Mark had done in his presentation to him. He then cryptically said, 'Things are kind a tricky right now, dog Now's not a good time to be talking to my guy about laying out some hard cash, you know what I mean?'

'No dude, I don't have the slightest idea what you mean, so why don't you try telling me?' Knoxx barked back, looking agitated.

Bezerk tried to hold onto the information, but he knew he had to tell him. Mark had done so much for him already, so Bezerk got down to laying it out for him. 'We got some problems dog, in our crew. We got hit at the border two days ago and lost a big ass load that was meant for upstate. A lot of homeys are gonna go down for this fuck up, you know what I mean?'

Bezerk swigged on his beer bottle, while Mark sat up in his chair, on point. He began to probe him further, asking, 'All right, go on, there's got to be more to it than that?'

'Yeah well, we think we have a rat on the inside. The coke got taken down by an F.B.I. taskforce at the Otay Mesa border, fifty million in blow, man.'

'Holy shit balls! Yeah, that does sound like a problem, dog,' was all Mark could muster as his reply, and he thought he had problems. As Jay-Z had said in one of his songs, 'I got ninety-nine problems but my bitch ain't one.' Knoxx could only envision the fallout from it. He had seen the movies, watched the documentaries, and had actually lived it in prison. He knew how it would all shake out; bodies would be falling from the sky, as the big homeys didn't take too kindly to losing anything, let alone losing their product to the cops because of a rat.

'Homeys are gonna be in body bags over this one, dog. Belieeve thaatt, yeess siirr.'

Bezerk let out a nervous, low-pitched laugh, but Mark hadn't seen anything funny in what he'd heard. Staying focused on his problem, he knew he had to make a play, plain and simple; the biggest risk of all is in taking no risk at all. Pulling a notepad off from the table, 'Tell me what went down, from the top. I want to know who, when, how and why,' He said.

'Oh yeah, boy, Knowledge is in the house, plotting again, yeess siirr. You know what I mean?'

'Just tell me everything you know, and everything you think you know.'

They then went over Bezerk's story a number of time until he got bored and irritated at having to repeat it so many times. He complained that Mark was interrogating him like a cop, but Mark held firm. He promised that they would soon be out on the town, scoring some chicks, as long as Bezerk finished telling him everything he'd heard from the word on street. He used up every sheet of paper making his notes, drawing out some charts with dates, places and timelines on them. Bezerk told it as he had heard it, and gave Mark all the juicy material from inside the Southsider organization, making sure to remind Mark that they could easily be killed if word got out about what he was telling him. Knoxx just rolled along with it, reassuring him and coaxing him along until it felt like they had everything straight. Sometime later, Mark had a list of names, dates and places. He had also narrowed down the field for who the four best candidates were for being the rat.

37

Mark made good on his promise and they soon got busy chasing all the trim with Bezerk doing what he did best, going berserk, drinking and hitting on a variety of low-rent skanks, dragging Knoxx into a number of down trodden watering holes throughout the backwaters of San Diego. Mark held his own, having done time in prison gave him the knowledge of how Bezerk ran his game, but it was clear that he wasn't from their world, and that they weren't from his. They got down to partying by drinking, dancing, flirting and getting in some heavy petting with some local Latin chicks. Mark sat back and watched how intense Bezerk became when he noticed a redheaded girl who had been in one bar with a group of friends. He noticed that Bezerk had a strong, perverse desire to have her at any cost. It seemed he never wanted to leave her alone, even while she was in the company of her boyfriend, who he threatened, ruining everyone's night in the process.

Knoxx tore through the night with Bezerk, backing his dog up at every juncture. But in the midst of all the drinking and bullshitting around, while he sat on a bar stool, he had only one thing on his mind. How was he going to get next to Big Smoke? Thinking about how the two of them were playing the bait and switch game on all the pussy they were chasing, gave him an idea. He laughed at the thought of it and at its simplicity, blowing it off, thinking he must be drunk.

It had been a long night and an even longer morning, having got back to the hotel around five thirty in the morning with some girls. A few months back, Mark and Bezerk had been leering out of their cell window at the drunken partiers across the street getting it on, not realizing they could be seen on the hotel's rooftop. Now it was their turn to return the favor to their brothers in lock across the street at M.C.C. and they laughed in their drunken state at their inside joke, as they played with the girls on the roof.

Knoxx woke up with a wicked hangover and, from the looks of them, two wicked babes too, and not in the good way. Mark woke the girls up and gave them cab fare that was far more than they needed, but neither one complained. After they left, he did his best to get his act together and his head straight by jumping in the shower. He spent the rest of the morning lying on the bed with pieces of note-paper strewn about. Different day same station. He knew he had something. It was all buried in the margins in his notes; he just had to figure it out. He remembered that he had had an idea the night before about how he could get back in the game and get back in the money. He fell back onto the bed and gazed up at the ceiling. His body began to feel cold as he lay there drying off with a towel around his waist. He exhaled, thinking, *Maybe it was all lost.* His head hurt, both of them, and now he was getting a headache just by thinking about it all.

Getting up from the bed, he meandered over to the window and looked at the same scene he had watched for the past eighteen months from his cell; only now, he was looking at it from a different angle. It was all as he had remembered. Everything was as he had left it. Picking up his coffee cup, he slowly sipped it, enjoying its warmth, while he scanned the streets of San Diego below. He watched everyone going about their daily tasks, watching the U.P.S. van bumping across the train tracks, the Yellow Cabs pulling up to the front of the Marriott Hotel, the airplanes coming in on their flight paths over downtown to land at Lindbergh Field airport. Everything seemed so ... what was the word ... coordinated. Everything had its order of things and each one seemed connected in some way. Taking another sip of his coffee, Knoxx brightened some, thinking, *That could be it.* The opportunity may have presented itself in the order of things. For something to seem so right, maybe, it could be just wrong, just as he and Bezerk were, and yet together they could lay their game on anyone using their bait and switch game. In between sips of coffee he whispered, 'Huh, bait and switch.'

Having slept most of the morning, Knoxx woke up to the crunching of sound of papers that he had left on the bed. They were the notes he had taken from the day before. He felt invigorated once he had woken up properly; remembering he'd had a dream. After a moment, he realized he had a plan, and the best part of it was, was that it was cunning, daring and exciting, but dangerous, and yet, he loved it. He stretched across the bed and called Bezerk's room. Bezerk answered it sleepily, listening to Mark telling him to get his fag-ass out of bed and to come to his room as soon as possible.

Bezerk strolled into Mark's room about forty minutes later as if he had been to Hell and back. With his hangover still lying heavy on his head. Mark had already arranged for room service to deliver a late morning breakfast. Throughout the rest of the day Mark explained his plan to Bezerk, having to run by it a few more times as each time he had lost him in the explanation.

Bezerk finally said with some humor, in the afternoon, how mad he was to think it would work and that Big Smoke would never go for it.

Late in the afternoon, after Mark had explained it one

more time to Bezerk, with him finally telling Mark that he must be mad to think Big Smoke would go for it, Mark handed Bezerk his cell phone, saying, 'Well there's only one way to find out if he'll go for it or not, puto. Call him and tell him I'll pay him five million dollars to talk about getting his coke back.'

Knoxx could see Bezerk was stalling because he didn't understand it. Mark smirked, trying to get Bezerk to lighten up, and pushed him along by saying sharply, 'Boy, don't bring out the devil in me.'

'Oh this is gonna be good, yeah real good. He ain't gonna go for it, I'm tellin' you, dog.'

'Well, he won't if you don't call him. So shut up and dial the friggin' number already.'

'Uh huh, yeah alright, fool, try me, culo, and you'll see what happens,' Bezerk said, taunting Mark as he began to dial the number for Big Smoke.

Mark said, 'Just say it as I told you bro', okay?'

He looked at Mark as if he was looking at him like he was stupid or something. He replied, 'I got this. You do you and I'll do me, you feel me?'

Bezerk had been speaking on the phone for around ten minutes and now it was his turn to listen. The voice on the other end seemed to be just as animated as Bezerk had been when he had given his scripted presentation. Bezerk answered tentatively, 'Uh huh, yeah aa'iight.'

Whatever he had been told by Big Smoke it had made his eyes pop. Mark could feel the intensity in his voice. Bezerk had gone over the same story, explaining it three times in a row, and each time it felt as if he was giving a different version than the one before. It sounded like he was getting further from the story he had been told to say, but there was no turning back now. It was now or never. Bezerk finally went quiet, as if waiting on a final decision being made. Mark could feel the edges of time slipping away, falling off the hands on a clock. Everything hung on this and he was clinging to his only life raft.

'I heeaardd thaatt!' That was all he needed to hear, to know it meant that Bezerk had heard some good news. Bezerk's eyes went to Mark's, confirming it as he replied, 'Yeess siirr, belieeve thaatt. Yeah, he's one fucked up crazy white boy, that's for sure. Whatever he's got up his sleeve, I'm sure it's gonna be a lot of laughs, you know what I mean? Uh huh, okay, we'll be there. I got you, big homey.'

Bezerk laughed again, at whatever Big Smoke had said. He disengaged the call and threw the phone at Mark, telling him, 'Yeah booyy. You're on for ten o'clock tonight and you better have it all squared away or you and me might not be coming back. You know what I mean, faagg?'

Knoxx got up from his chair. He stepped over to the bedroom window to watch the late afternoon glow bouncing off the water in Coronado Bay. The street lights began to turn on. Mark looked over at the tower of pain, the M.C.C. draped in its dark, gray walls with the burning, bright white light strips cutting through the window slats. Mark looked down at the grid pattern of the streets below, envisioning how it would all play out in his head. Then he had a second thought. What if he didn't pull it off? He'd be back in prison or end up lying in the street, dead. But he felt this was his time somehow, his destiny. Everything he had learned to date, who he was, was meant for this. For some reason he just knew it. He believed it. Looking at the streets below, he knew that he knew them better than most, and he knew he could use it. His knowledge.

38

Bezerk drove through the bright lights of San Diego, southeast towards Otay Mesa and then into Del Sol, into Southsider turf. The cars began to thin out and the gang signs began to thicken on all the walls of the buildings as they rolled through the streets. Mark sat quietly in the passenger seat, concentrating on his presentation to Big Smoke. Bezerk took every opportunity to get him all stupid with worry by telling him that, because he was a white guy in a new rental car, he could be killed for driving through this area. They then began to bullshit with each other like they used to, dumb and dumber, possibly driving to their deaths.

Mark knew, seeing all the strapped gangbangers who had an overall look of murder on their faces, that this was the place. They were hanging out on the street corner as they drove past them up to a house in the middle of the street. Looking out of the car window, wishing it was bullet proof. He knew he had reached the point of no return. Bezerk laughed at him when he heard Mark say, 'Fuuckk.'

'Yeah boy, be careful what you wish for. Come on, let's roll. Come meet my peeps. Don't be scared, faagg,' Bezerk joked.

Knoxx took a deep breath and forced himself to open the car door. He began to walk over to the house, a step behind Bezerk, noticing that everyone was looking at him, the white boy.

Bezerk strolled up to his crew and Knoxx listened to the round of greetings between them. 'Waassuupp, fool.' 'Waassuupp, homey.'

The words rang-out all around them as they cut their way through the throng. All eyes looked behind Bezerk as a nod of waassuupp was offered up, but none was given back. A tall, thin, sleeved-up tattooed gangbanger stepped out in front of Knoxx, blocking him off from the house. The Sureño soldier hissed in his face, 'Hey esse, I don't know you, homes.'

'Yeah that's right, you don't, and you don't wanna know me, you know what I mean?' Knoxx hit him back, mad-dog style with his face hardened and his jaw locked. It was stare-down time, one-on-one. The banger sucked on his lip and let out a gruff snort in a putdown way, but backed up slightly to let him move on. He caught up to Bezerk, and then as they reached the top step up to the house, they were both summarily padded down for weapons.

Stepping through the door, Mark said goodbye to the world he knew and set his eyes upon a new world. One that never in his life did he think he would see, but then seeing is believing. The living room had cocaine baggies strewn about that were being weighed on triple beam scales by young Latino girls who were all standing at the tables in thong bikinis. Some were drinking beers, while others were smoking reefers. Mark noticed that a couple of them were being man-handled by guys from behind. The scene was like something out of a movie, *Un-fuckin' believable,* he thought. Music was rocking out throughout the room and the television was on a music video channel. A number of Southsider soldiers were sitting around the room, draped on low-rider couches and chairs. The air was thick with the smell of cigarette smoke, weed and booze. Saturday night was party night, and from the look of things, the night was just getting started in here. As the two of them walked through the living room, all eyes fell on the white boy. Some of the guys looked at him as if they wanted to lay him out, while some of the chicas looked as if they wanted to lay him.

Knoxx was led down a narrow corridor. As he walked down it he looked in the bedrooms whose doors were open, and saw that each one had two girls sitting at a desk in bikinis. One girl was flattening bank notes out and putting them in piles of ones, fives, tens and twenties; the shortest stack being the hundred dollar bills. The other girl was putting the money through a cash counting machine. The girls looked up at him as he passed by. Some of the doors were slammed shut by a Sureño who was watching the girls work. One of the rooms had a fat chick in it on her knees, giving head to some esse, who let out a wry smile as Knoxx passed by, with a thick plume of smoke rising up from his nose and mouth; he was a happy guy, getting a happy ending.

Knoxx was given the signal to stay in the hallway while Bezerk and their escort entered a room at the back of the house. Looking back along the corridor Mark saw a couple of esse's were watching him. No one spoke to him; they just stood there and watched him.

A door opened beside him and out stepped a big-breasted, heavy-hipped, long-haired Latino girl. She stepped up to Mark, letting out a slight, girlish laugh, like a cat who had stolen the milk. Laughing in a light, curious way, she stepped up to him real slow, closing half the gap between them to press her breasts against his chest. She smiled happily at him, knowing what she was doing. Without warning, she grabbed him by his crotch, causing him to jump slightly. Feeling awkward, he heard her say, 'Ay pappy, buenissimo. I'm just checking you for hidden weapons, baby.'

She broke out into a strong, long sarcastic laugh, and moved her face up closer to his to plant a kiss on his lips. Knoxx instinctively moved his head back away from hers, hitting it against the wall behind him.

The door that Bezerk had stepped through, opened abruptly; loud talking and laughing came from inside it. In an instant, the young girl tried to move on, but the heavy set gangbanger grabbed the back of her hair and pulled her back towards him. In a gruff Spanish accent, he told her to get back to her post. The girl gave Mark a quick look, and then walked off down the corridor looking at the floor, clearly afraid. The Sureño mad-dogged Knoxx, bristling at the sight of him, but Mark could only stand there looking at him, caught somewhere between the lands of determination and uncertainty. The man motioned with a swift wave of his arm for him to enter the room.

Sweeping into the room, Mark quickly scanned it. There were four Southsiders in addition to Bezerk, and a small framed, heavily tattooed Mexican sitting at a table in the middle of the room. Knoxx surmised that this was Big Smoke and extended his hand across the table. Big Smoke took his time to shake hands, not bothering to look at him as he did. There was a moment of unsettling silence. Mark felt it wasn't his place to speak first, and so Bezerk spoke up for him, saying in his street lingo that Mark had a plan to get back the cocaine and flush out the rat. Big Smoke just sat back raked in his chair, fingering a cigarette in his ashtray, not making eye contact with anyone, just listening to Bezerk's ramblings. Mark could tell Bezerk was nervous as he stumbled over himself a couple of times, and had lost count of the number of times Bezerk had said, 'You know what I mean?'

Big Smoke raised his right hand as a signal for Bezerk to shut up, which he did. Mark knew he was The Man if he could do that. Big Smoke finally looked up and turned to look at Knoxx for the first time. Knoxx saw that Big Smoke had a lazy left eye and a scar running up the left side of his number one-buzzed cut skull. He had the tattoo of a teardrop under his left eye. A sign that he'd done major state prison time, even though he looked no older than thirty.

Big Smoke began with an empty greeting. 'Waassuupp, homes?'

Mark answered with the same, 'Waassuupp.' Saying it laced with his English accent. The room erupted into a chorus of loud, raucous laughter at the unique sound of his accent. Looking around the room at his hombres, Big Smoke asked, in a putdown manner, 'Fuck homes, what's that shit from?'

'I'm from England, mate. You know, across the pond.'

Knoxx heard the thugs sitting around and behind him, follow up with a round of, 'Shiitt!' 'Fuck yeah, homes,' and 'Fool's a fag.'

Big Smoke warmed up to Knoxx. He sat up in his seat and

said, 'Well, at least you ain't one of those punk-ass pussy Americans.'

A chorus of 'Fuck that homes' and 'Hell no, fool', went up around the room in agreement.

'I hear you did time with Bezerk here?' Big Smoke said. Knoxx nodded, answering curtly, 'Yeah.'

Big Smoke asked, 'You got something, 'bout how I can get my coke back?'

'No, I don't,' Mark replied firmly.

Big Smoke looked at Bezerk, questioning him, 'What's this? You bring a fucking pig in my house, fool?'

Bezerk looked just as lost as the rest of them.

Big Smoke picked up his cigarette and took a hard drag on it, and then blew the smoke in his face, while he stared hard at him. He asked, 'So, what you got?'

'What I got is a way to flush out your rat so you don't go around smoking all the wrong people. If it's done right, you might even get him alive, so you can get information from him on who he's been talking to, and see if there's anyone else inside your crew who's fuckin' you over. And I think I might have a way to get back the load you lost, too.'

Knoxx leaned through the cigarette smoke to send the message that he didn't give a shit about Big Smoke being a hard-ass. Big Smoke dropped his cigarette in the ashtray and looked at the smoke plume rising up from it. He sat quiet for a minute thinking about what Mark had told him.

Mark respected him for that. Big Smoke might be a stone cold murderer, but he seemed to have some smarts. Big Smoke looked up at Mark and asked, 'What do you get out of this?'

'I get an investment in my company from which you'll get a healthy return, and your guys can be employed running the security at the clubs.'

Big Smoke rolled his cigarette in his ashtray some more and then asked hard, 'How do I know you can do this shit, you say you can do?'

All the homeys in the room sat still, listening, watching the chess match playing out between the dueling players.

Knoxx replied, 'Because the five mill I'm prepared to put up, says I can.'

Big Smoke smiled and then laughed hard. Looking at Bezerk, he said, 'Fuck yeah, you were right, B'. He's one crazy white boy!'

Laughter erupted in the room; only this time everyone was laughing with Knoxx. The atmosphere, which had been like the moon, was now all very earthly. Big Smoke leaned back in his chair to speak to one of his crew in Spanish, who promptly got up and left the room. He quickly came back with some ice cold Tecate beers. Knoxx cracked the pull tab and took a swig from it. He then looked at the can, while Big Smoke took a deep drag on his cigarette. Big Smoke took a swig of beer and then asked flat out, 'How you gonna do it?'

Knoxx had thought about this moment on the ride over, thinking at the time, it was going to be the most sensitive part of the meet. He put his beer can down on the table and looked Big Smoke straight in his eyes. He said straight up, 'You got a rat in your crew. I don't feel comfortable talking about it in front of everyone.'

All the homeys fidgeted, and began to get angry as they muttered a round of, 'Fuck that.' 'Punk.' 'Puto.'

Big Smoke stared at Mark without reacting or flinching at his comment. He then spoke in a harsh voice, saying, 'Out. Everyone out,' not looking around at his crew, who hadn't moved yet. He repeated his command, 'I said, out! Get the fuck up outta here, all of you!'

They all started to get up from the couches and chairs to begin leaving the room, clearly pissed that this white boy had got the better of them in their own house.

'Bezerk stays,' Knoxx stated.

Big Smoke nodded for him to stay. Big Smoke then picked up a pistol from under the table, and with some ceremony pulled back the slide to chamber a round in it. He placed it quietly beside his left hand, and then calmly said, 'Okay, let's hear it.'

The three of them sat in the room for around two hours, with Big Smoke shouting out twice, once for some more beers and then again for a pack of smokes. Mark kept them enraptured in describing his plan, explaining it a number of times until they each understood their roles. He used the power of his smooth accent and his knowledge to sway them into following it.

Big Smoke had liked everything he'd heard up to a point, but had asked Knoxx about the five million, and Knoxx was no fool, even for a white boy. Bezerk had led Big Smoke to believe that he was going to stroll in with five million dollars in cash, which wasn't the case, as there was no case in sight. Knoxx explained that he would place the money in escrow at any nominated bank, and when the sting had been successfully completed, the funds would be released. Only by then of course, he would be twenty million better off, so theoretically, he wasn't putting any money up for the privilege of getting in the game. Mark had thought that by the time he was finished laying out his plan, the focus would be on finding out who the rat was and getting back the coke, and not on his cash.

The awkward moment ended when Big Smoke said unexpectedly that he had to make a phone call. He still hadn't returned after ten minutes, leading Mark to ask Bezerk in a hushed tone, 'Does Big Smoke have a boss?' After a quiet minute, Mark said, 'He's getting the okay to move on my plan.'

Knoxx then spent the rest of the time convincing himself that Big Smoke was getting to make a move on his plan. Bezerk didn't know what to say; he seemed more concerned that Big Smoke and his boys were busy digging two holes in the back yard.

Big Smoke finally stepped back in the room like Napoleon, all king-shit like, with his gun jammed in the front of his belt. He had obviously received some good news. Mark asked him if things were going to move forward, as Big Smoke dropped a slip of paper on the table in front of him. Mark picked it up and read it. It was the bank wire instructions for the bank that would hold the five million in escrow. Mark realized what it was, and reacted immediately by saying sharply, 'I'm not doing that.'

'What'd you say? What's that you say, pinche puto?' Big Smoke replied, reacting just as sharply. He stood up from his side of the table.

Knoxx said aggressively, 'I've changed my mind. I'm not giving you my money without getting confirmation this's a go from your boss. I want a cut from the coke too, if I manage to get it back.'

Big Smoke launched his taught, wiry body across the table, whipping out his gun in one movement. He took a hold of Knoxx by his head and pushed it down hard onto the table. He rammed his gun down on his temple, hollering. 'You a piece of shit cop, homes?' The door opened and his posse of Sureños looked in on them. 'Get the fuck out, I got this!' Big Smoke shouted hard at them, more to raise himself.

Mark did not move or flinch. He just kept his breathing low, slow and steady. *Ride out the storm, just ride it out*, he kept telling himself, feeling the barrel of the gun on his temple. He was down, bent over across the table facing Bezerk, who looked at him the same way, with a cold, hard expression.

'You a cop, punk, is that it? You come up in here with my boy as cover and try to get inside us, homes. Is that it?' Pushing the barrel down harder, twisting it further into Knoxx's skull, Big Smoke hissed, 'I ain't got no boss, fool. I is it. I is El Jefe, comprende?'

Big Smoke jabbed him hard with his pistol before taking some of the pressure off. The first wave of attack had subsided and he had survived it. This was the open ground that he had been waiting for.

Big Smoke checked Bezerk, angrily asking him, 'What the fuck's up?'

'I dunno,' he replied curtly.

With his head jammed against the table, Mark took his

chance to reason with Big Smoke. 'I'm only going to put my money in escrow, once I know I have confirmation from your boss that I'm covered on the backend. You can shoot me now and then get back on the phone and tell your boss that you just wasted the guy who was going to pay him five mill! How many eight balls of coke do you have to push on the street to make that kind of money, huh? I don't think it'll be too long before you join me in whatever lime pit you guys have ready for this kind of thing.'

Big Smoke put his hands - one of them still holding the gun in it - with his trigger finger itching, behind his head. His fingers slid down the back of his skull, feeling his scar, remembering how it had felt getting shot. He let out a frustrated growl in anger once he realized he had no choice. Knoxx had somehow found out and called his bluff. Big Smoke knew he could not off him. He pulled out his cell phone and dialed the number, and then in a fast, agitated way, spoke in Spanish. He finally stopped talking. It was several minutes before he suddenly and begrudgingly handed the phone across to Knoxx without a word.

'Good evening Mr. Knoxx. Your first name is Mark, is it not?' the voice on the phone asked in a rich, calm, baritone voice. It was heavy with a thick Spanish accent, laced with a hint of humor.

Knoxx responded, 'Hi, yes, I'm Mark. And you are?'

Knoxx put his elbows on the table and stared at Big Smoke, waiting for the other man to answer. It was all sunny skies again. Smooth as a hot knife slicing through butter, and butter sticks to bread, here he was, talking to the man who controlled all the bread. Mark heard the man on the phone tell him, 'My name is Roberto, Roberto Madrid. You may have heard of me, no?'

The skies turned cold and gray. Talk about an understatement. It was like asking an American Football fan if he knew who Tom Brady was or an Englishman if he knew who David Beckham was. In the world of the news and those who made it, Roberto Madrid was known throughout South and North America as the modern day Pablo Escobar. He was on the United States' Most Wanted list as one of the most wanted drug lords in Mexico, and hell yeah, he'd heard of him.

Unsure on how to address Madrid at this point, Mark answered timidly, 'Hi Roberto, um yes, I've heard of you. It's a pleasure to make your acquaintance.'

'It is a pleasure to talk to you too, and I must say, I have come to admire you, about what I have heard of your idea. I hope we shall soon meet. Now, how can I help you in this matter? How may I, how you say, be of service?'

Feeling disarmed by Madrid's calm manner and charm, It

made Mark feel better for having called Big Smoke's bluff. He went on to gain clarification by explaining, 'I just wanted an assurance that, when my money's put in escrow, as you can respect it's quite a sum, that I'll be covered on the backend, if I'm successful in getting back your coke and delivering the rat to you.'

'I respect that. You are a business man, and so I am also. We shall undertake business together, yes. You have my word that what I say is written in blood. Should anyone not abide by my wishes or impede you in any way, or not come through with the terms of our agreement, then they will pay in blood. I assure you of that. Does that meet your concerns?'

Knoxx offered up a weak reply, 'Uh, yes it does, thank you.'

'You are most welcome. I don't anticipate any problems on my end of our agreement. Although I have to say, from what I've been informed of what you are wanting to do, it does seem that you will be losing five million dollars. Nevertheless, I admire a man who is willing to take such risks to win such rewards. But is it wise for you to undertake such risks?'

'I think it's an acceptable risk. One I'm prepared to take, as it can set me up for life.'

'Or put you away for life,' Madrid answered, quick on the draw.

Having the chance to speak with Knoxx, the two of them went over his plan in detail making sure nothing was left to chance. Talking in a methodical way, breaking down each phase of the plan, Madrid was able to add some interesting insights on a few aspects of it and came up with some angles that Mark hadn't considered. After some time discussing it, they were both satisfied that it was a good plan, and now, they both owned it.

Feeling empowered by his conversation with Madrid, Knoxx stated firmly, 'I just want to confirm, Roberto, that if I get the rat, I receive ten million dollars and if I'm able to get back the cocaine, I'll receive a further twenty million, free and clear. Is that the deal? Are we clear on that?'

'That we are clear on, Mark; in fact, I look at it the other way around. This rat, this scum who inflicts so much pain on me and my family, is worth far more to me. You do this for me and I will be indebted to you. Should you successfully complete your task, it would be an honor to have you visit me and stay as my guest, I insist. Then, maybe we can expand upon our friendship.'

Madrid's words sent a chill of fear through Knoxx. He realized he was in a dangerous situation; one that was becoming more dangerous the more he was becoming involved. They finished their conversation and said their polite goodbyes. Madrid then asked him to hand the phone back to Big Smoke, who, for the most part listened, while he smoked a cigarette. He was clearly not happy about what he was being told, but he acknowledged that he would do as he was ordered. He hung up the cell phone and said, 'It's all you, homes. Whatever you need, just ask, it's yours. We got your back.'

39

'I don't have to tell you how much of a fuck up this all is. Each of you knows what's at stake. All our lives are on the line here, fools. Today's the day. If we don't come through, then we'll be taken out, and our families will suffer for our fuck-ups too.'

Four men were standing in a line looking at Big Smoke. Their eyes followed him as he stalked up and down in front of them. He had been speaking to them for nearly five minutes, getting them pumped up and motivated for the day ahead. The day they would either get back the cocaine, or the day they would all be killed. Bezerk and a handful of Southsiders stood aimlessly about the warehouse that sat inside the razor wire chain-linked fence, where they had all been summoned to be at this morning, the morning after Mark had met Big Smoke. The men looked like they were trying to not too look scared at what they were being told.

Big Smoke stopped walking and looked at one of the four men, who was one of the suspected rats, shouting in his face, 'Is that what you want?'

He jabbed his face in the Sureño's face. The Sureño looked blankly back at him with no emotion, while Big Smoke continued, shouting hard, 'You want to die, homes? Come ten o'clock tonight, I'll watch while you get a bullet in your head from El Jefe, before I get it too! Yeah, you heard me right. El Jefe's gonna be here tonight with his number one west coast buyer to prove the pipeline's secure and give his assurances that we can deliver on future shipments. If we don't come up with a load to replace the one we lost, we die and our families die. It's that simple. You're my captains and so you gotta shoulder the blame and the pain too. We need a new fifty million dollar load by ten tonight. Whoever delivers the largest shipment gets a million dollar bonus, and the one who comes up with nothing, gets dead. My head's on the block and so's all of yours.' Big Smoke then looked at the men, and confessed, 'I ain't going down for this. You guys gotta come through for me, for yourselves and for your loved ones. Do this and all your dreams will come true esse. Fail and those dreams will be your worst fucking nightmares!'

Big Smoke pulled out his gun from his belt, mad-dogging each one. He walked away, leaving Bezerk to clean up. Bezerk nonchalantly sauntered up and down the line, while he pulled out a pack of smokes. He said, 'Waassuupp, how you doin'?' He joked, 'Shiitt,' breaking into a laugh. He offered the guys a cigarette trying to ease the tension between them. While each one pulled out a cigarette from the packet, he said, 'I know we can do this shit. We own this fucking state, right? You know what I mean. We gotta get our hustle on, that's all. You know how we do. I'd go get the load myself, only I have to stay here and do some other shit, getting things ready for El Jefe tonight, but shiitt, fifty mill ain't shit and you esse's ain't shit neither. You guys pick a ride and drive it to wherever you gotta go and go get back some coke. Whoever gets the biggest load gets to keep the ride too, along with the mill. Just get out there and get back that load.'

The men dropped out of line to walk over to the four black Mercedes-Benz S600's that were parked by the far wall of the warehouse. They all knew who Big Smoke and Bezerk had been referring to as El Jefe. None of them had ever met him, and all of them knew enough to know that they never should. Nobody used his name even if they knew it. Speaking his real name was enough to get them killed. He was known as Juicy, or just as El Diablo, the devil.

Bezerk laid his arm across the shoulders of one of the suspected rats, Guerro, and said, 'You'll get what's coming to you.' Stepping off to the next man, he said with humor, 'Belieeve thaatt, homes.'

He let out a big belly laugh while each of the men picked out a car. As each guy got in a car, he called out something about it to the other gangbanger. It was the first time they had ever smelled new leather in a new car. Bezerk looked in on each of them and took his time to talk to them, stooping in to give them a last minute pep talk while they played with the settings in the car. They knew why Bezerk was there, and they knew, come ten o'clock, he would probably be the one who'd be putting a bullet in them if they failed. But no one wanted to go there yet. One by one, the cars fired up and began slowly rolling out of the warehouse. The guards at the compound's perimeter fence opened the gates for them to cruise out with each driver knowing what he had to do and what was at stake. Bezerk stood at the warehouse doors, watching them drive off.

Big Smoke then stepped up to him. Bezerk said to him, 'Fuck, man, that was some funny shit.'

'Yeah, wan' it just. You don't think I over did it, do ya?' Big Smoke asked in a serious way.

'Fuck no, homes. You're a natural, yeess siirr.' Bezerk slapped him on his back while the two of them watched the cars pick up speed, racing away from the compound. Both of them began to laugh, reminiscing at how each of them had played their role.

Big Smoke then spoke up, 'Come on we got some work to do. Let's do this.'

Rallying Bezerk, the two of them summoned the other

Southsiders to come inside the warehouse, and they each told them what they needed them to do. Each Sureño picked up some paint and a roller on a pole, and then walked off to find a window to paint over. No one had any idea why, and no one dared to ask. They all painted the windows in a different way, but over the rest of the day, each one finished his allotted quota of windows. Bezerk had been clear from the beginning, telling them to leave the window facing the south side and the west side unpainted. He oversaw the work, in between hitting a couple of reefers and sinking a few beers, while Big Smoke sat in his Cadillac El Dorado, immersed in watching something. Bezerk walked over to him periodically throughout the day, and they became locked in debate at what they were watching, sometimes smiling, laughing and then sounding like they were getting angry.

Once each gangbanger had finished his task, he was told to go and get a bite to eat. No one was to come back inside the warehouse without either Bezerk's or Big Smoke's approval. Bezerk said, in a low mean growl, meaning every word, 'This place's on lockdown. Anyone comes back in and I'll fuck 'em up for good, belieeve thaatt!'

The word went out and everyone stayed out. Bezerk and Big Smoke worked on the last two remaining windows on the west and south side of the warehouse, making sure that they left the top right hand corner of each one unpainted. They laughed their asses off while they painted them, talking about what could happen next. Both were amazed that it might actually happen, and even more amazed that, so far, it was happening just as he said it would. Knowledge had told them that the first instincts of the rat would be to check in with his handlers and get a take on what they thought. Knoxx had explained that the rat and the cops would probably follow the first two rules of business that were simple ones to follow: fear and greed. Fear of missing out on the money and the greed in capturing Madrid.

Knoxx had played his card and it had come up an ace. The first part they now knew. They knew who the rat was.

40

The heat coming through the windshield from the sun helped to lift his spirits as he stepped on the gas. Guerro began to laugh hysterically as he rode it hard, firing along the 5 Freeway, heading north from San Diego. He turned the stereo up and hit the gas pedal again, letting out a whooping sound in delight. He didn't have a care in the world. Even after being told, less than ten minutes ago, that if he and his compadre's weren't successful in securing the dope, they and their families would be murdered. He called the other Sureños from the car and each one was real scared, not having a clue where to go and how to begin collecting up such a vast stash of cocaine all in one day. Guerro listened to them whine on about the pressure they were under, listening to a couple of them say that they were going to go collect their families and use the car to take off and disappear. Guerro told them to cool it and just do what they could to make up for any short fall, telling them that he knew some vato's up in East L.A. who might come through with the whole load.

It was already pushing eleven thirty in the morning, and this deal was scheduled to go down in approximately ten hours. The clock was running on whether he would end up looking at the inside of an empty warehouse and then be murdered. Guerro checked his mirrors, thinking he might have a tail, and then began to slow the car down before making his next phone call. Guerro held the phone to his ear nervously, while it kept ringing, until eventually his connect answered with a simple disconnected greeting. Guerro gave his codeword and the person on the other end of the line confirmed his. Guerro then rammed it home, saying excitedly, 'Listen man, we need to meet right away. You ain't gonna believe what I got for you, homes.'

The guy on the phone said something that passed for a grunt as his reply.

'Yeah, believe me, you gonna wanna know this one. My word's good, right? You know what I did for you last time on the snow coming over the border. I'm telling you for reals, this one's even bigger!'

The elderly man's voice stayed monotone and even uninterested, asking for a hint on what Guerro was talking about.

He gave it up in a heartbeat, answering, 'Juicy's coming into town. I deliver some coke; I get out of here for good. You hear me? You get Juicy and I get out of the life for good.'

The voice spoke off the phone and then came back to Guerro, saying he would meet him at the usual place.

'Yeah, I figured that. I'm nearly there now,' Guerro answered.

Ten minutes later, Guerro pulled into the parking lot of the diner at Mission Beach. His black ride stood out as he maneuvered it into the parking bay. Two F.B.I. agents scanned the parking lot as they walked over to examine the car. Being such a slight, short man, standing only five foot four, Guerro seemed to fall out of the car; it seemed too big for him. Both agents smiled at the sight of this gangbanger getting out of the car.

'Nice ride, where'd you steal it?' F.B.I. special agent Patrick Connelly joked. His partner, special agent Darren Nicholson, caught the door to get a look at the interior. The black Mercedes sat absorbing the heat from the sun like a magnet. Agent Nicholson's heavy, black, bodybuilder frame, looked more suited to the car than little Guerro's.

Guerro replied, 'Naa, I ain't had to steal nothin'. This here's mine for being a good guy. After tonight, I'm gonna be living like this for reals. Believe that.'

'Sounds like you got it all worked out,' Pat Connelly said sarcastically. He didn't share the enthusiasm and confidence that his confidential informant, Guerro, was radiating, just as bright as the morning sun. He went on to say, 'Well, let's go inside and you can tell us what's going on. Then we can tell you what sort of life you'll be living after that.'

Guerro laughed nervously while Nicholson closed the car door. He pressed the button on the key fob to activate the car's alarm, not wanting the car stolen by some punk.

Having gotten settled in at a table in the Endless Horizons restaurant, the two agents listened while Guerro explained it all as fast as he could. Feeling the pressure, he continually checked his watch throughout their discussion. Connelly, however, had all the time in the world. It was not his life on the line and he made Guerro go over his story one more time, slowing him down during parts of it so they had it right. Agent Nicholson sat beside him, taking notes, asking a smattering of his own questions. He was being prepped to take over from Connelly when he retired at the end of the month. After about forty minutes, which seemed way too long for Guerro, the agents now had it down cold. From what Guerro had told them, Madrid had obviously taken a big hit when the Feds had busted his last shipment of cocaine, and now he had to prove to his buyer that he still had control of the Mexico - U.S. border.

Connelly put it aptly, explaining that Madrid was proving he was still in control of the border by being at the compound tonight. With Guerro agreeing and pushing

142

Connelly along with encouragement at every turn, Nicholson was the first to say it. 'Sounds too good to be true.'

Connelly sat back and stirred his coffee. He said, 'Yeah it does, doesn't it, but then you know what?' He continued, 'Truth can be stranger than fiction, but fiction can sometimes come true.'

He allowed himself a chuckle at how apropos he sounded. Guerro responded squarely by saying, 'I'm telling you, boss, even Big Smoke was sweating it coz he knows he's the one who's fucked. That load getting taken down at the border, thanks to me, he knows it's his neck on the line and he knows he's got to come through on this one. If you'd seen him, you'd know. Tonight's the night, homes. I'm telling you, one night, one deal, one bust, you can get 'em all, and I can get me and my family out of the life for good.'

For a small guy, Guerro had made a big impact. Having worked in the F.B.I. for twenty years, Connelly had heard it all, and this one did sound too good to be true. But how could he pass it up? He only needed to get lucky one time. It all sounded too good to be true, and yet, it did make sense. Juicy was taking a big risk by coming into the U.S., but his whole business was based on taking big risks to stay at the top, and Roberto Madrid was at the very top, and yes, he was a very big prize indeed. For Connelly, this would be the apex of his career. This one, last big bust would make him. He could even write a book and go on the book tour circuit. He had a thought. *What a way to go out.*

'One night, one deal and one bust, hey?' Connelly snorted while Guerro and Nicholson sat in their chairs, waiting on his final decision. After a moment, he looked at Guerro. In a philosophically smooth, even tone, he said, 'Well, let's see what we can do about crashing the party.'

41

'Yeah, uh huh, I know, I got you, fool. We got it from here,' Bezerk replied on his cell phone.

He lifted up a foot and placed it on a mover's box that was sitting beside the desk in the office. He sipped on a Corona beer and dug into a foot-long Hoagie. He then let out a deep laugh, nearly spitting out his food.

'Culo! You piece of shit, say it don't spray it!' Big Smoke said gruffly, laughing with Bezerk as he chunked on his own foot-long sandwich.

Bezerk then shared a joke with the caller, and afterwards listened intently as the next set of instructions came through. He checked that he had got it all straight, and then asked a couple of questions. He giggled some more, replying, 'You're a faagg, uh huh, yeah I got it. See you then.' Bezerk hung up the phone and jokingly remarked to Big Smoke, 'Knowledge, man, he's a bad man.'

They had received a delivery of two large boxes that had been sent down from Los Angeles. After taking care of the contents, they settled in their seats to huddle around the laptop. They talked about what they were going to do once they got their hands on the rat. They were both getting crazy mad and crazy in anticipation thinking about what was going to go down later that night.

Bezerk went over the final details with Big Smoke. Big Smoke checked his watch, saying he'd make his call in about fifteen minutes. It looked like it was all coming together now. Who would have believed it? Only Mark Knoxx. That was because the one thing he knew best was fear and greed. It can make or break you, and he intended it to be the making of him and the breaking of the Feds. Having instilled inspiration in Bezerk, he sat chillin' and illin' like a villain, knowing all he had left to do now was to wait for ten o'clock to roll around. For Showtime.

42

'I don't believe it. It doesn't sound right, Pat.'

'I know, I said the same thing myself but look at it this way, maybe it's been made to look too good to be true so that we'd take a pass on it and miss this opportunity. Maxine, sometimes what looks good on the outside is just real ugly on the inside.'

Agent Connelly was doing his best to persuade his boss, F.B.I. special agent Maxine Dobro, head of Southern California Drug and Organized Crime Taskforce. She sat stoically, thinking about what he'd said. Connelly had realized that he wanted this bust before his retirement but he needed her to back him on it even more than that. Maxine Dobro was a fearsome competitor who hated to lose, but even more, she hated not being in control of the situation. She sat at her desk across from Connelly and Nicholson listening to Connelly's plan. Her blazing, dark eyes held no deception in showing them that she didn't like his plan and she had been fighting him every inch of the way. Standing up from her desk to indicate that the meeting was over, the agents noticed her tight, taught body, honed from years of working out her frustrations in the gym; it created cutting angles that were sharp to look at. She wore a sharp business skirt and a tight and form-fitting shirt. Summarizing her thoughts just as sharply, she said, 'This is on you, Pat. I'm only going to let you run with this if you tell me you're going to vouch for your informant and for the cocaine. A honey trap, hey. So you want to use bait to catch a fish. Well that's a lot of bait you want to use and you better reel in a really big fish or I'm going to be casting you out on a really long line for the remainder of your time in this department. Do I make myself clear?'

Leading them out of her office, both men felt like schoolboys being reprimanded by their school principal. Pat Connelly answered in an obscure way, saying, 'Yes, Maxine. Crystal.'

Dobro caught it. Spinning on her heels, the fire from a burning cauldron, deep inside her toned body spewed forth as she venomously replied, 'Listen up, Pat. You work for me and no matter how many years you have in, that's how it is. This is my decision to make, not yours. Remember, I've warned you. Madrid is no fool, so don't underestimate him. You want to use the impounded cocaine against him. Fine, make sure S.W.A.T. and our department fully secure it and the location, because if you lose it or him, you will lose your job!'

Connelly quickened his pace to match hers; his white, tired skin that wore his age, looked even more pale than usual. He looked at her in a sage fatherly manner, with his paunch riding his pants low and his suspenders fully flexed around his thin shoulders. He caught Maxine by her elbow and she finally stopped walking, waiting for him to compose himself. He adjusted the frames of his glasses and framed his next statement. 'Maxine, please, understand the situation on this one. I know you're the future of this department and I realize my time and influence has come and gone. I'm happy to be moving on soon, I am. But I'd like to have one more big arrest under my belt, and I believe this is it. We've been fighting the gangs for how long now and have we really made a difference? Have we even made a dent in any of their organizations? I don't believe we have. I have this last chance to make a statement, to make a stand, to show the gangbangers that we won't give up. Things may be okay, but I'm not okay with things as they are.' Connelly sensed that he was getting through and so he softened his approach. Moving in closer to start a detailed recap as if he was still teaching her a thing or two, describing what he had planned, he explained, 'Our confidential informant has assured us that the head of the Mexican cartel, Juicy, will be coming to San Diego to meet with his number one West Coast cocaine buyer. Roberto Madrid needs to prove that he has control of the border. Our informant's the one who gave us the information on the cocaine that we scored in the first place, and now he's telling us this deal's going down tonight. I'm telling you, it's going to go down tonight. One meet, one deal, and for one night only, Juicy is within our grasp. We'll manipulate the situation to our advantage by supplying the honey trap, using the impounded shipment of cocaine against them. We'll control the whole thing because we know where and when the drop's going to happen in advance.' Taking a beat, he bored his eyes into Maxine's, closing the deal, saying with conviction, 'It's ours to lose, and we won't lose.'

43

'Where you at fool?' Big Smoke's voice could be heard on the phone asking.

Guerro immediately came up on point, sitting across the table from Nicholson. Already nervous about what he had instigated, he had crossed over the line and now he had no options left but to play it all out. There was no going back now. Guerro was lying and dying with every word from his mouth, pretending to be upbeat. Connelly entered the interview room, giving Guerro the thumbs up to indicate that they were definitely on for tonight. Guerro replied, 'Yeah waassuup Smoke? Man, I was just getting ready to call you.' Making his voice sound as excited as he could, he continued, 'I came up big! I'm coming through on the whole load! Don't get it twisted though; I still have to make sure I can get it from some esse's up in East L.A. It was meant for some fools in Vegas, but they said they'll offload it on credit to help us out.'

He heard the relief in Big Smoke's voice and could tell that he was real happy. Big Smoke laughed, saying Guerro would be set for life and that he'd be getting what was coming to him if he could bring it all in.

'Man, I'm gonna buy me two of them rides, Smoke,' Guerro answered, laughing with Big Smoke. He looked across the table at the agents who were recording the conversation. Neither one of them was smiling while they both watched him acting out his part, getting his money. Things took a turn to the serious side of the drug game when Big Smoke reminded him that if they didn't come through with the load then Juicy would have them all killed. This was all the F.B.I. agents needed to hear as it confirmed that Madrid would be present tonight. Connelly scratched out a message on his notepad and shoved it across the table. Guerro leaned over to read it and then nodded in understanding. He asked, 'What time's the buyer coming in? I need to make sure I got enough time to get the snow down to you.'

Big Smoke responded, 'Midnight.'

Guerro, making his play, candidly remarked, trying to catch Big Smoke off guard, 'How's he coming in?'

Big Smoke answered reflexively, 'By boat.'

The two agents looked at each other, both thinking the same thing. They had them.

44

At precisely 9:15 p.m. Pacific Standard Time, the big-rig truck rolled out of the F.B.I.'s La Jolla headquarters. A Latino undercover police officer who had been drafted in from Los Angeles at the last minute for security reasons, was driving the big-rig. An armed escort of six GM Chevy Suburban's were rolling at the front and rear of the truck. A G.P.S. tracking device had been placed inside the fifty million dollar load of cocaine. Guerro sat beside the driver in the big-rig while another police officer drove his car until they reached the point of no return. Guerro was then transferred back into the car to lead the big-rig truck in. Close to fifty F.B.I. agents with D.E.A. and S.W.A.T. officers were already positioned around the Southsider's warehouse. Connelly sat inside the high-tech operations control center positioned in a parking lot, close to a mile away from the Southsider compound. He had all the bases covered and had at his disposal, computer technicians, street cameras and a police helicopter that was tracking the cocaine. Nothing had been overlooked or left to chance.

'Like shooting fish in a barrel,' Connelly remarked.

The S.W.A.T. officer in charge looked back at him, stating disingenuously, 'We still have a long way to go.' He turned his attention to his own men, keying his radio to speak to a sharpshooter, 'Red One, what's your status? Over.'

Two S.W.A.T. sharpshooters had maneuvered themselves into a shooting position after two hours of sneaking around the perimeter of the compound. One of the snipers had found a spy hole into the warehouse at the south side and the other shooter had found a similar view from the west side. Both S.W.A.T. snipers had reported that apparently, someone had missed painting over a small pane of glass that allowed them to see inside through their riflescopes.

'Twenty-twenty, eyes good,' the report came back from both snipers.

'Copy that,' the S.W.A.T. captain confirmed. He then looked at Connelly, asking, 'Too good to be true?'

'Stranger things have happened. Even the best fall down,' he replied nonchalantly.

Connelly turned away to watch the monitors, which showed the F.B.I. convoy barreling down the 5 Freeway entering the San Diego city limits. Guerro made his phone call to Big Smoke while he drove towards the compound with the big-rig rolling behind him, snorting hard as the driver kicked it down a gear. He told Big Smoke they were about ten minutes away from the compound. As he had said it the police instantly noticed activity on the monitors as a number of armed Sureños came out of the warehouse shouldering various weapons. The S.W.A.T. snipers called it in, relaying everything they saw as to the type of weapons and the number of Southsider soldiers. From what they were describing this was going to be it and tonight was going to be the night. Connelly licked his lips. He could taste it. He picked up a can of Coke to quench his dry, nervous mouth. It tasted sweet. He looked at his watch, thinking, *Two hours to go*. They had the Sureños surrounded and after the shipment arrived they would close the net in around the compound. From then on nothing could come in or leave without them allowing it. Police officers sat nervously inside tractor trailers, cars and buildings, sitting low to the ground, waiting for the go.

'Eyes on principal targets,' one S.W.A.T. sniper said.

'Roger that, eyes on targets.' The other sniper confirmed that he had also identified Big Smoke and Bezerk when they had walked out from inside the warehouse. The lights went out inside, save for maybe two or three naked light bulbs hanging in the rear of the building, the interior of the warehouse was thrown into a dark light.

Connelly's cell phone chirped. He picked it up and looked at the caller I.D. It was Dobro checking in on how it was going. Ten o'clock and finally, this was it. He confirmed that everything was under control, saying firmly, 'We've got all the exits covered and the coke's entering the compound now.'

He went on to tell her that they even had eyes on the inside of the warehouse and that he had agent Nicholson heading up an F.B.I. team stationed at the harbor, waiting on the arrival of the buyer. Not sounding convinced, Dobro said she wanted a report every fifteen minutes from him, as she once again reminded him of what was at stake. He responded to her veiled threat, confidently stating, 'All we have to do now is wait for midnight and we'll have Juicy, his top buyer in California, and one hell of a headline in the morning. You'll see.' Connelly signed off and then exhaled a deep, satisfied breath, while he watched the big-rig reversing into the warehouse on the monitor, knowing they had them. It was all just a matter of time.

45

'Boy, look at you, you doogg!' Guerro heard Bezerk saying as he exited the Mercedes, having been told to park it next to the other three. The truck had reversed inside the warehouse into position using day glow sticks that had been laid along the floor like a runway. The big-rig's air brakes gave off a loud screech as it came to a halt. Once the engine had been turned off, two armed men stood by the driver's door to escort the driver out. With Guerro in tow walking next to him, Bezerk shouted, 'Everyone out!'

The big-rig was left sitting alone in the dark light of the warehouse, as everyone came out into view of the S.W.A.T. snipers. They watched silently as Bezerk slammed the massive, heavy doors shut and locked them tight with a heavy lock. The cocaine was sealed inside and now the Southsiders were sealed inside a ring of cops. Everyone was waiting for two people to arrive: Roberto Madrid and his cocaine buyer. All the police officers surrounding the compound knew that any mistakes now could mean a high price was going to be paid. These Southsiders were the hard-core gangbanger gansta's who would fight to the death once they realized they were surrounded. Connelly stood beside the S.W.A.T. captain, who was now feeling the heat too, standing there impatiently watching and waiting for something to happen.

'What's your twenty, Hill Two?' the S.W.A.T. captain asked in a pensive tone.

The sniper replied, 'I'm positioned on the west-facing building, approximately two hundred and sixty yards from the corner of the northwest block. I have twenty-twenty vision on the ball, sir. It's clean and green, nothing's moving in there. Over.'

'Copy that.'

The S.W.A.T. captain looked at Connelly and both men looked relieved. He then repeated his question to the second sniper, who reported that he was positioned at the south side of the compound and that he could see the cocaine too. A quiet storm was waiting over the endless horizon. Everyone was waiting for the main event, waiting for one thing and the same thing. The arrival.

Darren Nicholson had been dispatched with a small force to the Marriott Hotel at 333 West Harbor Drive, San Diego to watch for the arrival of the buyer. Looking out to sea, he watched with trepidation as a dark shape began to loom over the horizon. He called it in, reporting what he'd seen. A yacht. Connelly asked in a strained voice, laced with anticipation and pent-up excitement, for the U.S. Coastguard to identify it. Nicholson watched in awe as a silhouette stretched out across Coronado Bay, coming closer by the minute in the dark of the night. Five minutes later he reported that he estimated the yacht's length to be around a hundred and twenty feet, while he watched a launch being lowered from it. Nicholson then reported he could make out two males and one female. No one could afford to make a single mistake now. This was it. One night, one deal, one bust.

Connelly checked each monitor, time and time again, and each time, everything looked how it was meant to look. Bezerk was standing outside the warehouse bullshitting, laughing and joking with his crew, the undercover cop, and Guerro, who had been wired for the occasion at the insistence of Maxine Dobro. This had been the compromise to get the green light from her, and Connelly had pressured Guerro into it. Nothing was being left to chance. When everyone went down, the case would stick because they would have video and audio evidence, along with Madrid and his biggest cocaine buyer on the West Coast in irons.

Connelly licked his lips and took the last swig from his Coke can and then thought about tomorrow morning's headlines. He would be made for life from this career bust and he would be famous for bringing in an internationally hunted drug kingpin. One more round of radio checks and everyone it seemed, including the bad guys, were all waiting on the arrival of the big boss and his partner. The snipers on the two roofs were silently keeping watch; federal agents and S.W.A.T. were positioned around the compound, waiting to collapse the ring in tight. Everyone was itching to pull their guns and go charging in to take them down. Minutes that had turned in to hours had slowly eked away the officer's adrenaline. One officer who had been cramped into the back of a ninety-two minivan checked his watch. It told him it was 11:42 p.m. Showtime.

46

Bezerk had been on top form, cracking jokes as if he did not have a care in the world. He had no idea what was out there waiting for him. He had told a series of jokes, coercing the undercover cop into telling some of his own. Everyone laughed and bullshitted as if they were on a boy's night out. A handful of the Sureño guards stayed on point, patrolling the perimeter, but for the most part, everything was normal. To look at them you would never have thought that fifty million dollars worth of cocaine was sitting inside the warehouse. Now that Guerro had come through with it, Bezerk kept reminding everyone that he was going to get what was coming to him. He just loved saying that, and of course, 'you know what I mean.'

Big Smoke had filtered off from the pack. He was seen lighting up a cigarette as he got into Guerro's car, being tracked through a sniper's scope. The sniper watching him said it looked like he was listening to the radio. After a couple of minutes he got out and strolled back over to the rest of the guys, giving Bezerk a look that kind of froze him for a moment. He gave a nod back in an understanding kind of way as Big Smoke walked past him. Big Smoke then summoned everyone to come over and gather round as he checked his watch. 11:42 p.m. Time for the show to begin.

Everyone huddled around him. Guerro huddled in too, his wire picking up every word while his eyes scanned the circle of soldiers thinking, *Not long now, and I'm free. Free from the police and free from the gang life.* His eyes skirted the circle of men and came back around to Bezerk, who was already looking at him with a mad-doggin' kind of look. In the dark light of the compound he looked like he was a mad, rabid dog. Big Smoke gave the order and everyone snapped into killer mode, looking awesome. They were his best gangbangers. Each of them was a killer, and now, they were all on high alert. The wire hidden underneath Guerro's shirt picked up Bezerk saying to him, 'Come on, fool, you coming with me. I'm gonna have you meet the buyer, since you got all this done, homey. All this here's for you.'

He put his arm around Guerro's shoulders and they laughed in unison walking over to the cars, with Guerro talking about what he was going to spend his money on, and Bezerk saying he was going to come and rob him if he stayed in San Diego. They both arrived at Guerro's Mercedes. The four cars lined up behind the razor wire fence of the compound. Guerro and Bezerk were the first car, Big Smoke and three soldiers in the second car, and eight more Sureños in the two rear cars. All eyes were on them.

Connelly was pacing the length of the operations center while the monitors filled up with movement. The technicians were all busy recording everything. Nicholson radioed in. Barking into his radio, Connelly replied, 'Yeah Darren, go ahead.'

Standing with his hand on his hip, he listened while Nicholson described what he was watching. 'We got two males. First one's Caucasian, approximately five-six, a hundred and seventy pounds, dark hair. Second male's African American, bald head, six-six, two hundred and eighty pounds, looks like security. And one female, looks like she's light-skinned African American, might be Asian mix, five foot eight, long black hair, around a hundred and fifteen pounds.'

'Copy that. Where're they headed?'

'They're in a launch, coming in to the Marriott's marina.'

Connelly had a quick thought and asked one of the techs just as quickly, 'Any word on the boat and who owns it?'

The convoy of cars rolled out from the compound and raced up the street. As they did, Connelly had to make a decision. It was now or never. This was his decision to make and his career on the line. The captains and officers looked at him for the word.

The Coastguard finally reported in, saying that the yacht was called What A Waste. The manifest stating that it had been chartered by a Los Angeles-based company called Exile Corporation. Connelly had to act. The worst decision is not making one.

'Okay, we know where they're headed and our man is with them. They're on their way to the hotel to pick up the buyer, right?' he said, but in an asking kind of way as if he wanted confirmation from his colleagues. But no one responded, not wanting to put their neck on the line. It was Connelly's show and his call to make. Having reached a decision, he keyed the radio and said, 'Let 'em roll. All units, hold your positions. Hold, I repeat, hold your positions.' Looking over at the San Diego police sergeant, in a quickened pace, he said, 'I want them tracked all the way down to the Marriott and back again. Don't lose them.'

The sergeant began passing on the information to the airborne officers in the police helicopter, while Connelly explained his thought process to the assembled officers in the ops center. 'They're going to pick the buyer up and bring him back to the warehouse. We wait for Madrid to arrive, and then we'll take them down.'

The four Mercedes drove along the 905 freeway. As they did they began to shuffle their positions in the line of cars, but the main thing was that they were still heading west towards the Coronado Bay area. As the convoy raced along the freeway, the pilot radioed in with an update every two minutes. Nicholson was back on the radio to provide his blow-by-blow commentary, saying that the three individuals at the Marriott's marina had now exited the launch and were making their way up the rear gardens to the hotel.

The ops center was a hive of activity with every person now working at full speed. The sheriff was on his radio, making sure that none of the patrol units on the freeway was going to intercept the convoy, even if it was breaking the speed limit. He then ordered all the remaining police units in the general area to drop back and give them plenty of room, as the convoy was seen dropping into downtown San Diego and hitting the surface streets from the police helicopter's camera. Connelly checked his watch, 11:57 p.m. The arrival was scheduled for midnight and everything was going to plan. His plan. Guerro's wire was coming in loud and clear, and all he had been talking about was what he was going to do with his million dollar bonus for bringing in the biggest load. Bezerk had been joking with him until they came to the stoplight at the corner of West Broadway and Union Street, which stood beside the tower of pain, the M.C.C.

All four cars lined up behind each other below the Metropolitan Correctional Center with their engines purring, looking like four black cats. The stoplight changed to green, but still they waited. The helicopter held its position, laying back high in the sky with the pilot relaying the scene below.

Nicholson and his team were set. They could take the buyer down as he entered the hotel with his female escort and bodyguard. All the radios and television monitors were alive and racing with action.

'What are they waiting for?' Connelly said, pondering a thought. He held his radio at the ready, looking at the monitor, watching the line of stationary cars from the helicopter's point of view, muttering to himself again, 'What are they sitting there for?'

Nicholson came on the radio, sounding nervous. Unsure of what action to take, he asked, 'The three subjects are entering the hotel. What do you want me to do?'

'Hold your position. They're seven blocks away on Union Street.'

'Copy that.' Nicholson answered.

Connelly then said as an afterthought, 'They'll pick the subjects up and drive them back to the compound. Get as many photographs as possible.'

'Copy that,' Nicholson confirmed, and his team went to work on reconnaissance at the hotel. The cars sat in formation, looking awesome while they stood with their engines quietly purring, waiting. But waiting for what?

The answer came like rolling thunder. The big fog horn roared and the ground began to shake. Sitting behind the lead car with his cell phone to his ear, Bezerk checked his watch. 11:59 p.m. and still he waited.

The panoramic view from the police helicopter showed the whole scene from above like a horror movie being played out in slow motion; you already knew the ending but you had to watch it anyway. Connelly realized all too late.

'Go! Fucking go, go, go, go!' Bezerk screamed into the phone. The lead car raced out of the blocks from the stoplight and abruptly took a right turn. Bezerk raced ahead. The car behind him screeched its tires as it made a u-turn and doubled back with the last car making a hard left turn. The helicopter's night vision camera showed the scene as each car separated and veered off at high speed in a different direction.

'Whoa. What was that all about?' the pilot exclaimed, reacting to the scene below him.

'Nobody panic. They're probably just running some counter-surveillance. They'll meet up again at the hotel. Everyone hold your positions,' Connelly said in a commander's voice, commanding his troops.

Bezerk raced towards the closing railway crossing gates. The loud 'ding, ding, ding, ding' from the alarms on the gates bellowed as the Santa Fe Train's fog light began to illuminate them. The train screamed towards them along the train tracks. Gunning the heavy S600 harder, he launched it across the train tracks as the railway gates slammed down behind it.

'Which car do I follow?' The pilot asked, unsure what to do next.

Unsure too, Connelly answered, 'Hold your position.'

'Sir, you better look at this!' a young technician shouted above the din.

Connelly squinted at the monitor he was pointing at, and his voice rang-out, 'No, no, no, it can't be! What's going on down there?'

He looked mortified as he saw that the undercover cop was being beaten to the ground. He then watched as the gangbangers began running into the warehouse. Simultaneously, he heard Bezerk's voice over the speakers in the ops center, saying, 'Yeah boy, I told you, you was gonna get what's coming to you, you fucking piece of shit rat!'

Connelly checked with an officer standing nearby, and then looked at the S.W.A.T. captain, asking, 'Did you guys hear that?'

The sound from Guerro's wire went blank and now there was only static on the line. Connelly shouted, 'What's happening, people? Talk to me! I want to know something, now!'

*   *   *

Bezerk jumped on the brakes, stopping the car in a screech of tires and the two of them fell forward from the abrupt halt. He pulled a gun and pointed it at Guerro's head. He said, 'Yeah boy, I told you, you was gonna get what's coming to you, you fucking piece of shit rat!'

Bezerk leaned across and ripped out the wire from Guerro's chest, all the way down to the inside of his pants, tossing it out the car's window. The car's rear passenger door opened quickly, slamming shut behind him. One of Bezerk's homeys; Tavo, got in and took over holding the gun to Guerro's head. They had their rat. Guerro knew he was dead; it was just a matter of time. Bezerk bent over and ripped out a tape recorder from under the driver's seat. Looking at Guerro, he showed him the tape recorder that he had taped under the driver's seat earlier that morning, taunting him, saying, 'Fuckin' faagg, it's all on tape, asshole.'

He then stepped on the gas and drove slowly up to the intersection of West Market Street and West harbor Drive.

*   *   *

'What's happening at the hotel?' Connelly barked.

Nicholson answered that the subjects appeared to be checking into it, telling him, 'They're not heading for the entrance of the hotel.'

'Damn it! Do we have any visual or audio on our man?'

The tech turned from his post, shaking his head, replying ominously, 'None, sir.'

'What's the status on the cocaine?' Connelly barked, marching up to the S.W.A.T. captain.

'Sniper team says it's still in there.'

'Thank God for that. How could they have known about our guy?' Connelly said it to no one in particular, but he finally saw it for what it was as soon as he heard the S.W.A.T. captain say, in an offhanded remark, 'Bait and switch? If they knew about your informant, then they must've set this all up, don't you think?'

As soon as the words had passed the S.W.A.T. captain's lips, Connelly had a moment of clarity. Then, in an instant, he wilted, having seen it for what it was, realizing it was all a show. A show put on for him. Dread came over him. The Southsiders were holed-up in the warehouse and their confidential informant was lost. What the hell was going on?

'Take 'em down!' he barked into his radio. He turned to the S.W.A.T. captain, who had been waiting for the word from him. He gave it dejectedly, saying in a lowered, more

156

ambiguous tone, 'Take them down.'

The S.W.A.T. captain lifted up his radio and stated, 'You have a go.'

All everyone could do now was watch the video game play out, with people filling the screens from every angle on every monitor.

Nicholson was the first to approach the trio, who were shocked at being surrounded by F.B.I. agents barking orders at them and detaining them in the hotel lobby by the check-in counter. Nicholson raised his leather wallet, showing them his F.B.I. credentials. He soon lowered it and his tone, once it became clear that they were businesspeople in town for the following two days for a string of meetings. Nicholson confirmed who they were: Matthew Tamban, the lawyer for a venture capital firm called Exile Corporation; Olivia Marbela, the company's marketing and promotions vice president. They were being escorted by the company's head of security, Quincy Taylor. Their hotel reservation had been made the day earlier and their scheduled meetings were still being looked into. A relatively breathless and harried Nicholson relayed over the radio to Connelly who listened while he watched the video feed from the compound. S.W.A.T., F.B.I. and the assisting law enforcement agencies were entering it and not one Southsider could be seen. The snipers reported that they still had eyes on the cocaine sitting in the center of the warehouse, so at least he could breathe easy on that one. He said symbolically to Nicholson, 'They wanted to flush out the rat.'

S.W.A.T. secured the area and all the police officers moved in to secure the warehouse. All Connelly could pray for now was that none of the officers would be killed in the impending shoot out when the gangbangers realized they were cornered. While he watched the cops enter the warehouse on a monitor, he asked an officer seated at a computer, 'Any sign of our C.I.?'

'None. A patrol unit's found the Mercedes abandoned on the other side of the train tracks at the Circuit City parking lot. They're running parallels and we're trying to set up road blocks and a perimeter.'

'Jesus, it's all going to shit! I'm in Hell!' Connelly roared, realizing it had all gone from sugar to shit. Then it went all to Hell.

Over the speakers, everyone could feel the tension in the lead S.W.A.T. officer's voice from inside the warehouse. He stated coldly, 'I think you'd better come down here agent Connelly.'

'What is it?' he answered abruptly.

The officer simply replied, 'You're going to want to see this for yourself. There's no one here.'

Connelly checked the faces around him and asked, 'Say again?'

He had heard it right. The S.W.A.T. officer simply stated that he had better come down to the warehouse now, not wanting to report it over the radio. By now, television helicopters and news reporter' vans were encircling the area. Bright lights enveloped the compound. Whatever secret operation had gone down here, it was all out in the open now. The secret police sting was now going to be made very public. Connelly left the ops center, accompanied by some other agents and stepped into a waiting GMC Suburban that drove them off towards the compound.

Pulling into the warehouse he could see that all the officers had shouldered or holstered their weapons. They were all standing around in the middle of the warehouse, which had two large heavy drapes that were hanging from the metal beams above; one drape faced south and one faced west. All eyes turned to him and the mob of cops all fell silent as he approached. They began to part and back up from the hanging drapes as he stepped up closer. Walking through them, his eyes adjusted to the dark light inside. He quickly recognized what was printed on the hanging drapes as being two camera-ready-digital photographs of a stack of cocaine sitting on a pallet. Connelly felt his eyes begin to water and his throat begin to close, as his next step got even heavier. Approaching the middle of the room, he began to see what the cops were now staring at: a huge, ragged hole in the floor behind the hanging drapes.

'Looks like they've been hard at it all night right under our noses the whole time,' a random cop remarked in the crowd.

Each cop jumped as the ground shook and trembled under a low thud. One cop said, 'They just blew the tunnel shut from the other end.'

*   *   *

Having transferred Guerro into a Ford Explorer that Tavo had arrived in, at the parking lot of the Circuit City store, they pulled away from it. Looking south as he began to turn north onto West harbor Drive, Bezerk could see all the way down the street to the Marriott Hotel. 'Faaggss,' Bezerk said with some pride, as he and Tavo laughed. Guerro had been stuffed into the car's rear foot well, handcuffed behind his back. Bezerk then shouted wildly at him, 'Yeah booyy, you gonna get yours all right. We had you the moment you pulled off in the car, homes. It's called SATNAV, fool!'

Howling wildly and full of adrenaline, he laughed again as he slowly pulled away from the corner, making an easy turn north to drive away from the Marriott. Soon, he saw his destination beginning to come into view. Lindbergh Field. The airport.

*   *   *

Back at the warehouse, a haze of dust enveloped the cops.
'Do we have anything to go on?' Connelly limply asked.
'It's all gone. The cocaine, the informant, everything's gone.'
It was as if everyone was attending a wake and they were all looking at a dead body. And in a way, they were. Connelly felt all eyes falling back to him while all the cops stood around him. His cellular phone began to chirp as if on cue; the final eulogy would soon be given at his funeral. His career was dead. What was supposed to have been a career-making bust was now going to become a busted career. He would be known as the police officer in charge who lost fifty million dollars worth of cocaine while they all watched it happen. The bad guys had been able to get one back.
'Where do we go from here?' one officer offered up. Connelly simply replied in resignation, 'We go home.' He knew that's where he'd be headed before tomorrow ended. 'Wrap it up and try to get what leads you can.'

*   *   *

A jet was sitting on the runway with its engines running and its stairway lowered. Bezerk came to a stop about five feet from the bottom of the stairs. He gave Tavo his instructions on how he wanted the Explorer disposed of. He then got out and opened the rear door to pull Guerro out of the car. Forcing Guerro at gun point, he began to take the stairs up into the plane.
'You're late, fag boy. What'd you do, stop off for a manwich?'
Bezerk laughed hard with relief as he laid eyes on Mark Knoxx, sitting casually in his seat with a glass of champagne in his hand.
'Uh huh, keep it up, fool. I'll smoke your ass.' Both of them began laughing hysterically. Knoxx had done it. Got back the cocaine and captured the rat.

An Envious Life

47

Knoxx handed a chilled flute of champagne to Bezerk. Looking flushed with success, Bezerk said with excitement in his voice, 'To the great escape, my man.'

The jet quickly pulled up to its cruising altitude of twenty-two thousand feet. In three minutes it crossed the U.S. - Mexico border.

Smiling a bright smile, Bezerk said proudly, 'Man, I can't believe we did it, doogg. What a plan, Knowledge.' He said it in a sarcastic but proud way. 'You did it dude, yeess siirrr!'

Bezerk held up his champagne flute to give Mark a salute. Like it was the best beer he had ever tasted, he quickly downed it all, letting out a long satisfied sigh afterwards.

Mark replied, 'Easy money, bro'.'

Knoxx returned his own gesture, downing his glass with some relief. It tasted sweet. The sweet taste of victory. They laughed uncontrollably again, as what they had achieved finally began to sink in. Momentarily turning his attention to the rear of the plane, and to the little forlorn-looking Mexican seated there sobbing, Knoxx asked boldly, 'So this is the piece of shit that caused all this?'

'Yeah, that's the piece of shit, puto; you can believe he's gonna be one dead mutherfuckaa by the time I'm done with him, yeess Siirrr.' Bezerk scowled at him, saying, 'Believe that, puto, belieeve thaatt.'

Both men glared at Guerro, both wanting to get their hands on him.

Bezerk's pent-up aggression and adrenaline getting the better of him, he spat at him while Guerro sat handcuffed in his seat. Bezerk then fired at Guerro, saying hard, 'Told you, you'd get what's coming to you, didn't I, and now you will, you punk-ass bitch.' He laughed in a taunting way and began to whip himself up into a murderous frenzied mind of death and destruction. Bezerk's tirade was becoming more deadly and fearsome by the second, as he continued saying, 'You fucked us all over, homes. Your brothers, how many have sent down coz of you? How many are in prison coz of you, you piece of shit. Well, it's all caught up to you now. You gonna get what's coming to you alright, I'm gonna make sure of that. You best belieeve thaatt!'

Knoxx realized he had heard enough. Guerro seemed to be

in a trance, sitting comatose, muttering to himself, crying small tears.

'Bro', come sit down with me. We'll get information from him one way or another. Think about it. The Feds have good Intel from this guy on who's involved in all your operations. They know what loads to hit and who to arrest to make the most impact. So maybe this piece of shit can turn the tables for you?' Knoxx sipped on his champagne and took a moment to think about something. He explained, 'Sun Tzu in *The Art of War* says. "The supreme art of war is to subdue the enemy without fighting. All war is based on deception." Don't worry about it, just enjoy the ride. The hard part's done. Soon you can bask in all the glory.'

Easing back into the leather chair, he looked back at his soldier in a sarcastic mode, one that his old bunky knew all too well. They both began to laugh as all the tension finally fell from Bezerk and he said happily, 'Hell of a night, dog, you know what I mean?' Leaning over to refill Knoxx's flute, Bezerk remarked, 'Man, I couldn't believe it! I was laughing my ass off, once I knew we had him and the coke back. Oh, man, when I looked up at M.C.C. that was the best. I thought yeah booyy, that boy Knowledge, fucking Mark, always plottin', yeess siirr. Man, I never want to cross you! We did it, doogg. It's all down to you. Always plottin'.'

Bezerk once again offered up his champagne flute as a toast and the two carried on reflecting back on the night's events. Bezerk relayed the ins and outs of all of it for Mark to envision. They talked openly in front of Guerro, knowing it didn't matter as he'd be dead soon. They howled in delight at how the Feds could have been so stupid.

In fits of laughter, Bezerk said, 'Man, I'd loved to have seen the look on them Fed's faces when they realized we took our shit back right from under their noses and walked away with their rat at the same time, yeess siirr, you know what I mean?'

48

'There had to have been a huge number of people involved in this. Someone somewhere knows.'

'Ya think?' was all Maxine Dobro could reply.

Connelly had been sitting humbly in front of Maxine Dobro for around thirty minutes, sucking it up. He had to be the one to lay it all out for her, listening to her tell him, 'You got taken, Pat. Plain and simple. You got taken down by one of the oldest cons in the book. Play to someone's ego, fear and greed. Whoever was behind this certainly knows how to play the game real good, coz he sure as shit played you and this department.'

Dobro was in Rottweiler mode and was in no mood to mince her words. The only thing getting minced today would be the officers who had screwed up. Maxine was charismatic, attractive and alluring; she had recently turned fifty-three, but this in no way reduced her sex appeal. Always well-dressed and smelling good, Maxine had lived the good life, having been married to a big shot lawyer, and had two children. She was a career mom first, but she always remained a woman. Attractive with attitude, it was it was a great combination that she carried with ease upon her five foot eight inches tall frame; she had thick, brown wavy hair, and peering out from under that, were her dark caramel eyes. Maxine had a razor sharp wit and was smart as a whip too. She ran the Federal Bureau of Investigation's Drug and Organized Crimes Taskforce for Southern California as a hands-on take-no-shit, bad-ass leader. Her superiors summed her up easily as being brilliant, charming, funny and ruthless, and she was all of these things with a bag of chips thrown in today. They had lost a lot of chips the night before, and the F.B.I. wasn't in the business of losing.

Maxine asked Pat, 'How could you be so stupid, Pat? You've lost your edge. How could I have been so stupid allowing you to do this? I did this for you, Pat. Your last big case, wasn't that what you told me?'

Maxine looked at Pat in a way that told him this was still his last case. She had explained to him earlier that she would be catching fire and brimstone from everywhere today from her superiors, and even worse, from the media.

'Our confidential informant was clearly feeling he was in danger for his life. The way he explained it to us, it all made sense. One night, one deal, one man.' Connelly tried his best to make some sense of it, trying to make it add up.

Dobro hit back, saying, 'You only thought of yourself, Pat, and that's what they used against you. You wanted it to be true. You wanted to make this your career bust and that's what they used against you. They used your age and career against you. They dealt you the hand and you played it, and then they turned it around on you and played you.'

Dobro looked him squarely in the eyes as he sat looking despondent, having been humbled throughout the night, morning, and again here in her office.

'You're right about one thing,' Dobro nonchalantly said as she shuffled some papers around her desk, beginning to write something.

'Yeah, what's that?' Connelly answered, upbeat, looking for some solace from her.

Maxine looked up and stated, 'Your confidential informant? He probably is living in fear for his life now.'

She hit him with everything she could convey with her eyes. Connelly sighed. As he slumped back in the chair, defeated and tired, Maxine lifted up a cookie tray from under her desk and asked, 'Brownie? I made them this morning. I figured today was going to be a long one.' Dobro decided which brownie she was going to pick. She picked up the cookie tray and offered it across the table to Connelly. 'Want one?'

'Uh, no, no thanks,' he remarked, clearly thinking he was walking into another trap.

She pushed them further across her desk until he took one. She said warmly, 'C'mon, Pat, think of it as some comfort food for today.'

Sensing a little humor in her voice, he summoned up half a smile as he took one, and heard, 'You're gonna need all the comfort you can get today.' Ouch. Dobro sprang her trap and it had stung. Dobro's mood darkened, then she demanded, 'I'm going to have to give a press conference soon and I'm going to need some answers, some leads, something to go in there with. Then after that, we'll talk about your future. How's the brownie?'

49

The early morning hues from the rising sun lit up the desert's tan sand. From the jet, Knoxx could see the sun hitting the windows of the waiting convoy of cars that were lined up along the airstrip that was about ten miles east from the coast of Cabo San Lucas, Mexico.

Knoxx had spent most of the flight telling Bezerk that Guerro was now expensive cargo. He explained that Guerro was probably more valuable to Madrid than getting back his cocaine, and now they were in a position to ask him for practically anything. For Knoxx, he knew just what he would be asking for. Knoxx had explained that, at the end of the day, it was just doing business. Take the emotion out of it, focus on developing a relationship, and then build trust. What had seemed like a chapter closed for Bezerk was just the beginning for Knoxx. Bezerk figured that by returning the coke and having flushed out the rat, it was back to business as usual, slingin' dope. For Knoxx though, this was the opening of his resume, his chance to show what he could do and prove what he was prepared to do to rise to the top. He had proven himself with the top man. He had proven that he was a man who could make things happen and most importantly, a man who could deliver. He had made a point to deliver both packages back to Madrid for two reasons. One, he still needed twenty million dollars to form the Envious Group. Two, he needed a like-minded partner who shared his vision, and who had the foresight and courage to act upon that vision.

Knoxx had explained things to Bezerk on the plane, while Bezerk laughed in delight at what he was hearing. 'You're one sick fuck, dog.'

Bezerk took to the role that Mark wanted him to play, reinforcing the fact that Bezerk was his dog now. The way Knoxx had described it all, Bezerk soon began to realize that he was close to realizing his own dreams, belonging to something that made sense. Chris Wright was now so close to having it all - real money, real power and real respect - and it was Mark Knoxx delivering it to him, not the Southsiders. The plane descended at some pace and then landed on the small airstrip. Mark gave it his last shot in landing Bezerk, by saying sharply, 'From here on out, Bezerk, it's you and me, dog. You feel me? It's no more me and them. It's you and me, and them. You understand what I'm telling you? If you want it all, then I'm the one who'll give you it to you, but I want you all in with me. I need to know, you got my back?'

The plane wound down as it came to a stop. This was

Mark's last stop. He listened to Bezerk answering as only he could. Plain and simple, saying, 'C'mon dog, let's do this.' Bezerk growled out a laugh while he got a hold of Guerro. The plane's door opened and he quickly said, roughly, 'You know how we do! I got you; I'm your dog now.'

Knoxx stepped down regally from the plane, sliding his Armani shades on to cover the morning glare. Bezerk followed him from the plane with a tight hold of Guerro by the scruff of the neck, he tossed him down the stairs like an unwanted piece of luggage. He lay there in the dirt, crying, until he was roughly picked up by a group of Uzi-wielding gunmen and taken away to a waiting Range Rover.

'Welcome gentleman. Mr. Knoxx, it is a pleasure meeting you. My name is Alan. People refer to me here as Big Al for obvious reasons.' A strong smile came across his friendly face, and Knoxx got the joke. Big Al was anything but big, standing five foot five, tall.

'Please follow me.'

From here on out, it was all Knoxx. As instructed in the plane, Chris brought up the rear, speaking only when he was spoken to. He took up the position of bodyguard to Knoxx, even though they were amongst Bezerk's handlers, the EME, the Mexican Mafia cartel. Knoxx was shown to the middle car of a five-car entourage. The cool air from the air condition inside the Mercedes S600 helped to relax him.

'I trust everything's accounted for?' Knoxx enquired of Big Al.

'Yes, thank you, Mr. Knoxx. Everything has been accounted for. If there is anything I can get for you to make your stay with us here more pleasant, please do not hesitate in letting me know.'

The convoy kept its tight formation and its speed at around fifty miles per hour, while the two exchanged pleasantries about Mexico and the immediate area. The jet had taxied, turned around, and taken off up into the sun-filled sky, while the convoy of cars drove away from the airstrip, leaving a plume of desert dust that shot up from the cars and dispersed behind them.

50

'So c'mon, let's think this through.' Maxine said in a hollow voice, looking for someone to help make her life a little easier, and then, maybe just a little more bearable, having to face the media in an hour.

The media had got a hold of some of the meat off the bones about how things had gone down the night before. The La Jolla Federal Bureau of Investigation's building was now besieged by a throng of reporters. Satellite poles were extended and news producers were sitting in their news trucks, at the ready for what Dobro was soon to tell them. On the what, why, who and where. At this point, she had the, what and the where, and a pretty good idea on who was going to go down for this. She looked at Connelly with an impassioned face, listening to his hollow ramblings as he explained, 'We have nothing at this point, but it's still early in the game. We'll dig something up. Guerro's family's disappeared. They've either gone off on their own, or they've been taken forcibly. Either way, they've gone.'

He sounded like he was a drowning man, still doing his best to tread water. Dobro seethed, looking like she wished he was gone to.

'Is that so?' she said in a tone that conveyed to Connelly, 'you're so fucked.' She followed up with a curt, 'What else?'

Still holding out for a glimmer of hope, but in reality, not expecting much, she listened to Pat say, 'The tunnel was probably used for smuggling drugs and people across the border, which was why they picked it as the location for the drop. They obviously had planned this in advance.'

'Uh huh,' Maxine forced out through pursed lips, having to listen to him stating the obvious. Feeling this meeting was going nowhere, she pushed further, saying, 'And, what else?'

Choosing his words carefully, Pat decided to tip-toe his way through this minefield by stating, 'They had a lot of help and they'd planned it all down to the smallest detail, managing to use some executives as a decoy.'

Connelly now ran through this part in a somewhat automated fashion, having run it through in his head so many times all morning. He seemed numb to it, but Dobro seemed to perk up, questioning, 'What do you mean? Executives were used as decoys; tell me what you mean by that?'

Connelly explained the events in more detail, and then Dobro took him back through it, now listening to him; it seemed for the first time. She pumped him full of brownies and pumped him with more questions. Connelly finally capitulated and said, 'I don't get it?'

Connelly was clearly tired from his long night, and now, long morning. He needed sleep and he needed to be out of this room, but Maxine continued badgering him. Sounding out her thoughts, she laid it out for him, saying, 'Well, how would the Southsiders know to put word out in the morning that their buyer would be coming in by boat around midnight, and then low and behold, a boat arrives in the bay fitting the description at the right time? How would they know to put out that information to give us as their diversion, unless?' She searched Pat's face for some kind of interaction

He quickly responded, saying, 'You're saying they knew? You're saying these executives were in on it? That they knew they were part of a drug smuggling ring? No way, I don't see it.' Connelly was seemingly coming to life for the first time all morning.

Maxine responded, telling him, 'I know, Pat, you don't see a lot of things, do you? Look, they knew about our confidential informant in advance and they used him against us. They used his relationship to you to get you to play along with their timing in all of this. This whole thing was a smoke and mirrors sting from the start, right? Keep us looking one way while the real action was going down right under our noses.'

Maxine knew she had out stepped him, outwitting him again. He answered her abruptly and assuredly, 'We interviewed them extensively and they all checked out. We checked their alibis for being here in town; they were here for a series of meetings with companies that have offices here.'

Connelly felt as if this was going to be his last stand. Even if it might be his little Big Horn, he'd make it, standing firm in his belief.

'What's the name of the company they worked for?' Maxine asked him.

Getting to the correct part in his notes, he gazed up at Maxine and replied, 'Exile Corporation. They're based up in Santa Monica. They're some type of venture capital company, involved in buying of a number of nightclubs across the country.'

'And who owns Exile?' Dobro asked, not taking any crap from Connelly's approach, staying the aggressor, driving him forward.

Looking blankly at her and full of dread, he then referred to his notes again. Looking back up at her, he said, 'Aah Knoxx, Mark Knoxx. He lives in Marina del Rey.'

Dobro took a moment to gather her thoughts, and then she summed it all up for Pat. What she summed up seemed no coincidence at all.

'So we had this mythical West Coast cocaine buyer coming

down from L.A. We just happened to have a boat coming in off the coast of San Diego, with the launch coming ashore at the right time, conveniently fitting the timeline and the M.O. of what we were waiting on?'

'Right,' Connelly answered, swinging in his chair.

Maxine had him again, exclaiming, 'Wrong! This is so wrong. There's too much coincidence in this boat appearing at just the right time with these executives coming ashore right in the middle of our sting. They may have been duped themselves, I don't doubt that but someone in that company knows something, call it woman's intuition. I'm authorizing you to begin an investigation into Exile Corporation. I'm just not buying it. It's all too neat and I'm not buying it.'

Dobro's mind became convinced that this was it. This was the lead they needed to follow.

She then confirmed her thoughts by saying hard, and with conviction, 'That's our lead. Look into Exile Corporation and check this Mark Knoxx guy out.'

51

The convoy pulled off the dirt road and continued along a private track road for a while, seemingly a road to nowhere. Then an oasis in the desert appeared. Manicured lawns and cameras surrounded the perimeter wall. The motorcade fired up the main entrance, and standing there before them was a twenty thousand square foot monument rising up out of the desert, a sprawling red and beige Tuscan terracotta-style fortress.

'Welcome to The Landmark,' Big Al proudly announced.

'Yes, it certainly is,' Knoxx replied, moving in his seat to get a better view of the mansion and the grounds, while the cars blitzed in to the courtyard. Swinging around the centerpiece fountain was a statue of the Gods, Mars and Venus intertwined. The God of War and the Goddess of Love, two conflicting symbols with two distinct passions that can kill and that people kill for. The huge gates closed immediately behind them as the cars came up to an abrupt halt. Knoxx's car came to a halt in front of the main entrance to the house's double doors, as if he were attending a celebrity event, only at this event there were no cameras, no reporters and no red carpet. The entourage disembarked as soon as Big Al opened Knoxx's rear door. As if on cue, the heavy door to the mansion opened and two hulks walked out to survey the outside, their eyes shaded by their sunglasses. All the guards and escorts fanned out. Everyone was strapped, everyone except Knoxx. He coolly stepped out from the car and stretched just a touch. Heat plumes were coming off the flowers and shrubs from the early morning heat. He gave the courtyard one quick sweep and noticed that Bezerk hadn't been let out of the car behind him. Knoxx was once again, alone.

A huge frame of a man strode out into the daylight - six foot five, muscular-framed and big in every way, striding like the God he was. His imposing posture left no doubt in Knoxx's mind who he was, The Man. His hair was pulled back tight in a ponytail and he was wearing black Versace sunglasses with a cigar in his right hand. He wore white linen pants and an open, long-sleeved print shirt made of Egyptian cotton, pulling on his cigar as he walked. The two hulks walked a half a step behind him on either side of him. From about ten feet away, wearing a big smile, he joked, 'Knowledge.'

Releasing a big grin, Knoxx returned the favor, exclaiming playfully, 'Juicy.'

They both smiled and then laughed at the irony of them

meeting. Shaking hands warmly, Roberto Madrid then embraced him. Juicy put his cigar hand on Knoxx's shoulder, eyeing him strongly, taking him in as if he was searching his inner character. He then said surprisingly, 'I am Roberto. Please Mark, su casa es mi casa mi amigo, please, this way.'

Roberto Madrid, the overlord to the Mexican cartel, extended a wave of his arm towards the mansion and led Knoxx in to The Landmark. The convoy of cars moved off, leaving the two of them there while the cars holding both Bezerk and Guerro slowly disappeared around the corner of the mansion.

'I trust you had a pleasant flight and ride to my house?' Madrid asked in a friendly, warm voice.

Knoxx nodded in the affirmative, answering, 'Yes, thank you.'

'If you require anything, please do not hesitate to ask,' Madrid offered, clearly happy to oblige his guest, who had already done so much to make him happy, by returning his cocaine and a captured rat.

∗   ∗   ∗

'He will be staying with us in the guest quarters,' Big Al told the armed guards. 'Make sure he stays in his quarters.' Big Al stepped up to Bezerk, eyeing him with utter contempt and distain, ordering, 'Your weapon.'

Bezerk hesitated, but then thought better of it. With some showmanship, he duly obliged as he unchambered his gun and removed the clip with some ceremony. He handed it over to Big Al.

'Ah, a showman, I shall remember that.' He spun back around to return to the mansion.

Bezerk asked, 'What about that piece of shit rat?'

'He's our property now and we will be taking good care of him. Now get some rest, don't give him another thought.'

The bodyguard motioned for Bezerk to get inside the hacienda, but as he walked in, his eyes caught sight of a Range Rover across the courtyard with two guards pulling Guerro out of it; Guerro freefell out the back, sailing down onto the hard tarmac with a loud crack. To everyone present, it was clear he had broken some ribs.

Bezerk shouted at him happily, 'Yeess siirr, that's what I'm talking about. Pinche rata puto!'

Bezerk continued watching while Guerro lay on the floor, crying in pain. He chuckled contently, looking for confirmation from his guard about what they'd seen.

The guard didn't register anything, as if he hadn't heard him, and then asked in a bored but obedient manner, 'Is there anything I can get you?'

While Bezerk walked in the house, looking around it in awe, he replied, 'Serio?'

The guard did not answer, as it was redundant.

'How 'bout a boat load of Carne Asada, a crate of Tecate and two fine-ass bitches, you know what I mean?' He laughed a boyish laugh.

The guard nodded in confirmation, answering, 'Right away.'

He left Bezerk to walk from one room to the next, shouting out in excitement, 'Yeah boy!' He said in disbelief, 'Mutherfuckin' Knoxx boy, mi vida loca babbyy!'

Within a few minutes, the patio doors opened, opening up Bezerk to a whole new world.

'Yeess siirr, woo hoo!' Bezerk laid his eyes on two of the most gorgeous Latin babes he had ever seen in the flesh. Both of them were covered in tight-fitting Sarongs and tight bikini bras that only just covered their ample breasts. With their taught nipples pointing at him, they glided into the room, smiling and sizing him up. Both of them were for him. He laughed wildly, shouting, 'Mark, you're a faagg.'

Bezerk laughed hard as he took one on each arm. Loving these two girls, already loving his new life with Knoxx, he said, 'Aahh, the spoils of war. This way ladies.' He led them off towards the Jacuzzi, everyone smiling and giggling, all knowing what was to come and, come again, all day long.

*   *   *

Knoxx entered the main foyer with Roberto Madrid leading the way in a relaxed manner, passing through a vast open-air lounge with exotic flower arrangements, thick cushioned couches, and deep pile carpeting. Madrid led Knoxx past a pool table in a games room, walking out onto the veranda. Sitting high atop an atoll, the view, for as far as the eye could see was of a vast expanse of desert, shimmering in the morning's sun. He caught sight of a loan eagle that was soaring high on the warm currents. This was Roberto Madrid's land, The Landmark.

Madrid seated himself at the patio table while Knoxx sat respectfully on the other side. Madrid started to make small talk as part of his opening repertoire. Knoxx looked out over the open, desolate desert below, and his eyes picked out a faint dust trail coming up from a group of horses galloping at full speed across the lightly tanned, arid hot land. Madrid pulled on his cigar and gave an order to one of the hovering servants in Spanish. In an instant, a humidor was brought forward and opened in front of Knoxx. Watching as Mark picked out a cigar, Madrid then exclaimed, 'Aah, Opus X, good choice.'

Knoxx cut it, lit it, and drew hard on it, taking a moment to savor the taste, absorbing the moment of where he was and who he was with.

Madrid then said, 'Mmm, an acquired taste, like all things, you have to acquire the taste.'

Both men chuckled lightly at its meaning. Knoxx replied, 'And you have certainly acquired many beautiful things, Roberto.'

'Beauty is in the eye of the beholder, Mark. I am but the purchaser. The real beauty shall be returning shortly.' Madrid's eyes panned down at the dust trail of horses that were racing toward the compound. He continued, 'Everything around you, this house, and its surrounding grounds were designed by my wife.'

'Well, you and your wife are to be complimented, as this is a true reflection of everything that's beautiful.'

'We thank you for your kind words. Please, help yourself to breakfast and refreshments, if you wish.'

Both men carried on several topics of conversation over the next hour, covering subjects as diverse as, cigars, cars, boats, planes, sports and homes, then moving onto heavier topics, such as real estate, investments, the state of the stock market, geo-politics and the ramifications of it in the world. Both men covertly tested each other in a light-hearted way, and it was clear that they shared a kindred spirit. They were evenly matched in both their views and in their arguments, but more importantly, they had proven they were both well-educated and highly motivated in their chosen fields. Talking about some of the women he had dated in the past, Mark quipped, 'You know, women tell me that they're not interested in money, telling me, "Oh honey, love makes the world go round," and I tell them, "Yeah, but money keeps it spinning."'

The two men fell into a long, deep laugh, clearly enjoying each other's company, which helped to make the morning pass quickly. They then began to get in to deeper discussions. Madrid was opening up more to his new friend and Knoxx had developed a sincere respect for the man, the God of the land he ruled over. While Madrid talked, it was clear to Mark that he had class. He spoke in a low and confident tone; every word seemed to carry its own meaning and measured weight. He came across as a thinker, very spiritual, and a loving family man. He talked about owning vast tracks of real estate in America and throughout the world, along with several companies. He had been groomed to take over the Mexican drug empire from the age of ten, but he seemed far removed from what it was: a network of killers, drug traffickers, and prostitution rings. He controlled the flow of cocaine from South America for the Colombian drug cartels up into the U.S., overseeing the Southsider street gangs as his own personal army.

It seemed surreal that he was sitting with Madrid and Knoxx found himself forgetting this was the boss of death, destruction, and mayhem. At only thirty-seven years old, it seemed unreal to him that this calm and well-educated father of three could be the man who dispensed so much pain and suffering to so many people. Knoxx sat out on the veranda, laughing and joking, in the company of such a charismatic guy. Madrid had it all. He was living an envious life.

'Buenos Dias Cariño. Good morning, my love,' the golden voice rang-out in a distinctive Spanish voice, laced with girlish charm. A truly spectacular specimen had sauntered onto the veranda, still wearing her riding outfit, looking radiant through her dusty complexion as she laid a soft kiss on Madrid. She looked no more than twenty-nine, with long, buttermilk, golden blonde hair and deep brown eyes. She had the outline of a Miss World and she probably had been, standing so poised and regal at around five feet ten, in her riding boots. Madrid announced, 'Yessica, I would like you to meet Mark Knoxx.' She looked at Mark.

Knoxx half-stood up to give her hand a light handshake, as she extended it across to him. He felt himself blush as he met her eyes, while he hoped he had not been too obvious. Madrid smiled in amusement, having caught the look on his face.

'Pleasure to meet you, Mark.' Jessica Madrid slightly tilted her head, looking inquisitively at him.

'Pleasure to meet you too,' Mark answered.

Madrid then said, 'We have two guests who will be staying with us for dinner this evening. Please invite our usual guests to join us too.'

He said it in such a way that indicated his wife had no clue about anyone's arrival, but she still dutifully said, without missing a beat, 'Oh good, we'll be having a dinner party tonight,' she happily sang out. Jessica gave her final courtesies to the men and another kiss to Roberto, and then gracefully retreated, saying, 'Until this evening, Mark. Adios.'

She turned and left, as positively bright as the sun. Her radiance stayed with Mark all morning, leaving him thinking about her throughout most of the day. Madrid spent the rest of the morning sharing his plans for Mexico and life in his own region. He had purchased large parcels of land along the coastline, approximately a hundred and thirty miles south of Tijuana, where he'd been told by his sources in the central government that a new U.S. - Mexico, seven billion dollar development deal had been struck. They would construct and operate a commercial port at Punta Colonet, on the Baja California Peninsula. It would be used to carry the overcapacity for goods being imported from Asia and the Middle East, goods that the Los Angeles/Long Beach International Harbor could not handle. It would also be the harbor used by Madrid for the importation of his drugs for the United States, and for this, he had invested heavily.

Knoxx had spent his time wisely, listening and learning, because he realized Roberto Madrid already had the money, the power, and the respect. Knoxx needed an angle if he was to have a shot at getting Madrid to partner up with him. There was no fear or greed angle to be played, however, because Madrid didn't fear anyone. He not only had cash, he had cash flow. He was an astute businessman and a great strategist, but above all else, Knoxx reminded himself, he was also the head of an empire of stone cold killers and oversaw an army of drug traffickers and drug dealers. Knoxx realized he'd have to come up with something unexpected.

52

Maxine Dobro looked fired up as she strode through the doors, entering the briefing room while camera flashes lit her path. All eyes were on her making her way to the podium. She held them off for as long as she could by dragging out her opening speech. She then went into detail regarding the investigation on the perpetrators, also explaining that an internal investigation would be carried out too. Dobro closed out her segment strongly by saying, 'Whoever's behind this, we are going to find them, and we will prosecute them to the fullest extent of the law. I will be relieving special agent Connelly from this case. I will be heading up the investigation from now on. We have a strong suspicion that there may even be only one individual behind all of this. However, since this is an ongoing investigation, I cannot name this individual.'

This last statement sent the assembled media into a frenzy. Dobro tried to put a positive spin on it but it just wasn't happening. They wanted someone's head served up on a platter, and Maxine was going to waste no time in providing one after the interview. The media took great delight in embarrassing her at the podium in front of the television audience. Larraine Scott, a pretty, brunette reporter, asked, 'So, your sting. How did you get this information about this one night, one man, and one drug deal going down?'

'We had a confidential informant inside the gang who confirmed that this transaction was going to happen last night at midnight. So we put plans in motion to counter the gang's successful completion of this exchange.'

The reporter snapped back, 'So it was your plan to lose fifty million dollars worth of cocaine?'

'No, that wasn't in our plans.' Dobro choked out to the reporter.

'And this confidential informant, has he been able to shed any light on where the drugs might be now or who the mastermind was?'

She took half a beat to answer. 'Our confidential informant is no longer in our protective custody at this time. Thank you, that'll be all for now.'

Dobro snapped her folder shut. She gathered up her papers while the television cameras whirred, Flashes from photographer's' cameras followed her all the way back to the door. She remained stoic all the way, with the team of special agents following her out.

As the door slammed closed behind her, she snapped, 'I don't want to hear from you or see you in front of me for the foreseeable future, Patrick Connelly! Who knows, twenty-four hours from now, you might not be a special agent, or even an agent for that matter!' Slamming her office door behind her, she left a froth of foam in her wake.

Everyone in the hallway looked at Pat, standing there in his red braces with his jacket tossed over his shoulder, standing in no man's land. He had aged all too quickly over the past twenty-four hours, and the next twenty-four now looked as if they were going to be his last as an officer of the law.

'So much for my career bust,' Connelly shrugged. 'More like my career busted,' he whispered to himself. Through the glass window of her office, he watched Dobro smack her files down onto her desk. Her face said it all. She was in a rage, and someone was going to pay. She picked up the phone to take a call and fire began to rain down from her mouth.

'They've managed to embarrass this whole damn department and me, personally. I won't allow it, not on my watch, you'll see. I'm going to turn this thing around, and I assure you, whoever was behind this, I'm going to grind his balls into dust.' Dobro fired off her salvo on the phone, speaking to her boss in New York, who had obviously just been watching her on the news. The sound-bites were being beamed all over the United States and into some foreign countries.

The media had put their own spin on it, saying the bad guys had won one back for their team, beginning to sound as if they were rooting for them, giving the whole affair a snappy name, calling it The Get Back. One news report had said that the Fed's had been outplayed at their own game; even with all their technology and all their available manpower, they had been outwitted by a bunch of wet backs. Big Brother had been shown up and made to look ineffective, even after the attacks of 9/11. Everyone up the chain of command was now feeling the heat.

'Yes, yes, I know. Yeah, we do have a couple of leads that we're chasing down. We're looking into the business dealings of a company called Exile and its owner, Mark Knoxx, up in Los Angeles.' Dobro answered, now doing her best to stay focused. She gazed at her other phone line blinking on her phone console, knowing only two people had that number. She answered the person on the phone, telling him, 'Of course, I'll keep you up to speed, yes, no problem. I'll call you back at three o'clock my time. Okay, speak to you then, bye Kev.' She immediately dropped the call and hit the button for the other line. She instantly felt the curl of a smile as she answered the caller, 'Hello darling, is everything okay?'

Maxine's motherly instincts went into overdrive at the sound of her daughter's voice on the other end of the line,

'Am I okay? Are you okay is more like it. I saw the news.'

Her daughter, Danielle, whom Maxine affectionately called Dolly, was studying Law at the University of California Los Angeles, UCLA. She'd been living off campus in Westwood Village for around nine months now. The mother hen had let her little chick spread her wings and fly the coop but the bond between mother and daughter was still as strong as ever. Now, being concerned for mom, Dolly had called to check in on her. Even though Maxine could shoot an adversary down from fifty yards with one flash of her eyes, she always melted at the sight and sound of her children. Dolly was twenty-two and her son, Harry had just turned twenty-one.

Dobro was the present day Elliott Ness of the F.B.I. She was fearless in her pursuit of the bad guys, but she was still their mom and their guiding light, doing her best to shield them both from all that she knew to be bad in the world. Black cannot exist without white, but opposites are beautiful. When everything is gray, well then, you may as well be dead. For Maxine, her children were the only thing that was good in her life. They had paid their own price for Maxine wanting to further her career; they had been raised in two different homes by parents who hardly spoke to each other. Yet through it all, they had remained happy kids. In addition, when Maxine squeezed the juice, it came out as happy juice that always brightened her day. The two girls got caught up on how they were doing. Dolly perked up once Maxine said she'd bring Harry with her the following weekend, when she would drive up to see her in L.A. Maxine finished the phone call by signing off, saying, 'It's a date. See you then. Take care, and if you need anything, call me okay? Love you, Dolls.'

If only for a few pleasurable moments it had all seemed worth it. Maxine looked up from her desk, through her office window, and her eyes fell on Patrick Connelly, hovering like a paternal grandfather outside it.

'Pat! Come in here!' Maxine shouted, and motioned with her arm for him to come in. The rage inside her had returned.

53

The Landmark had been quiet for most of the afternoon. Knoxx had retired to the bedroom as requested by Madrid, and had spent most of the time surfing the news channels. He watched the F.B.I.'s representative, Maxine Dobro, give her statement to the reporters. Knoxx, and it turned out later, Madrid, had laughed at the ineptitude of all the police officials, who seemed to have no real clue about how it had all gone down the night before. Knoxx reveled in delight at the fact that the two main players in all of this were here, at The Landmark. It had all been undertaken for the one man that Knoxx wanted to get next to, and now here he was, lying in one of his beds, in one of his guest rooms, in Mexico. Knoxx heard a polite knock and was told that his presence was required in the games room in thirty minutes.

He got dressed and made his way through to the games room. Entering it, he saw Madrid chalking up his pool cue, carrying a wicked grin, as he joked, telling Knoxx, 'No one beats me on my own table, in my own house. House rules.'

'Well, it's not always a beautiful day, but it sure is a beautiful ride. If you're gonna be a gangsta, then you make your own rules, you don't follow them. So let's get it on,' Mark joked.

They toasted each other playfully and then got down to business.

'Double or nothing? Let's say, twenty million?' Madrid said with a wry smile as he chalked up his cue, after having lost the first game of pool.

'No thanks, my game isn't that tight, and it'd be rude of me to beat you twice on your own table, don't you think?'

Both of them laughed at Knoxx's remark, but Mark realized the real game was now in play as Madrid had mentioned his payment. Madrid was eyeing him, and Mark got the feeling that he was being tested. One of life's games, no one ever played it straight.

Madrid replied, 'What was the amount you've earned again? Aah yes, you have earned my whole hearted respect and my trust, and I salute you for what you've accomplished last night.' Madrid took on a solid look of awe on his face. Being serious, he raised his glass in gratitude and respect to Mark and went on to say, 'And you have both Mark. Otherwise, you wouldn't be here with me, and seeing as how you are here, who's running Hell?' He let out a belly laugh, as he said it.

'Hell's closed for business today.' Knoxx leaned over and cracked the pool balls to start a new game. 'And it's thirty million.'

'Do you need reminding of the house rules again?' Madrid quipped.

Both men laughed again, becoming fast friends.

The second game was Madrid's and they both decided to finish it as a draw. Madrid said, upbeat, 'Come, let's take a walk, and talk about continuing our business together.'

Walking the grounds of The Landmark Madrid was never out of sight of his personal protection unit; they walked a respectful distance out of earshot, but Knoxx always felt their presence. Knoxx explained his vision for the Envious Group, and the idea he had for Chris Wright handling security for all the clubs. The two of them stopped walking periodically and stood to speak in animated terms, while they worked out the details on how it was all going to work.

Madrid wanted to control and administer the payroll for the security, thereby taking a cut of the action, of course. He then went onto expand Knoxx's overall idea in his own eloquent way, explaining, 'It's a fact, Mark that drugs go hand-in-hand with the nightclub culture. It will go on inside all of your clubs, whether you agree with it or not. It's just a fact of life, drugs cannot be stopped. It is simply a matter of supply and demand, or, to put it another way, where there is demand, there will ultimately be someone who will fill that demand. People either want it or need it.' Madrid stopped and stood squarely to Knoxx, eyeing him intently. He then said, with just as much intent and determination in his voice, 'Drugs will be sold and distributed in your clubs, Mark, with or without your participation. That is a fact. I propose that it be with your knowledge and your approval and, more importantly, with you participating in the profits. So here is what I propose. You require twenty million to complete your purchase of all the clubs you want to buy, correct?'

Knoxx eyed Madrid in a way that had remorse written all over his face, helpless to stop the tidal wave that he felt was now drowning him.

'And I owe you ten million for the capture and return of the rat, Guerro,' Madrid said with mischief in his voice and smiling.

'Yes, that's right,' Knoxx answered coolly.

'Then I will arrange the transfer of funds first thing in the morning to your nominated bank account, and we will be partners from here on out. I will provide the security to all the clubs. My security staff will control the flow of drugs being bought and sold, and you shall receive your percentage from the sales each month. Simple, no?'

Knoxx felt he could only do one thing. Smile in agreement and nod in acknowledgment as Madrid then happily slapped him on the back with his big, heavy mitts.

'Good! Then it's settled. Whatever you need to make this happen let either Bezerk or Big Al know and I assure you, it will be done, as you require. Anything you need, they will take care of it. You are a good man, Mark, and we shall do good things together, big things.'

Mark had a feeling he had been outmaneuvered. In the pit of his stomach, he felt it, but what could he do? He had walked unwittingly into it and fallen for the soft sell. Roberto Madrid, the most wanted drug kingpin in the United States, who headed up a thirty thousand strong army of Mexican and American Southsider gangbangers, had smoothly maneuvered himself into a partnership with a highly visible, polished and driven executive. Mark could provide him with a legitimate front to distribute his drugs throughout the U.S. Madrid understood the ways of business, keeping it simple and efficient. Up until now, Knoxx had thought he was following his own destiny, but now he had taken on a powerful partner who would funnel untold millions into any bank account he desired. He spent the next thirty minutes, while they walked and talked, rationalizing it in his mind. He finally concluded that it made sense and Madrid was right. It was going to happen anyway, so why not profit from it? Madrid continued to sway and cajole him, explaining the method of distribution and how much money they could generate in profits.

They came upon an opening in the hedgerow, which led onto a courtyard to some stables. As they began walking across the gravel courtyard, one thing came to mind and Mark asked, 'Roberto, do you mind me saying something? I have a concern.'

'Please Mark, feel free to tell me.'

Knoxx hesitated, thinking about how best to approach it. He then said, 'I just want to run it by you, bring it to your attention to see what you think, that's all.'

Madrid slowed up, not looking at Mark, saying smoothly, 'Go on.'

'Well, I feel uneasy at this point. There's one man who can tie me to you, who knows you and I have spoken and probably have had a meeting.'

Madrid instantly got his point and barked, 'Who, Bezerk?'

'Bezerk? No!'

'Who then?' Madrid asked, giving him a confused, blank look.

Knoxx softly spoke the name on his mind, 'Big Smoke.'

Madrid's eyes misted over in thought, as soon as the name was uttered. He answered, 'Aah yes, I see.' It took no more than a few seconds for him to understand. 'Yes, you are right.'

Two steps later, Madrid turned and spoke in Spanish to one of his guards, who then stepped off to carry out his command. Madrid barked, 'Wait!' The guard immediately stopped in his tracks and looked back at him. 'Anything else?' he asked, looking subtly at Knoxx.

'No, only I think Bezerk should be the go-between between you and me.'

Madrid let out a small grunt and a nod, and then waved on the guard, who picked up his step once again. 'Consider it done. Big Smoke will not be a worry to you any longer, come.' Madrid said, as he picked up his pace. And that was it, no more Big Smoke.

Knoxx was now thirty million dollars richer, and he now had a new partner in his Envious Group nightclub venture, and he was in the drug dealing business, whether he liked it or not. What Knoxx had just witnessed made his whole body want to shake with fear. Madrid had given no thought to Big Smoke, no doubt a loyal soldier on the streets of San Diego and a good money earner. He'd been the gatekeeper to Madrid's empire along the border for years, but in the grand scheme of things, he had become a liability. Madrid had made a business decision, weighing up the pros and cons of keeping Big Smoke around. It hadn't added up, and so, Big Smoke had to go. Madrid had a new business partner now, one that needed protecting. The value that Mark brought to his empire far outweighed what Big Smoke could ever bring in from running dope on the streets. Knoxx picked up on this quickly thinking, *Once you've outlived your worth to Roberto Madrid, you've outlived your life.* And worse, it had been brought about by him bringing it to Madrid's attention. It was as if he had pulled the trigger and had murdered Big Smoke. Knoxx was getting in deeper and deeper by the minute. They strolled across the gravel courtyard at a leisurely pace. Madrid still led the way as they ambled across, their shoes crunching on the gravel, stopping to stroke some horses standing in their stalls as they went.

Madrid, seemingly speaking with a heavy heart, said, 'One thing Yessica and I like to do is ride out to nowhere and forget ourselves, you know? Leave my demons behind.'

Knoxx interjected, 'There's a heavy price to pay for having so many beautiful things, so much suffering and so much pain at times. If a man is to succeed, then he must do what the next man won't.'

He caught the horse as it nuzzled its head in his palm, searching for a carrot. Each man understood the other.

Madrid quickly replied, saying, 'Aah yes, naked ambition. Come let us see this ambition wasted.'

Madrid motioned for Knoxx to follow him, his guards shadowing them as they walked across to the coach house. Madrid strode in with newfound conviction, walking in as a strong leader. His men seemed to snap to attention the minute he entered, Knoxx keeping in step with him, a half-step behind.

Knoxx immediately stopped, maybe seven paces inside, feeling his heart jump into his mouth. Terror and dread came over him. Somehow, he could sense and smell death in the air. The whimpering of a man slowly being tortured to death in one of the horse stables also gave it away. Knoxx already knew why Madrid had led him here and who was in here with them: Guerro, the rat.

For all of his ambition and drive in trying to get ahead in life, he hadn't prepared himself for this. Never in his wildest dreams did he ever expect to come this close to a dying man, or get himself in a position where it could've been him who being killed. The world he had known as a businessman was a world of 'do the best you can do, make the best deal you can.' He had definitely been living in a world where the sun shone every day, but now he had passed over to the dark side, the side where you don't lose your shirt in a bad business deal, you lose your life. Knoxx had undone his own destiny, and he had wandered into this new life, totally unprepared. His own passion for money, power, and respect had led him here to this place and to these people. The Legion of Doom had a hold on him now, and it seemed he was standing shoulder to shoulder with the devil himself, and his real name was Roberto Madrid. Mark Knoxx had danced with the devil and the devil had changed him too, for Knoxx was in league with him now. He had delivered Guerro to him, and now Guerro was just a shell of blood and bone. The devil's work was being done before his eyes. He watched Madrid's men carving their way through his body while they interrogated him. He wanted to vomit right there on his Ferragamo loafers. Guerro was strung up like a piece of meat, with his arms hanging from a beam and his body weight extending his naked torso for them to carve.

Knoxx chose not to enter the horse stall. He stood rooted to the floor, taking it all in, in this house of horror that was in motion before him. Three guards were taking turns to pick at Guerro with knives, hot irons and beating him with sticks that had nails in them. Whatever these men chose to use, they had been using them expertly for some time. He had been walking through the grounds with Madrid for most of the afternoon, deep in conversation, all the time building admiration for this man who was eloquent, charming and witty. They had been walking aimlessly, enjoying each other's company, while all that time, a man's life was hanging in the balance, strung up from the rafters. Madrid's men were busy hacking away, slowly extracting all the information they needed, slowly killing him.

'You are right, Mark. Success is only temporary if one is

not willing to do what the other man is prepared to do. One must be prepared to do more than the next man, or a man, such as yourself, will step in to replace the one who is perceived to have become weak.'

Knoxx looked like he had the weight of the world on his shoulders as Madrid's words hit home. He stood stock-still and realized that no one knew of his whereabouts and no one would ever find him. He had never experienced this feeling before. Was this all a test, or was he going to be killed too? Maybe Bezerk was dead already. He had been outsmarted, outplayed and now he was outgunned and totally out of his league. He must have been out of his fucking mind to come here. He just stood in front of Madrid and his men, in stunned silence. His eyes were fixed on Guerro dying in front of him. Each breath Guerro took began to get weaker and he had his eyes firmly fixed on Knoxx's face, as if he knew that Knoxx was the man who had brought him here to this Hell.

Madrid looked back at Mark and said proudly, 'Mark, Guerro is the prize that is worth thirty million to me. Thank you for delivering him to me.' He then turned back to his chief interrogator, asking him, 'Has he been cooperative?' he said it in a way that brought a little smile to both men.

'Yes, he's given us more than we could've hoped for. He rats on us and now he rats on them.'

Madrid laughed a happy laugh at what the interrogator had said, and at the irony of it.

'He stinks like a rat,' Madrid said in a scathing way towards Guerro.

Knoxx hadn't moved from his spot or hardly breathed. He couldn't take his eyes off Guerro, hanging there like a slab of meat before going in to the butcher's freezer, covered in bruises, blood, and gore. He had stayed standing near the coach house's entrance, somehow refusing, in body and mind, to take those extra steps into the horse stall. He remained on one side with the living and the free, thinking, so this is what really paid for the finer things in life, all the expensive toys, and The Landmark. Mark was now seeing firsthand the real business that Roberto Madrid was in: drugs, destruction, and death. Everything funneled its way back up to Madrid, even death. He was in complete control over who did what and who gets to live or die. Since Mark had been in his company today, two lives had been deemed to be of no consequence to him. Knoxx had the ambition to rise to the top in his profession, which had already landed him in prison. He had then used the contacts he had made in prison to help get him out. He knew he had taken a life to win one back, but he had been far removed from that, the wet work. Now, however, he was standing in front of death itself. Be careful what you wish for, you just might get it. Knoxx had sold his soul to the devil, and now the devil had come to pay him a visit. Knoxx learned in prison to roll along to get along. He had found Satan's Army in the Southsiders, who had the power to set him free.

Madrid was proving he was a man who was hands-on in every aspect of running his business. Knoxx believed he was making his point. He could be the perfect business partner and host, a gentleman and a scholar. Or he could be Juicy the drug overlord. He could unleash his Legion of Doom and come grab Mark from the City of Angels, if he wished, and Mark would be wiped off the face of the earth at will. Black does not exist without white. Guerro was the past and Knoxx was the future.

Madrid had hardly taken his eyes off Guerro, as he asked the interrogators a series of questions about the information he had given them. He finished his conversation and said warmly to his men, 'Very good.'

They had stopped what they had been doing for some time now, but they soon began to look back at Guerro with some intent. He seemed to know what was coming, because he began to whimper at the thought of the pain he would be forced to endure once again.

Madrid asked, 'Do you believe he has more to tell us?'

'We have more than enough to move on those who work against you, Patrón. I will provide a full report in the morning,' the chief interrogator relayed in a proficient manner.

'Well, cut him down and clean him up. Give him some food and water and put him in some clean, dry clothes.'

Madrid used a tone that conveyed to Mark that he was somewhat displeased with his men for having gone so far in their torture. Madrid stood casually with the group of guards, as if they were discussing a sports game.

Juicy finished his final sentence, at which, all the guards smirked. Knoxx thought he'd heard him say, 'I want him alive and well enough to know that I have killed his whole rat-infested family.'

54

Mark had told Bezerk in prison, that their meeting had been destiny. From where Bezerk was lying, it sure felt like it had been. He had never been given so much by one person. Lying in bed in the guesthouse with these two beautiful girls, he felt like his own destiny was now being fulfiled. Knoxx had been true to his word and so far, it was all good. Here was Bezerk, a gun runnin', dope slingin', gangbangin' street hustler, livin' large and lovin' life, laying it down in his Patrón's mansion. But here he was with his bunky, who'd made it all happen. *Mi vida loca, my crazy life*, Bezerk thought. He had been given a blank page to draw on each day, as he wanted. Bezerk sniggered, thinking about how his life would be unfolding from this point on, saying softly, 'Fuckin' Mark.'

He rolled over on the bed to wake up the girls again from their sleep. They had both grown tired of him, but he managed to raise some cooperation from them eventually, while he roughly manhandled them into position, both of them duly complying in their own way. Just then, much to the annoyance of Bezerk but much to the delight of the girls, someone knocked loudly and firmly on the front door. As he got up to answer it, the girls took the opportunity to get up from the bed. Bezerk opened the door to see Big Al standing there. 'Yeah, waassuupp?'

Sucking his lip, it rippled through Big Al's bones, he said, 'You are required to be dressed for dinner in one hour. You are to help yourself to the clothing in the closet in the bedroom. Discreet and casual, if you can manage such a thing? I'll be back for you in fifty minutes. Don't be late.' Big Al looked beyond Bezerk in to the guesthouse. Raising his voice, he commanded, 'Ladies! Come with me.'

The girls collected their things and scurried out past Bezerk without a look in his direction or saying goodbye.

'Anything else you need?' Big Al said in a condescending manner.

'Nah, I'm cool.' Bezerk smacked the front door closed.

Reaching the closet, Bezerk slid back the mirrored doors to reveal an array of clothing, all neatly lined-up and color-coordinated.

'Fuck yeaahh!' Singing out in a childish way, like a kid in a candy shop for the first time, he muttered, 'Destiny man, fuckin' destiny.' He whooped and hollered, knowing his life had finally begun. Compared to the life that his fellow Southsiders were living back in San Diego, he was now truly living an envious life.

55

It had been one long day and one long headache for Maxine once she finally got to cross the threshold of her home.

'Thank God,' she allowed herself to say.

Keeping her sense of humor helped keep her sane and allowed her to get through days such as these. She thumped down her house keys on the entrance hall's side table. She was immediately greeted by a crescendo of 'Meows' from her two cats, Jax and Chloe, circling her feet. Pirouetting around her as they looked up to her, letting her know that it was feeding time in the Dobro household, what with Dolly at UCLA full time and Harry living for the most part with his dad, Gary. All Maxine wanted to do tonight was eat, chill out in a hot bath and then snuggle down with the cats on the couch to watch the news, and not be the one making the news. She had, it seemed, spoken to the world throughout the day, having had to talk to her F.B.I. bosses in Washington and New York, and both the Los Angeles and San Diego chief of police.

The headline news covered the car bombing of the Israeli Ambassador, murdered in Israel just two weeks after he had been in Switzerland. Vice President Tasker, was standing at the podium in the Rose Garden of the White House, declaring that the United States would help in any way it could to find whoever was behind this atrocity. The government will provide any assistance it can to Israel, he said. Joshua Simmons was as great Ambassador, and he was a great friend to this country. He will be missed, Tasker further intoned.

Switching channels to the local news, Maxine watched as her favorite news reporter, Larraine Scott began her detailed report on The Get Back, as it was now called by the media. Larraine Scott delivered her report succinctly, saying the Mexican drug dealers had duped the F.B.I. into providing their own impounded cocaine as bait, only to have the very same drug dealers steal it back, right under their noses. Her in-depth report went further to address the fact that the U.S. and Mexico border was still as porous as ever, regardless of what Homeland Security might say. Drugs were still coming in with ease, she noted, and obviously going out, she remarked. In closing, the news reporter said that a private yacht, chartered by Exile Corporation, a company owned by Mark Knoxx, based in Santa Monica, had had its employees caught up in the sting. Going further, she said, 'The F.B.I. and the San Diego Police Department are investigating any possible ties that Exile Corporation might have to The Get Back case.

The reporter stated that the station had tried to contact Exile Corporation to get a statement but at this time, none was available for this report. Maxine sipped her coffee and gave her girl Chloe a good scratch behind her ear, as she watched from the couch. She said softly, 'You're on my radar now, buddy.'

Having leaked that part of the story to the reporter Maxine had maneuvered Exile and Knoxx to the front pages. Now she could watch, listen, and learn while the news reporters went to work. Feeling good about the evening, she went to bed, expectantly thinking about how it would all play out in the morning and over the next few days now that she had taken the offensive and had started bringing it to Knoxx. One way or another, she would know soon enough if Mark Knoxx had had any involvement in The Get Back or not, as someone, somewhere would talk eventually.

What Maxine couldn't have known as she got settled down for the night to sleep with her two cats, was that someone had already talked. Names, places, times and events had all been documented by Madrid's chief interrogator back at The Landmark, and Maxine Dobro was now on Roberto Madrid's radar.

56

'Let your heart lead you, even if it takes you somewhere you may not wish to go, for your heart will never lie to you and no one can take it from you, only steal it, as my beautiful wife can each day. My heart belongs to you, my love, and to our beautiful children. Salud,' Madrid said while he looked at his beautiful wife, Jessica Madrid.

Everyone raised their glasses in a toast with Roberto standing at the head of the table, smiling wide while all the guests smiled and laughed too. Some of the women cooed and looked warmly at Jessica. This night was to celebrate a happy event, as all the men knew that the cocaine was back in their control and they were about to make more millions from reselling it. The twelve guests were engrossed in animated discussions, enjoying each other's company. Mark had been seated across from Jessica, and for some time, he had found himself transfixed by her. Catching himself, he looked away before it became too obvious. She was unaware of him staring at her while she was happily gossiping with her workout and shopping partner, who was married to Roberto's accountant, Luis Lopez. Madrid's other business associates were also there with their wives: Jorge Gonzalez, from Guadalajara, the president of Banco de México; General Señor Salvatore Francisco of the Policía Federal: along with an American, Chase Hughes, one of Madrid's drug importers into the United States.

These people were connected and they were all on Juicy's payroll, the third generation Colombian son of a drug baron. He had inherited a powerful network of money, people, and power, and bankrolled the EME. And now, Knoxx was sitting next to the seat of power. He overheard Jessica commenting to her friend, Larissa, that she and Roberto were putting their Miami home up for sale in South Beach, feeling that it had become too pretentious. They were buying a new home on the coast in the Caribbean, probably in Aruba or Bonaire, he heard her say.

Knoxx interjected, 'If the Miami home is anything like this one, then I'd love to view it. And if I bought it, think about the commissions you'd be saving.'

From there on out he was held hostage by the two girls, extolling the virtues of the Madrid's home, called, The Grove. Jessica went into detail describing the happy times her family had had there and that their two girls, Sury and Sophera, had been born there; Santos, their youngest, had been born at The Landmark. She said it was a must-see and she used all her charm and talents to sell it to Mark at the

188

bargain price of twelve million dollars. Knoxx had been sincere in asking to view the South Beach mansion and contact details were exchanged.

He asked, flippantly, 'Have you ever thought of taking up a career in interior design, Jessica?'

As soon as the last words fell from his lips he knew he had said the wrong thing. His mind screamed, 'stupid fuck!' He had broken one of his own cardinal rules. Never ask an open-ended question if you don't know what the answer could be, and certainly not to a drug kingpins' wife while he was seated next to you. Knoxx felt the air freeze over for the briefest of seconds. He could feel Madrid slightly turn his head to look at him, but he didn't register that he had heard the remark.

Jessica sidestepped it and saved Knoxx with the delicacy of a ballerina, answering, 'Maybe, a long time ago, but now I have so little time. It's just more of a hobby really, and it pleases Roberto.'

Her words trailed off with her thoughts, and for a moment, she was somewhere else. Knoxx nodded in acknowledgment, but he quickly disengaged himself from any further conversation on the topic. While he sipped on a glass of wine, he knew the damage had been done. He then had a thought about prison. Maybe prison comes in all forms. Many people walk around tortured by their own form of prison in their mind. Not everything that glitters is made of gold. A gilded cage is still a cage.

All-in-all it had been a successful night as everyone had shared jokes, points of view and passed along anecdotes, some being funny and some just plain boring. It had begun to get late, early, when Roberto spoke up, 'Well gentlemen, may I suggest cigars and drinks out on the veranda, while we take care of a little business, and then maybe a quick game of pool. House rules still apply!'

All the men laughed, Bezerk laughing with them, not quite sure why he was laughing. All the guests knew their invitations came at a price. Obedience. They would know when it was time for them to leave because Madrid would tell them. The women left for the sitting room to talk of vacation homes and resorts, schools and children's troubles, just like any other moms in a normal family environment. The husbands went out onto the veranda to discuss the order of business. How the shipment of cocaine would be divided up, discussed over drinks and shooting pool. The men waited until it was time for Madrid to speak, then they fell into line to hear what he had to say on what had taken place over the past twenty-four hours.

'Gentleman, friends, I wanted you here this evening to share in my victory today. As you are all aware, the United States was embarrassed last night by the daring raid against them, by men who had the courage to take them on and win back our cocaine for us. Not only were they successful in getting back the cocaine, but they also managed to flush out a rat amongst our ranks and deliver him back to me,' Madrid said proudly. Checking each of the men's faces, he continued, 'I would like to introduce you to those men who are here with us tonight, who dared to win, and won the day! I once again, introduce you to Mr. Mark Knoxx, and one of our own Southsider soldiers, Bezerk. Please, my friend.'

Madrid motioned for Knoxx and Bezerk to take their places next to him. He shook hands with Knoxx, embracing him, and then he backslapped Bezerk, while the four men clapped in acknowledgement.

Knoxx said, 'I can only say that if you don't stand for something, then you'll fall for anything. And believe me, I stand with you!'

The men erupted into a full crescendo of laughter at his joke. He then introduced Bezerk and stepped aside to give him his time in the sun, letting Bezerk them the story about how they had pulled it off. Knoxx was happy to stand back and watch Bezerk be Bezerk, revelling in seeing how the men were warming to him. He laughed with them while Bezerk described the events that had happened, playfully mentioning Knoxx's prison name, Knowledge. Taking his storytelling in good fun, everyone was enthralled by The Get Back, and at how Knoxx had thought it up. It was Bezerk's night though, just as Knoxx had promised him, and he had strung the story together terrifically, explaining it all to the sounds of, 'No way,' 'Cool,' and 'how funny.'

The men listened to every twist and turn of the plot, but no one was left in any doubt as to who the real mastermind was. Madrid kept a watchful eye on Knoxx, while Bezerk wrapped up the story, with everyone loving the part involving the yacht decoy. Señor Chaves said that the Fed's involved were probably applying for baggage handling jobs by now. Madrid laughed with everyone, making jokes at the F.B.I.'s expense. Everyone was happy because Roberto Madrid was happy. Everyone congratulated everyone else on a job well done. Madrid raised his arms to settle them down and the laughing quickly began to subside.

Madrid got down to business, saying, 'I want you to know that, in part, because of what Mark has done and because it is a wise business decision to so. I have decided that we will be going into business with him in his new venture, to build a chain of nightclubs, called Envious. In addition to being involved as silent partners, Mark has also been gracious enough to allow us to distribute our product throughout all of the nightclubs, which shall be overseen by our new captain, Bezerk.' Madrid eyed each of the men standing in front of him and hardened his tone. 'Each of you will be required to invest ten million dollars. This won't be a problem, will it?' Madrid stated ominously.

Each of the men nodded with agreeable headshakes, answering in various ways, 'Okay,' 'very good,' 'no problem,' and 'excellent.'

Knoxx could only stand next to Madrid biting his tongue in disbelief, only hours earlier he had struck the deal with Madrid for thirty million, and now here was Madrid, covering his own position and making a profit of ten million dollars. Knoxx's mind raced, as it shouted, 'Man, I should have asked for more!'

'Agreed?' Madrid questioned in a booming voice.

'Agreed!' The ensemble shouted back, as each of the men raised their glasses to toast the new venture, all looking at each other and smiling broadly on making such a good deal. Each of the men then took his turn to shake Madrid's hand, while saying, 'Thank you, Roberto. Thank you.'

Madrid, being magnanimous, replied, 'You are most welcome,' as he graciously accepted their praise.

Madrid stole a smile at Mark who could only look on in awe at how he had been outplayed. The play that Madrid had pulled was a classic Knoxx maneuver that he'd used over the years. Only one thing came to mind as he stepped up to Madrid to say, 'Nice one, my man, couldn't have done it any better myself, mate.'

Madrid got busy introducing Knoxx personally to his guests. Some of them shared a joke about how it had all gone down. Once they were away from the group, Mark playfully said, 'Gotta give props to the big guy.'

They hugged playfully and then they toasted each other again. Knoxx tilted his glass in salute, while Madrid smiled back in a rueful, sly manner, happy in the knowledge that he had outsmarted Knoxx. He quipped, 'My house, my rules.'

They broke into a long belly laugh. Then Madrid left him to speak with his partners, explaining the finer points of the deal and how each of them would benefit.

Bezerk sidled up to Knoxx while the guests talked to each other. He sensed this was his opportunity to ask Knoxx about making their move on the next part of the plan, which Knoxx had described on the flight down from San Diego. Somehow, Knoxx seemed to sense this in advance. As if he already knew what Bezerk was going to say, Knoxx cut him off abruptly, saying aggressively, 'Leave it. Not now. Let it slide for tonight. We'll get him tomorrow.'

This was all Knoxx allowed himself to say, hiding his mouth as he raised his glass. He walked away from Bezerk as quickly as possible so as not to attract attention to themselves. The assembled guests began to offer their respective good nights once it became clear that the night was over, with Madrid making remarks about wanting things to wind down. Knoxx retired back to his suite and Bezerk was escorted back to the guesthouse.

The morning sun came up all too quickly.

57

'Señor Knoxx?' Mark heard as he was woken by a knocking at the door. 'Nine o'clock, Señor!'

Knoxx decided to get up and get dressed. He'd been lying in bed for most of the morning anyway, thinking about how the day might work out. It came as a welcome relief to have a reason for getting up. After taking a shower, he stood at the window to gaze out over the panoramic views of The Landmark and its seemingly endless horizons. It was vast and riddled with mirages, even in its deserted barren emptiness; it was truly awe inspiring in its powerful beauty.

Mark placed a phone call to L.A, telling Matthew Tamban that thirty million dollars was going to be deposited into the British Virgin Islands account. He told him to prepare the documents for the purchase of the remaining clubs. Matt asked, with some inflection in his voice, joking, 'Do I even want to know how you pulled this off?'

They both knew it was a loaded question, with Mark not wanting to answer and Tamban not wanting it answered.

Tamban told him that he, Olivia, and Quincy had all been interviewed by the F.B.I. in San Diego. He went on to say that they'd be finishing up their business meetings today and taking tomorrow off, stating, tongue in cheek, that they deserved it. Then he asked, 'So I'll see you back up in L.A. in a couple of days, okay?' Matt's voice sounded concerned as he let Mark know, 'The Feds want to speak to you and some of the newspapers want to interview you too, but hey, look on the bright side, there's no such thing as bad publicity. Especially in L.A. It'll all work out and I'm sure it'll be good for the Envious Group's launch too, as long as you come out of this thing all right. You will, won't you?'

Knoxx replied in an upbeat voice, saying, 'Well, I guess I'll just have to make sure I do. Just keep going with the acquisitions and let me worry about the next couple of days, okay? I'll see you soon. Don't worry, catch ya later.'

Bezerk's wakeup had been a lot different. The guards walked into the guesthouse and shouted at him to get up.

He shouted back, 'Fuck yoouu!' He rolled over, getting deeper under the nine hundred thread count sheets, but he suddenly remembered where he was and decided he had better get up with one final rally cry of, 'fuck you, you faaggss,' throwing back his duvet cover.

Knoxx and Bezerk arrived out on the veranda at around the same time. The three of them began to eat some breakfast, which was much like their conversation, light. The morning sunshine was already burning bright and bringing some heat to the day. Knoxx thought he'd inquire about the whereabouts of Roberto's wife, but thought better of it. Mentioning her might bring some additional heat from Madrid, thinking back to his comment the night before. It still gnawed at him to think that he had said something wrong. He managed to come up with a better way of asking about her, by asking, 'Your Miami home sounds great. The Grove sounds like just the thing I'm looking for. Do you have any idea when I might be able to view it?'

Madrid seemed annoyed at Knoxx's remark. He eyed him coldly. 'I don't concern myself with such matters. Yessica handles all household concerns, as she told you last night.'

Knoxx realized he had hit a nerve last night and Madrid had now said what he needed to say.

Madrid then lowered the portcullis by reflecting on his former home, remarking, 'Good memories in that house.'

Knoxx quickly jumped in to raise the mood by saying, 'And long may those memories continue here.'

'Let us hope that is the case,' Madrid stated in a cryptic way. All three paused for reflection, two of them feeling somewhat uneasy in each other's company.

'Well gentlemen, on to today's business. We have lots to cover and you cannot stay here forever now, can you?'

Madrid put the emphasis on the word 'forever', and for some reason, it sent a chill down Knoxx's spine. Both Knoxx and Bezerk chose to let out a small chuckle, as if it were the funniest joke in the world.

Madrid leaned forward in his chair and said with venom, 'I like the fact that I don't have to instruct you on how to run the business.'

Mark immediately felt this line sounded like a threat. He knew Madrid had chosen the line for a reason, and his words had a purpose. He was testing Knoxx's fortitude and resolve. He replied with some attitude, 'That's one thing you won't have to worry about. I'm my own man and I'll only base my decisions on what I think is right, and what will be profitable for both myself and my partners, but I will be the one to make that decision. If I don't think it's worth the risk, then we won't risk it. I'm loyal to those who are loyal to me. The one thing I learned from prison is to trust no one. That's why, with all due respect to you, I work for no one but myself first and foremost, because I trust no one but myself, first and foremost.'

They were evaluating each other through the words they were choosing, and Knoxx felt he had driven his point home, having made his own position clear. He understood where this exchange could lead and if he wasn't careful, he could end up dead in a ditch. Still, he realized that under no circumstances could he end up being under Madrid's grip as if he were the hired help. He had better head this off here and now, sooner, rather than later he thought. His instincts told him something ominous was on Madrid's mind. He didn't seem as playful this morning as he had been since his arrival. One of his staff walked over to Madrid and leaned down to whisper something in his ear. Madrid nodded along with him as he spoke to him. Looking over at Knoxx, he told him, 'The funds have been transferred to your account. You may use the house phone inside to confirm the funds' arrival.'

Madrid had said it in a tone that was not asking but telling. A guard stood by Mark to indicate that he was to follow him, leaving Bezerk seated with Madrid at the breakfast table.

Twenty minutes or so later, Knoxx returned to the table to see Madrid finishing a discussion with Bezerk in Spanish, and from what he could see it had been a heated one. Knoxx seated himself back at the table and quickly noted that Bezerk's body language had changed abruptly. He looked agitated, and didn't want to make eye contact. Madrid pulled on his heavy Maduro cigar and said, 'Ah yes! Everything is as it should be, the order of things, I think you will find, Mark, no?'

Knoxx thanked him profusely for the bank wire of thirty million dollars.

Madrid quickly turned his attention back to Bezerk. 'I've just been reminding our friend here, that we have the luxury of working with our friends in this business, because if you are to survive this business then you must choose your business associates as you would your friends. Choose them wisely. As you say, Mark, trust and loyalty are at the top of that list if you wish to make business or any friendship work, wouldn't you agree?'

Knoxx flicked his eyes to Bezerk, trying to read him, but he only smirked back at him in a strange way. He realized all wasn't well here and it felt like this was some kind of trap waiting to ensnare him. Knoxx took a slow sip of his morning coffee, buying time to think. He conveyed the poise of a man in control, just waiting for his dog, Bezerk to make his move.

'Come. Let us take a walk before you leave,' Madrid said with a hint of sarcasm, as if he had sensed they had something planned for him. Knoxx knew they were going to segue into another line of conversation. A conversation Madrid didn't want to have. The one that Knoxx had outlined for Bezerk to give when the time was right, but now, that time had come and gone. Madrid's house, Madrid's rules.

The three men made their way out of the mansion and began to walk through the grounds of the Landmark, shadowed by four heavily armed guards, Knoxx noticed.

Madrid kept the conversation light-hearted, but it quickly took on a darker tone when he said, 'The time has come to re-evaluate my business ties and partners. In order to move forward one must be prepared to cut himself off from the past, as old partnerships become outdated and partners become fat and lazy, or worse, greedy and envious. It makes sense to trust your instincts and to proceed with a tight number of people who are loyal to your vision and your cause. By utilizing a small number of highly motivated and resourceful professionals, you can achieve great things in a short time.'

Madrid seemed invigorated and energized by his words. Knoxx recognized that the route they were taking was the one to the coach house. Bezerk walked with his head held low and his shoulders slumped, as if he had something weighing heavily on him.

Giving his words life with every step, Madrid said in a commanding manner, 'Let us go see the past. Then we shall cement our partnership for the future.'

Changing his direction and his pace to begin walking directly towards the coach house, he extended his arm subtly for Knoxx to walk on in, saying happily, 'Let's see how our friend is doing today.'

'Yeah, let's see how that piece of shit is,' Knoxx said, speaking up for Bezerk. He looked at him and all Bezerk could do was offer up a weak smile back at him.

Madrid spoke up, saying, 'You know, Mark, I have read over the transcripts of what Guerro has told us. You'd be surprised to see who your friend is, and who is really your enemy. You must be careful to see the difference, because they both dress and speak the same. You must be able to distinguish between the two. Like you explained, when picking companies to buy, you must evaluate the source, the message, and the motives behind them. That's the difference between those who are ordinary people and those who are people doing extraordinary things. And in order to do extraordinary things one must be prepared to go to extraordinary lengths to fulfill one's own destiny. To do things that another man isn't prepared to do.'

Madrid led the way into the coach house and it became all too apparent what was going on. His final test had come as the group of men walked in; Knoxx began to feel his breakfast hit his throat. There was Guerro strung up again. Bezerk growled at him, seeing him for the first time up close and personal, like a lion stalking a staked out lamb for the slaughter.

Madrid carried on talking nonchalantly. 'This is the past, and now I wish to know how far you are prepared to go to become a part of my future plans, Mark. How bad do you really want all of this? Are your words just empty rhetoric, or do they in fact carry true conviction? You say you learned a lot from prison and that your intentions are for the greater good. The wind can pass you by without you ever feeling it upon your face, but it can turn into a hurricane that can visit you at any time and kill your whole family in an instant.'

Madrid clicked his fingers. Snap, and just like that, Knoxx got his point in a snap. He was talking about how he could reach out at any time and kill him.

Madrid finished by saying, 'Do not try to reach out and catch the wind, for it has already passed you by.'

As he said his words, Madrid took up a menacing stance squarely to Knoxx. Knoxx noticed that he was being encircled by Madrid's guards, while Bezerk stood quietly off to the side. Knoxx realized he was on his own.

'This is your time now. Reach out and try to catch the wind, the wind of change. How bad do you want it? Everything you want is in this room. Everything you desire, everything you have dreamed of is here. It is here for you. Your future, it awaits you. My question to you is: do you want a future? Because in order for you to live your future, you must kill the past. In order for you to live, you must kill Guerro.'

Madrid let his words sink in, while he made his way into the horse stall. Guerro twisted and turned in terror as Madrid came up to him. Juicy, El Diablo, The Grim Reaper, head of The Legion of Doom had come for him, and today, he would be taking his life. The whole building fell silent. All the guards were standing on edge, weapons at the ready and alert. It was just Juicy and his former soldier, Guerro, mano a mano. Knoxx now knew once and for all who this man was. Roberto Madrid was the head of a drug empire, and he was Juicy, the drug trafficker and murderer. A ruthless leader and a ruthless killer; he was the boss of a multi-billion dollar operation because he was well-educated, street smart and all unforgiving. All Knoxx could do was stand there and watch the maestro weave his baton and watch his work play out, as if he was watching an opera. And like all operas, there was a hero and a villain, and the villain always dies at the end.

Guerro whimpered as Juicy came up close to him.

Juicy shouted, 'Silencio!' 'Silence!' Juicy then told Guerro to lift up his head and look at him. Juicy said something in a low, sharp tone to a guard and Guerro was lowered to the floor. He immediately scampered away to a corner of the horse stall and balled up, bringing his knees up to his chest with his eyes not leaving Madrid's for a second. Madrid walked over to him in and crouched down in front of Guerro, asking, 'Cómo estás?' 'How are you?' Guerro began to cry. Juicy continued slowly and softly, 'I wanted you to hear this from me. You have nothing to fear from me. I have not come here to kill you; I have only come to explain to you, myself, what you have done to yourself and to your family. I thought I should be the one to tell you how you killed your wife, your four children, your mother, and your children's grandmother.'

Guerro's eyes overflowed with tears as he fell into an increasing circle of pain, torment, and fear for his family and how they had died.

Madrid just looked at him and waited silently for his crying to wane. The coach house was deathly silent, with everyone's eyes fixed on Guerro and Juicy.

Juicy then said in a morose tone, 'Because of actions you took against me, they have paid with their lives, but I want you to know, I did not kill your family, carnal. You did.'

Guerro became inconsolable, as he laid his head in his hands and wept. Juicy extended his arm and laid his hand on his head, extending his condolences for his loss. Knoxx wanted to burst into tears and throw up, feeling like he wanted to be anywhere else in the world but here.

Juicy went on to say with some pace, while his voice started to sound firmer, 'I was told that your wife, Juanita, bled out from the shotgun wound in her belly. Your son, Jesus, took more time to die because he was suffocated in a plastic bag. The rest of your relatives living in Mexico were shot in the head, burned, and buried out in the desert right here. All because of your actions. Because you were selfish in your greed, selfish in not thinking about your brothers; your hermanos, and we were your brothers. All of us here, even I was your brother. Now you have no family, no mother, no wife, no children and no brothers. No one. Everyone you love is gone; everybody has died for your disloyalty!'

Juicy slapped Guerro hard across his face. Guerro's face was now firmly fixed on Juicy's; his eyes were on fire, and they were filled with hatred.

Juicy explained, 'I am going to let you live the rest of your days, knowing you have killed everyone you love. They are all gone and you will live with that for the rest of your life. For your disloyalty to me, they have died and you shall live.'

He placed his big heavy hand on Guerro's shoulder. Guerro winced at its touch, the hand of God, or the devil sitting on his shoulder. Only Guerro knew which one it was, and now he began to cry again.

Juicy said, 'Or, you can join them today. This man here is willing to help you. He will kill you and help send you to them. Is that what you would like, carnalitos? Would you like that, little brother?'

Knoxx caught Madrid's glance. He was referring to him. Knoxx felt his whole body vibrate with fear as his jaw began

198

to tremble. He noticed a vein in his right hand was throbbing. Guerro only nodded in the slightest way, indicating to Juicy that he knew what had to be done. He was ready to die.

Madrid glared back at his guards, who encircled the horse stall, closing in around Knoxx. Mark looked wide-eyed at Bezerk who stood there as if he was in a trance, with his eyes fixed on Guerro, looking agitated at not being able to get to him. His eyes were darker than the blackness of Hell.

A small voice could be heard amongst the sobbing, 'Just kill me, just kill me, please.'

Juicy stood up and walked away from Guerro. He turned back to him at the horse stall entrance, saying with some humor, 'Enjoy your time in Hell, Guerro. I will visit you there one day.'

Speaking in a hard tone to his men in Spanish, the rope went taught as Guerro was strung up again from the beam. He sobbed hard, coming to terms with knowing this was it; this would be his last moments on earth. All he knew for sure now, was that this stranger who had brought him here, would be the one to send him to Hell. Hanging from the beam, Guerro just waited, whimpering at the thought of his family being murdered because of him. Madrid closed in on Bezerk with his guards backing him up, and spoke to him in hard and fast Spanish. They briefly looked over at Knoxx, making it clear they were talking about him. Mark quickly understood what was unfolding. They were talking about how Guerro was going to be murdered and, who would be the one to do it, and his name was at the top of the list. *Un-fucking-believable*, was all he thought about what he was watching, lions fighting over a piece of meat.

Madrid raised his hand to indicate silence. He then looked over at Knoxx, and he instantly thought, *Oh fuck, now what?* Looking at him ominously, Madrid said boldly, 'I hope I see you soon, Mark. Sometimes, in life, it is better to ask for forgiveness afterwards, than to ask for permission before you are to do something that you know you should not do. You know what has to be done.'

Madrid and his men walked out and left Mark and Bezerk in the coach house. Guerro began to scream and howl in fear, realizing it was now Bezerk who had been given the honor of killing him. Now it would be a painful and slow death. Bezerk let out a low-pitched growl while he stalked into the stall. Some horses kicked and snorted as if they knew what to expect. A horrifying death. Guerro had been the rat who had helped send a lot of his brothers to prison, and now Bezerk could return the favor by killing him slow, without mercy.

Bezerk looked over at Mark and gave him a slight nod that indicated he wanted him to come into the stall. The horses seemed to sense his fear and instantly began to nay wildly and kick out. Mark forced one foot in front of the other, choking on the bile that had built up in his throat, realizing that he was in the lion's den now.

'Yeess siirrr, I'm gettin' me some get back today, booyy,' Bezerk growled, as he picked up a massive butcher's knife that had some weight to it. Guerro wriggled, twisted, and turned in sheer terror, once he saw the weapon that Bezerk had picked up. Bezerk taunted him by saying harshly, 'I'm bringin' out the devil in you today, boy.'

Bezerk's motioned for Mark to come closer. Mark could feel his eyes welling up as he did, knowing Bezerk was going to hand this cleaver to him, and he knew what he was going to have to do with it.

Like a man possessed, Bezerk screamed, 'You're in this now, you know what I mean? You know how we do! It's our code, dog, everybody dies!'

Taking a hold of Mark, Bezerk forced the knife into his hand, turning his fingers around the handle; he made sure Mark had a hold of it. Mark now knew that Bezerk was still a Southsider, and still loyal to Juicy, not to him.

'He's gotta know, dog. This is all you now, you put all this together, you made it all happen; you got him here, and now it's gotta be you to send him on his way. You're gonna do this with me, or it could be you, like this piece of shit, real quick. You know what I mean?' Bezerk shouted in Knoxx's face, standing in front of him in a fighting stance. Mark had thought he knew Bezerk well, but obviously he had been wrong about him. Bezerk looked hard at his face with a look of murder and mayhem written all over his. Mark was looking into the eyes of a raging lunatic. A madman who needed to kill, right now, as if he was craving it. Bezerk commanded, 'We gonna do this, dog. You gonna do this, you can belieeve thaatt.'

'What the fuck am I gonna do? What the fuck are you talking about?' Knoxx screamed back at him, adding, 'I'm no murderer! I can't kill anyone!' Fighting back his tears and fears, he continued shouting at Bezerk, 'I've done my part, more than my part in all of this.' Dropping the knife, it stuck in the wooden floor. Guerro wailed at the sight of the knife and its thickness, knowing it was for him.

Bezerk fought back, saying, 'No dog, this is your part! Right here, right now, and this fool right here is your part in all of this. You're gonna help me kill him, belieeve thaatt.'

Mark couldn't hold back anymore, realizing what Bezerk was telling him. This was all there was and no one had his back. He was on his own and, in order for him to live beyond today; he would have to kill Guerro. He would have to get hands-on and put in some wet work. He would have to become a murderer or end up being the one murdered.

Bezerk shouted, 'Juicy wants me to tell him that you did your bit. He needs to know you got it in you, that you are what you say you are, a soldier, and that he can trust you. He says he has to know you're all in, and if you ain't, well then - .' He couldn't bring himself to finish his sentence, because he knew he didn't have to. Bezerk picked up the knife that had been standing tall, stuck in the floorboard, and stood up with his chest pumped up.

Mark replied, 'Fuck yoouu and fuuckk thiiss!'

He tried to find some solace in Bezerk, but none was given. He stepped up to Knoxx with the knife firmly in his grasp. His saucer-black eyes looking right into Knoxx's very soul, he said, 'Oh don't worry, doogg, I'm gonna be doin' the heavy liftin'. I'm just gonna need you for a bit on this bitch, that's all.'

The future was now. Everything Mark had thought he'd wanted in life, or thought he did, could all be lost. Now all he wanted was to live through this day.

'Snitch on us, you fucking bitch!' Bezerk growled. He took his first steps towards Guerro.

Knoxx instinctively wanted to step in and help Guerro because he wasn't a killer. He was a regular guy. What did he know about murdering anyone? He had paid to have someone killed, yes. His own rat had been exterminated because he could not face being in prison for the remainder of his life, or at least the best part of it. There had only been one way out, but that way out had now led him here to this place with Bezerk and Guerro. Now, he was face-to-face with death, and he would either be taking part in it, or his life would be taken, and it would be his old cellmate and friend, Bezerk, who would be the one to kill him. Knoxx was at the abyss. It was his day to choose if he wanted to live or to die. He could only watch, breaking down in tears at being helpless to stop what was going to take place.

Bezerk was up on Guerro, taunting him. Guerro was already howling. Those howls turned into screams as Bezerk lifted up the knife to his face, showing him the blade up close and personal. He said, 'Yeah booyy, you and me are gonna have a good time together, you feel me? Uh huh, ha, ha, ha, you will soon enough, yeess siirr. Scream as loud as you want. No one gives a shit about a fucking rat! I told you, you were gonna get what's coming to you, fool; only it weren't gonna be no million dollars. I'm gonna get to chop you up into a million fuckin' pieces!'

He bent down, and in a flash, hacked off Guerro's left foot at his ankle joint. Bezerk screamed, Guerro screamed, and Knoxx screamed. There was no turning back now. Mark had stepped across from the light into the dark. He was a part of this now, and he promptly threw up.

Bezerk screamed wildly, laughing as he spat in Guerro's face, showing him his own foot. Turning the blood red knife in his hand, it glistened in the morning light while he spat out, shouting, 'I fuckin' hate you, bitch!'

He hacked again at Guerro, chopping into his right thigh.

He shouted wildly, 'Yeess siirrr, that's why I'm gonna kill you slooww. I'm gonna bleed you out, fool.' Truly mad, in a mad, mad world. He looked at Mark, saying, 'Mark! C'mon up here, fool. Time to come get your money, boy!' Bezerk's face was covered in blood and his hair was all flayed out. He was in his own world, living in a mad world. He had gone mad in his thirst for blood, for revenge, and for the taste of murder. Bezerk said coldly, 'Blood in blood out, that's how we do this. You either gonna do this shit or I'm gonna do you. You know what I mean?'

This was it for Guerro, the beginning of the end for him. He simply screamed, in his own world while Mark looked at him. *What the fuck can I do?* Mark's mind screamed; his mind spinning wildly out of control now.

Bezerk spun Guerro around, taunting him some more, saying, 'Oh yeah, boy, you're gonna like this.'

He yanked Mark roughly and pulled on him until he got him into the position he wanted him in.

'Take this, fool,' Bezerk growled, handing him the knife.

Knoxx took a hold of it. His eyes were out of focus as he looked past the knife to the floor. Guerro was screaming in terror at not being able to see what was going on behind him. Bezerk punched him hard in the kidneys, shot after shot raining into him like he was a punching bag.

'Fillet this fuckaa, now!' Bezerk shouted, as he held Knoxx's hand, showing him what he wanted him to do. He indicated by the line of his hand, showing Knoxx that he wanted him to peel Guerro down his spine.

'Fuuckk yoouu!' Knoxx shouted, openly crying while his body turned to stone. He was blocking out all thought and all noise now. All his senses felt dead, trying to block it all out as if it wasn't happening.

'This's your show, dog, and it's your time to show us what you got. If you don't do it, then you'll get some of the same as this bitch. I mean it, Mark. I love you bro', but you gotta do this for reals, homey. You got to choose. Juicy's ordered it and I can't not do it or my own family's gonna die. Do it, Mark, and do it now! I gotta be able to tell him you did it. If I lie, he might find out, and then we die. That's how we do this. So dig it in and pull it down, now! I got you from here on out, belieeve thaatt, we ride 'til we die. Now peel this 'fuckaa before you get us both killed,' Bezerk shouted wildly with tears falling from his eyes, seeing that Mark was in so much pain.

Mark's tears were flowing fast, crying at the thought of being hands-on. From now on his life would never be his own. He would belong to Juicy, and his soul would belong to the devil. Knoxx began to scream in tormented pain. Guerro screamed a death howl as he felt the long blade cut deep in his back just below his neck. The first slice. Then, as the blade took hold, digging into the first ridges of the spinal column, the heavy blade stuck in it. The horses nayed and kicked wildly as the whole coach house reaching a crescendo. This was it; no one could turn back the hands of time. The time had come and no one could save him. Knoxx closed his eyes as he gripped the handle of the knife tight in his hands. He began to put his weight into it, leaning down on it, but still the knife refused to move. Guerro could not move. All his breath was being ripped from inside him. He was in shock as the pain took him to another place and time. Knoxx leaned his head onto his hands, feeling the handle of the knife as it nudged a millimeter and then it moved abruptly. Guerro found his scream. The horses kicked out against their stalls again and Bezerk howled in laughter, shouting with feeling, 'From here on out, we ever go to war, I'm with you. It's now or never, Mark, do it doogg.'

The knife jerked as it crossed the first disc in Guerro's spine, the bump of it forcing it to dig in again as it hit the next disc below. The knife then picked up from Knoxx's body weight pulling it down, as it sliced down Guerro's spinal cord. Knoxx kept his eyes closed and screamed as he felt the knife lowering itself along Guerro's back. He put his left hand over his right, clamping down on the knife, pulling it harder, the knife slicing faster, the screams becoming louder. In an instant, Guerro became ghostly quiet as Knoxx continued to lean into it using his elbows as leverage. Guerro's back peeled open as he went. Zip. He could feel the hot blood running down his elbows as it ran down onto his face. He could taste what death was. It tasted sweet.

'You know how we do!' Bezerk shouted wildly like a man possessed while he watched his boy Knoxx putting in work on Guerro.

Knoxx leaned his body forward until he was practically bent over at a ninety-degree angle. His work was done in a matter of seconds. Seconds that changed his life forever. He felt the blade lodge in the back of Guerro's pelvic bone. He pulled the knife out and stepped back from Guerro while his work now came into view. Guerro's back looked like a row of pale white teeth stacked on top of one another. Guerro's spinal column looked back at him, seeping blood from either side of the cut. The cut ran from just below his neck all the way down to the top of his ass, exposing his pelvic bone.

Guerro just hung there in silence, bleeding out.

'Give me that fuckin' thing,' Bezerk shouted, as he grabbed the knife from Mark's frozen hand. He quickly jumped around to the front of Guerro. He drove the knife into Guerro's stomach without any hesitation or thought. He looked deep into Guerro's eyes, burying the knife right up to his knuckles. Bezerk pushed his face in Guerro's face, shouting, 'Biittcchh!' at the top of his lungs while he slowly twisted the knife from left to right in his belly.

Bezerk felt Guerro's last breath on his face. He smiled happily at him and broke into a laugh, spitting in Guerro's face as his last act of revenge.

He looked at Knoxx, saying proudly, 'Yeah booyy, you my dog for reals now! Yeah, you alright, fool.' Bezerk walked over to Mark and began to shake him roughly back into this world, laughing uncontrollably while he looked at Knoxx's frozen face. He began to handle and shake him more, grabbing and cuddling him at the same time, as he said, 'C'mon, dog, it's okay. I'll let you live.' He laughed more out of relief that it was done now, and that he did not have to kill his friend.

'You know how we do, fool. Everybody dies,' Bezerk hollered.

Both of them had Guerro's blood dripping off of their hands. Bezerk draped his arms around him to give him a big bear hug that practically lifted him off the floor; he laughed, thinking how wild the whole experience had been. But Mark did not feel a thing. His whole body was numb, having gone into shock. Shock at what he had seen, and shock at what he had done. He had made his choice, and now his life would never be the same again.

58

Mark Knoxx had said it was his destiny to meet Chris Wright, and Chris Wright had turned out to be Bezerk. Now Mark knew his life was not his own, knowing his life could have been taken in the most gruesome way. No one would have ever known how he had died or where his body had been buried. He'd have been murdered by Bezerk, under orders from Juicy, and both of them knew that his order would have been carried out.

Mark had gotten out of Madrid's grasp. He had left The Landmark as a loyal ally to Juicy. Roberto Madrid now knew that Mark could be trusted.

Knoxx got out of Mexico and back to the relative security of Los Angeles, and his home in Marina del Rey, California. He had breezed through the interviews with the F.B.I.'s Maxine Dobro, L.A.P.D., and San Diego Police Department. He had his alibi and he had his way of communicating it in an easy, disconnected way that conveyed he knew nothing about what they were asking him, because the person they were now interviewing was dead. Knoxx was dead. He had lived his life in the beauty of the black and white, right and wrong. He had known which side was which, but now, all he had was a life of living in the gray. Behind his smile was the gray of what he was living with inside. Death. Every smile had to be forced and every upbeat conversation had to be pushed out through his lying lips.

Maxine Dobro at the F.B.I. knew she had her man. She just could not prove it, yet. She kept him at the forefront of the news for as long as she dared, before his high-priced lawyers slapped a lawsuit on her so quick, it would be stuck to her ass the next time she took a dump. It had been a tactic that had worked out though, for Mark Knoxx. His lawyer, Matthew Tamban had been right. There was no such thing as bad publicity. It propelled Mark Knoxx to the forefront of the television news, newspapers, and the tabloids. The way he carried himself was with an air of confidence, and brashness, like a guy who could do bad things to bad people. Tamban was also right in that it had helped put the Envious Group on the map. As each nightclub, restaurant, and strip club opened, the media covered every event, each one drawing more moths to the flame. More media meant more celebrities, which meant more coverage, where NVS and Knoxx began to be mentioned in the same breath.

Madrid had been wrong. There was no point in asking for forgiveness after the fact; it was too late, as Mark could never forgive himself for what he had done, and for what he had become. Inside, he knew the truth and the truth was that with every opening of an NVS club, it meant that another distribution outlet for Juicy's drugs had just been opened. Another group of Southsiders took up their positions to secure a club, running security and running drugs, each one paying Knoxx around thirty thousand dollars a week. He had opened an offshore bank account and named it Endless Horizons, so he would never forget that day he had looked out over the vastness of the open desert at The Landmark, with its big morning sky, that could have been one of the last things he would have enjoyed as his last day alive. The day that had ended up being the day he had put work in and helped murder a man.

The media and the F.B.I. eventually stopped badgering Knoxx because they had other problems. Big problems that had escalated, it seemed, since the day Knoxx had returned to Los Angeles. Within a week of his return, the drug wars had begun. It started with a drug dealer being shot dead. A gunman had pulled alongside a Southsider gangbanger in broad daylight, in a busy tourist area known as The Gaslamp District in San Diego. Having shot the gangbanger in the face, the gunman got out of the car and stood over the body of the slain man to continue pumping an additional five bullets into his body. He had been murdered, execution style, while a number of tourists watched in horror as it was done. The body of the dead gangbanger was later identified as Big Smoke. One week later, in an upscale community far from the bright city lights, a man was found slumped in his car at twenty minutes past six o'clock in the morning, with one round shot through the temple of his head. The news coverage was intense for the following two weeks as the media circled the F.B.I.'s and the San Diego police department's headquarters, searching for answers on who had been behind the execution of retired, special agent Patrick Connelly.

Knoxx watched every report and read each newspaper article. He knew what was happening; Madrid was working through Guerro's list. In Mexico, it had gotten even more brutal. Where a wind had blown up from the south into California, a hurricane tore through Mexico. Madrid had reaped his whirlwind of vengeance on those who had plotted against him. If your name had been on Guerro's list, then it wasn't long before Madrid got around to crossing your name off it. The news had reported that two decapitated heads had been tossed out from a vehicle onto the City Hall steps in Mexico City. One head was that of the Chief of Police, Salvatore Francisco. The other head was of one of his deputies, who had policed the Tijuana and Otay Mesa border crossings.

206

An American tourist who had been crossing the Tijuana border in to San Diego had been sent to the secondary holding area, as the drug-sniffing dog had indicated there might be drugs in the car. Chase Hughes did as he was instructed by the U.S. border agents. Once several of them had began searching the car, it exploded with him sitting in it, killing everyone. A man had been on the bridge connecting Tijuana to San Diego, making a call on his cell phone. He had simply watched and then walked away, running his fingers through his long, black hair. The drug wars were leaving a long trail of destruction in their wake. The public now lived in fear, as did law enforcement officers.

Knoxx knew he could be on that list one day. Madrid had killed all his old allies and formed new ones with people who had never met or known the name, Mark Knoxx or Exile. Mark made good on the promise that he had made to Bezerk on their bunks one morning, back in prison. Over the next two years, Knoxx focused on two things: getting paid and getting laid, doing his best to drink every bar dry and sleep with every woman in the world. There was no end to his acquisitions, both in business and in beauty. Every event saw him with the latest model or actress of the moment. Life was to be lived, for tomorrow was not guaranteed, as he knew all too well now. His life was not his own anymore, and behind all the glitz of Hollywood, he knew it was all fool's gold. He had tasted the champagne, the fine wine and the finest Hollywood starlets, models and California babes, but they all tasted like coal in his dry mouth. He had dreamed the genius and he had witnessed the madness. Knoxx knew that if he stayed in the heat of California under the bright sun, he would get burned soon enough.

He decided to retreat to Miami, having purchased The Grove from Madrid. He had been so gracious on the terms of the purchase, Knoxx knew it would have been showing disrespect to turn him down; he knew better now. He immersed himself inside the fortress walls of The Grove, only allowing inside those who were close to him. He had his own soldiers parading the perimeter, and he had chosen his staff from friends back in England. Each of them were handpicked because he felt he could trust them. His number one ally and confidante, Jane Mears, stood shoulder-to-shoulder with him. Alisha Ellington, a former girlfriend who was good with numbers worked as his accountant, and Matthew Tamban, Knoxx's lawyer operated as his conduit to the offshore banks. Working with Tamban's young protégé, Olivia Marbela, she would be surreptitiously keeping tabs on Bezerk in her reports from the West Coast each week while she worked at NVS. Knoxx also brought back Andrew Matthews, Sam Malton, and Brian Meserve to make up his security team, the pride of lions protecting their territory. They were battle-hardened and they were now getting prepared for the day Juicy might come for Mark. They were ready, with Meserve often saying, 'We'll kill 'em all and let God sort 'em out.'

Had Knoxx taken the ten-year prison sentence, he would have been close to getting out, but now he was in for life. It was all too late, for his life was not his own anymore; it was on loan to him from Juicy. Mark Knoxx never spoke to Bezerk directly ever again, knowing that he would have murdered him back in the stables. Everyone knew Knoxx was a genius in business, but they could also feel his madness. He carried stone in his heart and granite in his fists every day.

'You've achieved so much, more than anyone could ever have dreamed of. Tell us, Mark, how did you do it? How did you get to live such an envious life?' the sexy television presenter, Helen Stacey, inquired, while Knoxx flashed a smile. Both enjoyed each other's company and laughed while they stood outside the NVS nightclub in New York on opening night.

Knoxx replied, joking, 'I could tell you Helen, but then I'd have to kill you.'

V.I.P.

59

'There's more to these murders than just drug territory wars, Kevin, I'm sure of it.'

Dobro had been going at it for nearly fifteen minutes, but she still hadn't been able to explain why she thought Mark Knoxx was involved. Still, she was in no mood to back down yet.

'Unless you have hard evidence or an informant, there's really nothing I can do, is there? You've based your theories on raw emotions, Maxine, on your "woman's intuition", as you like to call it,' F.B.I. Deputy Director Kevin Christie replied, while using one of Dobro's own tried and tested tricks. He began shuffling his papers on his desk. He then picked them up and looked at his watch to indicate that their meeting was over.

Maxine bared her teeth, giving her best Rottweiler glare, but she held her fangs in her mouth. It wasn't the best idea to go toe-to-toe with the suits in Washington or New York. Dobro had been summoned to New York for a briefing on the current state of the drug wars. Kevin Christie would then brief the Secretary of State, Graham Stewart, known along The Beltway as The Pelican. Maxine had found herself in a minority of one, however, in her belief that Mark Knoxx was not only involved in drug trafficking with Roberto Madrid, but that he posed an imminent threat to the U.S. with his latest venture, called HEAVEN. Christie had to pull her out of the briefing and rein her in after she'd gotten herself worked up and even he hadn't been able to calm her down since then. As Christie got up to leave his office, a thought came to him as he looked at Maxine.

He said, 'Here's what I'll do. Come with me, I have someone for you to meet. Maybe she can help you?' He began to walk out of his skyline-windowed office with Maxine chomping at his heels. She noticed his citations and awards lining the walls, photographs of him with senators, and world-renowned businessmen. Maxine got the point. He could make things happen or not, if he chose to. Two years had passed since The Get Back case, and Dobro's fire still burned hot, thinking that case had held her back. It had cost the lives of colleagues of hers, and that just didn't sit well. She had become Knoxx's nemesis. Taking an interest in where he was and who he was with, watching him on television attending The Oscars, charity fundraisers and state events in Washington, reading magazine articles about him, and seeing a photograph of him with the Vice President of the United States, taken at a charity clay pigeon shoot.

She was going nowhere and he was everywhere creating a buzz for his latest project, HEAVEN, which stood for, Hospital Evaluation and Authenticated Vitals Encoded Navigator. She felt sick in her stomach when she read about it in magazines, in *The Wall Street Journal*, or watched a television program about it. It just seemed wrong to her, but she the only member of a club who thought that Mark Knoxx was a bad guy, and a very dangerous one at that. She had watched his rise, gaining money, power, and respect, while her own life seemed to disintegrate. She'd separated from her husband Gary after he'd become disenchanted with their marriage, and she had lost touch with her children, Danielle and Harry. Dobro had been left behind and she knew who to blame. Mark Knoxx. All roads led to Exile and they were always dead ends.

Maxine found herself looking up to Heaven for help while she followed Christie along a series of hallways until he reached a glass door. He had to swipe his clearance card over a magnetic pad to open it, and then they walked into a secured wing of the F.B.I. building. Walking up to a door, he swiped his clearance card again and entered the secured room. Dobro saw that the room was filled with computer monitors and massive television screens that were tracking bank wire transactions throughout the United States to and from overseas countries. Christie walked up to a woman sitting at a computer terminal. He said to Maxine, while he looked at the woman. 'I'd like you to meet special agent, Teresa Hadley.'

Christie went on to say, 'Teresa's one of our best, Maxine. She heads up FinCEN.'

60

'Getting to the root of the problem, the heart of the divide. if we, as a society, cannot agree on what the gold standard approved source of medical information is, then that just reveals that we have even more problems to solve.' Knoxx took a moment to look at the audience from the stage and continued, 'If the patient isn't given all the facts, simply because the attending doctor does not have them available to him, then that is playing a dangerous game with someone's life, isn't it? Patients have been misguided in the past, sometimes through honest mistakes, sometimes due to lack of up-to-date information, and sometimes criminally so. I understand, no one can live forever and maybe not many people even want to, but I do believe that everyone wants to live their lives as best they can, for as long as they can. Nothing in life is guaranteed, except death and taxes.'

Bringing a ripple of chuckles throughout the auditorium, he went onto say, 'however, I do know this. Tomorrow isn't guaranteed, but I can guarantee you of this. For everyone admitted in to a hospital where HEAVEN is administered, patients will receive a four hundred dollar deduction from their health insurance or hospital expenses. Both the hospital and the patient will benefit from an up-to-the-minute diagnosis and a faster recovery time. It seems to me that the science of medicine is becoming more about caretaking than it is about curing. The big pharmaceuticals are becoming richer, while the world becomes sicker and certain countries become poorer. The public wants the facts. Give them all the information so that they may make better, healthier choices.'

Knoxx walked to the front of the stage, seemingly off script, speaking with fluidity and emotion. 'They can come after me all they want. It won't stop me from doing what I want to do, doing what I feel is right. You can't turn back the clock on any mistake like it never happened, I know that. The choices we make have consequences and God knows medicine isn't easy, and nobody pretends it is. But if there's one thing we ought to be able to rely on in our time of need is that the doctor isn't just playing hunches on what they think is the best course of action to take. There is still as much art as there is science in medicine, and as hard as we try, there is still the sovereignty of God. I believe God should be the one in control of who gets to live or die; only I do know differently. I've created HEAVEN to ease the pain and suffering for the patient and their families, so that they'll know the best care was provided, using the latest, most accurate data available from around the world. HEAVEN can only serve by providing the information; the results are still in God's hands.'

Knoxx now picked up the pace, trying to lighten the mood as he came to the close of his presentation. He picked up a swagger, making eye contact with a few hospital representatives.

'I know one thing for sure. You can't raise a hundred million dollars at two thousand dollars a pop'. No one has that many friends.' Knoxx said playfully, referring to the cost of the seats at this evening's dinner. Then he said, 'And if you're going to start a revolution, then you'd better have a snappy slogan.'

The big screen behind him sprang to life on cue, showing the HEAVEN logo. The audience cheered, rising to their feet in applause for Knoxx's presentation. He gave them a rousing wave and pointed to a few of the delegates as he began to walk off stage. Jane Mears and Alisha Ellington were waiting for him in the wings along with his security team, Andrew Matthews and Brian Meserve.

Moving out like a Secret Service detail, the Exile team moved as one. A convoy of cars were already waiting at the side entrance, that immediately whisked him off to The Hôtel Ritz, located at 15, Place Vendôme, in the heart of Paris. Knoxx had been on the road for six weeks giving presentations throughout Europe, extolling the benefits of HEAVEN to everyone within the drug industry, medical field, and hospital administration departments. Knoxx was becoming the new rock star in an industry that was unused to being at the forefront of the media's attention. He had now put HEAVEN on the front pages of *Newsweek, Businessweek*, newspapers, television documentaries and news channels. It was catchy and it had generated the publicity he'd hoped it would. It hadn't hurt that he had come from the world of venture capital and now he was becoming known as the guy who could save the healthcare industry. Mark Knoxx had helped to bring some celebrity to the stoic world of medicine and blown it wide open. In his eyes, it was vastly undervalued as a mainstream financial vehicle. It was always overlooked as a trendsetter and yet, next to air, it was the most important thing in everyone's lives. The money was rolling like the Santa Fe Train and Knoxx was on his way to becoming a billionaire. With HEAVEN, the sky was the limit as to what it would bring him.

61

'Move out,' the Secret Service detail moved as one. The President of the United States walked inside the pocket of Secret Service agents from the G-8 Summit being held in Paris. Both the President of the United States, John 'Jack' Blackmoor, and Vice President Stephen Tasker, were in Paris to reinforce the United States' resolve to contain the war in Iraq, and to move the peace talks forward between Palestine and Israel. It seemed that wherever the administration went, so did the war. President Blackmoor had won his second term election and was secure for his remaining time in office. All he needed now was to secure his legacy as a president who had left some seeds for continued growth, prosperity and security in the world. But that didn't seem to be happening. Most of the world seemed to know that John Blackmoor's presidency was a lame duck, in part, due to Vice President Tasker, who seemed to run the presidency like his companies, hard and fast, squeezing everyone and everything in his path. Tasker had arrived in Paris three days earlier before President Blackmoor, and that's when the real players were in town, looking to make deals with him.

The real game was with Vice President Tasker, who was married to his wife of nineteen years, Lynn Tasker. They had two young girls, Ruby May Tasker, seventeen, and Molly Rose, now fourteen, and one son, Tommy Tasker, eight. Stephen Tasker epitomized the American values. Study hard, work hard and use everything within your sphere of influence to make things work to your advantage. Tasker had used these fundamentals and a whole lot more to accomplish his dreams and aspirations. At fifty years old, the world knew that his time was rapidly approaching to take over as the next President of the United States. That's why the world's power brokers and wheeler-dealers wanted to align themselves with him early on in the game. The Secret Service call sign went out to indicate that the Vice President was safely dispatched in the car, 'Pinky is secure in Cadillac two.'

The cavalcade was on the move, much like Tasker's career, and his plans for the world. Tasker was a man on a mission, but his mission didn't necessarily include the wellbeing of his United States of America.

62

'Private equity firms are starting to take heavy positions in HEAVEN.'

Knoxx listened to Andrew Matthews while he relaxed from another long day, drinking tea in the vast sitting room of The Ritz. He took it all in with some distraction, checking out the Parisian females walking around the lobby and through the sitting room. Matthews carried on speaking knowing that Mark was listening in his own way, while Jane Mears sat beside him reading contracts for HEAVEN. Matthews continued, explaining, 'The big boys are heading into a headlong crisis and they know it. Over the next five years, around seventy pharmaceutical companies will be losing their patent protections, and when that happens there'll be a hole in lost revenues that'll be divided up between other companies totaling around a hundred billion dollars a year.'

Knoxx took another sip of his tea, eyeing Matthews. He then appeared to be looking over Matthews' shoulder, *checking out another babe*, Matthews thought. Mark asked in a blunt, uninterested way, 'What's our NNT rate to date?'

Mathews looked back as if he was unprepared for Knoxx's question, asking, 'Our Numbers Needed to Treat, count?'

Knoxx nodded back. 'Yeah, our numbers; what's our NNT rate?'

His eyes still followed a model while she sashayed her way across the lobby to the elevators. Matthews pulled up his laptop and fired it up. Knoxx waited and sipped the last of his tea, just sitting there killing time. He had nothing but time. Matthews stated, 'Okay, here it is. Our NNT is currently around one in five. Five people being treated with the same drug for it to save one life. Our worldwide count's around two hundred and ten million online.'

Putting down his teacup, Knoxx replied in a nonchalant manner, summarizing his thoughts, 'So that gives us a projected market cap of approximately forty-five billion dollars at the opening bell. And if the public markets don't value us as strong, I'll make damn sure the private equity markets will. Okay, we're done here.' He checked his watch, indicating that he was finished with this conversation. He looked over at Meserve and Malton, who walked over to him as he got up from the couch.

The double doors of The Ritz opened and in walked the Secret Service, while Knoxx had stood up and straightened his Armani suit. The Secret Service cleared the immediate area, and in walked Vice President Stephen Tasker. Meserve, Malton, and Matthews had already formed a perimeter around Knoxx, who was preparing to make his way towards the elevators. The Secret Service was walking in unison towards the bank of elevators themselves, enveloping the Vice President. Knoxx Acquiesced his position as they walked through the lobby. Vice President Tasker noticed the security detail around Knoxx and released a smirk as he passed by. Tasker gave a respectful nod in Knoxx's direction and he obliged with a nod of his own. Both men seemed to give the other a nod that said 'how are you,' having recognized each other. The only thing different between the two groups was that one group had neat earpieces while the other one probably had more kills to their name.

Knoxx had been to all the right charity fundraisers and had hosted all the right events to get himself noticed. Now it seemed, in the slightest of chance meetings, he had just been recognized by the one man who mattered most in the world, the next most powerful man on the planet.

'Damn, that was close,' Matthews said, beginning to laugh.

'Yeah, I thought we were gonna have to pour some mud in their asses and stomp 'em dry!' Meserve said in a joking, but hard way.

'Slags,' Matthews concurred.

Knoxx laughed with them as they started to walk over to the elevators, and then got back to business asking Jane, 'Make sure you get a hold of Cameron and confirm he'll be there tomorrow.' As the group arrived at the elevators, Knoxx continued, 'Tell him I'll meet him at the Hyatt in Serbia at five o'clock tomorrow. You and Alisha can have the next two days off, honey.'

Mark Knoxx had built an empire that encompassed commercial properties, office buildings, nightclubs and manufacturing plants in America, England, Europe, Russia and Hong Kong. The money was flowing twenty-four hours a day. Just as business relied on relationships to get deals done, so did governments around the world. Some legitimately and some not so legitimately, but doing business was doing business, and people in power-play positions had to find a way to make things happen. Both Knoxx and Tasker were in the business of making things happen. Some of those deals the public got to see get done, and some they didn't get to see or hear about.

A few years back, Tasker was being investigated in an insider trading scandal that ended, thanks to the untimely death of the Department of Justice's Attorney General, Alistair Collinger, who had been killed in a head-on collision with a semi-truck. The case was suppressed and Tasker's career continued. Since then, one of his friends and business colleagues, who had helped with that problem, William Baltizar the Third, had been appointed the Attorney General.

It seemed that both Stephen Tasker and Mark Knoxx's paths were one and the same. A butterfly had beaten its wings.

Where Knoxx had been investigated and subsequently faced a prison term for his insider trading scam, Tasker was never indicted. But then, Tasker was a member of the Rub a Dub Dub Club, a consortium that had been formed while he attended The Wharton School of the University of Pennsylvania, as a kind of joke. Only now, those same members were no joke, having become wealthy Internet, media, real estate and industrial moguls, and all of them were world-class players. And now the group's aspirations had become more sinister. They wanted to see their own man in the White House, and Vice President Stephen Tasker was now only nineteen months away from that goal's realization. He had the full financial backing of his influential and powerful friends. He had a veil of powerful brokers surrounding him, planning his every move. Each photo opportunity and every sound bite was man-managed to the point of manipulation. He was guarded not only by the Secret Service, but also in his own thoughts and chosen words. Everything was measured and reserved. The truth couldn't be told or shown to the world, not yet.

Tasker had at his disposal the N.S.A., C.I.A., F.B.I., and D.E.A., all working under the guise of defending America's way of life and its borders from terrorism and any other threat. At the same time, the U.S. assisted in destabilizing the third world's economy and allowed countries to produce drugs if they assisted them in the fight against terrorism. Which is the greater evil? Dance with the devil; the devil does not change, the devil changes you. America was at war on several fronts in numerous countries. On the home front, there was an ill-wind blowing. It was the wind of change. A new generation would soon be sweeping into The White House. Tasker's real aims and aspirations weren't yet being made apparent, and neither were those of his backers who wanted him there. The wind would blow across your face and then it would gain momentum, becoming a hurricane. Mark Knoxx and Stephen Tasker were worlds apart in their upbringing, schooling, friends, and stations in life, but they were headed in the same direction, only from two sides of the street, worlds apart.

63

'What you got on my forty, fool?' Bezerk said, breaking into a wild laugh with one of his homeys in the V.I.P. lounge of NVS on Sunset Boulevard and Vine Street. Bezerk was living large and loving life, just as Mark Knoxx had promised him he would. Bezerk had everyone and everything at his beck and call, as he rolled with his crew of Southsiders: Tavo, Beaver, Coco, and Jester. Bezerk treated them well and everyone was healthy and wealthy, living their life in Exile.

'Booyy, shiitt, that ride out there, let me tell you, it rides so tight. When I drove over a quarter, I could tell if it was heads or tails,' Bezerk said, laughing happily, referring to the black-on-black Ferrari F430 spider he had bought for himself. Christopher Wright was living an envious life all right. Only one thing still bugged the shit out of him, and he always came back to it most nights. His boy Knoxx wasn't with him. Knowledge had moved on to bigger and better things without him. Bezerk was envious of him now. Chris knew he'd made it happen for Mark, having arranged for the rat on his case, Jason Burne to be murdered. Knoxx was living large and loving life, getting all the media's attention, and he had left Bezerk behind. Even though Wright had it all, it wasn't enough. And now that he had tasted the finer things in life, mediocrity and anonymity just left a sour taste in his mouth. Bezerk had also found out, all too quickly, that money could only buy so much in life. It can only buy material things, and once they'd been bought, then what?

Bezerk wanted more from life and he wanted more from Mark, acknowledgment and respect. The crew were partying each night, either in NVS or at other L.A. clubs, or they were flying to Las Vegas for an all-night event of cocaine, strip clubs and hookers, with Bezerk always searching for his favorite redhead. He was being tormented by his dreams of what he had wished for, only to arrive in the reality and find out it was nothing like he had dreamed. After years of parties and V.I.P. promotions, Bezerk now knew that Knoxx had been right after all, years ago back in prison. They were all maggots. They were just fucked up people with fucked up problems just like him and he had finally realized that living life as a media-generated celebrity wasn't real.

64

The private jet landed at a nondescript airport six miles south of Kać, Vojvodina in Serbia. Knoxx and his party disembarked.

'Mark,' Romney said, giving Knoxx a small nod in acknowledgement. Adrian Romney was well paid for his services as the pilot and for his silence on trips such as these. He could be counted on for that and a whole lot more, being a former Special Air Services military specialist in the British armed services. Ian 'Springer' Hickes and Drew Yarward were waiting to pick up Knoxx at the airport. They were ex-military and now they were ruthless mercenaries – hard-core, bad-ass killers. On a trip such as this, they were certainly the kind of accessories that Mark wanted to bring along in addition to Matthews, Meserve, and Malton. Knoxx was rolling strong on this trip. He took a moment to check his watch, exhaled some cold air, and looked around. His bleak surroundings were much like his outlook on how this trip was going to go.

He then said, 'Well, Adie, if all goes according to plan, we'll be in-country around twelve hours. I'd say we should be back around six thirty in the morning. Will that be a problem?'

'No problem, Mark, I'll take us out through Serbia, across to Malta. We'll refuel and submit our flight plan from there, and head back to Rimini, Italy.' Romney explained.

'Sounds good,' Knoxx replied. Then he looked at the small invasion force that was encircling him, all waiting for their general to give the command. He said, 'Okay guys, saddle up.'

The two Toyotas filled up with the heavily armed men and then headed south towards the Hyatt hotel in Belgrade to pick up a package named Cameron Pope. Knoxx hoped this trip would be worth the risk and the effort, because according to Pope, it was a meeting that was worth seventy-five million dollars to him, if he came out of it alive. Mark Knoxx was attending a secret meeting with a very important person.

65

The air was frigid and the buildings looked just as cold. This was a war-torn country. Having had several invading armies march through it over the past few centuries had left its people just as cold towards foreigners. The Toyotas pulled up at the front of the Hyatt Hotel at Milentija Popovica 5, Belgrade in Serbia. The hotel stood defiantly in its brisk shade of gray windows in the Belgrade square. The Toyotas had seen better days by now, having gotten muddied up from their journey, which had been part road and part off-roading. Knoxx stayed in the warmth and security of the car, while Hickes and Yarward got out to survey the immediate area for potential threats. By now, all eyes were on them from the stallholders and merchants around the square. The crew had already noticed quite an impressive cache of weapons adorning some of the merchants and hanging from the posts of stalls. They were now definitely in the Wild Wild East. The security detail got out and formed a skirmish line. Knoxx received a final nod from Hickes and he quickly strode into the hotel without so much as a look, left or right.

Cameron Pope had been waiting for some time for his friend, and hopefully, future business associate, to arrive. Cameron was affectionately called 'The Silver Fox' by Knoxx, due to him being a wily old fox in his way of thinking. Cameron was a happy, portly old chap, and yet, at fifty-eight years old, he still carried his shoulder-length, gray hair and beard in a regal way. Knoxx called him 'The Silver Fox' for the way he conducted his business dealings too. Pope was a cool guy; a painter and a good sport, but he was also connected. He lived in London, where he owned several wine bars and art galleries that afforded him the luxury of meeting and dealing with some savory characters throughout Europe. Mark and Cameron had met in London, both being involved in the nightclub business. Knoxx had quickly picked up on Pope's overtures, letting it be known that he had more to offer him than fine wine and art. Knoxx had made contact with his old friend, Ivan the Russian, back in M.C.C., and he had been given a contact name to call in Serbia. Knoxx had passed that name on to Pope to act as the go-between and see if a deal could be done. Cameron had wined and dined the Serbian to the point where a meeting was set with a man he knew, who required Mark's services. And today would be the day that Knoxx would come knocking with his opportunity.

'Good to see you, Cam, you old fox, you,' Knoxx said, greeting him happily, smiling brightly as he entered the Hyatt

Hotel's lounge.

'Alright Mark. Good to see you, pal,' Cameron replied, as he got up from the deep couch to give Knoxx a warm embrace, the two men having a genuine affection for each other.

Mark said quickly, 'We're running a little late, Cam. And from what you've told me about this guy's problems, I guess we'd better make up for lost time and get this show on the road. I'm not here for the entertainment bud. I know we're in show business, but you're the show dude and I'm all business.'

'Oh, you are a one, you are, Mark,' Cameron replied mischievously, laughing at Knoxx's meaning.

Knoxx then said, 'Come on, you old fox, let's get going and we'll catch up in the car.'

The Toyota's engines were still running out front, as the security team reversed their procedures until Knoxx and Pope were packaged up neatly in the back of the rear S.U.V. The group began to set up for the ride out to the meeting point. Ian and Drew were the last to get back in the lead car, and then the convoy took off towards the Montenegro border.

A lone figure stepped out from a stall at the south-end of the courtyard to look more closely at the passing cars. He took a long, hard drag on his rolled-up cigarette. His gnawed and knotted, rough-hewn hand flicked it away while he adjusted his Kalashnikov AK47 automatic rifle on his shoulder. Finally, with a slight yawn and with little regard for anyone, he continued to watch the cars as they exited the square. He took out a satellite phone - its thick antenna bent over back against the handset - and keyed it into life. Speaking in a gruff, hard manner, he spoke while he watched intently for the direction that the Toyotas turned. 'They have just left in two gold-colored Toyota Four Runners. The lead car's carrying three men and the V.I.P. is riding in the rear car with two guards. Da, da! Yes, yes, they looked military. I'd say they are armed, da. They're taking Holdenhurst Road heading southwest. Good luck, comrade.' He hung up the phone and melted away.

66

The cars had been on and off the road for around four hours, with everyone taking turns to nod off, in between shooting the shit and listening to Russian-type music on the intermittent radio stations. The Toyotas kept in tight formation as they passed everything from burned out tanks, military convoys, and old men riding donkeys. The night's rain made the trip even more boring and dangerous. Cameron had been filling Mark in on the man he would be meeting, and the reason why he needed his services. Then Mark explained why he wanted to meet the man in question. The two cars began to maneuver through a pass, cutting through a desolate mountain when Hickes saw a set of headlights lighting up the road ahead of them. He couldn't quite make out if it was on the right or left side of the dirt road ahead of them.

'Asshole! Pick a fucking side, you slag! Any one'll do, you half-wit!' Drew Yarward shouted harshly, but then quickly realized it wasn't a car at all. It was a Ukrainian T-84 main battle tank and it was sitting dead center in the road. He had nowhere to go. Drew shouted, 'Oh shiitt!'

He brought the Toyota to a sliding standstill on the muddy track; Meserve reacted behind him, doing the same, having to stomp on the brakes of the car.

'We got some maggots up front,' Hickes barked into his radio, telling the guys behind him what he was looking at, while Malton locked and loaded his Heckler Koch HK MP-5 sub machine gun. The security team in both cars brought their weapons to arms. A resounding click from guns being loaded went up inside both vehicles, as they all realized what this was. An ambush.

Hickes stood behind the open passenger door, shading his eyes trying to find someone to focus on in front of the tank's blinding lights, but all he heard was shouting in Serbian, and a collective report of weapons echoed around him. The standoff lasted about two minutes with everyone standing on point with weapons raised, both sides shouting instructions to each other and at one another. Heavy machine guns were moved from side to side, sweeping for any advancing enemy. Knoxx's guys were up for it.

'Come and get some, then!' Andrew Matthews shouted out defiantly.

'Come on then, you fuckin' slaaggss!' Meserve barked, backing up his partner.

'Anyone wants to step up, let's get to it or step the fuck off! You get my meaning, Boris?' Hickes shouted from the car in front.

The battle tank fired up its engine and the turret began to lower in front of them. The whirring noise from its engine was deafening. The turret lowered at some pace, telling them all the same thing, but Matthews summed it up nicely, saying, 'We are so fucked.'

A Serbian accent spoke up above the din, shouting at them, 'We mean you no harm! I am to bring only one of you with me from this point on!'

'Like fuck you are, slag!' Meserve shouted across the road. His partners stood firm beside the cars. Knoxx sat in the rear Toyota with Pope listening to the mêlée expectantly. Meserve shouldered his machine gun tighter in his shoulder, locking it into the side of his jaw for a firing position. He shouted, 'These maggots gonna take our boy? No fucking way, right or wrong?'

They all knew what time it was. It was time to get their money. Get busy and get down, because they weren't going to lie down.

Knoxx slid out from the rear seat. He knew what time it was too. Time for him to speak up before this standoff escalated into open warfare, knowing that the war was won before the battle had even begun. Getting out from the rear Toyota, he shouted towards the tank, 'I understand! I am who you want and I will come with you!'

His crew began to scream obscenities again, more at each other than anything else. They knew they were helpless to stop the inevitable. One way or another, this was going to go down as a loss. They knew they couldn't protect him. The battle tank in front of them told them that, as its heavy engine continued to spew out acrid smoke as it lurched forward, teasing them. Knoxx picked up his laptop case and put on his heavy winter jacket. He checked his watch. It was getting close to eleven o'clock at night. Doing the mental math in his head, he had approximately three hours to get it done.

'Listen bud, if I'm not back by two, you've got to take off and get the fuck out of this shit hole,' Knoxx said in a resolute tone to Matthews, who was standing with him beside the Toyota.

Matthews nodded quietly, responding with a soft, 'Yeah, okay.'

'I'm sorry, Mark. I don't know what to tell you,' Cameron said from inside the car.

Knoxx leaned in and gave him a hearty handshake, answering, 'Don't worry. You know how we do.' He chuckled, causing Cameron to laugh, not knowing what he'd meant by it. Mark continued, saying with boyish charm, 'The adventure doesn't begin until something goes wrong, mate.'

He slammed the car door closed and picked up his pace across the track. Eventually, he disappeared into the bright, blinding lights of the tank. All the crew could do was watch, listening as a crescendo of Serbian voices rang-out and various commands were given. The hustle and bustle of movement came from many more armed guards than Knoxx's crew had thought there were in the darkness, surrounding them. The tank's lights extinguished abruptly and the noises died down to peace and quiet. Not one thing moved in the still, cold air of the night. The night was blanketed in darkness again. The crew stood down as their fears kicked in. Knoxx was gone, lost to them.

'Oh, this is cute, don't you think?'

'Yeah, that's really nice. You should try that on,' Alisha replied.

Jane had a little black number held up to her neck, looking in the mirror. Then the two girls meandered from one clothes rack to the next. Both Alisha Ellington and Jane Mears had already amassed a pile of clothes to try on. The girls were in heaven, charging through the clothes stores of Paris, busy spending their hard-earned cash. The morning had been filled with bank wire instructions being e-mailed to numerous brokers, pharmaceutical purchasers, and hospital administrators, who all wanted a ticket to HEAVEN. Knoxx had woven his magic tale across Europe and the audiences had been mesmerized into buying shares as fast as the girls could offer them. Even though it was an official day off for them, both Jane and Alisha knew there was really no such thing, living a life in Exile with Mark.

'Money does not care where it lives or who it sleeps with, as long as it's earning sixteen percent a year, so you'd better stack it high,' he had always joked to them.

Both of them had learned their lessons well, and now Jane and Alisha were living an envious life travelling the world as V.I.P.'s wherever they went with Mark. But they were still girls, and they did what all girls loved to do, shop and gossip. Jane Mears had been seeing a guy on and off for around eighteen months in Los Angeles, when she had taken meetings with Matthew Tamban and Olivia Marbela, and when she had to check in on Christopher Wright. Jane was always saying that she felt Dave Kenshaw was playing her, and that she didn't see any real future in them becoming an item. Still, she called him frequently to let him know what she was up to with Mark and where she was in the world, in the hope that they could maintain a long-distance relationship.

Alisha had her own man troubles too. She had been seeing a dude from Australia who lived in London, named Greg Hammond, but she'd found it difficult to maintain a long distance relationship. Both girls were missing out on the one thing that money could not buy. Love.

'Hey, if Mark and I are both single by the time we're forty, maybe we'll end up getting married,' Alisha remarked playfully over dinner in BIZEN restaurant, at 111 Rue Reaumur in Paris. But Jane instantly thought, *Not in this lifetime.* She hid her scowl under her glass of Pinot as she lifted it up to her mouth to take a sip.

'I'd have to say, in response, that interest rates are still low, which makes cash unattractive, investing in companies whose holdings are influenced by any number of events, such as mergers, regulatory changes or even hurricanes. They can cause hard currency to be earned or lost just as easily in market movements. If we knew where and when, or if we know how or what will cause those markets to move up or down, then we could make huge sums of cash, that's all I'm saying.' Andrew Pierce stated disarmingly.

'I think I've found a man who'll play ball with us,' Tasker replied with some ease. He sat back in the deep sofa in the West Wing at the White House. Crossing his legs, he waited for the other shoe to drop in response to what he was suggesting. A new addition to the Rub a Dub Dub Club, that had grown into what some people called The Skulls; they now called themselves The Firm. Vice President Tasker had been receiving donations like no other presidential candidate in history, averaging twenty-five million dollars a quarter from party voters, well wishers, lobbyists, big business, and friends connected to The Firm.

Graham Stewart, known as The Pelican for his unrelenting, voracious appetite in acquiring distressed companies, was the first to retort Tasker's statement. Stephen Tasker's guest at the White House, interjected, 'I think oil and gas will keep bouncing around as long as we keep the Iraq War and the Middle East in turmoil for a while longer. I'd say they're about done in this cycle. In my opinion, we should be looking to the underlying demand in high grade industrial metals in emerging markets, such as India and China.'

'I see the same thing for REITS investments. Unless you're thinking of going overseas to invest in Real Estate Investment Trusts, I'd say they were pretty much played out here at home too,' Pierce, Tasker's real estate investment partner and property tycoon stated.

Tasker replied firmly, 'Well, if I'm going to hit a home run in the elections, I need something that'll benefit the people. I say we appeal to the gray dollar and go with the retirees, promoting healthcare for all.'

'My apologies for the treatment you received on the highway, Mr. Knoxx.'

'No problem, general. Please, call me Mark.'

'Only you must understand, things in my country are not yet, do I say, stable?' the general explained.

Knoxx answered plainly, 'Yes, I think that would be a fair assessment on the current status of the region, but I dare say, comrades such as yourself will one day bring it into line with the vision of the West.' Knoxx had said it in such a way; hoping the general would catch the sarcasm in his voice.

There were some blank stares for a moment throughout the room full of guards, who were looking at General Draganovic. Draganovic blinked, and then laughed hard as he got Knoxx's twisted joke. 'Very good, Mark, yes, I see your meaning.'

The big, burly Serbian general laughed a big, deep, bear-like laugh. It helped to ease the tension and the stink in the room that reminded Mark of a place he knew well, prison. General Draganovic, known throughout the Balkans as General Dragon, had been on The Hague's, Most Wanted list, for war crimes for around eleven years now. The problem the Western diplomats didn't realize when they were thumping the podium at the United Nations and in Brussels, was that he was both loved and feared by his people and the military in the region, who numbered in the tens of thousands. The West would have to mount a major offensive in military assets if it really wanted to bring him to trial.

Knoxx was sitting in an eighteenth century, gold leaf, high-back chair in a cave, some one hundred and ten feet below the ground, somewhere in the Balkan mountain ranges. He was alone again, finding himself seated next to power. Sipping on chilled nineteen eighty-seven Perrier Jouet champagne, a wry smile came over his face as a thought came to him. No one knew how to find him, and no one would ever know where his body was buried. He whispered, 'Huh, déjà-vu.'

Looking into his flute of champagne, he thought back to his time with Juicy in Mexico. He quickly snapped himself into gear and got his mind focused. He put on his game face, looking around at the artwork, exotic cars, and furnishings around the cave. He then saw five Fembot-looking Pamela Anderson clones hanging off of various furniture items in a back corner. Knoxx could tell he'd better move this one along and get back to basics. ABC, Always Be Closing. Knoxx flashed his patented, gold plated smile and began by saying disarmingly, 'Thank you for taking the time to see me, general.'

The general nodded in agreement.

Mark remarked, 'Please send my regards to your friends who're enduring the harshest of conditions.' He was referring to the Russian Mafiya members and Oligarchs that were in prison. He nodded again. Knoxx kept to his own S.O.P.: Standard Operating Procedures, breaking down the client, establishing a trust and building a friendship.

The general relaxed some and said, 'Please Mark, call me Dragon.'

His heavy, thick paw beckoned one of the Pamela Anderson lookalikes over from a chair. He made her stand at his side while he stroked her ass before pulling her down onto his lap. Mark was still going through his warm up but the general interrupted his opening without any regard for what he'd been saying. All Mark could do was bite his tongue, although he felt himself flush up in angst at how the meeting was going so far.

'I have heard many things about you, and many things about your playboy lifestyle.' Dragon forced out a gruff, low, hard tone as he began to eye up his Fembot babe, saying it in such a way that it sounded like a disrespectful jab at Knoxx's character. He turned to look at Mark, to check his reaction.

Knoxx lowered his champagne flute and leaned out from his chair to get a better look at Dragon's bloated head, as he held his stare and replied, 'The reason I'm in your magazines and on your news stations is because your country chooses to become more Westernized in its culture. The things they buy are what they've seen on television and in magazines. The young celebrities, actors, and models help drive those sales of merchandise, just by going to all the right nightclubs and staying at all the right hotels. This makes for very good business, yes?'

He looked deep into Dragon's face, waiting for his reaction. He looked wide-eyed, dissecting the words Knoxx had spoken. Mark cracked the slightest hint of a smile. Dragon brightened; his cheeks flushed at the nerve of it and then he let out a hearty laugh. The Fembot moved up and down on his lap while he laughed hard, his big hand repeatedly slapped her ass cheek hard. Knoxx quickly followed up by joking, 'The youth is wasted on the young, don't you think?'

The two laughed. Knoxx was breaking him down, chopping away at the big oak tree. 'The young, they all want the same things: clothes, bags, watches, and of course, the right car,' Knoxx said cheekily, while he glanced over at the row of expensive exotic cars. He then quipped, 'Everyone wants to be a star, even in Serbia.'

They laughed warmly again. Dragon was beginning to warm up to his guest. He raised his glass and Knoxx did the same in response. They toasted each other with a hearty smile. The oak tree was beginning to fall.

Knoxx said, 'And we get rich from making them all look and feel like stars, don't we, Dragon?' A raucous laugh rang-out around the room from the Serbian Bear.

'Why, yes we do, and as you can see, I have my very own star right here!' he replied, pulling at the Pamela Anderson look-alike. She was clearly used to being pawed by him; she gave no hint of any emotion. She was the perfect Fembot.

Knoxx took on a more serious, somber tone as he went onto explain, 'Having a high profile lifestyle affords me access to people who can help me with my businesses and are influential in helping me to grow my HEAVEN project. I'm a known and trusted face in America. Thanks to the media. I'm accepted by those in power. The American people wouldn't believe that we have met, because the media would not believe it, because my powerful friends would not allow them to believe it.'

'This has worked very well for you, Mark, yes? You are known by many influential politicians, businessmen and celebrities, no? You have dated many beautiful women – many - actresses and models.'

The general asked in a way that meant he clearly had something on his mind. He then went on to drink his vodka heavily. He pushed the Fembot off his lap and she dutifully returned to the chair with the other four Pamela lookalikes, who were sitting quietly, looking bored.

'What is it, Dragon?' Knoxx inquired in a low tone.

Dragon asked in a soft, childlike manner, 'I was wondering if you know Pamela Anderson?'

He looked at Knoxx like a six-year-old asking his mother for some candy.

Knoxx gained his composure and did his best not to let a smile slip in embarrassment.

Dragon then let slip. 'Mr. Pope said you probably did, and that you could get her to come visit me.'

Knoxx delayed his answer and thought about what Dragon had just said. What Cameron had said about him could be very dangerous. He answered loosely, 'Well, I've met her a few times; I guess you could say I know her. I'll tell you what. Maybe I can invite her to a club opening I might have here, and then I can arrange to introduce her to you.'

Dragon's eyes lit up like a Christmas tree, envisioning meeting his girl. His face flushed as he moved in his chair to take another hit of vodka. He then sat forward, drawing Knoxx in closer. He asked in a hushed tone, 'Please, Mark, I feel you are holding back. If you do not mind, I would like to hear more of your life in America.'

Glances were exchanged during a pregnant pause, but then Knoxx began to weave his magic, setting the scene. It was lights, camera, action. Show business. He spent the next twenty minutes swinging away at the oak tree, spinning stories about the women in America, enthralling Dragon with tales of Hollywood parties, giving him the inside stories on who was doing who. Dragon interrupted Mark occasionally to ask questions about how it all went down in New York, Miami, and Los Angeles. He knew he'd never be able to leave this cave, let alone walk amongst the stars in America. A look of pure delight and awe emanated from Dragon in wonder and amazement at how Knoxx was living his life. Knoxx described it all, and then finished up by making a joke, saying, 'Livin' mi vida loca.' 'Livin' my crazy life.'

Dragon's face looked at him in disbelief, asking, 'Do you really think you can introduce me to Pamela?'

Mark gave him a confident smile and said that it might be possible. Dragon looked over at his young charge standing against the wall, ever diligent and watchful, holding a pistol by his side. Knoxx glanced his way, seeing the young man stood at attention in his Chinese-made camouflaged uniform. He was in his mid-twenties, looking like a blond American hunk. He was General Dragon's Spetznaz Special Forces-trained bodyguard. He gave no acknowledgment that he'd heard most of what Mark had said, but inside, he wanted to go to Hollywood too, to see it for himself. Knoxx and Dragon raised their glasses. 'I can't believe it,' Dragon exclaimed with some excitement.

'Believe it, as you should believe in HEAVEN,' Knoxx calmly replied. Dragon immediately straightened in his chair. Knoxx had managed to segue into HEAVEN, and now he steeled his mind for the reason he was here in the first place.

Dragon immediately rebuffed his remark by answering, 'I should? You ask a lot to believe in. Most beliefs are handed down from generation to generation.' Looking inwardly perhaps, Dragon went further, explaining, 'Beliefs are about something, about a Cause. If you don't stand for something, then you'll fall for anything. A Cause is worth dying for, if you believe in it.' Filling his chest with pride, he looked over at his guard who filled his lungs and stood a little straighter, feeding off the general's words. He then said, 'Belief, Mark, is something one cannot see, hear, or touch. It is just a belief. A belief that what one is doing is right and just.' His voice trailed off reflectively, maybe thinking about his own path in life that had led him here, living in exile, living his life in caves because of his beliefs. He looked at Knoxx with some disdain, speaking in a harsh manner. 'You. I can see, hear, and touch. You are but a man, an ordinary man.'

He sank back in his chair. It seemed boredom was sinking in and he had run out of energy for being with Knoxx. Or was it just the realization of where he was in his life?

Mark hit back. 'You're right Dragon. I am an ordinary man. I'm no different than you or anyone else. I love beautiful things, like you do, and we share the same tastes in cigars, cars, and in our choice of women.'

Bringing a small smile out of him, Knoxx continued, 'When I was a young child growing up in a small town in England, I dreamed of such things, never thinking it would become real, when I had nothing but my dreams to comfort me at night. Do you remember your dreams?'

Dragon blinked, wondering where Mark was going with this statement.

Mark continued, 'I am an ordinary man. That is true. I'm just like you, but, we have both done, and shall do, extraordinary things together, if only you dare to dream again. But first, you must believe. You talk about belief. I believe that beliefs come from stories and legends that are handed down from one loved one to the next, to serve as warnings or guide posts for the younger generation to learn from. But how do we know these stories and legends are true?'

Dragon was now totally absorbed in what Knoxx was saying. Even the wrong words rhymed as he kept his words soft and his tempo steady. Waving his baton from side to side, the soft tune played in Dragon's head while he danced along with Knoxx to the tune of destiny. Mark had all the time in the world. He just wanted to close out the show. Allowing his thread of words to weave their way around Dragon, so they could hang him on his earlier words, Mark closed him strong, saying, 'because, we believe in the source, don't we?'

Dragon knew Mark had him and softened his look, giving him his own brand of acknowledgment by way of the slightest of nod in agreement accompanied by a gruff snort. He realized where Knoxx was taking him on this journey. At least he thought he did.

Knoxx pulled out a one dollar bill from his pocket. He held it up for Dragon to see, and then he snapped it tight. It made a crisp, snap sound as he held it in his hands between both his thumbs and forefingers. He stated, 'The almighty dollar. It is nothing but colored paper, yes?'

Dragon nodded along as he spoke. 'Yet people all over the world crave it and desire it, wanting to accumulate as much of it as possible.' Turning the bill over in his hand, Knoxx read aloud what was printed on it. 'In God We Trust. Yet no one can see, hear, or touch God, can they? Yet they can see, feel, and hear their delight at what the dollar can bring them.

Pleasure. People wish to collect the dollar, just like you, but why?'

Dragon looked vague at this line of questioning, but he sat motionless, staying on point, listening intently to every detail so as not to miss a word, just as Knoxx had planned.

'Because, as you believe in the dollar as a trusted currency, you believe in America and its economy. This one dollar bill represents the power of the United States as a world leader and that America promises to make good on this piece of paper. But why do you believe that? You, yourself know the state of America's economy. You know that its trade deficit is out of control, and you know that America is failing in the war in Iraq and in Afghanistan.'

Mark then passed the dollar bill to Dragon. All part of Knoxx's show, but now it was time for the business half of his show business routine.

He asked, 'You believe in this currency, don't you? You believe in what it represents and that it has remained the trusted currency throughout this last century. You know the reality of what it represents, and yet you still trust it. Why? Because you trust its source. You believe America will make good on its promise to pay, knowing what you know, more than most, about America and its policies. Yet you still choose to believe in such a thing?' Lowering his voice even further, he caused Dragon to listen more intently to every word. He delivered his final sermon, the death of the American economy, continuing by explaining, 'All because of this piece of paper? That's a lot to believe in, general, isn't it? The only thing constant in the universe is change. Change starts with one person's belief, with what they believe to be true in their heart. Then this belief is passed onto a loved one, and so on, down through generations, and over time it's just something we simply believe. HEAVEN will change the way people live and die. You can believe in that.'

General Dragon opened up a cigar box and lit a cigar, offering one to Mark. He declined. Dragon exhaled his cigar and then took a hit of vodka. He thought about the words that Knoxx had threaded together to weave the magic jacket that was now draped over his broad shoulders, weighing heavily on him.

Cameron Pope had told Mark that a rogue general in The Balkans was looking to invest some gold bullion into a secure venture that would return his investment in U.S. dollars to any designated bank in the world. This general, Cameron went onto say, could not travel and the gold could not be sold on the gold exchange. Therein lies the problem, Cameron had explained. Mark had given it some thought and had soon come up with a solution to the problem, only he'd have to meet the general in person to explain his proposition.

Pope eventually told him that it was General Draganovic who needed the gold moved. Mark did his research in advance of meeting him and discovered that he was one of the last Empire holdouts from the Cold War; Draganovic had waged his own war against The West during the Serb-Croat war throughout the nineties. He had led the race in ethnic cleansing and was now on Interpol's Most Wanted list. General Dragon was reduced to being a criminal at large, running his private army in the pursuit of his survival. He represented the interests of the Russian Mafiya families, controlling the flow of drugs to The West; he had also helped himself to over a hundred million dollars worth of gold, cash, and art from various wealthy landowners along the way, over the past decade. With an army to pay and feed, Dragon needed to move the gold and Knoxx was looking for funding in HEAVEN. The two were a match made in heaven.

'Cameron has explained some of your plan Mark. I have to say, I am intrigued by your plan to convert the gold into a debenture note that can then be used to underwrite the development of a property in London. Cameron told me you were bright, and I have to say, I am in agreement,' Dragon imparted. Knoxx decided to shut up and listen, nodding along in all the right places, while he let Dragon talk himself into the deal. This was another one of Knoxx's rules. No one likes to be sold, but everyone likes to buy, and right now, Dragon was buying it. He said, 'Cameron told me that you two are partners. He also let me in on your other business.' With a dry, smug smile scrawled across his face, he asked, 'Maybe you can introduce me to your cocaine supplier in America? Maybe I can be a source of distribution for you here throughout the East?'

Knoxx nodded back warmly with a soft smile. While he looked like he was considering the offer, but inside, a hurricane raged, tearing through his mind, knowing he'd never spoken to Pope about his ties to Juicy. Cameron had no business meddling in his affairs, and definitely had no business passing along any information he'd found out about him to anyone, especially to a guy like Dragon. Knoxx held a stiff upper lip, being the consummate British gentleman; he let Dragon continue talking himself into the deal, thinking, *one thing at a time, ABC.* Knoxx blinked as though a light breeze had washed across his face while he listened to the general's ramblings. Dragon was unaware that he had given Knoxx a key piece of information. Mark answered a couple of mundane questions, realizing that Dragon had bought into the deal but he didn't want to look like a lay down in front of his men. So Mark obliged him, while they went through the motions of getting to the close.

Mark said, 'I'll arrange to have the gold smelted, and then

get it stamped under a new bank code. I'll then have it placed in a friendly bank's vault, where it will sit for the next hundred years. The bank will use the gold as an asset at its next valuation, where it will then receive additional funding from The World Bank. The bank will then extend a line of credit against our collateralized loan for the construction of a property in London, which will coincidentally amount to the seventy-five million dollars that you have given me in gold. Once the property has been bought, refurbished, and sold, I will then funnel the money through to HEAVEN as an investment, for you to make more money on.' Cracking a smile, Knoxx continued, 'Once this final transaction's completed, you'll have liquid funds that can be sent to any bank throughout the world.'

Knoxx was aware that the clock was running. He finally heard the buying statement from Dragon that meant he could seal the deal. 'I like what I've heard. I think we can do business.'

'Don't just think you'd like to do business, Dragon. Dare to dream, and you'll love doing business with me even more,' Knoxx replied firmly. He could see that Dragon had shaped a smile on his face in agreement.

Dragon replied timidly, 'Okay, let's do it.'

Mark quickly leaned across from his chair to extend his hand. Gripping Dragon's big paw, he said, 'I'd say you've just bought yourself a ticket to Heaven.'

'Damn good to see you, slag!' Matthews shouted, once he saw that Knoxx was making his way back across the track road from behind enemy lines.

Knoxx happily answered, and then asked, 'Walk in the park, mate. Had a lovely chat with a cuddly bear. Now, can we get the fuck out of here?'

They all walked back to the cars, patting each other on the back as they realized they were going to come out of this in one piece after all. Knoxx was walking back to the rear Toyota with Matthews and Meserve, when he pulled back on Meserve's arm, asking bluntly, 'You got a pistol?' Meserve nodded affirmatively. Mark said, 'Give me it.'

Knoxx slid into the backseat of the rear Toyota and got comfortable. He sat next to Pope who was looking relieved to see his safe return. He asked gingerly, 'How'd it go? I told you he was an interesting fellow, didn't I?'

'Yeah, he sure was, and I got some interesting things from him that I didn't think I'd get,' Knoxx answered cryptically, as the cars took off into the night, heading back to the airplane. After approximately one and a half hours of driving through the wind and rain, Knoxx told Meserve that he needed to pull over for him to take a leak; Meserve said he could do with one too. Flashing the car's headlights at the car ahead, both cars pulled up to a stop.

Knoxx asked in a disarming manner, 'You stretching your legs for a minute, Cam?'

'Sure. I'll grab a quick smoke.' Pope replied.

He slid out from the car and quickly walked around to the back, and then stomped his feet, using the Toyota Four Runner to shield him from the wind. Knoxx slid out from his side of the car and walked around to meet him at the back. When Cameron Pope looked up from lighting his cigarette, he was looking at the business end of a nine millimeter Beretta that Knoxx was pointing at his face. Mark said hard, 'You should read the warning label on that pack of smokes, mate.'

Pope went to speak, but as he began to open his mouth, Knoxx pulled the trigger. Pope was killed instantly. Knoxx turned to Matthews and said, 'If he'll tell you a small lie, then he'll tell you a big lie.' He then looked down at Pope's body, and said disingenuously, 'Smoking can kill.'

'Mark, you know the benefit night's coming up in two weeks, right? Have you got a date for the night; someone who'll actually know something about you, and not just stand there all night smiling as per her contract?' Jane asked sarcastically.

Mark had hung up the phone, having just said his goodbyes to his mom and dad, Maggie and Danny, back in Bournemouth, England. Jane was having a good laugh at his expense. He began to mash together a breakfast he'd had delivered from Clarke's restaurant on 1st Street to the Exile offices in Miami Beach, which overlooked the Intercoastal Highway. Jane leaned across the table and picked off one of his bacon rashers. Mark took it all in his stride, knowing it was how he and Jane worked together in life.

He said, with some fun in his voice, 'How about I take you as my date, seeing as how that twat Dave Kenshaw you're supposed to be dating probably won't turn up anyway. I'll get you something special to wear for the night. God knows, you've needed some new gear since we got back from Europe a couple of months ago. I think I've seen every outfit you've bought from there.'

'Shut up, pig!' Jane answered sternly, looking just as sternly at him, breaking out a swift punch to Knoxx's shoulder. For all of Jane's fierce stances and strong-willed scowling that she put out for the world to see, she was still a girl, and Jane could easily be hurt by the smallest of things, especially from Mark. It felt like pure white snowflakes falling from Heaven that had landed ever so softly, melting on her face. The smallest of things meant the biggest of things to Jane, and Mark knew it. She brushed him off, telling him not to be so silly, inviting her as his date, but inside, Jane loved that he had asked her. Mark didn't make any dates for that night, even though she kept blowing him off over the next few days. He knew Jane better than she knew herself, at times, and Mark knew that she was just playing hard to get, saying that she didn't even know if she'd be going. Mark knew she'd be going to the 9/11 Charity benefit at NVS in New York, and he knew she'd end up going with him as his date.

The briefing room stayed quiet while Teresa Hadley described the findings of the forensics accounting she'd undertaken on Mark Knoxx and Exile. His had numerous joint-ventures and investment positions in layered offshore companies. Hadley had been finding it difficult to stay on track herself, describing them, much less making her colleagues understand what it all meant. Most of the companies were blind trusts in offshore accounts that were out of the United State's jurisdiction. Under the instruction of Maxine Dobro, Teresa had done her best in pushing home the point that it all meant that Mark Knoxx was involved in criminal endeavors and that, at the very least he was involved in evading income taxes.

'So we can get him on income tax evasion. That's what you're telling us Agent Hadley?'

Looking around the table at his colleagues, Deputy Director Christie asked in an agitated voice, 'Why am I even here? Why not just hand this case over to the I.R.S.? Then we can move on to bigger and better things.'

He swung around in his chair, looking to get out from under the table. At around forty-nine years old, Christie had managed to keep his boyish looks. He still had a boyish charm up to a point beneath his jet-black hair and eyes. But when he was annoyed, as he was now, those looks turned darker. Maxine leaned over to catch his arm. Yet again, over the past two months, she had managed to coax him into taking another meeting on Knoxx and Exile, affording her one more trip to New York. Christie had said, in an earlier conversation, that this would be the last time they would be meeting to talk about this case.

'There's simply nothing here to warrant tying up our resources on him or his companies. If it comes down to tax evasion, then we have to let the I.R.S. have it. Let them have it Maxine. They'll get him. Hell, if you want him that bad, why don't you come along to his 9/11 benefit at NVS tonight and ask him yourself if he's involved in some international conspiracy,' Christie said in a derogatory manner, while the other agents snickered at his sarcastic remark.

Teresa spoke up for Maxine, saying coolly, so as to make sure the invitation would include her, 'That'd be great; I'd love the opportunity to ask him about the bank accounts and what they're being used for.'

Maxine's eyes sparkled, as she chimed in to add, 'Great, then I guess we're in!'

Even before the Maybach had pulled up to the curb, a wall of strobe lights was already immersing the car, bathing it in a bubble of white light. The Maybach's license plate had given it away as to who was in the car, with the plate reading, EXILE. Mark Knoxx stepped out, looking every inch the movie star, wearing a black designer suit, black shirt, gray tie, with a touch of deep red from a strategically placed silk handkerchief in his breast pocket. The camera flashes continued as he turned back to help his escort out of the Maybach. Jane Mears exited the car and stood up while a sea of white light drowned her from camera flashes. She did her best to stay composed and not laugh her ass off and lose it in front of the paparazzi. It all seemed so silly to her, as she began to walk up the red carpet on Mark's arm, giggling like a naughty schoolgirl who had snuck in on someone else's prom night.

'This is cool, isn't it? Strike the pose, c'mon, Madonna style!'

Jane stopped for one more paparazzi love fest, doing her best to maintain a model-type pout, all in good fun. Mark knew she was making fun of them and of him, which was why he knew he loved Jane. She never cared for the bright city lights or the big paydays; Jane only cared for him. He stood off to the side to watch Jane strike the pose. He laughed while he watched her enjoying every second of her time in the sun. He knew she would, once he had finally talked her in to coming with him as his date. Mark managed to get himself into the mood of the evening, which was to give somber praise for the men and women from the police, fire and rescue services, who had lost their lives in the World Trade Center, 9/11 tragedy. He spent the better part of ten minutes giving interviews and extolling the bravery that they and their families had shown.

Upon Knoxx's arrival, the evening got underway. The 9/11 benefit held at NVS in New York was a star-studded event that would raise millions of dollars for the victims' families, but it would turn out to be an evening that would change history, and his story.

74

'I've lived the best part of my life in the pursuit of my own happiness. But the men and women of the emergency services give so much of their own lives to others that they are the real heroes. In today's society, our kids look to all the media-generated celebrities as their heroes, and they aspire to be like them, but our real heroes are the unsung nondescript, everyday people we pass on the street. I like to say, it's not what you know or who you know, but who knows you, and that's the opportunity we're all being given here tonight, the opportunity to get to know these wonderful men and women from the fire, police, and medical services. Thank you, Helen,' Knoxx wrapped up the interview with one of his favorite reporters, Helen Stacey, who followed his every move on the celebrity circuit. Knoxx then moved inside with his entourage.

'Now I know why you pay those models. My bloody feet are killing me! Don't ever ask me to be your date again,' Jane said, in a joking but firm manner. 'C'mon, let's get a drink.' She leaned on Mark's arm as they entered the huge space that was NVS.

Olivia Marbela was one of the first people Mark picked out as he arrived inside. He walked over to her table to congratulate her on doing a first class job in getting all the right sponsors and celebrities involved. He looked at Matt Tamban and asked him, in a curt manner, 'Everything good back in L.A.?'

'Everything's good. No problems,' Matt replied, meaning that Chris Wright was behaving himself.

'This way, Mark.' Knoxx was shown the way to his table by Hickes, who was there to keep an eye on him with his partner Yarward. Mark and Jane walked across to their table, where various guests were already seated. Everyone greeted them with smiles as Mark and Jane arrived, while Mark made his way around the table to greet each one.

They had been strategically placed around the table by Alisha Ellington, who had seated herself immediately across from Mark. He leaned down and gently placed a soft kiss on her cheek, saying warmly, 'You look great, Ali, real good, honey.'

Jane watched Mark intently from her chair, while she choked down on some Pinot Grigio white wine.

75

Another set of eyes had been watching the circus roll in to town. Choking down on her glass of wine, Maxine Dobro sat a few rows back from the V.I.P. section. She and a few of New York's F.B.I. heavy hitters were there, as was Teresa Hadley. Most of the evening had been spent gossiping about the who's who that had sauntered by, or about a celebrity that had been spotted. NVS was filled to the rafters with the movers and shakers from the business world, the entertainment business and political figures who'd been flown in for the event on Exile's dime from the West Coast and overseas. Mark made a point of spending some time flirting and charming his way into the good books with Pamela Anderson. She had been flown in on the Exile Jet and given a suite at the NVS Hotel in Midtown Manhattan. Mark was soon working Pamela in a way that let her know there was no such thing as a free lunch. He soon got around to asking her if she wouldn't mind making a phone call to one of his friends. He spent a full hour speaking with the mayor of New York, the police chief and the governors for both New York and California. Maxine noticed from her table, a very brief, seemingly innocuous chat at the bar between Knoxx and Christie. Both of them smiled as if they were sharing a joke. Knoxx then squeezed his forearm in a familiar way while they shook hands, she thought, as she watched them say their goodbyes at the bar.

Jane had resigned herself to drinking a few more glasses of Pinot, and by now, she was wishing she had stayed at home. She spoke to people she had never met before or could have cared less to meet, while her eyes scanned the room to pick out her perfect Mark. Having caught his eye, he could tell it was time to spend some time with Jane. She had always done so much for him; she knew so much about him, he knew she loved him.

The opening act got underway. Mary J. Blige came on the stage and got the crowd jumping. The night's top billing, Bruce Springsteen, closed out his set. Two hours of Heaven. Jane had worked herself into a happy place and loved the night's entertainment. Alisha Ellington shook her booty at the front of the table, making sure that Mark noticed her. He felt the heat from Jane's piercing eyes, making sure his eyes were on the stage and not Alisha's ass. He played along, mockingly staring at Alisha's gyrating body, earning himself a quick fire punch from Jane and then laughter, kisses and squeezes, as they both knew it was all just a put-on by Mark to make Jane laugh.

During the intermission, there was enough of a lull for Knoxx to make a round of the club and say 'Hi' to the guests who really mattered this evening, the families of the 9/11 heroes, who were seated at the tables with invited guests from the police, fire and medical services. He stopped at each table, speaking, joking, and having his photo taken with them. Each table had a place card on it, so everyone knew who they were seated next to, and Knoxx was now walking amongst the New York Police Department. If only these everyday cops knew who they were having their picture taken with, and shaking hands with. While Knoxx smiled, he was shadowed by his hired killers, Ian Hickes and Drew Yarward. Ever the showman, he regally laid his hand on a guest's shoulder, causing him to look up to see him ask, 'Good evening, I just wanted to say hi, and make sure you're having a good time.'

The man shook Knoxx's hand in a happy, two-bottles-of-wine, four-whiskey's kind of way, thanking him for a great night. Everyone was having a good time, waiting to shake his hand as he made his way around the huge, circular table. He glanced up and caught someone's eye seated four seats ahead of him around the table. An attractive brunette exploded into a radiant smile with stunning laser-like, hazel eyes that watched him in action while he worked the table, moving closer to her. Knoxx felt instantly excited by her; he liked her look and he liked the way she was looking at him. He finally edged his way around to her seat. He watched her move her chair out slightly to get a better look at him. For what felt like the millionth time tonight, Mark began to make his introduction, but at the last minute he decided to change it up, as an electric tingle shot right through him as they shook hands.

He hovered for a second while she held his stare unfazed, fixed on his eyes for what seemed an eternity, before he gave it his shot, asking, 'Hi, I trust you have everything you could've wished for. Your wish is my command.' She chuckled politely while Mark changed his tack and asked, 'Seriously, though, are you having a good time? Because if there's anything I can do to make your evening more enjoyable, you only have to tell me and I'll do whatever I can to make it happen.'

The woman replied, by asking in good fun, 'How about your name for starters, then we'll see.'

He duly obliged her wish, answering sharply, 'Now that I can do. The name's Knoxx, Mark Knoxx.'

He said it in such a way that it sounded like he was emulating the man himself, turning on his elegant British accent, trying to lay down his A-Game. The brunette giggled, only now she seemed to be laughing at him and not with him.

'Very James Bond, I must say. You sound like you're a real secret agent, having people killed, involved in underworld activities, owning secret offshore bank accounts. I'd love to hear all about your 007 escapades, Mr. Knoxx, I really would.'

She began looking in her purse for something while Knoxx hovered over her in no man's land, unsure of what to do and what to say. 'Aah, here we are.' She then looked back up at him, to say sarcastically, 'Maybe you've heard of me? Special agent Teresa Hadley with FinCEN, the Financial Crimes and Enforcement Network. I'd love to spend some time getting to know you better, do you think that'll be possible?'

Teresa Hadley's eyes remained steady and assured. She may have been in Knoxx's lair, but he had gotten caught in her web and she had caught him off guard. Hadley sat with her eyes locked onto his while she waited for his reply.

He answered coolly, 'I'm sure you know all you're ever going to know. All that 007 stuff is for the movies, but remember Bond always gets the girl in the end. Some other time then. Don't worry; I know how to find you.'

He handed Hadley her business card back and gave her a wink with a small trigger finger salute. He began to move off, all smiles as if he did not have a care in the world. He glanced past Hadley's seat and fixed his eyes on her, two seats ahead of him. Knoxx had seen a ghost. Maxine Dobro had him squarely in her sights and there was no hint of pleasantry on her face. He flicked his eyes to the name badge on the table that told him he was at the F.B.I.'s table. His rage consumed him once he realized this was all a set up and he had been trapped in his house on his night. Smiling a million dollar smile, he gave Maxine a small nod in recognition. She did the same, with no smile accompanying it. Teresa's words stung as he heard her shout over to Maxine, in an even more sarcastic tone, 'He thinks he's James Bond!'

Hadley, Dobro and some F.B.I. agents laughed as if they were mocking him while Dobro did her best to catch his eye one last time. Mark couldn't bring himself to acknowledge that he had heard the remark, as that would have given them the upper hand. He felt embarrassed and angry. The rage and torment welled up inside him, as he thought, *I've come so far and achieved so much, and now I'm giving so much back to the world through HEAVEN, and this little pea-ant bitch is ruining it all.* He thought of himself as the King of New York. Who was this nobody, fucking his night up, trying to destroy his life? No pencil neck, nine-to-fiver was going to bring him down, no way.

'Mark! Mark! Can we get a photograph with you?' he heard as he walked away. A new group of police men and women had lassoed him. Knoxx dutifully obliged and let them lean on him for a photo. He looked as smooth as silk and acted as cool as ice, posing for the photograph, while only one thought screamed inside his head. *I'm going to kill the bitch.*

NVS had been jumping all night and those who had not been able to get tickets for the night's event were truly envious. Those inside got to dance and schmooze with those they wanted to meet or to bend an ear on certain issues. Everyone who needed to be there was there. Knoxx got up on stage to give a rousing speech about the amazing qualities of the men and women of the fire, police and medical services.

Coming to the end of it, he said, 'who get up every day and face death at every turn. Sometimes, it can be one of your own.' He picked Dobro out at the F.B.I.'s table as he said it. 'But for the most part, it's other people's lives you are trying to save. Their lives are in your hands, hanging on a thread. In your arms, lying in an Angel's arms sent from Heaven. Many of us will never know the names of these faceless heroes who aren't just around for the huge disasters like 9/11, but are here to help us all every day. All it takes is seconds for them to save a life. That's all it takes, seconds, between life and death. Please, everyone, raise your glass and stand to salute our heroes.'

The crowd erupted into a chorus of shouts, whistles and applause, while Knoxx was joined on stage by the mayor of New York, Matthew Senior, and Halle Berry to hand out awards, accolades and some surprise vacation packages to the families of those first responders who had died in the 9/11 tragedy. Mayor Senior then got down to the business of the auction to raise money for the victims' fund.

'Now, let's get this party started, right! We've got some more dancing to do!' Halle Berry shouted in the microphone after the auction finished. The crowd began to get up from their seats and walk towards the stage, as the next performer kicked off the final act of the evening. The curtains drew back, and under a single pinpoint spotlight, out stepped an hour-glass figure with long tresses of blonde hair, wrapped up in a tight, electric pink dress. The singer's name was Nicole Young, and she had the voice of an angel. She sang a soft Sade number as her opening song that brought the crowd to their feet. Knoxx gazed up at her and she brought him to his knees. In an instant, he knew, she was the one.

The entertainment channels were beaming the NVS benefit throughout the U.S. Some of the tabloid shows were analyzing what the guests were wearing, and who was seen with what star from the celebrity world of actors, musicians, and models. Mark Knoxx was shown speaking to Helen Stacey, a tabloid entertainment reporter, before going in to NVS for the night's event.

'Fuckin' faaggss. C'mon, we gonna have our own party.'

Bezerk leaned over a glass coffee table and took two lines of cocaine, snorting it hard through his nostrils. He then fell back hard against the back rest of the couch beside his date for the night. Some girl he didn't know the name of, having picked her up in NVS the night before. Her eyes were vacant under her long, fiery red hair, as if she was sitting in God's waiting room. Tavo and Beaver were already high, as they took their own hits of cocaine. They were in Bezerk's Hollywood Hills home on Oak Glen Drive, overlooking the bright city lights of Los Angeles sitting in a five thousand square foot mansion that had cost two and a half million dollars. Bezerk got up and walked out to the pool. Howling at the moon, drunk, high and wild, he was mad at the moon, mad at the world, mad at himself and mad at Mark.

'Fuck man, is this it? Pinche puto, you know what I mean?'

Having heard him shouting, Tavo ventured out of the house after him, asking, 'What's up, homey? Fuck, dog, look around you fool. What you gotta be so pissed about?'

Ambling out to the patio, Beaver asked, as he leaned up against the patio doors, 'What the fuck can be so wrong? Look where we come from, this's gangster's paradise, man!'

Bezerk looked around at them in a wild-eyed way, high as heaven. Then he leaned back until he almost fell backwards, while he was holding a bottle of Quervo Gold in his hand. With his arms spread wide, he howled at the moon, shouting his heart out, 'Yeah booyy, I'iiss gonna fuck you uupp for reeaals! Yeess siirr, belieeve thaatt!'

'Naa, fuck that, man, we've done enough scores in this town, and it's gettin' too hot.'

The four men were either sitting or standing about the penthouse suite at the Palms Hotel and Resort in Las Vegas, Nevada. It was getting late, both in the hour of the day and in the time that they could safely stay in Vegas. After nearly an hour of heated discussion, their leader, Joel Casa was beginning to run out of patience with his hot headed Club Bangers crew, with Nick Zacarro drawing most of the heat. Joey ignored what Nick Zacarro had been saying, and said matter-of-factly, 'You and Nick head to L.A. Me and Franz are gonna go case the Cabo Wabo joint down in Cabo and see if there's a shot at us taking it down. Then we can all move onto Cancun and get ourselves some Señoritas, then we can retire and live like Kings.'

'What the fuck?' Nicky Z responded like a spoiled kid, going on to say, 'How come he gets to go to Mexico and I gotta go to L.A.? No disrespect, J-Rock, but hey, Mexico beats L.A. hands down!'

J-Rock didn't take any offense as he thought the same thing. Casa took back control of the room once again, explaining it to them one more time.

'Listen, paisano, we're too hot for all us to go together right now. We can still pull off a couple of good scores in L.A. before we drive down to Mexico. Besides, I got a hook-up on a crew in L.A. that can help us score some guns and new I.D.'s. And they can point us in the right direction on what clubs to take down. I got some things to tie-up. Me and Franz are going down to Cabo and you and J-Rock are heading to L.A. and that's how it's gonna be, you gotta problem with that?'

Casa stepped away from the bar, and Zacarro stepped down.

The Club Bangers had been working nicely together for nearly two years now, but they had all felt it. Felt it on their collars, felt in their gut, and even felt it when they took a piss. They all felt the end coming. They had been feeling the pressure, knowing every State Trooper had their photograph from having hit so many banks, bars, and nightclubs as they made their way across the country. Joel Casa and Nick Zacarro were childhood friends and had worked their way up through the ranks of the Cherry Hill, New Jersey mob, committing petty crimes, working their way up to becoming hired guns for the New York Mafia. Joel Casa carried himself with a number two-buzzed haircut atop his six foot three, two hundred and thirty-two pound, muscular frame. His cool, breezy charm and cool-as-ice blue eyes helped him to score chicks any place, anytime. Casa was born to lead and his partner, Nick Zacarro, was born to follow him. He was only one year younger, but seemed much younger because of his lack of world knowledge. As the younger, slightly shorter and leaner of the two, Nicky Z took up the role of younger brother, and like a younger brother, needed his older brother to help him out in a jamb.

One such time was nearly two years earlier in a bar called Breeze, where Nicky Z had taken a liking to a young, hot, blonde singer named Nicola Cowper. She had finished her set and gone back to her boyfriend and his two friends at their booth. Nicky Z sent over a chilled bottle of champagne that was quickly followed by his drunken presence. Confident in the TNT he carried in both hands, all three men soon found out they had their hands full, as soon as the boyfriend protested at his arrogance in coming over to their table. When a fight broke out, one guy moved it up a notch when he made his move and pulled a gun. Nicola Cowper could only watch in morbid horror as things quickly turned from bad to worse. Only seconds before, she had been wearing a smile, but now she was wearing her dead boyfriend's blood sprayed across her face. Having seen the fight, Casa had stepped through the crowd just in time to see the guy's gun being drawn. In the heat of the moment he had drawn his gun and slain the three men. They had grown up watching Mafia movies, and now they were starring in their own. Nicola Cowper's boyfriend was the son of a New York Mafia made guy, causing Joey Casa and Mike Zacarro to beat their feet that night, or have to face the consequences.

They were destined to live a life in exile from their friends and family, on the run from their New York crime family. Nicola Cowper disappeared that night, too. She would never forget Joel Casa. And Joel Casa would never forget Nicola Cowper.

79

'Guess what?' Mark said to Jane excitedly, having hurried back to sit down next to her at the table. He thought a moment; *Take care of the ABC's*. He'd take care of those bitches soon enough. Now though, his mind was only on one thing. He was acting like a love struck puppy as Jane laughed and asked him, 'Yeah, what?'

Mark took a swig of wine while he savored the view on the stage in front of him. Finally, he leaned in to Jane to say, with a smile on his face, as if he was going to break into a laugh, 'I've just seen the future ex-Mrs. Mark Knoxx, honey.'

Jane laughed hard, having heard that line many times over the past twenty years. She replied, as if she did not believe it, 'Oh yeah, where?'

Mark didn't answer her. She just followed his stare up to the stage and her eyes looked again, this time more deeply at the singer while she moved about the stage, gliding effortlessly, holding the audience's gaze. Her songs ranged from Sade to Alicia Keys, Beyoncé, and then on to some old school Elaine Page classics. Nicole Young panned her eyes across the audience as part of her stage act, which had been honed at an early age. She had worked on the cruise ships to get away from her old life, turning up as a marquee act in the top hotels along the West Coast. Nicole found her eyes drifting back to table number one, back to the number one guy sitting at the table while she sang on stage. She recognized him as Mark Knoxx.

'Mark, you always say that,' Jane said as she held onto Mark's arm.

Answering thoughtfully, 'I know. But hey, you know what? I need a sunrise right about now; I'm tired of only seeing sunsets.'

Jane gulped back hard and put her sweaty hand on Mark's, gripping it tightly, understanding what he meant. She always knew, replying, 'Aah honey, I love you. Everything will be alright.'

Jane knew they had checked in at the gates of Hell, and had read the sign hanging there: Come Back Later. Jane looked at Mark and realized he would never love her the way she wanted him to. She would forever be cast as Cinderella, never getting to go to the ball with him as her Prince Charming and live happily ever after. Jane searched Mark's face, and then she turned away and looked up again at the stage, and said with a heavy heart, 'She's very beautiful, Mark.'

'Are you having a good time? Let me hear you say, yeah!'

Nicole Young shouted to the crowd and they shouted back, 'Yeeaahh!'

Her routine was tight, her set was tight, and her tight ass had Knoxx mesmerized. She moved around the stage, making eye contact with members of the audience and pointing out to some of them. Nicole Young was working the crowd, working them hard. And that was just what Knoxx was feeling between his legs, watching her from his seat. He summoned the waiter over to the table. After taking the order from the boss, the waiter quickly walked over to Olivia Marbela's table. She looked over at Knoxx while the waiter relayed his message to her. She gave Mark an understanding nod, and then got up from her seat and walked off into the crowd. Knoxx wrote a note on a napkin:

You can have one dream come true, and if you're gonna dream, then dream big!
Thanks for putting on a great show.
I look forward to seeing the next one.

Mark Knoxx. Xx

The note was partnered up with twelve pink roses that were delivered to Nicole Young's dressing room. All the guests danced along with her as she belted out the hits for the next hour. She carried them through the 80's, 90's and then onto the current hits of the day. All the tables had emptied out as the audience got up onto the dance floor to dance, clap, and sing along with her. Jane had got up from her chair and was enjoying the evening, bouncing along happy in her own way. Alisha and the rest of the Exile team did the same. Knoxx leaned back in his chair to stretch and looked out across the dark expanse of NVS from the V.I.P. section. His eyes fell upon the outline of a figure seated in the darkness that was looking at him. From where the table was located, he determined it could only be one person: Maxine Dobro.

He felt himself becoming angry again, in spite of it all. As hard as he tried, he felt himself becoming consumed with hatred and vengeance for this woman who had the balls to bring it to him in his own house. He motioned for Ian to come over. Then he got up to go to the restroom to cool off, thinking, *I'm gonna handle my business. They'll be sorry.*

'See what you can do about getting table 268 taken out of here, would you?'

Hickes promptly stopped thirty paces from the men's room while Knoxx continued walking through the empty void. He didn't care how it looked to anyone else. It was his night and his show, and he wanted her and them out of here. Thinking about how he was untouchable, he muttered, 'I'm King-fucking-Kong around here. I always handle my business.'

As he approached the men's room, his mind was racing with several different thoughts flashing through it. A male figure stepped out into his path, cutting him off. He had crystal blue, piercing eyes and dishwater blond hair, with a hint of gray in it. The man made his presence felt, as he intended, by cutting Mark off. Knoxx immediately caught his vibe and tensed up. Knoxx put the man at about fifty. He had caught him by his bicep, gripping it in an authoritative way. Looking hard into his eyes, he said sternly, 'Mr. Knoxx, we need to talk.'

He tried to get Knoxx to walk with him in some other direction, but Knoxx dug in and stood stock-still, determined not to walk in any direction. He immediately looked back at Ian, who had been speaking with one of the security team. Upon seeing this man confronting his boss, Ian began a brisk walk towards them. Knoxx looked at the man and said, 'It's time for you to be leaving too, asshole.'

The former British military Special Air Services specialist and kick boxing bad-ass, Hickes, arrived and immediately broke the man's grip on Mark. He stepped in between them, saying, 'Anything I can do you for, mate?'

The man paid Hickes no mind. He still seemed to carry a coy smile as if he was amused by the scene. He replied by speaking directly to Knoxx, saying, 'I can assure you, seeing me now is in your best interests. Or I'll just go and drop a file I have with me, somewhere here, on the F.B.I.'s table with the photographs of Cameron Pope, before and after, if you like?'

Standing at around five foot eight, and weighing in at around a hundred and eighty-five pounds, he was clearly no match for Hickes or Knoxx, but he seemed to take delight in standing toe-to-toe with them. With conviction of purpose, his piercing blue eyes looked at Knoxx without any hint of doubt. He took out a business card and seemed to offer it up as some kind of token peace offering, extending his hand to Knoxx. He stepped out from behind Hickes and accepted it.

It was an ivory white card with black embossed lettering on it. It had printed on it:

MMI Enterprises, Inc.
Paul Deavins
0012 1067 285 3219

'You can make an appointment with my personal assistant. She'll make sure you get to see me,' Knoxx stated in an offhand way, doing his best to sound dismissive.

Deavins replied, 'Funny you should mention Jane Mears, Mr. Knoxx. She is looking lovely this evening, isn't she? I'm not sure if she'd look as good in a tan jumpsuit though, do you? You remember what it was like to wear a prison jumpsuit, don't you? Aah yes, actually, that makes two files I can drop off with your good friend, special agent Maxine Dobro. One on Cameron Pope and another file that brings us all the way back to Jason Burne.'

Both Knoxx and Hickes rose up in the heat of an impending battle. They had the superior firepower, but at this point they were powerless to do anything. It seemed this guy Deavins held all the cards, and he certainly held the files that could easily destroy Knoxx. Whoever Deavins was, he was good. Deavins held his arm out, extending it in such a way to indicate that he wanted Knoxx to walk with him. He remarked with some humor, speaking at steady pace, 'Oh, don't worry. I'm not here because of them, or for Jane Mears. I'm here for you. Shall we?'

He was professional, in control and clearly in the know. The only thing Mark could do was follow him. Hickes walked step-for-step with Knoxx, while he leaned in towards him, listening to him giving him some rushed directions. Hickes nodded aggressively while he listened, understanding what he'd been told; his eyes never wavering from Deavins while they walked. The three of them cut through the stragglers standing around the apron of the dance floor, like a hot knife through butter. Knoxx had removed all hint of playfulness from his face now. Jane noticed him walking with Ian and a third, unknown man, as she happily waved to him. Mark waved back, smiling briefly, but Jane stopped dancing immediately to watch the three of them. She could tell by Mark's face that something was wrong, as they disappeared into the crowd.

They arrived at the NVS office door, and as soon as they came to a stop by it, Hickes said roughly, 'Against the wall,' and began to pad Deavins down.

'Easy on the jewels,' Deavins playfully said, while Hickes continued his rough handling of him.

'Give me your phone, watch, pen, everything you're

carrying. I'm keeping everything until you come out.'

Hickes began to take everything from Deavins, who slowly but surely got to the task of emptying out his pockets. His fine, dark blue, mohair suit hung beautifully off his shoulders, hardly making any sound as he fished through its pockets. Hickes then padded him down again.

'He's clean,' Hickes confirmed, looking at Mark. He then opened the office door and waved Deavins in. He checked his watch as Deavins passed by him; he flexed under his designer suit and said, 'You've got five minutes. Five minutes, and then I'm tossing you're arse out, mate.'

Mark gave Ian a reassuring nod as he walked past him to enter the office. Ian closed the door behind him. Sitting down behind the desk, Mark looked hard at Deavins. He laid his elbows on the arms of the chair. He raised his arms and entwined his fingers, resting them on his lips, thinking. He then leaned forward and placed his elbows on the desk, saying bluntly, 'Begin. You got four minutes and eight seconds.'

Deavins sat in his chair, casually resting his arms on either side of the armrests totally at ease, while his piercing blue eyes did their work. He said ominously, 'I know all about you, Mr. Knoxx. I mean, I, as in *we* know all about you. I feel as if I've spent time with you, as if I'd been by your side all these years, doing your business deals, and doing your time in prison before that. I wish I could've been there the day you met your friend, Christopher Wright, or better yet, the time you got to meet an even better friend, Roberto Madrid.'

Knoxx just blinked and breathed smoothly, knowing how it worked, show business.

'I'm guessing there's a punch line coming?' Knoxx said in a whimsical tone.

Deavins did not miss a beat, not wanting be taken out of his game plan. He replied in a similar fashion, 'Well, I'll get to the punch line shall I, so you can get back to your last night of freedom, or worse.'

Knoxx chose to lean back in his chair. This was getting testy now, so he chose to listen a bit more intently.

'Shall I continue?' Deavins asked. He knew it was a rhetorical question.

Knoxx merely nodded in the affirmative, saying lightly, 'Go on.'

'You have a pipeline for distributing hundreds of millions of dollars worth of drugs throughout your NVS nightclub chain, and you've been laundering millions of dollars worth of stolen International Monetary Fund's gold bullion, meant to help the war torn people of the Balkan States. You're involved in some heavy business dealings with men who are wanted by various law enforcement agencies throughout the world, men who you're not afraid of doing business with, regardless of the consequences.'

'This is pure fantasy,' Knoxx replied, leaning forward to meet Deavins' smirk.

'Fantasy?' Deavins retorted. Having trapped him, he asked, 'Kind of like HEAVEN? Is HEAVEN a fantasy too?'

Knoxx was quickly becoming irritated by this line of questioning and Deavins' threatening behavior. He got on point by asking aggressively, 'Look, I don't even know you and I want to kill you myself, so you'd better get to the point. Are you some kind of reporter looking for some kind of scoop because if you are, they're gonna be scoopin' your ass off a freeway underpass real soon, believe that.'

Knoxx checked his watch to see how long was left. He checked Deavins again, feeling he was getting the upper hand back, when Deavins replied, 'No, Mr. Knoxx, I'm not a reporter. I can assure you of that. But in a way I'm kind of like a reporter. I'm more of a facilitator of information, or a suppressor of information. It all depends on what my associates tell me to do with the information I've collected.'

He left the words he'd used to dangle. They hung cryptically for Knoxx to nibble on. Mark could tell what it was; it was a gate that was to be opened for the next show and tell. Knowing that was what he was meant to do, he asked, 'Okay, your associates, who are they and what do they want with me?'

Deavins smiled, knowing he had Knoxx back under his control again. Compliant.

'You think we want something from you? Like money, some kind of extortion? No, Mr. Knoxx, you're to be congratulated on a job well done to date. You own so many diverse and integrated companies that control the flow of data, all for your eventual use in HEAVEN, simply brilliant.' Deavins spoke in a mocking, controlled and predetermined tone. Knoxx knew there was more to come. Deavins screwed him down tighter, when he quipped, 'With HEAVEN, if you can cure it, then you can kill too, right? You can either cure it, or kill it, isn't that the saying?'

'What's your point?' Knoxx replied, sounding agitated. For the first time in a long while, he felt his life was in jeopardy. Feeling his pulse quicken, he needed to know what Deavins really wanted from him.

Deavins answered, 'My point is, that we have let you do what you do, to see how far you'd get. And quite frankly, we're impressed by your resourcefulness and your single-minded determination. We're impressed by your success to date, in your illegal business dealings. We feel we couldn't have done any better ourselves in creating such a solid criminal network. Considering your past military record, we think we might have a use for you.'

Knoxx clenched his jaw, slamming his teeth tight, knowing there was more to come. Better he just listen and learn, he thought. Now was the time for him to gather information and not give any away.

'I don't understand?' Knoxx calmly stated, even though a fire raged inside him at this game of Russian roulette bouncing back and forth between them.

'You will soon enough. I'm simply here to feel you out and see how you are in person, and so far so good. From what I can see, you are secretive, emotionally strong, highly motivated to succeed, and you've manufactured a highly visible false persona for yourself. And, let's not forget your best trait: Your willingness to kill anyone who's either in your way or a threat to you. We couldn't have built or trained you any better ourselves. You're a natural.'

Mark began to focus on what this envoy's message was, and who it was from. Knoxx knew it was up to him to force the play, and so he picked up the gauntlet. He fingered Deavins' business card again, trying to find some understanding from it. He asked, 'What do you want with me and who's this "we," you keep referring to?'

Whoever this guy was, he thought, he had him cold. Knoxx's game was good, but this guy's game was tight and on a whole other level.

Deavins replied, 'People out in the world might refer to them, no one really knows who they are for sure, but they are, for the most part, known as The Firm. And as long as I approve it, then you'll get to meet them tomorrow.'

'And if I don't want to meet this Firm?' Knoxx threw his line out there to see how it sounded, while he tilted back in his chair, trying to make it sound like he was being asked.

Deavins quickly clarified his position by saying, 'Then you will simply be exposed or eliminated.'

Deavins looked like he was done with Knoxx, standing up from his chair abruptly. He did not need any more time to get his point across; he knew he already had.

'I'll be sending a car for you at nine o'clock tomorrow morning. You're not to tell anyone where you're going or when you might return. If you're there, well, that'll be good for you. If you choose not to be there, then that won't be so good for you. Until tomorrow then. We'll see if this is your real destiny calling, shan't we? Enjoy the rest of your night.'

With military precision, Hickes opened the office door while Deavins held Knoxx's stare. He got up from behind the desk and walked around to meet Deavins and held out his hand. They shook each other's hand timidly, while they eyed each other, still measuring each other for any sign of weakness, while neither man showed any signs of doubt.

Knoxx said, cryptically, 'Until tomorrow then.'

Deavins left him in the office. He walked out of NVS with another security guard shadowing him on his way out.

Hickes closed the door to check on Mark. He looked deep into Knoxx's eyes and with some real concern in his voice, he asked, 'How are you? You got any holes in ya?'

'Not yet I haven't. But hey, it's getting late, early. But I'm still in the game, and speaking of game - .'

Knoxx and Hickes walked back out into the expanse of NVS. Mark swept his eyes around the V.I.P. section and quickly found what he was looking for.

Laughing and smiling, while her eyes shone under the bright lights, Nicole Young tossed her long mane of thick, blonde hair back over her shoulder, revealing her sensuous facial features. She pouted her thick, pink lipsticked lips, while she talked with a man standing close to the bar. Knoxx did not take his eyes off her while he moved like a lion stalking his prey in the dead of night. Nicole stood in the light. He walked around her in the shadows with his prey firmly set in his sights. He stopped at the bar and ordered two glasses of pink champagne. Then he moved in, just off to Nicole's left, just enough for her to catch a glimpse of him walking towards her as he intended. She saw him. Even though she was engaged in a conversation with a suitor, as soon as she caught Knoxx's eye, she moved her stance slightly, to open herself up to him. Smiling in anticipation as he approached, he looked every inch what he was. Professional, polite and prepared to kill. She broke into a smile that positively beamed with ecstasy as the attraction being relayed between them was clear. Knoxx broke off and walked out of range, and out of her field of vision, as if he'd been walking over to someone else. Nicole quickly got back to eye contact with the man she had been speaking to, her smile wiped from her face. It quickly returned once she saw that Knoxx was standing on the other side of her, with a wide-eyed cheeky grin on his face. He said, 'Gotchya.'

She released a naughty laugh in delight. It caught the man speaking to her off guard, wondering what she found funny. He realized the main man was standing next to him, holding two glasses of champagne. He quickly made his exit, leaving the two of them in a close quarter conversation.

Knoxx handed Nicole her champagne, both of them radiating heat from their sexuality. He joked, 'You know, if I wasn't gay, you'd sooo be mine.'

'That's the best compliment a girl could ever get!' Nicole jokingly responded, giggling hard. Like a laser-guided missile, his opening line hadn't missed its mark. Nicole fell forward in laughter, helping to light up her scintillating, sharp green eyes in expectation. She loved his opening line, she loved his look, and it did not take too long for her to love him. She had the perfect smile, perfect sense of humor. She was the perfect girl. The two of them were inseparable from that night onwards. Mark invited Nicole to sit at his table, where he introduced her to Jane. She spent some time talking to Jane, and after ten minutes, Jane indicated to Mark that she liked her. After that, it did not take long for Mark and Nicole to find their way onto the dance floor, where they became oblivious to the guests around them. They slowly nuzzled each other, touching each other, until finally they met each other's lips and kissed. They searched each other's soul through their eyes. As each minute passed, it became clear that they both adored each other and that they wanted each other. Mark was looking cool and Nicky was running hot, Yin and Yang.

Two million dollars had been raised for the 9/11 fund. The event had made all the right headlines in all the right publications for the following day, and for the rest of the week. Exile, NVS and Mark Knoxx were everywhere and it seemed, inseparable. Everyone had come away from the evening with something. Maxine Dobro had managed to keep up the pressure on her number one suspect and nemesis, Mark Knoxx. Teresa Hadley had got into the mix, getting noticed by her new boss as a team player, while also getting herself noticed by Mark Knoxx. The Firm, whoever they were, had now made themselves known and had let it be known that they had noticed Mark Knoxx.

Mark's envious life now seemed to be catching the attention of people who were in a position to destroy his ambitions and his destiny. They might also be in a position to help him achieve them. The Firm sounded like they had their own destiny to fulfil, and that they wanted something from him, letting him know that he was a very important person in their eyes.

Tomorrow morning, he might just find out how important he might be to the aspirations of The Firm. But tonight, there was only one thing that was important to Mark Knoxx. She was to become the V.I.P. in his life. Nicole Young. Mark had tried to see the good things in life, but they had been hard to find, trying to do things right. Things just had not worked out like that. Maybe things would be different this time around.

Envy

82

Sitting comfortably inside the sleek seventy-five million dollar Gulfstream G650, Knoxx just relaxed and enjoyed the ride. He had come to the plane with the attitude of 'what will be, will be', since he knew he really hadn't had a choice anyway. When the car had arrived at the private airport, he had noticed the logo on the jet's fuselage: Squared Agency. He knew it was an international logistics and support company that provided services to the U.S. Government.

The saber-rattling from Deavins had been relatively light on the way to the airport. At least Knoxx had shown up this morning, and it seemed to him, Knoxx was in good spirits too. Deavins didn't know this was due to the night he had just spent with Nicole Young, exploring her body, and then they had spent most of the early hours of the morning kissing. Getting settled in for the flight, Mark inhaled and smelled Nicole's scent on him. He pictured coming home to her later in the day and finding her still in his bed. Deavins had been explaining that he was, in effect, a head-hunter in more ways than one. Those people who didn't meet the standards, or didn't comply, were either exposed as being frauds, made to look as if they were involved in criminal activities, or at the very worse, they simply disappeared.

'Well, it's not where I've been but where I'm about to go,' Knoxx replied with some amusement, knowing he'd just quoted a line from a Jay-Z song.

'Sometimes, looking back at where you've been, can tell you where you're headed,' Deavins retorted tactfully.

Both men were beginning to relax in each other's company. It was approaching twenty minutes into the flight, and from the cabin window, Knoxx surmised that they were headed in a south-westerly direction. He got around to asking, 'What does MMI Enterprises stand for?'

Deavins' eyes glinted. He replied, 'It stands for Me, Myself and I.' Both of them laughed and Deavins continued, 'Because I work alone, no one really knows what I'm paid for, and so it just seemed appropriate.'

While Deavins spoke at length about his role, Knoxx kept reinforcing his own belief in his head, that whoever he was meeting, it was going to be a good thing in the evolution of Mark Knoxx. He finally let his anxieties fall from him, thinking of one thing: starting his life over with Nicole Young.

Deavins seemed to sense a difference in him, and so he brought himself up closer to him to say candidly, 'Does the term RED mean anything to you?'

Knoxx gave him a blank look, finding it hard to register what he'd been saying, having been thinking about what Nicole had been wearing, oh so pretty in pink, when he had left her at the apartment earlier. He shook his head and then noticed the music playing in the background. It was an Alicia Keys song that made him smile.

Deavins continued his line of conversation. 'RED is an acronym for Rapid Engagement and Defense. You've never heard of it?'

Again, Mark shook his head, replying, 'No, I haven't.'

'The people interested in meeting you are, I guess you could say, involved in making sure it continues to thrive and prosper. You might be aware, that the American armed services are currently operating in over one hundred and twenty countries worldwide, all requiring operational services and support each day? To put this in perspective, the cost to provide security to one oil and gas producing plant in Iraq runs at around eighty million dollars a year. The group you'll be meeting shortly could be described as, crisis and risk management specialists.' Deavins released a small, knowing smile, and then continued, saying, 'And that's where you come in. One quarter of the world's wealth is held between Bill Gates, Warren Buffet and Paul Allen. We live in an age where multinational corporations can wield more power globally, and have a wider reach than any country's government could ever hope to have. The world's top three percent of the richest people hold ninety percent of the world's natural resources and publicly traded company stocks in their portfolios. Their reach and influence is everywhere, and it's a very exclusive club to be in. People kill to get in it. Overall, I'd say you were a good guy, all things considered, and the world's short on good guys these days. From here on out, you must face your demons or stay chained to them. Killing people in the thousands may not be the best option, but it's still an option, and like it or not, we as a country have chosen our path to self-destruction. It's all just a matter of time.'

Knoxx sat in the chair absorbing it, not understanding what Deavins was trying to tell him, but he understood the words. He asked, 'What do they want with me?'

'Oh come now, you do yourself a disservice with your modesty. You know what you're capable of. You know what you've done in the past, and we know what you have created. We know you know, too. War is a dirty business, Mr. Knoxx, but it's still a business. Someone somewhere gets rich from it, and I'm sure you wouldn't mind it being you, now would you? You know how it works, fear and greed, the fear of war and the greed from the spoils of war. When war breaks out, everybody in the know makes out. Energy companies, telecom companies, information and technology companies, heavy industrials and financial houses. Everyone makes out from war, if you're in the club, of course.'

'How do I become a member of this club?' Knoxx asked, trying to sound naive and inquisitive at the same time.

Deavins was already onto him and his game. Laughing lightly and carefree, he replied, 'Oh, all in good time, all in good time. We're nearly there.'

Seven minutes later, the plane began to descend. Looking out of the window, Knoxx could see some black Lincoln Navigators lined up, waiting for their arrival. He was ushered out from the plane and escorted at a brisk pace to one of the cars. Within minutes, the convoy was driving off at speed, winding through tree-lined avenues. The cars soon pulled up at a pair of wrought iron gates that had burly guards standing behind them, with Rottweiler dogs under their grip. The dogs did their work, sniffing around the cars, while I.D.'s were shown by the drivers before being waved on through by the guards. The convoy drove up the gravel drive towards a huge, Gothic mansion. As it came into view, Knoxx thought that wherever he was and whoever he was meeting here had it going on. *Big time people doing big time things,* he thought. The cars came to a stop at the front of the house with a very, Juicy, beginning. *Déjà-vu,* he thought, as he got out of the car.

83

Death is for certain, life is not. As Knoxx was led through to the great hall of this great mansion, he was uncertain about who wanted him here and why. He was shown to a chair that had been placed in the middle of the room. As he sat down, he was uncertain whether he'd be leaving this place, alive.

Two well-tailored escorts stood about twenty paces behind him with two more positioned off to his right. Other than that, he was on his own. He took in the banquet hall that was draped in fine art, with a cathedral window facing him that was dripping in the morning's daylight, Knoxx could hear himself breathing lightly and he did his best to slow his heart rate. *Be cool*, he thought. Over the next few minutes, that's all he had to focus on, being cool, while he watched the light beams slowly creeping their way across the wooden parquet flooring. The brighter the light, the deeper the shadows. He was definitely in a place that had a lot of secrets hidden within the shadows of these rooms.

The door opened and in walked several men. Knoxx recognized some of them from the political and financial world. He exhaled, trying to relax. Why he was here, he did not know yet. Show business. Like several times before in his life, he would have to kick back, listen, learn, and let it all unfold. The men found their positions at a chair facing him along the banquet table. One of the men Knoxx recognized as the media titan, Clive Robbins spoke a verse in Latin, "Benedictus, Benedicat per Jesum Christum Dominum Nostrum," meaning "Blessed is He and blessed is this food through Jesus Christ, Our Lord." The men seated themselves, leaving the seat in front of Knoxx empty.

'It's a pleasure to meet you, Mr. Knoxx. I'm glad to see you decided to meet with us here this morning,' William Baltizar, the United States Attorney General, said lightly, implying that he knew Knoxx hadn't had much of a choice in the matter. Knoxx merely nodded in agreement, as Baltizar went on to ask, 'Do you know why you've been asked to join us here this morning?'

Knoxx simply shook his head, saying calmly, 'No, I don't.'

Baltizar moved on, asking him, 'Do you recognize anyone here with me?'

Knoxx let out a muted, 'Yes.'

Baltizar and the others sat squarely at the table, with none of the men showing any reaction or emotion. Baltizar looked in his dossier and then said, without looking up at Knoxx, 'Good, then introductions won't be needed, but what is important, Mr. Knoxx, is that we know you, and that may turn out very well for you, or very bad. So let's get started, shall we? What we know to date is this. You have built a cocaine distribution network with Roberto Madrid throughout the United States, using your nightclubs as a cover, isn't that right?'

Baltizar looked up at Knoxx in a matter-of-fact manner. He let it sit, while a moment passed.

Knoxx answered simply, 'Yes, that's right.'

For the first time in years, he'd finally given it up and let the words pass his lips. The funny thing was, it had felt okay to say it and finally admit it, but what was even funnier was that nobody seemed to care about it. All eyes were on him, but no one spoke.

He continued, 'You've been smuggling gold bullion, stolen from The World Bank, intended to help ease the suffering of the people of the Balkan States. Isn't that correct?'

Knoxx felt his heart miss a beat as it rose up into his throat. All he could do was nod, as he coolly replied in a low tone, 'Yes, that's correct.'

Keeping eye contact with Attorney General Baltizar, he merely nodded in appreciation. Knoxx felt strange, as no one seemed to care about his illegal activities. They all sat in their chairs, with some of the men making brief notes. After a deafeningly quiet moment, Baltizar summed it up in an impassive manner, 'Very good, Mr. Knoxx.'

Baltizar picked up a telephone handset, putting it to his ear and pressed a button. He then spoke for a minute in a quiet voice, while some of the other men along the table spoke to their neighbor in hushed voices. Knoxx was unable to distinguish anything that was being said. He looked at them while they were talking, taking each face in. One man he recognized as Gordon Forrest, the Under-Secretary-General of the United Nations, and Allen Sanders from the International Atomic Energy Agency: the IAEA. One more face he recognized, the man seated next to him, Israel's Minister of Foreign Affairs, Jake Head. Knoxx then set his eyes upon John D'intino, the industrialist, and oil and gas magnate. As they talked to each other, some of the men looked at him. The United Kingdom's Secretary of State for Defense nodded at him in acknowledgment.

Baltizar ended his telephone conversation and the other men quieted down while their eyes fell back to Knoxx. Baltizar said, 'Mr. Knoxx, I should tell you that by having confessed your crimes, the United States can prosecute you to the fullest extent of the law. As the U.S. Attorney General, it's my duty to inform you of your rights.'

Baltizar was speaking in the regal tone that Knoxx had heard so many times before when he'd watched CNN. He knew he was in deep shit, and yet, he felt calm and quiet inside. For some reason, he felt this wasn't the end.

He quickly followed up by saying, 'But I don't see the need for that quite yet.'

As if on cue, the door to Knoxx's right opened, and the men sitting along the table simultaneously stood up and looked towards the door. The two security escorts seemed to straighten, as if they were standing to attention, as in walked the Vice President of the United States, Mr. Stephen Tasker, saying, 'Good morning, gentlemen.' He seated himself at the empty chair and looked at Knoxx, giving him a quick nod, and then followed up with, 'Good morning, Mr. Knoxx. It's been a long time coming, our meeting. Good things come to those who wait, but only those things left over by those who hustle.'

Everyone at the table politely laughed. Even Knoxx couldn't help but release a smile and a little snort at the remark.

Tasker allowed himself a chuckle while he unfolded his leather dossier and asked, 'Well now, everyone's gotten acquainted. I trust everything's out in the open on where you and we stand?'

'Yes,' Knoxx answered.

At this point, he didn't dare ask why he was still sitting in the chair and not getting his ass hauled off to the nearest firing squad. Tasker rolled right along with him nodding, expecting the answer. His commanding presence filled the vastness of the banquet hall. He was the Commander in Chief, heir apparent, and he wasted no time in getting on to what he wanted to say. 'When it comes to thriving in a competitive marketplace, my belief is that playing it safe is no longer playing it smart. In an economy that is defined by overcapacity, oversupply and overspending, where everyone already has more than enough of whatever it is they're buying, one needs a truly distinctive idea. The idea should clearly convey what they are selling and where they are headed. Leaders take action and action causes reaction. You are being given the opportunity to take part in our action, where you can reap the benefits of that reaction.'

Never once taking his eyes off of Knoxx, Tasker searched for any doubt in him, probing him with his prose, his saber like words cutting into Knoxx's very being, testing him. Knoxx sat stock-still with nowhere to go and nothing to say. He just sat, watched and waited.

Tasker then said, 'And so, you bring to us HEAVEN. I myself am a big fan of it and what it can do, helping to sweep me into office this coming November.' He emptied some water out of a blue bottle into a glass, while a low rumble of sniggers from the assembled men resonated. Tasker looked along the row for the first time, catching John D'intino's eye.

Looking back at Knoxx, Tasker's mood changed to stone, 'I believe HEAVEN can pave the way to bringing about stability, peace and order in an efficient, economic and effective manner. It's the American way.' He took a beat. 'Or I should say, it was once.'

The pregnant pause, left by Tasker's reflective mood, left an opportunity for Knoxx to clarify things. He took a breath and figured that now was as good a time as any to see if he was on the same page, asking, 'Forgive me for asking in such a blunt manner, but am I right in thinking you and your colleagues want to have access to HEAVEN?'

The air around Knoxx took on a decidedly colder chill as all eyes fixed on him in a look of disdain. Tasker was quick to clear up any misunderstandings. 'No, Mr. Knoxx. We don't wish to have access to it. We intend to own it. As we own you, so we will own HEAVEN.'

Knoxx felt some heat rise in him, his own headstrong pride beating him over his head. A thick lump was choking him in his throat, but the words he wanted to say just wouldn't come. He knew he'd be dead for sure, if he said what he really wanted to say. He let the words fall from his mouth as calmly, evenly and as smoothly as possible, asking, 'And, what's in it for me?'

'Well, you're still breathing, aren't you?' Tasker quipped, dismissively.

This seemed to sum it all up quite neatly. All Knoxx could do was give a light shrug of his shoulders, as if to agree.

Tasker took the initiative to step on his throat a little harder in closing the deal, following up, saying, 'Let me say, none of us here in this room want to harm you in any way. We only want what's best for you, and what's best for you will be what's best for us. And what's good for us, is good for our countries and the freedoms we enjoy. You enjoy your freedoms, don't you?'

Knoxx looked blindly at Tasker's mesmerizing eyes, nodding in confirmation and resignation, knowing he had no freedoms in his life. Not anymore.

'We're at war and it's an all-consuming world war. We are in World War Three. It's just that the people haven't realized it yet. It will be a war that will rage for generations. We haven't inherited the earth from our parents, we are simply borrowing it from our children, and all of us here in this room must take action. And in war, the first casualty of war is the truth. I would give everything for happily ever after, Mr. Knoxx, I would, for my own family's sake and for the people of this great nation, but everything's turned from sugar to shit, and America is dying. We are in trouble, but none of us want to be the one to speak up and say it publicly. If we as a nation go down, then these gentlemen here today and their respective countries will go down too, and we just cannot, nor will we, let that happen. America is fourteen trillion dollars in debt. We have committed ourselves to a war against a people who have been at war themselves for three thousand years. We are in a place in time that we should never have found ourselves in, and now, we have to turn this thing around. Sometimes, doing the right thing is the hardest thing to do. It's a battle I'm prepared to never win, but by God, I'm willing to fight, and die trying. I can tell you this, Mr. Knoxx, to take responsibility is a heavy burden to bear and the journey travelled is one of sacrifice, but I, and all of these men here today, believe it is better to fight for hope, than to hope for change to come and save us. Hope is not a strategy; you take care of today and tomorrow will take care of you. That is what we are fighting for, a better tomorrow. We are capable of such amazing, wonderful things, and yet, we can create such horrific nightmares, but it's our own choices we have to live with in life, which path we choose.'

Knoxx chose to let Tasker's words fill him up. All he could do was sit in despair and sink further into helplessness at where he was being led. Tasker spoke his words eloquently, looking every inch the next President of the United States of America.

He noticed the change in the climate, the electricity that hung in the air around them as Tasker summarized his thoughts succinctly. 'The American people are beginning to smell the shit, and I'll end up being the one to clean it all up when I get into the White House. Then I'll end up being just another president who's inherited someone else's mess. It'll be one more president's term in office wasted. The American people don't want to blame themselves for any of it; they've been fed the shit that's been dressed up as sugar, over the past fifty years.' He poured out some more water from his blue-bottled, Ty flat water, emptying it in his glass. He looked at Knoxx and said reflectively, 'What goes around comes around, and in time, it all catches up to you.' Looking at the bottle's label, absent-minded, as if the answer to all his troubles were on it, Tasker then looked back up at Knoxx. He said, 'You know this better than most, don't you? And this is where you come in. Your whole life has been a lie, and you, yourself, are a beautiful liar. Some things are so obvious, they don't need to be questioned. You have been living inside your own lie for so long that you don't even know that you've created a false persona. You probably think you're in control of your own destiny. Let me ask you, when do you know you've made it? You know, when you have arrived?'

Resigned to being just a puppet in the play, Knoxx flippantly retorted, 'I'll let you know when I get there.'

Feeling slighted by his remark, Tasker immediately struck

back to confirm, 'Oh, I can assure you, Mr. Knoxx, you have arrived.'

Knoxx began to feel his temper flare. He had been made to sit in the middle of this room and eat this wordplay. He had begun to realize that whatever they wanted from him, it was surely important enough for them to have revealed themselves. Mark felt emboldened and so he released his own wordplay by taking the fight to Tasker and defending himself the only way he knew how, by attacking. 'I see The West fighting the same army that Rome faced two thousand years ago, the Mahdi army in Persia. Rome got too big for its own good as the lone superpower of its day, and it ended up bankrupt, imposing its will on the conquered people, educating them to their Roman, higher standard of living, telling them that their way of life was a righteous and civilized way to live. But only through instilling fear and military might was Rome able to control the so-called barbarians, who only wanted to live their lives their own way. And Rome soon found itself defending its own way of life on all fronts from the people it had either subdued, coerced or conquered. Rome was faced with smaller armies fighting unconventional battles, because they were desperate to win back their own existence and way of life. And guess what? Rome lost everything. War losses were quickly followed by bankruptcy, and then inevitably, collapse. Rome didn't welcome outsiders just as we don't today, until the outsiders outpaced them, but by then, it was too late. So let me ask you, what about us? Are we too late?'

Tasker and the other men looked at him with a look of new found admiration, beginning to realize they'd now found what they had been searching for, one of their own. His words had given them food for thought and once again, there seemed to be a void that needed to be filled as each side thought about each other's point of view and profound meaning. But most were now thinking of what the future held for them as individuals and for the world at large.

Vice President Tasker once again stepped up as the leader to put it all in perspective for Knoxx. With a softer voice, he aired his thoughts, asking, 'Are we too late? Well, time and the tide wait for no one, and even though we're running out of time, it's time for the tide of change to carry us all to a better place. It just depends on which way the tide is carrying you.' Leaning onto his elbows, Tasker transformed his stare into an intimidating glare, 'Every day, the people of the world, the regular world citizens, just want to see the world as it once was, or how it will be. They want to see change. They wait on the world to change, for things to get better, or they are happy reminiscing about how good the old days were, but they do know change is coming, for better or for worse. What they see and what they're told is what they believe. And it's us, here, who ultimately bring about that change. We have the power to bring about the changes throughout the world. The freedoms we provide are a luxury, and they're not to be squandered. Never compromise on luxuries.' Leaning back in his chair Tasker then interlocked his hands, resting his finger tips on his mouth while he drilled his eyes into Knoxx. He lowered them and got his final point across, 'There are those who wish to take everything we have built from us, Mr. Knoxx. You know that, and you probably know most of the major players off the top of your head. Make no mistake, you are in a war. It's raging all around you, and you could easily become a casualty of war. There are two sides fighting this battle. You just haven't picked a side yet.'

84

'Hmmm ...' Stretching, releasing a long drawn out sigh of contentment, Nicole Young took in the smell of man that was on her, as she draped herself across the sumptuous California King bed. She let out a small giggle, thinking back to Mark's opening line the night before. She playfully rolled across the bed to check the clock, five minutes to one in the afternoon. Groaning at the time of day, her thoughts changed to the room she was in. She saw that on her side of the bed, sitting proudly on the bedside table, six, moist, long-stemmed pink roses. Nicky widened her bright, white smile and let out a little girl laugh at the cheek and the charm of it. She bounded up to the vase to check for a card and, sure enough, embedded in the flowers, there it was. Her eyes and her heart beamed while she grabbed at it like a six-year-old on Christmas morning. She opened it in anticipation as she quickly read it, and then a second time to gain its meaning. The card read:

Six roses for the six hours of complete happiness you've given me. Dreams do come true, because mine brought me you. Live your dream, baby, and if you're gonna dream, dream big!

Mark xx

'Aahh,' a giggle quickly appeared that turned into a little inward look, as if she might cry. Snuggling up in bed, pulling the duvet up, she took a long deep breath. Nicky allowed herself a long sigh, thinking it had been a dream, because it had been the perfect night with the perfect man, her perfect Mark, and now, she had been given the perfect card. Now, it will probably come to an end, as Nicole Young was well aware of Mr. Mark Knoxx's reputation as a playboy, slick operator, life and soul of the party, along with being one of the most eligible bachelors. She gave a thought to her own station in life. Who was she, really? Just a scared girl, trapped inside the body of a beautiful woman, always mindful of how her looks and perceived sex appeal attracted men, the majority of them unwanted. Her looks had cost her dearly, two years ago when her boyfriend had been gunned down. She'd run away from the scene and from her life, and she'd been trying to run away from herself ever since, riddled with guilt about what had happened. The phone beside her rang, causing her to jump. Her heart skipped a beat as she leaned over to answer it, sheepishly asking, 'Hello?'

'Good afternoon, Ms. Young? My name's Tobey Brewin. I've been instructed by Mr. Knoxx to call you at one o'clock.

I hope I haven't disturbed you?'

Nicole answered, 'No, you didn't. It's okay.'

Tobey Brewin took her cue and continued, 'I'm calling from the concierge downstairs to let you know that whatever you need, I'll be happy to arrange for our personal shopper, Nikki Dunne, to pick up for you and deliver it to the apartment.'

Nicole had found her smile again. She was embarrassed by the forethought, but excited at how thoughtful Mark was. He'd proven that he was an English gentleman and full of surprises. The dream was real. Taking her prompting from Tobey, Nicole pressed on and ordered up some food and some casual wear, also arranging to get herself pampered by the beauty treatment staff. After she'd hung up the phone, Nicole managed to fall out from the bed. She sank herself into the massive Jacuzzi bath, along with a long-stemmed flute of chilled, Perrier Jouet grand brut champagne. She situated herself in a position so she could gaze back into the bedroom and look at her roses. All of her heartache and troubles melted away in the heat of the bath, while she dared to dream of her life with Mark from this point on, thinking, if only it could happen. All the roads she had travelled, it felt like they had led her here. Last night was one of the great ones. Last night, she was made to feel like she was a princess. But while she lay in the bath, she decided to stay strong and hold her feelings in check. It did feel like it was a fairy-tale, but last night was probably all an act, for all she knew. Maybe it was how Mark played all his women, with a well-honed, tried and tested formula that worked well. But she was here now, and now was just fine with her, as her mind began racing and scheming. Maybe she could end up being the one to tame the ladies' man. Nicole giggled at the naughty thoughts now racing through her, while she began to scheme on how she would ensnare her man. Others might want to be where she was, but she was here right now. Nicole slid down under the bubbles in the bath, and then rose up to spit out some hot water, with her eyes bright, her body warm and her heart on fire. Nicole Young wasn't going to be put out so quickly. This was where she was meant to be, and everything she had done in her life had led her to this time and place. She laughed and then screamed playfully. She had a plan. Singing along happily for most of the day and lounging about on various chairs and couches, her mind began to think about Mark. Where was he and when would he be coming back? Time was moving on.

85

'Time is moving on, Mr. Knoxx, and we don't have too much of it left. We have to change our way of thinking. We have to become strong again, financially, spiritually and militarily. Our children are a generation of MTV and iPhones, voyeurs of other people's lives and soap operas. They only look up to celebrities and movie stars. Our children have never had to look into the darkness and find their way home. I feel sorry for them; they'd be better off if they had. So, here we are, and here you are. Make no mistake about our collective resolve. We realize that we may not see the benefits of our commitment in our own lifetimes, but we are going to begin to sow the seeds, and then we are going to hoe the row. Now's the time to take action and we will do so. We won't cower behind the rhetoric, like those politicians who are always the first to stand up to be heard, but are the last to stand behind action. We are going to begin trimming the fat, the gutless, the boring and the useless, and those who plot against us, which brings us back to you, and RED, Mr. Knoxx.' Tasker took a drink and then blankly stated, 'RED is our key to turning this around, Rapid Engagement and Defense. We will use it to funnel funds to you for the worldwide distribution of HEAVEN. RED provides around sixty billion dollars a year in reconstruction aid to countries that we are deployed in. It also props up forty-eight thousand private military operatives in a hundred and eighty-one countries, where it disburses some thirty billion dollars a year to our own private mercenary force, that's second in size only to U.S. forces. What we are proposing here today is that we supply you with the funding, support and logistics, through the shell companies that we control, to complete HEAVEN. Use the funds for whatever purpose you see fit, with one requirement from you.'

Knoxx didn't move or blink. Up to now, it had all been sizzle, but now, here it was, the steak. When it all came down to it, it was a trade off, someone wanting something from someone else. A thought flashed through his mind; they wanted him, but they needed HEAVEN. It was time to get down to business. For the first time, the thirteen men seated at the long banquet table seemed pensive. Some adjusted themselves in their chair, as they knew the time had come for Knoxx to pick which side he was going to be on.

'And what would that be?' Knoxx asked in a firm voice, knowing the time had come and the real purpose of this meeting was about to be realized. He felt a little more in control of his emotions and in his resolve, knowing they could only get to HEAVEN through him.

Tasker replied, just as firm, 'Simply, a yes or no, are you going to join us? It's your choice to make and you must decide here and now. Everything you've done to date and everything you have the potential to achieve in the future, everything we have come to know about you, tells us that it would be good for you, for us, and for our Cause, if you were to join us of your own free will. Only you can know what is in your heart and how far your heart will carry you. Maybe you carry a heavy heart, where you're worst fears lay, your nightmares. Maybe you've come as far as you can go.' Knoxx watched as Tasker paused, taking his time to pour out some more water into a glass. 'Life isn't about the amount of breaths one takes. It's about the one moment in life that takes your breath away. You have the chance to become one in a million, and not be one of a million, by joining us, the Illuminati.'

Knoxx was aghast. He felt his jaw open and his chin quiver, trying desperately to maintain his posture. Knoxx had read about them. He had seen a few television programs and read magazine articles about them. They operated under a number of names: One World Order, The Company. But the two names that were most infamous were The Skulls, and the all powerful, Illuminati.

The Illuminati dated back to the formation of the Vatican in Rome. In Latin, it means, The Enlightenment Era. They were said to be a secret society, comprised of a group of immensely rich and powerful elite men and women who had sway over any country's government. They were originally the covert special-ops force for the Catholic Church and for Rome, centuries old and passed down only to the rightful heirs. Those in power, the chosen ones, the modern day members, were chosen as young adults in the highest echelons of the best private schools throughout the world. Those who showed early promise of becoming great were embraced in the warmth of the light. The Enlightenment Era had, however, over time become the dark light. The handpicked men and women were then taught the ways of the Illuminati. Inducted first into The Skulls, their real schooling began when the network of older members were made aware of who these young people were to become, with each member playing their part in providing every opportunity for them to work at their companies. The special ones were put on the fast track, onto bigger and better things, becoming captains of industry, real estate tycoons, oil and industrial magnates, communications and media titans, prime ministers, and even the President of the United States.

People all over the world knew the story of the Illuminati, but no one knew if they really existed. No one really, believed. Now Mark Knoxx was seated before them, listening to them persuading him to become a believer. Believe in them and believe in their Cause, to right the wrongs of the world, to fight the ultimate enemy as they had been doing for centuries. To take up the fight against those who fought against the Church and people who lived a just life. The enlightened ones were fighting against Satan's Army, and they wanted him to join them in that fight. Today. Bring the wrath of HEAVEN upon them to land soft, kill quietly and kill them all.

'Do I really have a choice?' Knoxx asked, hoping to hear a summary of options, but none was given.

Tasker responded quickly, 'What's it really like to have a choice between life and death? Did you provide a choice to Mr. Burne or Mr. Pope? Did Mr. Connelly have that luxury? Really, who gets to choose who gets to live and who gets to die? We do, that's who. Where things end is usually dependent upon where it begins. We're here today, simply offering you a new beginning. For one life to end, a new life can begin.' Tasker sat up in his chair, taking on a look of regal posture. Eyes front, his powers of persuasion were clear and defined in delivery. Economical, efficient and effective.

Knoxx replied reflexively, asking, 'And in order for me to join you as a member, I must give up my old life, give up control of my life to you and control of HEAVEN?'

Tasker allowed himself the curl of a smile, turning the glass of water in his hand. Gazing into the glass, he then looked up at Knoxx, replying tacitly, 'Not quite. You'll be free to continue your life, as you know it, but understand, the greatest form of control is when one provides the illusion of being free, but in reality, you are being manipulated. We own the greatest form of manipulation ever invented. It's in the hearts and minds of hundreds of millions of people throughout the world. We own all forms of media, and the number one propaganda delivery system sits in the living room, continuously mind-washing everyone. It streams our messages out subversively to the world every day, twenty-four hours a day. It's called the television. We will tell you what we want you to do and how you are to do it, and you'll do it without question. You'll then sell it in your own way and in your own style. You'll sell our message to the people and you will do as we deem necessary. You'll be our messenger, our envoy, one of our enlightened soldiers. You'll be called upon to use HEAVEN to kill those who plot against us. We will require you to terminate specific targets that we've deemed to be enemies of the state and you will use HEAVEN to eliminate them. We will then, over time, spread fear, eventually bringing about order, and ultimately, winning back compliance and control. The people need an enemy,

Mr. Knoxx. Don't you make one of us. Even the longest rope has an end. You'll be free to live your life, only we will control those freedoms you'll enjoy. Like I said earlier, what goes around comes around, and everything you've done in the past has now caught up with you. It's time to choose your destiny.'

Tasker sat back against the back of the chair, knowing he had done his best to sway Knoxx. All the men believed the words and the rhetoric that Tasker had recited. They believed their Cause was just and righteous, each one having chosen of their own free will to join in the fight for that Cause. For joining, they received and enjoyed wealth, power, and the unlimited freedoms provided by being a member of the Illuminati.

Knoxx thought a moment, pondering it all, and then he somberly said, 'I've wished for a lot of things in my life. The way I feel right now, I don't wish you well. I don't know if you're really doing the world a real service or if you're the ones who are slowly, but surely, bringing us all to our eventual demise. I know that everything dies, and as a human race, we are dying. I just hope you're not the ones responsible in expediting it. I am in this, as you say, and I am in this up to my neck and, I guess it was inevitable that I would finally feel the roughness of the noose around my neck one day. So what choice do I really have? None.' With complete resignation, he said, 'Tell me what you need me to do. I'm in.'

86

'I'm in fool! You know how we do! BET! Watch me take all your money, and then I'm gonna put you out to work as my ho', biaatch.'

Everyone at the table laughed as Bezerk taunted Beaver while they waited on the turn of the last card. Bezerk and his crew had been playing cards, drinking beers and smoking reefers all afternoon to take the edge off. The turn of the card came and it turned out to be a king.

Bezerk jumped out of his seat, already knowing he'd been had, shouting, 'Fuuckk! Son of a biittcchh!'

Everyone laughed hard, seeing Bezerk losing what he'd believed was his for the taking.

'Yeah, that's how we do this, bro'. You know how we do.' Beaver replied, while he leaned across the table to scoop up the cash.

Coco's cell phone rang. He answered it in an unassuming way with the long drawl of a tired and bored, 'Yeah, waassuup?'

For the next two minutes, he mumbled his way through a coded speech, making a deal and securing a time and a place for the drop. His final sortie finished in grinding out the highest amount, while having to disconnect himself from the tirade of profanity that Bezerk was still ranting, while he tried to intimidate Beaver into giving him his money back.

'Aa'iight, we cool. See you there, fool. It's all good. Don't make me wait. Later, dog.'

The deal was done. Bezerk was getting a chance to get his money back after all, as some shooters in town from Las Vegas wanted to buy clean straps. A hooked-up bartender that was in the know had offered up Coco's number at the Voodoo Lounge in Las Vegas. Coco had gone through the usual channels to confirm that these guys were cool, and sure enough, everything had checked out. Word on the street, was that this crew from New York were hot and needed some heaters before they could disappear to who knows where. Coco had closed the deal and the meet was set. They'd all make out nicely, as it was quite a list of weapons they wanted. All told, the handguns, ammo, rifles and one RPG, rocket propelled grenade with three missiles would all come in at around fifty grand, a good score, seeing as how Bezerk's crew had stolen the weapons. Coco shut off the phone and informed his big homey about what he'd just hooked up.

Still annoyed from his loss, Bezerk barked, 'Cool. Let's go fuck these fools up.'

Nicky Z had been told by Coco that everything was cool

and the meet was set for later that afternoon. They'd be back in business before the night was out. Nick Zacarro and Joel Casa got down to business on how it was all going to go down. One hour from now, they would meet on a dirt track road underneath the Hollywood sign, leading up to Sunset Ranch.

'You and Franz go together. Me and Nick'll cover you,' Casa told J-Rock. With a small nod of understanding where their respective positions laid within the crew, he knew if anything were to go wrong, he would be the first to be gunned down before Zacarro and Casa could retaliate.

'We're gonna get going and get set up. You won't see us, but we'll be covering you, okay? Don't worry, brother.'

Joey Casa, as always, was bringing about calm and instilling confidence into his young guns. He was a fearless leader, knowing who was expendable and who wasn't. Joel and Nick set off, getting the jump on the Southsider crew who would be selling the guns to them. If all went well, it would go down in a matter of minutes. Both sides knew what was at stake. Both sides could lose a lot if either side decided to come down strong. Casa wasn't about to give up fifty thousand dollars to anyone, and he figured the other side wouldn't want to lose their guns either. Both sides knew how the game was played and if the game picked up, then they could lose their lives if the deal went bad.

Bezerk ordered his Sureños to move out, having called up a small Brigade of gangbangers. His turf, his rules. Not bothering to ride along, he left the heavy lifting for Tavo and Coco, telling them at the house, 'See you fools soon. Call me when it's done, dog. If anything looks wrong or feels wrong, smoke 'em all. You got this, okay?'

Bezerk hugged Coco and Tavo. The Sureños thugged out of his crib. They wanted to use their overwhelming force to intimidate the buyers into giving up more cash at the last minute. That was the plan. Leverage. They had the guns and they had the superior numbers in soldiers, and these buyers were in their territory. It was a tried and tested formula that had worked for them numerous times in the past and no one could see a reason for it not working one more time.

Casa had spoken to his guys about it because he knew the score too. If the roles had been reversed, he would have been looking to do the same thing, being a matter of supply and demand. It's whatever the market will bear, and Joey had told John Rockhound, nicknamed J-Rock, what to say. Joel Casa had also come up with some leverage of his own, and now both sides were ready.

'Pull in here a minute,' Franz said, having a dry mouth in expectation of what lay ahead of them. J-Rock pulled into the Seven-Eleven convenience store on Santa Monica Boulevard between La Brea Boulevard and North Highland Avenue in Hollywood. They had been shooting the breeze about everything but where they were headed, knowing they would soon be meeting a tough gangbangin' crew.

'Get me a Big Gulp coke and a pack of Marlboro's,' J-Rock mused. Franz hopped out and entered the store. They were twenty-two minutes away from the meet. J-Rock checked his watch for the twenty-second time, the fifty grand was stuffed in an envelope squared away in the glove box. Both guys were carrying heaters, strapped to their sides. J-Rock listened to some hip-hop and pulled on the butt of his cigarette, forcing the smoke out through his nose; he then ass-flicked the cigarette onto the parking lot tarmac. He eyed a skinny, junkie-type guy, who had stopped at the low cinder block wall, hooking one leg over followed by the other in quick succession. Yeah, a fucking junkie whacked on smack, J-Rock thought to himself. He watched the guy, who looked like he was high, noticing that he was around the same age as him. He seemed to be in a real hurry with nowhere to go. It began to amuse J-Rock, as he continued to watch this fuck-up saunter along to the front of the store.

*   *   *

Franz had scooped up the items and had drunk some of J-Rock's Coca-Cola. He looked unerringly bored as he handed over some bills to the cashier, who looked just as bored. A minute passed by while she opened the cash register and went about getting him his change. Franz smiled as she handed him his change. He walked out, chugging on the Big Gulp, looking at J-Rock in the black Navigator.

The junkie had stopped at the pay-phone close to the front door of the store, rummaging deep inside his pocket; he extracted two dollars and eighty cents in loose change. He picked out two dimes and a nickel. Pushing them in the payphone's slot, he hit the push button keys aggressively, while he stole a quick look inside the store as the phone began to ring. He looked at the reflection in the window and noticed a big guy with shades on sitting in the driver's seat of a black S.U.V., and another guy walking out of the store. They looked like cops. He decided he'd wait a minute before going in.

'Man, what the fuck's this shit? Why's my cup so low?' J-Rock ripped out.

'Call it a service fee, dude,' Franz casually answered. The two gunslingers backed out from the Seven-Eleven parking lot. They quickly turned the Navigator onto Santa Monica Boulevard to begin their drive towards the meet above Hollywood. As J-Rock stepped on the gas to pull in to the street, he gave one last glimpse in his rear view mirror to check on the mook, the junkie, while he carried on cursing at Franz for drinking half his drink.

The junkie had hung up the phone and was quickly pushing his way inside the store. His thin, long and lanky frame didn't need to open the door that far while he seemed to slither inside. J-Rock gunned the Lincoln Navigator to catch up with the traffic's pace. They were the first car to be stuck at the stop-light at the corner of Santa Monica Boulevard and North Highland Avenue, where they waited for the light to change, still arguing about the drink.

*   *   *

Having replaced the phone's receiver after getting no answer, the junkie waited a brief moment to collect his change, needing every single coin as he was dead broke and it was no joke. He was desperate for a little money, a little food and a big fix. Reggie Carringdon, called Curly, by his friends and family, had begun his downward spiral into despair when he'd been fired from his job for failing a random drug screening test. He had been a recreational user, much like most of Los Angeles, it seemed, taking a little pot through high school, and then moving onto cocaine. Next, he'd progressed to heroin, and after losing his job, he became hooked on crack cocaine. It had cost him his job, and then his wife and child. Now, here he was in the streets, having to fight for an existence every day. He still held onto the idea that his wife Donna, would take him back, saying to himself that he didn't really have a problem. He could, after all, stop anytime. He had been calling Donna all day, but she hadn't answered, and because of that, his rage had been building in angst all day. He desperately needed to speak to her, and he desperately needed a fix to set him straight for the rapidly approaching night. Donna hadn't answered her phone because she had been at the Silverlake Police Station for most of the day securing a restraining order against him. Curly had nowhere to go and nothing to lose. All he had was change.

Picking out a pack of gum from the front of the store counter, Curly gave the store a quick scan. The girl behind the counter was instantly on red alert from the moment he had walked in. She had a feeling he was no good. Curly handed the girl a fistful of change, hopping from side to side while he waited for the thing to happen. Simultaneously, as the store clerk hit the register's open tab on the cash register, Curly pulled a Taurus 850 CIA: Carry It Anywhere, .38 handgun from behind his back. In a fit of fear and from being nervous at this being his first hold up, he mistakenly squeezed the trigger. The loud boom of the handgun filled the whole store. At point blank range, the bullet tore through the cashier's body, imploding her Seven-Eleven, light green, polyester shirt just below her name tag: Sonia. The bullet missed her heart by a heartbeat, knocking her off her feet. She hit the floor hard.

Curly now had the opportunity he needed. He jumped the counter, landing on Sonia's ankle, nearly turning his ankle over in the process. He placed his feet on either side of her legs while she lay on the floor with blood bubbling up from her chest. Her eyes were glazed and weary. Her breathing was already soft and gurgling, as the air bubbles were being trapped by the blood flow from her heart. Curly had reached the point of no return. He was in shock and chose not to look at the girl lying quietly on the floor. The silence was deafening while he got busy grasping at the bills from the cash register. There were plenty of them and so it would be worth it. Tonight, he'd get high one last time and tomorrow he'd go find Donna and make it all alright with her again. Curly wouldn't know until later that night that his takings amounted to one hundred and seventeen dollars.

Sonia Bright's divorce had cost her dearly. It had cost her life, and now her son Guy had no mom, and a dad he barely knew. Guy was playing soccer with his friend Ben when the police turned up at the Vista Views Apartments on Laurel Avenue. Six years old and growing up fast, he was a happy kid who had been learning to read and write fast these days. His mom would have been there to help him finish reading *Thomas the Tank Engine* tonight.

Sonia Bright had taken four minutes to pass away on the cold, tiled floor, alone. Her last thought was about what Guy would eat tonight and who he would read to now.

89

'What we got Mike?' Detective Caron Smart asked.

'Female: one shot to the chest. Caucasian, twenty-five years old. I.D. shows her address as 1554 Vista View Apartments on Laurel Avenue. She had a picture of a young boy in her wallet. We're sending a black and white over to check on him.'

Detective Caron Smart and her partner Mike Adwell maneuvered their way through the Seven-Eleven store. Smart calmly gave some of the uniformed cops some things to do, saying that maybe the perp' had cased the place out first, before going in. Caron was a good cop. She and Mike Adwell had been partners for four years, longer than her marriage to her husband Jeremy, from England. Caron Smart was small in size and in her foot print, being a petite blonde, but she packed a big punch. She loved her job and she was great at it. She and Mike had the highest arrest rate in the Hollywood Robbery and Homicide Division.

Hollywood is known throughout the world as Tinsletown. Hollywood is paved with stars, along its Walk of Fame. But like the movies it makes, it is pure fantasy. The City of Hollywood is small compared to its neighboring cities. The tourists visit Hollywood by day, but the locals own the night. Hollywood is empty and has an empty soul. It has killed more innocent people in the lure of its gold-paved streets than any war. Lives have been lost through the realization that not everyone has what it takes, having to come to terms with the fact that not everyone is blessed with the stardust. The harsh reality is, that these aspiring actors must start to live their lives beating a trail, just like everyone else in any other town in Main Street U.S.A., with their dreams crushed. The characters in this saga arrive with no skills and no money to support themselves. In the long run, their fragile egos lead them off the brightly lit dreamscape path that is Hollywood Boulevard, into the back alleys of the darkened boulevard of broken dreams.

Caron Smart worked these boulevards and had become accustomed to the body count. As the sheet was pulled back on Sonia Bright, Caron looked down for a moment, thinking, *She kind of looks like me. We could've been sisters.* She snapped back into detective mode, saying sharply, 'Okay, let's see how much was taken.'

She pulled on her latex gloves and began to step over the body, asking, 'You can take her anytime you're ready. What's the caliber?'

'Looks like a thirty-eight,' the coroner answered as he

dropped the sheet back on Sonia's body.

'Any witnesses?' Caron asked the uniformed cop who'd been the first on scene. He and his partner had followed procedures by rounding up everyone within a one block radius as soon as they had arrived.

The cash register chugged out a receipt. Caron stood over it, watching as it sputtered out the subtotal.

'A hundred and twenty-eight dollars in the register, we probably got about five bucks in change here. She was killed for around a hundred and twenty bucks,' Smart said in a harsh disconnected way.

'We got a couple of independent witnesses. Both of them saw a black Navigator pulling out and haulin' ass towards Highland,' the uniformed officer answered her, looking at Smart for a response.

She didn't bite, replying, 'No one driving a Navigator's going to hit this place for a hundred and change. What else?'

'Same thing. The driver who pulled in to the store, who called it in, says he saw a black Navigator pull out before he pulled in to the lot, says he didn't see anyone else go in or out of the store.'

Caron looked at Mike.

He just shrugged and with a coy look, said, 'Maybe it's stolen?' He added, 'Maybe they needed gas money?'

Caron looked around the register booth and took it all in. What did those last minutes feel like? She looked in the cash register draw. She had seen it all too often. Now, her only emotion was a desire to get home each morning and to make sure she caught as many bad guys as she could. She looked back at Adwell, with the uniformed officer standing next to him. She looked at the receipt print out one more time. The last ring-up was for a seventy cents pack of Juicy Fruits. The one before that was for a Big Gulp, a Coca-Cola, two Almond Snickers bars and a pack of Marlboros. Caron focused her thoughts on the task at hand, saying, 'You said the Navigator turned east on Santa Monica?'

The uniformed cop nodded in the affirmative, with his hands on his hips. One palm rested on his gun and the other one sat on his Billy club.

Caron turned to Mike, and simply said, 'Call it in. Get ten minutes before the time of the shooting, and ten minutes after, from the traffic stop-light cameras at the corners of Santa Monica and La Brea, and Santa Monica and Highland. Tell them to print every license plate and face of every driver in a black Navigator. Now let's pull the store's security tape and see what went down.'

90

The sun was setting on Hollywood. The sky was filled with hues of orange as the big ball of fire retreated over the Santa Monica Mountains. The early twilight was a perfect time for this kind of thing. The shadows were long, allowing for good cover while still being able to see the terrain. The first thing he saw was a black Navigator come up the dirt track. Its black body-work gleamed under the dirtied tires as it stopped in a spot of open ground; it looked like it had plenty of room for a quick exit, should one be required. It slowly turned around to face back down the hill, giving the driver a clear view of Los Angeles' Westside. The Navigator cut its engine and everything became calm, while it sat proudly above the din of Los Angeles. No one got out and no one could be seen inside.

A few minutes later, a low rumble and a heavy roll of wheels crunching on stones and dirt could be heard. An armada of cars rolled up, fanning out at various points on the hill. Two cars raced up above the parked Navigator and then turned to face looking down on it from the higher ground. The Navigator's driver's and passenger doors opened. Two well-framed, burly, six foot plus men got out from it and walked a couple of feet to the front of the car. Doors opened from six cars and numerous men of all shapes and sizes jumped out from their rides, most showing their weapons in plain view, tucked in the front of their belt straps. They were tattooed and all of them looked like they wanted to shoot the other men right off the bat. One of the Sureño gangbangers walked up towards the two Club Bangers, stopping around four feet in front of them to say something dismissive. The exchange was underway.

Joey Casa kept his hunter's rifle trained on the head of the gangsta who was standing in front of J-Rock, with his finger poised on the trigger. His breathing was cool, calm and collected; just a touch on the trigger and the gangsta's head would pop open like a smashed grapefruit hit by a hammer. He watched the homey in his scope become animated in his conversation.

Both men looked hard at each other, as the gangbanger pulled something out from his back pocket. Joey exhaled and concentrated on his target. The young Sureño tapped the keys on his cell phone, briefly speaking on it; he hung up abruptly. Both men seemed to be in a Mexican standoff. Then, just as abruptly, the Southsider turned away from J-Rock and shouted to his men, who went into action. Franz had never moved from his position, covering his partner.

Joey didn't allow himself to be distracted by the noise emanating up from the track below. He followed the gangbanger in his sights back down the hill to his car, where he was handed a heavy duffle bag that he opened and checked. Then he dropped it on the floor and a Sureño soldier picked it up. He began walking back up the hill towards the Navigator with the other gangbanger carrying the duffle bag. Casa reversed the same procedure, hoping his partner Nicky Z was doing the same from his own vantage point. Zacarro had ventured off on the other side of the track to find his own sniper's position earlier. Both men met in the middle of no man's land. The heavy duffle bag was thrown forward and landed heavily. J-Rock handed over a yellow manila envelope that the Sureño roughly tore open and looked in, with his own soldier standing a few feet from him to counter Franz's position. Joey was still locked on the head shot, but he could see that a discussion was taking place.

Then it was done. Both men gave each other a pound of their clenched fists, knuckle-to-knuckle. The Southsider abruptly turned away and walked back down the hill towards the cars. Once the gangbanger was safely inside, the other gunslingers returned to theirs. A loud noise of car engines picked up and shot through the quiet of the Sunset Ranch dirt track. Joey followed his target until he was out of sight around the bend. He swung his rifle back over to the Navigator to see that his own guys were safely back in their ride. He watched them descend the dirt track. He decided to wait for about ten minutes before slinking out from his position, just in case the Southsiders had secretly positioned their own snipers, and to make sure there wasn't any tail, thinking they might roll them for the guns back at their digs.

Joey was done. From where he sat, things looked like they had gone according to plan. His plan. The sellers had tried to change the deal at the last minute and J-Rock had countered with his own offer, one that Joey had figured would be appealing to a crew like this one. It had all worked out and no one had got hurt. Everyone had gotten to go home, and from what Joey could tell, it was an evening's good work.

'Good work,' Mike said, as he snapped his phone shut while he walked over to Caron. She was sitting in the police car writing in her crime scene dossier. He told her, 'Only one Navigator came through at the time immediately after the shooting. The plates came back registered to a Michael Donne, and get this, Michael Donne's a white; fifty-two-year old taxi driver, living in Las Vegas. He reported his Ford Expedition stolen eight days ago from there. I just got off the phone with him; he's been at work all day.'

Caron looked at Mike, questioning him, 'In Las Vegas?'

Knowing it was a rhetorical question, he answered, 'Yep, viva Las Vegas, baby!'

This was getting better and better. Caron Smart had, only minutes earlier, put out an A.P.B: All Points Bulletin on a Caucasian, male, five feet ten, with long, black curly hair, weighing approximately one hundred and sixty pounds, wanted for the murder of a store clerk at precisely 7:10 p.m., three blocks from the corner of Santa Monica Boulevard and North Highland Avenue in Hollywood. The fugitive is armed and dangerous; use extreme caution in apprehending him. He is described as a homeless, dishevelled-looking, drug user.

Having watched the videotape at the crime scene, it was obvious who had done what. Only the merest of seconds had passed between the two men; while one walked out, the other had walked in. Detective Smart had originally wanted the man in the Navigator as a witness, having been the last man to see the store clerk alive as the junkie walked in. That man's testimony could have put it all together for the District Attorney to put this scum down for the rest of his miserable life. She had expected to be taking the driver's statement within the hour, but now things had taken a turn for the worse. Now Caron Smart had two cases. One was a first degree murder. The other, for now, was a federal offence of Grand Theft Auto across state lines, and who knows what else? The first forty-eight hours were critical in any homicide, especially involving a transient. Caron would let the black and whites cruise the back alleys of Hollywood, rousting their informants and hustling up the pushers to see what Intel they could come up with in the streets of L.A. Caron now turned her attention to a bigger target. She put out a B.O.L.O: Be On the Look Out, for a black Lincoln Navigator that had peeled out of the Seven-Eleven parking lot. But more importantly now, and what she wanted to know was, why did it have fake plates?

'Yeah, we cool. Everything's like you said. Yeah, they were pro's,' Coco said, reliving the details of the deal. He spoke to Bezerk on his cell phone while being driven back to Bezerk's pad in Hollywood Hills. Coco had taken a couple of lines of coke; he was high from the adrenaline rush of being face-to-face with a potential enemy. Coco never knew that he wouldn't have even seen Franz pull his pistol; all he had to do was put his arm up in the air and Coco's skull would've been split in half by the high caliber round that Casa would have fired. He continued with his rap, telling Bezerk, 'They gonna come down to the club this weekend. He seemed cool; but said he didn't run shit. His man wants to meet you, said he wants some lines on which joints to take down while they're in town. Dude said they didn't want to hit the wrong ones. Said they'd cut you in on the scores. No shit. Yeah, I know. Cool, huh?'

Coco laughed as he heard a low-pitched giggle ringing out in his ear from Bezerk. Bezerk was being Bezerk. Always thuggin', he'd keep thuggin' 'til the Fed's come get him.

*　　　*　　　*

Curly had made his getaway through the side exit that led onto North Orange Drive. He walked two blocks, then cut over to North Highland Avenue, and caught the thirty-eight bus up to Hollywood. He was close to two miles from the murder scene and he could taste the cocaine. Reggie Carringdon walked another half a mile or so along the south side of Fountain Boulevard, one block below Sunset Boulevard. He then cut along Laurel Avenue, keeping his head low and his pace sharp, once he noticed a black and white police cruiser parked ahead in the dark. It was parked in a red zone outside the Vista Views Apartments. Giving it a quick, timid glance, Curly kept hustling up the hill, moving seemingly faster with every step, feeling he was getting closer to his hook-up and his fix. Tonight, he was going to celebrate his last night of being a junkie. He'd throw all his cash in the pot and buy a speedball, getting what's known in Hollywood as a Belushi, and it would be a righteous high. Then tomorrow, he'd begin again, reborn. Clean. But tonight, just to see how it felt, he'd go all the way and get himself a forty/fifty to shoot up, forty percent cocaine and fifty percent heroin. Yeah, tonight would be like going to heaven. He'd get himself so high; that he'll be looking down on Heaven.

93

'HEAVEN, Mr. Knoxx. That is what we require you to do.' Tasker held Mark's gaze in a stern look, not yet satisfied that he was actually in, as he had said. 'We require you to carry out specific orders that will be communicated to you, sometimes daily, weekly or even several months apart, requiring you to follow the orders to the letter, without question.'

With that remark, Tasker looked over at a Secret Service agent, who then walked up to the table. Tasker looked at John D'intino, seated four chairs along from his left. The Secret Service agent stopped in front of D'intino, where a short interaction took place. D'intino handed a white envelope to him and he walked it over to Knoxx, promptly handing it to him.

Tasker said, 'This is your first assignment. We expect it to be carried out to the exact requirements described inside.' While Knoxx began to open the letter, Tasker continued, 'Input the instructions into HEAVEN. We will make sure the target is placed in one of the hospitals that are trialing it. I trust this can be done?' He asked in a not so asking way, watching Knoxx's face while he read the two lines that were typed on the pearl white paper.

Knoxx reacted immediately to what he had read. 'You've got to be kidding me?' He looked up to face Tasker in utter disbelief. He read the letter again, realizing he'd read it correctly. His eyes flicked back up to Tasker, questioning him. 'This is for real? You're really going to take this guy out? But I thought he was a friend of yours, of ours, one of our allies. I don't get it, why?'

'It's not for you to ask or to reason why, only to do, and you are required to do this. We are starting you out in this grand fashion, so that we'll know for sure that you are, as you say, 'in,' so I'll ask you again. I trust this can be done and HEAVEN can complete this task, flawlessly?'

'Yes, I'm sure it will, but why? Why this guy?' Knoxx answered with the same question again, his voice taking on more of a pleading tone. His heart felt wrenched again, being caught in the middle, being asked to participate in the murder of a seemingly innocent, good man. Tasker showed no such remorse or hesitation as he once again rose to the challenge thrown down by Knoxx. His one word summed it up, saying bluntly, 'Leverage.'

Knoxx looked blankly at him. His eyes seemed to dull, as once again, he was in a place that he didn't want to be. In a dark place, in a dark light, with the enlightened ones. That was all they would allow him. The explanation was complete. Knoxx was being drafted into a war that had been raging for two thousand years.

Tasker asked again, 'HEAVEN can do what we think it can do, correct?'

Everyone in the room believed it was up to the task. Assassinating presidents.

Knoxx replied, 'Yeah, it can do it. It can be activated from anywhere in the world. I can input instructions and upload them into the DRAM: the Dynamic Random Access Memory, on the web. The information is tamper-proof and is primed to set a worm into any hospital's healthcare records throughout the world. As soon as the records are activated or updated for the targeted patient, HEAVEN will activate its download protocol and modify that patient's records. As it has no host drive, portal or Internet Service Provider, it can't be switched off. It'll sit embedded in the net, lying dormant, constantly searching millions of computer terminals all over the world. Basically, it's a highly mobile worm that's transferable between the Internet and web-enabled phones. The hybrid program can be morphed into whatever weapon required. It can kill instantaneously or it can leave the patient in a variety of states, such as a coma, stroke, memory loss, heart attacks of any strength, any number of ailments, leaving the target incapacitated. HEAVEN can decide who gets to live or die, and I have absolute power over it. It can lay dormant, with your name in the program. Then years later, if you have to go into hospital for any reason, and you're on the list – the guest list, I call it - then your number's up and you're on a stairway to Heaven.'

Knoxx ended ominously but with pride, feeling a rush of excitement streak through him, knowing he'd got his point across. Anyone who messed with him could be the one who had bought their ticket to Heaven. Even though he may be dead, years later, so would his enemies. It was a message that was delivered crystal clear to the thirteen most powerful men in the world. They had their man. The one they had chosen was the best candidate for the job. The firmness of his voice and the confidence in his delivery led Knoxx to believe that he was, now in fact, in. Having heard his own words, he was quickly becoming intoxicated with the feeling of power he'd be able to unleash. He would be the ultimate judge and jury.

'Very good, Mr. Knoxx,' Tasker stated approvingly, now looking at him as one of their own.

The Secret Service agent repeated his path to Knoxx with what looked like a cellular phone. He handed it to him. Knoxx studied it sitting in his left hand. It didn't look like any phone he'd seen before, thinking, *where's the keypad?*

'My name is Michael Midway; I'm the deputy director for

MI6.' Knoxx knew the man's accent well, having been born in Bournemouth, Dorset on the South Coast of England, about one hour's drive from London. Michael Midway leaned forward to rest his heavy arms on the table. His belly, Knoxx knew well too, thinking, *fish and chips, washed down with several pints of beer, no doubt.* Midway looked and spoke every inch a cockney boy from East London. He said next, 'The phone in your hand is an Israeli-designed, level five, military prototype. It's designed for maximum security and emits no pulse to cell towers that require an electrical signal for telephone transmission, so your actual location can never be zeroed in on. Any phone conversation will then take place piggybacked over a phone line that will convert to another phone line every two minutes or so. We're working on reducing this timeline, but the objective of the phone is to provide a seamless, hacking-proof capability. The caller can place a phone call and be in any location without the fear of leaving any footprint emitted by the phone itself. You might recall the C.I.A. mission in Italy to capture and remove a high-level Al Qaeda terrorist. The agents were successful in capturing him. They flew him out from Aviano air force base in northeast Italy to Egypt, where he could then be tortured legally. Their undoing however, was the electronic pulses that their cell phones emitted. Checking the local Italian cell phone towers proved the operatives were in the country at the time of the abduction. It all got very messy after that, C.I.A. agents operating illegally in an ally's backyard. Once you imprint your fingerprints on the phone's screen, it can only be accessed by you. It's called biometrics, and it's completely tamper-proof. I won't bother you with the details. It's yours, fire it up. Hold your palm, or any part of your hand, on the phone for five seconds. It will read your fingerprint or palm print randomly and, once it's confirmed in its memory, the phone can only be turned on by you. You can make calls to and from just about anywhere in the world, and all international calls are free.'

Midway allowed himself a cheeky grin towards his fellow Brit as he'd said that. Knoxx smiled back as he watched the phone light up.

'Whoa,' he sighed. His eyes danced across the screen as it filled up with numerous icons as if he was looking at a computer screen.

'Try it out later; the phone is called a SWIFT phone: Secured Wireless Internet Frequency Telephone. Once you've dialed any number, the phone will automatically store that number with the name and location of the person you've called, having searched the telephone exchange for that country. You can also reverse lookup your caller while you're talking to them, so you'll know where they are while they're talking to you. Anyone you want to have your phone number, simply give them a five digit code. Yours is 26 1 88. 26 1 88, that's it. You can figure the rest out. There's a twenty-four hour hotline that you can call anytime for any reason, and I do mean for any reason, from anywhere in the world. If you need to know something, or you need our assistance, use the phone, you understand me? This phone's classified. Don't, under any circumstances, lose it.'

Midway turned decidedly cold. Knoxx gave a familiar nod, understanding his meaning. His message was clear: don't fuck up. Mark was doing his best to absorb it all and to understand his position in it all, and the ramifications of him being a party to this.

Tasker moved in to close the deal, saying, 'In our lifetime, we will be in an all out world war, probably over oil; maybe it will be over technology, or even over clean drinking water. God knows we've certainly had our fill of wars being fought over religion. We live in uncertain times, Mr. Knoxx, but you can be certain of one thing: we will win. Even if it takes another thousand years, we will win. And now that you've accepted your destiny, to become a soldier for good, joining us in that fight, I will also tell you one other thing that is certain. You must kill to get in, and you will have to die to get out.'

94

'Get out, no way! I don't believe it!' Caron exclaimed excitedly in response to what she'd heard. Her face became a picture of disbelief, when she quickly followed up with a staccato of, 'Uh huh, uh huh, okay, yeah,' and an excitable, 'all right!'

Caron Smart looked across the squad room to find Mike Adwell. When she did, she gave him a big emphatic wave to get his attention. He stopped his conversation and came back over to her in his big ol' self way. He looked down on his hardened crime fighter, sitting at her desk, and asked, 'What you got?'

Caron retorted excitedly, 'You know the B.O.L.O. I put out on our Navigator.'

Mike nodded. 'Yeah,' waiting for the rest.

'Well, we've got a hit on it! Awesome, hey?'

'Yeah, babe, that's real cool. Where is it?' Mike responded enthusiastically.

'A black and white picked it up, cruising along Hollywood Boulevard. It's just crossed Hollywood and Vine, heading west. I've just ordered up a sheriff's helicopter to come over and follow it. You never know, maybe they're on a job,' Caron answered.

She looked up at Mike for encouragement, listening to him reply, 'Sure thing, girl, good looking. Man, you're one hard-ass girl; you got the killer instincts. I'm glad I'm on your team and not one of the bad guys. Ain't no one getting out from under my girl,' Mike quipped. He fell back in his seat at his desk, laughing a long and slow chuckle; he then asked his own cop question, 'Hey, any news on the photo printout from the traffic stop-light camera?'

'Oh yeah, thanks. That reminds me, I really need to get my desk organized. Hmm yeah, I'll call down now. Hang on a minute.'

Mike did as he was told. Caron was the hard charging, office type. He was for the street stuff, rousting up the pimps, hustlers and shakers, shaking them down and intimidating them. He got right up close and personal as Caron's three hundred pound gorilla. When she put him onto someone, he was on them to break them down and bust them up. Mike swung back in his chair and kicked back, watching his girl do her thing.

The little blonde dynamo whirred into action again, forcing the play and not letting the computer tech, big-ass tattooed Russ Hay, blow her off. Big Russ always had a coffee mug beside him that everyone swore was laced with gin. His tattoos portrayed every nuance of his crazy life with an array of girls that had come and always gone. Caron had managed to bully big Russ into pushing her case to the top of the hit list. She reasoned with him that, as she was on the phone with him, he might as well deal with her now. She coerced and cajoled him along, slowly eking it out of him, until she blasted out, 'Are you kidding me?' Caron stood up from her seat and quickly followed up with, 'No way! Are you shitting me?'

Adwell sat up straight, knowing this had to be real good, seriously good if Caron had used profanity. Her face told him that it would soon be time to saddle up and get going. His face turned to stone while he waited some more. Caron scratched at her desk, looking for a pen; she snapped her fingers at Mike who produced one, slapping it into her hand like a surgeon's scalpel.

Caron roughly wrote her notes. She said in a hurried manner, 'Russ, this is priority one, okay? The guys in that car are on our watch list. They're wanted for a string of murders and robberies from coast to coast. Track the car from the central computer through the traffic flow cameras, just in case we lose them on the streets.' She listened, giving Mike a look of, 'fucking hell, I just want to get after these bastards.' She said hurriedly, 'Okay great, thanks, Russ. Love you, baby!'

She slammed the phone down and then looked at Mike. He said in good humor, 'Looks like someone's licked an ice cream cone?'

Caron beamed at him while she picked up her gun and shield. Then sliding on her coat, she said, 'Come on. Let's go.'

'Let's go.' With that command, the plane leapt forward from its standing still start. The roar of the plane's twin Rolls Royce engines propelled them up and away. Neither one spoke at this point. Each one felt the back of his head being pushed into the headrest of the soft leather chairs. In a short minute, the plane had reached its cruising altitude and had leveled off for the return trip back to New York.

Deavins broke the ice with a quip, asking a rhetorical question, 'Things went well then? Otherwise, I guess you wouldn't be here now, now would you?'

Pulling out a chilled bottle of champagne from the cabinet, a wry smile filled his heavy-jowled face. His ice blue eyes came alive and warm. He laughed at his joke, while he began to rip at the covering on the neck of the bottle. Despite knowing little of the meeting, Deavins knew he had done his job well by bringing Knoxx to meet The Firm. He was obviously pleased with the outcome but he was more pleased with the outcome for himself, knowing he'd receive praise and a big bonus.

Mark wasted no time in getting into it with him, asking pointedly, 'Can the Illuminati really be the savior of humanity?'

Deavins hesitated at pulling the cork and lowered the bottle of Perrier Jouet between his knees. His posture lowered too, along with his voice. 'I refer to them as The Firm, Mr. Knoxx. From where I sit, it's very profitable being in business with them. Like I told you on the way in, I'm just a facilitator of information. They make the final decision on whether they wish to proceed with any candidate. I work alone and that's how I prefer it. But I'll tell you this. I think The West has become as soft as the grass we walk on, bending under pressure, always choosing to lean towards the warm sunlight while ignoring the weeds that are growing in the garden, choking out the grass, infesting it until it withers away.'

Deavins' simple analogy left Knoxx in pensive thought. Deavins proceeded to pop the cork on the champagne and began to sink the fine wine into two flutes. Knoxx felt reflective, thinking of happier times. He had wanted all of this, hadn't he? But it did seem to be true. What goes around comes around, and you damn well better be careful what you wish for. You just might get it.

Be careful what you wish for, you might just get it. And right now he was smack in the middle of getting it. Putting the bottle of booze tight to his lips, he sucked it hard, down to the bottom. He pushed the syringe in deep, sending the crystals in to race through his veins and give him the rush of a lifetime. Curly had gotten what he wanted, what he had killed for, and now he was reaping the benefits. Pure bliss.

The Belushi, a mixture of cocaine and heroin, hit his veins like hard driven snow, and the high hit him instantly. His mind and heart were happy, content and totally free and clear. It had turned out to be the best idea he'd had, and definitely worth all the hassle he'd had to go through to get it. Now he was able to enjoy the fruits of his labor. The roller coaster high had sent him so damn high that he really was looking down on Heaven. But then, just as quickly, the pressure from coming down felt as though he was descending in tight circles, forever falling from the sky ever so fast. His whole body had gone weightless, with the needle still hanging from the inside of his elbow. The vein throbbed from the overload his body had just endured. Curly had a fixed smile on his face but wore eyes that were dead. He was falling in slow motion, covered in a clean white light. It bathed him in disco lights that were turning in tight circles, keeping him entertained and calm. Everything was going downwards at hundreds of miles per hour. Yet everything felt like it was in slow motion, as if he was suspended in a deep, dark ocean that had begun to pull him down as he floated in it. Alone and freezing cold, he was too tired to pull his face up, listening to his heart beating along with his slow breathing. It was like he was being born. He was stripped bare and his soulless body was totally white, bathed and cleaned in a white light. He was at peace and very happy. He sat there, limp and lifeless, with a warm tear on his cheek and a smile on his face, free of all sins. His head rested against a 1st Waste Management sticker.

The two L.A.P.D. police officers, Jay Colter and Alistair Elwins, stood over him in the dark alley with their hands on their hips, just watching. Their radios crackled. Their crisp uniformed outlines cut silhouettes out of the blinding white light from the searchlight on the police cruiser. The emergency lights on top of the car gyrated quietly in tight circles. The cops watched him slip away from this world to the next, slumped beside a trash container, ready for the morning's trash collection. The police officers were both thinking the same thing about this guy. Poetic Justice.

'Poetic justice.' The group laughed with Maxine and Teresa, as Maxine continued, 'That's what I call it.'

Dobro recited the series of events from the night before. Each time, her story became more elaborate in its description of how her girl, Teresa, had got the better of the man she despised, Mark Knoxx. The portrayal ended in a fit of laughter when she told the assembled few that they'd been asked to leave by Knoxx's security.

Maxine had been in high spirits all day. She knew she had found a sidekick in her newfound friend, who was, in her eyes, heaven sent. Both girls laughed at times during the day, reliving the look on Knoxx's face as he'd had to retreat from their table. Maxine just loved recounting Teresa's line, 'He thinks he's James Bond!'

They both knew they had some serious work to do though. Maxine train of thought was that, after last night's events she was sure Knoxx would try to do something to impede her investigation, some kind of bogus harassment suit maybe. He had all the right moves and he always seemed to be one step ahead of her. Teresa, Maxine, and a few other agents got down to forming a strategy to mount some kind of attack.

Teresa took the lead in the conference room with her hair pinned back, giving her dark complexion a high-cheek-boned look. Wearing a figure-hugging suit and tight pearl white shirt, she began her presentation in a tight format, explaining, 'Investors are like cattle. You just need the right cattle prod to push them along with, and Knoxx seems to have found the right type of investor; one who isn't worried about capital gains or tax write-offs. I think he's being paid percentage points for laundering illicit funds; maybe he's cleaning drug money? One thing's for sure, he must have the basis for a high octane investment platform as the capital his companies seem to be burning through each month will need to be returned at a high rate of interest.'

Everyone in the room looked at each other not knowing how to approach this obstacle. Knoxx looked as if he was buried in deep.

Dobro was looking radiant herself today, with her hair shiny and her face radiating like the sun itself. She was on a par with Hadley, only her hair was dark and full as it lay down either side of her face. Maxine, being no shrinking violet, forced the meeting along by joking, 'Well people, it's better to go in with a half-ass plan, than no plan at all. So let's find us some leverage.'

Leverage. That's what Tasker had told him. That's right. That's what they had on him, and what they had used against him, he thought, while he sat in the plane. They'd got him to comply and now they had control.

'Everybody has a secret. It's what makes them unique. Something they can hide within themselves. You just have to find it, and then, when you do, you have them, and then you have leverage,' Deavins said matter-of-factly as he tipped his head to Knoxx, finishing their conversation.

Relaxed in the knowledge that he was nearly done with all this espionage stuff for the day, Knoxx sipped the last of his Perrier Jouet, allowing himself a little smile as the plane began its descent. Just last night, he'd been accused of sounding like James Bond, and now, here he was James Bond. He had been admitted into a shadow world of espionage, geopolitics, becoming involved in the assassinations of influential world figures. He was carrying his first mission inside his jacket pocket, two lines of typed instructions that held such power. Now he carried that unbridled power inside him. His mind filtered back to the night before. The bitch.

The bitch Dobro and the new one, the new bitch, special agent, fucking Hadley. Yeah, he'd heard of her, and had heard that she'd been assigned to his case, but now, she was too good for her own good. She had shown him up last night. Taking his time to relive the moment, he remembered her saying, 'He thinks he's James Bond.' He remembered how they had all laughed at him.

He felt his anger returning again and felt a flush of vengeance in his heart. Knoxx had developed a dark heart. He knew how to fight, because he was a student of *The Art of War*. The devil is in the details. He only needed one thing to finish this war with Dobro, and as it came to him, he whispered the word. 'Leverage.'

Breaking his silence as the plane began to come in on its final descent, Knoxx asked, 'What leverage can I use on anyone who's trying to fuck with me?'

Deavins looked at him in a nonchalant way. With no real thought, he replied, 'Whatever protects you, will in turn protect us. Every one of us is expendable. No one is a ruler. If you're in any doubt, when the time's right, just use your phone to clarify things with The Firm. They're most agreeable and will give you quite a bit of latitude, as long as you're a worthy soldier. So, as you so eloquently put it. If anyone does, "fuck with you", then use as much leverage as you like to simply, fuck them back.'

Knoxx mulled it over, his blue eyes turning a shade of gray, as his thoughts proceeded to turn darker. There would never be anymore white for him; he lived in the black now. The black-book operations of the Illuminati, where there was no going back to a world of ignorance. A world of knowing the true lies of good and just men. Now he knew the secrets, and everything he thought he knew were lies. The leverage he had been searching for came to him in an instant, and it caused him to slither out a slow smirk at the thought of it. It was further than even he thought he could ever go to hurt someone, but he was in a fight, a fight to the death, and he sure wasn't going to go down without the other side knowing that they had been in a fight too. He drew upon Tasker's words, 'When you have secured the leverage, you have compliance, which ultimately leads to control.'

A sly, dark smear razed across his face once he realized he knew what to do. From his own investigation into Dobro life, looking for her secrets; the chink in her armor, he now realized he knew what it was. He would manipulate the scenario to make it work in his favor and then, once it was complete, he would have her. Knoxx savored the thought. He would have two things from Dobro, eventually. Compliance and control.

The plane glided into the hangar effortlessly and sidled up to the demarcation point. The plane shielded any view from the outside world while the hangar doors closed in on them. The bright daylight from outside faded to gray inside. The men disembarked and stood in the shadows. Paul Deavins took Knoxx by his arm and closed the gap, saying assuredly, 'Man only has two things in life to live by. Dreams, and the courage to live them out. It doesn't matter what you do in life, people will always condemn you for what you've done, but at least you've done, something. Someone has to do the good, the bad and the ugly. You are now on your way, Mr. Knoxx. This is the beginning of The Enterprise.'

99

The enterprising fashion that L.A.P.D. detective, Caron Smart always employed in her style of police work, more often than not, paid off. Although she put it down to ninety percent motivation and ten percent perspiration, the other detectives called it luck. Caron and Mike had the highest arrest rate because she was willing to look at the edges of the crime, where the clear lines blur into the gray area of the unknown. It was called the back-story of a crime, which was where Caron thrived in her job, investigating the details. Most of the time it paid off handsomely, and tonight it was looking more like this investigation of a two-bit, nickel and dime convenience store shooting was just about to go off the hook, big time. Caron had scratched at the borders of a crime and had come up with a big cockroach. The light was now on the cockroach, only this particular one didn't know the light was on him.

'Okay. He's turned west onto Sunset now. He's in the second lane and staying within the speed limit. Everything seems normal. Over.'

The Sheriff Department's police helicopter had the black Navigator painted with its laser designator. No matter where the S.U.V. turned the laser had the car glowing in the dark like a glow-worm in a sealed box. And that's what the L.A.P.D. now had it: in a box. Detective Smart had called for backup. Now the Navigator was being tailed by seven unmarked police cars, with some running parallel to it above and below on Fountain and Hollywood Boulevard. The detectives from the Hollywood Robbery and Homicide Division had responded to the call. Uniformed black and whites were seconds away from the scene for additional back up and S.W.A.T. was suited up, sitting in a truck, awaiting further instructions. None of them knew what they were up against at this point, but no one was taking any chances. The unit was working seamlessly. The helicopter pilot had confirmed through his infrared scope that the Navigator had two individuals riding inside. Smart had confirmed who those two individuals were.

One was John Rockwell, a.k.a. J-Rock: white male, six foot, two hundred and twenty-two pounds, aged twenty-nine. Individual number two was Franz Bochetta: white male, six foot one, two hundred and twelve pounds, aged twenty-nine. Both were wanted in connection with three counts of murder, armed robbery and Grand Theft Auto. 'Use extreme caution, code 10-30,' Smart said, reading their criminal records over the radio.

'Okay, we see 'em. This is Richmond 2 taking up the lead position. All units, be advised, hold the perimeter and let the Beverly Hills P.D. know we'll be coming through their backyard. Tell them to hold off their black and whites. We don't want these guys getting spooked, and then have us runnin' and gunnin' with them before we're ready. Over.'

Dan McGann spoke succinctly into the radio while he sat in the passenger seat of their unmarked police car. His partner, Richard Keets was driving tonight. They laid back a healthy five cars, never changing lanes to catch up; knowing the eye in the sky had The Club Bangers locked down. All they had to do was sit tight and run with them for maybe two or three miles. Then the next unit would take over, probably Detective's Ray Tombs and David Blisset, who were now sitting further along Sunset Boulevard in front of them. Everyone was on point and on top of their game tonight. They had all worked together for a long while now, and like most offices, they had their office politics to deal with, but when something like this came down, they came together to drop the hammers down on the bad guys. Each officer knew the other one had their back. They were always going to be the top team in this town: Hollywood Robbery and Homicide were the team to beat.

The Navigator stayed on a straight line, weaving its way through the beautiful, serene multimillion dollar mansions, stretching back up from Sunset Boulevard through Beverly Hills. Detective Dan McGann radioed that they would stay on its tail in case they cruised Sunset all the way down to the coast to Pacific Palisades. The net was becoming tighter around the Navigator. Smart and Adwell had now joined up with the other units. Caron waved across to one of her good friends, Richard Groome, affectionately referred to by all the cops as Groomie, was driving with Detective Roy Bowen. Caron instructed them to move on ahead and cut down into Westwood, which was where the vast majority of the UCLA students lived.

'They might turn in to Westwood Village from Sunset.' Caron said, trying to guess their route while trying to cover all the angles.

Groomie responded, 'Roger that.'

Their car veered off to take up its position ahead of the Lincoln Navigator. A few minutes later, while the Navigator drove through the tree-lined Sunset Boulevard, that's exactly what happened. Moments later, the Navigator came to a stop at the front of the W Hotel at 930 Hilgard Avenue, just north of Westwood Village. One male stepped out and spoke to the driver who kept the engine running for a minute. The passenger closed the door and the male, now identified as John Rockwell, walked into the W Hotel. Ray Tombs and

David Blisset, parked up further along the block and walked back to the hotel. The Navigator pulled off from the hotel.

'Take him down at the next light, three blocks from here. It's a dark residential spot.' Caron got on the radio to tell the other officers, 'All units, be advised, we're moving in on the subject at the intersection of Hilgard and Le Conte Avenue to take him down.' The time had come to spring the trap. Caron knew this was going to be her best opportunity, while the driver was alone and obviously unaware that he'd been made. Caron was a take-no-shit, hardened street cop, and when the tough decisions had to be made, she left no one in doubt that she was more than capable of making them. She made the call, saying in her radio, 'Go, Go, Go!'

Cars screeched in from all sides. Groomie's police car slammed up against the drivers' door to prevent it from opening. Within a second of the first car pulling up next to the Navigator, around eight weapons were rapidly being leveled at the driver from all directions. Commands were ringing out in unison. A huge spotlight from above draped everyone in a thousand-watt-arc-light. It seemed as if Heaven itself had fallen in on Franz Bochetta. Only a minute earlier he'd been listening to the KISS FM radio station and now he'd been caught driving a stolen Navigator with illegal weapons stashed in the trunk. Before he could react in an aggressive manner, it was already too late. A blond, six foot two, heavy set dude was already up on him, with his nine millimeter Smith and Wesson pistol shoved in his face, ordering him to put his hands on the steering wheel. Some other big, dark-haired guy had a shotgun pointed at him through the windshield, standing on the hood of the car that had pulled up in front of him. Franz was done. Caron Smart called it in on the radio, '10-15.' Letting everyone know that they had the prisoner in custody.

Franz was pulled out of the car and manhandled onto the tarmac. The sheriff's helicopter moved off. All the other units went about their regular work of patrolling the streets of L.A. One black and white unit, driven by officers Jay Colter and Alistair Elwins, decided they'd hit a few back alleys and see if they came upon Carringdon, the suspect in connection with the Seven-Eleven shooting. Maybe they'd get to wrap this whole thing up tonight. Their patrol car rolled off and began snaking its way back up through West Hollywood towards Hollywood.

100

Bochetta was toast. He had an arsenal of weapons in the car and his criminal jacket was thick and heavy with crimes, and that would be what they would use to drown him.

McGann and Keets pushed Bochetta into the back of their police car. They were known as two tough dudes in Hollywood and they'd be perfect for the ride back to begin the routine that all the cops knew well: breaking down the suspect, getting him to crack and then get him to turn on his partners. What they wanted was manipulation, compliance, and then control and Dan and Richie were the best at doing this. No one really knew how they did what they did, but everyone knew they were the go-to-guys. They were known as The Westside Pimps. Most cops liked them and their style, while some didn't.

Franz was cuffed and strapped down tight to the hook on the rear seat. Dan gave Caron a high five. Who would have believed it, and who could have known that it would fall into place like this? It was only because of Caron's dogged police work that she had brought in a whale.

The last of the police cars drove off and silence fell upon the sleepy street again. Dan and Richie spoke with Caron, and it was agreed that they would sweat this guy first to see what they could get from him before pulling in J-Rock, who still had no idea that the cops were on to him. Detective Dave Blisset radioed in that J-Rock was sitting at the bar in the hotel, trying his luck with a couple of babes; a couple of good-looking ones at that, he had reported.

For Franz, his night was over. For the Hollywood Robbery and Homicide Division it was just beginning. They had him cold. Franz was going to be put away on ice for life. With his brand new attorney sitting by his side, Franz Bochetta cut himself a deal. Dan and Richie had done their thing through a combination of being slightly mad themselves, they let Bochetta know that they'd turn him loose on the streets right now, and put the word out that he was their snitch, or that they'd come looking for him and kill him themselves. Whatever their tactics were, they usually worked.

The detective's back at the house gave Caron her props. She was the star of the show and promptly invited them for drinks at Barney's Beanery, the cop bar on Santa Monica Boulevard. Up to that point she had them, but then, by saying she would sing karaoke, she lost them.

Franz Bochetta's deal was simple. He'd wear a wire and be cut loose for forty-eight hours under strict supervision. He'd have to secure another meeting with the Southsider crew and find out where and when The Club Bangers' next takedown was going to be. Then they'd talk about a deal. The guns were disabled and put back in the Lincoln Navigator, and within an hour, a task force was sent out to cover the remaining Club Bangers. All of them were going to go down. After that, they were going to take out a vicious Southsider gang that had been operating in Hollywood for some time now. A name popped up; one that McGann and Keets knew all too well: Bezerk, also known as Christopher Lee Wright. Franz was put back in the Navigator and allowed back on the streets, only things were decidedly different now. *How the fuck did they get on to me?* was the one thing on his mind. He ran through all the different scenarios on what might have tripped him up, with each thought becoming more complex. Little did he know that it was just a simple little detail that had changed his life forever: wanting to stop for a Coke and a pack of smokes. That choice had cost him everything. The devil lives in the details. Franz had the radio off now. All the way down to Venice Beach, he never saw them, but he knew they were there. His cell phone was ringing. He had to answer it, and worse, he knew they would be listening. He already had thirteen missed calls on the caller I.D. Each one had been from the ruthless Joel Casa.

'Where you been, man? I've been calling you for hours.' Sounding somewhat relieved, Casa continued, 'Christ, dude, I thought those peisas had caught up to you, you alright?' He sounded more controlled now.

Franz did his best to sound light-hearted by answering, 'Yeah, I'm okay Joey. Sorry, man, I couldn't remember your number, seeing how it's always getting changed.'

'Yeah, what else?' Joey asked, like he wasn't buying it, while Caron, Mike, and the rest of the squad listened in on their earpieces.

Caron gave Mike a quick glance while they drove behind Franz. 'He ain't buying it!' Mike said coldly.

'He's got to,' she replied.

Detective Smart prayed for her luck to hold out. All of The Club Bangers were now accounted for and they had a tail on everyone accept Joel Casa. They were trying to get a fix on him now. The cops heard Bochetta say, 'I stopped in at Fantasy Palace to see my girl Pasha, you know, just trying to kill time and blow off some steam.'

Franz had gone off script. Staying on script was part of the plan. He might have blown it now. The sting and his deal.

101

'The deal is, we're going to put together all that we have on Knoxx, Exile, and the Envious Group and look into HEAVEN, and then take this up The Hill for an indictment, right?'

'I don't know if it's enough, Maxine,' Hadley announced, having mulled it over in her head in a cold factual way, just as Maxine should have. Teresa knew this was personal for Maxine, and that she was running on her emotions.

Maxine replied hard, 'You let me handle that. You just make sure you come in there with me and give them hell.'

Teresa could only nod in a half-hearted, agreeable manner, knowing that her friend needed her. She needed someone to believe in her and someone to back her up when the going got rough. Teresa was beginning to feel that she shared a kindred spirit with Maxine, respecting the type of person she was: a strong, independent woman who had been standing on the edge of the world, but was still taking up too much space. Maxine still held a belief that Mark Knoxx had been involved in The Get Back case two years ago, and she also believed that he was mounting another deadly scheme with HEAVEN. How she knew it, she didn't know, and she couldn't explain it to anyone. Somehow, she felt she just knew. She just simply, believed it.

'Alright!' Teresa replied, forcing it out.

Maxine kept her stare laser-painted on her, but then broke the hint of a smile. Her posture changed a little, saying softly, 'Sorry.'

She pulled a plastic container up from her bag on the floor, full of homemade cookies, while Teresa said sharply, 'Just be careful what you wish for Maxine. You just might get it.'

Maxine stiffened. She reflected on the words. Teresa was becoming a trusted ally. Maxine had grown to like her and had noticed her rising to each challenge. Her confidence and her style were changing into that of a 'thinking out of the box' rebel. Teresa was a beautiful flower blossoming before Maxine's eyes, following her own strong leadership skills. Maxine had garnered a real affection for her now. Maxine finally admitted, 'I just want to get some respect around here, you know, and to get it, well, it's a hands-on kind of thing. I guess I've just come to terms with who I am. I'm just trying to live my life my way now. Love me or hate me, it's up to others to decide. I don't care anymore. I am who I am, and it's better to be hated for who you really are than to be liked for someone you're not.' A touching moment, with the two of them sharing their thoughts. She finally admitted, 'I know the word "hate" is a strong word. But I do hate Mark Knoxx.'

'Listen, hun, the more you leave behind, the more room you have for the new,' Teresa replied. She leaned across the conference table to take Maxine's hands in her own.

Refusing to let herself deteriorate further, Maxine held her head high and began to compose herself again. Trying to take back some of the lead, she joked, 'Yeah, I know. For one thing to begin, one thing must end, and all that. All that bullshit about who controls the present, controls the past and influences the future.'

Both girls fell into a fit of giggles.

Maxine said, 'It's all bullshit! Words work. It's not what you say, but what people hear, and trust me, I've got the loudest friggin' voice here!'

They both laughed. Maxine was back in command of her feelings. She looked into Teresa's eyes. Only this time, her eyes glistened like black stones with a ripple of water teeming over them.

Maxine was back, and back in the game, remarking, 'I'm telling you, remember this day. You heard it from me first. All of this here,' her arm waved over the papers strewn across the table, 'this is all an illusion. P.R., bullshit, that's all it is, and I'm betting Exile Corporation is an illusion too. It's all in here, hidden in the notes in the margins, I know it. And you're the only one who can help me find it. I think there's a lie in here that's keeping some kind of conspiracy hidden. I know Knoxx is involved in a conspiracy; I just can't prove it yet.'

Her eyes sparkled at Teresa. Maxine changed her tack, lightening up in her explanation, 'We need to find something in here that we can use against him. He has a huge ego, I'm sure, and the way he made a move on me last night, he sure does like being the center of attention, doesn't he? Did you see him dancing with that girl who was singing earlier?'

'Well, you could hardly miss her, could you!' Maxine replied in a disapproving manner.

Teresa continued her thought process by saying, 'Well, if I can find something on him or one of his companies, to use as leverage, then maybe we could manipulate it to get the Attorney General to approve an indictment. Then we'd own him. He'd have to comply with our subpoena, and then we'd control the way the game's played.'

Maxine replied enthusiastically, 'Teresa, you pull this off, and I'll make you a star!'

102

'Where's my star!' Mark shouted as he sauntered in to the lobby of the duplex apartment above Manhattan. He picked up his pace and almost jumped the stairs, taking them two at a time. He paced into the master bedroom and gave it one quick scan. He found her looking unbelievable and she instantly stopped him in his tracks at the doorway. Mark stood there, not knowing what to do.

'I bought you this. I hope you like it?' Nicole asked, in a cute and playful way, knowing the answer already. She sat seductively on a mountain of throw cushions and pillows at the head of the huge bed. Her hair was shiny and its blonde ringlets were perfectly curled, highlighting her high-cheek-bones, her lips a perfect pout of pink. Her eyes seduced him, cutting him to the quick.

All Mark could muster was a lame reply, 'Oh yeah, I love it!'

Nicole was laying her long, toned legs along the bed, with her tight-ass-banging body, lightly covered in a pearl white studded corset and garters, wearing a cat mask and a long tail. Every inch of her oozed sex appeal and she knew she wore it well. It wrapped her like sugar loves candy, and Mark looked at her like she was his favorite flavored candy bar in the whole wide world. So good, he didn't know where to begin unwrapping her.

He answered, 'I've died and gone to Heaven!'

They both broke into a fit of laughter. Knoxx still stood in front of her, not knowing what to do next. What a day it had been. Life was certainly full of surprises, and from where Mark was standing, looking at his shining star, there were no surprises for guessing what was about to happen next.

'Come over here, you! You've been a bad-boy today, haven't you!' Nicole commanded, playfully admonishing him.

Quick in taking up his role, Mark played along with her, replying, 'Oh, you have no idea how bad I've been! Yeah, I've been a bad, bad boy.'

He laughed, knowing the truth was stranger than fiction, knowing he was not lying to her. Nicole answered, 'Yes, you have!' She pulled him down onto the bed towards her. She continued, 'You've left me here on my own all day, wondering where you went and who you went off to see. You're a naughty little devil, Mark, and I'm one hot pussy. Now come here and start stroking this hot, little pussy.'

103

Mark and Nicole spent the rest of the night in bed, and most of the following day too. She made good on her promise to severely reprimand him. They cuddled in each other's arms, with Nicole resting her head on his chest. Mark allowed himself to think of his future with Nicole; he didn't want to leave her on her own again. They whispered sweet nothings throughout the following morning, and then watched a DVD in bed, *The Bridges of Madison County*. It caused Nicole to cry, but then she wanted to make love, and that, in turn, caused Mark to just simply fall in love with her. The simple details made it happen. Her look was one thing, but it was how she looked at him, reading him so well. It was as if they had somehow found each other in the here and now. Her musk electrified him, and with each intake of breath, Mark soon began to breathe easier. The past seemed to have caught up to them. They had been searching for the same thing and found it in each other. For the first time in a long while, in his whole life possibly, Mark was okay with that, accepting it for what it was. Love.

She told him her stories about her past life, and went onto explain why she had left Cherry Hill, New Jersey in a hot minute, not wanting to get caught up in a Mafia killing. She hated violence and could not even watch it in a movie. As she let her story unfold, she told him that her real name was Nicola Cowper. It just felt right to tell him all of it. He was the perfect gentleman, her perfect Mark. She could sense the darkness and somehow knew he had some mystery in him too. He had an edge that she loved about him too. Nicky was inspired by his intelligence and she became hot for him, listening to his English accent and how he strung his words together.

She came to understand his wild, playful, playboy image, and to her, he was a loveable rogue who was always flirting and complimenting the fairer sex, but she knew he was hers. When he held her tight, he was soft but firm and she melted when he was in her. For Nicola, she knew that first night when they'd met, that she had just had her first and last kiss. She believed in Mark and she believed that he would love her the way she needed to be loved. She finally felt that life had come and saved her. From that first morning on, Nicola knew she didn't want to be without him. She never wanted to be alone again. She had secretly prayed for a moment like this, and now she felt her prayers had been answered from Heaven above, because finally, she was in love.

Nicola decided to suspend singing at night, as her new man

had been surprisingly quick to offer her a set of keys. He asked that she come and go as she pleased and to treat his place as her own. Knoxx pulled out all the stops to make it a home for her and in the end, it just turned out to be too inconvenient for Nicky to go back and forth from her apartment across town, and so she moved in with Mark after a few weeks. They became an item, and when Mark rolled, Nicky rode along as the beautiful woman in his life. A man is measured by the style of woman he carries on his arm, and Nicky carried herself like the woman she was, an angel sent from Heaven.

At all the events and dinner parties, she was flawless and everyone just loved her. Nicola Cowper was a shining star that complemented Mark's dark light. They decided to stay with her stage name, Nicole Young, because it made her feel better, and so it was Mark Knoxx and Nicole Young attending events from coast to coast and overseas. Nicky was blissfully happy and Mark had made good on the note he'd left in her dressing room. He was doing his best to make all her dreams come true. Mark had allowed himself a managed happiness too. Yet he knew that no matter where he went throughout the world, The Firm knew how to find him, and it felt like they were always watching. With some regularity, wherever he was, a sealed courier package or a white envelope was delivered to him. He never opened any of the envelopes in front of Nicole. She asked him about the envelopes one night in bed, for the first and last time. He replied in the best way he could with his heart crying inside, answering, 'There's only ever bad news in the mail.'

At all the parties, charity events, dinner parties and receptions, there was always someone pulling him aside and planting a business card in his hand and asking, 'How's The Enterprise coming along?'

Illuminati. They were always encouraging him and pushing him further to the end of the rope, building him an empire, with all roads leading to Exile Corporation. He was always amazed at who was a member, or someone sympathetic to the Cause. A willing participant in murder, and in the future destruction of humanity itself. All they ever wanted was more money, power and respect, and they made sure that Knoxx was being given all the right connections for him to distribute HEAVEN. He could never let Nicole know the man he really was. Each time they went to yet another star-studded event, she happily said, 'There's a lot of stars out tonight.'

104

'There are a lot of stars out tonight,' Adwell remarked, while drinking from his coffee mug, sitting next to Caron in the unmarked police car, yards away from the Yellow Box Storage Company's entrance in Venice Beach.

Caron answered, 'Yeah, I know. It's lovely, isn't it? God, I hate this job sometimes, you know? We always seem to be wasting time sitting on a stakeout, waiting for something to happen, while the bad guys make things happen. I'd love to be a movie star for a night, get all glammed up, and go to some big event like The Oscars or something.'

They both laughed because it was complete bullshit. Caron loved her job, and she was always putting herself right in the middle of the action.

Mike replied with a laugh, 'It's okay, girl. You're a star to me.'

The two cops were the best of friends; they knew how to do stakeouts, keeping each other entertained. Caron replied joking, 'Yeah well, I'm not here for your entertainment, so don't mess with me tonight!'

Being the karaoke queen, she sang a tune from one of Pink's songs. They laughed again, when Caron's radio chirped with her call sign. It was Groomie, covering the rear of the lockup with his partner, Roy Bowen. He keyed his mike to check in as per police procedures, every ten minutes.

'Go ahead, Groomie.'

'All clear, everything's quiet here. Over.'

Bochetta had been speaking with Casa while he drove through West Hollywood, West L.A. and then turning onto Venice Boulevard. Joey had asked him what time he had stashed the S.U.V. and how he had made his way back up to Hollywood. All the while, Franz was making shit up, getting himself deeper in the shit. Joey told him that he was on the Sunset Strip at the Skybar and that he was to make his way over to him. It was a trip that would be impossible to make in the time that Joey expected Franz to arrive, considering he hadn't even dropped off the Navigator yet. He knew he was screwed, and so did the cops. They had two choices. Take them down now, or get hands-on and drive Franz up to Hollywood. Caron called Dan McGann and asked him to check out the Skybar. Caron had some tough decisions to make. If they took them all down now, at least they had one bad-ass crew off the streets, but if they played their hand well, they just might get some more luck. But Caron didn't know that her luck had just run out.

Franz pushed up the roller shutter door to the storage unit. He quickly got back into the Navigator that was now fitted with microphones and a G.P.S. tracking device. He eased the S.U.V. into the darkened Unit, checking his side mirrors and his rear view mirror as he eased it in. He stepped on the parking brake and switched off the engine. There was silence for a blissful second, but then he jumped at the sound of a quick succession of repeated taps on his driver's side window. He looked to see Joey Casa holding his index finger up to his lips with a gun in his hand. Casa opened the rear door and got inside behind him, while Franz just sat frozen in his seat. Joey put one foot up on the running board, and in one fluid motion, he pressed the Glock into the headrest behind Franz's head. He pulled the trigger, instantly shattering Franz' C5 disc at the base of his skull, severing his spinal cord. Within a second, Franz was dead, sitting upright in the driver's seat, in the dark light of the storage unit. Casa eased himself out from the seat and softly pushed the rear door closed. He calmly walked to the back of the S.U.V. and unloaded the guns. He marched out of the storage unit across to the far end, where another smaller unit's door was already open. He calmly dropped the duffle bag holding the guns on the floor in the unit, and then picked up a four foot long, pipe-like-cylinder.

Joel Casa had learned a long time ago that the only way to stay ahead of the police and the mafia was to always mind the details. He knew the devil was in the details, and that's why he was always prepared for the unexpected. Fail to prepare, then prepare to fail. Joey Casa was ruthless because his life depended on it. He had been waiting all night for Franz to arrive. After the exchange, Joey had driven down to the storage unit to inspect the weapons he'd bought. He knew Franz had been lying to him. Everybody lies. So, he had manipulated the conversation with Franz to catch him in a lie, and once he had, he knew he had him. He didn't know why Franz was lying and he didn't care. One way or another, Franz was going to do to him what Joey had just done to Franz. He justified it in his head as poetic justice.

Joey lifted up the dark green tube and hefted it up onto his right shoulder. After some eight seconds, he fired the AT-4 shoulder-mounted rocket launcher. It could shoot a missile nearly 1,000 feet through buildings and tanks. Joey fired it into the storage unit. It lit up the night sky in a fireball of white, hot flame and a deafening bolt of thunder. Joey looked on in awe, saying excitedly, 'That's hot!'

106

'That's hot, maybe too hot, baby,' Knoxx jokingly said, playfully ribbing Nicole about the outfit she planned to wear to The Oscars that evening at the Kodak Theatre on Hollywood Boulevard. Nicole stepped over to Mark and planted a light, sticky lipsticked kiss on his lips. They embraced tighter than she would have liked in her dress, her full ample breasts pushing on Mark's chest. They began to kiss passionately, like it was the last kiss they were ever going to share. Mark said, 'You always know how to get to me, babe.' They shared a loving look. Her bright, teal green eyes shining back at him, he continued, 'You know, babe, you're like the sun and the moon to me. You know that?' He gripped her body tight again, in a big bear hug.

They giggled playfully while Nicky replied, 'Hmmm, hold that thought for later.' Nicole gripped him low between his legs. He let her go and then walked over to the full length mirror to get a look at himself, wrapped up in a designer tuxedo. Knoxx turned to the door of their hotel suite, having heard a knock at it, leaving Nicole to freshen up in the bathroom. As he opened the door, Nicky heard that voice again, 'Hello honey, how are you? Aah you look nice, Mark.'

It seemed to Nicole that no matter where they were, Jane was always close by, always on call and, it felt, always watching. Nicole had come to the frustrated reasoning that she knew her place when it came to Jane Mears, second place. She realized that Mark and Jane shared a special bond that she would never be able to break, or understand. Mark always seemed aloof when she tried to get a better understanding of their relationship. When she was in the company of Jane, they had awkward moments, but Jane soon realized that Nicky was no passing fad, and so she had to warm to her.

When she saw Nicole glide out, Jane complimented her effusively, but always checked back to Mark, asking if he was alright, as if some impending doom hung over him. Nicole had come to know one thing about Jane. She had Mark's back. He was her perfect Mark, and he always did his best to keep Jane happy, because she seemed so highly-strung.

As Nicole continued getting ready, she noticed the same routine that she knew by now not to ask him about. Mark handed Jane an envelope. Nicole would never get to know who the envelopes were for. Jane left, saying she would see them later that evening.

107

The night's event was a success, Mark and Nicole had made headlines. He'd made it in Los Angeles, New York and Miami. Main Street loved Nicole and Wall Street loved Mark. They were the hottest couple on the red carpet. Mark Knoxx had indeed, arrived. Over the next five or six months, the M.O. was the same. Mark and Nicole partied and lived the lifestyles of the rich and famous. He slowly but surely maneuvered them around the world, one country at a time, on the yacht, What A Waste, which he'd purchased to give him a sense of freedom. Still, he always took along his security detail, consisting of Matthews, Meserve and Malton. He made sure he was livin' mi vida loca, living my crazy life, living each day as if it were his last. Over time, it practically drove him crazy with this crazy life he was now living, because he couldn't tell a soul about his real life.

The genius of it all, was that the lies were everywhere for everyone to see, if they knew what to look for. Knoxx was heading up RED and he had huge amounts of money flowing through the Exile accounts, all being funneled into HEAVEN. Exile Corporation was the holding company for the Envious Group that was rolling over hundreds of millions of dollars in illicit drug money. Then there was Envoy Developments in England that was still in the gold bullion smuggling and money laundering business. Mark had now broken ground at The Strand in London that Envoy was developing, which would pay back General Dragon from the profits it generated once the new hotel was built.

It was the small lies that ate him up. Every day, it just seemed to drip on him like Chinese water torture, dripping his very soul away. Mark knew that HEAVEN was out there somewhere, hunting. The Dynamic Random Access Memory was designed to be a hunter killer, and as each envelope kept turning up, so did a dead body. Someone had lost a husband, a wife or a mother, a daughter, a son or a father. HEAVEN didn't care and did not care to know who they were or what they'd done to get their name on its guest list. It was a program designed to kill and it was a very efficient assassin. Knoxx never knew the majority of the names he had typed into the guest list. Pawns in a chess match, expendable in the grand scheme of things. In a war, the nameless and the faceless die in their thousands. Sometimes, he did recognize a name. Sometimes he knew the face, and sometimes the names added to the guest list were names of queens and kings on the chess board. Genius and madness. The madness of it was knowing that he was playing a part in having people murdered every day. HEAVEN was doing what it was designed to do - efficiently, effectively and economically. Once your name had been put on the list, you were as good as dead, and that knowledge was now killing him. The genius of it had been in the planning; the madness was in its execution. Every day, his team continued with their execution of the day-to-day business, growing the Exile empire deeper into enemy territory.

Exile Corporation controlled the Envious Group, Envoy Developments and HEAVEN, each, in its own right, were making Knoxx a wealthy man. Wherever he went, it seemed that someone recognized him. He was a role model for young aspiring businesspeople. No one realized what he really was, and what he was really doing. Knoxx was a drug trafficker, money launderer and a monster, a global killer. Each of his companies were in the business of hiding those facts. Slowly but surely it began to surface, eating away at his very soul, killing him slowly from the inside like a cancer. Knoxx's mood began to swing from calmness to rage, from a blissful happiness and carefree spirit, to a dark and threatening manner. One minute he exuded genius in the master strokes of his business dealings, but then the madness would take over, with him lashing out at his staff, friends, and at himself. He was tormented, cursed with his knowledge.

Nicole had learned to read the signals by now. When to approach him and when to stay away. Staying away seemed to be the better option, and so Nicky endeared herself to Alisha Ellington. When the opportunity arose, the two of them would jump ship to shop, lunch and laugh in each port of call. Jane opted to stay with Mark onboard, always mindful of his burdens. The burdens they both shared.

Knoxx had been drunk the whole day. Nicole had become accustomed to sleeping on her own more often than not. Mark had been watching the news religiously over the past forty-eight hours. The coverage had been intense, as Nicole watched it from the relative safety of the bedroom. The President of the United States had been on television for most of the past two days. In this latest report, he said, 'It's a great loss to a great nation. He was my friend and a great ambassador for his people and for peace. Israel will miss its son. President Roberts was a force for good. The American people send their best wishes to his family and to his countrymen in their time of need.'

Knoxx knew the name. It was the first name they had given him at their one and only meeting. As he watched the news, he knew the truth. As he looked around at all the sheep following the wolf, a thought came to him, which soon turned into anger. One word came to mind at how blissful their ignorance must feel. He was filled with envy.

The Gold Shield

108

What have you done for me today?' he asked, pausing to look at the crowd. 'That is what you should be asking your government each day. For I believe that is what your government should be doing for you, working for you, the great people of this great nation of ours!'

The crowd erupted. Raising his voice with conviction, he said, 'That is what government should be doing, answering to you!'

The cheers and applause rose to a massive din around the stadium, as all the supporters waved and swayed as one with the banners. They all shouted the same thing after each rousing segment he offered up for them to devour.

'Tasker for president! Tasker for president! Tasker for president!'

Tasker raised his arms high and wide, to quiet the crowd so they could listen to his words. He said, 'As you know, I am a man who is trying to do the right thing for his country, for his people and for our children. I'm going to mention this with humility, because all of you are my friends here, and so I must let you know something. I want you to know, come January, you should all dress warm, because it will be quite cold in Washington, standing on the steps of Congress, as I am sworn in as your next president of these United States of America!'

Another loud cheer rose up from the fifteen thousand strong crowd, knowing he was not wrong. Stephen Tasker was all but assured victory in November. The world was waiting for him. He was just a handful of months away from becoming the forty-fifth president of the United States. The crowd knew it, he knew it and the opposing party knew it.

Stepping away from the podium for effect, Tasker continued quickly by saying, 'What am I going to do for you? That is the question you may ask of me. What have you done for me today? Well, this is what I will do for you. For too long, this country has been in the hands of caretakers. People who are too afraid to take any decisive action. A leader cannot always be liked, but he must always be respected. I believe we have lost that respect as a country, and that we are running out of time to hold onto what little influence we have left. We are the richest nation on earth, but are we truly wealthy? Now is the time for change, for change is coming, whether we want it or not. Time is running out for us, as a people, to change. And so, to all of you out there, watching this broadcast, I give you my word. I will make this nation great again. Strong again, for all of us. A strong nation built tough from within. A strong nation that can lead from strength, that can bend in the wind without breaking under the weight of being put to the test from those who wish to us harm. What have you done for me today? That, my friends, is what you should be asking yourselves, for you are the country that binds us all together as one. You are the ambassador, as a citizen of this country. I'll be the first to admit, I cannot do this alone. I will need your help. If it were easy, well then, it just wouldn't be worth doing. But I love this country with all my heart. My blood bleeds red, white and blue!'

A huge roar erupted again.

He waited a beat for the crowd to settle down and continued, 'I am willing to lay my life down for my country. That is what I am prepared to do, but the question is, how far are you, every one of you, prepared to go in building our nation into a great nation, a world leader once more? We have all had it far too easy, for far too long. And now someone has to pay the tab and that someone is us, here and now, before it's too late for our children and our children's children.'

Tasker began engaging the audience further, as if taking his cue from a movie producer; he unbuttoned his tie and stepped out towards the crowd, moving closer to them as if he was sharing a secret. His audience was enraptured by his motion on stage. They listened intently as if each one were the only one he was speaking to.

'Only when the last tree is felled, the last animal shot and the last fish dragged from the seas, will we realize that we can't eat money. Only then will we realize that paper doesn't take our breath away, like all God's amazing gifts that he has given us in our world. We cannot continue as we are. People of the world, take note. We are all at sea together on this lifeboat that we call earth. We must take care of it, or we shall sink into a black ocean of space. Extinct. If only we had the strength to change, for as the world turns, so must we turn from what we are, into something better for all humanity. It will start this coming November nineteenth, when I become your next president of these United States, and united we shall stand!'

The crowd roared, waving banners, shouting in approval of their new leader, while Tasker stood with his arms raised in acceptance of their adulation. The crowd was with him every lock-step, marching to the beat of his drum.

Tasker lowered his arms and signalled for the crowd to quiet down and said, 'Do not test the will of the people of this great nation, for it was born out of tyranny and dictatorship, and we shall never bow to any form of terrorism. Ever!' A huge roar served as his backdrop. 'I warn those of you who aim to bring terror to America and the world at large. If you want a war, then by God you shall have one!'

This prompted the biggest roar yet, with banners jumping up and down in a tide of arms waving about. The sea of people moved back and forth in unison, all following his lead in a kind of mass trance, all becoming programmed to Tasker's message, listening to him say, 'We didn't start this war, but we will finish it. We do not wish for war, but we will not run from it, for we know what it's like to start a nation. We will not be bullied or brow beaten by anyone, for we are America, the home of the brave and the land of the free!'

He lowered his tone and the crowd became quiet, as he began to bring his speech to a close. The banners stood still. On cue, the cameras moved in for the close-up shot of the future president's face.

All for effect, his face filled the television screens at home. The audience watching at home listened as he said, 'My friends, my fellow Americans, we are the lone superpower, that is true. We are the world's leading economy; that is also true. And we are still enjoying our quest for life, liberty and the pursuit of happiness. But if we are to continue being the world's ambassador, then we must be the first to show other countries how we can live in harmony with our planet. We must deal with the issue of our oil dependence. The U.S. consumes over twenty million barrels of oil each day. The world is consuming eighty five million barrels a day, and by 2025, China will be consuming ten million barrels a day.'

Lifting his left arm up to his shoulder, holding a blue bottle of water, he poured the water into a glass that he held in his right hand by his waist, while he said, 'This is unacceptable. Time is running out. We, as a nation, have been living each day without thinking about tomorrow, but tomorrow is here, today. It is said that the human race carries an enduring soul. I believe that the vast majority of the six billion people on this planet would agree with the notion that the enduring soul is just another word for humanity. We must all stop looking outward to others and look within ourselves to know what is right. What is right for us, for our children, for our fellow man and for our mother, Mother Earth. The farmer in Brazil cuts down a tree in the rainforest in order to survive. Have you heard the expression 'that when a butterfly beats its wings, it can cause a typhoon to rage on the other side of the ocean?' In the end, will humanity itself survive? We have to find a way to stop the wars, famines and diseases throughout the world. We have to begin to heal ourselves, to find a way to educate people and assist in bringing medicines and technology to those who are less fortunate than ourselves, because that is the American way.'

He paused to drink the glass of water. The masses swayed in a sea of hope and unity. Their boards were raised high at the thought of a future-thinking president, coming into office to lead them.

Tasker gripped the podium. He smiled confidently, looking presidential and in control. He said with confidence, 'I will bring forth change. Change in thought, change in attitude, change through action. I will change the environment and the education system. I will bring tougher justice for those who break our laws and provide more law enforcement and security for those who wish to have it. I will also provide more opportunity for our young adults, for it wasn't too long ago that I was one myself.'

A ripple of laughter reverberated throughout the stadium. The Secret Service agents stood tall with their chests out, listening in their earpieces, while others spoke into their wrist handsets.

'I will fix our broken healthcare system, providing better care for the sick, the weak and the elderly. I am one of you, a baby-boomer. I have come to terms with getting old, but I, like you, still crave quality of life. That quality of life shouldn't be given to only the few and the privileged. I know the fears we face. I know that in January, the month I am sworn in as your next president,' the crowd cheered, as he continued speaking, 'seventy-six million people shall begin to retire at a rate of ten thousand a day, for the next twenty-five years. This is a tide that is rising, and time and tide wait for no one. It's not that a rising tide raises all boats, but it's which way the current flows that matters. We must take action now, for the tide of change will sweep us up and carry us. No matter how hard we might try to swim against the tide of change, it will overtake us and swallow us up.'

Waving his arms, he indicated that he wanted to be heard. Bringing relative silence once more, controlling the crowd and the tempo, he explained, 'Whether you restrict supply or increase demand, prices will rise. The price of money is interest, and so I will provide new tax incentives in all areas of business, because I know that what's good for business is good for the country. I intend to stimulate growth in our economy and in the job market. I intend to help the poor, the ill-educated and the under-privileged who make up the bulk of our people. Those who are the last to be hired but the first to be fired. I will lower their taxes to stimulate higher earnings. That will help in increasing tax revenues from the goods and services they will be able to purchase by having more disposable income. What have you done for me today, you may be asking? Well, that is what I will be doing for you.'

The crowd were hanging on his every word. He waved at them as if he knew some of the people personally, waving in a presidential way. He had been groomed his whole life for this moment, to manipulate and bring about compliance, and then gain control. All over the world, men watched with the knowledge that they had helped put him on that stage, because he was one of them, and he would do as they asked. Each of them were proud to be one of the special ones, Illuminati.

They heard him say, 'Ask and you shall receive. Well, you have asked for a strong leader, and now, one has appeared. You have asked for change and change is coming. And you have asked to be a great nation once more, and I will do my part to help make us great again! But the question I put to each of you is this: will you do your part?'

109

Lifting her head up at the sound of the phone ringing, Jane dropped the rolled up hundred dollar bill on the table.

'Yeah, okay. Keep 'em there at the front. I'll be right down,' Bezerk growled in the phone and hung up. He looked across the coffee table at Jane Mears, while she wiped the white powder from her left nostril, telling her in a hard tone, 'Two pigs are downstairs. Fuckin' faaggss.'

He stood up from the couch, and straightened himself up. Roughly wiping off his nose, he got ready to go and head them off. Wright looked down from the office window and saw them slouching against the bar near the entrance. *Assholes*, he thought, fucking McGann and Keets. It seemed like they had put him on their shit list for the past ten months or so, since the whole missile thing in Venice Beach. He had told them that he didn't know anything about any guns, or who had blown up half a city block, but they kept coming back to fuck his shit up, and now here they were again.

'Don't let them see me here,' Jane demanded. Her eyes became fearful of the fallout from being caught with Bezerk by the police, not to mention Mark, especially if what they were up to, got out.

He answered, 'These pigs ain't got no business here fuckin' with me. I have a good mind to go down there and stretch them two fools out.' He sucked on his lip while contemplating the thought, but then, thinking better of it, he allowed himself a small laugh, telling her, 'You hang here and chill. I'll be nothing but a minute with these two fags.'

'I can't afford to be seen here,' Jane barked at him, reinforcing her awkward position, 'And put this away!' she handed him the envelope she had delivered earlier. Jane began getting herself together for a quick exit. The L.A.P.D., she could probably handle, but having to explain it to Mark, that was another story altogether.

Bezerk took his sweet old time sauntering down to the two cops, who had now become a major pain in his ass. He made a point of scratching his ass as he approached them, throwing his line out there in an offhanded way, 'Waassuup?'

Detective Dan McGann and Detective Richard Keets had both helped themselves to a beer, looking at him while he walked towards them. Bezerk didn't bother riding their asses about them drinking on the job, as he knew their routine by now. They were loose cannons, and like him, they were dangerous.

'Yeah, waassuup?' Richie Keets replied in a putdown way,

smirking as he said it, looking at his partner, Dan McGann.

McGann jumped in, in a sarcastic reply, 'Waassuupp witchyaa.'

Bezerk quickly said with venom, 'Uh huh, yeah real funny. Yeah, I got ya. You know, the only thing keeping me from whoopin' on your fag-asses is them gold shields you fools carry, you know what I mean?'

Dan looked at Richie, saying sarcastically, 'Does that sound like a threat to you?'

Both of them smirked at the game they were playing on Bezerk, eating up his time and his patience. Their intention was to grind Bezerk down and make him give up some information on something or someone. The boys had been at it for a number of months now, doing what they do best, wearing down their opponent over time, handing out some street justice.

'You know, if I really wanted you to throw down, well I'd just put this shield up on the bar.' McGann unclipped his gold shield from his belt, where it had been sitting next to his nine millimeter Smith and Wesson pistol in its holster. He stood up away from the bar to face Bezerk, squarely saying, 'Then I'd say, "Go for it."'

Bezerk stood toe-to-toe with him, sucking his top lip, mad-doggin' McGann squarely in his face. Neither one looked like he was going to give ground. After he'd taken a deep swig from his beer, Richie spoke up. 'You know, I think we have ourselves a Mexican stand-off.'

'Yeah well, we just call it a stand-off,' Taking Richie's cue, Bezerk answered, letting some humor cut into his voice, which helped to cut the tension.

Dan let out a snigger, saying, 'Some other time, then.'

'Yeah, you best believe that, fool,' Bezerk responded hard, allowing himself to stand down from his battle stance.

Dan said, with a mocking tone to his voice, 'You know, Bezerk, we're not gonna get off your back until you give us something, so you may as well throw us a bone, coz if I was you, I'd want us out of your life, because I don't have one. So I'm going to keep riding you hard, until you either fuck up or you decide to fuck someone else up. But trust me, either way, I'm gonna be taking something from you. We'll be back tonight, so hook us up with some V.I.P. action and a couple of your best girls.' Staring down Bezerk, who answered in a pissed mood, 'Man, fuck yoouu,' being the one thing he could give up to them right there and then.

Dan and Richie leaned back against the bar. Richie leaned over it to pick out another beer. Both cops looked like they were settling in for the long haul, and that was unsettling for Bezerk, especially with the person upstairs, waiting to get out of there. He sat himself on a bar stool and ran his fingers through his hair and began to pull on his goatee, thinking. His face was giving it away. Dan could tell that this might finally be the time, after all the months of digging into his life and working the NVS club, making life hard for their number one bad-boy on the Sunset Strip. Dan, Richie, and most of the cops in Hollywood, figured that Bezerk was involved in some real bad shit. Word was out that he was moving major weight on the street. And they hadn't forgotten that he was the main player in connection with the guns exchange and Franz Bochetta's murder, which had originated from the case now known as The Happy Face Killer shooting of a Seven-Eleven store clerk.

Caron Smart and Mike Adwell had paid a high price on that one, taking a chance on leaving The Club Bangers out on the streets. All of them had disappeared at the same time when a missile had taken out half a city block, nearly killing detectives Richard Groome and Roy Bowen in the process. The case had made headlines and had nearly cost them their heads in front of a police procedures hearing. It had caused Caron and Mike and most of the division to back off for a while until things cooled down; due to that, so had the leads on Joey Casa and the rest of The Club Bangers.

Dan and Richie, however, being the Westside Pimps, didn't adhere to normal procedures, and it seemed that the police division's powers that be, liked it that way. They seemed to like it that these two operated outside the box, getting results their own way. However they got it done, this looked to be one of those times. Getting it done.

Dan took the opportunity to hammer home his resolve by telling Bezerk, 'Look man, we're in the ass-kicking business and business is only going to get better. We know you supplied the guns to that Club Bangin' crew. You just got lucky they're gone.'

Bezerk gruffly replied, quick with wit, 'Yeah, just like that punk-ass bitch rat. I heard he took a stealth bomber up his ass!' He laughed as he envisioned it. He summarized a thought, saying, 'Heard you were the ones who turned him, got him to rat out his crew.'

Dan's face turned to stone. He responded brutally, 'You heard wrong.'

'Yeah, whatever,' Bezerk answered, quick to discard it. Sucking on his lip, he continued, 'I liked the way that boy handled his business. Got to respect that. You know what I mean?'

110

'You have to respect the fact that a lot of man hours have gone into this report, sir. I'm sure you'll find it conclusive in its findings. Our investigation points to hidden assets and secret bank accounts, and in my opinion, there are many illegal activities being undertaken, both in the Unites States and abroad in several sovereign nations, allies of ours, some of whom have been cooperative, as you'll see in the report.' Dobro took a moment to gather herself. 'The Government Accountability Office states in its own report that Squared Agency was awarded a two hundred and ninety-seven million dollar Pentagon contract to provide services to our armed forces. After having been awarded a contract that was said to be eighty-five million dollars over and above the nearest bid, the company then contracted the work out to another company for the billing, data storage and backbone support for the Internet data pipeline. That company was Endless Horizons, a subsidiary of Exile Corporation, wholly owned by Mark Knoxx.'

The person sitting behind his desk let out a gruff snort as he listened intently, taking notes. Teresa Hadley and Kevin Christie were listening to Maxine give her all. She had pushed hard for months to get this meeting, and now, her time was here, today. Maxine had taken the lead in the presentation on behalf of the F.B.I. Special agent Hadley was present for technical support, sitting beside her.

'We believe Knoxx is laundering drug money throughout the world's banks. He may also be laundering funds on behalf of companies involved in defrauding the U.S. of millions of dollars through bogus bids in Iraq and Afghanistan. This system was intended to help save money in the War on Terrorism, not steal from it or help to compound the problem even more,' Maxine said.

She also presented their findings on the paper trail that Agent Hadley had uncovered, from thirty tons of Bulgarian arms that were impounded at the border of Sierra Leone. An obscure waybill had led Hadley to discover a contract for Macbine Consultants that had, in turn, outsourced that contract to supply arms to forces in the Balkans, that company being another subsidiary of Exile Corporation.

'The evidence is overwhelming and concise, as you'll see,' Maxine remarked. She lowered her tone, sounding as if she didn't want to say the words that were following her thoughts. But today was the day, and nothing could be left out in the hall for tomorrow. She showed no fear in following her heart when she said bluntly, 'The C.E.O. of

Macbine is Stuart Rawkins. He's the former deputy director of the C.I.A.'

Looking squarely across the table, her host did nothing other than wait for more from her and showed no emotion or condemnation for what she was implying.

Teresa Hadley tactfully took over the reins, feeling that Maxine had run out of material and that they needed something new to move this mountain. She interjected, 'Exile Corporation was awarded a contract to manage the government's mainframe computer, maintaining its infrastructure and billing processing. Squared Agency provided security for a gold mine in Papua New Guinea, but the government there called in their own troops to oust them from their country when it became apparent that around two hundred and thirty million dollars worth of gold bullion had gone missing from the mine. However, Exile still managed to collect forty-two million in fees. That contract was awarded to Exile by the brother of the Under-Secretary-General of the United Nations, Gordon Forrest, who it so happens, knows Stuart Rawkins from the Gulf War One and Bosnia. Forrest served in the French Foreign Legion back in the eighties, and in the early nineties he was the personal bodyguard to the Aga-Khan. Within this accountability study you'll find that all the bank wires weave their way across continents and through several of the world's top fifty banks, all leading back in some shape or fashion to one company and one man, Exile and Mark Knoxx. He has seven satellite offices in five countries and employs some seventy well-trained and specialized staff. He has an inner circle of about five people that he talks to directly on a daily basis. That's what we have. What do you think?'

Teresa and Maxine held their collective breath.

The United States Attorney General, Mr. William Baltizar the Third, leaned forward and said cryptically, 'You've certainly shed a lot of light on things.'

111

'You've certainly shed a lot of light on things, senator.'

'It's appeared to me that the Iraq war was never about war on terrorism or even against Saddam. I've always believed it was a test, run by this administration in how to privatize a war.'

The interviewer responded quickly by asking, 'And why would this administration want to do that?'

The camera flipped back to Florida's senator, Emma Spitzer, who replied, 'Well, quite simply, Operation Iraq Freedom wasn't an invasion against a foreign nation but an invasion against the people of the United States from its own government; an invasion against the federal budget. You only have to look at the facts and crunch the numbers. Oh, we're in a war, all right. It's just that our enemies are the fat cats up on Capitol Hill who are getting wealthier with every gunshot. It's in their best interests to keep this war going for as long as possible.'

'How can you make such allegations, senator? You don't really believe that this administration, or any of our own representatives, our president, would send our children to war, to die for profit?' The interviewer responded with concern, pursuing the senator hard for all its worth. She knew this would be worth a lot to her own career. The senator from Florida wanted to make her own mark and needed no such prodding. She had been a lightning rod for controversy for the past two years, always being an outspoken voice against the war and the Blackmoor administration.

Senator Spitzer announced, 'I'll prove it to your viewers, how this administration is profiting from war in clear violation of our Constitution and the Geneva Convention.'

'Please, go on senator,' the interviewer asked, prompting her further.

Senator Spitzer went on to say, 'It was probably one of the worst ideas in the history of this country to go to war in Iraq. But you know what? The work there is great and the profits to be made there are even greater. And all you have to do is show up. If you can make it to Iraq, then you've made it. One of the first things this administration ordered was for twelve billion dollars in cash, on one pallet mind you, to be flown into Iraq. Imagine that for a moment, if you will Belinda? Twelve billion dollars, one hundred thousand dollars, wrapped in plastic bundles, each bundle handed out, most with no regard as to what the money would be used for. I have the General Accounting Office's own report saying that it has no idea where most of the money has gone. I have records that show, on most occasions, a twenty-four-year-old corpsman signed a receipt, approved by the oversight assessor on site, approving a blind bid contract within twenty-four hours. I have reports of contractors, with no previous experience, providing security or support for our troops in the middle of a war zone, bidding on cost plus contracts. It was common knowledge, stick around long enough, and bid enough times, and your turn will come around. You just have to know how to play the game and by whose rules.'

Belinda Vittali, the host of her own show, The Queen B Show, couldn't resist pushing the controversy even further, just as she was known for pushing the ratings of her talk show through the roof. Her interview tonight was the culmination of months of background research on her team's part. The Queen B Show was one of the highest rated business investigative report shows in the country. Belinda was a celebrity in her own right, often making headlines in the tabloids for her outrageous comments and for her style of partying in Hollywood, Las Vegas and New York. She knew her show would bring the heat to an already hot topic, which was why she had cajoled Senator Emma Spitzer to appear on her show, making it the number one show in the final weeks before the presidential elections. The queen of the talk shows didn't let anything pass her by. She continued to fuel the flames under the senator's seat, knowing that it takes one match to start an inferno. She asked the loaded question, 'And tell me, Senator Spitzer, who are these companies that are taking advantage of this war, and our young men and women being sent overseas to risk their lives?'

Belinda sat regally, holding her posture in anticipation of the answer. Every question had been planned in advance to feed to her guest, all for maximum impact.

The senator answered succinctly, 'The companies that are helping themselves to our taxpayers' money Belinda are companies such as Macbine, Squared Agency and Exile Corporation. They have collectively been awarded some ten billion dollars worth of business. Everything from meals to underwear, music, e-mail and even mailing home birthday cards each day. One contract alone was worth seventy-five million dollars; the building of the Iraqi police academy that was later condemned and pulled down, but Exile still collected a twenty-two million dollar consulting fee.'

112

Exile was dialed in. Mark Knoxx had the phone numbers and contact details of everyone who was either Illuminati or was inside the inner circle under the dark light. It seemed to him that everyone he'd met, or that had been steered his way to imprint his palm with a business card, was connected to someone within The Firm. He knew they were consolidating their power worldwide. Just as Tasker had vowed some time back at their one and only meeting, he was trimming the fat, eliminating with the blade of a surgeon's knife, the weak and the meek, and it was being done through HEAVEN. The Enterprise was firing on all cylinders, becoming more powerful with every success in eliminating another enemy of the state. The Firm was becoming more brazen in their assassinations and in their demands of Knoxx, raising the pressure, slowly twisting the screw. In the months that Knoxx had been a part of The Enterprise, he had come to terms with his place in it and the hold they had over him. He was getting to live a charmed life, free and alive.

The majority of the murders had been on faceless, nameless men and women who had the ear of the people in power. The power brokers, arms dealers, bankers, mid-level politicians, people who wouldn't be obviously missed or make headlines, except whenever absolutely necessary, such as the President of Israel, who'd had to be sacrificed to bring in the more hard-line vice president, who within sixty days of coming into office had forced an issue in Palestine and promptly invaded the country. That was what The Firm really wanted, anarchy and fear. Knoxx read the newspapers every day, watched the news and listened to his own voice of reasoning. He knew the truth now. The real truth, buried behind the lies. A heart attack here, a coma or a stroke, and all the families were left with was an explanation of how their mother, father, son or daughter had died peacefully while they were in the hospital, all neat and tidy and very quiet. But Knoxx was becoming anything but quiet. The inferno was raging inside him. A firestorm of unrest tore through him, wondering if he was really fighting on the right side after all.

The Enterprise, The Firm and Exile, they were everywhere and could find you anywhere. They could kill you any time they liked. It would be blamed on a bad diet or a stressful lifestyle. Everyone was expendable, with no back trail and plausible deniability. Mark Knoxx had the innovation and the motivation to proceed with HEAVEN. The Illuminati had found the perfect assassination tool when they had been able to program Knoxx into the perfect soldier to do their wet work, doing their murdering for them. But Mark Knoxx was imperfect and he lived in an imperfect world. No matter what computer programs are written, all programs have bugs in them. Just like HEAVEN and just like Mark Knoxx. That's why Knoxx employed some of the brightest and best minds in the computer industry to support and maintain the mainframe algorithm for HEAVEN. Just as it hunted for its programmed targets, so they hunted for the bugs within the program, the ghosts in the machine.

The bug in Mark Knoxx's program was called a conscience, something he had seemingly lost a long time ago, but since finding his new life with Nicole, he had been fighting his demons more and more each day. The battle over right and wrong was now raging inside him; the black and the white. The bright light of the media shone on him but he lived under the dark light of the Illuminati. As regularly as each envelope was delivered to him, he knew it was becoming wrong for him to be a part of this. He knew too many details. He knew that he knew too much and he knew that if he ever did fuck up, someone else would be receiving an envelope or taking a phone call on their secure cell phone and his name would be on that guest list. Someone, somewhere would eventually whisper his name and he would, he knew, become expendable.

Each day, Knoxx was given the Numbers Needed to Treat. The NNT was rising rapidly and HEAVEN was now embedded in eight hundred million computers worldwide, hunting down the names that were on its guest list. HEAVEN was the real lie. It had been so successful in programming hospital organizational charts, schedules and patients' visiting times that it was a huge success worldwide, having streamlined the industry and helped to save thousands of lives each day. 'It's a miracle!' Those words were being said numerous times a day by a family member who had received the good news from a doctor. HEAVEN played a big role in providing real-time, downloaded information for that particular patient's requirements, cross-referencing its databases from six hundred and nineteen million patients' records that it now had access to. All Knoxx needed was his password to change any patient's record and with one keystroke, change the smallest detail and the target was either disabled or eliminated while they were lying in their hospital bed. Knoxx was becoming as rich as God, along with everyone else inside The Enterprise who had assisted in leveraging the stock price to an all-time high. They were making millions. Exile Corporation grew through mergers and acquisitions, and so did Exile's, along with everyone's bank accounts.

Listening to Alisha and Jane most days, and watching

Nicole go about her daily life, Knoxx had become filled with envy, because they all had plausible deniability about what he was doing. He knew they knew, because they knew him. They could not help themselves from knowing, being a part of the life he was living, living their life in Exile. They saw some of the documents, typing drafted contracts and taking some of the phone calls. They each had their own ideas about Envoy, Endless Horizons, Squared Agency, Macbine, NVS and Exile. Each one had its own life within the organization and each one helped in covering up the lie, each one serving its real master. Mark Knoxx was ruled and watched over by HEAVEN. No matter how much money he had or where he went in the world, they could always find him. And kill him.

He would often find himself lying on a beach with his posse, everyone taking in the sun and enjoying themselves, oblivious to the murders taking place somewhere. The manipulations and the control. Knoxx would be listening to music on his I-Pod, but his mind was elsewhere. *Maybe in the long run we'll all be better off. Maybe in the long run we'll all be dead,* he constantly thought. No matter how many Jack Daniels and cokes, beers, or glasses of champagne he washed down, and no matter how many reps he pushed out in the gym, he couldn't escape The Enterprise and he couldn't escape his mind. His own thoughts were killing him and he finally came to the conclusion that seemed to help him. Inevitable.

It was inevitable. His own end was coming. He felt it. Every envelope he opened - sitting at his laptop, or even easier, inputting the instructions into his phone - had become harder. Each keystroke was inevitable. He had realized his name could be on a list somewhere and combat warriors in dark fatigues without eyes, would come for him and eliminate him. It was kind of calming, in a way. He liked that word, Inevitable. That's why Mark had sent Jane to deliver envelopes on his behalf to the one man he knew he could stay clear of, and who would be free from them waving their dark light over him. At least for a while, as his contact was naive to The Firm's plans and too far down the pecking order to be of any threat to them. All their best laid plans were now running hot. Those events that weren't controlled by The Firm were either left to luck or nature. Knoxx only ever listened to half of what he heard and let his eyes believe only half of what he saw, but today would be the day that that he didn't want to believe would happen. They would come for him.

113

Lying on the beach with the Exile staff, Knoxx heard his phone ringing, not his regular phone but his other phone. Their phone. Even though he had carried it with him every day for the past thirteen months, it had only rung seven times. This was the eighth. Alisha stole a quick look. Nicky stopped talking to Jane, and he felt everyone look at him. Everyone knew the importance of the phone, as Mark never went anywhere without it, yet none of them had ever seen him talking on it. They listened as he answered it timidly, greeting the caller, 'Hello, this is Mark. How are you? Huh uh, yeah?'

Knoxx turned his head away from the group, who had continued their conversations a bit quieter, trying to pick up on the line of conversation. Nicky heard him raise his voice, saying, 'No fucking way!'

Mark stood up and walked a few paces away from them. Matthews and Meserve got up and followed him to an empty part of the beach, standing off from him at a respectable distance. Everyone stole a quick look at Mark as he became more animated.

'I can't believe they're coming after me. How do you know?' he asked.

Knoxx listened to the voice. The voice of the facilitator of information, Paul Deavins, explain, 'They met with the Attorney General last week. You remember him don't you?'

Knoxx merely grunted out a weak, 'Yeah.'

Deavins continued talking evenly and concisely, explaining, 'The information they've compiled is quite detailed and Ms. Dobro seems to have garnered herself a capable ally in a FinCEN agent, Ms. Teresa Hadley. Both of them seem dedicated in bringing you down, and you know we can't allow that to happen, or rather, we won't allow that to happen. One way or another, we will put a stop to this.'

Knoxx interjected, with hate in his voice, 'That bitch Dobro, she just won't let up on me.'

'Apparently, they plan to embarrass you in the media one week before you take HEAVEN public. And that's the same week as the presidential elections, which will be even more of an embarrassment for our future president, now wouldn't it? I'm sure some of the fallout from you being indicted will eventually fall onto our new president, and I can assure you, Mr. Knoxx, that is totally unacceptable.'

Knoxx swiftly responded, exclaiming, 'She's like a rabid dog with a bone! What am I going to do with her? I want to kill her.'

'You were told, I'm sure, at your initial meeting, that

whatever's bad for you, may end up being bad for us. And I'm actually calling you with two pieces of bad news, I'm afraid.' Deavins lowered his tone, having to deliver the next piece of information.

Knoxx replied, 'Yeah, go on, what?'

'It's concerning you friend, the senator.'

In an instant, Knoxx felt the hairs on the back of his neck stand on end, knowing who Deavins was referring to, having had a brief fling with the divorced senator. They had remained friends, but it had been rumored around West Palm Beach that they had remained friends with benefits. He knew this wasn't going to be good news, especially if it was coming from Deavins. Knoxx simply said, 'Go on.'

'He wants her made a top priority. She's been on the Queen B show and practically laid out our whole Enterprise organization for the whole world to see. It's as if you, yourself, told her in the pillow talk moments of your special friendship,' Deavins remarked, trying to make light of it, but at the same time making a point. Knoxx was quick in making his own feelings known, answering harshly, 'No fucking way! Are you trying to say I told her? I don't tell anyone about our arrangement. Got it? No one. Not even Jane.'

'Well, someone knows too much and someone's been talking. Whoever it is, they seem to have talked to your senator friend, and we've heard enough from her. She's to be targeted as a top priority. Today. We'll get her into a hospital. HEAVEN may not even be needed, but as a precaution, input the details I'll give you now, just in case she survives.'

Knoxx's heart missed a beat, as he felt his blood begin to boil from the pressure mounting inside his chest. He either wanted to kill Deavins himself, kill anyone in the immediate area, or just break down and cry at how helpless he was to stop the tide that was rapidly engulfing him. He felt like he was drowning in his own despair. He asked with dread, 'What do you mean, if she makes it?'

Deavins was swift and accurate in his reply. 'You sound like you care? What's this, you actually care for this woman? Do you care more for her than Jane or your girlfriend, Nicole? We're committed to this all the way, and you need to be too,' Deavins said in a taunting way.

'No mate. You guys need to be committed because this is madness. You're all mad! Stark, raving mad!' Knoxx said.

'Just so I understand, you're saying that you won't input Emma Spitzer's name in HEAVEN, is that what you want me to report back?'

Deavins' words were even, with no emphasis on any of them, wanting to make sure that Knoxx understood the ramifications, should he not comply. Deavins waited silently for his answer. Knoxx stood in his board shorts in the morning's bright sunshine on the beach in Nice, in the South of France. He put his hand on his hip dejectedly and let out a long, hard sigh, while he felt his insides tighten. He turned his feet in the hot sand, and then looked back over at Jane reading her magazine with her baseball cap pulled over her eyes. She glanced up at him and smiled. Then he looked at Nicky, who was leaning over to Alisha with a magazine in her hand, locked in hot debate. Everyone looked happy and content. He could only look down at his left foot, thinking about his next move. He turned his kicking foot in the sand, thinking that he wanted to kick it right up Deavins' ass. He answered softly, saying, 'No. I'm not saying no. I'm just saying, when will this all end?'

'I expect that once our man's in the White House, things will calm down a bit. But until then you're to do as you're told. I'm sure things were explained clearly to you, Mark,' Deavins replied, saying Knoxx's first name for the first time. 'Love and hate have moved more people through their feelings into action than any ideal or presentation ever has. That's what nine-eleven did.'

'What are you telling me? You guys did that?' Knoxx said, jumping in with shock.

'What I'm telling you is that you have to follow your mission parameters to the letter. Otherwise, through your own emotions, you'll get others killed. Those you love. If Nicole Young knows who you are, then she deserves you, doesn't she? And if that's the case, then she's a willing participant, a combatant, and she will be killed, along with Jane Mears of course, if you don't comply with our wishes. It's down to you. You have to end it yourself, for yourself. We want you to take care of the F.B.I. indictment problem and we want your senator friend gone by tonight. We'll do our best to relieve you of any further pain by completing the mission ourselves, but just as a precaution you have to initiate HEAVEN. Do you understand?'

Mark simply answered with a heavy heart, 'Yeah, I got it. I understand. It's done.'

114

After taking the instructions from Deavins, Mark dropped back onto his sun lounger. His mood now blotted out the sun, its warm rays doing nothing to warm him. Mark looked at Jane, who momentarily looked at him as if she knew what he was thinking already. She gave him her look and he melted. Picking up the SWIFT phone, he methodically thumbed in his password, Hollywood and Coco, for the two cats that Jane had owned years ago when they had dated as teenagers. Checking it twice, he pressed 'send', and then once the screen read back 'message sent' he dropped it in his bag. It was done. He knew he had just sent a good person to her grave; it was all just a matter of time before the inevitable happened. Knoxx pulled on a baseball cap and sunglasses, while Nicole leaned over to check on him, but he brushed her off, dismissing her. He put on his earphones and lose himself in a sea of destruction. He listened to his I-Pod, thinking about his life that had been for nothing, because he owned nothing and he made nothing. It was all based on destroying other people's lives through deceit. He realized he was The Enterprise and there was no hiding from him, just as he couldn't hide from himself. After a few hours at the beach, he decided to get himself lost in a sea of booze. By mid-afternoon, he had managed to upset Nicole. He had practically fired Alisha, and he had asked Jane to accompany him to the hotel bar for drinks. Meserve and Matthews knew they were in for a long night.

'Never leave a wounded dog alive, Jane, otherwise it'll come back and bite you in the ass. Remember that, honey. You might not like where I'm going or where I've been, but at least you'll always know where I stand,' he solemnly said, as he then took a long drink on a Long Island Iced Tea, sitting at the bar of the Sandbanks Hotel.

Jane grabbed a hold of him, tugging at him, pulling him into her for a hug. She then said warmly, 'Come on, honey. What is it? It'll all work out. You always know what to do, Mark. I love you and there's nothing you can ever do to change that. If anyone's trying to hurt you, then you have to fight back. You've come so far. You know, people read too much into shit. Success lies in miles and miles of bullshit. You can't keep running. Sometimes you've got to turn around and fight. You know how to do that, right?'

Letting out a laugh, helping Mark to laugh too, she helped to pull a small, tight, wicked smile out of him. Mark gave it up, answering wistfully, 'Yeah, I know how to get down alright.'

The two of them were content to spend the next few hours together. No one else mattered. Deavins was right. He would never trade Jane for anyone or anything. No amount of money in the world. They kept laughing and drinking into the early evening. Nicole had tried calling him without getting any answer. Becoming more frustrated with him for ignoring her phone calls, she switched tactics by calling Andy Matthews' cell phone for updates on what the two of them were doing, asking him when he thought Mark would be returning to their room.

Mark decided that afternoon he was going to fight, all right. He was going to bring it to them. Just like he had once thought of Tasker, he now saw himself as King-fucking-Kong too, thanks in part to spending time with the only person who really mattered to him. He realized he could never live without Jane, but he couldn't live with himself. Taking another long drink, he said remorsefully, 'There's nothing left to choose and I have nothing left to lose, except you, and that's just too much to pay. I've lived my whole life looking for the one person I can live with, but you're the only one I can't live without.'

Jane soaked it all up. She was always Mark's rock in his time of need. Now more than ever, he needed her, she thought. She felt that she just had to sit with him and let the toxins fallout, that were eating him up. As they embraced in a drunken-fuelled moment, he saw her, working her way through the early evening dinner crowd. Nicole had got dressed and come down to join them poolside. She knew she hadn't been invited. She was intruding on them. Even though there wasn't a cloud in the sky, the temperature being eighty-seven degrees, Mark had a face like thunder. She caught his eye and the air turned ice cold when he saw her walking towards them.

Mark instantly looked over at Matthews, who was seated a short distance from them. Nicole had made it through the cordon and did her best to act natural, trying her best to brighten them both up in the hope that they would sober up. Jane gave her a look as if she had just walked over her grave.

Mark summarily dismissed Nicky, looking at her while saying to Jane, drunkenly, 'Look at this bullshit, what a fucking joke! What complete bullshit.' Looking at Nicky with disdain, telling her, 'You don't love me. You're living a lie, and you lie to me every day. Everyone lies, babe, it's alright. I'm not mad at you. We're all playing our parts. We're all acting; all of us. We're all actors in one, big stupid bullshit play. Some crappy movie, where some of us are playing the good guys and some of us the bad guys, some of us are the pimps and some of us are the whores. That's how life is. Random. Only the ones who write the play, that produce the crap, they're watching all of us and they get to say who stays in the movie and who gets written out. You're just my bitch. That's all. So don't get it twisted, thinking you're anything else.'

Sitting smug on a barstool, Mark looked away from Nicky to pick up his drink. She quickly closed the gap and struck him hard across his face. The slapping sound was heard across the pool's dining area. Most of the diners were now looking at them. Jane sat stock-still in her seat, looking at Nicky with an inimitable, shocked gaze, just as Mark was. It seemed as if time itself had come to a stop and Nicole stood in no-man's land. The welling up of her eyes betrayed the fire in her heart.

Mark only took a moment to recoil, before he set himself to attack back by shouting sarcastically, 'That's it? That's all you got? Fuck! Damn girl, you don't even have it in you to make it hurt. And that's coz you don't give a shit. Do you!'

Knoxx gave her the look he'd learned in prison that told the other guy he was a punk-ass bitch. She picked up on his look and broke out into full-fledged tears of anguish at having to suffer the public humiliation, not knowing what had caused the abuse she was receiving. Nicole was seeing it all fall apart. Her eyes were wide and bright, shining from the wet moisture in them, doing her best to fight both her feelings and Mark and Jane, together a formidable force. Jane held a gaze that carried a look of a slight snigger on it, laced with arrogance. She knew how this would unfold from here, another one of Mark's girlfriends going down in flames. Mark had struck a match that had ignited an inferno inside him, and those who were unlucky enough to be in its path were going to get burned to a crisp. Jane knew to stand aside and let the fire roar downwind of her. As Mark rose up from his stool, the sting of the slap from Nicole helped to spur him on to the final licks of fire, slapping it back across her face, while Jane listened, 'Whatever you want, I don't give a shit. You can have it.'

'What are you saying?' Nicole asked with venom of her own, now digging in for the fight, not giving any ground. If this was going to be the place and the time, then here and now would be where it would be done. She bore her determined eyes along with her very soul, into Mark's eyes. His eyes seemed to be in another world, dead as ice, shining back at hers, cold as ice. Unknown to Nicole, they were as thin as ice too, and could be easily smashed, for behind them laid a man, broken.

Tasker had been correct in his description of Mark when they had met. He had told him that he was a beautiful liar. And he was right. As Mark stood in front of Nicky, he knew every word was a lie. 'We're done. It's over, got it? Go get your shit and get the fuck out. I don't want you anymore. You bore me. That's what it is. I'm tired of you now. I'm gonna go out later and buy me a new piece of ass. Don't worry, I'll arrange for Andy to drop you some cash for your time, thanks for the memories. Get the fuck out of my face.'

With that last remark, four hotel security guards stepped up to move in on Knoxx. He immediately put his drink down and turned his attention to them. Nicole wiped her tears away, but she still seemed fearful for Mark, still loyal to him. Jane picked up her glass and sucked on the straw of her drink, watching it all unravel. They both listened to Mark menacingly say, 'Boy, you better know how to bring it if you're gonna try putting your hands on me, you know what I mean? You think you're tough? Man, I've cracked more heads, drank more beer, pissed more blood and banged more pussy than all you maggots put together.'

Stepping into the security man's face, while Meserve and Matthews now took up their positions, Knoxx let out a raucous burp in the man's face, trying his best to antagonize him into making the first move.

Then somebody made the first move. As if a seemingly uncontrollable three-hundred-pound Rottweiler was being held on a tenuous leash by a cute, ten-year-old girl, Jane yanked on the lead. Putting down her drink, she pushed off from her bar stool and walked over to stand next to Mark. Taking him up by his arm, she said, 'Mark, enough. Come on, let's go. Come on, honey, everything'll be okay, let's go.'

Immersing her eyes in his, Mark seemed mesmerized by her and began to stand down from his battle stance. With one little shove, he moved. Jane had moved a mountain and she began to step off with him in tow. The crowd parted as he began to move with her.

She looked over her shoulder, trying to pick someone out. She found her, telling her, 'Come on, you're coming with us. Come on, he doesn't mean any of it, let's go,' giving Nicky a wistful, knowing glint from her eyes.

Jane had slain the dragon. She knew that whatever had happened today on the beach, it was all finally becoming too much for him. What had gone around was now coming around back to him, and to her. Throughout the day, as it had been for weeks now, Jane had been watching Mark die. The man she knew, was changing inside. What he was changing into, though, she had just gotten a glimpse of.

Upon returning to the suite, Knoxx walked directly into the master bathroom and promptly threw up all the toxins that needed to come out. Not just the booze, but the hatred he carried inside for them. All of them. The Feds, the cops, The Enterprise and The Firm. But most of all, as he lifted his head to look in the mirror at his bloodshot eyes, with streams of tears rolling down his cheeks, his face told him that he hated himself the most. He wanted to die, right there, alone.

'You are sooo fucked,' he told himself, not knowing if he was actually saying it to them, or to himself, as he defiantly banged both of his hands down on either side of the sink. After wiping off the tears from his face, he calmly washed it. He began to put all the pain behind him, but when he opened the bathroom door, it was all very much in front of him, standing in the middle of the bedroom. Nicole's eyes were red from crying and her face dropped in despair. She began to cry as soon as she laid eyes on him. She seemed a stranger, standing in the middle of a strange room, looking at a stranger before her. Doing his best to put on a bright face, as if he had done the right thing down at the pool, Mark asked curtly, 'Hey, you alright?'

'I don't know if I'll ever be alright,' Nicole replied. She slumped down on the bed and began running her fingers through her thick ringlets of blonde hair. She wiped away more tears, becoming angry with herself for crying. So she decided to aim her newfound anger towards Mark, asking, 'Mark, tell me what's going on. What did I do?'

Wiping away a falling tear, she sniffed hard to retreat the oncoming flood. Mark walked around her to the cabinet, not looking at her. He picked up a water pitcher and poured some water in a glass and then shook out two aspirins onto the palm of his hand. Holding them in his hand, ready to swallow, Nicole heard him say, 'We're done. I don't want you anymore.' He slipped the pills into his mouth and drank the whole glass down. His head tipped backwards, helping to hold his own tears in check to stop them from falling. He swallowed hard and then said hard with determination, 'I never thought I'd get to really love someone. It always seemed like it was someone else's dream. Only dreams are just fairytales and not all fairytales have a happy ending.' Managing to steel himself for the final lie, he said, 'And trust me, babe, this one doesn't have a happy ending.'

He turned and gave her his mad-dog prison look, and then he saw the hurt-filled tears fall from the one he loved. Mark walked out of the bedroom, thinking, *For one thing to live, another must die.*

115

'Hmmm ...' he murmured lazily. He felt sore and his head hurt like hell, but whoever that was next to him, it sure felt good having them there, as he snuggled with her on the couch. Nicky smelled sexy and like pure snow. Mark began to take her in his arms as she forced a little prod of her tongue into his mouth, as a scout to see if it would be well received. Nicole instantly knew it had, feeling a hard prod against her belly. She lowered her hand and softly pulled on him, as another muted 'hmmm' came from him, having not yet opened his eyes to look at her. She didn't care what was going on inside his head. The only thing she wanted, was him inside her. The birds could be heard chirping outside while the world still slept. The early morning light beamed its way across the floor; each ray of light was a single beam of hope for Nicole. Hope that today was a new day and a new beginning. She kissed Mark lightly on his forehead, waking her sleeping prince as she nuzzled in further to whisper in his left ear, 'You're like the sun and the moon to me.'

They both let out a small, muffled giggle, neither one wanting to fully wake up to the reality of the new day. Lifting up her head away from Mark, she studied his face. He didn't answer her, but she carried on without waiting for him to reply, softly whispering, 'Mark, you know last night, you told me I could have anything I want?' He still didn't answer or even looking like he was listening but she continued by saying sweetly, 'Well, what I want is to make you scrambled eggs on toast in the morning. I want to make you breakfast and dinner from, time to time.' Hesitating, she then said, 'And I want to make you a baby boy, or a little girl, if you like.'

Nicole fought back the tremor in her voice, knowing in her heart she was seconds away from breaking apart. Mark opened his eyes and looked into Nicky's crystal clear, teal green eyes. She was open to him in every way. Stripped bare before him, he felt the warmth of her pulse beating on him, as he gazed deep inside her eyes, studying her face. He realized she was close to breaking point and she couldn't hold on.

Finally, she said, 'I didn't ask for any of this and I don't need any of this. All I need is you.'

She felt herself wilt under the strain of holding herself up, and from her heart breaking. She began to lie back down on top of him, but Mark flexed, and gripping her tight, he held her high. His eyes now dark and gray, he finally responded, 'Over time, even the hardest edges are smoothed out. You're out of touch and I'm out of time.'

His eyes glazed over, sensing the pain he knew she was feeling. She looked back at him as if he had thrust a blade through her beating heart, looking at him as if her heart had just stopped. Her lower lip began to tremble harder and the first drop of a tear fell onto Mark's chest. She quickly wiped her eye and he could see that she had clenched her jaw tight. She was so beautiful and brave. He motioned for her to move over to let him out from under her. She only moved after he gave her a nudge.

He said smoothly, doing his best to provide a little comfort, 'You make me smile, honey.'

After getting out from under her, he became firmer in his resolve to do what had to be done. He knew he had to do it. He had to save her. 'All my promises are gone. I lied to you all the time. I know you don't believe that, but you will. I don't know anyone who's done what I've done or seen what I've seen. I don't even know how I've survived it all. I guess there's more work for me to do here, but we are done, hun.'

Looking down at Nicole, it now took all his strength to keep it straight in his head. Nicole had tried to give herself to him one more time. Here she was, the love of his life, and he had to turn her away, forcing her to leave him. Nicole had pulled a throw-blanket over herself. She looked like an angel as the sun kissed her long, blonde tresses with her light green, saucer eyes looking at him for some understanding, under long streams of tears that she didn't bother to hide from him anymore. Through her own will, she managed to stifle a tear and fought with everything she had in her, saying as she snuffed out another tear, 'I believed in you, Mark. I believed in the man you said you were. For the first time in my life, I believed I'd found what I'd been looking for. You. I'd walk across a fire for you. If I go, when I'm gone, will that make you happy?'

The dam burst at the words she had heard herself say. The realization that this was going to happen; she would be leaving him. They were over. Mark leaned against the back of a chair to support himself, both visually and emotionally, to reply, 'Hun, sometimes the hardest thing and the right thing, are the same thing. And you're going to have to prove to me that you do love me, by leaving me.'

Nicole stood up with the throw blanket wrapped tightly around her. She moved to walk past Mark, but then she stopped and leaned on him. Then after a moment, she quietly walked away from him to enter the bedroom, where she closed the door behind her to begin packing her things.

116

Knoxx was immersed in watching the television, even though Nicole was in the bedroom for most of the day, collecting the remnants of her things that she now called her life. Not once had Mark come in to save her. She could only rely on life itself coming to her rescue, as Nicky had now woken up to the fact that Mark was a fraud. He had lied to her, and now he was done with her. And she still didn't know why, but whatever reasons she could come up with, they just did not add up. Everything seemed fine up until this time yesterday. Everything in life seemed sweet and she was in love with the only man that mattered. Up until he had got that phone call. *Yeah*, she thought, *that phone call?* And Mark had turned to the one person who only really mattered to him. Not her, but Jane. Nicole started to move a little faster and with more determination as she began to piece things together. Mark and Jane. Always Mark and Jane.

She had known all along that they shared a special bond. Plenty of people had told her about it. Alisha Ellington was always extolling their special relationship, making it known in her own way that she was somewhat jealous and envious of it. What had she been thinking? It was all bullshit and Mark was the king of swing, throwing the bullshit around like it was money. When she stepped out of the shower and began to get dressed to leave the hotel, Nicole heard her voice in the next room, recognizing the voice of her nemesis, the special one, Jane.

Nicole opened the bedroom door and looked over at them. They were quietly huddled on the couch; it looked as if Jane had quickly pulled her hand away from Mark's. Mark kept watching the television, not once glancing her way. Old news, Nicky thought, as she held her look, expecting him to acknowledge her. *So that's what you pay a hooker for,* she thought. *You don't pay her to spend the night; you pay her to leave in the morning.* She fired herself up for the task of putting on a brave face, having to walk out on Mark and her life. Again.

Nicole stepped back into the bedroom, put the television on, and checked the same news item that Mark and Jane were watching. The CNN report was of a fatal car crash involving a senator from Florida. She had been an outspoken critic of the war in Iraq and Afghanistan, and the U.S. government's policies on it, the news reporter explained. Nicole recognized the woman immediately. She knew that Mark had had a relationship with her in the past. Nicole sat on the bed and watched for half an hour. The reporter said that Senator Spitzer had died instantly when a big-rig truck had lost

334

control on a freeway, crashing into her car, killing her instantly, cutting her in half. And that's how Nicole felt right now, sitting on the bed: cut in half. Just a few feet away, Mark was sitting in the next room, seemingly a world away, being comforted by the one woman who truly owned him, because she owned his heart.

*   *   *

'Janey, I'm gonna have to end this one way or another, honey. You were right last night. I have to turn around and face my fears and fight. I can only do my best and try to end it,' Mark told Jane, with his eyes wetting up while Jane held his hand tight, gripping it to the point where her small knuckles began to turn white. Her face turned white from the fear of knowing what lay ahead of Mark, and her. Fear of the unknown.

Jane let it all pour out when she said, 'I know, Mark. I know how hard you've been fighting it, fighting them out there and fighting it all inside you. I love you. If you go down, then I'm going down with you. I'll never leave you on your own, you know that.' She stroked his hair as if he were a child that needed reassuring. Jane always knew what to say and do for him, her perfect Mark. She asked him gently, 'What did they say, Mark? Yesterday, come on, I'm not stupid. It's okay. I'm in this with you. I know something happened yesterday. Tell me.'

'It's because of her,' Mark simply said, brushing away a falling tear. He pointed at the television.

Jane asked, trying to make sense, 'What's because of her? What do you mean?'

'They always make good on their promises. They said they'd kill her,' Mark mumbled.

'Who, Mark, you're friend? The one who died in the car crash?'

'No. Nicole, and you.'

Mark and Jane just sat quietly together, safe in an angel's arms, because they were together.

Jane reflected on it. She squeezed his hand again and then looked closely into his ocean blue eyes with her own lush, moist, strong green eyes.

'I guess it's kind of inevitable, really, isn't it?' she kind of quipped, while she shrugged, carrying Knoxx along with her. 'Well, you did say we were going to be together forever.' Allowing himself a grin, they both laughed and embraced. Leaning into each other on the couch, they hugged each other tight. Finally releasing her own tension, Jane said quietly, comforting Mark, 'Love you, honey.'

'I love you too, Janey,' Knoxx whispered back, fighting the

urge to let out all the hurt inside him.

As they separated, Jane ran her hand across her eye. She steeled herself for the next question, asking it in a more serious manner. 'What are you going to do?'

Taking her cue, Mark leaned back on the couch and fished out a gun. Holding it up to the ceiling, he pulled back the slide and chambered a round. The motion filled the air with a loud click. Jane almost jumped from her seat at the sight of Mark holding a gun locked and loaded. Mark set his gaze back at Jane. Jaw squared off, back straight up and down like six o'clock, he then confidently stated, 'Be first, be fast and hit 'em hard.'

'Mark, you can't do that. They'll kill you!' Jane replied breathlessly. Beginning to break into a tear-filled gaze, she grabbed his forearm, her hand was hot and sweaty with fear. Her nerves were becoming ragged as she swallowed hard, like she was choking down a jagged little pill, bitter to the taste.

Mark did not hesitate. He did not flinch or look as if he had any doubt as he cast his cold, steeled eyes at Jane. He waited for her to compose herself, rolling the pistol in his hand, the gray steel catching the light. Jane sat almost in a trance with her mouth slightly ajar, catching flies, as Mark went on to say, quietly with confidence, 'I'm already in the ground, so I might as well put as many of them in the ground with me. I can't let them get away with it any longer. If I'm going to get the chance to be a good person, then this will be the one, good thing that I can do before I leave this place, and that one thing is going to be getting to them. So that's what I'm going to do. I'm going to do the one thing I do best. Cause some mayhem and fuck 'em up.'

Knoxx lowered the gun and softened his pose, giving her his wry, cheeky smile. He was back. The Mark that Jane had loved her whole life unconditionally. His eyes glinted and he gave her the only thing she ever needed from him. The truth.

'I don't regret this life I chose. I only regret having to see myself live it. I wanted to marry Nicole, you know? I always thought to myself, marry someone you'll be proud to walk into any room with. And I was. And now, there's just you and me, as always. I need to ask you something. I need you to do something for me.' He confessed.

'What, honey? You know I'll do anything you ask. What do you need me to do, Mark?' Jane replied eagerly, as she began to cry.

Mark held up his hand to hold her little face that was such a beautiful, fresh face on a cute little frame. She was packed and wrapped so tightly, a bundle of nerves, energy and TNT. He glanced over to the bedroom, saying, 'I need you to look out for her. The tighter I hold onto reality, the more I feel like I'm losing my grip on it. The further I am away from it, the closer I feel I am to it.'

Gripping his hand tight, she asked, 'To what, honey?'

Dazed and confused, her eyes reached out to Mark in desperation for the truth, for some understanding. She listened as he said, 'I feel like I'm getting closer to the real unknown. Death. There's nowhere to run to anymore, and you're right. It's time to stop running, so I'm going to do this. You need to do this one thing for me. Take Nicky with you for a couple of weeks to L.A. I have one more envelope for you. Give it to Chris. He'll know what to do, and then, just keep Nicky safe with you, okay?'

Jane wiped the tears that were falling down her face, using her sleeve. She nodded and said simply, 'Of course, Mark. Just do what you have to do. Do it quickly. Take everything from those assholes. Just come back to me, okay?'

She froze in thought. She then said, 'You have to tell her!'

'No, not right now, it's better for her, for you and for me. I don't want her to worry too. It's better that she hates me, then I can stay focused on what I need to do without having to look out for her. If she's with you, then I know she'll be okay. They're mad, Jane.'

'Who, honey, who?'

'All of them out there, the ones who watch us; they're always watching me and you. They know about us. Everything we think we have, it's all bullshit. We have nothing. Not even our own lives. I was given the opportunity to work with some people a few years back, not that I had a choice really. And if I did what they wanted me to do, then you and me, we could live our lives free; stay alive, only for others to die. They're contaminating everything and everyone, Janey, even you and me. We're not the same. We've both changed. Forever. Keep Nicole with you and as far away from me as possible. It's already too late for me. But maybe I can get to them first and make it all right for you two. I'm the only person to blame for my mistakes. Nicky doesn't deserve me and she doesn't deserve to be hurt because of the choices I made. How much pain and suffering can love buy? How much is my life worth to her? How much is hers to me? I'll gladly trade my life to save yours.'

They hugged tightly again and Jane went about straightening herself up. Mark looked at the television with the volume turned down. He saw Vice President Tasker, speaking in front of the United Nations in New York. The caption below read that the U.S. had just approved four billion dollars in funding to the African Nations for humanitarian causes. The man standing next to him, graciously accepting the funds on behalf of the African people, was Gordon Forrest, his real representation being the Illuminati. Knoxx knew that Tasker knew. He also knew that the time had come. It was time to go to war.

The bedroom door opened and in stepped Nicole, with Mark and Jane watching her every step, shining bright in her summer dress, being herself, brave and beautiful. She stepped lightly into the foyer of the suite, pulling a roll-along suitcase. No one said a word. Nicole halted in front of the suite's double entrance doors. She finally met Mark's eyes, while she stood regal and defiant. She had risen to the challenge, the ultimate challenge that life throws at you: disappointment. She managed to say softly, 'There's nothing left.'

'If I find anything, I'll have it forwarded on to you,' he replied.

'That's not what I meant.'

Knoxx got up from the couch, having placed the pistol behind a cushion. Jane could see it from where she sat, and a cold chill ran over her. She gave herself a slight jolt and picked herself up in one fluid motion, trying to brush off the reality of what was happening. Mark was lying to Nicole because he loved her, and she was beginning to hate him because she thought he didn't. Jane could only stand and watch Mark, the beautiful liar, close out the show and seal her fate with one last lie. 'Count your blessings because now you know, there's no such thing as forever. Our first kiss that night at Envious in New York, it was always going to be our last. I took a chance on letting you into my world, but now, you're out.'

Nicole looked at him with wet eyes, holding her breath, fighting it every step. Mark picked up the remote and turned away to watch the television. It was done. Nicky gave it one last shot by asking Mark, 'When you're all done, getting everything that's important, Mark, how can you not see you've already lost everything that was good in your life? Isn't happiness the only one thing that's really important?'

117

'Yeah, how you doin'? Talk to me,' Joel Casa asked the caller.

'Listen, the heat's on me, man. You need to move on, so I can get back to doing my thing. You know what I mean? It's time for you to beat you're feet, fool, before you get us all pinched. I'm got one more club on La Cienega and Sunset called The Forty Deuce Club, owned by Ivan Keane. He's an old friend of a guy I fucked up a few years back. I want his club taken down, then everything's squashed and we can all go back to livin' our lives.' Bezerk then let out his famous deep baritone laugh.

Having kept Casa and Zacarro low-pro' in one of the Southsiders' safe houses, Bezerk had come to the conclusion that the only way to off load these guys was to get them one last score, or to set them up. That way, the cops could find a new set of balls to break, as long as they weren't his.

Wright had fallen back into his old ways from some time back. You can take the man out of the hood, but you can't take the hood out of the ma, and the one thing Bezerk wanted to be was The Man, having learned from the man himself, Mark Knoxx. Bezerk had realized that Mark would never send for him to be at his side in the corporate world, where the real action was. So he decided to descend back into the world he knew best, a world where he could do the one thing he did best, being a Thug. He was wheeling and dealing everything from coke, guns and ho's along the Sunset Strip. Even though he was raking in millions a year, he'd always been a junkie, and it was a habit he couldn't break. He wanted more of it every day. Only this time around, thanks to Mark Knoxx, Bezerk was now a junkie, high on money and power, but now he wanted respect from the streets.

Marbela seemed to be running the Envious Group more these days, always covering for him. Chris Wright knew how to work her, with perks like hotel penthouse suites, a day at the spa, buying her lavish gifts like expensive perfume, clothes, watches and shit. Girl shit. Bezerk didn't give a shit. It was all free money to him. He played both sides of the street and now he had decided to play Joey Casa and his Club Banging crew. It was inevitable, after all. Bezerk had to give McGann and Keets something or someone if he was going to get his life back.

118

The girls spent the day talking, having drinks and sharing stories about the last few months, laughing at some of them. There had been a lot of good times, before the bad times had come along. Jane had done her best to tread the minefield lightly, holding back her tears while she watched Nicole fall apart throughout the day. They shared a couple of intimate moments and tears. Nicole cried because she had lost Mark and didn't know why. Jane cried because she knew why. Nicole thought he had thrown her away because he didn't love her anymore. Jane knew that Mark was sending her away because he did.

Jane could only offer up one slice of hope, telling Nicole that Mark had told her that they were to go to Los Angeles on the Exile jet. They would stay there for a couple of weeks while he worked some things out. She said that she thought things would eventually work out okay between them. To Nicole, this all sounded like bullshit. Once again, Jane was covering for her perfect Mark, who could do no wrong; he was never to blame for his actions. The way he had thrown her out, supposedly the girl he loved. It felt like it had happened on the flip of a coin. Tails, she'd lost. Jane worked at endearing herself to Nicole, and eventually, they bonded. Nicky would have preferred Alisha to have been with her but she felt that there must be some truth to what Jane was telling her as she was the one that Mark had picked to accompany her. Maybe they could patch things up after all. By holding onto that thought, Nicky soon found herself smiling, driving and stopping for a beer.

Knoxx met them at a private airport just to the north of Nice International. He stepped out of his black-on-black, bad-ass Lamborghini Gallardo, draped in jeans and a white, Joker t-shirt. He walked over to Jane first, saying something briefly. He turned and walked up to Nicole, giving her a warm embrace, eventually kissing her neck and smelling her perfume. They eventually kissed and then held hands. She knew there and then, that Jane had been right after all. He said, 'You know, that first morning back in New York after we'd met, I had to be on a plane and I heard an Alicia Keys song playing. It made me smile because I thought of you. You're like the sun and the moon to me, babe.'

She gripped his hand. Nicole couldn't help it. Tears began to fall as she felt herself slowly, softly, mouthing the words, 'I love you.'

Mark didn't respond. He fell into her and they kissed. Letting his hands fall down the back of her shiny, honey blonde hair, he kissed her as if it was the last kiss he could ever give anyone. Then he was gone. Knoxx walked back over to Jane without even looking back at her. Always Jane. She was the one he always turned to, first and last.

Nicole could only stand under the hot sun, feeling the hot jet-wash from the waiting plane. She watched Mark pull out from his jeans' back pocket an envelope that he handed to Jane. Her face looked as if she had just faced down the devil himself. Jane's face told Nicky there was more to this than she would ever be allowed to know. Jane and Mark held a tight discussion, oblivious to the waiting world. Once again, locked together in their own world. Mark passed along his final instructions to the one person he truly trusted in the world. After a few minutes, Nicole watched as they embraced, seemingly with more morbid importance than Nicky and Mark had. She noticed Jane had begun to cry. What was happening? Nicole began to cry, while Knoxx held Jane by her thin, toned arms. Whatever he was telling her, it looked to be definitive. Jane shrugged him away and wiped the streaming tears from her face. She stepped away, but suddenly turned back to him, returning for a harder embrace, like it was the last time she would ever get to hold him. She cried openly, looking up at him. She then kissed him long and hard. Then, as fast as she had cried, she stepped away from him without ever looking back. Jane strode towards Nicole with her head held high as if she had just won an Oscar. Walking confidently, passing by her, she said in her best Breakfast At Tiffany's voice, 'You alright, darling? Come on, everything'll be alright. Let's get going. We'll have some martinis.'

The girls watched from the plane's windows, each for their own reasons. Mark was leaning up against the bad-boy car with his shades draped over his sore, reddened eyes, hiding the pain he was enduring. He gave an easy, long wave to them. Stepping into the Lambo', he peeled out a five-hundred-and-forty degree spin, carving up the runway, engulfing himself in smoking tires. His own set of smoking guns would be running hot soon, once he'd begun to blaze his way through the guest list. His own guest list.

The plane picked up speed, taking off as it began its trek across the Atlantic and onto Los Angeles. Knoxx was now free of the two people he loved the most, and free to do what he knew he had to do. He was going to try to kill them all, the members of The Firm. He had sent the two most important people in his life to a place where he thought they would be safe. Back to his private army, the Southsiders, but he had forgotten the first rule from prison that Pauley had taught him. Trust No One.

'We have agreements in place for when you become president. In spite of the embargos put in place by your predecessors, we've manipulated the rules through an arrangement with the honorable Mr. Forrest, allowing us to ease them. Libya sits on thirty-nine billion barrels of proven oil reserves. It has huge potential for economic growth, and if we can gain a foothold in that region, then we can influence the whole Northern African peninsula.'

Tasker sat in his high-back leather chair, rocking slightly while he listened to the sweet tune of greed and total control. Tasker knew he had it all. His final play was in motion and the men seated across from him were all playing their parts in perfect harmonious tune.

Stewart, continued, 'Over the next five to eight years, Libya could end up being the top oil supplier, pulling us out from under the Saudi's and the Middle East's grip. We estimate a further sixty-five billion barrels have yet to be discovered there.'

Tasker took a slow drink from a familiar blue bottle of Ty water. He flipped forward in his chair. Letting out a sick chuckle, he voiced a thought. 'So, this cluster-fuck we created in Iraq. We can pull our asses out of the fire, having made it all look so bad that we can sell this to the American people? I like the thought of putting it all in play, the enemy of my enemy is my friend, and all that.'

'Absolutely,' Stewart replied, confirming, as he too, laughed.

'And once we've sent the whole Middle East into another thousand-year war, while they concentrate on exterminating each other, we can recoup our war outlay, withdraw our troops, save our economy and secure a new oil supply with Libya?' Tasker asked.

'Yes, sir,' Stewart confirmed, meeting Tasker's eyes firmly.

Tasker tipped back his chair. Smiling, he said, 'Fan-fucking-tastic.'

Everyone laughed at the inside joke. While all the focus had been on the War on Terror, Iraq, Afghanistan, Tasker and his men had all been filling their pockets, and then negotiating a back door deal to make amends with the American people. Tasker would come out of it as if he had pulled America out from under the most horrific war that America had ever gotten itself entrenched in. In the new era of his presidency, he'd be the one to secure a hundred years of oil supply from a former enemy, Libya, who by comparison to Iraq, was as easy to control as a puppy.

The girls spent the first two days at The Peninsula Hotel in Beverly Hills, sleeping for the most part and then laying out by the pool. The early October sun was still hanging bright in the Los Angeles sky. Nicole had been able to sleep on a diet of V1 Vodka and Soda and plenty of pink champagne. Jane kept her light in the head, so she could fend off any further questions like the ones she had endured on the plane coming in. Jane pretended that she was sleeping most of the way over from France, to keep Nicole from finding out the truth.

The drinking had also helped to dull the hurt that Jane carried inside. The truth was that Mark was going to be locked in a war against the men who had controlled him for too long, the men and women he had told her about. As the plane rose from the Azure Coast of France, taking them both to safety, Jane had looked down at Mark; her feelings had told her that it would be for the last time. She just knew. It was woman's intuition, she guessed. She carried the knowledge that her best friend in the world was preparing to give her the best and the worst gift she had ever been given in her life. Mark had told her, before she kissed him goodbye at the airport that he would love her forever; he had always loved her, but now it was too late. Time had run out. She remembered him telling her, 'Smile when you feel the wind brush your face, coz that'll be me, touching you to let you know that everything's okay. You'll always be the wind beneath my wings.'

In a townhouse at the back of the hotel, Jane cried and slept, then cried some more, but she knew she had to keep her end of the bargain. She had to play her part, because Mark's best and worst gift to her was that he was going to trade his life to save hers. He was going to war and he had asked Jane to help him win. She had to get Chris Wright to do what Mark needed him to do, but what Mark wanted done was the worst thing Jane had ever heard. How had he come up with it? He'd summed it up by telling her, 'for one thing to live, another must die.' In war, there were going to be casualties. He had then given her the envelope before she had boarded the plane for America, telling her, 'Deliver the envelope and make sure it happens this weekend.'

He had been firm with Jane at the airport. Knoxx, being the general, was now bringing out his army of Southsiders to join him in the fight, and it was going to be fought on all fronts. He just wasn't prepared for his number one foot soldier, Bezerk, blind-siding him.

'That's what he told me to tell you, and you have to make it happen at the latest by this weekend.'

'Shiitt, I dunno,' Bezerk said in a vague tone, pulling on his goatee. He rubbed his hand on his belly, having gotten fat from living the good life, partying most nights, sleeping in a soft, fifteen-hundred-thread-count Egyptian cotton bed at his two and a half million dollar mansion in Hollywood Hills. It had all been provided by his old cellie, Mark Knoxx, and now, here he was mulling it over in front of Mark's number one fan, Jane. She knew how badly Mark needed this; their survival depended on it getting done.

'What's to think about? What do you mean, you don't know?' Jane answered, exploding in anger.

Bezerk mad-dogged her and immediately slapped her hard across her face.

'Fuck you! I ain't no punk-ass bitch, and ain't no bitch gonna be telling me what I can and can't do. Get the fuck over there and suck up some of that snow. Ain't no one telling me what I gotta do anymore. I call the shots around here, you best belieeve thaatt!'

Jane recovered from the sting of the slap. Never one to back out of a fight, she would stare down the devil himself, kick him in the balls, and send him on his way to stoke up the fire. She knew the fight she was in. Mark had told her what to say if Bezerk was on the fence, only it seemed to Jane that he wasn't even near the fence, let alone on it.

'I don't need any of that shit! What I do need is for you to do this here.' She stabbed at the crumpled up, typed letter that Bezerk held tightly in his hand. She argued, shouting, 'This isn't for Mark. He's not telling you to do it for him. He's giving you the heads up on this. Otherwise, you'll probably end up going back to prison. Mark's letting you know that the Feds are on your ass. If you can get her into the hospital, Mark will help you out with the rest. Then you can go back to doing whatever it is you do? That's what he told me to tell you. He also said that if you didn't do what he's asking, then he'd go to Juicy.'

Upon hearing this, Bezerk went berserk. Grabbing her by the throat, he threw her against the wall, saying, 'Fucking bitch, I'll kill you!'

Following up quickly, he lifted her body weight up against the wall. His mad, black, dilated, eyes told her what he was going to do, as he began to squeeze down on her throat. He looked deep into her eyes while her eyes began to pop while she felt her breath leaving her. Trapped inside Bezerk's grip, smelling his hot breath on her, feeling the air inside her trapped, she began to see black spots in her eyes. She felt the seven seconds of squeezing catching up to her, listening to Bezerk gurgle deep in his throat like a lion, saying sarcastically, 'Have your boy come himself next time, if he's a real man. Don't send a sheep to do a wolf's job.'

Jane's small knuckles tightened. Her eyes squinted, looking hard at Bezerk. A look of sheer will came over her, summoning up all her hate and anger. It came from her determination to succeed, not from fear. Her head jammed down onto Bezerk's iron grip, allowing her to catch the smallest of air in her lungs. Jane then drove her right knee hard up into Bezerk's balls. In an instant, as he released his grip to suck in some air, she drove a right cross across his face, catching him on the bridge of the nose. He moved away slightly with the momentum and the shock of actually being hit by her. Jane then kicked him in the shin. She moved swiftly to her left to create some distance between them and then quickly launched an almighty Hail-Mary kick, right up into his balls again, sending him to the floor writhing in pain. Jane coughed and wheezed to clear her lungs, but only for a second, gasping for fresh air. She knew she'd only have the upper hand for a fleeting second, as she glanced at Bezerk, who was beginning to gather himself. Jane staggered, half-jumping with adrenaline, as she meandered her way across to the other side of the blood red couch in the middle of the office. Bezerk pulled himself up, using the end table, shouting, 'Bitch! I'm gonna fuck you hard, make you bleed, and then I'm gonna fuck you up!'

Bezerk fell to the ground, knocking off a picture of a Sureño standing in front of a razor wire fence at the California-Mexico border. He had drawn it in prison years earlier, to remind him of where he had come from and where he could end up, back in prison, if he didn't stick to the game plan, as he had promised Knoxx he would.

Jane had been in the office many times during the past year, delivering Mark's envelopes, and she knew exactly what she wanted. And so did Bezerk. Jane opened the end table and hefted it out, her long, sinuous forearm tightening under its weight. She repeated what she had seen Mark do, days earlier. Bezerk heard the heavy click from the slide action, and it stopped him cold in his tracks.

'He sent his number one bitch to come handle his punk-ass bitch!' she shouted at him, while she began to gather herself and steady her breathing, pointing the dark gray, steel Glock pistol at Bezerk's dick. Then in a harried, breathless, mocking tone, she said, 'You know how we do! You want me to go tell your boys you just got your ass kicked, or are we gonna come to an arrangement?'

'Fuck you!' Bezerk shouted, rubbing his balls.

'You better say goodbye to your little friends then.'

Jane stepped forward and aimed the gun at his balls, letting Bezerk know that she would go down with Mark if she had to. Bezerk could tell that she wasn't bluffing. He had gotten to know Jane well over the past couple of years, and knew how strong her loyalty to Mark was. She was broken and weakened from the stress of carrying so many of Mark's secrets, getting involved in taking cocaine, but she knew when to draw the line, and right now, she and Bezerk were both standing on opposite sides of it. Jane would always fall on the side of Mark, and right now, Bezerk knew it. He held up the palm of his hand to indicate that he had seen enough, saying in surrender, 'Alright, I got you. Fuckin' bitch. Put the gun down, we're cool. I'll do it.'

'When? Tell me when and how you're gonna do it?' Jane asked matter-of-factly, jabbing the gun at him, showing him who her bitch was now.

Bezerk sat upright, resting his elbow on one knee with his head in his hand, trying to bring his breathing back to normal. Finally, seeing the funny side to it, he sat on the floor and pulled on his goatee, thinking about how it had all come to this. He shrugged, as if he was going to laugh. Looking up at Jane from the floor, he quipped, 'Fuckin' Knowledge man, fuckin' faagg. Got one over on me again, huh.'

Bezerk knew she would do it too, shoot him dead, no question. Jane jabbed the pistol at his face one more time and said forcefully, 'Well?'

'Okay, listen,' Bezerk answered. Searching for inspiration, pulling on his goatee, he started to let it tumble out. 'We put on a V.I.P. night, some kind of ladies night. Then I'll get the D.J. to call up some girls for some prizes. The girl you want will be one of them, and then, when she comes up on stage, we'll know who she is. When she goes to the bar, I'll make sure her drinks are spiked with some special juice I got handy. After one or two sweet drinks, that fuckin' bitch'll be done. You know what I mean?' He began to laugh, the more he was thinking about it. Saying it as some kind of sick joke, laughing a sick laugh, he then sang out, in an easy way, 'Yeah, she's done. No problem, I'll get it done this week. Come back at the weekend and kick it with me. We cool, babe.'

Bezerk was now back on point and back on the team, rolling along to get along.

'What you got for me?' Dan opened up abruptly, greeting the caller while he and Richie were cruising the Sunset Strip.

It was Bezerk. He finally had something and it sounded good. Months of riding his ass and picking through the trash of his life was finally paying off for them, but Dan being Dan didn't want to take the credit for it. He and Richie were always working multiple cases in Hollywood; Bezerk was just one of their play things. Someone they wanted to fuck with, to let him know who the real players were in town: them, the Westside Pimps.

Dan McGann and Richie Keets had been working a serial murder case that required them to cruise the strip joints and bars of Hollywood. Yeah, it was brutal work, but hey, someone had to do it and the Westside Pimps were just the guys for the job. Dan, being single, took full advantage of the situation, picking up chicks all over town. Richie was out with him like a man possessed, as if he was young, free, and single too, which he most certainly wasn't. But Richie seemed different over the past three weeks, like he did not care about his family, his job, or his future anymore. Dan, as yet, hadn't been able to put a finger on it, or drag it out of Richie. He had, however, been able to drag out a young, happening babe from one of the strip clubs. They had been visiting Fantasy Palace on Pico and El Segundo Boulevard, where Dan had worked a hot babe who called herself Pasha, on stage. She had given up her real name to him though, Amanda Linsay, along with a key to her apartment on North Gale Drive, half a block back from Wilshire Boulevard.

Dan listened intently to the ramblings of a mad man. Bezerk kept his flow strong and his reason for doing what he was doing strong, ramming home the concessions he wanted for himself. Dan agreed to them but had no intention of keeping his word to a guy like this. He listened to him frustratingly repeat, over and over, at the end of every sentence, 'You know what I mean.'

Dan eventually picked up the phrase and began ending his sentences with, 'You know what I mean,' and, 'yeess siirr,' mimicking Bezerk. It became the inside joke between him and Richie when they trolled their way along the Sunset Strip, hitting the clubs and bars of Hollywood, trying to catch the serial killer. At the end of the call, Dan told Bezerk that Detective Caron Smart would be contacting him to go over the details of the sting. She would get another crack at The Club Bangers, courtesy of Bezerk.

'What do you mean, it's inconclusive and circumstantial - evidence? How can that be? Even a blind man with A.D.D. can see that we have him dead to rights.' Dobro smashed the palm of her hand on the desk at the message being delivered to her.

She had Hadley on a conference call with their boss, Kevin Christie, who explained, 'You gave it your best shot. I can't fault you at all. I thought you'd nailed it and the information Teresa provided sold me. But he's the ultimate boss with the final decision. He says you got to put together harder evidence if you want him to sign an indictment.'

Maxine took it hard and responded just as hard, shouting in the phone, 'I don't believe this! Something's not right! What do you think, Teresa?'

Speaking on the speakerphone, she was looking for some support from Teresa when Christie, beating her to the punch, kicked in his thoughts before Teresa had the chance to respond.

'Maxine, I know you think this is all some kind of conspiracy, but it's not. You just don't have it yet, and you don't have him.'

Maxine did not miss a beat, asking, 'Teresa, what do you think about all of this?'

'Well.' There was a pause on the line, leaving both parties hanging on her answer. She said, 'I guess we could find an actual link that proves there's a direct connection to Knoxx's personal bank accounts.'

'There. You see?'

Christie jumped in all over it, screwing Dobro down tighter than a zebra's hide on a bongo drum. It resonated through her, the low vibration as the drum-beat marched to the sound of her getting royally screwed again by her colleagues, and in some way, by Mark Knoxx.

She said in disbelief, answering, 'I can't believe this. Okay, I want Teresa on the earliest plane out here. I want her to look through all the accounts one more time. Only this time, we'll go way back and we'll focus on the one thing I know best, drugs. Let's lower our sights and follow the trail of drug money coming up from Mexico into California. I know that's real. No one in their right mind would dare try covering that up. I give you my word, before this year's out, I guarantee you Knoxx is going down. I'm going to be the one to tan his hide, watch me! See you out here in a couple days Teresa.'

124

'Oh God, please no, God no! When? Where did it happen?'

Maxine had been woken up early in the morning, or late at night, depending on which way you lived your life. She answered the phone in mid-second ring. In her business, she was used to getting calls at odd hours, but if she was getting one at twelve minutes past three in the morning, then it was bad news. Bad news came with the job.

Already in tears at the grim news she had received, she jumped out of bed, paying no mind to her cats, Jax and Chloe, who looked at her as if she was crazy. Chloe began to lick the base of her paw, while Jax lazily dropped his head back onto the soft, warm duvet. Maxine was crazy all right. She was blindly banging her way around the bedroom, having difficulty seeing what she was doing through a thick flood of tears, openly crying at the hopelessness of it all. She moved like lightning, getting dressed, but then she faced an agonizing two hour drive from her apartment in La Jolla to Cedars Sinai Medical Center, located between Beverly Boulevard, and San Vicente Boulevard in West Hollywood. Maxine had to go right away. Not as a police officer, but as a mother.

Jane had been woken up to a similar phone call around an hour earlier. She had bolted upright in anticipation of getting every single detail right, knowing that Mark would want to know all the details of what had happened when she called him in the morning. Mark lived his life in the details; since it had been his plan, he would want to know that it had been carried out in every detail. Jane listened with morbid fascination, but her heart fluttered and she felt herself stifling her tears, listening as a woman. She felt for Maxine and for what she must be going through, but Jane managed to stick to the program. Mark was doing what he did best, plotting. He had the program that would keep them all in line. The HEAVEN program. His assassination program. She sat up in bed and listened to the deep, excitable voice on the other end of the line; it spoke with every other sentence ending with, 'You know what I mean.'

Jane knew it was done. She realized it had begun. The art of war.

Maxine had spent all morning sitting in the waiting room. The hospital was known for being one of the best in the world. All the movie stars were taken to Cedars, as it was referred to by the residents of Los Angeles. Maxine had been able to see her for a few minutes, but her little darling was in no shape to know she was by her side, gripping her hand while she whispered soothing words to her. Maxine was broken. Everything she had thought was important in her life was all bullshit. She was a mother to two great kids whom she never saw enough of, and now that Dolly had slipped into a coma, it might be too late to make it up to her.

The sunlight did nothing to warm her bones. She was wearing a Juicy Couture tracksuit that she had thrown on and some oversized black, Chanel sunglasses. Sitting bundled up in a black, Burberry overcoat; it seemed as if God himself was spearing her through the heart with ice bolts from Heaven. The fierce lion that was special agent Maxine Dobro, just sat quietly. She gripped a cardboard coffee cup for comfort in the hospital's cafeteria, thinking that if she ever got a second chance, she would make it right between her ex-husband, her kids, and with The Almighty himself.

An above average-looking waif of a woman sat down at a small metal coffee table next to Maxine. Maxine didn't notice her; her eyes were open, but they didn't see anything. The dishwater blonde sat quietly for a minute, seemingly in her own world as she too began to sip on her cup of coffee. She snuck only the tiniest of glimpses at Dobro, with Maxine sitting at a right angle to her. She stole another look at her, noticing that she looked dazed and confused. Maxine was unaware she was being watched.

'Excuse me, are you okay?' the woman said, as a gesture of goodwill for another woman's anguish. Maxine turned her head slightly to acknowledge the remark. She vaguely recognized the woman from somewhere, but it didn't register. Maxine just shrugged in some appreciation, but no words came from her. She had lost the will to speak and even live at this point. Only one thing mattered to Maxine, and that was whether her daughter would live to see another warm, sunny day, so she could hug her and tell her that she loved her more than life itself. The woman spoke up for her, in a distinct and perfunctory, perfectly formed British accent. Hitting Maxine dead center, she said, 'Maxine, your girl, Dolly, she can survive this, you know.'

126

Jane spent the rest of the week with Nicole doing the rounds on Rodeo Drive, Brighton Way in Beverly Hills, and on Melrose Boulevard. They were having a good time, leaving their troubles behind, having made a silent pact not to discuss Mark. Only Jane did know. She knew everything, having been sent on a seek and destroy mission. She was looking to cut the heart out of the devil, one piece at a time, and she had delivered on her end of the bargain, after having threatened to blow his dick off. Delivering the envelope to Bezerk however, had turned out to be the easier part of the bargain.

NVS had spread the word throughout the UCLA campus that it was party central and that the University could come and get their groove on. Only one girl in particular hadn't known that from the moment that she and her friends had entered NVS, a freak was watching her. Now Maxine knew the truth. Jane had delivered it to her. Knoxx had put her in play. He had manipulated the play, having learned of his enemy's weakness, and shown her that she needed to be compliant to his wishes. He had ultimate control over who gets to live or die. This, Jane had found, was much tougher than she had expected, having to relay it to Maxine, but she believed in Mark and she believed that, in war, there were casualties. Jane delivered the well-honed speech that Mark had drilled into her. Even though she knew Maxine was the head of the F.B.I. for California, she now realized, as Mark had betted on, that she could drop the documents in Maxine's lap and simply walk away.

The war had begun, and Mark was hitting them first, fast and hard. It was now all in Mark Knoxx's hands. The next card to be played was his. Jane could now relax and just enjoy some time with her new friend, Nicole. They made plans to shop, do some sightseeing, go to dinner, and then do some clubbing at NVS this coming weekend, before Jane had to move onto the next phase of her mission while she was in Los Angeles.

Mark had been driving hard and fast along the highways of France and Spain, and then hauling ass back to Monaco, breaking the speed limit while his mind raced too, plotting.

Pulling up outside the Sandbanks Hotel in Nice, in a canary yellow Porsche 996 twin turbo, he checked his Breitling Bentley watch and decided that it was time to get some beers out on the patio. Not one to shy away from any opportunity for female company, he called Alisha Ellington to join him. She told him that she'd be down in twenty minutes, which of course, being a woman, looked suspiciously more like an hour, according to Mark's watch before she stalked out onto the patio to join him. Mark blazed a warm, million dollar smile. With his biceps round, full, and tanned, he took off his shades to get a better look at her tight, dancer's frame. Alisha was dressed as a predator, looking like a sleek panther. She smiled and leaned over to kiss him, giving him a look right down the low cut, plunging opening of her black shirt that was accentuated with black, boot cut jeans. Mark immediately rose to her challenge by delivering his best material throughout the evening. She laughed in all the right places and as more drinks came, so they came closer together, the predator slowly moving in on its prey for the kill.

Knoxx was a reader of self-motivation, positive mental attitude, philosophy and human history. He was a student of Wall Street and had become a banger on Jump Street. Everything he found important had, in some way, been passed down in time from one person to the next through their own experiences, whether they knew they were telling him something he found useful or not. During his rise to wealth, power and respect, every signpost was there for him to see. Danger. But more often than not he always seemed to miss it. The last phone call he'd taken was from the man he was now going to war with, Paul Deavins, who'd warned him, 'Love and hate have moved more people through their feelings into action than any ideal or presentation ever has.'

Mark was blessed with genius but he was also cursed with madness. As the night began to draw in, Alisha had drawn him into her. They had kissed passionately several times, with Alisha letting out a low, enticing growl. Knoxx was going to war tomorrow, but here he was, doing what he did best, getting paid and getting laid. In a cute, drunken, giggling way, he closed the deal, saying suggestively, 'Fuck it, let's fuck.'

'Yeah boy, you a sight for sore eyes!'

'Yeah, whatever, man. Let's get this done so we can get the fuck out of here, comprende?'

NVS was jumping and Bezerk had been flying high all week, throwing his boys plenty of flash cash. Everyone was loving life and living large. Olivia Marbela had done her job fabulously, having come up with the Simply Gorgeous Fashion Night in mid-week that had ended up being a terrible night for one girl who had collapsed and had to be rushed to the hospital. Other than that, the event had been simply fabulous.

'Listen fool, I'm the one doin' you a solid, so don't go get it twisted. You're in my fuckin' town and in my club, belieeve thaatt,' Bezerk growled.

Bezerk and Casa were standing by the office window that overlooked the dance floor of NVS. The office was party central. Most of Bezerk's crew got some level of action from the girls they had with them, while Nick Zacarro and John Rockhound busied themselves with some young honeys. Bezerk stood at the mirrored window, drinking from a bottle of Corona, with both of them looking at the hot pussy gyrating down on the dance floor. Bezerk's eye caught something, just as Joel Casa's had, looking at the same thing but at two different girls. Bezerk let out a little gruff, grunt to himself in recognition of seeing someone familiar; she waved up at the office as she walked through to the V.I.P. section. Joey Casa immediately lit up, his eyes blazing as he began to rip into Bezerk. He took a half-step away from the window, saying dramatically, 'Who the fuck's that? Can she see me?'

'Who, that chick? Na man, she's part of the crew. She knows I like to stand up here watching, that's all.' Bezerk let out a chuckle at his own, sick, inside joke.

Casa replied, panicked, 'No man, not the one that waved, the tall blonde that's with her. Who's that?'

Joey seemed alarmed, while Bezerk looked annoyed and a little confused. He answered, 'Her? She's my partner's chick. She lives in Miami. Her name's Nicole Young; she used to be a singer. Now she's hooked up living in the lap of luxury, fucking her way round the world. Gotta be some major piece of ass.' Bezerk searched her out, laughing at his twisted humor, and how he'd meant it.

Casa replied, 'Yeah, that's some piece of ass alright.'

With a look of terror on his wide-eyed face, he now stood squarely to Bezerk. He looked like he wanted to off everyone in the office.

Bezerk looked at Joey, mad-dogging him, and asked, 'What?'

Casa didn't respond. He just looked over at Nicky Z and barked, 'Nick, get the fuck over here!'

Zacarro looked up from the couch with a young, wanna-be-model sitting on his lap. He smiled at Joey, trying to let him know, 'Not now dude.' He recognized the pissed look on Joey's face and got around to leveraging himself out from under the chick, leaving her on a promise. Getting his ass over to Casa and Bezerk, he asked in an annoyed voice, 'What the fuck, man, I'm getting down with that chick. It's in the bag, man.'

Casa ignored him and stayed on script. Flipping it, he asked him, 'Fuck that. Look the fuck down there and tell me who you see?' Joey pointed directly down at the V.I.P. section. Nicky Z took a moment to get a fix on where his finger was pointing, but it only took him two seconds before Joey and Bezerk heard him say, 'Fuck me! Say it ain't so?' He let out a small laugh, both in the disbelief and in horror. Joey and Nick both let their eyes do the talking.

Bezerk just watched them, while he kind of sniggered, asking, 'What? What the fuck's up?'

'That blonde chick down there, the one that's dating your bro', the one who came in with the one who works for you,' Casa stated.

Bezerk's eyes searched the girls out, looking at Jane Mears and Nicole Young. He asked, 'Yeah, waassuupp?'

'That chick ain't just some chick that's fuckin' your partner. Her real name's Nicola Cowper; she's from our home town back in New Jersey. She can finger us for three murders,' Joey said in no uncertain terms.

'It's because of her that we're in this shit in the first place,' Zacarro followed up. Both men were filled with dread and hatred towards her.

Bezerk drank on his beer, and then summed it up for them. 'Shiitt, I guess what goes around comes around.'

Oblivious to the action in the office, because the real action was downstairs in the V.I.P. section, they each watched in their own way.

Bezerk was the first to speak up. He looked back across the office to catch the eye of each of the coke-sniffing whores and guys from his crew, telling them in a pissed, hard way, 'Get the fuck up outta my house! Come on, fools, I ain't fuckin' with ya. Everyone get your shit out of here! You know what I mean. Move it!'

No one spoke. Nick Zacarro, Joey Casa and Bezerk all waited for the room to empty. Tavo and Beaver were the last to leave.

Bezerk then sipped his beer and swilled it in his mouth. He

giggled some more on his thought, and then said ruefully, 'Leave it to me. I got this, belieeve thaatt. You fools sure do fuck things up for yourselves, huh, yeess siirr.'

Casa rode it out, waiting to see what was coming next, while Zacarro became agitated, saying, 'What the fuuckk! What we gonna do?'

Bezerk took over, saying, 'What we gonna do is get you guys the fuck outta here as quick as possible. Those two bitches have the run of the place, you feel me? So here's what we gonna do. We'll get some chicks to hang on your arm as you leave. And me, I'm gonna fuck these bitches up for you. Sweet fucking payback's the way I see it. Anyway, I got a gold plated shield on me. You know what I mean?'

Bezerk let out a grumbling belly laugh at how it had all come back around, saying, 'Go on, get the fuck out of here. We'll still be on for next weekend. Don't worry, I got you.'

Bezerk picked up the phone and gave the orders. Within minutes, some hot babes were by the door to the office with Tavo, Beaver and Coco to escort The Club Bangers out. The strategy paid off. Jane and Nicole were too busy drinking with Matt Tamban and Olivia Marbela to be looking around at anyone outside the V.I.P. section. Bezerk watched from his crucible, repeatedly pulling on his goatee, looking like Lucifer himself. Plotting. He was filled with hatred, revenge and envy. Finally, he picked up the phone, while he looked down at the V.I.P. section. He watched as Jester picked up the phone from behind the bar. Bezerk told him what he wanted done. Jester looked up at the mirrored windows high above, unsure of what he had heard him say, Bezerk confirmed it by telling him, 'You heard me right fool! I said the blonde in the black dress, got the pink feather shit round her neck. I said, juice her up, hit her up and call me back when it's done. Yeah, I know who the fuck she is. I know who owns her ass. She belongs to Knoxx. Just do it, or the last thing you'll be worrying about is your piece of shit job, you know what I mean?'

Within thirty minutes, it was done and the hot poison was already running through her veins, beginning to kick in. Nicky felt hot and began to run a fever, so she decided to visit the restroom, doing her best to put on a brave face while trying to giggle it off. Jane ribbed her, saying that she was a lightweight and that she should have had more stamina by now, having been drinking for the better part of two weeks straight. Nicole managed to steady herself. Her eyes were stinging now and she was beginning to feel her pulse literally beat out of her skin. It was beginning to feel like Hell itself was trying to pull her down to the floor. Nicole said firmly, 'I'll be fine. I'm going to get some air. No, you stay here. I'll be back in a few minutes.'

Patting Jane's hand away; Nicky got up from her seat to go to the ladies' room. Jane watched her and laughed with Matt about her. Jane then checked back Nicole's way. Something. It was just, something. It just didn't feel right, in some way. Mark had specifically asked her to watch over Nicole for him. Jane allowed herself a small glimpse at her watch, taking a mental note of the time, thinking she'd give Nicole around seven, maybe ten minutes, tops.

*   *   *

Nicole was gripped by her arm and picked up under her elbow as soon as she began to stagger. She was losing her footing with each step, each one becoming heavier. Her eyes looked up in a gaze of pure joy and happiness at the heavyset guy with long, dark hair and a goatee who had a hold of her. He was laughing a long, happy laugh, and so Nicole laughed. It felt like fun. She felt like he had picked her up, high off the ground and she was now flying without a care in the world. He looked kind and very handsome. Was it Mark? No. Mark didn't have a goatee. Over the loud, low base beat rhythm of the nightclub music, she could hear him saying her name. This strange face seemed to know her, telling her calmly, in a warm, friendly way, 'Everything's cool, Nicola, belieeve thaatt, baby. I Gotchya.'

The man laughed again, causing her to laugh along with him; only now, Nicola didn't feel too light. She felt herself becoming heavy. The weight on her chest was so unbearable; it seemed as if the sound and the lights were now muffled. She felt like she was underneath a dark light.

Nicola couldn't move. Her face could only feel the light warmth of a single crocodile tear that was slowly tracing its way down her cheek from the outside corner of her left eye. Her eyes were blank but her face faced a picture sitting on an end table in the quiet office, a picture that had the sun coming up from behind razor wire, with what looked like a Mexican gangbanger in sunglasses and a heavy moustache drawn in it. She felt herself smile inside, but she couldn't breathe or move. She felt free, somehow. Her eyes focused on the picture, frozen in time. She could feel the tug on the zipper of her dress, listening to the deep growl of a belly laugh, and the words from a man, roughly getting on top of her. 'Yeah boy, I'm getting my money tonight.'

*   *   *

Marbela and Tamban were having a great time, just as they had been for the past few years. Everything Mark had promised them had come true. They were in the middle of all the action and were living an envious life, heading up their departments and making plenty of money along the way. Most of the time it had been a pleasure in bringing so much pleasure to so many people throughout the country. The Envious Group had become them. They lived out their dreams through it every day and most nights, either hosting or being invited to a mega-party for the rich and famous. Now, here they were, entertaining Mark's jewels in the crown of his business portfolio, Jane and Nicole.

Olivia had noticed how Tavo, Beaver and Coco were all huddled around Jester at the bar. Jane had noticed too, and got up to join them. She became animated in her actions, and stepped into the middle of them, pointing her finger aggressively at Tavo. There seemed to be a moment between them. One thing was crystal clear; Jane had put them on notice. Tavo seemed to give Beaver a shrug of his shoulders. A few words were exchanged, then all of them took off through the V.I.P. section, with Jane not even bothering to mention anything to Matt or Olivia. Matthew Tamban, ever the lawyer, said to Olivia as he refilled her glass of champagne, 'Whatever it is, I guess we're not supposed to know about it.'

Jane marched hard and fast with Bezerk's boys. Beaver and Tavo took the lead, forcing their way through the crowd of night clubbers who were dancing to the hot, rhythmic beats of the club. Every eager step they took, cutting through the crowd, seemed like they were wasting agonizing seconds. With every second wasted, it felt like they would be too late. Bounding up the stairs, Jane was already shouting Nicky's name. Only Tavo could hear Jane shout, because the noise from the music drowned her out. She felt herself begin to cry already about what was happening up in the office, shouting in desperation at Tavo, 'Come on! Get in there!'

Tavo pushed on through the door to the office and everyone fanned out throughout the room. Jane hesitated. Beaver pulled his gun, Tavo pulled out his gun, then Coco too. All of them aimed their guns at Bezerk. Jane stood stock-still, looking at Bezerk. He stood there with eyes that wide and wild with his shirt undone, and his jeans undone. Nicole's eyes told them all what their fate would be, but Jane confirmed it by steadily stating, 'Everyone in this room's dead. All of us.'

Art of War

129

'Heads up, guys.' The two other men sat waiting on their black, Ducati Desmosedici RR, one thousand CC super bikes, already aware of the oncoming car. The three of them sat in the darkness of the early morning's night air, which even for Florida in November was still quite humid. They sat in a column, waiting and watching in silence. The biker sitting last in the column watched the car as it approached the turn and came to a stop while it waited for the gates to open to allow it to proceed up the driveway to the house. The Mercedes-Benz S600 sat for a few seconds, and then smoothly transitioned into the driveway, its headlights never picking up the leather-clad bikers sitting ninety yards away along the dark road. As the headlights disappeared into the driveway the three superbikes' engines ignited into a low-pitched purr, barely audible in the still of the night, while the residents of Las Olas, Fort Lauderdale slept. They sat patiently while the rear biker watched the car coming into view on his cell phone's screen. The biker pressed the, 'send', button on his phone and watched to confirm that the electronic pulse bomb had done its work, disabling the car in the driveway. A second later, the rear biker spoke into the headset in his helmet, calmly saying, 'Let's go.'

The three motorbikes erupted into a chorus of whining as they ripped up the road. All three riders yanked back hard on their twist grip throttles to command the motorbikes to eat up the tarmac in the blink of an eye, red lining the bikes and running hot. They leaned across the huge gas tanks as they raced up the road with their lights turned off. The air was now thick with the motorbikes' roar. Within seconds they were riding low and hard, quickly turning into the driveway in a reverse triangle formation. The two lead bikes stopped at the gates, where each one leaned his bike against a gate to ensure it stayed open for their escape. The third biker at the rear continued up the driveway, smoking towards the disabled Mercedes. The driver turned to see the bike tearing up towards him while he stood by the car wondering why the electronics had failed.

As fast as the biker tore up the driveway, the driver was fighting to pull his weapon from its shoulder holster, realizing there was more to it than he had thought, all too late. The rider shot him from close range in a close grouping. Swinging the back-end of the bike around into a sliding skid, the rider quickly kicked down the bike stand and in one fluid movement stepped off it. He walked confidently across to the open driver's door. With his arms relaxed by his sides, he pulled the trigger and spat out a hot round from his silenced, nine millimeter Beretta as he stepped over the bodyguard lying on the ground, not bothering to look at him; the guard's body jerked from the bullet.

With the low purr from the bike's engine in the background, the only sound was from one more spit from his gun after he had leaned inside the driver's door, shooting into the darkened rear seats of the car. A low, high-pitched wail could be heard from inside the car, while the gunman coolly pressed the door latch and opened the rear passenger door. He stretched in over the rear seat and roughly pulled on the man until he fell out onto the hard tarmac, his own body weight doing all the work. The executive cried out in sheer terror and pain, as he tried to look up at the helmeted gunman. He began to crawl away from the car, while the gunman returned to the bike to take off his helmet. He calmly placed it on the bike's seat, paying no attention to the bleeding executive crawling away from him.

The gunman turned around and began walking briskly back towards the injured executive. He stowed the pistol inside his leather jacket and then crouched down over the crawling man, as if to study him, looking him over in detail, focusing on his matted gray hair. His whole body was shaking and mad with fear as he ranted, cried and whimpered for someone to save him. The biker knew the gate's surveillance cameras would not save him, because he had inserted a video-loop an hour earlier, along with the electronic pulse bomb. Anyone watching the security monitors would be watching the boring video of a dark and empty driveway.

He had all the time in the world, and he would use all of it on this man. The biker stood up and promptly kicked the crawling man with all the venom of a UFC fighter. He nearly lifted the old man into the air, which expelled all the air from his five foot five, slight build, forcing him over onto his back. Holding his stomach with both his hands in severe pain, he met the eyes of the biker, whom he realized now was here to kill him. His eyes told him that he knew his killer. The biker leaned down and roughly drove a knee into his chest, breaking the smirk of a smile once he knew the executive had recognized him. He said in delight, 'Hello John, how are you, mate?'

The executive tried his best to expel some words, but the terror of his impending death and the shock at who his assassin was had left him speechless. He was looking up at

Mark Knoxx.

'I'm just gonna work on you a bit first, okay?' Knoxx said sarcastically. He drove his leather-gloved fist into the sixty-four-year-old man's face, time and time again, in a fast and furious manner. His left fist hammered down into the dying man's face; within fifty seconds, it was a contusion of bone and flesh, draped in blood. Knoxx pulled the broken face up from the asphalt, closer up to his own blood-spattered face, searching it for any signs of life. A small groan came out from the face that wasn't recognizable now. He leaned in further, getting closer to the man's face, so the man could hear him better. He heard Knoxx - in a dark, quiet tone, with conviction in his voice - say ominously, 'I'm just gonna hit on you for a little while longer, John.'

He viciously rained down more huge punches into the already cracked and disfigured face of his victim, who no longer reacted or moved from the onslaught. Knoxx finally stood up to catch his breath and wiped his gloved hand across his blood-smeared face. He slowly reached inside his leather jacket and pulled out his gun. He stood over the body, placing his rider's boot on the man's chest and raised the gun. Aiming it at the man's head, he said, 'When you see that slag Tasker in hell, tell him this was for Emma.'

He cut loose three shots in rapid succession, tap, tap, tap, one bullet through each eye and one through the forehead - three dots; the mark of the Southsiders. Knoxx leaned down to the body and roughly went through its pockets, taking everything out and placing the contents inside his jacket pockets. He walked calmly back to the car and pulled out a briefcase from the backseat. He returned to the motorbike And secured the briefcase on the seat. He slowly placed his helmet back on, and then swept his eyes around the scene, giving his work one last look over. Sitting back on the bike and revving it hard, he kicked back the kickstand and then stood it up. He said, warmly into the headset in his helmet, 'Good job guys. Let's roll.'

He torqued the accelerator grip hard, causing the bike to wheel-spin as he swung the motorbike back around to face the gates. In his earpiece, he heard, 'Fucking maggots. Let's get to killing them all, boy.'

Meserve's words warmed him. He rode past Meserve and Matthews, who were now turning their bikes around to leave the driveway.

130

Having slept soundly for most of the day, he now rolled over to turn on the television on in the master bedroom. The news channels were covering the headline of the day. Soon, the Vice President of the United States was on television, giving a eulogy for the man who had died in the early hours of this morning. Knoxx sat up and shook his eyes out, rubbing his face to wake himself up as he began to take it all in. It was just as he had expected it would be. Vice President Tasker was a showman, standing behind the podium in the Rose Garden of the White House, extolling the virtues of his mentor and dear friend for over twenty-five years, John D'intino, the industrialist, international businessman and oil magnate, who had sat on the Foreign Intelligence Advisory Board. 'John D'intino died in his sleep early this morning in Fort Lauderdale, Florida,' the news ticker along the bottom of the television screen was reporting. Even though he had been his lifelong friend, and even though Tasker must, by now, know the truth about how his close friend had been murdered, he didn't flinch from his scripted speech. He knew it would be political suicide to reveal the truth, only three weeks away from becoming the forty-fifth president. The storm of publicity would have shed unwanted light into why he was murdered in such a way and what, if any, involvement the vice president might have had in his death.

Knoxx knew that Tasker knew, and he knew that Tasker would want to come for him now. But what he also knew was that the lie was so deep, he could bury Tasker in his own shit. The press had been all over the story all day and they would continue to dig into the background story on John D'intino. They would investigate his fundraising, business dealings and brokered oil deals throughout the Middle East. It wouldn't be too long before all the shady deals would come to light, eventually shining so bright that it would begin to blind one man. Stephen Tasker. The press had also asked if Tasker would be attending the funeral of his good friend. Seeing as it was so close to the presidential election, wouldn't it impede on his campaigning for the final votes? one reporter asked. Knowing the political mines, Tasker told the press that his loyalty to his friend and mentor was far more important to him than votes. This was also something Knoxx had planned for, knowing he could never get close to Tasker in Washington, but out in the open he stood a chance. He had a small chance, of killing him.

Having showered and eaten a light lunch, Knoxx chilled out on the patio to go through D'intino's personal effects.

He took his time to review the documents that were in the briefcase, and then after he'd read them, he laid back to begin a relaxed nap by the pool, without a care in the world. The Grove was filled with hired guns inside its walls. The Grove could only be approached by bridge, which had a guardhouse posted at the entrance or by the water. It had once been Juicy's fortress, protecting him from his enemies. Now it was Mark Knoxx's for the same reason, knowing that if Tasker or Deavins were stupid enough to come for him, then whoever they sent would suffer a high rate of casualties. Tasker and Knoxx were at a standoff, both waiting on the other guy's move. Knoxx was roused from a blissful nap by his SWIFT phone ringing. He rolled over on the sun lounger to answer it. He then lay back, once he heard her warm opening greeting. 'Hello darling, how are you?'

In her fresh and upbeat way, Jane managed to stay positive in her opening delivery, but her voice didn't take too long before it turned dark and serious. Mark righted himself to listen for a minute, while he worked out the angles, trying to decide which parts he believed and which parts were bullshit. Out of loyalty to her and her judgment, he agreed with her summary. Jane had told Mark in no uncertain terms, that she would be returning to The Grove tomorrow with Nicole. Knoxx ended the phone call, noting the phone's G.P.S. that Jane had called him from St. John's Medical Center, located in West L.A. He fell back on the sun lounger to soak up some more sun and to digest what Jane had told him. He closed his eyes, thinking, *it's not the words that are spoken, but which words are heard that's important.* And what Mark had heard in Jane's message was one word. Trouble. He drifted off back into his nap, thinking of all the possibilities, and then plotted some more while he worked on his tan. His mind drifted back to the task at hand. Tasker. Now that he had drawn first blood, Tasker would want revenge, but where would they strike?

131

Earlier that morning, when Knoxx had returned to The Grove, he had called Paul Deavins at MMI Enterprises, telling him what he had done. He went on to tell him that he had inputted their names into HEAVEN. If The Firm did try to kill him, then HEAVEN would be activated by him not logging-in at his pre-assigned time, and so whether he was alive or not, HEAVEN would kill them all, eventually. He had made it crystal clear to Deavins that he would prefer them to be dead sooner, rather than later. He had another thought while lying on the sun lounger. He got up to speak to one of his assistants, and while he was speaking to her, Alisha walked out from the house. Even though it was Monday, it felt like a Thursday, because she had legs for days as she sauntered across the patio in the hot afternoon sun. Knoxx watched her cat-like-strut as she walked up to him. She bent down over him to plant a sticky, lipstick kiss on his lips, with her eyes suggesting what her body wanted. They exchanged some pleasantries and Knoxx saw to it that she got what she asked for, in the way of refreshments. While she got settled in the chair, he turned his attention back to the assistant, telling her to tell Adrian Romney and Drew Yarward that he wanted them to fly to Los Angeles to pick up Jane and Nicole. Jealousy and envy being potent emotions, Alisha didn't take the bait on what she had just heard. Keeping her feelings hidden, she brightly asked the simple question, 'Are Jane and Nicky coming back?'

'Yeah, they'll be here tomorrow morning,' Mark answered, keeping his thoughts close to his chest.

Alisha managed a happy tune, but inside, she knew that she would be relegated to the third spot again, behind Jane, who she could do nothing about, but Nicole, who knows? Maybe she could. Jealousy and envy are a killer combination; wars have been fought over them and thousands of men have gone to prison for them.

Mark turned his attention back to Alisha and the folder she had carried in with her. They sat in the afternoon sun, arranging the final bank wire to General Dragon. Knoxx had been wiring seventeen million dollars, every thirteen weeks for the past fifteen months to him. The general was receiving eighty-five million dollars for the gold that Knoxx had smelted and arranged to have dispersed with the gold he'd stolen from the Papua New Guinea gold mines. The gold was now safely placed in the vaults of a friendly, and now, very wealthy, banker in Belgrade. He called Dragon to confirm the bank wire details. The general was effusive in his description about his phone conversations with the one and only, real Pamela Anderson. She had called Dragon, just as Mark had asked her to, paying her a reasonable fee for doing so. Dragon repeated his promise that should Mark ever need anything from him, he should call him anytime. Mark had made out like a bandit on the deal too; forty-two million from the sale of a property in London, and a further sixty-eight million from the gold that had been stolen from the Papua New Guinea gold mines. He ended his call on an upbeat note, jokingly saying, 'It's all one long party when you're young and rich. You're funny, smart and handsome too, but who's got your back when it's all done? Yeah, that's right Dragon, me, that's who. I'll catch up with you soon. Have yourself one beautiful day. Love life and live it large.'

132

'Come on, let's get you back to the hotel,' Jane said with some concern, while she helped Nicky to walk; now taking her up in her arms.

'Thanks, Dave,' Jane said, as her part-time lover in L.A., Dave Kenshaw, stepped in to help. She still seemed a little sore and walked slightly bent over from the stomach cramps, as she gingerly walked out from St. John's Health Center at the corner of Twenty-Second Street and Santa Monica Boulevard in West Los Angeles.

Two nights before, Jane had stepped into the NVS office with a look of murder on her face, when she had first laid eyes on the scene. Nicole wasn't moving on the couch and had no signs of life in her eyes, while Bezerk looked like a madman possessed. He had moved away from Nicole when they had all entered the office, laughing when Jane had exclaimed that everyone in the room was dead. Bezerk had jokingly said that he was only playing and that he'd had second thoughts about going through with it. He just wanted to scare her. He wanted to get back at Mark by telling him that he could've fucked her if he'd wanted to.

Jane had been quick to move. She was short on discussion and long on taking action. As soon as Beaver, Tavo and Coco had escorted Bezerk away from Nicole's immediate vicinity, she had splashed water on her face and then repeatedly slapped her hard across her face, while she shouted for Nicole to wake up. As soon as there was a look of fear and loathing in Nicky's eyes, Jane stood her up and got her to walk over to the office's bar to bend her over the sink, promptly sticking her fingers down her throat. Nicole threw up repeatedly until her throat was bone dry. Jane gave the order that she and Nicole were leaving. She called Dave Kenshaw, who arrived to help, entering the office and giving Bezerk a nod. Jane never did notice that familiar nod. She was too caught up in the emotional moment of saving Nicole's life. She knew it would have killed Mark to lose her in such a vile way. Jane had shouted at everyone standing about the room, 'Anyone ever talks about this again, I'll see to it that you die in the worst fucking way, and so will your family! Got it?'

Everyone stood around not knowing what to do. Bezerk couldn't help himself, laughing as he said, 'Yeah boy, I was this close to gettin' me some prime princess tail. You know what I mean?'

Just as the last, sick, sarcastic word fell from his mouth; Jane dropkicked her left foot into his nuts. All the guys cringed as Bezerk crumpled up on the floor, holding his balls in his hands. Jane had taken the precaution of booking Nicole into the hospital in West L.A. Even though the Cedars Sinai Medical Center was nearer, she could not take Nicole there and run the risk of bumping into Dobro.

Jane had spent the night with Dave Kenshaw, not telling him too much, but just enough for him to understand the overall scheme of things. Just enough for him to understand his place in all of this. He had worked his way into Jane's bed when she had visited L.A. and now he was in her heart. Jane never realized that things, which can seem so insignificant or innocuous, could really be the most important of things to watch for. Over the past two years they had been seeing each other; Kenshaw had become accustomed to the pattern of Jane's life, and in turn, the details of Mark's operation. Nothing it seemed, was ever as it seemed. Jane had called Mark to tell him that she and Nicole were headed back to Miami. Even though she had some more work to do in Los Angeles, she had to deliver Nicole back to him safe and sound.

When she'd called Mark, knowing he was on a secure phone, she would not allow herself to be drawn into explaining the details of it all. She said that she wanted to see him face-to-face, and said that she needed to know she'd returned Nicky to him in one piece. He knew it was bad from the way Jane sounded on the phone. *Shit*, he thought. He had needed things to go well in L.A. with Dobro. Maybe he'd overplayed his hand with her. Maybe she had told her friends at the F.B.I. and had given them the package. Jane needed the plane ride back to straighten out her story with Nicky, getting her to understand that they couldn't tell Mark what had happened. Not right now.

Mark knew Jane well too, having been her best friend all her life. He knew her better than she knew herself, sometimes. She always thought she was the one looking out for him, but really, it was Mark who looked out for Jane.

As Mark had hung up the phone with Jane that afternoon on the patio, one thing he knew for sure was that she wasn't being straight with him. Whatever the reason he didn't care right now, but he had learned enough to believe half of what you hear and half of what you see. He knew Jane was always the one trying to protect him, either from others or from himself. She would have to tell him what happened in L.A. when she got back. Whatever it was, Knoxx would have his own crack squad of former military specialists, Drew Yarward and Adrian Romney, in position to take action upon his orders if they were needed. The Exile jet left Miami with the two mercenaries on board, to drop off in L.A., returning to Miami with the girls.

Focusing on the priorities, Mark got himself back on track, taking care of business, working through the day into the early evening with Alisha. She knew when to be the loyal worker and when to be the friend with benefits. She still loved Mark in her own way, and in his own way, Mark loved her. She had always pushed to become the surrogate Jane to Mark, but it had never happened. Many had tried, but they had all failed. There was only ever one girl, constantly in Mark's life. Jane.

They ate dinner and talked about various topics, before Mark asked her to watch the news with him. They snuggled down, toe-to-toe, end-to-end, on the couch to watch the television. Alisha knew her time in the sun had passed, as tomorrow, Jane and Nicole would be back at the mansion, and she'd be on the outside, looking in.

Mark watched Tasker being interviewed on the Queen B Show. It was a last-minute taping that the vice president had agreed to do, before the untimely death of Florida senator, Emma Spitzer. Tasker had wanted to go head-to-head with her on the issues of the Iraq and Afghanistan wars and to address the rumors that U.S. companies were getting rich from them. Only now, of course, that wouldn't be possible. Belinda Vittali, the tall, hot, blonde kept the action going in her own unique style, never one to shy away from the bright light herself. It was as if Senator Spitzer was communicating to Belinda from the grave, due to her taking every opportunity to bring Tasker down a peg or two. He used the show to raise awareness about what he had already achieved, seventeen days before his expected presidential inauguration. He announced the signing of a joint-venture partnership with Mexico to build a natural gas pipeline and a commercial container port, thus securing the delivery of gas and goods to the West Coast of America.

'The reason I'm so successful, Belinda is one word. Focus. I am an operator and I intend to operate this country as if it were a business. And I'm in the business of making this country great again.'

Knoxx had to laugh at his statement, knowing Roberto Madrid would be the one in control of all that, not Tasker, and not America. Sure, they'd get to spend their money building it, but Madrid would be the one who'd collect millions from importing drugs and collection protection racket pay-offs from the shipping and oil companies.

133

'What we got?' Dan McGann asked. He stepped under the crime scene tape. The crime scene was lit up by the mobile night-lights belonging to the Crime Scene Investigation unit. McGann and Keets had responded to the call as it looked like it was the Modus Operandi of their guy the serial killer. And it sounded like their guy had struck again.

The officer on scene gave them a quick rundown on what the first officers had come across. They had secured the immediate area around the dirt track road leading up to the Sunset Ranch above Hollywood Boulevard. The officer informed them by saying, 'We got a single female: Hispanic-white mix. I.D. in her purse has her listed as five foot six, two months short of her twentieth birthday. Looks like she gave the perp' one hell of a fight in there.' He looked up towards the car while he continued, 'She's on her way to Cedars now. Word is, she's in critical condition. Doubt she'll make it through the night.' He said it as he lowered his head slightly.

Not fazed by this show of emotion, Dan moved right along, asking, 'Is she listed as a hooker in the database?'

'No, she came up clean. She's a dancer at The Bodyshop on Sunset,' the officer replied.

Dan and Richie gave each other a little look, as it became apparent to them that they might recognize the girl. Having obtained most of the relevant facts from the police officer, they turned their attention to the area nearer the car sitting on the dirt track. Taking in the scene, the car was facing down the hill, with both of the front doors open and its headlights on. Richie reacted to what he'd noticed. 'Shiitt, how long have they been here?'

The officer turned to see what he was referring to. He kind of smiled, replying, 'Who, them? Oh, only about ten minutes. They're acting like this is their crime scene already. You two have fun now. See you later at Barney's?'

'Yeah, okay. Thanks, Ali, see you there.'

Dan and Richie left Alistair Elwins behind and walked up the hill towards the car. They immediately met the irritating sound of Detective's Ray Tombs and David Blisset shouting at them in a disparaging manner.

'The ranch'll be open in about another five hours, dudes!' Ray Tombs said sarcastically, releasing the first salvo.

Blisset, opening up his flow, interjected, 'Maybe you guys were coming up here for some alone time, and didn't know we were here.'

The two of them laughed. It was a long, mocking laugh

that had been going on for far too long in Dan's mind. Blisset followed up quickly by joking, 'The way you two look, you look like a couple of midnight cowboys.'

They both laughed while Dan took his final step up to Blisset. Without any warning, he sweep-kicked his legs out from under him, knocking him to the ground, he fell to the floor hard, knocking all the sarcastic and snappy comments out of him. Dan then stepped over to Tombs. Getting up in his face, he grunted, 'Do you really wanna go there? I mean, really?'

Ray stood toe-to-toe with Dan, bearing down on him, while the other officers stood around, not knowing what to do. Blisset got up and dusted himself off as he unleashed a crescendo of abuse. A couple of cops held him back while he shouted a number of profanities at Dan. Dan and Richie laughed and then began to walk across to the victim's car. Tombs shouted at their backs, 'This is the Westside Pimps' show now? What a fucking circus, man!'

Richie stopped and turned back to them, yelling hard, 'Listen man, if you know what's good for you, you and your girlfriend better get on with doing your job, or go back down the hill and stick to chasing purse snatchers, before I whip your ass and turn you out as my trick on The Strip!'

Not reacting to the ranting behind him, Dan looked menacingly at one of the C.S.I. officers and then at a police officer, telling everyone in the immediate vicinity, 'Let's get to work! We got a live one, and if we can put together enough of a detailed I.D. on this animal, she might be able to finger him for us. Get me something to work with. She's in the hospital fighting for her life and we're fighting amongst ourselves. So you two, shut the fuck up. And the rest of you get me something I can use, so I can nail this son of a bitch. I promise you, whoever's doing these girls, if I get the chance, I'll drill his ass!'

The crime scene became a hive of activity. The police officers got focused back on the job at hand, which was catching the bad guys. That's what McGann and Keets were known for doing, bringing them down any way they can, dead or alive.

They both worked at a feverish pace, but it was slow in coming together: the chain of events, how the pieces of the puzzle fit together like links in a chain. As in all investigations, it was only as strong as the weakest link. The details were what make or break any cases, and this case had been full of details from day one, always the same type and age of girl, they were all, tall, young, pretty with Latino features, and long, red hair.

Dan and Richie worked through the night up at Sunset Ranch, until the early morning's sun began to light up

Hollywood. The hustle and bustle from the morning commuters began to take up the quiet of the new day. Dan felt they had gathered enough information; for now, they would have to hope that the girl would pull through in Cedars. Dan planned to catch some breakfast with Richie, and then stop off at his girl Amanda's pad to catch a shower. Then he would cruise over to Cedars to see if they could interview the victim. Dan and Richie made their way back to the station and said their goodbyes. They arranged to meet up in two hours at Edies Diner, before going down to Cedars from there.

He gave some thought to Richie while they were standing in the parking lot. He caught him before he walked off to his car, which seemed more like skulking off with heavy boots to Dan. Maybe he had problems at home, because he did not seem to want to go home. Dan asked him in a light way, 'C'mon Pikey, what's up? You've been acting weird these past few weeks. Who knows you better than me? And if something's up, you might as well let me in on it. No matter what it is, bud, I got your back, you know that. So come on, give it up. What's up?'

'Nothing's up, I'm fine. I'm just handling some shit, that's all, family shit, nothing for you to worry about,' Richie replied, filling his chest with air. He stood in a way that led Dan to believe that, whatever it was and however close they were, Richie did not want to give it up, not yet anyway. Dan could tell there was more to come, but for now, he'd ride hard with his best friend. He would push harder in a few days though if Richie hadn't either snapped out of it or had told him.

Dan also had some things on his mind too. He needed to have a talk with his chick, Amanda, having become concerned for her safety. She was in a dangerous profession as it was, but now it was made even more dangerous by having this serial killer running loose on the streets of L.A. Dan had hooked Amanda up, working the morning shift at Edie's Diner on Sunset Boulevard, in the hope that she would transition out of the nightlife scene into a regular day-to-day routine. Dan had noticed that the allure of the big money on The Strip as an exotic dancer was too much of a pull for her, or Pasha, as she was known in Fantasy Palace. Dan felt that he needed to have a talk with Amanda about it. And the day was only just getting started. But as he drove to her apartment, he found himself resigned to thinking he'd talk to her about it another day.

134

Maxine had no time to waste. Time was precious and she would never get it back. If she didn't do as she was being told, she'd never get her baby back. She had only looked at the outline of the slight, waif-looking woman through a haze of confused tears, listening to her explain, as if she might cry herself, that if she did as she was told, Dolly would be released from her coma. 'Dolly's being watched over by Heaven now,' the woman had told Maxine.

The woman had explained that she had control over the outcome of her daughter's condition. If she did as she was told, it would all be over soon enough. In a brightening English accent, the woman tried to lift Maxine's spirits by saying that Dolly wasn't the primary target. 'You'll see in this package what's really going on, and all you need to do is help. By helping us, you'll be helping yourself. If you do as you're told, then no harm will come to her. I'll see to that, I promise. Just do everything without question, and you'll get your girl and your life back. It's all in here. Don't show the information to anyone and don't tell anyone about it. You'll receive further instructions soon.'

The woman had placed a padded manila envelope on Maxine's coffee table. All Maxine could do was sit and watch in a haze of tears as the woman, her lifeline, began to bounce away with her hair swinging in a ponytail. She bobbed along, merging in with the traffic of people going about their morning's business, coming and going in the foyer of Cedars Sinai Medical Center. Was she being watched herself? Would the way she reacted decide whether her daughter lived or died? Maxine was numb. Numb from the pain of what her daughter was going through upstairs, and numb from the fear of what she herself was going to have to go through to ensure that her daughter lived. Maxine had watched the woman leave, becoming enveloped in a heat-haze, while she walked outside into the bright morning sun of West Hollywood, never to be seen again.

Maxine needed to gather herself. She couldn't allow herself to fall apart, because Dolly needed her now, more than ever. Maxine knew she would have to follow the rules of the game in order to win, and by the sound of things, this game had an end in sight. Maxine would be getting back the one thing that was truly important in her life - her young, beautiful daughter. Dabbing her eyes, she began to compose herself, getting it all straight in her head. She had to assume that she was under surveillance, by whom and why, at this point, she didn't know or care to know. She picked up the envelope and firmly gripped it with all the hate she could muster, ripping back the fold and pulling out its contents. In an instant, she knew who had sent it and what it contained. She couldn't believe what was happening and she couldn't believe the reasoning behind it. Everything she read told her that she had been right all along. She held all the evidence she ever needed in her hands. She held her hand up to her mouth to stifle a yelp of disbelief, and fear, as she settled in to read the cover letter.

Reading the second paragraph, she quickly looked up, feeling that eyes were upon her, watching her. She then recovered her wits and read the cover letter again in detail. Reading it again, one thing was clear: these were serious people and she was now playing a serious game of life and death. She knew the people named in the package. Some she knew well, too well. She had one task to do and the letter said it was to be completed today. Maxine was now in play. She had a list of things to do and each task was to be completed to the letter. If she did not comply, Dolly would die. Only a few hours earlier, Maxine had prayed to God himself that if she were given a second chance, she would do things differently. Now, she had her chance. From this day on, things would be a whole lot different. Her life, and Dolly's life, were now not their own, realizing that Mark Knoxx owned them. And just when Maxine thought things couldn't get any worse, they did. Her phone rang. She answered it, trying to push back the fear in her voice. A bright, happy, if somewhat tired voice greeted her. 'Hi Maxine, you didn't forget me, did you? I'm here, waiting for you at LAX.'

Teresa Hadley had landed at Los Angeles International airport to begin the investigation into linking Mark Knoxx to any drug trafficking crimes.

'Oh my God! I totally forgot. I'll be there as soon as I can,' Maxine answered, trying her best to react just as brightly. Maybe they were watching. Maybe they had the capability to listen in on her phone conversations. She had been instructed not to tell anyone, and she had to do exactly as instructed. She began to collect herself. She shuffled up the papers, forcing them back into the envelope. She folded it over tightly into thirds, stuffing the envelope in her purse while she chatted to Teresa, apologizing profusely. She panicked at the thought of having Teresa in her company, to start the investigation on Knoxx. If he found out, maybe he would make good on his promise to punish Dolly severely. As per her instructions in the package, Maxine had one thing to do today, and she needed to do it now. She offered up a lame excuse, saying she would be there as soon as possible. She suggested that Teresa make her way to The Hilton Hotel on Century Boulevard, just outside of LAX Airport and wait for her there. Maxine carried on a conversation with Teresa while she walked through the hospital, doing her best to keep her voice calm and steady.

Teresa, however, had already noticed something in her voice. She asked, 'Is everything okay, Max?'

Maxine froze. Sheer terror taking over, she realized she couldn't give an inch of ground. They were everywhere, watching. She managed a curt reply. 'I'm fine. I'm pissed about running late. I'll be there as soon I can hun.'

She promptly disconnected the call. Maxine subtly glanced around while she marched across the rooftop parking garage towards her car, picking up her pace to reach the safety of it. Sitting in the driver's seat, she checked her face in the rearview mirror, and then went about putting her game face on. In the heat of the morning sun, Maxine felt cold, as she again picked up her phone from her purse. At the sight of the envelope in it, a cold rush of dread raced through her veins. She steeled herself to complete her task for the day. Maxine dialed the number and began to take part in the play that was being orchestrated by others. Feeling sick inside, she talked her way through the layers of departments. It went against every principle she lived by, to uphold the law. As each sentence came out of her mouth, she wanted to throw up in disgust at how she was being manipulated. She had begun her lie. The web of lies that would have to follow could never be undone now. Maxine started her car to make her way to the F.B.I.'s L.A. headquarters at 11000 Wilshire Boulevard, where she needed access to their computers.

135

The temperature was blistering hot when the girls arrived back at The Grove. Yet the atmosphere surrounding the mansion was decidedly chilly, and the reception they received from Mark was even colder. Nicole was amazed to see so many men at the house. To her, it looked more like a fraternity house than a home, only these boys didn't look like they were in a party mood. Nicole realized that Mark had surrounded himself with men who were armed to the teeth. This only added to the tension she already felt, in addition to what she had gone through over the past three days since Bezerk had tried to rape her. But at least she was home, or what was left of it. In a moment of panic at coming face-to-face with Mark again, she decided to go straight upstairs, picking out one of the guest rooms for herself.

Jane walked through the house and out onto the patio to greet Mark, who was busy speaking on the phone. He made her wait. He looked her over, not in as warm a manner as she might have expected, after having flown across America to be by his side. Being the dutiful and beautiful best friend that she was, Jane patiently waited, pulling faces as she did. Mark studied her, thinking about how he was going to begin his line of questioning when he finished his phone call with his banker in Monte Carlo.

Once he'd hung up the phone, his first question to Jane was about Nicole. Jane explained that she had to deliver the news herself and wanted to get a better understanding of what exactly it was that mark needed her to do back in L.A. She told him that she didn't feel comfortable leaving Nicky alone, as per his instructions. Jane went on to tell Mark that Nicole had been having a terrible time in L.A. and that she feared for her safety, thinking she might have even been thinking about harming herself. This was the cover story that Jane had talked Nicole into agreeing with, to buy her some time to recover from her ordeal with Bezerk. Jane had managed to talk Nicole into not telling Mark the truth yet. Jane had fought Nicole all the way across America, while Nicole had tried her best to pry out of her what was really happening with Mark. Eventually, what Jane had explained, had made sense to Nicky. In her current state of mind and the fragile state of her body, she realized that she needed to return home and try and patch things up with Mark.

Jane would take Mark's initial wrath alone. She knew he would want to know every detail of what had happened back in Los Angeles with Dobro, Bezerk, and with Nicky. Mark had reiterated to Jane that this was the wrong time for them to be anywhere near him, let alone staying at The Grove. Jane didn't waiver in her commitment to Nicole, never giving Mark any other version than what they had agreed on. For both their sakes. Jane knew that, for all of his mean spirited stances, Mark had a good heart. She couldn't stand for him to be torn between what he had going on right now and knowing what had really gone down in Los Angeles with Bezerk. He would have been forced to retaliate in some way, that could start a new war on the West Coast against the Southsiders. Jane had decided that she needed to protect him from that.

Mark transitioned from one subject matter to the next. Jane felt slightly more relieved when he began talking about his plans for the future, which meant they were getting further away from the lie. Finally, they got to the one subject that mattered most, at least to Jane. While they were talking about it, Jane saw Alisha meander out from somewhere inside the house, looking like the cat that had stolen the milk. She walked over to Jane and gave her a peck on the cheek, accompanied by a hug. Jane smiled through gritted teeth while they greeted each other with Alisha knowing that Jane was irritated, but she carried on with her happy greeting anyway. She then walked over and stood, closer than Jane would have liked, next to Mark, asking him where Nicole was. Jane answered for him, saying that Nicole was tired and had gone up to bed. Alisha pretended not to hear Jane, as she looked deep into Mark's eyes. She told him that she would be with Nicole in her bedroom. If he needed her for anything - she accentuated the word 'anything' - then he should let her know. Jane narrowed her eyes and targeted Alisha with every long-legged step away from them.

Jane wanted to launch into Mark with her own interrogation, but he quickly moved back to the details of what had happened with Dobro. After twenty minutes of discussing Maxine, they talked about what he wanted Jane to do back in Los Angeles tomorrow night.

Mark told her that Adrian Romney and Drew Yarward were already there, setting things up for her. He then asked about Nicole again. Only this time, the questions were coming at Jane in rapid fire succession. Jane was under fire. When Mark finally finished with her, she felt like some of the shots had hit their target, and the seeds of doubt had been planted in him. She felt her story had changed somewhat since the first time.

The warm evening had drawn in and Mark had been on his own out on the patio for some time now, thinking about his life. Smoking a cigar and swigging on a bottle of Corona, he knew he couldn't put it off any longer. It had been around five hours since they had arrived home, and he hadn't been up to see her yet. *Nicky's home*, he thought. This is her home and he had no right to force her out of it, or his life. He knew she was his life.

He readied himself to begin the long walk up to her bedroom. Alisha had gone home and Jane was in her bedroom asleep. It was all quiet at The Grove. As Mark walked through the house, he passed through the living room, which had CNN on the television, watching for him. Tasker was right where he was supposed to be, looking presidential as he spoke on camera. Knoxx always knew where Tasker was and where he was going to be, because he was on the campaign trail. Mark knew that he could, if absolutely required, disappear. Tasker could never do that. Mark felt warmed by the fact that he could always find him. And if all went as planned, he would soon be living in a really big, White House, on Pennsylvania Avenue, being driven around in a cavalcade of black limousines.

Mark stood in front of the television and watched with a smile, because none of it mattered. All the grandstanding and speeches were for nothing, because they would both be dead soon enough. But tonight, there was only one thing that mattered, more than anything else, and she was probably a bundle of nerves, having waited all day to see him. He just wanted to hold her hand and say 'hi', and that would be enough to make his day. He politely knocked on the bedroom door. After hearing a small 'Hello?', Mark opened the door and laid eyes on Nicky for the first time in two weeks. It was the longest time they had been apart in nearly two years. Nicole wiped a tear upon seeing him; she seemed scared to death. She curled up her knees under the duvet and began to dab at her eyes, while Mark walked in lightly and sat at the end of the bed. They talked for over an hour, neither one venturing to say the words that they each desperately needed to hear themselves say to one another. Finally, Mark said, 'I love you, honey.'

As those words fell from Mark's lips, Nicole fell into a world of despair and doubt, for her heart already knew what her head was telling her. She had become frightened of him.

136

'Who's that you're talking to?'

It had become all too familiar. Each day he was questioning Nicky, and each day it had become more aggressive in its tone; all it was doing was pushing her further away from him. Nicole had been crying on and off for the better part of a week now, and it had become too much for Mark to understand anymore. No one inside his camp was talking. In spite of everything else that he had going on, this was the one thing that consumed him. The sale of the property in London was now under contract and the final gold bullion run was underway, being smuggled out of Serbia. The Envious Group was posting record profits, both on and off the books. HEAVEN was now approximately two weeks away from being taken public on the New York Stock Exchange, which was anticipated to be one of the largest Initial Public Offerings of the past decade. Exile Corporation was gearing up to raise eighty billion dollars for it.

Both HEAVEN and Knoxx were everywhere, on the covers of business magazines and on news reporters' lips. It seemed to the whole of America that the race for the White House was embroiled in a competition for airtime too. As one segment ended on Vice President Tasker, another one started on HEAVEN, Exile Corporation, and Mark Knoxx. The two of them seemed to be locked in a battle over television ratings.

Mark had heavy hands, and now, he carried a heavy heart. His workload was bearing down on him, and when he looked to Nicole for some support and good loving, she just weighed him down further. He couldn't touch her without her cowering, or worse, nervously breaking down in tears. There were always tears. They were talking, but just not saying what needed to be said.

'I feel like I'm walking on broken glass and I'm getting cut to ribbons. I'm living in an empty room in an empty house, with a man with an empty heart,' Nicky had said, wiping a tear away the night before.

Mark was still seating himself at the foot of her bed each night before going to his own bed. This was their ritual now. It had become the norm. Mark had replied in a low, reflective tone, 'I don't know if I've ever really been loved. I have nothing left to fear hun. I'm not a perfect person, and there're many things I wish I hadn't done. Things I never want you to know about me. I just wish I could catch your tears, baby. I'm sorry that I hurt you. I never meant to.'

Nicky sniffed out a tear and managed to reply, 'Nothing

makes any sense anymore, and I can't accept that we're going nowhere, Mark. All of this, us, we can't be wrong. I feel like you just take me for granted and that you've got used to pushing me around. I always feel like there's a whole other side to you, another you, that you'll never let me see, never let me know. And if that's how it's going to be, then how can I love you, when I don't even know you?'

All Mark could do was accept that she was right. He could never explain himself to her, because she was the light and he was the dark. She was beauty and he was the beast. She was a simple girl who wanted to live a simple life, but his life was anything but simple, living multiple existences. All of his different lives were coming to an end soon, he thought. He told her, 'Sometimes, I've wondered how I've made it, how I've survived life, how I've made it through life. But then, I'd look at you and I'd know that I could do anything. When you smile, your smile's like a ray of sunshine, shining through a cloudy day, baby.' Leaning forward and resting his arms on his knees, he thought for a moment, while the two of them sat in silence. He then continued, saying softly, 'You say you love me hun, but you don't know who I am. I'm torn between where I've been and where I stand now. I just feel like I'm standing on my own, alone, and I'm okay with that. I think I need to be alone. That's why it's probably better if you let me go.'

Knoxx deftly rose from the bed, giving her a warm look; he then quietly walked out of the bedroom to make his way down to the patio, to think some more about what he had planned, and to drink. Two hours later, he was livid. The sky was black, with flashes of electric white lightning off in the distance over the Atlantic. But in the immediate vicinity, in Mark's dark heart, the hard thunder inside tore through him like a hurricane as he became delirious and utterly mad at himself and at the world. And at Nicole. No one understood him. No one would understand. He also understood that he couldn't even begin to try to make anyone understand who he was, because he didn't even understand himself. And that made him sick to his stomach, and angry. As he gulped down the last of his Jack Daniels, his thoughts became twisted. In his mind, he thought of her. How she had failed to understand him. Everything he was facing, he faced alone.

He rose from his chair and looked upstairs. That was what he wanted. The difference between wanting and needing is that one comes from a desire and the other comes from a basic requirement. Knoxx picked up his pace, forcing himself up the stairs, moved by desire. The drunken state, the passion and the madness in him filled him up, forming a hurricane that swept right into the guest bedroom where Nicole was fast asleep. Rushing through the door and striding heavily in towards her, she immediately awoke and bolted upright in bed. Coming up beside her, he pushed her back down onto the bed, holding her by her shoulders. She kicked at him, yelling for him to get off her, screaming for help, but no one would be coming to help her. She caught the look in Mark's eyes, the deepest blackness she had ever seen. The light from the landing backlit him as if it were the moon and he was a werewolf, growling and howling in sick delight, having caught his prey unawares. Nicole could only think of one thing. Bezerk.

'Baby, please stop. Mark, don't! Let go of me! Get the fuck off me!'

She shouted as loud as she could, but still he pushed and pulled at her, and then began to rip and tear at her shirt like a man possessed in the pale moonlight. Mark and Bezerk, one and the same after all.

'Shut the fuck up! I want you baby, c'mon. I fucking need you Nicky. Give it to me!' Mark commanded, his voice becoming more aggressive.

He didn't care that he loved her or that he was hurting her. He had her head firmly in his grip now, as he pushed her head into the pillows. Nicole feared for her life. Her eyes were wide, and Knoxx now had her legs just as wide.

'Bitch! You're all the same. Don't move. Don't think about fighting me,' he growled in a menacing tone. He gazed at her for only a second. One second that was the last time he would ever love her. He dipped down and licked her face to taunt her, nuzzling over her face to force his tongue into her mouth, his hand moving onto her throat. This was really happening. She had barely survived one madman, only to find another one living with her. He pushed Nicky's head deeper into the pillows, grabbing her by her long, blonde hair, turning her over onto her front. He immediately forced himself inside her from behind and began finger-vibing her underneath. With each stroke, he thrust harder in her. After a while, it began to sound as if they were whimpering in delight and shared ecstasy. Finally, with some softer strokes, softer words came from Mark. He spoke lustfully in her left ear with some warmth, with Nicky replying softly, answering the same.

'Love you, baby.'

'Love you too.'

137

'There will be a time when wars are fought, when we can't or won't send our troops. I feel that we, as a nation, cannot afford to be the world's police anymore, based on the economics, and in the collateral damage to our young service men and women, for causes they don't even understand.'

'So, you're saying there's a firm timeline for a phased withdrawal of our troops in Iraq and Afghanistan?'

The one-on-one television interview with Larraine Scott, on Hardline Report, had been going for some time. Knoxx was gripped by its content because he knew it was all bullshit. Knoxx sipped on a beer, as he'd been doing for most of the day. In his own world, far removed from anyone and even further, it seemed, from Nicole. Once again, he could only smirk in quiet contentment while he watched the television, watching his prey. Knoxx was consumed with checking every sound bite and every movement, every day. This was the only thing that was important to him. The countdown clock to doomsday was becoming louder and louder in his head, causing him to feel like he was going mad.

Tasker smiled at the question. Derisive in his tone, he answered, 'No, I'm not saying we should abandon these people, but I am saying that, once I become our next president - .' He paused, with a glint in his eye, the interviewer going along with him, smiling. He continued, 'I will look seriously at alternative energy resources, even if that means entering into discussions with other countries - and who knows, even with former enemies of ours – in order to secure a brighter future. The security of this nation comes first, and if that means a phased withdrawal, then so be it. The Iraqis and Afghans will have to learn to live with each other. We cannot become an occupying force indefinitely. Words can only get you so far, but action is what really makes the difference.'

Feeling that the subject was now closed, Larraine Scott moved on to the next segment, the rapidly approaching election date, asking Tasker what was happening next in his campaign. He replied, 'Well, Larraine, I'll be heading down to Florida for my dear friend, John D'intino's funeral. He was a great man, a great teacher, and a great husband and father. I will miss him and so will this country. Then, from there, I'll be heading across to California, where I have strong support for my ticket and for my party. And I can assure you, California is always one, long party.'

'Thank you, Mr. Vice President for this interview. Only eight days to go, and then, I may be changing that title, I think,' Larraine Scott remarked, signing off her interview with Tasker in good spirits.

Knoxx sauntered out from the living room, having laughed at the program. Everyone on the patio seemed to curve away from him as he walked out.

'Fuck him,' Knoxx muttered to himself, as he put his beer bottle down on a patio table. Across the pool, he spied Nicole wearing oversized, black sunglasses, but he could feel her looking at him and he sensed that she'd been crying, again. *Fuck her*, was all he thought while he walked around the pool in a stalking fashion. *My fucking house, my fucking rules. No more fucking crying*, he shouted inside his head, while he bored his eyes into her. *I'm King-fucking-Kong*, sang in his head while he walked around the pool in his board shorts. His body was lean and taught, with tight, pumped muscles. His prison tattoos gave him a hardened edge, letting the world know what he really was. A Thug. He mad-dogged Nicky. It was the first time he had laid eyes on her since last night, and what he noticed made him mad and angry. Again.

'Who's that you're on the phone with?' Mark shouted as he approached, not caring that Nicky was talking on the phone. She sat on the sun lounger with her knees up, a pen in one hand and the phone in the other, resting a notepad on her knees.

Nicole lowered the phone slightly from her mouth to answer, 'I'm on the phone!'

She went back to talking on the phone, trying to ignore him. Knoxx picked up his pace and walked around behind her, trying to intimidate her. He looked down over her head. As he did, it felt like two bullets had been shot right through his eyes. It was beauty that had killed the beast. Knoxx faltered a step, but then walked away from her. His heart hit his chest firmly, certain about what he had seen.

Mark had recognized the doodle that Nicole had been drawing on the notepad. He would recognize it anywhere, because it had been the one that Bezerk had drawn when they were cellmates, all those years ago. Knoxx remembered instantly; Bezerk had said he'd look at it when he fucked the Hollywood chicks, joking that it wouldn't be any work for him, nailing them. Knoxx realized this had been the lie. Nicole had come back home all right, but only after she had got one over on him by fucking Bezerk, and Jane knew. He knew there was something they had been hiding, a secret they had from L.A. Bezerk had fucked his girl. Or had she fucked him? His mind told him he was right, *Fucking bitch! Fucking Bezerk!* shouting in his head. Knoxx was turning himself inside out with his twisted thoughts, not believing that Nicky could have been invited up to the office for drinks with Jane, thinking, why wouldn't have Jane told him about it. There was more to it, and now he had found out what it was. They had all been conspiring against him.

Mark felt he needed to cleanse himself, and so he dove straight into the pool and began to swim under the water. He let out a long, air-filled bubbled shout of death. Staying under for as long as possible, he then surfaced to do some long, deep, strong strokes to the other end of the pool. Wishing he could keep swimming away forever, one stroke after the other became more aggressive and more assertive. He touched the far end, and with that touch, he was back.

Mark lifted himself up out of the pool with all the grace of an Olympic swimmer, and then wiped his face down. He set his jaw and then set his mind to the next task at hand. His mind became as clear as the pool's water. All his sins were cleansed, for others had sinned too. Others had lied to him. Everything was a lie. Everybody lies, he realized. He knew what he had seen. The face of a man with the shades on, Knoxx knew, was a Southsider, with the sun rising up over razor wire. It was all there and it was definitely Bezerk's drawing; it was one of a kind. Mark was never one to react right away. As smooth as the concrete paving, he padded his way over to Nicole. As he did, he noticed she moved the writing pad away from his view. He calmly and coolly asked, 'Sorry, baby, everything okay?'

She gave him a short nod as her reply. As if she was filled with fear. He bent down to give her a kiss. His first with real hate, and her last with real love.

Mark abruptly and menacingly said, 'I need the phone.'

He picked it up without waiting for any approval. He nonchalantly swaggered away from Nicky, dripping in his board shorts, with his back showing his tattoo: Only God Can Judge Me, with an avenging angel in chains below it. He pressed redial on the phone while he crossed the threshold to the downstairs office. After two rings, a voice he knew well answered. He summarily asked who it was on the phone, to confirm he had it right. She answered, saying, 'Oh hello, hi honey, how are you?'

'Meet me at China Grill in an hour. We need to talk. And Ali, don't make me wait, one hour means one hour.'

Nicole had been speaking with Alisha. She had been talking to the wrong person. With Jane gone, Nicky had told Alisha. In the past, she had spent the most time with her, and so, Nicky had gravitated her way, to share the horrific experience that she had endured in L.A. two weeks earlier. Alisha shared in her hurt and provided her with some much-needed support. The girls had circled the wagons to protect Nicole and Mark from each other. Alisha had intimate knowledge of what had happened, and now it was going to be her turn to face the firing squad, just as Jane had the day before.

138

'What's wrong? Is everything okay?' Teresa asked. It seemed that every time her phone rang, Maxine looked at it with unbridled fear. She had looked like death on wheels over the past three or four days since Teresa's arrival, and their bond seemed tenuous at best. No matter what Teresa had been doing, working on the Knoxx case, or trying to communicate to Maxine as a friend, Maxine seemed distant and even uninterested in what Teresa was doing or saying. Maxine had been spending most of her time on the phone out of earshot, but Teresa had been able to ascertain that there was some kind of problem with one of her kids. Maxine was being evasive in her answers, saying that it was a personal matter. Only by now, Teresa had thought there were no personal matters between them.

No matter how long the hours that Teresa had put into compiling her reports, it was not good enough. Not good enough for Maxine and not good enough for Kevin Christie. He had dispatched agent Hadley with the specific caveat that she call him at the end of each day, New York time, to keep him up to speed on the developments. What Christie didn't know, was that Maxine knew. She knew that he was one of the special ones, because Christie's name was one of the names on the list in the package that Knoxx had given her. The Enterprise was everywhere, watching and listening. That's what Maxine had come to know now, and so, she purposely held back on becoming engaged in any discussions about Exile, Mark Knoxx, or any of his known associates. Maxine was too scared to speak up for fear of retaliation. Dolly was still in a coma at Cedars Sinai, now being watched over by her dad and her younger brother, Harry Allsop. Maxine had to temper her emotions and gauge her weighted dialogue each day, always mindful of who might be watching and listening. She chose every word carefully because it could mean the difference between life and death for Dolly. After four days, Maxine was close to breaking point from not being able to tell anyone, and even more at her wit's-end because of her close proximity to Teresa.

The new Maxine seemed tearful and timid most days. She had become a mystery to Teresa. She'd known Maxine for around fifteen months now, and each time they had been in contact, she had always been full of energy for her job and for life itself. But now, she was different. Hadley had flown in from New York with all the expectations of a school kid going away for the first time to college. Teresa finally felt that they were going to hit pay dirt on Knoxx, now that they were bringing it back to basics in the area that Maxine was renowned for, working the drug trafficking gangs in Southern California.

Teresa had brought with her the forensic accounting findings from the overseas accounts that she had been able to uncover. She had expected to get deep into the drug cases of Southern California, specifically the Southsiders, which she knew, even from New York, ran the West Coast importation and distribution of drugs, guns, and everything else in between. She had become frustrated with Maxine and had come to feel that it was all a complete waste of time. It also felt like Maxine was hindering the investigation by not providing any linkage to her own case files. She didn't want to sit down to discuss some of the names that Teresa had uncovered that were possibly linked to Knoxx, inside the Southsiders.

One name that Teresa had become accustomed to seeing in a number of the Southsiders' criminal files, known as jackets, was one Christopher Lee Wright, also known as Bezerk. Upon mentioning his name to Maxine, she almost jumped across the table, unleashing a torrent of up-to-the-mark abuse at her. Agent Hadley noted in her evening report, in front of Maxine, that this drug dealer from Del Sol, Christopher Wright, might have some connection to Knoxx from a past life. Maxine could only listen stone-faced while Teresa spilled it all to the very people that Knoxx had warned her about. And now, sitting across from her in the conference room in Los Angeles, it was all being offered up, by way of an innocent Teresa Hadley, to the inside man for The Enterprise, Kevin Christie, and there wasn't a damn thing that Maxine could do to stop her. She cried inside, as she was sure it would get back to Knoxx, and he would be furious at her, thinking he would punish her by killing Dolly.

The days were long and hard, but the nights were even longer. Most nights and every weekend, Maxine visited Dolly, sitting with her at her bedside. Each visit, a doctor came in to see to her, and each time, he placed a HEAVEN Navigator on her wrist to check her vitals. Maxine held her breath. The MP-3-type device instantly checked its Internet database, cross-referencing millions of hospital patient's' records to determine the correct dosage of drugs and in what order they were to be administered. Every milligram was automatically digitally encoded into that hospital patient's records. The Navigator was cool and cutting edge, aiding the doctor by doing most of the work automatically. Every dose had already been downloaded into the database, and all the doctor had to do was place the Navigator on the patient's' wrist and let the technology do the rest. Every doctor in the U.S. wanted one now that the testing phase had finished.

HEAVEN Navigators were being boxed up in their millions, ready for shipment worldwide, beginning in ten days to coincide with Exile's Initial Public Offering. Sitting in her chair beside Dolly, Maxine read articles about HEAVEN. She quietly cried, wondering what she had done to deserve this. How had it come to this? How had he gotten to her?

There had to be a way. There had to be something she could do to fight back and release her girl from this Hell, and send Mark Knoxx there in her place. In all her years as a police officer, she had never come up against such a ruthless adversary. And in the past few days, she had come to learn most of their lies and their secrets. She needed an edge, one to cut them with, so she could get her revenge.

Sitting there, alone in the quiet of the hospital room, under the dark light, her phone suddenly rang. It was the call. She jumped out of her chair and almost ran into the hall, while her throat literally jumped from her neck. She forced out a simple, timid greeting, asking, 'Hello?'

For the first time in nearly five years, she was listening to his clear, crisp, acute British accent, cutting her to the quick. Her breathing felt shallow, filled with stress, anguish and fear but she didn't want to miss a single word, listening closely while he imparted his knowledge to her in detail. Having manipulated her, he now controlled her, and so she listened to his instructions, not as enemies, but as allies.

139

The Rolls Royce Phantom rolled up to the curb. Quincy Taylor got out from the front passenger seat and scanned the street. A black S.U.V. that had pulled up some distance behind the Rolls kept its engine running. The men inside were heavily armed and they scanned the street to. Quincy gave them the briefest of looks, and then opened the rear door. Knoxx got out and stode into the China Grill restaurant at 404 Washington Avenue in Miami Beach to meet Alisha for a late afternoon lunch. Only Knoxx wasn't hungry for food. He was starved of information, and one way or another, he was going to get it today - the easy way, or the hard way.

Walking into the restaurant, he gave Alisha a brief sizing-up look before they kissed lightly, but the air between them was already frozen. Alisha had been quick to pick up Mark's vibe as she, like Jane, had known him well for most of his life.

As Mark took his seat, he had a thought. If she didn't come across with the truth this afternoon, then their friendship would be coming to an abrupt and messy end today. Mark got settled in and let the few minutes of nothingness wash over him. Getting the first round of ordering over with, Alisha noticed that he hadn't complimented her on how she looked. He had always been polite and respectful, but today that didn't seem the case.

He immediately put Alisha on point, asking point blank, 'What's up with Nicky? I know you know, Ali. I know Jane knows, and you know what, I'm pretty sure I already know too. I just want to hear it from you.' Looking at Alisha with a deadpan face, his first shot had hit her dead center. Knoxx had hit her cold with no warm up, no innuendos, and no smile. He fired another shot, telling her, 'I know about Bezerk.'

Alisha looked like a deer caught in the headlights. She could only look at him with a blank look, her face telling him that he'd scored a direct hit.

He closed out the show by telling her, 'It was just a matter of time before I found out. It's always the smallest things that end up making the biggest difference. You know what I mean? So come on, it's down to you. I expect nothing less than the truth. I know everyone's been lying to me up to now. If not lying to my face, then just not telling me what went on in L.A. So here we are, you and me, and you're going to be the one to tell me the truth.'

He said it in such a way that it got his point across. He was in a dangerous mood. They might have all been plotting against him, trying to keep the truth about what had happened in L.A. from him, but now he had them all. The three girls all thought he had gone weak, but really, he was a lion in disguise. His speech pattern was meant to intimidate her. He drank his orange juice and lemonade. No more being perceived as weak. No more booze and no more bullshit. It was on now, on all fronts. Picking up his steak knife, he turned it in his hand while thoughts of Guerro came to him; it warmed him, remembering the taste of his blood dripping down his arm onto his lips. Sweet. He lifted the knife and leaned forward on his elbows, looking determined.

Mark said menacingly, 'Just tell me what happened. Just tell me the truth.'

Alisha sat straight in her chair with her head held high and her lips, shiny and thick, with a shade of deep, red lipstick on them. Her eyes began to shine. A slight film of moisture was on them, while she breathed out and looked right into Mark's eyes, realizing this was the moment. Her moment.

'Mark, I'm sorry. I'm so sorry, honey. She was drunk. She felt bitter and was angry about how you'd dumped her. She slept with a guy in L.A. His name's Chris; I think they call him Bezerk. She just wanted to get back at you. But now, she's all cut up, and - .'

'Fuck that, and fuck them! They're both dead!' Knoxx cut her off, shouting. He smashed his hand onto the table. The other patrons looked over at their table. Meserve and Matthews made themselves known as they stood up from their table. Mark had vengeance on his face and a look of hatred towards Alisha.

She pleaded her own case, sounding like she was going to cry herself. 'Honey, I'm so sorry. I hate to have to be the one to tell you. Please don't hold it against me. I only found out myself today. She's really in bits over it.'

Alisha resisted the urge to get up and jump for joy at the irony of it. As she reached across the table to catch his hand, Alisha looked as if she was going to break into tears for Mark. She knew the pain he was in at having to hear the truth. Her truth.

Knoxx had been told a long time ago, by Roberto Madrid that he must look out for his enemies, for they all looked alike and dressed the same. Again, he had not heeded the words. Now, he was the one caught up in a Venus' flytrap. He was the one filled with jealousy and envy, and he was going to kill someone for it. Mark watched her face for any signs of doubt or any lie in it, but Mark and Alisha were made for each other, because she was a beautiful liar too. She held his gaze to seal the deal, and what a deal she had made for herself. She would now be in top spot, and Jane had delivered the opportunity to her, herself, by not taking care of business. Jane had made a mistake in her handling of Mark, and now Alisha took full advantage to make her move. Textbook play.

'I guess it was inevitable, something like this would happen, eventually. I knew it would. I just didn't see it coming, and I always thought Jane had my back,' Mark remarked despondently, his face turning ashen.

'Honey, c'mon. Maybe this was meant to be. Maybe it was inevitable. Look, you've got way too much going on right now to be pulled off course by this. You've got to ask yourself, 'is she really worth it?" Alisha asked him, in a warm and loving tone. She was doing her best to close the deal, while inside, her pulse was racing at being so close to getting it all. So excited, she felt a heated rush of adrenaline pump through her body in all the places that she liked Mark to touch her. Mark looked up at Alisha while she continued to support him, telling him calmly, 'No matter what, no matter where, and no matter when, I'm with you. You know that, right?'

Her dark, hazel eyes shone, she could almost taste the blood on her lips, the sweet taste of revenge. Revenge for always being the odd one out, always feeling like part of the entourage, but not being part of the group. Now, she was front and center and very much the center of attention, having the sole attention of the one thing she both wanted and needed at the same time. Mark.

Mark looked across the table at Alisha, having looked at her all these years, but not actually seen her. Maybe she was right. Maybe all these years, he'd had the right girl in her, but he had never seen her as the right girl. He always thought of Alisha as the right girl, for right now. But here she was, coming to him as a loyal friend, laying it out there, letting him know that she would support him through yet another failed relationship. He wanted to take her into the men's room and bend her over the washbasin, rip her panties to one side, and take her hard in front of the mirror, unleashing all his hate for Nicole on her, while she would love every minute of it. But Mark was back to being his old self. He was back to being Knowledge, and now he was armed to the teeth with it. And he only wanted to make two people suffer for his pain now.

140

Leaving Alisha at the front of China Grill, Knoxx made his girl of the hour feel real good. He promised to have a gift delivered to her the next day, for having been good to him, one that she would get a real kick out of, he told her. She took a chance by saying that he had no idea how good she really wanted to be. She flashed her eyes and giggled, letting Mark know that the thought he'd had earlier in the restaurant might have been on the cards after all. Using all of her charms and powers of seduction, she secured a promise from him that, once her present had been delivered, he would come by her place to collect his. Alisha felt light-headed and was loaded with orgasms as Mark walked away to get in the Rolls; his security team gave her the once over as they too began to clear the area. Wearing a mid-cut skirt that revealed her best assets, Alisha spun around on them and walked away from the restaurant, beginning to plan her future with Mark, happy that her lie had taken hold.

As soon as they were underway in the car, Knoxx picked out his SWIFT phone from his pocket and dialed the West Coast. During the last twenty minutes or so of their dinner, Mark knew the game Alisha was running on him, because he'd seen and heard it from a variety of girls over the years. He also knew how Alisha operated, because she, like Jane, felt that she could handle him. He had been thinking about two things while they had sat in the restaurant. He couldn't wait to get into the quiet of the car to begin putting his newfound knowledge to work in his favor. The phone was answered by a strong Birmingham English accent that belonged to Adrian Romney, who was in L.A. running counter-surveillance for Jane Mears as part of the best-laid plan that Knoxx had devised. He answered chirpily, saying, 'Hello mate, everything alright?'

The thing was, both Adrian and Drew Yarward would kill for the fun of it. Only, they knew it was better to get paid for something they were good at, so why not put their work out for hire? Knoxx answered in a pissed tone, replying, 'No dude, none of it's alright. It's all gone to shit, mate, and life's full of slags.'

Adrian laughed, thinking Mark was joking. Only Mark wasn't. he heard Romney reply, 'C'mon, Mark, it can't be that bad? We're all set here. Drew and me have been keeping an eye on things and Jane's doing great. I tell ya', she's a natural. Don't worry about her. We'll make sure she does it right and comes back in one piece.'

'I don't know if I want her back,' Mark retorted swiftly.

Romney hit back immediately. 'You what? Jane's your top girl, Mark!'

'Yeah, I know, forget it. I've got another job for you, while you're out there. Forget the one we've got lined up. We'll get him next time.'

Before Knoxx had even finished his sentence, Romney replied, 'Fuck that! We're in too deep now to pull Jane out, mate. I can't just walk up to her and tell her, "Sorry, Jane love, but Mark's changed his stupid, daft head on wanting the next President of the United States dead." Are you really that mad? Do you know how much time and effort's gone into planning it all, not to mention the risk that Jane's taking, for you!'

Knoxx had not counted on it being put to him so openly and honestly, or so graphically. It was refreshing in a way, and it kind of made sense. How many opportunities does a person get in a lifetime to make a real difference? He was so close to making one, through his planning and Jane's effort.

He was now consumed with the smaller issues, however. The pain he felt at being betrayed by those he cared for and loved so much. It was dragging him back to the one time and place that he did not want to revisit. Prison. The murder of Jason Burne. Once Knoxx had gotten to his current enemy, the Vice President of the United States, he knew they would retaliate by killing him. He could not leave this world for the next, knowing that Bezerk would still be breathing the fresh air of freedom, after double-crossing him by sleeping with his girl. He was living a crazy life, all right. He had everything, but he had nothing. His life was just an empty shell of material things, and now he realized that, if he was to end up with nothing, then so would Bezerk. With everything he had going on; he still had one more thing to do. He needed to know that Christopher Wright was going to pay for his sins too, just as he would be. By the time Knoxx reached The Grove, he was content, knowing that he had the man for the job in his back pocket. So he made the call. After hearing his happy greeting, Mark opened up with his own. 'Hi, Dragon. I'm fine, thanks. I'm calling for a favor. Can you send someone over to do a job for me?'

The conversation was upbeat and very easy to understand. Knoxx was thrilled to learn that General Dragon had just the man for the job. Even better, he fitted the bill of looking like an all-American boy; and that he would love to come to America and visit Hollywood. That he was coming over to kill someone, didn't factor into it. That was what he was trained to do. Knoxx ran it over in his mind, playing out all the different scenarios, working out the plays of the game, the final details of the plan, not wanting to be disturbed, and as Nicole didn't factor into his plans anymore, she probably didn't even know he was home. There would be no quiet talk tonight, and no need for a lust-filled visit to her bedroom. He was all business in the office tonight, busy handling his business, burning the midnight oil with only the desk lamp providing the light while he plotted away. His business tonight was to figure out how to murder someone clean. Life was hard, but so was Mark Knoxx. He had hardened to his task, furious in his mind, but calm in the execution of the plan. Some hours later, while the early dawn approached, Mark stood in front of the doors to his office on the patio. Looking out towards the rising sun over the endless horizon, everything just happened. It all fell into place. His mind was made up and the plan was set in stone. Everything had come back around to him and Bezerk, back to the beginning.

Within three days, Tasker and Bezerk would both be dead. As Mark lit up a cigar in the cool of the early morning's breeze, he found it calming to think that he would be dead soon after them too. The world would probably be better off without the three of them in it anyway.

He stepped back inside the office to send off e-mails. He sent one to Matthew Tamban, telling him to leave a Porsche in a parking lot in Beverly Hills. Then he sent one to Adrian Romney, telling him to be at The Kingshead pub and restaurant on Santa Monica Boulevard the following afternoon, to meet a young foreign student from Serbia, named Luke Watson. He instructed Romney to get him booked into The Viceroy Hotel on Ocean Avenue in Santa Monica, and get him equipped. Then, Mark did the one thing that made him great. He was Knowledge, and he used it well. He e-mailed Adrian Romney with a second e-mail, using the years of knowledge he had gained about Bezerk. The e-mail read:

Make sure you find and hire two stunning, young hot babes. Pay them cash up front for their time and for their hotel. I want them staying in the Sunset Tower Hotel on Sunset Boulevard for the next three days. Tell them to visit NVS on Hollywood and Vine, telling everyone they're in from Vegas. Very important, make sure one of them is around twenty years old, Latino-looking and has long, red hair.

141

'Vice President Tasker visited his old friend today. To say goodbye,' the television reporter said in a somber tone. The picture cut to the funeral of John D'intino, taking place in West Palm Beach, Florida. The television crews were held back at a distance from the funeral service. The Secret Service was on unusually high alert at this event, due to the fact that it was so close to the final voting day; Stephen Tasker was only a matter of days away from being called President-Elect Tasker. The cameras for the Associated Press captured the mood of the event. Tasker was attending with his tall, statuesque, former-supermodel wife, Lynn Tasker, and their three young children: Ruby, now seventeen, Molly, thirteen, and eight-year-old Tommy Tasker. D'intino's widow, his children and grandchildren, were all there to pay their last respects. And so was Mark Knoxx.

He watched every nuance of Tasker's movement. How he held his wife, and every short word he let go from his mouth. Knoxx was watching from the living room at The Grove. What he wanted to know was, did they know? Did D'intino's family know how he had been murdered? Kicked into the ground, and then ground and pounded into it some more, before taking the kill shots to his head. He would never be seeing his way through Hell, because Knoxx had taken his eyes. Thinking about it more, he thought, *how far could a lie go?* How far could it be stretched before someone says, no? The twist and turn of each lie, each one covering up the earlier one, how many people in D'initino's family could be entrusted with knowing the truth, everyone or no one? Knoxx had called Maxine to tell her, 'Check out the coroner's report on the John D'intino's death, if there is one.'

'He died a couple of days ago in Florida from a heart attack, didn't he?' Maxine had innocently responded from the hospital.

'No, he didn't. He died from an ass-kicking and three bullets to his head,' Mark had answered.

'How do you know that?' Dobro had wistfully asked.

In a half-baked laughing remark, the words cooked her raw as she heard Knoxx answer. 'Because I kicked the living shit out of him before I shot him. And I can prove it. Check it out. That'll prove to you I'm telling you the truth and they're the ones lying.'

Knoxx was keeping everyone on a tight leash, having them watched to see if any of them were trying to bring him down before he could complete his mission. For now, he felt that he was on a mission, and he felt he had now found his purpose in life.

Years earlier, he'd been sickened by what he had learned about Roberto Madrid. How he had made his decisions with no regard to the value of human life. Knoxx was now doing the same. He had no regard for his own life, so how could he possibly have any regard for anyone else's? He had put the one girl he knew he could trust - at least he thought he could - in harm's way for his Cause. Jane was on her assigned mission. Knoxx was now just as ruthless as Roberto Madrid had been, but he had come to terms with who he was now. Living life is sometimes about living in the extremes, being without guilt, without having to worry about tomorrow. Knoxx now understood what had kept Roberto Madrid in power, as Juicy. Fear. For fear brings out love, honor, and above all else, obedience. Fear breeds loyal subjects. The cost of being disloyal may only be a prison term, but the price of being obedient is a life sentence, for in one's own mind, fear is the ultimate unknown. And that was what Knoxx had planned for. He wanted to spread fear amongst The Firm. Each of them would be filled with it, and each of them would be stepping out into the unknown each day. Mark was going to make an example of one man, so that they would all become obedient again. Life isn't fair, and Knoxx was realizing that there was nothing to gain by playing fair in life, so he was not going to be playing fair anymore. There were no limits and no rules now. They had their elite Special Forces and police agencies, but so did he. Mark had learned his craft well. All war is based on deception. Don't be where the enemy expects you to be, hit them where they least expect it. Mark had been given the name Knowledge in prison, and he was now using all the knowledge he had gathered over time. Having watched and listened to the details of people's lives, he would use it against them. This was his genius, and his madness.

Mark could not tell anymore, which thought was real or just a mirage as he hardly slept and ate anymore. His mind was consumed with plotting their downfall, making sure he had every angle covered. His enemies and those people that were meant to be his friends; he couldn't tell which was which anymore because they all looked alike, were now under surveillance, their whereabouts being accounted for.

Alternating between his desk and being out the patio, Mark had nothing left to do but just wait. Everything was done and there was and no way to stop it now. He had been fighting the thought that he wanted to save himself from this nothing he had become. It was as if he needed to be woken up inside, like it was all back to being a dream. How had he come so far, yet had never even begun? He was in trouble again, only this time, big trouble. He laughed at the inevitability of it all, remembering that his only dream, all those years ago, was to come to America and become rich and famous. He was both of those things right now, but for all the wrong reasons, and by this time next week, he'd be famous all right. Within the next twenty-four hours, he would become infamous. Sitting alone, it felt like he was always alone, people saw him as having everything, but all he had now were his memories to keep him company. Nothing else mattered anymore. They were all just things he'd acquired, even his friends, and his girlfriend. *It's been one hell of a ride*, Mark thought. *I've been on more rides than an amusement park*. He let out a small laugh at his jumbled, crazy thoughts. At his meeting with The Firm, Tasker had said not to make an enemy out of them. But Knoxx had never told them not to make an enemy out of him.

As he sauntered over to the downstairs restroom for his early morning 6:15 a.m. piss, his mind drifted back to his time in prison. That's where this had all begun, and the irony of it was, he would be approximately one year away from getting out, had he been given that ten-year sentence. Prison had shown him that tough guys had to make tough decisions. He realized that he would be posted up in rain, snow, and the searing heat of the desert all day, every day, waiting on this day. For today was the day that Stephen Tasker was going to die.

Falling back into his office chair, Mark scribbled out some thoughts on a notepad. Names of people he wanted to see dead. Stephen Tasker, Bezerk, Dobro, Teresa Hadley, Nicole Young, Alisha Ellington and Dave Kenshaw. After a pause, he scribbled out, with a heavy heart, the name, Jane. Knoxx thought of them all dying. He scratched out ABC. Only this time, he wrote below it: Attitude, Belief, Commitment. Maxine Dobro was the one person he knew he could trust, because she was driven by love and hate. Love for her daughter and the hate she had for him. Maxine already had the attitude. He was making her a believer, and then she would be committed to his Cause. The belief that Mark was right after all, would be her driving force. They should all die. And as the day began to light up, he was left with one last thought. What a waste.

142

Giving herself one last good look in the mirror, she still found it hard to see herself, because she looked totally different. She stood back from the restroom mirror to smooth down the front of her waistcoat. She straightened her brushed metallic name badge that read: Kerry. With her dark hair brushed tight and combed over to one side with a hint of cherry highlights in it, she gave her look a final approval. Picking up her black tortoise shell, designer glasses, with some ceremony, she placed them on her face to view herself in the mirror. She let out a nervous laugh. Smoothing down her waistcoat again, she decided that she was ready.

Jane did not look herself, which was of course, was the idea. The hotel uniform made her demure, athletic body look plain. Not too ugly but not too pretty, she just looked, plain Jane. Tilting back her head to confirm that the glasses worked, Jane exhaled a long, deep breath. She ran cold water over her hands, for what seemed like the sixth time since being in the restroom. She checked her watch, knowing she had to get moving. As soon as she walked through the door, she was in the middle of a war zone. Everyone was scurrying about in all directions, with chefs and headwaiters giving orders as if they were generals in a war. Jane quickly blended back into the melee as she picked up a ticket and walked over to pick up a tray, to take into the restaurant.

Within the hour, they would be told about the V.I.P. arriving later that night. Jane already knew who it was going to be. Her general had given her his orders. She would carry them out later that afternoon. While Jane, or rather, Kerry, worked in the restaurant, the majority of the hotel guests and staff, knew that someone big was arriving. The Secret Service had closed the largest convention room and most of the hotel had been off limits for the past two days. The Secret Service had been doing background checks on the guests and each member of staff, including Kerry Greener, where no criminal record had showed up.

Kerry Greener. Her life was no more dull and no more exciting than the next person's, and to look at her, you could see why. She was bland and she lived in a bland world. A vanilla-tasting life, living in a vanilla-wrapper world; she lived alone and rarely dated, working from home as a website designer. She was vanilla herself, pleasant on the eye, but in some way, just not overly attractive. The Secret Service agent reviewing the file on Kerry Greener gave her the once over and moved on; the F.B.I. had nothing on her. She had been cleared to work the main event that evening. And the reason she had been cleared to work in the convention room was clear to those who had the knowledge. Her background was a ghost.

Kerry was now standing in a line-up with around thirty other staff members in the convention room at The Beverly Hills Hotel. They had been told that at 7:30 this evening, the Vice President of the United States would be hosting an event. The staff watched while boxes of glassware and cutlery were being delivered. They were being told that they were to be laid out on all the tables by five o'clock. Secret Service agents stood at every corner of the room, with agents posted at either end of the stage.

The men delivering the security-sealed boxes all wore their laminated I.D. cards that hung from their necks. Their overalls were blue and had the name Macbine on their backs. The boxes were labeled with the same name. Macbine was the supplier of goods and services to the U.S. Government. This company had been awarded the contract by another company called Endless Horizons, which was a sub-division of a larger entity named Exile Corporation. The staff went to work unpacking the plates, cups and saucers, cutlery and glassware. It was the standard operating procedure for the Secret Service, leaving everything to the last minute. The convention room would be sealed until all the guests were accounted for and seated at their assigned tables, before Vice President Tasker entered the hotel. Nothing was ever left to chance. And Knoxx had left nothing to chance, either.

Kerry went about her work while they watched them all. Every agent in the room was watching each person work, but they had no idea what they were meant to be watching for. But Kerry Greener knew. And through her bi-focal glasses, she saw it. The green, bioluminescent glow guided her to it. Kerry made her way over to pick it up from the table with the rest of the glassware. She deftly carried a server's tray that had six Waterford, crystal tumblers and two, large, empty water pitchers on it. It was surprising how strong she was, considering her small frame.

Waiting her turn, she walked up to the bottom of the stage for a look over by a Secret Service agent at the foot of the steps. He checked her tray and looked into her eyes, and then checked her laminated security badge. He waved her on, allowing her to make her way up onto the stage. Four other members of staff were busy laying out silverware along the long banquet table, which looked across the vast expanse of the convention room.

Kerry moved swiftly along the table - one, two, three, four - setting down every heavy-bottomed, crystal glass tumbler in the same fashion, with an empty water pitcher being set down with every third glass. She glanced through the lower-half of her bi-focal glasses. The iridium-coated lenses confirmed the glass tumbler she needed. She picked it out, seemingly at random, and set it down with an empty water pitcher next to the podium with the seal for the Vice President of the United States of America on it.

Kerry continued along the table, placing the glassware down until she had run out. Walking down the steps at the other end of the stage, she passed another Secret Service agent. She picked up another tray filled with glassware and continued laying out table after table throughout the convention room. All the worker bees slowly but surely building the hive. With the afternoon drawing to a close, Kerry walked back towards the stage to check that the honey trap had been set. It was sitting there neatly, silently glowing, right where she had left it, at the right hand side of the podium. Waiting. *The Art of War. All war is based on deception. The supreme art of war is to subdue the enemy without fighting.* Knoxx was its finest student.

Kerry Greener dined in the staff's dining room, chatting with some of the other temporary staff who had been brought in as servers for the night. They were excited at being a part of history, being in such close proximity to the next President of the United States. Everyone was running on adrenaline. It had been a long day already, and it was certainly going to be a long night. But it would be a night to remember, a night that would go down in history. Vice President Stephen Tasker was now, forty-eight hours away from becoming the forty-fifth President of the United States. He was, however, only twenty-four hours away from becoming a dead vice president.

143

The funeral service for John D'intino passed without incident. The high level threat that the Secret Service had thought it might have been, due to the intelligence they had received from their inside man, seemed to have been misplaced. But you never could tell how these things would shakeout. Since nine-eleven, a lot of things had changed, for better and for worse.

Homeland Security, the F.B.I. and the C.T.C: Counter Terrorism Center were all on high alert. The Secret Service had been on point all day in Florida but it had turned out to be just another day at the office. The office was now a secure thirty-four thousand feet up in the sky. It allowed the Secret Service agents time to get some shuteye before they were back on protective detail for this evening's event in Beverly Hills. Tasker had no such luxury though, having one more task to do, winning last minute assurances from governors in other States that he count on them for their support in him becoming the next President of the United States. All the polls showed him to be the clear leader in the early voting and everyone seemed to be comfortable with the finality of it all. Behind the closed doors of his private office in Air Force 2, however, Tasker wanted another finality. He asked, 'Where are we on the HEAVEN program, gentlemen?'

He cracked open a bottle of Ty sparkling water, pouring it into a glass. He looked at each of his men, who each paused for thought. Tasker then took a deep drink, allowing them time to think about their answers.

'We've encountered a slight problem. HEAVEN is encrypted with EBDIC code. I won't bore you with the details, but it's a code that has 256 different character references for each letter of the alphabet. As we destroy one code, another four new worms spread out from it and a viral infection code disperses over the Internet,' Tasker's National Security Advisor, Gary Mast, explained.

Tasker placed the glass back down on the desk. The hum of the jet engines provided a little impasse on what he might have wanted to say in response. He managed to temper it, and looked at David Vickers, the head of C.T.C., asking him, 'So, we're in a holding pattern in Florida?'

'Yes sir, we have a Ghost Recon Team in position at Bal Harbor to squeeze the immediate target area and we have a SEAL Team 45 positioned at the port of Miami. We're waiting on the 'go'.' Vickers answered, controlled and calm.

The Secretary of State, Graham Stewart, now added, 'We've cracked part of his Firewall passcode. So far, it looks like it's LOCO.'

Tasker mused, 'Loco, huh, yes it is.'

'We just need a little more time. We'll have it cracked soon, and then you can give the order to go in and take him out,' Agent Vickers interjected.

Tasker looked into his glass, as if he could see the future, maybe wanting to see his own. He pondered on it for a minute and remarked, 'Time is something we're all running out of.'

David Vickers felt the need to bring up one more point, saying with trepidation, 'We seem to have another wrinkle in all of this.'

Tasker gave Graham Stewart a brief look, and then looked at Vickers, inquiring, 'Go on.'

'Our Miami office was contacted this morning by an F.B.I. agent asking for the medical examiner's records on Mr. D'intino's death. The Florida office patched her through to our office, and she questioned why she was speaking with the C.T.C. when the reports were that Mr. D'intino had died from a heart attack.'

'Jesus, can this get any worse! What did they tell her?'

'They told her the files were classified under the National Security Act,' Vickers replied.

Tasker expelled some exasperated, hot air within the temperate confines of Air Force 2, jetting across America towards the Golden State of California. He evaluated the situation, and took it in his stride. Presidents have hard decisions to make, and this looked to be one of his first tests as President-Elect. Looking at Vickers, he asked, 'Do we know who the agent is?'

'We've monitored her for some time,' Vickers informed him.

Tasker laid his arms on the armrests of the chair, looking like a judge would look, before sentencing a murderer to death. He asked coldly, 'How much does she know?'

Vickers didn't hesitate. 'She knows too much.'

Tasker swung his leather chair around slightly to face his long-time friend - and Godfather to his son, Tommy - to get his point across. Presidential and perfunctory, he said, 'We have too much invested in this to allow everything to unfold now. We're so close I can taste it. Can't you?'

Stewart nodded, answering softly, 'Yes, Mr. President.'

Tasker allowed himself a small smile at the sound of that title, knowing it would be official after this weekend. His last official engagement as vice president was tonight, and then it would be President-Elect Tasker. His face turned solid and his eyes glazed over into stone, telling Stewart, 'I think you know what I'm asking of you, Graham. You must do your country, and me, this great service. We're all depending on you to do the right thing.'

Tasker lifted up his glass, trying to wash away the bitter taste in his mouth at what he knew he was ordering to be done.

Graham Stewart replied in a hollow voice, 'I understand. I'll see to it. I'll have it taken care of as soon as possible.' He tried his best to sound reassuring, nervously sitting in the front portion of his seat, thinking about what he was being asked to do.

'None of this can ever come back to me, you understand?' Tasker barked.

'I do. And it won't. You have my word.' Stewart confirmed.

'God damn it! I feel like we could all go down for this, right as we're about to pull it all off. Not because we've broken so many laws, or even because we've perjured ourselves, it'll be because we sold a war too well,' Tasker stated. He looked blank, thinking back to another time and place. Then that thought led him to ask Vickers, 'What about our inside man? He submitted a report stating that Knoxx might attempt an attack on me.'

'Yes, he did. The Intel we received indicated the most likely event was to have happened in Florida at Mr. D'intino's funeral, or even at his home, but that didn't materialize. Our watchers say he hasn't left his home in three days, except to visit a restaurant,' Vickers responded.

'So you're saying there's no threat from him directly?'

'I'm saying that the most obvious threat, where you were most vulnerable, has now passed. It looks like Knoxx is out of touch with reality on what his position in all of this is,' Vickers stated harshly.

Tasker retorted, 'Huh, reality. There's a good choice of words. What is real and what is fiction? Sometimes, the truth is stranger than fiction. All I know is I want him to pay for his disobedience, and for murdering John.'

'He probably sees it as an eye for an eye,' Stewart reactively remarked, letting his thoughts tumble out from his mouth.

Tasker was quick in his reaction, answering, 'And that's what he took, Graham, John's eyes! I don't want to hear about Mark Knoxx anymore. Just crack that code. Clean house and let's put all of this behind us.'

144

'Hello mate, good to meet you,' Adrian Romney said, while he extended his hand for a handshake. He sat in the front, right hand corner of The Kingshead Pub in Santa Monica. He had been waiting the better part of half an hour, eating a steak and kidney pie and chips with baked beans, washed down with a Budweiser. The tall, blond, clean-shaven and toned male sat down next to him on a barstool. He looked around the pub, noticing how tanned and relaxed everyone looked. The California sea breeze wafted in through the front door of the bar, while Adrian breezed on with his repartee, asking, 'So what'd they call you then?'

Happily moving along into his jovial routine, Adrian didn't care that this guy was a trained, stone-cold killer, and that his sole purpose for being here was to commit a murder.

'My name is Goran Milic, but my friends call me Gosja.'

'Huh, that's like Gotchya, hey?' Adrian replied, sniggering at his own joke as he lifted his pint glass up in a happy gesture, asking, 'Fancy a pint, Gosha?'

Goran Milic was twenty-seven years old, standing six feet tall. He had served in the Serbian military, after fighting for his own survival during the Balkans war, keeping low to the ground while living off the land during the ethnic cleansing that both sides were conducting. By the time he had reached fifteen, there was only one fate for young Goran, who by now was known simply as Gosha. He would join the military and join in the fight. He would fight to survive and he would fight for his people, so that they might survive as a people within a nation torn apart. Gosha had seen his family torn apart as a child when his father was dragged out from their village home onto the street and shot, with his mother soon sharing the same fate. Goran, their only child, watched while he hid in the bushes, crying stifled, terror tears.

Gosha had lost his parents, but had found a new father figure in an emerging Country. He was trained from an early age in how to kill efficiently and effectively, and he had no problem doing it. He and his young unit, comprising of child soldiers would go out on sorties dressed as young peasant boys, trying to lure the opposition in, looking for an easy kill. And it turned out to be easy for Gosha to kill. He quickly rose through the Serbian military ranks, to be trained in the Spetznaz Russian Special Forces. After the war, he became a hit man for hire. He was General Dragon's personal bodyguard. And now he was in Hollywood.

Romney took Gosha under his wing for the day, giving him the grand tour of Beverly Hills. They drove past The

Beverly Hills Hotel that had been cordoned by the Beverly Hills Police Department, due to some big event happening there. They managed to grab a quick look at 'the pink palace', as the locals knew it, driving along Sunset Boulevard on through to the Sunset Strip. Adrian drove Gosha through Sunset Plaza while he talked him through the steps, always saying Gotchya, when in fact it was pronounced, Go-Sha. Adrian knew it was beginning to annoy his younger charge, but he didn't care. With the sun beating down on them, Gosha loved the feel and the colors of Hollywood. And the women, they were everywhere. Gosha kept smiling at every one of them, and at every opportunity he waved to them, laughing, with some even waving back at him. Living in Los Angeles, he decided, was like living in Heaven. From that moment, he decided that he wanted to live in exile from the dark, dank surroundings of Serbia.

He had served his country well, and he had served his master well. General Dragon had lived in Moscow back in its hey-day and Gosha hoped that Dragon would understand, and that he would want the same for Gosha, to live free, in the land of the free. Gosha drove Adrian mad with all his questions, but Adrian was quick to point out that he was in L.A. to do the job first. Then after it was done, he would get to do some partying in the clubs. Romney said in an obtuse way, 'You'll have all the money you'll need soon enough, son.'

Adrian continued to fire Gosha up while they drove along Sunset Boulevard past the Sunset Tower Hotel, and then driving past NVS. Adrian showed him the route he would take in, and then out, after it was done. He explained that he'd be watching the club and would call him to let him know when the bait had been taken.

The two girls Romney had picked for the occasion had been staying in the hotel for two nights now, and had definitely made an impression in NVS. One of the hookers called herself Kimberly, although her real name was Heather. Her mom was a Latin beauty and her dad was an American. Heather had left high school, enrolling in beautician school to become a beauty technician, only to find out that her own beauty could get her to where she wanted to go much faster. She regularly earned eight thousand dollars or more a week at the age of only nineteen.

Adrian met with Kimberly and her partner Jacqui at the hotel bar each night to pass along instructions before they went out for the night, finishing up at NVS. And tonight, Adrian told them, 'Make sure you snag him tonight. Tell him it's your birthday and you want him as your present.'

The girls giggled at all the spy stuff they were involved in, having been told they were part of a Bounty Hunter sting.

Chris Wright was going be arrested on a number of outstanding warrants in the morning. Adrian told them that he wanted to catch Wright on his own, away from his friends so it would go smoother. All the girls had to do was to make sure they got him back to the hotel tonight.

Gosha was set and the timetable was set. He knew the route in, and out. He would then meet up with Romney afterwards, and Adrian would then drive him to Santa Monica Airport, where the Exile jet would fly him down to Cabo San Lucas, to sit out the fallout from Bezerk's murder.

Knoxx had communicated his plan to his silent partner, and his compadre did not hesitate in providing his support. He understood, saying that he would have done the same, killed for the honor and for the disrespect. Juicy saw no problem with it. He knew how to tie up the loose ends, agreeing with Knoxx that it had to be done, even though it meant he was losing a strong soldier.

'Keep your enemies close and your friends closer. If I can assist in any way, do not hesitate to call upon me. You have served me well, I will be there for you, should you need me to be, believe that. Don't leave anything to chance, or anyone alive who's not worthy to enjoy the luxury of breathing that you have provided them. It is everything or nothing, Mark. Take everything from them and leave them nothing.'

Madrid signed off, telling him to think on it. Mark said he would, but thought that he had everything covered.

Adrian had left Gosha at the Viceroy hotel to catch up on some sleep. He'd received a phone call late into the night, listening to Mark pass along his genius and his madness. A thought that had been consuming him for months now. Mark was asking Adrian to do one more thing for him. He gave him the name of someone who lived in L.A. Someone he wanted him to murder, leaving Adrian asking, 'Why this guy?'

'Because it's my job to find secrets and keep secrets. Everybody has one. That's who I am. It's what I do. And I want you to find him and kill him.'

145

The convention room had been filling up since 5:30pm, and now at 9:30pm, everyone had been entertained, wined and dined. Now they were all sitting and shuffling in anticipation, wondering when the main event was going to get underway. Kerry Greener had been in her flat shoes all day, having only been allowed to take three ten-minute breaks all day. The staff had all changed into new, crisp shirts and waist jackets for the night's event, but her feet and her head were killing her. Her only thought was *When were they going to get to kill him?* She just wanted it to be over, so she could get out of these clothes, have a long, hot shower, and then get out of L.A.

Drew and Adrian had been running counter-surveillance, making sure the F.B.I. had not made her. So far so good. With her dark hair and dark-rimmed glasses, Kerry blended into the background perfectly under the dark light of the convention room. She had been given tables nineteen through twenty-one to attend to, and she was ready to drop, having been working for thirteen hours now.

Then, the lights dimmed inside the vast room, and the tune that every President of the United States marches to, rang-out. The crowd erupted into applause and cheering once the spotlight fell on him. In walked Vice President Tasker, waving profusely at the audience and then clapping along with them, pointing out to a few people in the crowd. It was now or never. Kerry looked up at the stage with all the other people in the room, but then turned back to a guest who had been in the middle of ordering some drinks from her. *What will be, will be,* she thought. She had done her part, now it was all up to Mark.

'Whoa! Thank you, thank you. Wow! So this is where all the beautiful people are!' The crowd laughed with him while Tasker stood behind the podium, looking presidential and full of himself. He joked, 'I was in Sin City, Las Vegas the other night, and I said to the crowd there, 'Let the good times roll, just in case God doesn't show!'' Well, from where I'm standing, it looks as if God showed up here. Look at you! Beauty's in the eye of the beholder, they say, but hey, if there is a God, then he's been hard at work in this room.'

Tasker opened strong, segueing into a topic to begin his one-hour-and-thirty-minute prepared speech. This was business, and the reason why he was here; to close out the show. Jane worked her section with the air of a professional, handling each guest with grace, keeping her head low, while all eyes were fixed to the stage. Tasker was still going strong after an hour, lacing his commentary with highlights and jokes. The audience was being manipulated into thinking that he was the greatest guy they knew, but then, none of them really knew the man as he truly was. None of them knew his secrets. Only one man had come to learn a secret about him.

Jane Mears was beginning to lose her faith in the plan happening, her belief in what Mark had told her would happen. She remembered what he had told her: 'It's inevitable. It's just a matter of time, hun. You'll see. Keep the faith, Jane. It'll happen.' Having explained it the day before back in Miami, Mark had told Jane not to give it any thought, and to just continue to act out her role as a server. It was all academic, Mark had told her, after she had acted out her part in the play, she would be done with her part.

Now though, as much as she tried, Jane couldn't stop herself from thinking about it, and she did her best to catch a glimpse up at the stage. She had seen the vice president's personal detail come in an hour earlier to lay out the table with condiments, fill up the water pitchers, and of course, sit down Tasker's favorite bottled water. The distinct, dark blue, Ty Welsh spring bottled water that he only drank. Three bottles sat at Tasker's right hand side. Jane was too far away to confirm that the glass tumbler was still there. Her eyes were killing her now, along with her feet. She just wanted it all to be over.

It wasn't going to work out as Mark had planned, Jane thought. She resigned herself to getting her part done, getting home and then regrouping. They would have to think up a new strategy. As she stood against the wall, watching for the next eye to catch her from her section, she briefly thought of Mark back in Florida, wondering if Mark and Nicole had made up, and how Nicole was coping, having to keep her secret from Mark. Jane decided that once she got home, she and Nicky would sit him down and tell him what had happened. She had the distinct impression that Mark knew that something had happened, and she needed to be straight with him; she hated having to lie to him. Her eyes took off to another place. Lost from all this madness that all seemed so mad, thinking about how they were now living their lives, living a life in Exile. Jane then quickly refocused again, and her focus went directly to the stage. For some reason, she seemed to take note of what Tasker was saying, hearing him say, 'Friends, I cannot lie. I am excited.'

The audience were cheering and laughing. Tasker picked up a large blue bottle of spring water and snapped open the security seal on it. He was standing with the bottle held high in his left hand, holding the glass tumbler at his waist in his right hand as he continued, 'I'm excited about our future, this coming Monday, and for the next eight years!'

Everyone in the room stood up to shout their approval and applaud, realizing what he meant. Jane's view was temporarily cut-off by all the bodies moving about in front of her. She tried to catch a glimpse, but she didn't have a clear view right at that moment from where she stood. Had it happened? She couldn't be sure.

'If the terrorists win, they'll never let us remember who we once were. That we can believe in ourselves. I believe that's the only thing that keeps us from being a great nation once more; our own belief in ourselves. I get up every morning and check Forbes' Richest One Hundred list, and if I'm not on it, well then, I go to work.'

The audience erupted, laughing with Tasker, while Kerry, the server, attended to a guest again. Tasker paused and then continued speaking. Jane had missed it. He then said, 'Thinking about what is possible and making it a reality, is created by managing. Creative leadership, rather than crisis management, positive goals set today, can head off the future problems of tomorrow.'

Then he did it. He did the one thing that sealed his fate, his future, and his destiny. Stephen Tasker did the one thing he did. The one thing that Mark Knoxx believed he would do. If you know where to look, you will always come to learn the details of a person's life. One thing Knoxx knew for sure was that the devil lived in the details.

Tasker was a showman, much like Knoxx and tonight, he was at the center of the show business universe here in Beverly Hills, with all of Hollywood's celebrity elite loving the show he was putting on for them. He raised the bottle up to his shoulder for effect, as he had done many times before on the campaign trail, to make a point. He then poured the water into the glass that he held in his other hand by his waist. He said, as he did it, 'When money is flowing fast and free, in a free flowing and growth economy, it sure does feel good. But we must all be careful, because it could all too easily dry up.'

He took a long, deep drink from the glass, emptying the glass of water. He then waved at the audience while saying emphatically, 'Goodnight, Los Angeles!'

146

Launching the black Porsche Cayman S forward from the stoplight while giving the hot, blonde-haired woman behind him in her BMW a cursory wave, the executive drove along the soft camber of Sunset Boulevard towards his morning destination. Standing before him, gleaming in the mid-November balmy morning sunshine, was the Sunset Tower Hotel.

Guiding the Porsche into the hotel's driveway, he brought it to an abrupt halt as the parking attendant stepped up to the new arrival. Getting out from the car, he straightened his canary yellow linen jacket, which he wore with a white shirt and dark blue Rock & Republic jeans. The executive looked at the parking attendant, both of them in their mid-twenties, telling him, 'Keep it up front, okay. I'll be about fifteen minutes.'

He palmed a crisp, fifty-dollar bill into the attendant's hand.

'Sure thing,' the parking attendant answered enthusiastically, as he got into the car to drive it up farther along the hotel's driveway.

Standing for a brief moment in front of the hotel, the driver swept his eyes up and down The Strip, his eyes shaded by his Armani sunglasses. He was twenty-seven years old, six foot tall, with sun-bleached blonde hair and every inch a Hollywood player.

Walking up the entrance steps, he pulled back his shirt cuff to check his watch; it told him it was 8:54 a.m.

'In and out Smooth,' was all his lips betrayed as he sauntered nonchalantly into the lobby, to complete his mission.

What a Waste

147

The temperature in Miami was a blistering ninety-eight degrees with a humidity factor of about eighty-five, but at least there was an intermittent warm, crisp, breeze that swam into the large, austere home office through the open patio doors.

The deep, cherry brown, high-backed leather chair swung around to face the view of the one hundred and thirty foot long Sunseeker Predator moored at the bottom of the pristine, manicured garden. An electric blue circle of thick cigar smoke rose up from the front of the chair, a perfect circle every time. A voice could be heard coming from the chair. 'Get it done and make it messy. You know how we do. Yeah, he's gone, been a long time coming, really.' Carrying on after a pause, 'Now he's got to go, too. Yeah well, that's how it is. Tell Beaver not to worry about getting out; it's all been arranged in Mexicali. He's just got to get there, and then they can all disappear from there. Yeah okay bud. Speak to you later, Adrian. Thanks for taking care of this last thing for me.'

He hung up the phone and drew hard on his Avo cigar, savoring its taste while revelling in the spoils of war, thinking about what had gone down this morning. The man sitting in the chair was a happy guy. Swinging his chair around to face the cabinet behind his desk, he bent over, placed his encrypted SWIFT cell phone in the safe, and shut its heavy door. Spinning the dial to lock it, he then kicked the chair back around. He then noticed one of his favorite songs by Sade playing on the radio. It made him think about her, and the life he'd chosen. That got him thinking, *Mi vida loca.* He muttered to himself, 'My crazy life,' but then he said determinedly, 'Bad things happen to bad people.'

The phone on his desk rang. He answered it in a soft, warm tone, 'Yeah, Janey? Okay thanks, hun, it's about time he called. I got it, go get some sleep babe, okay?'

The girl questioned him about the caller with some concern.

He listened for a minute and then, in a rich English accent that sounded soothing, he answered by saying, 'It'll all work out babe, no problem. You worry too much. Now go get some sleep. I'll see you later.'

The girl's voice on the other end of the line said something that made him laugh.

He answered, 'Yeah, I'm glad you're home, too. Okay, little pop, don't worry. Love you, too. Put him through.' He stiffened up in his chair and straightened his back. He was the first to speak once he realized the caller was on the line, having heard him cough over the phone. He greeted the caller by saying, 'Good afternoon, Mr. Vice President, how are you today?'

'I've been a hell of a lot better, Mr. Knoxx. And you?' Receiving the anticipated terse reply, he casually continued with his own repartee, answering, 'Great, thank you. I'm just lovin' life and livin' it large.'

Mark Knoxx gave the caller his attention as they got down to discussing what had happened back in Los Angeles.

Tasker noted the sarcastic tone in Knoxx's reply, setting the tone of the phone conversation right off the bat, both men despising each other. Knoxx had been prepared for this call, as it had been just a matter of time in coming. Since leaving The Beverly Hills Hotel, Tasker had flown back to Washington overnight and had picked up some kind of flu bug that added to his already short temper. He was tired and he was definitely tired of having to deal with Mark Knoxx. A seemingly endless stream of a hacking cough followed. After he caught his breath, Tasker began his tirade. 'You think you can bring me down, bring us down? It'll never happen. I assure you, not in a million years. You'll never get to us. We're too powerful. We've been at this for a thousand years. Many have tried over the years and they've all failed. You try and expose me by murdering my friend and now you put on this petty charade in L.A.'

Knoxx could hear him take a deep drink over the phone to subside an oncoming cough. Taking it all in his stride, he waited for his turn. Knoxx could sense Tasker was worried. They were all worried. He knew they were attacking his Internet firewalls, trying to crack the HEAVEN code, and as they hadn't killed him yet, that meant they hadn't cracked it. He knew they had h-ll---o-a----co decoded. Soon, they would have it all: Hollywood and Coco. Knoxx drew on his cigar and continued listening to the dead man talking. 'We're everywhere, watching you and I promise you, you can't escape, Knoxx.'

Knoxx placed his cigar in the ashtray and then lent on his elbows, resting them on the desk. He spoke assuredly into the phone, replying, 'What makes you think I want to escape? I hope you've made your peace with God, because I know only God can judge me, and trust me, we'll both be seeing him soon enough.'

'What do you mean by that?' Tasker asked, following up with a hacking cough.

He heard Knoxx reply, 'I mean, I never intended to go after all of you. I only needed to get to one of you, and I have. I promise you, you'll never get to be president.'

Tasker rose in anger at Knoxx's arrogance. No matter how much pain his body was in, he wanted to take control of the conversation, his voice rising with conviction, 'Don't be so absurd. You'll never get to me. I am going to be president!'

'You're so wrong. I only needed to get to you, and I have. Remember when you questioned me about being all in? Well, I'm all in now, and guess what? I am committed. I'm committed to seeing you dead, which by my calculations, should be in around six hours from now.'

'Are you threatening me?' Tasker barked, bringing about another tirade of coughing.

Knoxx answered, 'No, man, I'm just letting you know, I have a new reason for me. I know what I'm supposed to do in my life now. I've realized the reason I was born and everything I've done to date was for this. It was to kill you. The space between right and wrong is where you'll find me hiding, and you know what? I'm no different from you. We might have different names and different blood running through our veins, but in the end, we're the same. You've always known what you were born to do, what you were going to become - only to lose it, just as you were about to get it. Me? I never knew who I was or what I was put on this earth to do, or what I wanted to do, really. Until now. I've found the one thing I was looking for. I found my reason for me being who I am, and that reason's you, because I finally did it. I made good on my promise to do one good thing, fulfiling my God-given talent. My destiny was to kill you, and I have.'

'You've gone absolutely mad! I should have seen this coming; I should have just had you killed when you murdered John D'intino.'

'Yeah well, it's too late for that, for him, and it's too late for you.'

After a short burst of anger, which triggered off yet another bout of coughing, Tasker relented. Feeling weak and wanting to end the phone conversation, he finally got around to asking what his fate was. All hopes of any reconciliation had faded, as Tasker knew that nothing could be saved. He would soon come to know, not even himself. He asked, 'What is it? What do you want to tell me? Come on, what are you trying to say? This is madness.'

Mark inhaled and then exhaled a slow, long breath. He fingered the cigar sitting in the ashtray, needing to frame it just right. The final repartee was his and he wanted to savor every moment. He knew that as soon as this phone call was done, so was he. 'You know, I did some dealing with the government of Papua New Guinea, providing the security and management operations for their mines over there, just north of Australia in the South Pacific Ocean, on an island called Bougainville.'

'Yes, yes, what are you saying? This is all just mere drivel.'

The phone line became thick with a hacking cough again. Knoxx didn't once remark on it while he waited for it to subside, waiting for the right time to close out the show. 'Well, that's why you're coughing so much.' He said with some humor, 'It's because of the gold mines; well, because of the by-product of the mine, really.'

'What's that? What are you talking about?' Tasker answered dismissively.

Knoxx took his time to answer, not wanting to be taken out of his game plan. 'I'm talking about a disease that's endemic to Papua New Guinea that kills thousands a year, especially around the gold mine area. I'm talking about Dengue Fever. It causes typhoid of the intestines, the first symptoms of which are - oh I don't know, say - fever, headaches, coughing, your eyes are aching, pain in your muscles and joints. Does any of that sound familiar?

'You son of a bitch!' Tasker barked, followed up by a severe coughing bout.

Tasker could be heard taking a drink again over the phone. Knoxx stayed on script. Making sure his last stand would be remembered, he answered, 'Yeah, I am a son of a bitch, but I just made you my bitch.'

'You're dead! You hear me, dead!' Tasker replied, rising to a high ground stance.

Knoxx brought him down hard, replying, 'I'm okay with that, are you? I've been carrying the devil on my back for some time now. I'm already in the ground, so I guess I'll be seeing you there soon too.'

Knoxx allowed himself to fall into a long, deep laugh. All he could hear was more agitated coughing, as the full horror of what was happening dawned on Tasker. Knoxx had got to him somehow.

Knowing he had him good. He tortured Tasker some more by telling him, 'Of course, I had to make sure. So that's why, at your last event as vice president, well actually, at the last event in your life, I juiced it up a bit. You know, if you look at someone's life long enough you can find their rhythm in it. The life people think is so random, not knowing that they do the same things each day, expecting different outcomes. I look for the details, and one detail I found out about you was that you love to drink from that bottled water, and you always liked to make a show of it. I knew you'd do it one more time. That's why I had your glass laced with poison, and just to make sure, I added Dioxin. You may know it, as you're in the business of the art of war, as STCOD, known as Agent Orange, you son of a bitch!'

Knoxx let out another laugh, above Tasker's coughing. Tasker sounded like he was dying right there and then on the phone, having to listen to Knoxx taunt him.

Knoxx continued, 'It can only be disposed of by intense heat. It doesn't degrade in soil or you know what else, water. And it's extremely deadly, used mostly in industrial waste.'

'You think this's over. It'll never be over, you bastard!' Tasker answered, shouting at the top of his coarse lungs.

Knoxx just felt content, as he chilled, kicking back in his leather chair. He calmly answered, 'Yeah, it sucks, I know. Life's like eating chow in prison. It's all a mystery meal. Sometimes it's okay. Other times, well, you just got to choke it down and move on. You know, you once said to me. "How will you know when you've arrived, when you've made it?" Well, you know what? I just have.'

He smacked the phone down, ending the phone call on a high note. He took in the brightest day outside in the darkest hour of the remainder of his life. Looking at the phone, he sagely said, 'My time may be up, but your time has come.'

148

Drawing on his cigar, he knew that he had done his best and given his all to do one good thing, and be a good person. He knew the inevitability of it now. They had him, but at least he had gotten to them, and it warmed him inside to know that revenge was best served cold. He had one body cold in Hollywood. He was racking up one in Washington D.C. and he had one more on its way, once Romney got around to it. It had been a good life, for all of its faults. Mark basked in the warm sunlight, and had a simple thought. A life not lived is still a life lost. He may be losing his life but at least he had got to live his life in his own inimitable style. One thing was for sure: however he had lived his life, he was sure going out in as much style. Happiness is in the journey, not the destination. He knew his final destination, and so, sitting back in his chair, he took some time to reflect on the journey he had taken.

Andrew Matthews looked in on him from the door to the office, giving him a 'what's up' kind of look. He walked in and sat down in front of Mark's desk, saying with trepidation, 'I think I've found something, mate. I thought I'd run it by you, seeing as you're Knowledge and all.'

He looked at Knoxx with some concern, but then cracked a smile. The two of them shared a close moment that brightened Mark up. Realizing he was still on his journey, asking, 'What's up?' Bringing himself back from where he had drifted off too, back into the here and now. He wasn't dead yet.

Matthews pulled out some papers from a file while he said, 'I think HEAVEN has hit upon a DNA string of some type. It's not random and it's definitely not localized, but it looks as if all the people share a common bloodline of some type. It's pretty awesome.'

'Show me what you mean,' Mark asked him.

They both walked over to a table in the office, where Matthews laid out the papers, saying while they looked them over, 'Damned if I know what this is all about?'

It became apparent that Matthews was onto something. The DNA string seemed to cover thousands of people who had emigrated from the southwest region of Egypt up through Turkey and on to the South of France.

'What are we looking at?' Matthews asked.

He looked at Mark, while he was still looking at the chart, trying to absorb it. Matthews continued his thought process by saying, 'We have such a huge database that this would've never have shown up anywhere else. Because HEAVEN can run all the cross-referencing on millions of patients' records, this has even shown up as a hit. It looks like, whatever it is, we were never supposed to find it. Heaven only knows what this could mean.'

Both of them looked at each other in morbid fascination. Matthews turned the top sheet over to show Mark the one underneath.

'What do you make of this one? The historical DNA chart we just looked at, now, compared with this chart, shows the majority of the names on the first chart all died well before their time.' Matthews inquired.

Knoxx leaned over the table and flipped from one page to the next, trying to get an understanding of them. He didn't know a damn thing about medical records or medicine through the ages, but he did know a few things about history and geography, and these historical records went way back in time. Studying them in detail, in a flash, the combination of knowledge and instinct struck him, as he exclaimed, 'Holy shit!'

Recognizing some of the dates and places, Mark felt his veins boil inside; the hairs on the back of his neck stood up in fear, excitement and anticipation. He wanted to laugh and cry at the same time. It was amazing. He laughed uncontrollably while he gave Andy Matthews a big shake by his shoulders and then ruffled his head, telling him, 'You, my son, are a slaagg.'

He laughed like a school kid again. He was hours away from death, but oh man, what a ride and what a life.

Knoxx ranted, 'This could be the bloodline of Jesus fucking Christ, mate!'

149

Nicole had slept in one of Mark's shirts for comfort, still needing his smell on her. The past few days had seen little improvement but she knew Jane had returned, and hoped they would be able to sit down with Mark and tell him what had happened back in Los Angeles. She felt that she should leave Mark alone, thinking he had more than enough on his mind right now. Nicky had spent the day busying herself. When she finally got around to putting on the news, it brought a new meaning to her life. Freedom. She had been set free from her guilt and freed from the chains of her fear of having to tell Mark what had happened, even though she had not brought any of it upon herself. The news had changed all of that. There had been a murder back in Los Angeles that had become known as The Bezerk Murders.

She watched as many news stations as possible. Even though the murders had been gruesome - because two innocent girls had been killed along with the assassin - the one man that had been causing her so many sleepless nights was dead. During the evening, she began to think about how the murders had taken place. The news reporters had begun to link it to some mysterious entity. The F.B.I. had made a statement, saying that there was possibly more to the murder of a local drug dealer than met the eye. Nicole watched as an F.B.I. special agent, Teresa Hadley came on camera to say, 'In the course of our conducting an ongoing multi-department investigation, we have determined that one of the victims, Christopher Wright, was linked to organized crime on an international level. This murder has led to FinCEN, the Financial Crimes and Enforcement Network, to uncover ties linking Wright to numerous offshore bank accounts whose account holders may be involved in criminal activities.'

She immediately thought of Mark. What if he'd had something to do with it? She could only wonder. It scared her, and yet it thrilled her at the same time, thinking he might have made it happen. Maybe he'd found out. She knew that was possible, but would he do that for her? Could he? Had Mark defended her honor in the worst way? Was that why he'd been so ill-at-ease lately? When she saw Mark sitting out on the patio eating his dinner, Nicole spent close to an hour getting ready. She decided to go down and start her life over with him, wearing her new, sexy chiffon robe and pink lace underwear.

150

Miami was in full swing, as it was seven nights a week with all the bars, restaurants and nightclubs banging and full to the brim. Having had sex a short time earlier, she looked radiant in her little black, Vivian Westwood number, while Mark whispered in her ear, 'You look stunning, babe.'

Putting his hand on the small of her back, she smiled at him and her eyes glowed. Knoxx was rocking in a white on white, Versace ensemble, which was the dress code for South Beach. As he led her into the club, Nicky looked hot and Mark looked cool, Yin and Yang.

From where Mark ate and slept right now, the air was filled with a feeling of invincibility that was intoxicating and all-consuming. Regardless of what his inner voice was telling him: it's all over.

In the V.I.P. lounge, the clubbers looked down periodically at the huge dance floor below filled with dancers having a good time. Knoxx and his party had everything at their beck and call, sipping on the best champagne, wine and liquor, while the dancers on the dance floor looked up at them periodically throughout the night, looking envious.

Having noticed Mark on his own at the bar, Alisha saw her chance to begin peppering him with questions, trying to make sense of what had happened over the past two days. Knoxx answered her questions cryptically, knowing she probably knew. But he knew that Alisha knew what was best for her, which was keeping her thoughts to herself.

Alisha had been questioned a few days earlier about why Nicole had been crying so often. She had given him the answer he had been searching for. Even though it was something he hadn't wanted to hear, he had rewarded her with a Porsche Cayman for telling him the brutal truth. She knew what she had told him and how he had taken it. He had told her what he wanted to do them to get revenge once she had told him what she knew, and it had been playing on her mind ever since. But she knew not to push it. She knew how he handled his business.

After having a disjointed conversation with him, she reassured Mark in an intimate way, saying, 'You know I love you, right? Whatever happens, no matter what, I'm here for you, okay? If you need to talk to someone, make sure it's to me. Just be careful, honey, please.'

'Hi babbyy,' Nicole said, handing him a chilled glass of Perrier-Jouet champagne. She planted a wet kiss on his lips that tasted crisp and sweet. As she wrapped her long, taught arm around him and got settled on his lap, she said, coyly,

'How've you been, baby? Have you missed me?'

He replied, 'Baby, I've been missing you my whole life.'

'Aahh ...' Nicky answered. They laughed and then they kissed, playfully nuzzling. Afterwards, she said, 'I love you, Mark.'

Nicky could only wipe away a falling tear while she hovered on his lap like a child. She nodded aggressively, choosing not to open her mouth for fear of saying the wrong thing. Mark then joked, saying, 'You know what? I'm gonna take you home and fuck you like a porn star, babe, and then tomorrow, we're gonna go shopping and live life like a rock star!'

That brought Nicky back to a fit of tear-filled giggles. While she dabbed at her eyes to dry them, she answered, 'Hmm, yes please, I like the sound of that.'

Mark then said softly, 'I'll be right back, honey. I need to use the phone in the office.'

Knoxx waved over at his bodyguard, Quincy Taylor, and when he got over to him, Mark spoke in his ear. Quincy then stood tall and barked at the crowd nearest them, 'Make a hole, people.'

Looking at his watch, checking the time zone difference, Mark knew he had made his mind up. It was time to put his final play in the game or risk losing everything. To not take a risk is the biggest risk of all. He sat at the desk and looked at the phone before picking it up, calculating how it would play out. Nicky's words hung in his mind, knowing how she meant it. 'Don't be too long, baby.' She was hungry for him. That had spurred him on. He was a lion when it came to protecting her, but it's the lioness that gets to choose which lion it wants to mate with and she had chosen him. To succeed, one has to be willing to fail. He had defended Nicole. Now he had to defend himself. Alone with his decision, he would be the only person to know what he was about to do. He knew he had to make the call. He knew the one person back in Los Angeles who would give him what he needed: inside information.

151

'I say again, coach. Eighteen seconds until the receiver is out of the pocket. Does the quarterback take the shot?'

Four blocks east of Barney's Beanery, approximately seven hundred yards away, they had been waiting for this moment for over two hours. The black-cladded sniper was locked on target and tracking his quarry with every step through his night vision scope. His spotter barely made any audible sounds as he spoke in his throat-mike over the secure satellite communications link back to his commanding officer. All they needed to hear were three words. The sniper soon heard them in his earpiece: 'Take the shot.'

The sniper exhaled slowly, moving his scope in step with his target. The Russian-engineered VAL silenced sniper rifle was locked back hard into his shoulder. He slowly squeezed the trigger. He felt the hard kick from the rifle-stock-butt as it released its nine millimeter subsonic heavy bullet, capable of defeating standard body armor. The concussion from the rifle recoiled hard while he kept his aim.

The thud of the bullet was not heard above the laughter and singing until Teresa Hadley cried out in mock horror. She had fallen forward, having miss-stepped in time with Richie and Caron who were singing, *I will Survive*. She had pulled Richie's head forward and down with her as he tried to counter her weight from falling to the ground. Teresa felt a searing heat brush past the back of her neck and simultaneously heard an impact thud. Just as quickly, she was on the ground. Only, for some reason, she had now turned from a mock cry of happiness to a cry of fear. She didn't know why, but she just felt dread and death.

The three of them tumbled to the floor, with Teresa falling first, followed by Richie falling on top of her and then Caron, who had her arm entwined with Richie, being dragged down to the ground by his dead weight.

*   *   *

The sniper unchambered the first spent round from the bolt-action rifle, calmly taking it and placing it in his coverall webbing. He then chambered another round while he and his partner waited and watched for confirmation. The spotter, looking through his binoculars, calmly spoke in his throat-mike, telling him, 'Hit it again.'

They had nothing but time as the sniper took aim, focused, exhaled and fired.

*   *   *

Screams rang-out. Teresa realized she was covered in blood, and God knows what else hanging off her hair and parts of her face. Sheer terror now took over as she realized that, under Richie's dead weight, she could not move. Caron also realized that something was very wrong. She screamed in sheer terror while Teresa wriggled under Richie's body lying across her. She instantly heard and felt the zing of a bullet. Its heat burned her right eye as it zipped by her head, ricocheting up off the concrete from where her head had been just milliseconds earlier. Caron slumped silently to the floor, as the plate-glass window behind her on the Niketown storefront shattered into a million pieces.

There was a fraction of a second when the whole world seemed as if it was at peace. Dan McGann, standing with Maxine Dobro, shouted in horror, once he realized that what he was seeing was not a movie, but was really happening. Running towards them, he was quickly accompanied by the loud screech of tires, as Adwell's Ford Expedition pulled up at the curb. Dan shouted repeatedly as loud as he could, 'Richie! Richie! No, Richie!'

*   *   *

'I don't have a shot. The vehicle's blocking my line of sight,' the sniper calmly said through his throat-mike.

'We're gone,' his spotter answered. The two of them reversed their route, moving low and fast off to the north side of the building. They repelled down the building's wall, yanking on the Kamikaze knot, causing the rope to fall back down to them. They got into a waiting black GMC Suburban that then sped off into the night.

152

Dan, Mike and Maxine were at the scene in a panic, not knowing who was hurt or how bad, but they could all tell who was dead. Dan crouched down to get a hold of Richie, to lift him up and hold him in his arms. Ray Tombs and David Blisset came running down to the scene, pulling up on their heels. They both quickly realized that what they were seeing had actually happened. Richie was dead. Mike Adwell was already shouting in his police radio, yelling, 'Officers down, officers down, we need assistance right away. Hell, we need everybody!'

Tombs and Blisset secured the area while Mike attended to Caron. The second bullet had been a through-and-through. It had ricocheted off the tarmac and ripped through her just below her shoulder blade. Dan had yanked Teresa up to her feet. He needed to know that she was okay, and because he needed to get a better look at Richie. He still had a small beacon of hope that he was alive, but it was soon extinguished when he did get that look at Richie.

He was now sat on the ground with Richie's body in his grip. He held him with his head cradled in his lap. It was as if Dan wasn't there with all the police and emergency services' lights now surrounding them. The perimeter was set up, but most of the officers were just standing around in shock.

Dan didn't notice any of them. It was just him and Richie, hanging out. Dan spoke to him as if he was in a trance, 'Come on, Pikey, you've had your fun. Come on, bud, get up now and let's get going. You're gonna be late home and you know how pissed Jo's been lately.'

Dan laid his hand on Richie's head. It gave him a shock of realization, as Richie's head was all matted and wet. He looked down at Richie again, not seeing through his own eyes that Richie only had half-a-head. His skull had been torn in two from the bullet's direct velocity head-shot.

The professionals got on with the job of attending to the victims and taking statements. They then got around to parting Richie from Dan. Teresa managed to compose herself, through crying eyes to speak with Dan quietly, gaining his trust and reasoning with him. They would go with Richie in the ambulance to Cedars, she told him, which was only a few blocks from Santa Monica Boulevard. Finally, amid a number of shocked and stunned officers, some wiping away their tears, Dan relented and let go of his partner, his best friend, his brother.

153

At Cedars, uniformed officers stayed in and around the hospital. Dan stood with Ray and Dave, Roy Bowen and Richard Groome, who took over as a protective detail, protecting one of their own. Officers Jay Colter and Alistair Elwins, not wanting to leave their brother, both good friends of Dan and Richie's, stayed close to their buddy. Everyone was in shock, no one knowing what to do or say. Elwins and Colter allowed themselves a tear, both hugging Dan periodically. Ray and Dave told Dan that whatever he needed them to do to get the guys who did this, he only had to say the word and they were with him. After some time, word filtered out that after a lengthy operation Caron was going to pull through. A round of hugs and backslapping went around the tight hall where all the officers were standing. Dan managed to release a tight smile, but his face told a different story. He wanted to hear that news about Richie, which of course he knew, by now, would never happen.

The media was camped outside. The news reporters were set up out front; it was lights, camera, action. In Hollywood, the show must go on. Captain Wyatt now stood out front, holding a press conference, announcing that an officer had died at the scene. The name of the deceased police officer would be released after the family had been notified. He went onto say that another police officer was recovering from her wounds.

The hospital became police headquarters for a time, and within the eye of the storm, stood a figure out of sorts. Maxine Dobro knew most of the shortcuts along the corridors of the hospital. She sat quietly off to the side, holding a lukewarm cup of coffee for comfort while she watched everyone around her fall apart, just as she had in the very same hospital a few weeks earlier. Maxine appeared to be in a daze herself and couldn't bring herself to look any of the officers in the eye. They all stood about her asking the one question that the city of Los Angeles would soon be asking when it woke up to the news.

'Why? Why Richie?'

The power-assisted doors opened and out came Teresa Hadley. She was ashen in the face with exhaustion and still in some shock. All the officers looked at her with pride and warmth, even though most of them did not know her personally. They all felt for her and were proud of the fact that she had survived. They all needed something from this. She immediately picked out Dan in the crowd and ran over to him. Falling into his arms, she released a cry of relief at finding someone she could lean on. Dan held her tight; both of them still had Richie's blood on them. They shared his pain at losing Richie, and her relief in being a survivor. Dan looked down at Teresa and she looked up at him, and they kissed.

Maxine cried inside while she watched them. She was terrified at the thought that she would be next, standing in the hallway with her family while they held each other, coming to terms with losing Dolly. She kept hearing the same round of questions, noticing that the police officers were becoming more agitated because no one had any answers. Except Maxine Dobro did. She sat in her chair, quietly drinking her coffee, fighting the urge to sneak up to the ninth floor to catch a quick glimpse of Dolly.

She began to realize a few things while she reflected on the man, Mark Knoxx. He had been one step ahead of them throughout her investigation. He was a ruthless killer; she had come to know that about him. She was in possession of everything she needed to bring him down, because he had given it to her himself: The Enterprise, Exile and HEAVEN. But so was Teresa Hadley. What if Richie wasn't the target? Maxine had come to the conclusion that the bullet wasn't meant for Richie. It was meant for Teresa. Maxine knew that she had told them everything, when she had reported her findings to Christie. Knoxx had warned her about him in his letter to her, and he had told her on the phone earlier that night, that The Enterprise is everywhere and they have eyes everywhere. It soon dawned on Maxine that if they wanted to kill Teresa, then they must also want to kill her.

154

After some prodding from Teresa, who seemed to be stuck to Dan like glue, he finally left Cedars and went home, being driven home by Colter and Elwins. All of them were now brothers in arms, torn by grief. It was becoming the dawn of a new day, alone for Dan, as he went about getting ready for his new life without his bud, Richie. He looked at his phone, half-expecting it to ring with the news that it had all been a mistake. Only his phone did not ring. After showering in the hottest shower that he had ever taken in his life, Dan put on a new shirt and some jeans, while Jay and Alistair waited outside in the police car. Dan stole a look at a photograph sitting on the side table of Richie, Jo and Elenoor, with him before leaving the apartment to go break the news to Jo.

As they pulled up outside Richie and Jo's house, Dan looked at Elenoor's bike lying on the grass on the front lawn. He thought about how much of a family home it seemed and how lived in it looked. Dan had a great family too, but Rich, Jo and Elenoor were as close to a family of his own as he would probably ever get.

Jay and Alistair said they'd come in with him if he needed them to. Dan didn't answer them while he opened the rear door and put one foot in front of the other, to begin the longest, hardest walk of his life. He rang the doorbell, feeling as cold as ice, thinking he could get through it, but once Jo opened the door, he melted, and they both lost it, just by looking at each other. Jo realized, seeing Dan standing on the porch without a warm smile, told her everything she needed to know, even though he hadn't said a word. Jo knew her new day had begun, and she too would be spending it alone. It was a new day that would last the rest of her life, and she would have to live it, alone.

Dan deftly stepped over the family home's threshold into a lost world. They hugged while they cried on each other. Later, they laughed a little at some of the memories they shared, and then they just drank some coffee in their own peaceful way. Jay and Alistair sat outside the home all day. For Dan and Jo, the day felt like it hadn't even begun. It was a day they would never forget for as long as they lived. Dan stayed with Jo, to wait for Elenoor to come home from school so they could both be there for her. They both needed, in their own way, to explain it to her. Dan loved Elenoor as if she were his own daughter. While they were breaking the news to her, they all cried. Later, they ate a little, and then they just talked, reassuring her that everything would be okay. Eventually, Jo was able to put Elenoor to bed and get her to go to sleep.

After Elenoor had fallen asleep, the final nail was driven into Dan's heart. Jo revealed to Dan that they were preparing to invite him over to dinner later that week because they had something they needed to tell him. Jo managed to keep her head held high and her voice strong. She revealed that Richie had been diagnosed with cancer. He had been given six months to live. Dan quietly cried, pulling on his tears, while Jo went on to say that Richie had wanted to spend as much time with him as possible while he could still function, but it had been weighing on his mind that he hadn't told him. The doctors were insisting that he begin the chemotherapy, but Richie wanted just one more week doing the job he loved with his best friend that he loved.

Dan tried to comprehend what Richie must have been feeling, what he must have been going through, having to deal with the disease that was eating away at him. Dan had been annoyed at his behavior and his mood swings, and all the while, Richie had been carrying the cancer inside him, coming to terms with how he was going to tell his best friend that he was dying. Dan felt his rage welling up inside. He hadn't told Richie that he loved him. Richie had been on his way to dying, but now he had been murdered, taken from everyone who loved him. Dan became filled with revenge as it all began to sink in.

Richie did not have too long left to say his goodbyes to all those who loved him, and now he was out of time. He had been taken from them, and now they were the ones left behind with too much left to say. Dan's mood changed. He had been filled with grief, but now he was a man resolved to feeling hate, anger, and wanting revenge. With his eyes darkened, Dan said ominously, 'Jo, whoever did this, I'm gonna kill 'em.'

155

Having been driven home, Dan found that he couldn't just sit around, not having anything to do, so he did the only thing he knew to do. Police work. He drove back to Cedars to check on Caron, who had made a good recovery since last night. Dan sat with her, letting her talk about her life and how she was doing. Both of them wanted to talk about nothing in particular, and especially not about Richie. Caron had come too close to dying herself to want to talk about the night before. Both of them now carried the imprint of the last moment of his life in their heads forever. Caron had said that, regardless of this being something that comes with the job, she'd been given a wakeup call to the dangers of it, one time at the missile explosion in Venice beach, and now this. She asked Dan, 'I guess the club bangers 'll get a pass tonight then?' referring to Joey Casa and Nick Zacarro, who had been on their hit list to take down later that night, before Richie had caught it.

Dan replied, subdued, 'For now, but they'll get what's coming to them. Like those bastards who did this,' rising in his chair, his voice rising in anger.

Caron cut him off, saying in a tired voice, 'Go home, Dan. Get some rest. I need to sleep. Tomorrow will be here soon enough.'

Dan leaned over the bed and gave her a hard, tight hug accompanied by a soft kiss on her head, and told her to sleep well. He closed the door to her room. With nowhere in particular to go, he walked down the hall, he thought, *why not?* He walked to the bank of elevators and pressed the elevator button. He rode it up to the eighth floor, to check in on the redhead that had been found brutally beaten up at Sunset Ranch. He walked up to the uniformed officer sitting next to the door. The cop offered his condolences and asked that Dan pass his respects on to Richie's family. Dan nodded but felt compelled to keep on going, asking, 'Anyone been in to see her?'

'No, her family's still on their way over from Pecos, Texas. The doctor's in with her now. They're trying something new, to try and bring her around, I think.'

Dan pushed on the door and stepped in the room. As he entered it, he opened up his jacket to show the doctor his detective's gold shield on his belt, inquiring, 'How's she doing?'

'Well, we'll know soon enough,' he replied, as he held out the redhead's arm to place a small cell phone-looking device on her wrist. He already felt the question coming and said in anticipation, 'It's a HEAVEN Navigator. We're one of the hospitals trialing it.'

Dan stood in awe. Talk about being dumbstruck. He didn't know what to say, thinking it felt like Mark Knoxx was everywhere.

The doctor said, 'There. We'll see what HEAVEN can do for her now.' He disengaged the Navigator from the girl's wrist, continuing his summarization, while he looked as if he was readying himself to leave. He remarked, 'Funny thing. We have another girl upstairs with similar vitals; both of them have the same toxins in their body.'

'Yeah?' Dan answered. It hadn't sunk in fully, still too dazed by the last seventeen hours or so.

The doctor's clear blue eyes seemed unfazed by Dan's vague response, saying, 'Yeah, this one has the same compound of drugs in her body as all of the other victims that I'm aware of with your case, but the girl upstairs has all of them except one. She probably had the same dealer. She OD'ed at NVS nightclub a couple of weeks ago. Still in a coma, too.'

Dan squared up and clenched down on his jaw. His eyes were now fully focused on the doctor. He told him in an agitated tone, 'Say all that again.'

'What?' the doctor answered, at a loss to what he had said.

'Say it again. What you just said, only this time, slow it down.' Dan asked, 'Go through it with me, step by step.'

The doctor had to stop in his tracks because Dan had taken on a menacing look and was now blocking the door. The two of them spent the next ten minutes getting it straight. And it was as straight as a bullet, and it all made sense to Dan. He instructed the doctor to take him upstairs. Dan entered the private hospital room on the ninth floor to see a girl who was maybe twenty-two, lying in much the same room as the girl downstairs. Only this girl had a full, thick head of long, black hair with features that instantly reminded Dan of someone. He unclipped the chart from the foot of the bed and aggressively flipped the pages looking for it.

The doctor, now wondering what was happening, asked in a disturbed manner, 'Is everything's okay?'

Dan did not hear him. He was too busy searching, until his tired eyes found what he was looking for on the second page of the hospital chart.

He quickly found what he was looking for:

Cedars-Sinai Medical Center
8700 Beverly Blvd. Los Angeles, CA 90048

Ref: Code – 012-10-1967 Room B-19

HEAVEN	trial patient: # 19-11-65
Patient:	Danielle Allsop
Father:	Gary Allsop
Mother:	Maxine Dobro

156

Hearing the incessant pounding at the door frightened her. It could only be bad news waking her up. She had only just fallen asleep, not that she really slept that much at the moment. She got up as quickly as she could, while the pounding on the door got faster and harder. She quickly pulled on her Juicy Couture tracksuit. Maxine took one brief glance through the spy-hole in the door to see Dan McGann. She shouted his name to make sure it was him. He answered her, 'Yeah.'

As soon as she'd begun to open the door, he was in, and had set upon her. A thunderous right hook knocked her down to the floor, followed up by a severe kick that sent her rolling back even farther into the room. Dan squeezed her up against the wall next to a table. Ripping the phone from the wall, he yanked out the phone cord from the phone and began to wrap it around her throat and hands. He quickly pulled it tight, while she fought for her first, and possibly, last breath. She tried to kick out but Dan gave her no such chance to counter-attack. He pulled his gun from its holster and rammed it into Maxine's mouth. He had her pinned tight against the frame of the table with her neck taught from the phone cord with his weapon jammed into her throat; both wondering what was going to happen next. Maxine had tears rolling hard and fast down both her cheeks and daren't even attempt to move or speak.

Dan steadied his breathing and then moved his head down to meet hers, staring at her squarely in her face as he pulled back hard on the slide of his weapon to chamber a round. He growled like a lion and said in an ominous, deep voice, 'I told my best friend's wife, just a few fucking hours ago, that I was going to kill the person responsible for killing her husband. And that's what I'm going to do.' Maxine tried to whimper some words, but Dan gripped her throat, shutting it tight. 'You twisted bitch, you set this up! You're in this with Knoxx, that Mark fucking Knoxx guy. He got to you, didn't he?'

Maxine's eyes widened, thinking her death was imminent and that her family would never get to know the truth.

Dan scowled in her face. 'I've seen your daughter, Dolly. I know she's in a coma. That's how he got to you and turned you against us, isn't it!'

Maxine felt the pistol bite inside her mouth as she tried in vain to speak. Dan watched her face, searching her eyes, seemingly still undecided about how he was going to kill her. Strangle her or put a bullet through her head.

'Why the fuck did he murder my partner? What's Richie got to do with this?' He asked.

With all the force Maxine had left, because she wanted to live, and she wanted to tell the truth - she knew she wanted to get to the truth herself - she managed to mutter a strong, 'Hemmaann.' She mouthed the long word that sounded all too familiar. She sounded it out more clearly the second time, saying, 'HEAVEN.' Her eyes then indicated that there was something he needed to see, nodding in the direction of the bed. As Dan pulled the gun from her mouth, she managed to mutter through the phone cord, 'I need to be untied.'

Dan pulled her up by her neck. His strong grip tightening around it, he growled, 'Try anything cute and I'll off you, got it! I'll bury you here.'

He jabbed her head back hard against the wall, and then released his grip to begin unwinding the phone cord. Once released, Maxine fell off to one side, gasping for air. She began breathing in the crisp, clean air while she sobbed, feeling every inch of her body had been beaten up. Dan stood over her, not giving her an inch of ground, not the slightest bit concerned for her status in the F.B.I. or for her wellbeing. He was a trained killer, and his only concern was who was going to get killed real quick and in what order, with Dobro being at the top of that list. Maxine coughed out, asking, 'Can I have some water?'

'No. What do I need to see?' Dan replied bluntly.

Maxine waved up towards her briefcase on the bed, as if motioning for Dan to get it. He did, never taking his gun off Maxine's head. He pulled it nearer to him and opened it. Shaking out its contents, all the papers fell out on the bed. A manila folder with sheets of paper fell out from it, while Dan's eyes fell upon some names he recognized. He sat on the edge of the bed, while seconds ticked by, with his gaze becoming more focused as his thoughts now turned from Maxine to the names on the pages. The letterhead on different pages read: Exile Corporation, HEAVEN and The Enterprise.

'What's all this shit?' Dan asked, not worrying about Maxine having to gasp for breath while he thumbed through the pages, studying each one.

Maxine replied eagerly, 'It's what this is all about. It's why Richie was killed; only they never meant to kill him.'

'Who's they and who were they after, then?' Dan barked. He raised his gun to her face, fearing some line of bullshit from Maxine, thinking she'd say anything to try and save herself.

'They were after Teresa and I think they'll be coming after me next,' she answered.

McGann sat for a moment, thinking. He lowered the gun

eventually. He'd had the same thought the night before. From his own sniper training, the drills were, one shot, one kill. Dan had quietly figured out that the sniper had probably missed his target on the first shot, which was why there had been a second one, the one that had tagged Caron.

'Why would Knoxx go after Teresa?' Dan asked disingenuously. He flicked through the papers, while continuing his interrogation.

Maxine sat up and leaned against the table. Running her fingers through her hair, she touched her face to make sure it was still there, answering fiercely, 'It's not Knoxx, that's what I'm trying to tell you,' getting her bearings back, she found her voice, explaining, 'He's not the one who did this. He warned me in advance. He told me to block the files on Wright, so that if anyone came looking for him, I'd be notified, and I was, when he turned up dead.'

'And you think it was this group of people?' Dan asked.

'I didn't at first, especially since he has Dolly, but then, after tonight, I'm beginning to believe him. I think we're uncovering a huge conspiracy, something that we can all be killed for.'

'Maxine, you've been had. Knoxx got to you and used you; he's used your daughter against you. You're too emotionally attached and that's how he's using you. You know Bezerk wasn't killed by any of the people listed in here. Richie and I were told in the lobby of NVS by Olivia Marbela, that the rumor around the club was that Knoxx's girlfriend slept with Bezerk. That's why Bezerk ended up dead, good old-fashioned jealousy and envy. Knoxx took out Bezerk for fucking his girl, nothing more. You know how it works. There's thousands of guys doing hard time over the same thing. You've been had. You wanted what he'd told you to be the truth, that's all.'

Maxine looked up at Dan, not wanting it to be the truth. Her mind thought back to all those years ago, when she had said those same words to Patrick Connelly. She then countered by telling Dan, 'But he warned me about them. I looked into it. He told me John D'intino didn't die from a heart attack in bed. He told me he'd shot him as revenge for them murdering his friend, Senator Spitzer. I had Teresa follow up on the lead to confirm it. She was given the run around, ending up at the Counter Terrorism Center, where they said it was a matter of national security that his medical records couldn't be released. Doesn't that sound odd to you?'

Dan answered her clearly and objectively by explaining, 'They said in the news that D'intino was on the Foreign Affairs Intelligence Board. So that could be why, I guess. You wanted it to be true, Maxine, for your girl, and you still do, don't you?'

Maxine laid her head in her hands. It was all coming back around to her, the same words and the same sting. She realized Knoxx had played her. 'Yeah, it does make sense, the way you're saying it. But then, you have your reasons for wanting it to be Knoxx too, don't you?'

They both knew what those reasons were. Dan needed someone to blame so he could kill them. Dan quickly rebuked her claim, saying, 'I'm gonna make damn sure it's the right guy, or woman, first. Listen Maxine, I know you're good at what you do, and I'm sure you never meant to get yourself in as deep as you are right now. Shiitt, maybe if I had a kid of my own, I don't know what I'd do, or how far I'd go to save my kid. I guess I'd have done the same thing.' Dan laid the gun on the bed, and put his elbows on his knees, to lean in towards Maxine and in a matter-of-fact way. He said, 'You're in this shit way too deep. If this comes out, then you're going to go to prison for a long time, so you better start paddling up shit-creek with me. When I was in the military, we used what we called soft propaganda, which was used to win the hearts and minds of our enemies' citizens. Counter-propaganda also played on the fear of the larger, more fearsome enemy. That way, what the people were looking at by having us around didn't seem all that bad. Does that sound familiar?'

Maxine could only look at Dan. Nodding in agreement, she thought about it all, and all that he'd said. She replied with a simple, 'Oh God.'

'Now tell me everything, so we can get this son of a bitch before it all comes out, because I promise you, I am going to kill him.'

Maxine began to get up from the floor, wiping away her last tear while she resolved herself to the fact that Dan was right. She had been used by Knoxx to do his dirty work, in a dirty war, that was being played out on a higher level, what the military called 'a fog war'. She poured herself a glass of water and then plunked herself down in a chair. She leaned her head against the wall, exhausted. She was tired of all the spy stuff, tired of having to figure it all out, and tired of crying for Dolly. Life seemed so much easier investigating the street gangs.

'Let's start from the top, then maybe we can both work this thing out,' Dan said with vigour.

Dan got up off the bed to put a fresh pot of coffee on while Maxine gathered herself, trying to put it all in order. She told Dan that she'd been given an envelope that had the names of people who were part of an international conspiracy to manipulate and control various countries. She went on to tell him that the charts that were shown at police headquarters, the network for The Enterprise and HEAVEN were given to her by Knoxx. She asked him, sounding as if she was defending Knoxx. 'Why would he do that?'

Dan answered, ignoring her question, 'Go on, what next?'

'I was given a profile that I was to input into the F.B.I. and L.A.P.D. database for someone called Kerry Greener, who had an apartment on Fourteenth Street in Santa Monica. Then I had a call from Knoxx telling me to block Wright's files because he thought The Firm might come after him, and he needed to protect him from them.'

Dan poured out two cups of coffee while he listened in detail. Maxine lowered her voice as if ashamed of herself. She quietly said, 'Then he called me yesterday afternoon, when I was in Wyatt's office, when I noticed you guys and Teresa looking at me. What have I done?'

She held her hand over her mouth as if to stifle an oncoming vomit. Dan was quick to ask, while he moved in closer to her, placing the cup of coffee down on the table, 'What? What is it?'

Maxine looked up at him with fear and shame in her eyes at what she knew she had to tell him. 'He told me I needed to get him his guest list. If you found it in your investigation, I was to get it. He told me I should suggest we all go out for drinks, that it would be a good idea for me to try to bond with you and get you to give it up to me.'

She managed to choke out the last words, but just as quick, that's what she felt, the choking sensation of Dan's hand wrapped around her neck. 'I told you it was him! You helped him, you fucking bitch! You and Knoxx, you both killed my buddy. And if it hadn't been Richie, you'd be happy enough for it to have been Teresa, if that's what it took to get your girl back, isn't that right? Isn't that the real truth?'

Dan banged Maxine's head against the wall. He released her from his grip, and then stepped back over to the bed to pick up his gun. He raised it up to her face, standing four feet from her with his feet apart in the classic stance of an assassin.

'Where's Knoxx now?'

'I don't know,' she replied aggressively, shaking her head in fear.

'Where's the guest list and what does he want with it?'

She shook her head again, beginning to break down, thinking this was to be her end.

'I don't know,' she answered, shaking with fear.

'Are you able to contact him?'

Maxine knew this would be the end of her if she answered truthfully.

'He's calling me later today. I have to have the guest list. He wants me to deliver it to him and then he'll release Dolly from her coma,' Maxine answered, having to think fast. She still had game, even under the most intense pressure. She needed to get to the bottom of this too, and she was determined to see Mark Knoxx in the ground.

Dan said hard and fast in a dismissive voice, 'What's all this bullshit about a guest list? That's all I hear about, this mysterious guest list. Olivia Marbela said Bezerk was always talking about it, only she'd never seen it.'

Dan lowered his pistol again. Maxine could tell he was thinking about something. It was there. They were on it, right over it; Dan felt it, standing in no man's land, working it all out in his head. Maxine sat still, quietly watching him. Dan then pondered on his thought by saying, 'So Knoxx knows something about intelligence warfare. He knows how to manipulate things to get control, so he can win complete obedience. That's how he got you to do his work for him. And Bezerk, what was he paid over two million dollars a year to do? Manage the guest list, or protect it? This guest list must be something, don't you think?'

He seemed to be speaking more to himself than Maxine. She remained quiet and subdued, not wanting to bring his rage back, giving him time to work things out.

Dan sat back down on the bed. He sipped on his cup of coffee, before deciding to share some information with Maxine. He offered up some of his knowledge, telling her, 'You know, I'm not just some run-of-the-mill detective. I used to be in the military before I became one of L.A.'s finest. I was in the Special Forces. I did some checking up on Knoxx, and what I found out sounded familiar. I think Knoxx comes from a military background too. From what I've been hearing, he served in the marines and was in the Falkland Islands war back in the early eighties. Then he fell off the radar, which is pretty revealing in itself.' Dan's voice lowered in its tone, as if he was talking to himself, working it out in his head. 'His military records and tax returns show that he lived in a town called Hereford in England.'

Maxine offered up her first interaction, innocently questioning, 'What's so important about that?'

Dan stared back at her, as if he was thinking about it, then thoughtfully replied, 'Hereford's where the S.A.S. is stationed, the Special Air Services, the British version of our Navy SEAL's. And if he did serve in the S.A.S., then he is something special because he's been playing us all the whole time. He's probably been playing both sides too. From here on out, we'd better be real careful how we go about bringing him down. Otherwise, we'll be the ones getting taken out. Knoxx obviously has some kind of death wish or he just wants to take as many people down with him before someone gets to him, and that makes him very dangerous to everyone around him. I wouldn't be surprised to see a psychological profile on him saying that he has some kind of personality disorder. One minute, the guy's hailed as a friggin' genius, yet underneath that smooth exterior, he's a mad man. And that makes him unpredictable, and that makes him dangerous. The guy's I.Q.'s probably off the chart, so don't try to outsmart him. Otherwise, if you try to go head-to-head with him, you'll think I'm a boy scout compared to him, you hear me?'

Dan used his intimidating look to make sure he'd got his point across. They both contemplated their next move, thinking about it all. Dan sat eyeing Maxine, as if the answer was somewhere in her face. Drinking his last sip of coffee, it came to him. Simple, yet genius, and at the same time, madness. He would've laughed if it weren't so sick. It made him sick to his stomach. The ending was the beginning. Both he and Richie had been looking at it right at the beginning, the one thing that was probably the cause of so many murders.

Dan looked at Maxine with clean eyes, crystal in his vision for what he had to do next. With his gun now back in his hand, he looked at her for a moment, thinking. Then Dan solidly said, 'I need to know that you're with me. If I get you this guest list, you have to understand that we're going to use it as bait. I'll get your daughter back alive and well, Maxine, but then I'm going to kill Knoxx. Just so we're clear.'

'That's all I want. That's all I've ever wanted, just give me back my daughter. If The Enterprise find out, what if they know that's what we're up to? He said they know everything. They're watching all the time.'

'Maxine, get a grip. It's all bullshit! It's just one man. And we're going to stop him.'

'Alright, tell me what I have to do. Promise me you'll do all that you can to save Dolly first. I can't do anything that'll jeopardize her life,' Maxine pleaded.

'But you were okay with jeopardizing the lives of Teresa, Caron and Richie though, huh?' Dan gave Maxine a look that said she was on board with this, one way or another.

'Okay, what do I have to do?' she replied.

'Tell him when he calls you that you have the guest list, and that you'll bring it to him. Ask him where and when he wants to meet you.'

'But I don't have the guest list,' Maxine responded.

'You will, because I'm going to go get it.'

'What do you mean? Where is it?' she questioned.

'The guest list's been hiding out in the open the whole time. It's looking back at everyone in the NVS office. It's hidden in all the drawings that Bezerk drew,' Dan replied.

Maxine envisioned it all, the nightmare unfolding before her, coming into view. As Dan flew out of the hotel room,

434

she flew into a panic. She didn't know how to contact Knoxx, and now, if Dan had really gotten a hold of the guest list, if he was right, then that meant that she could escape from this nightmare and be back with Dolly, safe and sound, in a matter of hours. She had to think. How could she get a hold of Knoxx? Mark Knoxx. Was it all really a lie? Was his whole life a lie? How could she have been so stupid? Had he really caught her in a moment of weakness and manipulated her to the point where she believed it all? Maxine sat on the bed and looked at one of the pages that she had been given by the girl, who she remembered was Jane Mears, Knoxx's best friend. Maxine pulled the sheet of paper around to the right side up to begin reading it again. As she did, she felt it had to be real. It all made sense. Why would Knoxx expose it all, incriminating himself along the way? She unfolded the page that she had folded over into thirds. The letter read:

The Enterprise. It is also known by other names. The Firm, being their chosen name but we know them as Illuminati, translated from Latin, it means, 'The Enlightened Ones.' Only they have chosen The Dark Light. The United States is part of the old heritage of Illuminati, dating back to its inception. Illuminati are as old as the Vatican itself.

The United State's one dollar bill proves their existence, designed by the Freemasons in 1782 by Charles Thomson, the Founding Father chosen by Continental Congress to come up with the final design for the Great Seal of the United States. The dollar bill carries an unfinished pyramid. In the zenith is an Eye in a triangle, surrounded with a glory proper. Over the Eye, above the pyramid, are the Latin words 'Annuit Coeptis' meaning 'Announcing the Birth Of'. On the base of the pyramid are the numerical letters MDCCLXXVI, and underneath, the following motto 'Novus Ordo Seclorum' translates into 'A New World Order.' Together, this means, 'Announcing the Birth of the New World Order.' The date, in Roman Numerals, is 1776; the year the modern Illuminati was born, the year of American Independence. The Latin 'E Pluribus Unum' means, 'One out of many,' which is the foundation for the New World Order's plan to unify the world's governments, the first test being the European Union's Brussels Parliament. The second will be the monitoring and controlling of the monetary systems. The third will be religion. Make no mistake, they are among us. And they are watching.

Dan arrived at NVS on Sunset and Vine and made his way up to the office, after telling a member of staff why he was there. In the office, Dan took in the scene that was much the same as before, when he and Richie were in it. The office looked professional and, well, clean. Now he could tell there was something about it in the way it was set up. Bezerk had it going on all right. He could keep tabs on everyone from up here. Then, whatever he wanted to do, he couldn't be seen by anyone. Just as he and Richie had done only two days earlier, Dan stood and looked at them. Only this time, he really looked at them. *Damn it*, he thought, *why didn't I see it before?* Dan began to feel sad, but then quickly turned angry. Sad that he hadn't seen more in The Bezerk Murders earlier and angry that he hadn't. Then maybe Richie would still be alive. As if déjà-vu was haunting him, a voice caught him unawares again while he looked at the drawings. Only this time it was a man's voice.

Matthew Tamban entered the room, saying, 'They're pretty cool, aren't they?' He walked up to McGann with a cock-sure attitude, asking him, 'I hear you want to take these?'

'You heard right,' Dan replied, steeling himself, knowing this guy was bad, and that he was going to give him some trouble.

'You know, these pictures are the property of the Envious Group. If you want to remove them, then you'll need a warrant to do that,' Tamban quipped.

'Oh, I don't think that'll be necessary,' Dan answered, while he opened up his jacket to expose his gold shield that sat next to his gun. Tamban seemed unfazed by the posture and was just about to spew his next slick line of shit, when Dan squeezed his arm tight and pulled him to his face to tell him, 'I don't give a shit about warrants and I don't give a shit about procedures. Not anymore! I know who killed my partner and why. You can shove your stupid little pompous T.V. lawyer crap up your ass! Anyone getting in my way is getting dead. So yeah, I *am* taking the pictures. You think you can stop me? Make my fucking day, I dare you.'

Captain Wyatt looked out from his office to see Dan sitting at his desk, across from Richie's empty desk, which still had papers, case files and his coffee mug on it. Dan looked up from his desk and looked over at Wyatt, as if he sensed he was being watched. Wyatt waved for him to come into his office. With a heavy sigh, he got up and made his way in like a petulant child, hearing Wyatt say in a strong voice, 'Dan, close the door.'

Wyatt straightened up his desk, more as a way of getting himself prepared for dealing with the next issue, on top of having to do the paperwork involving the death of a police officer. He started bluntly, 'I got a call from a Matthew Tamban, saying you threatened to shoot him if he didn't let you take some pictures. What's the deal? You going to throw away your career over this?'

Dan sat square in the chair, just waiting it all out, thinking about his next move; how he going to kill Knoxx.

'Are you listening to me? We've all been hit hard by what happened to Richie. He was a good cop, a great cop, and a great guy. We're all going to miss him. You know, I've needed to talk to you anyway. It's procedure to have you take a leave of absence, and now this thing with Tamban; he's that Exile Corporation lawyer, right?'

Dan nodded in agreement, answering a morose, 'Yeah.'

'I'm going to need those pictures back, whatever they are. Tamban says he's willing to let the whole thing drop if you return them.' Wyatt already noticed the complexion in Dan's face. It told him that it wasn't going to happen. Pete Wyatt continued, trying to explain his thoughts in a softer tone, 'We all grieve in different ways. Just take some time off and let yourself grieve. It's only natural that you want to take it out on someone, but Tamban's not the guy.'

'I know he's not,' Dan replied sullenly.

'I'm not going to get those drawings back, am I?'

Wyatt had ordered Dan to give the drawings back, but then, after not getting the response he was looking for, he told him to take a leave of absence. Since Dan had disobeyed both commands, Wyatt ordered him to hand in his badge and his gun, placing him on administrative leave for the next two weeks, pending an investigation. That suited Dan just fine. He thumped down his gold shield and his weapon on Wyatt's desk. He had plenty of guns at home, and as for his badge, he didn't need that for what he had planned. With Wyatt shouting after him as he left his office, he heard his last words, 'Just let it go.'

Dan slammed the door shut and walked up to Dave Blisset's desk. Leaning over him, he quietly but firmly told him, 'I need you and Ray to go over to The Sunset Marquis and keep an eye on Teresa Hadley and Maxine Dobro for me. Can you guys do that?'

Before anyone realized that Dan had just been relieved of his gun and badge, Richard Groome entered the squad room with a look of some trepidation on his face. Upon seeing Dan, he changed his original direction to walk over to him, saying excitedly, 'Hey Dan, you'll never guess what?'

He arrived at Dan's desk, not noticing that he was emptying it out.

Dan asked disingenuously, 'What?'

'Me and Roy, we took over the redhead case, you know, since ...' His voice trailed off.

'Yeah,' Dan replied with a vacant response, not paying attention to him.

'Well, it's a miracle! She was switched into that HEAVEN program and POW! Just like that, she begins to come around. After an hour or so, she's sitting up in bed drinking a Yahoo. We couldn't believe it.'

Not biting on it and not sharing the same enthusiasm, Dan looked perturbed. He seemed to become agitated, listening to Groomie while he kept his hands moving over his desk collecting up his things.

Groomie quickly realized that something wasn't right with him, and moved on by telling him, 'So we sit down with a sketch artist, and wouldn't you know it. It didn't take us too long to figure out who she was describing.'

Richard Groome slapped down the artist's drawing and the accompanying mug shot for one Christopher Lee Wright, a.k.a. Bezerk. Dan looked up at Groomie, who had the look of a young kid who had just found out that Christmas had come early this year. Dan picked up the artist's sketch and the mug shot, holding them in either hand. With surprise drawn over his face, he replied, 'Are you shitting me?'

'No shit, dude! She even had the THUG down for being tattooed on his chest. It's a small world, huh?'

'Yeah, too small, getting smaller every day,' Dan answered soberly, dropping the sketch and mug shot on the desk.

Nicole searched out some company while Mark was in the NVS office. She waved over at Alisha, motioning for her to join her.

'Hello honey, how are you?' Alisha greeted her happily, both of them kissing each other on the cheek.

Nicky was happy again. She had gotten her life back and she looked to be getting back together with Mark too. She felt free again. She was looking forward to making love like a porn star and living life like a rock star. Nicole said to Alisha, 'Here I am with a smoking hot boyfriend, and I have to keep an eye out for all the bitches trying to tempt him away from me.'

'A bitch is someone who looks like his last girlfriend,' Alisha jokingly replied.

Nicky fired back quick as a flash, laughing as she said, 'Yeah, God gave a guy a brain and a dick, but only enough blood to run one at a time!'

Both girls cracked up laughing and then continued chatting, joking and drinking. She finally felt at ease in herself, while Alisha felt uncomfortable in her presence.

Jane stood by the bar and as far away from any more potential drama. She was tired from the stress of the past few days and especially from the night before in Beverly Hills. Jane just felt dirty, knowing that she was involved in a dirty war, having played her part in murdering someone. Only this someone was due to become the President of the United States twenty-four hours from now. All Jane wanted was one night, free from it all. She stayed away from Mark after they'd spoken at the bar to enjoy having a quiet drink with Andy Matthews. She looked across the V.I.P. lounge periodically, to watch Nicky, and as always, to keep an eye on Alisha.

Knoxx dialed the phone number. It answered on the third ring. Maxine Dobro answered in a wavering voice. Knoxx had become accustomed to her being obedient. He had called her to give her new instructions, only to find out that she had some instructions of her own.

Wasting no time in taking the high ground, Maxine took the offensive, informing him, 'I have your guest list.' She felt emboldened, knowing that Teresa was sitting with her and that, together, they had worked out a plan to set the bait for Knoxx to bite on

She heard him answer casually, 'Really, so what do you want to do now?'

'I want to meet you face-to-face, so I'll know you've released my daughter from her coma. I want to be there when you make the call, or do what you have to do, to make it happen. If you don't want to meet me, then I guess I'll have to take my chances with Dolly. If she dies, then it will have been in God's hands and not yours, and then you'll never get your guest list.'

'Well, I guess we'll both be taking our chances, won't we? Come to Florida. Meet me at Coconut Grove tomorrow night at eleven o'clock. I'll call you at 10:30 to tell you where we'll be meeting, and Maxine, come alone. If you bring any of your friends with you and try to arrest me, I won't hesitate in killing your girl. I will kill her, believe that.'

Knoxx's voice took on a more sinister tone. Maxine held her breath and her tongue while she stood with the phone in her hand looking at Teresa.

'Yes, I understand,' she calmly replied.

She heard Knoxx say in a lighter tone, 'Now then, back to why I was calling you. I've been keeping up with the news. What's the status on Teresa Hadley? Is she okay? Is she still digging into the financial records I gave you?'

Maxine's eyes shot Teresa a look of sheer fright. Teresa looked back at her, not knowing that Knoxx had specifically asked about her. Maxine answered quickly and then asked, 'Yeah, she's fine, why?'

She thought back to what Dan had said. Was Knoxx the only man involved? Was it all smoke and mirrors? Why was he asking about Teresa? Was he fishing for inside information?

'When I heard about that detective getting shot in L.A. with all of you there, I figured it wasn't him they were after. It must have been your special agent Hadley they wanted.'

Maxine saw her opening to get some understanding and

jumped in with a question, asking, 'Why would they want her murdered? Why is she important in all of this?'

Knoxx answered in a humorous poetic prose, 'She probably knows the answers to the riddle, but she doesn't know that she knows them. I think, that they think, she already knows what they're up to.'

'What riddle? What are you talking about? I'm so lost in all of this.'

'God, Maxine,' Knoxx replied, mocking Dobro. 'Do I have to do everything? I'll explain it to you tomorrow night, if you behave yourself. Just let Teresa know that a few days ago when I was in Europe, I went and changed the slush fund accounts, the money's out in the open; the money that's used to pay all the senators and all the king's men. Tie it to the government's General Accounting Office. Tell her to look into a covert military operation, code named RED. See you tomorrow night.'

161

Maxine relayed what Knoxx had said to her to Dan on the phone. Dan then phoned Tombs and Blisset to confirm that they were guarding them. Dan had to make some phone calls of his own, setting up a meeting in Florida with some old friends from his Navy SEAL days. He'd been running on adrenaline for the past forty-eight hours and hadn't allowed himself to feel any grief; his only comfort was being consumed with revenge. He was running on a tight schedule now. No matter what his schedule was though, he had to find time for Jo and Elenoor, so Dan made his pilgrimage to see them. Here he was, back at Richie's house, confronted by the one thing that was driving him on, the look of pain in Jo's eyes. And from great pain, great beauty can be born, as Elenoor raced up to Dan for a big bear hug, standing in front of him at hip height. All of them tried as best they could to hold back their tears, hugging each other in the living room.

Standing off to one side was the family priest, there to prepare for Richie's funeral. It felt like only yesterday when he had presided over one of the happiest days of their lives, at Elenoor's christening. Now he was here to preside over the saddest day of Jo's life, the burial of her life and soul, Richie. Dan sat in a chair, listening to Priest Manuel Munoz. He had been in the middle of counseling Jo, and at forty-four years old, he felt her pain too, saying warmly, 'I found God when I was lucky enough to have survived a car crash twenty years ago. My grandmother always wanted me to become a priest, but I thought I knew better, and now, I do. Every day, I'm able to do the ordinary extraordinarily well, which is how your Richard lived his life, and should be celebrated for it. His calling in life was to serve and protect as a police officer. Now it's God's turn, and he will protect us all.'

Jo nodded in agreement, flashing a quick glance at Dan, who was looking somber.

Priest Munoz continued, 'Our path is often one chosen for us by others. God has a plan for each of us, whether we like his plan or not, but God is providence, where nothing is left to chance or circumstance.'

Dan lowered his head in thought, while the room was quiet for a minute.

Priest Munoz then turned to look at Dan. His black saucer eyes pierced him with his sincere look. Dressed in black with his white dog-collar, Munoz asked him honestly, 'And how are you coping, Daniel?'

Dan just merely looked back at him blankly. Checking Jo, he answered plainly, 'I'm coping, you know.'

Munoz, reading him well, ventured further, replying, 'Dan, revenge is sinful. An eye for an eye will make the whole world blind. I know you, and I know, in your heart you want revenge, but it's a sin.'

Knowing he had to be back in L.A. for Richie's funeral in four days, Dan knew he was running on a tight schedule. A schedule that had his own plan, not God's plan, in it, and he needed to leave to catch a flight to Miami with Teresa and Maxine, now.

Jo padded at her eyes. She did her best to stay focused while Priest Munoz continued speaking. 'There is cause for rejoicing here. You may, for a time, have to suffer the distress of many trials, but this is so that your faith, which is more precious than the splendor of fire-tried gold, may, by its genuineness, lead to praise, glory and honor, when Jesus Christ himself appears from Heaven.'

Priest Munoz rose to bless Jo and kiss her on her forehead. Dan, seeing his opening, also got up from his chair. Jo looked over at him, realizing that he was getting ready to leave. Dan edged her away from Priest Munoz, and spoke softly to her. Jo looked up at him in her own way, strong and sentient, her face holding on to every ounce of love she could muster.

'Jo, honey, you remember that promise I made you the other day?' Instantly welling up, Jo dabbed at her eyes with a handkerchief again. One little nod was all she could manage while Dan went on to say, 'Well, I have a chance to make good on it, but I have to go, now. I have to get it done my way or it might never get done, you know? I feel like justice is blind and there'll never be any justice for Richie. It's time to take the blindfold off. Are you okay with that?'

Jo fell into Dan's arms, doing her best to fight the fight inside her, the good, the bad and the ugly of it all. As tears fell from her soul, her voice trembling with fear, she said, 'Just make sure you come back, okay? Whatever you're going do, just come back to us.'

She and Dan looked over at Elenoor, quietly playing with her dolls on the floor. Dan replied with conviction, 'I'll do that, I promise.'

162

The Toyota Four Runner reversed into the garage, the red taillights indicating that it had come to a halt. Seconds later, the engine cut and the garage became silent. A hint of an opening in the driver's door allowed the interior light to come on while the driver picked up his things from the passenger seat. As he opened his door and stood out, his long, wiry frame and tight, short-cropped gray hair could be seen from the courtesy light inside the car, giving the assailant a perfect shot at him. Within seconds, the driver was on the floor, being choked-out silently from behind. The shorter, stockier man, crushed down on his windpipe, with his legs wrapped around him, holding on, waiting.

Adrian ransacked the house, finding files on Exile, Knoxx and HEAVEN. It seemed as if Kenshaw had been documenting and recording most of his meetings with Jane over the past four years. He had compiled quite a dossier on Mark. Romney cracked his fire-proof safe and pulled out all the papers from inside, briefly filing through them, he could see that some of them had the contact details for his F.B.I. handlers, some being his inter-department communiqués. This was what Knoxx had known about. How he knew what he knew, Romney couldn't begin to comprehend. He took a minute, kneeling in front of the safe with the files in his hands, and just kind of snorted in an ironic laugh. Knoxx was Knowledge, and Romney knew he would use all of this information to bury them all.

The drive from Admiral Avenue in Venice Beach up to Mulholland Drive was easy for the blond-haired, five foot ten, heavyset assailant. His S.A.S. training served him well, keeping his wits about him. He checked everything twice before making his move, taking his time, driving across Los Angeles. The other occupant in the Toyota was tied up and still unconscious riding in the back.

Romney arrived at the perfect spot he'd located earlier in the day. He pulled off the road onto the dirt track that overlooked both Burbank and parts of the Westside. It was a tranquil spot, high above the sprawling city lights of Los Angeles, with only the stars to light his way. Having cut his headlights, the black-painted Toyota mingled into the background. Opening the rear hatch, Romney roughly unhinged the tape around the man's mouth. His white, ashen face, bug eyes and flared nostrils said it all. Fear. He had pissed on himself. Romney pulled a Sig-Hauser automatic pistol out from his coat and asked him, 'What's your name, mate?'

'Davi - David Kenshaw!' the man shouted trying to sound convincing.

Romney replied, 'Wrong answer, dude!'

'Wait, wait, don't fuckin' shoot! I'm with the F.B.I.!'

'Yeah, and I'm with the Rub a Dub Dub fuck you club!' Romney shouted, as he pumped seven hard rounds into the man, who jerked and flapped around in all directions. Shooting him was as easy as shooting fish in a barrel from such close range.

163

Stirring from a deep, booze fuelled sleep and squinting out from under the duvet, Mark's eyes focused on Nicole sleeping contently. He watched her as if she were a little girl, listening to her faint breathing. Every day, it seemed as if he was seeing her for the first and the last time.

Mark leaned in and kissed Nicky lightly on her head. He then nuzzled in, softly kissing her lips and whispered, 'Love you, baby.'

Nicky returned a soft whimper of agreement as she snuggled in deeper under the duvet to carry on sleeping. The scent of sex still lingered on them both and she still felt the afterglow from the hard, passionate sex they had launched into when they had returned home from NVS.

He dropped away from her and got out of bed. Standing naked in the vast master bedroom, he checked the bedside clock that read 6:15 a.m. The morning's sun was already rising over the endless horizon. Standing at the window, he stood in awe, feeling its heat, remembering. *Old habits die hard*, he thought, allowing the curl of a small smile. He then waded across the plush carpet that caused his feet to bounce as he made his way to the master bathroom. Standing over the toilet to take his early morning piss, he thought, *what the fuck have I done?* His eyes stared at a picture on the wall above the toilet. Standing there in another place and time, he finally let a thought fall from his lips, saying in a hard way, 'Mutherfuckaa.'

He stood in the peace and quiet alone, thinking of how it all began, nearly five years earlier.

Mark then thought of Jane. How would she live in tomorrow's world? It was time to get everyone moving.

164

'Honey, wake up. Janey, wake up. I need you to pack some things that you need the most. I'll have the rest sent to you. You've got to go now, babe. Please don't ask me why. I just need to know that you're out of here and that you're safe. Go to the airport with Andy and go back home.'

Mark had woken Jane up in her bedroom. As soon as Jane had woken up, she began a tirade of questions, while Mark began to gather up some of her things around the bedroom. Jane wouldn't be moved so easily, however.

Mark explained as best he could, telling her, 'Look, hun, this is it. Our time's up. My time's up. I don't want you anywhere near me. So go back home and wait for me there. I've lied my last lie hun. I know you couldn't leave me even if you wanted to, but you have to, now. You can stay at mom and dad's. They'd love to see you anyway.'

Jane began to shout at him in rebellion, but her voice began to waiver. Mark just kept the pace up, not listening to her, moving her along, slowly but surely coaxing her along. He kept picking up her things, and after a while Jane realized that the time had come and today was going to be the day that he had said would come. Now, she needed to be strong for him. In a flurry of sobbing, within a whirlwind of movement throughout the bedroom, helped along by Mark, Jane finally had everything packed that she needed for tomorrow. How she would live in the unknown of tomorrow, with a new day and a new life, she didn't know. She steeled herself to look at Mark with shining eyes, holding on to the one thing she knew she would carry in her heart forever. Her love for him.

They came together and hugged for the last time. He knew it and so did she. Mark finally broke down. All the love he could ever carry in his heart and soul allowed him to say warmly, confessing to her, 'Don't be something, Jane. Do something. That's what I need to do, honey.'

'I know, I know. It's alright, Mark. You don't have to explain it to me. You never have to explain yourself to me. I love you for you, and I always will. No matter what, you know that,' Jane answered weakly, as she began to cry freely now. They hugged hard and kissed.

Mark began to fight his tears. Trying to shut off his emotions, he broke away from Jane in his own defense. 'I'll call you tomorrow to make sure you got there, okay,' he told her, trying to sound convincing.

'Okay, I'll talk to you then,' Jane answered, nodding profusely, knowing he'd just lied to her.

There wasn't going to be a tomorrow for him. Staying strong for him, she glinted out a small smile, to give him her strength. She then put one foot in front of the next, and walked out on Mark and their lives together.

Mark readied himself for the next wave of decisions he had to make. His phone rang, and Romney informed him that he had been right about Kenshaw; he'd been an undercover F.B.I. agent, getting information on him through Jane. Mark quickly disengaged himself from the phone call. In no mood for idle chat today, he kept himself in motion. The Grove was a hive of activity; What A Waste's engines were heard warming up. Sam Malton, Quincy Taylor and Brian Meserve were all on board setting up security measures. Knoxx then called Alisha, telling her to come to the boat.

He thought pensively about his next phone call. Staring at the phone, not wanting to pick it up. He glanced at the notepad where he had written out the names of everyone he thought would be dying with him. His eyes finally fell to the one name that brought fear into his heart. Jane.

He called his mom, Margaret, back in Bournemouth, England to explain to her in a heavy, choppy, monotone manner that he was sending Jane to stay with her, and that he needed her to be taken care of. His mom sounded scared and confused about the reasons why her son wanted Jane taken care of in such a way. He told her what he wanted done, realizing he was probably giving Jane a death sentence. Knoxx hung up the phone abruptly, after receiving assurances that she would do as he had asked, amid a flurry of tears over the phone. With a heavy heart, Knoxx had to think about one last act before leaving The Grove and his envious life behind. He got his act together and began walking through the house, making his way up to the master bedroom to see Nicole one last time.

Waking her up softly with a kiss, Mark started softly, telling her, 'Nicky, listen, hun. I have to go. I'm not sure where I'm going, or for that matter, where I've been lately,' trying to make light of it all. 'I'm done with all of this. I'll see that you're taken care of, okay? I have to go, babe.'

Nicky jumped up in bed and then just as quickly jumped down Mark's throat, saying, 'Taken care of? I don't want, or need to be taken care of, Mark. I only want to be with you, wherever that might be. I told you before; I don't need this, any of it! I just need you.'

Nicole spoke as a woman who knew what she wanted, and what she wanted, she was going to get. One thing was clear, she was Mark's girl and she wanted it to stay that way. Making her stand, she said, 'Do you want to go through life wondering what could've been? You walk out on me now and you'll always be wondering, what could've been. My life is with you, for better or for worse.'

Mark hit her back, saying resolutely, 'Yeah well, it's about to get a whole lot worse, I can tell you that. You have to make that decision yourself, babe, because I'm responsible for you. Like me, you'll have to live with your choice, because every one of our choices has a consequence. Believe that, Nicky.'

Nicole's mind was set. She knew, without being told, that this probably had something to do with The Bezerk Murders. She had her secret and Mark had his. Now they were one, entwined in a bond that would hold them together forever, just like a God of war and a Goddess of love, two conflicting symbols with two distinct passions that can kill and that people kill for. She sealed her fate, telling him, 'All I want is you. A little bit of you and a little bit of me, and we've got our own slice of Heaven.'

He leaned in and they kissed. She could never have cheated on him. Something inside told him that. Call it instinct, call it his inner soul of knowledge, but she seemed to have looked at him with pure, pristine eyes. And one thing Knoxx knew well, were lies. He could finally tell, he realized, that Nicole wasn't lying. He found warmth in her beauty and inner strength, and it lit a fire inside him to reign eternally with Nicole by his side, where anything was possible.

Doing her best to put on a brave face, she cracked a smile and Mark smiled back at her. She was making her own decision to stay with him. Perhaps, he had found true love after all. Unconditional love, for the person he was, just Mark, the boy from Bournemouth, not the Mark Knoxx that the media portrayed.

'I can't make any promises on how this is going to turn out, but if we can get through tonight, then we'll be on our way to starting a new life together, and I promise, it'll be a better life. I'm in a fight with Me, Myself and I, and I don't know if I'll make it, but if I do, then I'm all yours.'

He flashed a bright new smile, with mischief in his eyes. No matter what the stakes, Knoxx could fight off the downside, believing there was always a way. An obstacle is an opportunity in disguise. All he had to do was to find a way to get his guest list back, hold on to it and then disappear. As simple as ABC. For one thing to live, another must die. One ending is another beginning.

165

Dan was in position, watching Maxine. Teresa was sitting at a table in another restaurant with a laptop computer at the ready, on the phone with Cedars Sinai Hospital to confirm Dolly's medical condition. Maxine sat out front of The Studio bar and restaurant at the marina in Coconut Grove, Florida, waiting. Checking her watch, it told her that it was 10:58 p.m. Coconut Grove was throbbing with tourists and couples out for the evening, which made any real surveillance impossible. In Maxine's case, that was a good thing. She knew it would make any kind of standoff a bad idea as the place was crawling with cops who were making sure the pickpockets and drunks stayed away from the tourist trap. Maxine checked her watch again. As she looked up, Mark Knoxx was standing beside her table. She instantly fought the urge to look around to where she thought Dan might be, to make sure he had seen him. All she could do was look at Mark in surprise at how he had gotten to her unnoticed. He smiled an easy smile and asked, 'Hi Maxine, how you doing?'

Maxine found it difficult not to pull out her gun and shoot him right there on the sidewalk. She hated the man standing over her. She fought her tears welling up, for her hate for Knoxx and for the love she had for Dolly. She knew this monster standing before her, standing in blue jeans and a t-shirt, looking like an everyday guy, was the man that had put her daughter in a coma.

Knoxx sat down and got settled in. He picked at some breadsticks from the table. He wasted no time in getting down to handling his business. His eyes fell from hers briefly. His basalt, blue eyes came back up to meet hers. 'You know, Maxine, what a waste all of this is, you and me. All the pain and suffering. I'm tired of it all, aren't you? I'm sure you're wired and I'm sure you're not alone, and you're probably armed, so let's not bother playing nice. You know what I want and I know what you want. So let's get this done, shall we? I want my guest list and I'm guessing it's in there.'

He vaguely motioned down to Maxine's foot, where a large bag sat. Maxine answered just as shortly, questioning him, 'How do I know you'll do the right thing? How do I know you'll really let my daughter live?'

Knoxx seemed to sigh, somewhat inconvenienced, as he chomped on a breadstick. He flashed his blue eyes at her under his tanned face, asking her, 'You read my letter, right?'

Maxine nodded in the affirmative. 'Yes,' she answered.

'And you have the information I've supplied you?'

Maxine nodded, following up with a small, 'Yeah, I have it

all.'

Knoxx asked, in a questioning tone, 'Then why wouldn't you trust me on this? I told Jane to tell you, at the beginning of all of this, that I never meant any harm towards your daughter. It was you I needed. I needed you to believe me. I knew you never would, unless I forced your hand, to look through all the bullshit. We can escape this world, Maxine, but we can't escape each other. Just use your eyes. Everything seems right somehow, but then, when you look deeper, you'll see it's all lies. Our patterns can be the same, and they can all be found in our own pasts, but it's that one small moment of discovery that can make the grandest of changes. Just use a small paintbrush to pick out the details and you'll see it.'

'See it? See what?' Maxine answered, asking in dismay.

'See them, the ones who are shaping our lives and our future. We don't own them, they do. They want all the power and control, and they're well on their way to getting all the money, believe me. This is all about using ourselves against us. How we allow ourselves to be manipulated by the corporations. A little at a time, until it's too late. Then, they own us all.'

Maxine searched for the answer, but came up with nothing. 'But what does this have to do with me? I don't understand. All I know for sure is that you're a murderer.'

Knoxx seemed to become agitated, leaning in across the table with a look of darkness in his eyes. Flashing a shade of gray in them, he replied hard, admonishing her, 'You don't know me. Don't even think you do! You don't wear my chains or carry my scars. You'd have to feel my blood in your veins, then you might have some idea of what it's like to be me! I've given you everything I have to give. This time tomorrow, trust me, you'll believe me, and then you'll know I'm the only one who's been telling you the truth. The truth can be stranger than fiction, but sooner or later, fiction can sometimes come true.' Pausing to keep his oncoming anger in check, Knoxx quickly changed his tack. He said in a lighter tone, 'I'll tell you what. I'll go first. I'll prove to you that I want you, and the others you have here with you listening in on our little chat, to believe. You don't have to believe in me, but you do have to believe in The Firm. Fair enough?'

From his jeans pocket, he pulled out a HEAVEN Navigator, just like the one Maxine had seen back in Dolly's hospital room. Knoxx tapped on it a handful of times, almost playfully and with some dexterity, as if he was playing a computer game.

He then said with some pride, 'There, all done. She should be coming around in about half an hour or so. She'll probably feel sick, and she'll have one hell of a headache, but after that, she'll be fine.' He dropped the Navigator on the table, disregarding it as if it was of no use to him.

Maxine looked at him in disbelief and asked with doubt in her voice, 'That's it? I mean, that's it? You've done it? I don't believe you.' Doing her best to stay focused but finding her motherly instincts taking over, she released some excitement in her voice at the possibility of it all being over, at least for Dolly. She stifled a small smile, asking unconvinced, 'So that's it?'

'What? You were expecting some kind of big production? I said I'd go first and I have. You must try to start thinking about me in a different way, Maxine Dobro.'

Knoxx let out a small laugh because he could see that Maxine had lit up with hope at the thought of it all being over. She held up her hand as if to shut him up, and then indicated that she needed to use her cell phone. Knoxx fell back in the chair, checking his watch. He nodded his approval and waved at her in a friendly way, but then he quickly clarified his position, telling her sharply, 'I have specialists in the immediate area too. Try anything and they won't hesitate to use force. That's one thing you can believe!'

He watched Maxine dig through her purse, where she pushed aside her thirty-eight caliber handgun and fished out her cell phone. She called Teresa, who was seated half a block from them, asking her to confirm on her phone if there had been any change in Dolly's condition. Maxine listened while Teresa spoke with a doctor, whose words Teresa relayed back to Maxine. Teresa could be heard laughing on the phone as she relayed the news to Maxine, who also began to laugh, wiping at her eye, as she began to let it all sink in. Within minutes, Dolly had changed from being comatose to showing signs of movement. Maxine laughed, and so did Knoxx, feeling comfortable living with the knowledge that he had the power over who gets to live and who gets to die. He loved it as he heard Maxine say, softly in disbelief, 'It's a miracle.'

'I know. Now I think it's your turn,' Knoxx stated ominously. He turned his attention back to the bag, while Maxine hesitated. He remarked, 'I have plenty of these.'

Looking at the Navigator he had discarded on the table, Maxine wasted no time in pulling up her bag. She pulled out the rolled-up drawings, and one by one, put them on the table.

Knoxx sat upright in his chair to unroll one, taking his time to pore over it, his eyes focused and his mind razor sharp. It was as if all he ever wanted in the world were these drawings. He muttered to himself while he looked at the drawing, 'Yeah, that's what I'm talking about! You beauty, they're here. Nice one, Bezerk.'

'This is what this has all been about?' Maxine asked hard.

'Yeah, that's right.'

'And that's why you killed him; Bezerk?'

'No time for small talk I'm afraid, but hey, never say never. If I make it through to tomorrow, who knows? Maybe you'll get your chance to arrest me after all. But keep this in mind, HEAVEN will, after going public next week, generate around four billion dollars in revenue a year. The market space it's in is worth two hundred and eight billion dollars, but more important than that, is that it has access to millions of people's health records. Think about it, Maxine. We live in an age where the boxes are chipped to tell us where they need to go, and now we're testing RFID chips on humans. Ask yourself the one question I had to ask myself. Why? Nine-eleven did one thing. It forged one, universal thought into the collective thinking of a nation. We were united in that one thought. Revenge. Then what? It seems okay that the government has implemented more controls, conducting surveillance of our phone calls and monitoring our bank transactions. A war can be manipulated, it can even be invented, and if there's no real reason for going to war, then they'll find someone to play the bad guy. Create a lie, and repeat that lie enough times to enough people, and eventually, the people will own it. They'll pass it on to others as their own beliefs and their friends will believe it, because why would their friends lie to them? People don't go down for telling a lie too well; they go down because they sold a lie that was too good to begin with.' Preparing to leave, he flashed a bright, white smile. With his eyes blazing, knowing the trade was done, he said thoughtfully, 'No words of mine can ever persuade you. Only seeing is going to make you believe or understand what I'm trying to tell you, but believe me Maxine, tomorrow you will believe. Love life and live it large, babe.'

In one swift movement, he stepped away without any fanfare and was quickly lost in the crowd. Maxine sat for a moment. She had nothing left to do. Her role in all of it was done. She called Teresa again to tell her that Knoxx had left. Teresa said she'd come over to her. She joined her at the table after a few minutes, and handed Maxine her phone. Maxine heard the muffled, weak voice of her daughter, asking, 'Mom? Mom, is that you?'

Maxine and Teresa both laughed tears of joy, as they reached out to each other across the table. They sat and smiled, laughed and cried. Maxine joked with Teresa, and they talked about the miracle that had just happened. But after a while, Maxine found herself reflecting on something. Knoxx hadn't lied to her. She pondered on what he had told her: 'Tomorrow, you will believe.'

Maxine wondered for a moment what he could have

meant. Was it because he'd given her back her daughter? Had he given her another chance? She had promised God that if she were given a second chance, she would do better this time. Maxine had a second chance to start a new life. Was that what he'd meant? One thing Maxine did reflect on was whether Knoxx knew he wasn't going to be seeing tomorrow, because as he got up from the table, she knew he had picked up a tail. Whether he knew that his own choices in life had caused his own consequences, Maxine would never know.

166

'Sir! Sir! Is everything okay? We need to move him, stat!' the Secret Service agent commanded, after having been summoned by Lynn Tasker to their bedroom during the night. The vice president's coughing had become worse, coughing up blood; he was beginning to lose his faculties. His breathing had become shallow, erratic and unstable, and he was having trouble speaking. With one look at him in the dark light of the bedroom, the agents knew it was bad. The vice president, now only a matter of hours away from becoming the President of the United States, tried in vain to wave them off. The guard detail moved swiftly into action, producing a stretcher to place him on. Having strapped Tasker down on it, they hefted him up and moved him out while he frantically waved and thrashed about, seemingly in fear of having to go to the hospital.

The convoy sped Stephen Tasker to Bethesda Navy Medical Center, in Maryland. There, at 2:54 a.m., November nineteenth, the morning of the general elections - when he was to become the forty-fifth President of the United States - Stephen Tasker was pronounced dead. He had died from severe complications of the liver and kidneys, exacerbated by internal bleeding through the membrane walls.

His death would throw the political arena in to turmoil and the United States into a state of anxiety. Everyone was travelling down a road of unknown destinies. The scripts had already been written and the spin had already been spun. Now it would all have to be undone, and a new kind of spin would have to be written so as to not cause undue panic and mistrust. The people had to be shielded from the truth. All the king's men and The Firm got to work setting the history books straight on how Stephen Tasker had died. The fight continued and the Illuminati would continue, without one of its loyal subjects.

The Illuminati's grandfather, code-named Lovo, The Wolf, was informed of Tasker's death at The Vatican in Rome.

167

Knoxx reversed his course, while being shadowed by Meserve and Matthews. They had been instructed to undertake counter-surveillance measures on Dobro, so they stayed ashore while Knoxx took the launch back to What A Waste. He had the five mural drawings firmly in his grip as he entered the Predator yacht. It was now past two o'clock in the morning. The Monday that would see a new President of the United States come into office, a different one than had been expected Knoxx suspected. *So far so good* he thought, as he got settled in, having got what he needed. The guest list.

Nicky was lying on the sofa sound asleep. Everyone else was in bed asleep, and all was quiet. No one knew that a quiet storm was approaching just over the endless horizon. Mark began to take photographs of each mural on his SWIFT phone, meticulously writing down each of the names that were embedded in the coded pictures with a pencil. One by one he was decoding Bezerk's hidden code that he had shown him all those years ago back in prison. His boy Bezerk had done well, up to a point. There seemed to be hundreds of names connected to them, the Illuminati. Anyone who had mentioned The Enterprise had gone on Knoxx's guest list, for a time like this. It had been hidden in the most unlikely place with the unlikeliest of allies; one that few people, if any, would ever have thought was connected to him in such a way. It was all hidden in the details. It would take all day to decipher each drawing, but if that's what it was going to take, then Mark would get it done. Learn from yesterday, focus on today and prepare for tomorrow. He had done all three. Now, tomorrow was today. There was a slight dapple of rain around What A Waste as it lightly bobbed about in the early morning's dark light. No sound, no noise, just the quiet of the ocean as it lapped against the hull. It seemed to hold Mark in a trance, providing a comforting rhythmic beat that helped to keep him on track, searching out each code listed as a number of dots on a telephone keypad.

The swaying of the boat had helped to calm Sam Malton into a light sleep while he laid out on a sun lounger on the stern and it had also helped to lull Quincy Taylor into a sound sleep, stretched out along a bench on the bow. The rhythm of the sea had helped to rock everyone into a soft slumber.

*　　　*　　　*

Twenty meters off the stern to the southwest, a helmeted

head watched while it was mercilessly hit by raindrops and a small swell. The head jutting out of the water bobbed along with the rhythm of the yacht sitting in the sea, watching it. The arm of a black-cladded figure came up, while its elbow crooked for him to look at the Nite SEAL MX10 military watch. Its illuminated dial read: 2:52 a.m. Nothing was moving on the boat that he had been watching for some time now. The man in black scuba gear, treading in the black sea, masked by the blackness of the night, lowered his head into the water and began swimming closer to the stern.

Malton heard something, even though he felt he was asleep. Something had awoken him. It had been blissfully quiet, but now there was a small noise, and he had noticed it now. It sounded like it was coming from the back of the boat. Malton got up and cautiously approached the stern to look the nine feet down onto the transom deck. There it was - a noise that had a light rhythm with the sea, some kind of metal-on-metal tapping sound. Malton stood there lazily thinking about it. If it was going to continue all morning, then he wouldn't get any sleep. It was probably something that had washed loose and had caught on the propeller. He made his choice and suffered the consequences for it. He climbed down the steps and knelt down to get a better look and to hear better, trying to locate the problem. His face reflected off the black water.

A dark figure darted up, grabbing Malton by the back of the neck, while at the same time thrusting a knife through his heart as he was pulled back into the black water. A pull back and one more vigorous thrust of the knife deep into his chest, and Malton was kicked away and discarded to descend into the deepest darkest depths of the ocean.

The black neoprene suited-scuba diver surfaced, watching the yacht from approximately three meters. He listened to the rhythm of the lapping water against the hull, both bobbing in time to the beat of the death march. The scuba diver approached and put one hand on the transom deck. He then raised himself up onto What A Waste, slowly climbing the steps in a crouched position. He deftly stepped along the port side of the deck around to the bow. He pulled out a silenced MP-5SK suppressed automatic rifle. His footsteps were long and confident, his neoprene socks making no sound. He rounded the front, raised his weapon, and without warning fired a short silenced burst at close range, killing Quincy Taylor instantly.

The assassin knelt down on one knee, staying stock-still, listening to the rhythm of the rocking yacht. He let four minutes pass by until he knew it was all clear. He reversed his course along the port side to the back of the boat.

At precisely 2:46 a.m. November nineteenth, Paul Deavins of MMI Enterprises, was roused from a sound sleep, secure in the knowledge that all of his hard work over the years was finally going to pay off. Taking this phone call however, Deavins quickly realized that their best laid plans had all come to a whopping, big, fat zero as he listened to what the caller had to say. If God had a plan, then Deavins wasn't in it. He sat up in bed, listening intently to the voice on the phone that calmly explained to him that it was all over for them. Tasker was dead. He had died from some kind of poisoning. Their plans lay in ruins.

Deavins disengaged the phone and sat quietly for two minutes, before he concluded there could only be one man who had got to Tasker, before Tasker had got to him. He still had the phone in his hand, resting on his lap as he thought it all through, the choices and the consequences. Realizing the nightmare had come true. One name fell from his mouth. He whispered, 'Knoxx.'

He dialed the phone number for the SEAL's Commanding Officer. Two teams of SEAL's were on reconnaissance detail, watching Knoxx aboard What A Waste. They had two hard-bottomed Rigid Inflatable Boats, close to half a mile off the bow and stern of the Predator, each containing six, fully armed Navy SEAL's. The authorization code came through, telling them to move in and take everyone out.

168

As if he'd dreamt it his whole life, Mark watched as a figure, slowly ease back the sliding door and lightly slide into the room. Knoxx made no sound or movement, knowing it was always going to end this way, an assassin with no eyes, coming for him. The scuba diver smoothly closed the sliding door behind him. Knoxx still held his SWIFT phone in his hand. He calmly pressed the 'send' button on it, never once taking his eyes off the ninja-type warrior who had a machine gun pistol raised at him. The assassin blended into his dreamscape, stepping in gracefully with no rush, as if he had all the time in the world.

'Keep your hands where I can see them,' the assassin commanded. Knoxx smirked, not giving a shit about any commands. It was inevitable. It was always going to be his destiny to die this way. He had no intention of going out any other way now.

The strange voice did do one thing though. It woke Nicole up, as it had subconsciously threatened her. She immediately bolted upright and sat next to Mark. She was about to scream, when Mark lightly pressed on her thigh to calm her and then took her hand. She looked in his eyes and they were warm, almost happy. She listened to him say, 'Baby, everything's going to be alright. He's only here for me. He won't harm you. It's something I've known was coming for a while now. Please, honey, just be quiet and stay calm.'

The assassin hadn't said a word. He just looked at them. His right hand moved up to his hooded-diver's cap, and then slowly began to peel off the skin-tight hood.

Dan McGann stood before Mark Knoxx.

'You! You? McGann? What are you doing here! What are you doing?' Mark shouted at him. Having immediately recognized him, his demeanor changed just as fast.

Dan took both his hands and wrapped them around the MP-5SK, rolling his hands into a fist around the barrel and the handgrip. Both men stared at each other.

Dan replied firmly, 'What do you think I'm doing here, you sick fuck? I'm here to kill you, for killing my best friend!'

'Don't be so ridiculous! I didn't kill him. I had nothing to do with it. You've got it wrong, bud,' Knoxx answered him dismissively.

McGann itched to pull the trigger, while Nicole began to cry. This wasn't how it was meant to be, both men thinking the exact same thing. It was all sugar, but now it was turning to shit.

McGann got back on point, shouting, 'Bullshit! Everything

you say, everything you do, it's all bullshit. You were after Hadley because she knew too much. You meant to kill her, but you, or whoever you sent to do the job missed her and murdered Richie for no Goddamn reason, you piece of shit! Now I'm here to put a stop to it all. It's over for you! You hear me? Over!'

McGann lifted the gun up to his rib cage, getting ready to fire.

'You're here because you think I wanted Hadley dead. Why would I want that?' Knoxx responded defiantly as if he held the gun and was in control of the situation. The fact that McGann was here to murder him played no factor into it now. He was mad, and becoming angrier by the minute. All his plans seemed to have gone to shit, and it would now be some cop from L.A. coming to kill him, and for what? A misunderstanding? No way was that going to happen to him, not now and definitely not today. Knoxx now raised his voice in anger, and shouted at Dan, 'Listen, McGann, you got it all wrong. I'm telling you, I'm not the guy. I know you want your pound of flesh for your buddy, but I'm telling you, I had nothing to do with it. Who the fuck do you think tipped you off in the first place about Bezerk? I put you in the game, when I told you to meet me at Edie's Diner at nine o'clock that morning.'

'Yeah, like you had nothing to do with Bezerk getting iced too, hey? You killed Bezerk because she slept with him. I know all about it. Olivia Marbela told me.' McGann replied, acing him, knowing he had him on that one, standing over him, pushing his gun to the right slightly, pointing it at Nicole.

Knoxx felt as though the bullet had pierced his life force, as all his senses left him. He'd heard it, but it felt as if he'd gone deaf. The rage was so intense and bright inside him. He could not see any of his surroundings due to his anger being as intense and as hot as the sun. His life was over. Everything had been a lie, everything and everyone. The smallest thing can have the biggest impact, and that one remark changed Knoxx's destiny, history and his story. Without fear, like a fierce lion, he flew into motion before any bullet could reach him. Knoxx grabbed a hold of Nicole's thick mane of blonde hair and pulled her up off the couch, and stood her up in front of him. He gripped her hair tightly in his right hand, while he still held a pencil in his left hand. The pencil was now pushed hard against Nicky's exposed throat. He jerked her head back to expose the veins in her neck.

Mark looked as if he was possessed by the devil. His eyes were dark and his face was a menace to society. His face was fused to the side of her cheek as if they had been welded together. His body was protected by hers while he maneuvered her roughly into the position that he wanted her in. One minute, she had been in a restful sleep, but now her life was being threatened by the one man who had vowed to defend her and keep her safe. Hissing like a boa constrictor while he tightened his grip on the back of her hair, he scowled in Nicky's ear, 'So you fucked him, did you? Well now I'm going to fuck you! I'm going to fuck you up, you bitch!'

Knoxx was in an uncontrollable rage, pulling and tugging on Nicole like she was a Barbie doll. She screamed hysterically, not knowing whether to fight him or go with him while he backed away from McGann. McGann staying step-for-step with him.

Knoxx shouted hysterically at McGann and Nicole simultaneously, 'I knew it! I knew it! I fucking knew it!' Looking at her and then at McGann, as if he wanted him to agree with him that Nicole was a lying bitch. Knoxx stopped his juke and jive and stood tall, looking to the side of Nicky's face, jamming his pelvis into the small of her back.

McGann realized this was all wrong. His instincts were to protect life. His police training went into overdrive as he started to lower his weapon, knowing there was nowhere for Knoxx to run too. He began to try to reason with Knoxx by telling him, 'Look at me Mark. Look at me! I'm putting the gun down.'

Dan placed the weapon on the floor. He had his sidearm at the ready in its holster, along with the seven-inch knife strapped in a calf-muscle scabbard.

'Do you know the first thing I learned in prison was?' Knoxx growled while he continued looking at Nicky in his own sick world. Heaven and Hell were both calling him. His mind had left this world and he wanted to take one last person with him. Pulling her hair tight, her eyes went bug-eyed as she caught his eye. Knoxx was a wild lion, roaring over and over, as if it was his mantra, 'Trust no one! Trust no one! Trust no one! You fucking bitch! Trust no one! I trusted you and now look! Look!'

He thrust Nicole's head forward to face McGann. Dan stood with his arms spread at his sides and his knees flexed, ready for any opening, but Knoxx was prepared for his move. He jabbed the pencil at Nicky's throat. His eyes were wide and taut as he became keenly aware of his surroundings.

Nicole tried to speak, hoarsely blurting out, 'He tried to rape me!' Buried under an avalanche of tears, she tried to shout, 'He was going to rape me!'

Her words weren't registering with Mark in his wild state. Pushing her by her thick mane of hair towards Dan, he drowned her out, screaming over her words, 'Do you know why this guy's here? Look at him! He's come here to kill me, and do you know why? Do you, you bitch!'

Nicole couldn't find the words to calm him. She just found more fear and more tears while McGann watched Mark in detail, waiting for one chance, one small opening. Looking into Nicole's eyes, he tried to relay some kind of telepathic message while Knoxx continued his ranting.

'He's here to kill me because of you! Of you! Because you slept with Bezerk! You went and slept with him didn't you? Didn't you! This piece of shit cop is here for me because of you and your fucking lies, bitch! And I trusted you!'

With one mad move that could never be undone, while Nicole was opening her mouth, Dan realized he could see the move coming. He shouted as loud as Knoxx had while he moved in one fluid motion, to reach for his machine gun, but for everyone, it was all too late. Knoxx buried the pencil's tip and shaft deep into the side of Nicole's throat. Her blood instantly hit Knoxx in the eye, as she jerked in panic. Her body weight becoming too heavy for Knoxx to hold, he threw her at Dan, cutting off Dan's line of sight while he had begun to rise up with his gun in his right hand. Dan tried to catch Nicky as she fell forward onto him, with blood spurting profusely from her neck. He had to think fast and he had to act even faster. Catch her. Shoot him. He tried to do both while Knoxx turned, crouched down, and ran for the starboard side door, sweeping up his SWIFT phone as he did. Dan leaned over to his gun side, while he caught Nicole's body weight. The MP-5SK released a barrage of rounds that hit their mark in the general target area of the doorjamb, surrounding wall and through the open door. The bullets followed Knoxx out the door as he sprang through it.

*   *   *

'Use of lethal force has been approved and authenticated, gentlemen. Use extreme prejudice. I repeat, use extreme prejudice.' The SEAL captain kept his voice steady over the secure sat-com, while the two Navy SEAL Team R.I.B.'s raced towards What A Waste; both boats were expending all their horsepower as they cut through the cold, black ocean. All of the SEAL Team members were lying down in their assigned positions in the inflatable part of each R.I.B. while the boats bumped across the ocean towards the boat. Each SEAL commando was wearing black camouflage and had blacked-out face paint, and each one was heavily armed. In three minutes, they would be storming the boat and killing everyone on board; their briefing was that terrorists had infiltrated The Port of Miami. They had a dirty bomb on board. Everyone was to be regarded as hostile and extremely dangerous.

Dan kept his finger squeezed tight on the trigger until every round had been shot, the majority of the rounds had followed Knoxx out of the door into the dark light that fell out from the open doorway. Nicole was choking, drowning in her own blood and at the same time beginning to convulse as she went into shock. The pencil had hit the carotid artery that supplied the head and neck with oxygenated blood. Dan held her body weight in the inside elbow of his left arm. He was torn. All in the blink of an eye. Should he drop her to the ground, leaving her for dead and go after Knoxx? Seconds meant life or death. He did not know if he had even hit Knoxx. Was he dying from his wounds out on the deck? Dan looked in Nicky's eyes. She was trying to communicate something while her mouth tried to suck in air like a fish flapping on a boat deck.

Dan looked up at the door that Knoxx had run through. After hearing the hard splash of a deadfall over the side, Dan manically screamed out, 'It ain't over! It ain't over! You hear me? You better be dead, you mutherfuckaa, coz I'll kill you again! You hear me? This ain't over! I'll find you and I'll fucking kill you! It's not over!'

Dan began to focus on Nicole, his hands covered in claret, his face covered in her spurting blood. The rhythm of gushing blood pulsed to the beat of her heart, pumping straight up from her throat.

'Stay with me! Come on baby, stay with me!'

Black neoprene silhouettes began to stalk up the steps, each one covering the other. The first one pointed his machine gun at the patio doors. The SEAL's began forming up on deck. Dan looked through the door and saw one of the armed warriors. He immediately shouted out the code word used for the mission, 'Redhill! Redhill! Redhill!'

169

'Shocking news today. Vice President Tasker was rushed to Bethesda Naval Medical Center this morning, the White House citing stress. According to sources, however, the vice president suffered a stroke at his residence. His press secretary denied this, explaining it was simply a case of exhaustion. The vice president is the firm favorite to become the President of the United States today. An update on his condition will be released as any updates come in. We here at this station, as I'm sure the nation, wish him a full and speedy recovery,' Larraine Scott said.

She looked at her co-presenter, to hand over the next segment. He transitioned into the next news item, announcing, 'Well, they say, truth is stranger than fiction. They seemed inseparable at times, always in the news. It has been reported by the Associated Press that Mark Knoxx, C.E.O. of Exile Corporation and several of his staff, died early this morning, while sleeping on his yacht, What A Waste, off the coast of Florida. The U.S. Coast Guard responded to the scene after a fireball lit up the early morning sky. They recovered a number of bodies. It isn't known at this time if Mark Knoxx was among them, although it has been confirmed that he was on board at the time of the explosion.' The lead newscaster looked back at his female co-host, who raised her eyebrows in a questioning manner. He continued, 'Truly a sad day for all those involved. The search for survivors will go on throughout the day. The Navy's Search and Rescue is also at the scene. Authorities say, at this time, it's unknown what caused the explosion.'

Larraine Scott interjected, saying ruefully with a hint of conflict in her voice, 'Who would have thought, Vice President Tasker and Mark Knoxx, both on the same day. Our thoughts are with the families of those killed or missing.'

'And in other news.'

The presenter paused and then continued with the other news of the day. Another day had begun. Just like any other.

Belief

170

Three weeks after the events in Washington and Florida, the media storm had only gained in fury. The media focused on the relationship between Stephen Tasker and his connection to Mark Knoxx. The spin-doctors were working their magic, trying to down-play the accusations, but one thing they couldn't spin was the death of John D'intino.

The F.B.I. had released a statement at the time of his death, saying he had died in bed from a heart attack, when in fact, a video released on the Internet showed him being brutally attacked and then murdered in his driveway by Mark Knoxx. The media smelled a cover up and a huge conspiracy. The trail led back to one company and one man, Exile Corporation and Mark Knoxx.

Bank accounts were uncovered, with hundreds of millions, some with billions of dollars in them. Transactions from these accounts were beginning to be traced back to Senators, Congressmen, politicians, businessmen and shell corporations that had been operating in countries where the United States' armed services operated. The highest profile accounts being linked to Iraq and Afghanistan. A line in the sand had been drawn, and it was becoming clear that Tasker and D'intino had been involved in embezzlement, money laundering and tax evasion at the very least. Names were being named and people in power were being indicted, having to sit before a congressional hearing. Some were taking an early retirement or resigning. A hurricane was sweeping through Washington and in other Western countries, cleaning house along an endless horizon.

Upon her arrival back from Florida, Maxine had flown straight to Los Angeles to visit Dolly, smothering her with hugs, kisses and homemade brownies. Maxine had gotten her wish. The chance to start her life over. Her only goal in life now was to spend as much time with Dolly and Harry as possible. She found that by just being a mother to them, she was, in fact, loving life and living it large. As Mark Knoxx had foretold, when her tomorrow arrived, she would come to know the truth. Now Maxine knew the truth. Upon her return to California, she'd had an e-mail waiting for her. It had names and bank account details in it. The last thing he ever did. Each month, Maxine pulled out the letter that she had folded into thirds and had stuffed in her purse that first day at the hospital when Jane Mears had handed the envelope to her. At the time, she had read it as a threat, but now it seemed to read differently as she took her time to read it carefully this particular day. It read:

As we grow up, we learn that the one person who was not supposed to let us down probably will. You will have your heart broken probably more than once, and you will break hearts too, so remember how it felt when yours was broken. You will fight with your best friend. You will blame a new love for the things an old one did. You will cry at times, because time itself seems to be passing you by all too fast. Eventually, you will lose someone you love.

So take too many pictures, laugh too much and love like you have never been hurt by anyone or anything in your life, because every sixty seconds that you spend being upset, feeling let down, angry or filled with revenge is a minute of happiness you can never get back.

Dare to dream and dream to do. The difference between the dreaming and the doing is in you.

Do not be afraid that your life will end.
Be afraid that it will never even begin.

- Mark Knoxx
Chief Executive Officer
Exile Corporation

In Maxine's mind, Mark Knoxx was a monster, but he was her monster. One that would always remind her of what could have been, and what she had now. She had her life back. Maxine had come to believe in the conspiracy, and in them. The Illuminati. Having absorbed the reports in the media and having read most of the F.B.I. reports, Maxine now carried a belief inside her. A belief that the U.S. Government was not to be trusted and she now believed that any form of monitoring was a form of manipulation that gained control. It was her belief that she wanted to have handed down through the generations of her family. Maxine knew all the secrets. Some she kept, some she didn't. Over time, as if it were a slow leak on an inner tube sitting in the ocean, she leaked various names, bank accounts and information throughout the world. Information that had come from her archenemy, and now the foundation of her belief, Mark Knoxx.

*   *   *

Teresa Hadley had returned to New York from Florida to be briefed by her superiors at F.B.I. headquarters, with Deputy Director Kevin Christie overseeing the briefing.

Teresa Hadley knew the truth. She knew what, why, and how it had all gone down, and she could see that they were making it all sound and feel very different. The F.B.I. was involved in a cover up. Teresa believed the truth. The real truth. Believing what had happened should come out, but they made her sign documents to seal her mouth shut, threatening her indirectly with prison and with not being able to see her children. Christie was doing the bidding for his real bosses, Teresa now knew, because she knew that he was one of them, The Firm. Teresa quietly held her belief that they shouldn't get away with it. The cover up and lies that helped to shield the real monsters, the billionaires, multimillionaires, politicians and members of The Enterprise. The Illuminati. Teresa shared in Maxine's belief that the government agencies and the multinational corporations were involved in murder, manipulation and control.

Teresa and Maxine were both true believers in the existence of a New World Order and both of them were secretly fighting them. Together.

171

The car pulled up to the curb at Branksome Wood Road. Stepping out, the bitter, cold winter wind hit him hard. The early morning air was thick with salt from the nearby beach. He lowered his head into his scarf to fight off the chill that was usual for this time of year in Bournemouth, England. The gravel crunched under his feet while he walked into the Branksome Chine Horizons. As soon as he entered, he was met by the warmth and the smell of food and hot cups of tea being handed out in the dayroom of the convalescent home. He was greeted enthusiastically by some of the residents as he walked through, saying his usual greeting of, 'How are you today, ladies? You're all looking lovely this morning.'

He walked through, carrying a bouquet of daffodils in his right hand, with a copy of the USA Today newspaper tucked under his arm, along with a large bar of Galaxy chocolate in his left hand. He had sat with her for four days now, in the hope that she might let something slip about Knoxx.

As Dan McGann approached her room, a woman in her mid-sixties was leaving it. He had decided that he had to find the truth, believing that Maxine had it wrong. The woman deftly slipped a Navigator into her right hand pocket before turning away from the door. She looked up and smiled. Since meeting her and having had several conversations with her, she seemed familiar to him, but Dan could not place her. Her eyes lit up as she greeted him. 'Oh hello, lovey. Morning Dan.'

'Hi Margaret, how are you today?' Dan asked, putting on his best American accent, knowing she loved it.

'Are those for me? Coz if they are then I'm doing great!' she joked, looking at the chocolate bar.

Dan gave his answer by just standing there like a wet limpet.

'Always the bridesmaid, never the bride,' she joked. Margaret then said, as if imparting a secret, 'I'll be in to see her later, so I'll get one or two of them then. I've put on two pounds since you've been here, Dan.' His face searching hers, Dan asked reflexively, 'Maggie, do you think she'll ever remember anything? You know, since her stroke. Will Jane ever get her memory back?'

Margaret could only look pensively at Dan. Her own mood turned dark, thinking for a minute. She came to her own conclusion, replying cryptically, 'Oh, Heaven only knows, dear. HEAVEN only knows.'

Out of the night that covers me black as a pit from pole to pole, I thank whatever God there may be for this unconquerable soul. In the failed clutches of circumstance I have not winced nor cried out loud under the bludgeon of chance, my head bloodied and my head unbowed.

Beyond this place of wrath and tears, looms the horror of the shade. Yet, through the menace of the years, and shall find me unafraid. It matters not how straight the gate or how charged with punishment the scroll.

I am the master of my fate. I am the captain of my soul.

Invictus
William Ernest Henley (1849–1903).

As told to Mark Knoxx by:

Calvin 'Boozy' Dedrick
Federal Reg. No. 22165-038
Security Housing Unit
Super Maximum Penitentiary
ADX Florence, Colorado

Serving four life sentences

Born and raised in England, the author moved to Los Angeles, California USA in 1991 at the age of 25 years old. Training to become an Investment Securities Broker, by 1995, he was one of the most sought-after telemarketers throughout the USA. Upon the advent of the Internet, Mark joined an organization that then manipulated the burgeoning electronic age, eventually embezzling approximately $117 million by 1999. Fleeing the US in 2001, he was pursued as a fugitive by the F.B.I. throughout a number of countries. Eventually being extradited back to the USA in 2004 and brought to justice, he was sentenced to serve 4 years and 9 months in Federal prison. Mark wrote the book *Exile Corporation* partly based on his true story, his experiences, and people he met while in prison. He now lives in Bournemouth, Dorset England and works as a business consultant.

www.exilecorporation.com
exilecorpmark@gmail.com

Look out for the explosive, action packed sequel

LIFE IN EXILE
Running out of time
Time to stop running

For information and to purchase books
please visit:
www.exilecorporation.com